Five Couples Are Given a Second Chance at Romance

FOREVER
Yours

Andrea Boeshaar, Gina Fields, Joyce Livingston,
Kim O'Brien, Kathleen Y'Barbo

BARBOUR BOOKS
An Imprint of Barbour Publishing, Inc.

Castle in the Clouds © 2000 by Andrea Boeshaar
Familiar Strangers © 2000 by Gina Fields
One Last Christmas © 2004 by Joyce Livingston
A Wedding Renewal in Sweetwater, Texas © 2012 by Kim O'Brien
Major League Dad © 2003 by Kathleen Y'Barbo

Print ISBN 978-1-63058-887-8

eBook Editions:
Adobe Digital Edition (.epub) 978-1-63409-545-7
Kindle and MobiPocket Edition (.prc) 978-1-63409-546-4

Published by Barbour Books, an imprint of Barbour Publishing, Inc., P.O. Box 719, Uhrichsville, OH 44683, www.barbourbooks.com

Our mission is to publish and distribute inspirational products offering exceptional value and biblical encouragement to the masses.

 Member of the
Evangelical Christian
Publishers Association

Printed in the United States of America.

Contents

Castle in the Clouds

by Andrea Boeshaar

Chapter 1

Wren Nickelson's index fingers pecked laboriously at his computer's keyboard:

> *"You're crazy to even think about buying this ancient, falling down, gutted-out hunk of rock!" Joe told his twin brother, George, as the two of them ambled through the eerie gray-stone castle.*
>
> *"The price is right," George replied cheerfully. "The state of Saxony is only asking one German mark." He chuckled. "That's just over half a US dollar. For a castle! My very own castle!"*
>
> *Joe threw him a pathetic look. "Such a deal. It'll cost seven million in repairs!"*
>
> *George shrugged nonchalantly. His brother didn't know that money was no object. He had more than enough in his Swiss bank account. . . .*

Wren sat back and gazed at the last sentence he'd written. Running a hand through his dark brown hair, he wondered if the Swiss bank account idea was too farfetched. *Guess it is,* he decided. *Better make that seven million available through grants or. . .or God's provision. Yes! That's it!*

With renewed vigor he reworked the initial chapter of his first novel. Then he reworked the initial chapter of his very first novel. After another hour had passed, he decided there wasn't much else he wanted to change at this point. He liked his characters, George and Joe. Rather, he liked their names. Simple. Common. Strong. Not at all resembling his own name—Wren. Unique, yes. But odd. Disappointing.

His name was Welsh and meant "ruler," and his mom, bless her heart, had determined upon his birth that her beloved son would someday be a great leader. Instead, he'd become a mail carrier and aspiring novelist. But worst of all, he'd become a broken man whose wife had divorced him more than a year ago, stating that she couldn't live with him or his "religion."

Wren didn't completely understand Nancie's reasoning for ending their twelve-year marriage. What he did know, however, was that the woman who meant almost everything to him didn't love him anymore, a fact that still crimped his heart and seared his soul. Now he was a court-ordered weekend dad, and for the longest time, he had felt lonely and depressed over the divorce ruling. But amazingly enough, without Nancie and his two daughters—Alexa and Laura—around, he suddenly found the time to do the very thing he used to only dream about doing.

Write.

It was like God's blessing of encouragement, sent from heaven just for him. He'd lost so much—his house, his family—but the Lord had given him an outlet for his emotional pain. And for the past four months a Monday evening creative writing class and imaginary characters had kept him company. He was only too glad that Risa had suggested they take the class together. He probably wouldn't have done it on his own. But she was rapidly becoming a good friend, and that congenial push was all he had needed.

Maybe he'd even be able to upgrade his computer soon.

Wren shook himself from his reverie and glanced at his wristwatch. It was past midnight, and he had to be at the post office by 7:00 A.M. He stood, stretched, and decided to call it a night.

∞

Nancie Nickelson gently shook her two girls awake. "Time to get up. Mommy has to go to work."

Alexa, eleven years old, and Laura, age seven, groaned. After all, it was six in the morning.

Stifling a yawn of her own, Nancie walked across the girls' bedroom and opened the shades. Slivers of early-morning May sunlight quickly cut the darkness.

"Is it gonna be a nice day today, Mumma?" Laura asked, brushing blond bangs out of her eyes. "Maybe Mrs. Baird will take us to the park again."

"Yes, maybe she will." Nancie smiled at her youngest, recalling the fun Ruth Baird, the girls' babysitter, had described to her yesterday when she'd picked up the girls. Having three children of her own and committed to motherhood, Ruth was the perfect day care provider. And Nancie ought to know: She'd been through half a dozen babysitters in the past eighteen months before finding Ruth at the end of March.

"Come on now, girls. Get up and get dressed. Everything's ready for you—even breakfast."

Nancie left their bedroom, reflecting on her hectic lifestyle. Laying out clothes and loading backpacks were tasks she ordinarily did each night after Alexa and Laura went to bed. Next she routinely would wash dishes and tidy up their compact two-bedroom apartment before pouring herself into homework and studying for classes at the college she attended on weekends. When her fatigued body refused to accommodate her pace any longer, she collapsed into bed.

After five or six hours of sleep, Nancie would force herself out of bed before sunrise and begin a new day, which would be just as busy as its predecessor. She started off each day by preparing coffee for herself and toast and cereal for her daughters. By seven o'clock the rush was on, first to Ruth's house, just a few blocks away—her daughters walked to school from there—then to the sales department of a large manufacturing company, where Nancie had landed a terrific job.

And this morning promised to be as hectic as any other.

"Don't forget, your father is coming to pick you two up this afternoon," she reminded the girls after they arrived at Ruth's.

"Aren't you ever gonna be done with school?" eleven-year-old Alexa asked, her deep brown eyes glowering with something akin to resentment.

"I've got two years left to go. You know that."

"Seems like forever," the girl groused before turning and entering the Bairds' home.

"Good-bye, Alexa," Nancie called after her.

There was no reply, and Nancie felt terrible.

"She'll be all right," Ruth assured her, standing at the front door with a baby on her hip. Wisps of light brown hair blew onto her cheek, and with her free hand, she brushed them back off her face.

"This has been happening more and more often," Nancie confided. "Last night Alexa and I had a full-fledged argument. Sometimes I feel like she hates me." Sudden anger rose inside Nancie as she wondered what Wren was telling the girls. Would he stoop so low as to poison their minds against her? Nancie couldn't be sure. She knew her ex-husband was a Christian and that he wasn't ambitious by any stretch of the imagination. But Wren loved his daughters, and Nancie had an inkling he might be working behind her back, trying to get custody of them.

"Nancie, divorce is always hard on kids," Ruth said gently. "Alexa and Laura only get to see their father on weekends, and it's hard for them to get bounced between you two."

"They're not being 'bounced,' " she said, sounding defensive to her own ears. She toned down her voice. "It's a schedule like any other, and children are very adaptable. As for Wren, I think he's up to something."

"Like what?" Ruth tipped her head curiously.

"Like...oh, never mind," Nancie said hotly. "You're on his side. You Christians all stick together."

"That's not true. I'm not on anyone's side. But I care about the girls."

Ignoring the comment, Nancie gathered Laura into her arms and kissed her good-bye. She couldn't dally any longer—she had to get to work. And tomorrow she was supposed to give a speech on women's rights for her sociology class, so she'd have to do some last-minute preparation on her lunch break. It was going to be another long and busy day. She didn't need to start it off this way.

"I love you. You be good for Mrs. Baird," Nancie told Laura, squelching the hurt caused by Alexa's aloofness.

"I will," the child promised sweetly.

Straightening, she smiled at the woman whose lifestyle seemed so opposite to her own. But Nancie had made her decision, and being a "domestic engineer" would never suit her again. Actually, it had never suited her. She'd always wanted more out of life than staying home and raising kids afforded. Now she had it. And in a couple of years, after she finished college, she'd have it all.

"Bye, Ruth. Thanks."

"Have a good day."

With a parting nod, Nancie walked back to her car. Climbing inside, she started thinking about Alexa's recent antagonistic behavior and then wondered why Wren didn't just say something if he wanted custody—not that she'd give in to the request of course. But he could at least quit being such a coward and tell her face-to-face what was on his mind. But no, instead he used sneaky, dirty, underhanded tricks to drive a wedge between a mother and her daughter.

"Well Wren, you're going to have a fight on your hands if you're trying to take my girls away from me," Nancie muttered angrily, pulling away from the curb. "A fight like you've never known. . ."

∞

With two leather satchels strapped across his chest, Wren walked his mail route and thought about his novel, *Castle in the Clouds*. He hadn't told another soul he was writing it. The project was his secret outlet, much like a very private diary. It gave him a welcome sense of purpose, and amazingly, he felt as though his heart was on the mend. Maybe one day he would even get the book published!

Smiling to himself, he mulled over his plot. The story line wasn't at all complex. A divorced man, George, buys a castle in Germany, fixes it up, then kidnaps his ex-wife, Nan. Alone together within the confines of the castle walls, she has no choice but to face the fact that she's always been in love with him. The divorce was a horrible mistake. An American missionary, the pastor of a church near the castle, is summoned, and George and Nan are remarried. They send for their two adorable daughters, who had been with a babysitter in America. . .and then they discover the treasure buried within one of the castle's walls. However, George's evil twin brother, Joe, devises a scheme to steal it away from the happy couple and their young daughters.

Wren continued on his way, still pondering his great American novel until he finally finished his route. Once back at the post office, he punched out and then headed to pick up Alexa and Laura from the babysitter's house.

Wren couldn't say he minded the girls staying at the Bairds' home while Nancie worked. Ruth and her husband, Max, were wonderful Christian people. So far Nancie hadn't complained about their "religion" and Wren hoped she never would.

He pulled his older model Ford minivan alongside the curb in front of the Bairds' red brick house. Climbing out from behind the wheel, he headed for the driveway. Halfway there, he spotted Ruth and five kids—two of them his—coming down the sidewalk.

"Daddy!" Laura cried, running toward him.

Right behind her, Alexa smiled and waved.

Smiling broadly, Wren felt like he was in a Kodak commercial, celebrating the moments of his life. He wished he could forever etch in his memory the delighted expressions on his daughters' faces as they raced to greet him. As he opened his arms wide, the girls rushed into his embrace.

"Hi, Daddy!" Laura said, hugging him around the waist.

"Hi, baby." Wren placed a kiss on her blond head. Her hair felt feathery soft against his lips and smelled like sunshine.

"We're just getting home from school," Alexa informed him as Wren kissed her forehead.

"Guess I've got good timing today, huh?"

"Can we have pizza tonight?" his youngest asked.

Wren chuckled. "Sure."

By now, Ruth and her brood had reached them. "Happy Friday, Wren."

"Thanks. Same to you."

Ruth instructed Alexa and Laura to wait over by their father's car. "I think you should know," she began, once the girls were out of earshot, "that Nancie was a little upset this morning. She and Alexa still aren't getting along well."

"Hm. . ."

"Nancie thinks you're up to something."

Wren blew out a weary sigh. "Well, thanks for the warning. I'll try to talk with her Sunday evening, but I doubt it'll do any good."

"We'll be praying for you."

"I appreciate it."

Ruth's baby began squirming in his stroller, wailing for freedom.

"How much do I owe you this week?" Wren asked.

He settled up with her, then pocketed his wallet. As he strode toward his dilapidated vehicle, the irony struck him. Nancie got "liberated" and he got stuck with the day care bill. Perhaps he ought to talk to her about picking up the tab each week. Or even every other week. Wren grimaced at the thought of an encounter with his ex-wife. He wouldn't win. He never did.

Climbing in behind the wheel of his minivan, he wondered what his character George would do if Nan stuck him with the sitter's bill week after week. Wren smirked. George wouldn't take it for a minute. He'd confront Nan and tell her that she had to at least pay half. George wouldn't let a woman push him around. George was a man's man.

"Dad, tell Laura to move over," Alexa whined from the backseat.

Wren twisted around to settle the matter. "Buckle up, girls. . .and no more bickering."

"I hate little sisters," Alexa spat. "I hate everything."

"Even pizza?"

Wren couldn't help the easy quip, but it worked. After a roll of her eyes, Alexa smiled.

"Okay, who's hungry?" he asked, slipping the key into the car's ignition.

"I am!" Laura cried.

"Me, too," Alexa admitted grudgingly.

"Well, so am I." Wren grinned and stepped on the accelerator. "Let's go find some food!"

Chapter 2

Mary Wollstonecraft, an eighteenth-century feminist. Lucretia Coffin Mott, Elizabeth Cady Stanton—both pioneer activists in women's rights. Betty Friedan, the founder of the NOW organization..." Nancie paused, hoping for a dramatic effect. "What would these leading feminists think of us today? Women are still slaves in their own homes. Slaves to piles of laundry, dirty diapers, and their husbands' smelly socks..."

Nancie paused again as an image of Ruth Baird flitted through her mind. What would she do if she didn't have Ruth watching her daughters? Her conscience pricked her. Ruth, after all, said she liked staying home and taking care of her kids—and Alexa and Laura, too. She really ought to be fair to everyone.

Taking the pencil from behind her ear, Nancie added the word "some" and began practicing her speech from where she'd left off. "Some women are still slaves in their own homes...."

After she rehearsed her speech several more times, she finally felt confident enough to give it in class the next day. And then she'd get her semester grade. School would be over for the summer. Nancie sighed with relief. She needed the break. Working full-time and carrying a twelve-credit load at the weekend college was beginning to take its toll. She felt tired constantly. Crabby. Tense.

Well that's Wren's fault, she decided, crawling into bed. Her muscles groaned their relief as she settled between the soft sheets. *If he'd stop trying to sabotage the court order, I'd have less on my mind.*

Nancie wondered if that's really what he was trying to do—get custody of the girls. Wren had always been mild-mannered, easygoing, and sincere—part of the reason she'd married him. And divorced him. After twelve years she'd grown bored living with a spineless amoeba. The man lacked drive and aspiration when it came to bettering himself in the business world, although he was certainly the epitome of a mail carrier: neither rain, nor snow, nor sleet, nor hail. . .

However, Nancie had wanted—expected—more from her husband than mere faithfulness to a job. She'd envisioned his climbing the ladder of success, but he'd never been interested in advancement.

And then he'd found religion. It happened right after she'd given birth to their youngest. Nancie had had a troublesome pregnancy, and both she and Laura developed some problems after the delivery. Wren's fear for his wife and child had led him to what he termed "the saving knowledge of Christ," and he wasn't the same man afterward. He began taking the Bible literally and attempted to obey its every word.

When Nancie grew concerned about the change in Wren, she talked to her friends at the department store where she'd been working part-time, and they helped her see the real light. Her husband was adopting a philosophy right out of the dark ages, and he'd soon demand that she become some subservient creature. And to think Wren once had had the audacity to tell her the Bible said women should be "keepers at home" and "obedient to their own husbands." When Nancie heard that, it was all over. She had a right to her own life, for pity's sake! As for her children, she loved them with a mother's fierce, protective love, but she knew she could manage her career, college, and raising them, too. Wren knew it as well.

So would he really try to get the girls?

Nancie had to admit she didn't know her ex-husband anymore. Maybe he would. . .except the Wren Nickelson she'd been married to wouldn't have put up a fuss. He would have passively accepted his fate, claiming he was "trusting God." For nearly five years she'd lived with his "trusting God." But she had still hoped he'd take charge of his life and become more assertive. Instead, Wren preferred studying his Bible to reading the self-help books on success that she'd purchased for him.

What a disappointment. What a simple man!

Would he really fight me for custody?

Part of Nancie didn't want to believe Wren was capable of such a thing, but the other part didn't trust him. Frankly, she didn't trust men in general. She'd had a few dates since her divorce and had discovered men were all the same. They wanted women to act like deferential ninnies to bolster their macho egos.

Well, not her. Not Nancie Cunningham Nickelson!

∞

"Why can't I live with you?" Alexa asked.

"You do live with me," Wren replied diplomatically. "You live with me on the weekends."

"No, I mean all the time. Why can't I?"

Wren thoughtfully regarded his oldest daughter. Her small face was framed by long, light brown hair. Her cocoa-colored eyes beseeched him with the question she'd asked. "Why?"

"I take it you and your mother aren't getting along any better than last week."

"She hates me," Alexa said, pouting from across the dining room table. Wren's computer and a small pile of his work-in-progress occupied one end, while he and his daughters breakfasted at the other.

"Your mother does not hate you," Wren assured her. "Why do you think that?" He forked in a bite of pancakes and chewed, waiting for the reply.

"I look like you, Dad," the eleven-year-old stated precociously, "and Mom hates you." A little sob threatened to strangle her. "Now she hates me, too."

"Nonsense, Alexa." Wren set down his fork, stood, and walked around the table. Hunkering beside his daughter, he gathered her slim form onto his knee. She wrapped her arms around his neck. "Your mother loves you very much." He swallowed hard. While he knew he spoke the truth, it hurt to think Nancie hated him. What had he ever done to her? A hot, white-lightning anger, mingled with profound pain, caused his chest muscles to constrict. And for that moment, he hated her right back.

No. . .no, I don't, he thought, his reason slowly returning. He didn't hate his ex-wife. He despised the fact that she'd severed their marriage,

18

and he abhorred his oldest daughter's anguish—an obvious result of their divorce. But no matter what Nancie did or would ever do, Wren knew in his heart he could never hate her. Not only did he realize that that would equate to murder in God's eyes, but very simply, he had loved Nancie far too long and far too deeply.

He still did, although it wasn't always easy.

And that's why he continued to feel wounded—even after a year and a half.

"Dad, she's so mean," Alexa sobbed into his shoulder. "She yells at me all the time. Please, can't I live with you?"

Wren took a deep breath and had to wonder if hormones were at work in his oldest daughter. *Already?* He grimaced.

"Dad, please?"

"Shh, honey—you're wrong. Your mother loves you. But I'll speak with her. Maybe we can work something out." Wren glanced across the table at Laura, who happily ate her pancakes, seemingly unaffected by her older sister's outburst.

Alexa quieted and lifted her chin off of Wren's shoulder. "Do you promise to talk to Mom?"

"I promise."

The girl appeared somewhat mollified.

"Are we still going to the picnic, Daddy?" Laura asked, wiping her syrup-covered mouth on the sleeve of her pink nightie.

Setting Alexa back on her chair, Wren stood and smiled at the seven-year-old. "We sure are, so hurry up and finish your breakfast. Both of you."

Picking up his plate, he walked into the small kitchen of the lower flat he rented, silently dreading a confrontation with Nancie. She knew how to chew him up, spit him out, and make him feel about two feet high.

George wouldn't be afraid of his ex-wife, Wren mused as the image of his main character flitted across his mind. *George would stand up to her.* He grinned. *Better yet, George would grab hold of Nan, pull her into his arms, and kiss her until she came to her senses.* Wren paused, frowning. *Or would he kiss her senseless. . . ?*

"Daddy, I'm all done," Laura announced, bringing in her plate from the dining room.

Wren snapped to attention and reached for the syrupy stoneware. "Thanks, baby."

She smiled up at him adoringly. "Now I'm gonna get dressed."

"Good girl."

Alexa was next to bring in her plate. "I'll wash the dishes for you," she offered.

"Great. I'll dry."

They made a good team, and soon the task was nearly completed. Peering at his daughter as he dried the last of the utensils, Wren had to admit that Alexa did resemble his side of the family, while Laura looked more like her mother. But he highly doubted Nancie would ever hold her physical appearance against their oldest daughter.

Or would she?

Well, he thought wearily, *I'm going to have to talk to her and find out.*

∽

"Mrs. Fagan. . .about my grade. . .a D? How could you have given me a D on my speech?"

The instructor, a petite brunette, gave Nancie a tight smile. "I didn't think you conveyed the true purpose behind the women's rights movement. Mary Wollstonecraft advocated educating women so they would be better wives, not so they would shun their station in life. You said some women were slaves in their homes, but housework has nothing to do with women's rights and education. Housework is a part of life in general." The instructor lifted a brow. "I have to do housework, and I have a master's degree."

Nancie glanced around the classroom, relieved to see that most of the other students had gone and that those remaining were out of earshot. "I was referring to housewife mentality as opposed to a woman wanting a career outside the home."

The instructor shrugged. "I felt it was a weak argument and certainly not the cornerstone for women's rights. I know a lot of bright, well-educated women who run their households better than some business professionals manage their offices."

"But—"

"I'm sorry, Nancie. Your speech sounded more like it was based on bitterness than fact."

"Bitterness? I beg your pardon?"

"Look, I've got to go. You're welcome to discuss this further with the dean of our department and appeal the grade. However, I don't think your speech warranted anything more than a D."

The woman turned on her heel. Nancie stood open-mouthed, gaping after the instructor who was leaving the classroom. All her hard work. All her research. Her speech had been worth much more than a D—the information she'd provided was worth at least a B!

Feeling someone tap her on the shoulder, Nancie spun around and peered into the face of a middle-aged, heavyset woman with blond, frizzy hair.

"We call her Fagan the Dragon."

Nancie lifted a questioning brow. "What?"

"Our instructor. Her name is Louise Fagan. This is the second time I've had her for a teacher, and I can attest to the fact that she's earned the nickname Fagan the Dragon."

"Oh. . ." Nancie didn't feel like discussing the matter with another student and began shoving her text and notebook into her red canvas shoulder bag.

"So you're divorced, too, huh?"

Nancie gave the woman an annoyed glance. "How'd you know?"

"Takes one to know one, I guess. My husband left me for another woman ten years ago. I carried a lot of anger inside me for a long time. Who wouldn't?"

"For your information," Nancie replied curtly, "my husband did not leave me. I left him. And I am not angry or bitter, contrary to Mrs. Fagan's theory. . .and yours, too, obviously." Throwing her bag over her shoulder, she added, "And I'll thank you to mind your own business from now on."

"I'm just trying to help."

Nancie didn't reply, but marched out of the classroom.

"Deny it all you want," her classmate called after her, "but you're going to have to face your feelings sometime."

Oh, what does she know? Nancie thought with a huff as she left the building for the parking lot, striding purposely toward her car. *I don't have a resentful bone in my body. I'm just confident and successful and they're jealous.* Reaching her white sports car, she opened the door and threw her book bag into the passenger seat with more force than necessary before she slid behind the wheel. *I don't need them. . . . I don't need anyone. I'm going all the way to the top and no one is going to stop me!*

Chapter 3

Risa Vitalis saw him walk into the picnic area of the park with two girls and excused herself from the conversation she'd been having with one of her coworkers. She'd been hoping he would show up today at the annual postal workers' picnic.

"Wren!" she called, smiling and waving. She immediately took note of his light blue polo shirt and well-worn jeans. He looked good—real good. "I saved us a spot over here," she added, pointing to a table in the shade that she'd covered with a brightly-patterned plastic cloth.

Nodding, he strode toward her, while the girls took off in the opposite direction, heading for swings and jungle-gym apparatus. As he neared, Risa's smile grew.

"I'm glad you decided to come, Wren."

He shrugged his broad shoulders and easily swung the cooler onto the table. "I wanted to take the girls somewhere today, and seeing as the weather's so nice—"

"You mean you didn't come because you knew I'd be here?" she asked, with an exaggerated pout.

Wren gave her a sideways glance, but his tiny smile indicated the embarrassment he felt.

"Aw, I'm just kidding. But you knew that, right?"

"Yeah, I knew it."

And Risa knew it, too. . . . That is, she knew Wren Nickelson didn't share her romantic interest. He didn't ask her out on dates or lead her to believe he ever would. He'd made it clear—they were just friends. But that didn't stop Risa from dreaming about him at night—or trying to win his heart by day.

"Want a pop? I brought some."

Wren shook his dark brown head. "No, thanks."

He sat down on the bench, leaning his elbows on the tabletop. He gazed off in the direction of where his daughters were at play while Risa made good use of the moment and admired the man. His face was clean-shaven and already tanned from walking his route. His arms looked strong—from lifting and carrying heavy mailbags, she supposed—and Risa wished she'd one day feel them around her. . . .

Now if only he'd take off that silly wedding band, she thought as the gold ring on his left hand glinted in the sunshine.

As if he sensed the weight of her stare, Wren turned and looked at her.

She blinked. "So those are your daughters, huh?" she asked lamely in an effort to cover her enamored scrutiny. Clearing her throat, she sat down beside him.

"Yep." He fairly beamed. "See the one in the pink T-shirt? That's Alexa, my oldest. The little blond one in the yellow bibs is Laura."

"They're adorable—even at this distance. I can't wait to meet them." Risa scooted closer to him, then crossed her legs. "Have you done your description assignment for Monday night's class?"

Wren looked her way and his dark brown eyes twinkled. "Not yet. You?"

"All done. Want to read it?"

"Sure. You brought it along?"

"Uh-huh." She stood, found her vinyl tote, and pulled out the green folder. She plucked the neatly typed page of description from one of the pockets and handed it to Wren.

While he read, she reclaimed her seat and nibbled her lower lip nervously.

Finally, he looked over at her and smiled. "It's very good."

"Really? You wouldn't just say that, would you?"

"No."

Risa nodded. She believed him. Wren was honest to a fault.

"But I hope you don't mind my saying it is rather dark." He handed the paper back to her. "It reads like something out of a Stephen King novel."

"I was describing my stepfather. He's always reminded me of a reptile: beady eyes set too far apart on his wide face, thin lips. . ."

"Yeah, I get the picture." Wren tipped his head quizzically. "Doesn't sound like you're very fond of him."

"I'm not. He was abusive."

"Oh Risa. . .I'm sorry." Wren's tone was warm and sympathetic.

Somewhat embarrassed, she dropped her gaze to the page she held between her hands. Then she peeked up at him. "I'll bet you're a wonderful father to your two girls, aren't you?"

"I sure try," he said with a small lift of his shoulders and a weary-sounding sigh. "I wish I could be more a part of their lives."

"Divorce is tough. I was about twelve when my folks divorced. My mom remarried the next year and I hated my stepfather. Still do. I was his verbal punching bag."

Wren stretched a comforting arm around her shoulders, giving her a little hug, and Risa had to resist the urge to snuggle against him.

"Finally my mother felt sorry for me and sent me to live with my natural father. I went through a lot of counseling. For a long time I couldn't trust anyone. I didn't feel safe enough." She paused, hoping he would somehow understand the depth of the words about to pass through her lips. "But I feel very safe with you."

He didn't disappoint her. "Risa, I'm. . .I'm flattered you feel that way." She smiled. "It's true."

Wren brought his arm back to his side, much to her disappointment. "Well, I've got to give the glory to the Lord for that one," he said, gazing out across the expanse of plush green lawn.

"What do you mean?" she asked with a puzzled frown.

"You feel safe with me because I'm a Christian."

"No. I've met men who were religious and I wasn't comfortable in their presence at all."

"Risa, just because a guy acts religious doesn't mean he's a Christian. Being born again isn't about religion. It's about God's grace."

She replied with a shrug. In truth, she didn't want to talk about God. She was a little afraid of Him. She figured if she didn't bother God, He wouldn't bother her. "Well, anyway," she said, changing the subject back to her past, "the counseling helped, and I'm okay with everything now."

"Except you still hate your stepdad."

"Always will."

"Then you aren't really okay, Risa. You need to forgive him."

"Are you nuts?" She stood and put her assignment back in her folder. "What my stepfather did to me is unforgivable."

Wren didn't answer.

"I hope you noticed how calm I sound."

"Uh-huh."

"Well, that just proves I'm okay. I can talk about my stepdad, I can even write about him, and I don't feel angry or depressed anymore."

"That's a mark of healing, no doubt about it."

"But?" Risa sensed more was coming.

"But forgiveness is the ultimate test."

She shook her head before combing several fingers through her unruly, rust-colored curls. "I can't forgive him."

"No, you can't," Wren stated emphatically. "Not in your own strength you can't. But with God's help, you can." He suddenly chuckled. "Didn't think you'd hear a sermon on a Saturday, did you?"

With a little laugh, she sat back down next to him. "I'll take it from you, Wren, because I know you're not a hypocrite. I know you mean what you say." She grinned coquettishly. "Except I'd like to change your mind about a few things you've told me."

"Like what?"

His boyish innocence caused Risa to laugh. "I'm flirting with you," she stated emphatically.

Wren's eyes lit up with understanding. "I'm glad you pointed that out," he said as an embarrassed expression crossed his face. "Guess I'm a dunce."

"No, you're delightful."

He met her gaze for several long moments, causing the hope in her heart to soar unfettered.

"I think I'd better go check on my girls."

He stood and, before Risa could reply, three of their coworkers appeared, asking to share the picnic table. Much to her dismay, Wren gave them an enthusiastic welcome.

∽

Nancie barely made it through her classes Sunday morning—it was a good thing they only lasted until noon. As she drove away from the college, she felt the tension melt from her muscles. She was exhausted, so exhausted she could hardly think straight. But her final exams were now over. She'd completed another year of school.

As she maneuvered her car through the streets of Milwaukee, she thought about calling a few friends and celebrating this feat—two years of college, finished. But mulling over several names, she realized that she'd lost touch with many of her old acquaintances in the past eighteen months. Besides, some of them were Wren's friends now, not hers. Divorce had an ugly way of causing people to choose sides.

This is dumb, Nancie thought. *I have lots of friends. Why can't I think of a single soul to call?*

If her mother were alive, Nancie knew she'd call her. Mom would have been thrilled. She'd always said, "Women can have it all, but we settle for so much less." And Nancie supposed twenty-seven years of marriage to a factory worker and veritable "couch potato" had taught her mother that. As much as Nancie loved her father, she considered him something of a disappointment.

Like Wren.

"Well, I'm not settling, Mom," she uttered out loud in prayerlike fashion. "You'd be proud of me. I have a good job, beautiful kids, a comfortable apartment with new furniture. I'm bettering myself by earning a college degree. . . ."

Nancie frowned. *So why can't I think of some friends to call?*

Cruising along the lakefront and then down Lake Drive, she came to a halt at the stoplight on Capitol Drive in Shorewood. The village was one square mile in diameter and bordered Lake Michigan. Nancie hadn't enjoyed living in Shorewood. She'd wanted to live in Whitefish Bay, the neighboring suburb with more class. However, Wren had refused, saying they couldn't afford it. He never even tried. But after she dumped the guy, Nancie had gotten what she wanted—a Whitefish Bay address.

When they divorced, she was awarded the house in Shorewood, but promptly sold it and made quite a bit of money. Nancie bought the girls and herself some needed things—new clothes, shoes, bikes—and then socked the rest away in the bank for her college education. Of course, Nancie had a bit of savings left from which she occasionally drew in those times when her paychecks didn't quite cover all the bills, her car payment, installment on the new furniture, and the rent. But, thankfully, Wren paid child support. That helped.

She gasped in sudden understanding. *That's it! That's why he wants custody. He thinks he's going to save money.* Indignation swelled within her. *Well, he's got another think coming!*

Nancie turned off Lake Drive and headed for Wren's place, deciding she'd pick up the girls early and take them someplace special for dinner tonight—after she gave that ex-husband of hers a piece of her mind.

Whatever's left of it to give, she silently quipped. Moments later, she pulled up alongside the curb in front of his duplex.

She gazed at the house before exiting the car. It looked somewhat shabby even for a Shorewood residence. The yellow wooden siding had faded, chipped, and peeled. The brown trim was in need of paint as well, and the rickety front porch required attention—soon.

Why doesn't he find a better place to live? she wondered, making her way up the walk. She recalled Wren saying an investment company owned the building, and obviously it wasn't concerned with the property's upkeep. The neighbors must be furious.

She rang the doorbell. No answer. She waited. Nothing. Then, as she headed for her car, she heard giggles coming from the backyard. Soon Alexa and Laura came strolling around the side of the house, dressed in their Sunday best. Wren was behind them, wearing tan trousers and a navy jacket with coordinating tie.

Church. Of course. Nancie had forgotten.

"Mom. What are you doing here?"

She tried to ignore Alexa's frown, although it angered her. Wasn't her oldest child glad to see her?

"Hi, Mumma," Laura said, looking a bit confused. "It's not time for you to come yet."

Seeing her, Wren halted in his tracks. His expression was a mixture of their daughters', sort of an uncertain grimace. "Hi, Nancie. Did I miss something? Had you planned to pick up the girls early today?"

"Well, yes. . .except this is rather spur of the moment. I guess I should have phoned."

"I'm not going!" Alexa said crossly as she folded her arms over the red-white-and-blue plaid jumper she wore.

"Nancie, I think you and I had better talk."

"Yes, I think you're right," she said through a clenched jaw.

Alexa turned to Wren. "Tell her I don't want to live with her anymore. She's mean!"

Nancie's eyes widened in shock. "Alexa!"

"Tell her, Dad."

Wren gave the child a stern look. "I won't have you talking about your mother like that. What does the fifth commandment say?"

Alexa tucked her chin and grudgingly answered, "Honor thy father and thy mother."

"Did you just honor your mother?"

She shrugged.

"Lex?"

"No," she ground out at last. "But it's true."

Wren lowered his voice. "And didn't I tell you I would take care of the situation?"

"Yes, but. . ."

Alexa clamped her mouth shut as Wren narrowed his gaze in silent warning. Nancie had to admit to being somewhat impressed by the way he'd handled their cantankerous eleven-year-old. Inevitably, Nancie ended up losing her patience and raising her voice.

Pulling his keys from his pants pocket, he handed them to Alexa. "Take your little sister inside and make us some lunch, okay?"

" 'Kay." She took the keys. "C'mon, Laura."

The girl followed, but paused on the top step of the porch. "Daddy?" She glanced briefly at Nancie before looking back at Wren. "Can we still go to the birthday party this afternoon?"

"We'll see, baby. Oh, and here," he said, shrugging out of his jacket. "Take this into the house for me."

She nodded agreeably and entered the house.

Wren turned and faced Nancie.

She took a deep breath and prepared for battle.

"I understand that you and Alexa aren't getting along," he began.

"We'd get along just fine if you'd stop poisoning my relationship with her."

"Me?"

"Don't look so surprised. I know you're talking behind my back. You're hoping the girls end up hating me so you can take custody."

"That's ridiculous. I've never said a bad word about you to our children. To anyone!"

"You expect me to believe that?"

Wren thought it over a moment. "Yes!"

Nancie tapered her gaze, wondering if he told the truth.

"Have I ever lied to you?"

"I've never caught you at it, no."

Wren rolled his eyes and put his hands on his hips.

"What about the custody issue?"

"What about it?" he asked.

"Are you planning to take me back to court?"

"No. We're adults. We should be able to settle this without dragging it into court."

Nancie folded her arms, lifting a stubborn chin. "What do you suggest?"

Looking across the yard, Wren squinted into the sunshine. "I think Alexa should live with me for a couple of weeks. Maybe that'll alleviate some of the tension between you two."

"And where do you think this 'tension' is coming from?"

He brought his gaze back and considered her for a good measure of time. "Nancie, that's something you're going to have to figure out. I don't know what's going on with you. I only know what Alexa's told me."

"What's that?"

"That you yell at her. . .you're mean. . .that you hate her."

"Oh give me a break, Wren. That's crazy. I don't hate my own daughter."

"Alexa told me yesterday morning that you hate me, and because she resembles me, you hate her, too."

Nancie shook her head, dismayed. "I don't hate you, Wren. I hated being married to you."

A look of hurt flashed across his face, but Nancie ignored it. Wren needed to hear the truth. . .again. Perhaps he'd finally get it through his thick head and take off his wedding ring. It irked her that he still wore it. She'd sold hers.

Taking a step forward, Nancie glared into his brown eyes. "Marriage to you, Wren, was the greatest oppression I've ever experienced."

He didn't even wince. . .this time. "Well, you got what you wanted. You're free to do whatever you like with your life."

"And I'm doing it."

"So why aren't you happy?"

"I am happy," Nancie retorted. "I'm very happy!"

"You don't act like it. You don't sound like it. When I see you coming, I cringe, wondering if you're going to pick another fight with me. You're a bully. Don't you think the girls pick up on that stuff? Alexa especially, being the oldest. You can't fool them, Nancie. Our daughters see a very angry woman when they look at you."

She cursed, and this time Wren did wince. "For your information, I've been under a lot of stress. I work full-time and attend weekend college, and I have to manage my home and kids."

"Don't complain to me about that." He narrowed his gaze furiously. "And don't you dare take it out on my children."

Nancie suddenly felt like she was losing ground. Wren had never argued with her before. He always gave in to her demands. Why was he suddenly standing up for himself?

Because he's not fighting for himself, she soon realized. *He's fighting for his daughters.*

Inhaling deeply, Nancie decided on a different tactic. "You know, Wren," she began carefully and in a softer tone of voice, "the girls have it so good with you. You see them on the weekends, you play with them and show them a good time. I get them during the week and have to be the disciplinarian. I have to tell them to turn off the television and do their homework. I insist they help with the dishes, straighten up the apartment, and make their beds every morning. That's why Alexa thinks I'm 'mean.' Of course she'd much rather live with you."

"Then let's allow her to stay with me for a while and she can see what it's really like."

Nancie arched a brow. "And if I refuse?"

"Then you'll probably have to take Alexa kicking and screaming, because she's made up her mind that she's not going home with you."

She'd lost. Nancie knew it. She could take on Wren single-handedly, but she couldn't fight Alexa, too. However, her innermost fear was that Laura would follow suit.

"You know what, Wren?" Nancie said with a clenched jaw, "I think I do hate you."

He kind of shrugged. "I don't doubt it."

She turned on her heel. "I'll be back to pick up Laura at eight o'clock," she shot over her shoulder.

Without a reply Wren turned, walked up to the front door, and entered the house.

Chapter 4

Wren finished writing the next scene of his novel, then sat back in the dining room chair. He liked this next sequence of events: George and Nan just had a spat, and George emerged the victor. But George always did. Nan had nothing on him.

Recalling the confrontation with Nancie this afternoon, Wren was quite surprised by his own relentlessness. He'd stood his ground for probably the first time in years. Well, Nancie already hated him. What did he have to lose?

Lord, he silently prayed, *it's getting harder and harder to love that woman.* And yet Wren knew he did. There would always be a place in his heart for Nancie...although Risa had somehow found a place there, too. He enjoyed her company. She was a good friend.

Looking back at his computer screen, Wren suddenly wondered if he ought to kill off Nan and twist the plot so that George could marry Lucia, the redheaded Italian beauty who was crazy in love with him. He grinned. The scenario had definite possibilities.

Hearing a soft utterance, he glanced over his shoulder at Laura, who had fallen asleep on the couch. He looked at his wristwatch. Ten-thirty. Where in the world was Nancie? She should have arrived two hours ago.

Scooting the chair backward, he stood and walked into the kitchen, peeking into the girls' bedroom on the way in. He found Alexa in bed, sleeping peacefully. After grabbing a cold soda from the fridge, Wren strolled back to the dining room, where he intended to resume his writing.

Until the phone rang.

"Wren? This is Nancie."

"Where are you?" he asked impatiently. "I thought you were coming at eight."

"I know. I'm. . .well, I'm at the hospital," she said. Her voice sounded strained. "I got mugged tonight."

At once, Wren's agitation became concern. "Are you all right?"

"Yeah. . .except I needed a couple of stitches. Everything happened so fast that I don't even remember what I hit my head on. Whatever it was, it gave me a nice gash above my ear."

"Oh Nancie, I'm sorry," Wren replied sincerely.

"What's worse is that the jerk got my purse containing all my money, my keys, and my credit cards."

"Did you get a good look at the person who jumped you?"

"Not really. But I heard his voice, so I know it was a man."

Wren paused. "It could have been worse, Nancie. I'm glad all you got was a laceration."

"I know." She cleared her throat. "When I think how easily I could have been beaten or murdered. . .or raped."

A brief interval of silence lapsed between them before Nancie spoke again.

"Umm. . .Wren?" she asked carefully. "I wondered if you could pick me up and drive me home. The manager of my apartment complex said she'd let me in once I get there."

He hesitated before answering. On the one hand, he wanted to do Nancie this favor. On the other, he was still stinging from the hateful words she'd hurled at him this afternoon.

"The girls are sleeping. Couldn't you take a cab and pay the driver when you get to your apartment?"

She expelled an audible sigh. "All the money I had was in my wallet. My checkbook was in there, too. I don't have any cash at home, so I'll have to go to the bank tomorrow in order to make a withdrawal. The hospital is letting me make a couple of calls from the registration desk because the mugger stole my cell phone, too"

"Yeah, okay..." Wren didn't see any other options. "I'll be there soon."

"Thanks," she murmured before hanging up.

Clicking off the portable phone, Wren looked over at Laura's sleeping form. Then he threw a glance toward the girls' bedroom, in which Alexa slept. He hated to disturb them. They needed their rest. They had school tomorrow.

Just then a loud thunk above the ceiling caught his attention. Staring upward, he guessed one of his three neighbors had dropped something. He supposed he could ask Julie to stay with the girls. She was probably still awake and studying for finals.

Walking through the kitchen, he opened the back door and quietly climbed the back stairs. Two young women and a rather strange-looking young man lived up here. All were students of the university, but of the three, Julie seemed the most responsible. Wren felt confident she would watch the girls tonight, she'd done it before, and Alexa and Laura liked her.

Arriving at the door, he knocked.

⌒⌒

The cool night breeze caused Nancie to shiver as she stood outside the emergency room entrance waiting for Wren. But at least the throbbing in her head had dissipated, thanks to the doctor who'd given her a dose of pain medication. She hugged herself tightly, trying to keep warm, and decided that this had been the most frightening night of her life. She'd felt perfectly safe, walking to her car at 7:30 in broad daylight. And she'd been confident in her ability to take care of herself, having taken a self-defense course last year. How had that man overpowered her so effortlessly? How had he sneaked up behind her so quickly? Suddenly Nancie wasn't so sure of anything anymore. Even now, standing here under the lighted entryway of the hospital, she felt alone and afraid.

Just then she spotted Wren's car and sighed audibly in relief. She watched as he drove into the circular drive and pulled up in front of her.

"Thanks for picking me up," Nancie said, opening the passenger door and climbing in.

When Wren didn't reply, she gave him a sideways glance.

"You sure you're okay?" he finally asked.

Nancie conceded a little nod. At this point she wasn't sure if she was "okay" or not. Something had happened tonight—something that had caused her self-confidence to splinter like rotten wood.

"What happened? I mean, I know what happened, but how did it happen?"

"I was at a nightclub downtown. . .celebrating."

"By yourself?"

Nancie clenched her jaw at Wren's perceptiveness. "What makes you think I was alone?" she ground out.

"Well, for starters, you wouldn't have phoned me if you'd been with friends. I'm the guy you said you hated this afternoon, remember?"

She didn't answer. She couldn't. What he said was true. Once more that sinking, isolated feeling enveloped her.

"You want the truth, Wren? Okay, I'll tell you the truth." Her voice sounded hard to her own ears because of the hurt she felt inside. "Yes. I was alone. I've completed two years of college now and I wanted to celebrate, but I couldn't think of anyone to invite. I wanted to take the girls to dinner. . . . That's why I came over this afternoon."

"Why didn't you just say so, Nancie? We would have rejoiced with you."

"No, you wouldn't have. We hate each other." She folded her arms in front of her and stared out the window. There wasn't much traffic this late on a Sunday night. Even the nightclub had been sparsely populated.

"I don't hate you. Never have," Wren said softly after an interminable pause.

Nancie swung her gaze around and gave him a perplexing stare. "You should hate me, Wren. But that's your problem. You don't think like normal people."

"Is that why you phoned me tonight?" he asked, somewhat sarcastically. "Because, not being 'normal,' you knew I'd pick you up? I presume a normal person would have let you fend for yourself after what happened this afternoon."

Nancie closed her eyes briefly, swallowing her indignation. "Okay, Wren, I suppose I deserved that. You're right. I called you because I knew you'd come. And. . .well, thanks."

Silence filled the car for the rest of the drive to her apartment. Climbing out of the car, Nancie noticed the bright moon, clear sky, and sharp stars. Then she noticed something else; the lampposts surrounding the parking lot were off. An eerie premonition gripped her heart. Suppose the thief was in her apartment, waiting for her? He had her address, her keys. . . .

"Um. . .Wren?"

He was already out of the car, obviously planning to see her inside. She wasn't going to have to ask.

When they reached the small lobby, Nancie located the manager of the complex and obtained the spare key to her place. Wren dutifully walked up the steps behind her and followed her to her door. Frightened silly over the thought of her attacker possibly being in her home, Nancie's hand trembled as she tried to insert the key into the lock.

"Must be the pain medication the doctor gave me," she muttered to Wren. She hoped it covered her ineptitude, which embarrassed her terribly.

Wren took the key from her fingers and unlocked the door. He stepped inside first and, having been there numerous times, flipped the wall switch, causing the matching lamps on each end table to flood the living room with light.

No one had been lurking in the shadows, and relief filled Nancie's being.

Next, Wren walked into the small kitchen and turned on the light. He repeated the procedure in the hallway, the girls' bedroom, and Nancie's room before reentering the living room area.

"I think you'll be okay. I even checked the closets and under beds."

Chagrin washed over her, from her hairline down. She had to smile. "How'd you know, Wren? How'd you know I was scared out of my wits, thinking someone might be hiding in here?"

This time Wren looked embarrassed. "We were married for twelve years, Nancie. That's how I knew."

"But I'm different now," she argued. "How could you possibly have guessed I felt so frightened tonight?"

He shrugged. "I suppose some things never change."

Nancie glanced at the beige carpeting beneath her feet. "Perhaps not."

Then Wren surprised her further by stepping forward, placing his hands on her shoulders, and giving her a sound kiss on the cheek. Smiling into her eyes, he told her good night.

As she watched him exit her apartment, Nancie experienced a myriad of emotions. Anger because Wren obviously still cared for her when she didn't want him to. Relief that he did still care and was willing to be there when she needed him. Remorse over the way their marriage had ended. And most of all, disappointment—because Nancie realized tonight that she was not the brave, self-reliant woman she'd led herself to believe.

Chapter 5

Nancie made the appropriate phone calls to her credit card lenders and the bank the next morning to report her wallet stolen. Shortly before noon, a locksmith completed the task of changing the locks in her apartment and the door in the lobby. Then, spare car key in hand, she took a taxi downtown and retrieved her vehicle. By 1:30, she arrived at work.

Setting her new purse on her desk, she checked in with her boss before heading to the cafeteria, where she intended to purchase a can of cold soda. But as she neared the entryway, the sound of male voices caused her to pause there in the hall.

"Don't bother asking Nancie Nickelson," one of the men said. "She won't be interested. She never donates to our pizza lunches."

"Why not?" asked someone else.

"Because she thinks she's too good to eat with the rest of us," said the first man, and Nancie soon recognized his voice—it belonged to Bob Mitchell, a coworker.

"She doesn't have a friend in this entire company," said another man whom Nancie guessed to be Craig Harris. He and Bob were thick as thieves.

"So, she's one of those hoity-toity females, eh?"

"No, Nancie's more like a blond broomstick rider," came the reply before a whoop of laughter broke out.

Outside the door, Nancie fumed. How dare those imbeciles talk about her like that! She turned, preparing to enter the cafeteria and verbally blast them into orbit, but then she thought up a different plan of action. What if she killed them with kindness and made Bob and Craig look like the idiots they really were?

She grinned and decided to do it. Taking a deep breath, she walked through the doorway.

"Hi, guys," she said pleasantly, throwing them a quick glance.

Their laughter subsided.

"Oh hi, Nancie," Bob said. "Come over here and meet Pete Larsen, our newest employee."

After purchasing a soft drink, Nancie sauntered over to the large, round table at which the three men sat. "Hello, Pete; nice to meet you," she said in a friendly voice. Sticking out her hand, she gave his a firm welcoming shake. "I'm sure you'll enjoy working for this company. It's one of the best in the nation."

"Thanks," he replied, looking a bit uneasy. "I'm sure I will."

"So, Nancie," Craig said, sitting back in his chair and wearing a confident smirk, "wanna go in on our next pizza luncheon? It's scheduled for Wednesday."

She manufactured a velveteen smile. "Sure. That'd be great. Sign me up." Glancing briefly at all of them, she added, "See you guys later."

Dead silence followed in her wake and Nancie almost laughed out loud. What a bunch of losers.

With her head held high, she walked back to her desk; however, by the time she reached it, she had begun mulling over what she'd heard. *She thinks she's too good to eat with the rest of us. . .she doesn't have a friend in this entire company. . .a blond broomstick rider.*

Nancie signed into her her computer and wondered if what they'd said of her was true. Of course it wasn't. . .except she couldn't think of a solitary comrade here at work. She had her acquaintances, of course, but no one with whom she shared confidences.

Okay, so that part is true, she thought, feeling somewhat defensive. *But it's only because I've been so busy. With a routine like mine, who could find the time to make friends!*

She reached for a stack of papers on her desk and for no apparent reason Alexa came to mind. Nancie's heart ached as she remembered how her oldest daughter had called her "mean." Did Alexa really think her own mother hated her?

Sorrow filled Nancie's heart. She loved Alexa deeply. Sure, they'd had their scrapes, but they were a result of Nancie's attempts to correct her daughter's bad behavior, not to mention her lousy attitude.

"Blond broomstick rider." The cutting depiction of her character rang in Nancie's memory. Is that really how coworkers saw her? Is that how her own daughter viewed her? A wicked witch of some sort? Next she recalled how Wren had called her a "bully."

Uneasiness crept over her, but she did her best to ignore it, and she forced herself to concentrate on her work for the rest of the afternoon.

∽

Wren finished up his mail route and then picked up the girls at Ruth's house.

"You're early," Ruth stated with a note of surprise when she opened the front door. "The girls don't usually get picked up until about five-thirty."

"Yeah, I know. . . . I hope this doesn't pose any problems for you, but Nancie and I talked yesterday and decided Alexa would live with me for a while until the tension ebbs between the two of them. I figured as long as I'm picking up Alexa, I might as well get Laura, too. Nancie can pick up Laura at my place after work."

"That's fine. I could smell a change in the wind when you dropped the girls off this morning." She tipped her head as a curious expression crossed her face. "Did Nancie really agree to those terms?"

"For now." He couldn't help but chuckle at Ruth's incredulous, wide-eyed stare. In fact, he felt much the same way—awestruck—and the small victory had boosted his confidence by leaps and bounds.

That's how George would have handled things, he mused in the front hallway as Ruth rounded up his daughters. However, Wren knew in his heart that any battles won with Nancie stemmed purely from God's grace. Yesterday afternoon's triumph was, very simply, a blessing from heaven.

Shifting his stance, Wren leaned on the doorjamb. *I've got to make sure that George gives the glory to the Lord for his successes,* he decided, thinking over his story line. He was ready to begin writing chapter three, and his fingers itched to get to the computer keyboard.

"Da-ad," Alexa said, bringing Wren out of his faraway thoughts, "me and Laura are ready to go."

He smiled, feeling a tad embarrassed. "Great."

Together the three of them walked to the car. The sky was overcast, the air cool. Climbing in behind the wheel, Wren wondered what to do with Alexa tonight while he was at writing class. He supposed he could ask Julie, his neighbor upstairs, but he hated to bother her again.

He drove the half-mile from Whitefish Bay to Shorewood and parked in front of his house. The girls jumped out of the car, grabbing their backpacks and spring jackets, and dashed to the porch. Wren met them there moments later and unlocked the door.

"What's for supper, Daddy?" Laura said, plopping down on the sofa. "I'm hungry."

"To tell you the truth, I hadn't thought about it." Wren began unbuttoning his shirt as he headed for the shower. "Stick in one of those videos we got from the library Saturday, and I'll think about making you two something to eat while I'm washing up and changing."

Entering his bedroom, he heard muttered replies. Then, as he removed his uniform and pulled on a bathrobe, he mentally took stock of his cupboards and refrigerator. He hadn't gone grocery shopping in a long while. There wasn't much in the way of ingredients for a healthy meal, although he had dry cereal, milk, eggs, and a loaf of bread. Maybe he could make them breakfast for dinner.

After a long, hot shower, Wren shrugged back into his terry cloth robe and left the steamy bathroom. In his room once more, he dressed in blue jeans and a Wisconsin Badgers sweatshirt before stuffing his stockinged feet into white leather athletic shoes.

As he sat on the bed tying the laces, he suddenly smelled something—something good. Garlic. Tomato. Maybe pizza. His mouth watered.

"Alexa, what are you doing?" he called, leaving his bedroom and strolling to the kitchen. "Are you cooking?" He stopped short at the doorway. His eldest daughter was cooking, all right. Laura, too. But they had some help—Risa. Wren smiled. "What are you doing here?"

"I'm creating a Caesar salad. What does it look like I'm doing?"

He smacked his palm to his forehead. "Silly me. I should have known."

The girls giggled at the exchange, and Risa grinned. "Seriously, though, I made up a pan of lasagna last night," she explained, "and I thought I'd share the leftovers. When I arrived, Alexa and Laura told me they were hungry, so I decided to take liberties in your kitchen." She paused, and her hazel-eyed gaze bore into his. "I hope you don't mind."

"Not at all," Wren replied, looking away and focusing on his daughters. Boy, was he glad he'd picked them up this evening. They'd act as chaperons, of sorts. He enjoyed Risa's company, but he was beginning to enjoy it far too much. Sure, he was divorced, unattached by the world's standards; but he felt certain that dating and marrying any woman other than his ex-wife was not in God's plan for his life. The Lord had made it clear to Wren that he'd taken a vow "till death do we part," and now he had an obligation to uphold that promise. Besides, Risa wasn't a Christian. That was another reason he couldn't entertain thoughts of developing a romantic relationship with her.

"Dinner will be ready shortly," she said, flipping a thick portion of her curly carrot-orange hair over her shoulder.

"Great. Maybe I'll watch the news for a while."

Risa followed him into the living room. "Are you mad at me, Wren, for barging in on you like this?"

He pivoted. "Not at all." He shook his head, chastening himself for giving her that impression. Looking her squarely in the eyes, he added, "But I do think there's a guy out there, somewhere, who's more deserving of your culinary skills than I am."

"Oh yeah?" She tipped her head sassily. "Find him. I've been searching for years, Wren. You're the most decent man I've met so far." Raising a brow, she smirked. "And you're not bad-looking either."

A flash of chagrin warmed his face. "You sure know how to get to a guy."

"I'm trying," she replied impishly before spinning around and heading toward the kitchen.

"Risa..."

"I know, I know," she said over her shoulder with a backward glance. "We're just friends."

∽

Nancie stood on the porch and rang Wren's doorbell. She pushed up the sleeve of her blouse and peered at her wristwatch. Six-fifteen. She'd gotten out of work forty-five minutes late only to discover that Wren had picked up the girls. Consequently, she'd had to backtrack over here. An extra trip. . .and she felt so tired. What's more, her head was beginning to pound from yesterday's injury and the stress at the office today.

Suddenly the inside door opened and Laura gazed up at her. "Hi, Mumma."

"Hi, sweetie, can I come in?"

The little girl nodded. Nancie pulled on the screen door and entered the house. The aroma of Italian spices assailed her senses at once, causing her stomach to grumble with hunger. Then she spotted Alexa on the couch with her math book open.

"Did you two eat supper already?"

Laura was the one to answer. "Yep. Lex and me helped Risa make it, too."

"Risa. . . ?"

No sooner had Nancie uttered the name when out from the kitchen stepped a lovely redhead. In two sweeping glances, Nancie noted how well the woman's jeans hugged her slim hips and how the fitted green sweater, with its deep V-neck, complemented her full figure.

"Hi," the woman greeted her as she entered the living room. There was a slight edge to her voice. "I'm Risa Vitalis."

"Nancie Nickelson."

"I figured that's who you were. Wren's ex, huh?"

"That's right." Nancie knew her tone sounded flat, wary. Was this Wren's girlfriend or a very shapely babysitter? No, it couldn't be his girlfriend, she silently reasoned. Risa didn't appear to be the kind who would fall for a boring mailman. She must be a neighbor. . . .

"This is Risa, Mumma," Laura said.

"Yes, we just met." She looked at her eldest, who still hadn't uttered a word to her. "Hello, Alexa."

"Hi." The girl didn't even glance up from her textbook.

Nancie sighed. Why did everything in her life suddenly seem so hopeless? "Get your stuff together, Laura. Let's get going."

"Okay."

While Laura collected her belongings, Nancie chanced a look at Risa. To her dismay, the woman was eyeing her speculatively.

"Something wrong?" Nancie asked.

"No. I was just thinking." Risa sat down on the arm of the couch and forced a smile.

"Uh-huh. . ." Nancie couldn't have cared less.

At that moment Wren walked in carrying a dish towel, drying his hands with it. "Hi, Nancie."

"Hi."

"How's your head?"

"It hurts," she said curtly.

"Sorry to hear that." Nancie recognized his nervous expression. She saw him glance at Risa. "Have you two met?"

"Just did," the redhead replied with a genuine smile for Wren. And the way she gazed up at him left no doubt in Nancie's mind as to her intentions. She was definitely not the babysitter. The only puzzle was that Wren acted unaware of her adoration.

Nancie's curiosity got the best of her. "Are you two dating?"

"I'm dating him," Risa said with a small laugh, "and I'm striving for reciprocation."

"Knock it off, will you?" Wren replied with a chuckle before bringing his gaze back to Nancie. "We're just friends."

"How nice," Nancie muttered, although she didn't believe a word of it. Friends? Yeah, right.

Then she noticed that Alexa was watching Risa closely and wearing a fond expression. A stab of jealousy pierced her heart. It seemed to Nancie that the Italian beauty was destined to replace her in more ways than one.

"Say, Wren, why don't you ask your ex about tonight?"

The question captivated Nancie's attention. "What about tonight?"

"Forget it, Risa."

"Oh, just ask her. The worst she can say is 'no.' "

A dubious expression waved across his features.

"Ask me what?" The question escaped Nancie's lips with an air of indignation.

He shifted his stance and chewed his lower lip for a brief moment before explaining. "Risa and I have a class tonight and I don't have a sitter for Alexa. We could take her along—"

"Yeah!" the eleven-year-old exclaimed with glee.

"But it does run kind of late," Wren finished despite the interruption. "Besides, you'd be bored, Lex."

"You're taking a class?" Nancie hadn't gotten past that bit of information. It seemed too incredible. For years she'd nagged Wren to further his education in one form or another and better himself, but he'd refused. Now he was actually doing that very thing? Nancie wondered if the voluptuous woman in the snug green sweater had had something to do with it.

Again the pang of jealousy.

"I know you're still recovering from last night's ordeal," Wren continued.

"No. That's all right. I'll stay with the girls." She wasn't sure why she had volunteered so quickly, but Nancie sensed that she had to. For the sake of her relationship with Alexa, if for no other reason. Somehow she had to change her image in her daughter's eyes, and it had to top Alexa's opinion of Risa.

"Are you sure, Nancie?" Wren asked, a tiny frown furrowing his brows.

She nodded. "I'm sure."

"Great," Risa said as she stood up. "We should get going, too. Class starts at seven."

"The girls ate already," Wren stated informatively.

"Yes, Laura told me."

"There's plenty of lasagna left, so help yourself."

"Thanks."

Risa found her large black satchel and swung it over her shoulder. A few feet away, Nancie watched as Wren gathered up a stack of white pages that lay next to the portable printer on his dining room table. He carried them to the built-in wooden buffet and locked them in the top drawer. Next, he dropped the key into the pencil holder above it.

"What kind of class are you two taking?" Nancie asked.

"Creative writing." Risa looked at Wren. "Ready?"

"Ready."

Nancie had to keep her jaw from dropping. "Creative writing? Wren, I didn't know you could write. I didn't know you were even interested in writing."

"He is. And he's really good, too," Risa gushed.

Wren's expression was one of sheer embarrassment. He tried to hide it by kissing the girls good-bye and giving Alexa last-minute instructions.

"Dad, I don't want Mom to stay here," Nancie heard the girl whine under her breath. "Can't I come with you?"

Nancie fought against the billow of hurt and insult that came crashing at her. "Alexa," she all but pleaded, "let's get along tonight, okay? I love you and I don't want bad feelings between us."

Wren muttered something for Alexa's ears only, and she finally nodded in agreement. "Thanks, Nancie," he said, turning toward her. "Make yourself at home."

She summoned a tiny smile. "Sure. Have fun."

Risa told the girls good-bye and left without so much as a backward glance at Nancie.

Wren followed her out and closed the door behind them.

Chapter 6

By nine o'clock, Alexa had obediently crawled into bed, while Laura lay on the couch, watching a silly video about personified vegetables. Nancie had never seen the likes of it before, but Laura claimed her father deemed it appropriate, so it had to be. Wren was a fanatic about what the girls watched on television—another thing about him that drove Nancie crazy. How would their daughters ever grow up to be worldly-wise if Wren continued to shelter them the way he did?

She expelled an exasperated sigh and took her plate into the kitchen, depositing it in the sink. The lasagna had tasted delicious. At first Nancie had stubbornly decided against eating any, but finally hunger got the best of her.

After rinsing dishes, Nancie ambled into Alexa's bedroom. "Sleep well, honey."

"G'night, Mom."

Nancie smiled and turned away from the partially closed door. She and Alexa had gotten along very well tonight. Finally. A step in the right direction.

Walking back into the living room and passing through the dining area, Nancie paused beside the buffet and stared at the drawer that Wren had locked before he left. What were those papers he'd stuffed inside? Had he lied to her? Was he really seeking custody of the girls? Were those legal briefs?

She glanced at Laura, still engrossed in the video. She looked toward Alexa's room and felt confident that she would stay in bed. Quietly, swiftly, Nancie fished the key out of the pencil holder, then opened the drawer. With deft fingers she removed the pages. One quick scan told her they were neatly typed and printed, but not any kind of legal documents.

She began to read, staying close to the open drawer in case Wren should come home. Chapter one. . .

This is a story that Wren's in the process of writing, she soon deduced. It wasn't too bad either. Perhaps a bit sappy and nothing like the polished literature she was accustomed to reading for her college courses, but it was decent. A guy named George purchased a castle in Germany. . . .

She read to page three and met the character Wren had named "Nan." She bore a striking resemblance to herself, and Nancie wasn't sure if she should feel flattered, insulted, or alarmed. Several pages later, Nancie decided she was definitely offended. Nan was a villainess who thwarted George at every turn, but through it all, he still loved her.

Nancie snorted in disgust. Did Wren really see her as a "Nan"? Did he see himself as the macho character named George?

"You know you love me, Nan," George said. He captured her in a heated embrace.

Nancie rolled her eyes.

"Let go of me, you brute. I hate you. I'll always hate you."

"Prove it." George's lips fastened to hers, and just as he presumed, Nan responded to his kiss.

"Oh, good grief," Nancie muttered. "Wren is writing smut!"

She heard the front door open and quickly placed the manuscript back into the drawer, closed, and locked it—all in three smooth moves. Taking a deep breath, she met Wren in the living room. Risa wasn't with him.

"How was class?"

He shrugged. "Okay. How were things here?"

"Fine."

"Really?" Wren looked surprised.

"Really. Alexa and I got along great."

"Glad to hear it."

"I'm glad to report it," Nancie said emphatically. She folded her arms. "Tell me about the creative writing course."

Immediately, Wren appeared uncomfortable. "Nothing really to tell. I registered for it so I could keep myself busy last winter. The class is just about over now."

"Did you meet Risa there?"

He shook his head. "No. We both work at the post office. Risa's the station manager, in fact, but she's the one who talked me into enrolling."

"Do you like it? Writing, I mean. . .do you like writing?"

He gave her a nod before picking up Laura off the couch and setting her feet on the carpeted floor. "Time to get you to bed." Giving Nancie an apologetic glance, he added, "Sorry I'm so late. Risa and I stopped for a cup of coffee."

She arched a brow. "Just friends, huh?"

"Just friends," Wren said with an earnest expression.

"And pigs fly."

He narrowed his gaze. "What do you mean?"

"Do you really expect me to believe you've got a platonic relationship with a woman like her?"

"A woman like her. . . ?"

"Oh Wren, don't play dumb. Or are you blind? No man in his right mind would ever be content to be 'just friends' with a woman who's got a dynamite figure like Risa's."

"I don't allow myself to look at her figure, and I definitely don't think about it."

"Then what do you do?"

He grinned. "I write."

It was a reply to end all replies; Nancie couldn't think of anything else to say.

"Are you two fighting?" Laura asked, looking worried.

"No, baby. Your mother and I are just discussing something. But you two need to go now. It's past your bedtime."

"Mine, too," Nancie quipped.

Looking over Laura's blond head at her, Wren smiled. "Thanks for helping me out tonight."

"Sure. I owed you one, remember? But if you must know, my motives for staying with the girls tonight were purely selfish. I wanted to spend some time with Alexa."

"That's not selfish, Nancie. That's a mother's heart." Wren helped Laura gather her things and then showed them to the door. "Good night."

He hunkered down in front of Laura, and she hugged him around the neck before they exchanged kisses.

"I love you, Daddy."

"Love you, too, baby."

He straightened, and his brown-eyed gaze bore into Nancie. She held her breath, waiting for him to say he loved her, too.

But he didn't.

"Good night," he said.

" 'Night, Wren." With that Nancie led Laura down the walkway and to her car. She felt oddly disappointed, but immediately told herself that was nonsense. She didn't want Wren to love her. She didn't love him.

Once in the car, she pulled away from the curb and refused to look back.

∽

The rest of the week proceeded much like Monday had. Every day after work, Wren picked up the girls. Ruth said she didn't mind that he came two hours early now that the weather was getting nicer. She and her husband, Max, owned a sailboat and liked to spend evenings at the yacht club. The sooner her charges went home, the sooner the Bairds could go to the lake. Wren, too, was happy with the arrangement. He figured the girls would spend ten hours fewer in day care each week, and he would save some money. What's more, he got to spend extra time with his daughters, particularly Laura, and so far, Nancie hadn't balked at the change in routine.

She did surprise Wren, however, by showing up at his front door on Friday evening.

"I thought I'd bring a few more of Alexa's things over," Nancie said, handing him a small pink duffle bag.

"Thanks." Wren eyed her curiously. She hadn't been acting like herself for the past few days. "Everything okay? You seem down in the dumps lately. . .depressed."

"It's been a long week."

Wren nodded. He knew what those were like.

"Any plans this weekend?" she asked.

He furrowed his brow in thought. "Nothing special. How 'bout you?"

Nancie shook her head.

"Well, use the time to relax. You said you've been stressed."

"Yeah. . ." Turning, she descended the steps of the worn porch with peeling paint.

"Have a good weekend," he called.

She just sort of waved over her shoulder.

Odd, he thought as he reentered the house.

◠

Nancie's peculiar behavior bothered Wren right up until Saturday afternoon. That's when he remembered: *Tomorrow's Mother's Day!*

"Girls," he called into the backyard, where they were at play with some neighbor kids. "Come on inside a minute."

They did as he asked, and once he had their full attention, Wren announced that they were going shopping for Mother's Day gifts.

"Good thing you remembered, Daddy," Laura said.

"No kidding." Wren wondered how the date had snuck up on him this way, but at least he hadn't missed it altogether. He made a mental note to buy his own mother a gift while he and the girls shopped today. The three of them could visit her tomorrow afternoon—his mother always loved to see the girls.

"Last year Mom was at school," Alexa remarked as they walked to the car.

"That's right," Wren answered. "She took summer classes last year, didn't she?"

Alexa nodded. "I think she likes school more than Laura and me."

"That's not true, Lex," Wren said, opening the car door. "And you've got to stop thinking like that. It hurts your mother when you say those things."

"She says bad things about you," his daughter spouted.

"Like what?" Wren usually discouraged Alexa from tattling, but this time he thought he'd hear her out. Maybe if he allowed her to vent, she'd feel better.

"Mom said it's your fault that you guys are divorced. She said you weren't a good husband. You didn't make her happy."

"I suppose that's partly true."

Alexa's eyes grew wide with indignation. "No, it's not!"

"Look, Lex, I tried my best to please your mom, but I'm sure there are things I could have—should have—done better."

The child's face fell. "But I remember how she yelled at you that one night and told you to leave. I hate it that you and Mom are divorced now."

"I hate it, too. But being angry isn't going to change things."

Alexa cast her gaze at her feet. Wren cupped her chin and forced her to look back at him.

"Your mom needs the Lord. She doesn't know Him like you and Laura do. You need to show her the love of Jesus, and you can't do that if you're angry with her."

Fat tears pooled in the girl's eyes, so Wren pulled her against his chest and kissed the top of her head, rubbing her back consolingly. After several long moments he gave her a gentle squeeze and then steered her into the backseat of the car.

"Better now?"

Alexa nodded, albeit reluctantly, as she wiped her eyes with her palms.

"Good." He closed the door and walked around to the driver's side. Seating himself behind the wheel, he decided he had required that little lecture as much as Alexa. It was a good reminder. They were the "light" Nancie needed to see.

Chapter 7

Mother's Day.

Nancie forced herself out of bed, feeling hollow, empty. . .lonely. Knotting the tie of her white satin bathrobe at the waist, she padded to the kitchen and set a pot of coffee to brewing. She figured she had the post-semester blues—similar to the letdown some people experience right after Christmas. She'd been so busy for so long that now she felt isolated, which was especially depressing today.

Wren could have been more sensitive, she inwardly groused. But he obviously hadn't remembered the day's significance—that was evident on Friday night when she'd stopped over. She wondered if he and Risa had plans with the girls, although Nancie really had no evidence on which to base that notion. She'd questioned Laura, who claimed she'd only met the other woman twice—at a picnic last Saturday and then Monday night. Most likely, what Wren had told her about his relationship with Risa was true. But Nancie guessed it wouldn't be long before she'd be hearing about a budding romance, and she secretly envied them.

Coffee in hand, she walked to the door, opened it cautiously, and retrieved her thick Sunday newspaper. She still felt somewhat anxious from last week's mugging. As she made her way to her favorite, most comfortable chair, the doorbell sounded, causing Nancie to jump and spill the steaming liquid in her cup onto the carpet.

"Aw, man…" She hurried to the kitchen to fetch some paper towels. On her way back, she paused at the intercom.

"Yes," she answered.

"Happy Mother's Day!" her daughters cried from the lobby.

A twinge of guilt assailed her. So Wren had remembered after all….

Nancie buzzed up the girls, and within the time it took her to sponge up the coffee spill, they were knocking at the door. She opened it, and two colorful presents were thrust at her.

"How nice," she said with a smile.

Alexa and Laura entered the apartment, encouraging Nancie to open the gifts.

"We can't stay too long," Alexa added. "Dad is out in the car waiting, and we have to go to church."

"You don't have to, Alexa," Nancie told her. "If you don't want to attend church with your father, he can't force you to go."

"No, Mom," she said, shaking her light brown head, "I do want to go…it's just that we have to get going or we'll be late."

Nancie replied with a single nod. Ever since the divorce, Alexa had defended her father. While it didn't irk Nancie any less now than it had in the past eighteen months, she was making a concerted effort to hide her emotions in an attempt to salvage the relationship between herself and her oldest daughter.

"Thanks for the Mother's Day present," Nancie told Alexa, opening hers first. Under the bright, floral-patterned paper, she found a blank scrapbook and pretty paper. "Oh, wonderful!"

"I know how you like taking pictures and making scrapbooking pages about us." Alexa said.

"I do. Thanks." Nancie gave her a hug and kiss, thankful the girl allowed it. Perhaps Alexa was working toward harmony between them, too.

She opened Laura's then—a box of chocolate candy and a bottle of bubble bath.

"Thank you, sweetheart."

"Do you like it? Here…smell."

Laura unscrewed the cap, and Nancie took a whiff of foaming bath liquid.

"Mmm, nice."

Laura beamed. "All of us can use it, so we smell good."

Nancie chuckled lightly.

"C'mon, Laura, we gotta go," Alexa said. "Dad's waiting."

"Okay."

The girls kissed their mother good-bye, and Nancie thought Alexa seemed sincere with her affection and in wishing her a good Mother's Day. But as she walked them to the door, Nancie's heart sank. Once they left, she'd be alone again. *It's my fault,* she admitted. *I should have planned better. I should have told Wren I was going to switch the schedule so I could have the girls with me today.* Tears of remorse filled her eyes.

"What's wrong, Mumma?" Laura asked, catching a glimpse of her misty eyes.

Nancie quickly blinked her tears away. "Nothing, honey," she fibbed. "You guys have fun today."

"We're going to see Grandma," Alexa said. "Dad bought her one of those jigsaw puzzles she likes."

"I'm sure she'll appreciate that," Nancie replied, remembering how Wren's mother could sit for hours pressing together all those pieces. Simple. That's where Wren got it from, she guessed. But Nancie didn't dislike her former mother-in-law. In fact, they still corresponded from time to time.

After one more kiss and final waves of good-bye, the girls departed. Nancie looked over her gifts again, knowing Wren had most likely paid for them—and had miraculously removed the price tags. Nancie grinned ruefully. After twelve years of Mother's Day presents, he'd finally gotten that part right.

~

"What do you mean she was crying?" Wren inquired after getting Laura's report.

"She's sad, Daddy. I can tell."

"Maybe they were tears of joy because she liked your present so much," Wren suggested.

He looked at Alexa, who just shrugged. No help there.

Shifting his gaze back to Laura, he asked, "You really think she's sad? Should I see if I can find out what's wrong?" Wren knew it wasn't like Nancie to cry. That simply wasn't her style.

In response to his question, the child nodded her blond head vigorously.

"Lex? What do you think?"

Again a noncommittal up-and-down of her slender shoulders. "If you want to, I guess. . ."

Wren thought it over. "All right, you two. . .wait here. I'm going to talk with your mother."

In the small, locked lobby, he rang Nancie's apartment. After he announced himself, she buzzed him upstairs.

"Did one of the girls forget something?" Nancie asked, meeting him at the doorway. She was clad in a low, scoop-necked white night-gown and robe, which caused Wren's mouth to go dry. Suddenly he recalled the unique softness of her body—every freckle, every curve. . . .

Casting his gaze at his feet, he shifted his stance and scratched his jaw uncomfortably. Why did that memory have to surface now?

"Wren?"

"Umm. . ." He forced himself to look into her face—and only there. "Laura said you were crying and I. . .well, I thought I'd make sure you're okay."

She frowned slightly before setting her hands on her hips. "Don't you ever get tired of being a nice guy? Nice guys finish last, don't you know that by now?"

He drew back. "Well, I can see you're just fine," he said, struggling in vain to keep the edge out of his voice. "See ya later."

He turned and headed down the dimly lit hallway.

"Wren, wait. . . . I'm sorry. You didn't deserve that."

He paused and slowly turned back around.

Just then a curious neighbor from across the way poked his gray head out the door and stared at Nancie. She quickly waved Wren inside her apartment, and after he was in, she closed the door soundly.

"That guy is such a busybody. His wife is, too."

Wren didn't reply. He just stood there, still smarting from Nancie's retort about "nice guys."

She walked slowly toward him, and he looked away. Didn't she have any idea what a temptress she was at the moment?

"I've got to get going," he muttered, pulling the car keys from his trouser pocket. He wanted something to hold so he wouldn't be enticed to hold her, although he seriously doubted she'd allow him any such pleasure. She didn't love him anymore. She was fond of saying so. Why couldn't he get that through his thick skull?

"You're nervous," she said.

"The girls are out in the car. I don't want to leave them there too long."

He didn't see Nancie's reaction because he refused to take his eyes off the keys he continued to turn in his palm.

"Wren, I'm sorry for what I said before."

He nodded, although he knew that's what she thought of him. In her mind, he definitely was a loser.

"And if you must know, yes, I was crying," she continued. "I don't feel like being without my children on Mother's Day."

Wren sighed wearily. "Nancie..."

"I know. It's nobody's fault but mine."

"I won't argue with that," he said sheepishly.

Glancing at her at last, he saw her kind of roll her eyes.

"The girls and I have plans to visit my mother," he began, thinking Nancie expected him to alter his arrangements for her...again. He didn't want to, but maybe they could work out a compromise.

"Could I come with you?"

Wren blinked. He couldn't believe what he just heard. "What?"

"Oh, I suppose Risa is riding along, huh? To meet your parents?"

"Risa?" He frowned. "No. She's in Illinois this weekend visiting some friends. I told you, there's nothing going on between Risa and me."

"That's what you think," Nancie smirked. "That woman wants to make a husband out of you, Wren. I could see it in her eyes when she looked at you."

He conceded a slight nod, knowing full well that's exactly what Risa had in mind, even though he tried to tell her it could never be.

Nancie stepped closer to him, finger-combing back her shoulder-length blond hair. "If you let me come with you today, Wren, I promise I'll be nice. For Alexa's sake."

He peered down at her, noting the pert, freckled nose he used to love to kiss. "What about me?" he fairly croaked. "Do you really think I'm without feelings, Nancie? What do you think spending a day with you will do to me?"

"I said I'll be nice."

"Yeah, that's what I'm worried about." He shook his head and stepped around her, making his way to the door; but Nancie caught his elbow.

"Wren, please? My life is a mess right now. My coworkers think I'm a witch, so I'm trying to change my image at the office. Alexa thinks I hate her, but I'm working on remedying that, too. And I know you and I have been at odds for years, but—"

"Let's get one thing straight," he said, whirling on her. "I was never at odds with you. Everything you wanted, you got. My ambition in life was to please you, Nancie, and you were right when you called me a failure. I failed at making you happy and it still hurts. On the other hand, I admire you for taking note of all the wrongs in your life and trying to set them right. But don't kid yourself. You wouldn't enjoy spending an afternoon with me—even if Alexa and Laura were around."

She let go of his arm and turned away. "You're probably right."

Nodding, he walked the rest of the way to the door. "Treat yourself to lunch, Nancie," he suggested, his hand on the doorknob. "Go shopping."

When no reply came, he stood there scrutinizing her back as she stared out the large living room windows.

Then he saw her shoulders shake slightly.

"Nancie?" Curiously puzzled, he dropped his keys into his pants pocket and stepped forward. When he reached her, he carefully cupped her upper arm and forced her to face him. Tears were slipping from her eyes. "No way," he said in disbelief. "I haven't seen you cry since your mother died."

She practically dissolved in his hands. Soon she was in his arms.

"Oh Wren, I think I'm having a nervous breakdown," she sobbed against his shoulder. "It started after I got jumped last Sunday night. I haven't been able to sleep. I'm anxious. I'm depressed. Maybe I need professional help."

"Maybe you need the Lord," he replied, stroking her silky hair and reveling in the feeling of holding her body close to his. He felt a little guilty for finding any pleasure in her pain, but hadn't this been what he'd been praying for—for God to soften Nancie's heart?

"I just don't want to be alone today," she said with a sniff. Pulling her chin back, she glanced at his shirt before giving him an apologetic smile. "By the way, I slobbered all over your nice, clean Oxford."

Wren shrugged. It seemed a small price to pay for what had just occurred.

Nancie lifted an inquiring brow. "Can you finally iron your own shirts without scorching them?"

He shook his head and grinned. "Alexa irons them for me."

"Wren!"

"Well, she likes to," he said in his own defense. "She irons every Saturday night while Laura cooks supper."

"What?" Nancie backed out of his embrace. "You allow a seven-year-old to use the stove?"

"I'm usually right there." Sensing an argument on the rise, Wren made for the door. "Still want to come this afternoon?" he called over his shoulder.

A pause.

He swung around and lifted an expectant brow.

"Yes," Nancie replied, looking like a lost little girl as she continued to stand by the window.

"You can't try to pick a fight with me," he warned her halfheartedly.

"I won't," she promised, and Wren almost chuckled. She resembled Laura after a thorough reprimand.

"Okay," he acquiesced. "I'll pick you up after church...around noon."

Nancie nodded.

"Have you got a Bible around here?"

"Probably."

"Well," he said, opening the door, "if you've got time, read the Psalms. They'll soothe your soul better than any psychologist."

"Yeah, sure," she replied skeptically. "But I'll be ready at noon."

Wren left the apartment, and for the first time in a very, very long while, there was an airiness to his step and a swell of hope in his heart.

Chapter 8

Risa approached Wren as he prepared to leave for the day. "Did you have a good weekend?" she called from several feet away.

He smiled upon seeing her, and Risa's heart soared. "Yeah. How 'bout you?"

"Good. I spent time with some friends I hadn't seen in a long while."

"That's always nice."

Risa nodded and folded her arms. "What did you do?"

"Well, Saturday was pretty much an ordinary day," he replied, leaning up against a nearby doorjamb as they stood conversing in the back room. "Sunday after church," he continued, "I took the girls to visit my mother, who lives about an hour and a half north of here, and my ex-wife came along."

"She did?" Risa felt her eyes grow wide.

"Uh-huh. Nancie was on her best behavior, too." He chuckled lightly.

"I don't understand you, Wren. From what you've told me, it sounds like your ex has been extremely selfish throughout your marriage. She took you to the cleaners when she divorced you. She's mean and condescending. How can you act civil toward her, let alone spend an afternoon with her?"

He shrugged and his smile faded. "Nancie's going through a hard time right now, and I feel obligated as a Christian to be there for her."

"You're too good to be true," Risa declared with a wag of her head.

"No, I'm not. You just don't know me very well."

She grinned. "I know you well enough. . . . Say, are you going to class tonight?"

"Sure am. Are you?"

Risa nodded.

"Nancie said she'd stay with the girls again."

"Great." Risa took a step closer. "Can I bring dinner over like I did last week?"

"I don't know if that's a good idea," he said, growing serious. "Risa, I don't want you to foster any hope that—"

"Not to worry," she cut in. "We're just friends. But I happen to have a taste for veal parmigiana, and I hate to cook just for myself. Besides, Wren, I'm Italian. I love to feed people. You and the girls have to eat, right? Sounds like a match to me."

"Only if it's a platonic one," he quipped.

"Right."

Wren cracked a smile. "Veal parmigiana, huh?"

"I make the best."

"You drive a hard bargain, Risa. You caught me at a weak moment. I'm starved."

She laughed. "I just have to take care of a few things and then I'll come over to your place."

Wren gave her a parting smile before leaving the postal station.

Watching him go, Risa felt a bittersweet pang. While she might access Wren's kitchen this evening, she still hadn't gained entry to his heart.

⁓

The woman could definitely cook—Nancie had to give her that much. Never in her life had she tasted such a delicious meal.

"I think you should marry her, Wren," Nancie whispered to him as she carried several plates in from the dining room. They were alone in the kitchen, and he stood at the sink, washing the dishes. "You'd never starve to death."

He sort of smirked, but didn't look up from the silverware in his hands.

"Why don't you marry her?" Nancie asked, seriously now. She couldn't help it. She didn't understand him. Risa was gorgeous and obviously smitten with him. Wasn't Wren human?

"I don't love her," he stated simply.

A flash caught her eye, and she spied the wedding ring he continued to wear on his left hand. "Wren, we're divorced. You're free to pursue a relationship with Risa."

He finally glanced at her, shook the water off his hands, and reached for the dish towel. "Thanks for giving me your permission," he stated with a note of sarcasm. "But Risa and I are just friends, and that's the way I want it to stay."

"Why?"

"Because I personally believe God gave me one shot at marriage, and I blew it."

"Don't be so hard on yourself. Besides, chances are you wouldn't blow it a second time."

After a noncommittal shrug of his broad shoulders, he began drying and putting away the dishes. His lack of response irked her for some reason, and Nancie shook her head at him before leaving the kitchen. She found Risa in the dining room, clearing the rest of the table. Nancie picked up a few glasses.

"He's a lost cause," she told the flaming-haired woman. "Don't waste your time."

"I assume you're speaking about Wren."

"Uh-huh. He's behind the times. I can't imagine what you see in him."

"You want to know what I see?" Risa countered. "I see a wonderful, chivalrous, caring man who stands by his word."

"I've got firsthand news for you, honey. Chivalry is boring."

"And I've got firsthand news for you. Chivalry is refreshing. There aren't many decent men left in this world."

Risa walked into the kitchen, leaving Nancie to mull over the reply. Finally, she gave up and decided it was all relative. In the same way that one man's junk was another's treasure, Nancie supposed one woman's ex-husband could be another's knight in shining armor.

Well, she can have him, she thought cynically. *I certainly don't want him.*

Nancie strolled into the living room, where Laura sat reading a book and Alexa struggled through her math homework. She heard Risa's voice above the din of rushing tap water in the kitchen, and then Wren chuckled at whatever she'd just said. They'd make a good couple, Wren and Risa. Even their names sounded harmonic.

Nancie took a seat beside Alexa and offered to help her.

"No, that's okay, Mom."

She looked across the room at Laura and realized her daughters were growing up fast. Both had been in their glory tonight, helping Risa prepare dinner.

Her mind wandered. *Suppose Wren did indeed marry her. . .would Alexa and Laura want to live with them?* The thought sent a shiver of apprehension up Nancie's spine. If that happened, she'd truly be alone—and solitude was something she'd begun to fear lately. She never imagined herself growing old all by herself, and she certainly wasn't getting any younger.

Shaking off her melancholy, Nancie glanced at Alexa. "Are you enjoying living with your father?"

She nodded.

Nancie noticed Laura's wistful gaze. "Don't tell me you want to live with him, too?"

The child shrugged and turned back to her book.

"Okay," she said, exasperated. "Explain to me why it's so much better over here. Our apartment is nicer."

"We still love you, Mumma," Laura stated with a diplomatic air. "It's just that Daddy needs us."

Arching a questioning brow, Nancie looked back at Alexa. "Is that right?"

"I don't know," her oldest said, keeping her gaze on her arithmetic.

"I understand you iron his shirts and Laura cooks."

A tiny smile peeped out from Alexa's otherwise stony expression.

"You can iron and cook at our apartment, too, you know," Nancie offered glibly.

Before further comment could be made, Wren and Risa entered the room.

"We've got to leave or we'll be late for class," Wren announced. He bent over, cupped Laura's small face in his hands, and kissed her soundly.

"Bye, Daddy," she said, smiling up at him adoringly.

"Lex, get your homework done and I'll check it when I get back."

She nodded, before lifting her chin and puckering her lips to receive Wren's fatherly smooch.

He glanced at Nancie. "Want a kiss, too?"

"No, that's quite all right," she assured him, unable to keep from smiling.

"I'll take one," Risa interjected, a teasing grin on her face.

Wren swung around and laughed. "Out," he demanded lightheartedly, pointing to the front door. "We're going to be late."

Smiling, Risa waved to the children and did as she had been asked.

After he had followed her out of the house, Laura looked over and with a most earnest expression, said, "You should have taken the kiss, Mumma."

∽

George found himself in a quandary. He couldn't help but love Nan, except the captivating Lucia was working her feminine wiles on him again. Her soft-spoken, uplifting words were like a salve after Nan's hatefully spewed sentiments. The woman could be as cruel as she was determined.

Nancie felt her ire on the rise as she continued to read through the third chapter of Wren's silly novel. Cruel? Is that what he thought of her in real life? But a few pages later, the story took an abrupt turn, and her indignation dissolved as she lost herself in the action. She chuckled inwardly when George heroically saved Nan from a raging fire in her apartment building before rescuing other tenants. In response, Nan agreed to fly to Germany with George and give him an estimate on decorating the castle he'd bought.

She resumed reading.

George smiled to himself. Nan had thought being trapped in a raging inferno was horrifying, but she hadn't yet even come close to knowing the true meaning of the word. His dark, spooky castle, with its surrounding moat, wouldn't allow her to escape its confines. Once she was inside, Nan would have nowhere to run when the shadows frightened her. . .except into his arms.

"Oh brother," Nancie muttered. However, she had to admit to feeling thoroughly amused and somewhat intrigued. She wanted to know what would happen next.

She glanced over her shoulder to make sure she hadn't disturbed Laura, who had fallen asleep on the couch. Laura continued to doze peacefully.

She flipped over the page and begin reading chapter four.

> *The flight to Germany was enjoyable. George and Nan got along surprisingly well, which pleased their two beautiful daughters. At the last minute, George had decided to take them along.*

She continued to pore over the manuscript and decided the scene smacked of their Mother's Day outing yesterday afternoon. *Wren must have written this part last night.* She'd already noticed that when she and Wren were on friendly terms, so were George and Nan. When they weren't, Lucia began sounding more like the heroine of the story. This was obviously a cathartic project for Wren—and he'd all but admitted as much last week.

Suddenly she heard the front door open. She hurriedly tucked the loose pages into the drawer where she'd found them. It hadn't been locked tonight.

"Hi," he said, entering the living room and setting down his book bag. "Everything go all right?"

"I'm not the sixteen-year-old babysitter, Wren," she said facetiously, "so you can spare me the interrogation."

He grinned. "Sorry."

She smiled. "How was your writing class?"

"Good. But I'm dying of thirst." He headed for the kitchen, and Nancie followed.

"I noticed you have an old computer. Is that what you use to write your assignments?" She knew it was, but wanted to see if he'd tell her about his novel. Maybe then she wouldn't feel quite so guilty for reading it.

"Yep. I bought that machine at the Salvation Army store for fifty bucks." He took a healthy swig out of the orange juice container.

"Wren, that's gross. Use a glass." To his curious look, she shrugged. "Forget I said that. This is your house."

"Thank you."

"Why don't you buy a better computer? That would make your life simpler."

"Can't afford it right now."

"Oh."

He put the carton back into the fridge and closed the door.

"Do you write other things? Articles for the newspaper. . .anything like that?"

"Yeah, I fool around a little."

"Will you let me read something you wrote?"

Wren shook his dark brown head. "Nope."

"Why?"

"Because I'm not very good, Nancie. This is just a little hobby for me. Kind of like my mother and her jigsaw puzzles."

She opened her mouth, preparing to refute him, but closed it again. She had wanted to tell him he wasn't a bad writer, but she could hardly say such a thing without confessing to snooping.

"I think it's really neat that you've taken up writing," she said carefully. "I'm actually quite impressed."

"You are?"

Nancie nodded.

He stepped closer, then stopped, and stood before her with arms akimbo. Looking up at him, Nancie decided that Wren was still a nice-looking man. She could understand Risa's attraction. A warmth suddenly entered his dark gaze, a response that Nancie recognized.

"Wren, I don't want you to love me anymore."

His dark eyes briefly clouded with anguish. But a moment later, it was gone. "I can't help it. We were married for a long time. My feelings for you are deep-rooted and won't go away just because you changed your mind."

"Fall in love with Risa and be happy."

He narrowed his gaze. "Something tells me you wouldn't really like it if I did."

She arched a challenging brow. "I just suggested it, didn't I? Do you think I say things I don't mean?"

"Uh-huh."

Her palm itched to slap the smirk off his face. But before the thought could become a reality, the unthinkable happened. He backed her up against the kitchen counter and kissed her.

"Wren!" she cried in utter surprise. She gave him a shove, which didn't budge him. "Stop it. You're acting stupid." She thought he was behaving like his George character, and Nancie couldn't quite believe it.

Leaning toward her, he gently grabbed her resisting arms and kissed her temple, her cheek, her neck.

"Knock it off, Wren."

"You really want me to?" he whispered close to her ear.

She hesitated—why, she would never know. But it was all the encouragement he needed. In a heartbeat, Nancie found herself wrapped in his arms with Wren's lips slowly gliding across hers.

"Mom? Dad?"

The spell was broken.

Nancie came to her senses in a flash and pushed on Wren's chest. He moved away easily.

"Now you did it!" she hissed.

Wren turned around, and they both saw Alexa standing in the doorway leading from the hall. Her confused expression said it all; however, the question still tumbled from her lips.

"What are you doing?"

"We're not arguing, Lex," Wren said, a touch of amusement in his voice.

She looked from one to the other, obviously still uncertain.

"It's all right, Alexa," Nancie told her. "Go back to bed. Laura and I were just leaving." She shot Wren a look of derision before marching into the living room.

Within moments, she had Laura up and ready to go. Wren saw them to the door.

"If you're expecting an apology out of me, forget it," he said.

Nancie didn't reply. In truth, she felt as baffled as Alexa had looked. She had enjoyed that little tryst in the kitchen.

But she shouldn't have. They were divorced. There was nothing between them anymore.

"Good night, Nancie," he said after walking them out to the car and helping to situate Laura in the backseat.

" 'Night," she replied in a voice as crisp as the cold, damp wind.

But as she pulled away from the curb, she couldn't help but release a tiny laugh. There wasn't a doubt in her mind that next week she'd be reading this scene in Wren's book.

Chapter 9

"Kissing in the kitchen?" Ruth Baird giggled like a high school girl a few days later. Nancie bristled. "Alexa told me all about it."

"I'm sure she did," Nancie retorted. "I'm going to have to talk to that girl."

"Any chance of you and Wren getting back together? I know that's been his prayer."

"None—and prayers don't work on me. I'm not a religious person."

"Well, that's good."

Nancie blinked, suddenly puzzled. "Good? I thought you were one of those born-again people. . .like Wren."

"I am. But being born again isn't about religion. It's about having a relationship with the Lord Jesus Christ."

"Oh, right. Wren's told me that before."

"Did you ever listen?"

Nancie nodded. "One night I heard him out. I let him show me some Bible verses about sin and hell and how God sent His Son to die for us. But I just don't believe it. I'm an intellect, Ruth. I think all the religions of the world have merit. I find that studying them is fascinating. And you know what's interesting about it all? Each religion claims to be the right and only source of truth."

"But obviously that's not possible, so you have to choose which god you'll serve."

"Or choose no specific god at all, which is what I've done." Nancie glanced at her watch. She had to leave or she'd be late for work. "Ruth, look, I'm into the human experience. I believe that when we die, we'll each go to our own kind of heaven. You and I will have our own unique places in the universe."

"All by ourselves?" Ruth asked with a frown. "That doesn't sound like something to look forward to. I don't want to spend an eternity alone. There's no hope in that.

"My God says I'll share heaven with all His other children," she continued with a wistful expression. "We'll sing and rejoice together and worship the Lord Jesus Christ, free from the worries of this world."

"To each his own," Nancie replied, making her way to the door. "Have a good day, Ruth."

"You, too."

Walking to her car, Nancie felt rocked to the core. She'd never thought of it before. . .spending an eternity alone. That's the last thing she wanted!

But I won't be alone, she thought, squelching the anxiety that had quickened her pulse. *I'll be part of the universe. The moon. The sun. The stars.*

Driving away from the curb, Nancie put a firm halt on her musings. She didn't want to think about death and eternity—not when she had so much to live for!

∽

"Lex, I'm going to play basketball tonight with some of the guys from church. . .and guess what?"

"I have to come along," she replied with little enthusiasm.

"Right. You win the prize!" Wren chuckled.

Alexa rolled her eyes, but smiled all the same.

"Bring your homework if you'd like."

"No. I'll do it when I get back home."

Wren studied his daughter. "Do you think of this as 'home,' Lex? Or do you feel like you have two homes?"

The girl began her reply with a habitual shrug. "To me, there's Mom's home and this home. . .the one I like best."

"Why's that?" Wren probed, pulling on his spring jacket.

"It's got the furniture in it that I remember from our house on Cramer Street."

"Mm, I see." Wren knew that Alexa didn't like change and the divorce had really thrown her. She'd struggled in school for the past year, but had finally worked hard enough to get her grades back up. Now it seemed she was on the emotional mend, surrounded by things that comforted her—things that Nancie had discarded after she'd sold the house. However, there was something else Wren wanted to see happen in his daughter's life. "Lex, you can be happy anywhere—here, at your mother's apartment, or on the mission field, if God calls you there. You can be content wherever you live. You've got His Holy Spirit in you. You're saved by grace, but now you need to learn how to lean on the Lord and depend on Him. He's the only one who can help you roll with the punches—and, trust me, life comes with plenty of them."

She didn't answer, but Wren felt confident that she would at least think it over.

"Dad, are you and Mom going to get back together?"

Wren was momentarily taken aback by the shift in conversation. "I don't know," he said at last.

"She can't really hate you if she had her arms around you and was kissing you."

The grin on his face refused to be stifled, although he couldn't quite believe what had taken place in his kitchen—and he was even more surprised by the fact that he'd initiated the whole thing. "We'll keep praying, okay, Lex?"

She nodded.

"But there is something that would have to happen before your mom and I could get back together," Wren added, serious now. "She would have to become a Christian. Otherwise our marriage would be just as bad as before. . .maybe worse."

"Great. . . That'll never happen," Alexa muttered.

"God can do anything," Wren quickly reminded her. "He saved me, didn't He?"

Wearing her usual indifferent expression, Alexa shrugged.

Together they left the house, pausing on the front porch long enough for Wren to lock the door. Then Alexa pulled on his jacket sleeve.

"Dad, look who's here. . . ."

He turned to see Risa running through the rain from her car. She expelled an audible sigh once she reached them.

"This weather's incredible. It's been storming all week long!"

"Tell me about it," Wren replied. "I've walked my route in this stuff."

"As the station manager," Risa said, lifting her chin and giving herself a look of importance, "I'll be sure to note that in your file and recommend you for a wage increase."

"Promises, promises."

She laughed, and Wren joined her. Alexa watched curiously.

"Where are you guys off to?" Tendrils of wavy red hair were rain-plastered to the side of her face.

"Dad's playing basketball in the gym at our church."

"Oh, I'd like to see that," Risa said with an impish grin.

"Good. You can keep me company, 'cause Dad's making me go."

Wren felt that his fate had just been sealed. No point in arguing about it either—he'd never win. "All right, come on. . . ."

They stepped off the porch and walked briskly down the cement walkway. Just as they reached the car, Nancie pulled up to the curb and rolled down the window of her vehicle. She glanced at Wren before surveying his entourage.

"I have some shopping to do," she said, "and I wondered if Alexa wanted to come along."

Wren looked over at his daughter, who shook her head.

"You mean you'd prefer to watch your old man shoot hoops than spend money, Lex? What's wrong with you?"

She responded with a laugh and climbed into the car.

Wren gave Nancie a bewildered look. "I'll never figure out a woman's mind."

"Nope, probably not," she replied. "Where you going?"

"To play basketball with some friends. Lex and Risa are coming as spectators."

"Really? Well, in that case, how about taking Laura with you? She doesn't feel like shopping."

His youngest peered at him from the backseat. "Please, Daddy, can I come with you?"

"Sure, come on," he agreed.

Laura was out of Nancie's car and into his in a matter of moments.

"What time will you be through?"

"Maybe nine," Wren replied.

"Oh...well, I won't be shopping for that long. Where are you playing?"

"At the church."

Nancie nodded. "Okay, I'll pick Laura up there."

"It's a date," he said without really thinking about it.

She did a double take, casting him an annoyed look in the process, before driving off.

Way to go, he admonished himself. Nancie acted as though she hadn't forgiven him for taking such liberties in his kitchen, and now he had to go and mention the subject of dating, even if it had been in fun. No doubt he'd fueled her fiery temper. *I can be such an idiot.*

Getting into his car, he started the engine. "Everyone ready?"

"All set," Risa said from the passenger seat beside him. "I can't wait to see you play. I'll bet you're a very good ball player."

"Well, I don't know. . . ." He glanced at her and she smiled back; Wren noted the ardent gleam in her eyes. "I guess I'm not too bad."

ᗏ

The rain came down in sheets. Nancie began to wonder if it would ever stop. The whole week had been like this, some storms generating enough water to flood underpasses and highways. Tonight's weather seemed to be particularly intense. The wind tore through the treetops, and newly budded branches littered the streets and lawns as she drove away from the shopping mall.

Reaching the church, Nancie ran from her car and into the building. She knew where to find the gymnasium, since Wren had been a member of this particular congregation for the past five years. As she neared her destination, the sounds of a bouncing basketball and athletic shoes squeaking on the polished floor grew louder, as did the grunts, groans, and cheers of the six male players. She cast them a quick glance before making her way to the wooden bleachers where Risa sat watching the game; Alexa and Laura were fooling around down at the other end.

"Are we having fun yet?" Nancie asked Risa facetiously.

She smiled slightly and turned back to the ball game. "I'm enjoying myself. Did you have fun shopping?"

Nancie sat down beside her. "I don't know if I'd call it fun, but I found what I needed." Following Risa's gaze, she saw Wren—dressed in navy nylon wind pants and a red T-shirt—preparing to shoot. A moment later, the ball swished through the hoop.

"Nice shot, Wren!" Risa shouted encouragingly.

"Go, Dad!" Alexa called from the far end of the bleachers.

Laura jumped up and down. "Yea!"

Nancie rolled her eyes. "Wren's head is going to get so big, he'll never get it through the gymnasium doorway tonight."

Risa regarded her thoughtfully for several long moments. "You know what I wish?" she finally said. "I wish you'd get out of Wren's life forever."

"Excuse me?" Nancie couldn't believe what she'd just heard.

"I know your kind," Risa went on. "You're a user and abuser of sweethearted guys like Wren. You're only nice to him when it serves your purposes, otherwise you tear him down every chance you get."

Nancie lofted a brow. "It's none of your business what I do." She eyed the red-haired woman speculatively. "At least now I know where Alexa got her hateful attitude toward me."

"Not a chance," Risa replied with an amused grin. "You can't pin that one on me. Alexa is an intelligent girl. She sees you for what you are—a selfish, self-seeking individual who gives little or no thought to others."

Nancie stood and called for Laura. She wasn't about to stay and listen to any more of this nonsense. As her youngest collected her spring coat, Nancie almost smirked. She ought to tell Risa about how Wren kissed her the other night and said he'd always love her. The twit was wasting her time; Wren wasn't interested in her.

At that moment Wren walked over to the bleachers, accompanied by a dark-haired man.

"What's going on?" he asked, looking concerned.

"Ask your girlfriend," Nancie replied tersely. Grabbing Laura's hand, she left the gym and headed for home.

Chapter 10

$\mathcal{I}$m sorry, Wren," Risa said. "I couldn't help it."

He shoved his hands into the pockets of his wind pants and stared at his gym shoes. Risa could tell he was disappointed in her for spouting off to his ex-wife. The guy beside him looked somewhat concerned, too, which only increased Risa's discomfort.

"Well, look, what's done is done," the man said. "God can use this, too."

"Sorry," Risa stated once more.

Wren looked up, sent her a wink, and her insides began to quiet. He wasn't angry with her.

She turned and considered the other man. He stood a few inches shorter than Wren and had thick, jet-black hair and a dark five-o'clock shadow covering his jaw. His white T-shirt was stained with perspiration from his efforts on the basketball court. "Who's your friend?"

"I guess it's my turn to apologize," Wren said. "I should have introduced you guys. Risa, this is Mike Gerardi. Mike, meet Risa Vitalis."

"It's a pleasure," he replied, sticking out his right hand.

Risa gave it a shake. "Same here."

Folding his arms across his wide chest, Mike frowned. "Vitalis. Hey, you aren't related to Alphonso Vitalis, are you?"

Risa searched her memory. "Does he have a brother named

Joseph and a sister, Marie?"

"Yeah, that's him."

"He's my father's cousin." Risa chuckled. "Aren't all of us Italians related somehow?"

"I suppose so," he said with a charming grin. "Alphonso is a good friend of my family's."

Risa nodded politely before turning her attention back to Wren.

Mike did the same. "So, you think your ex will start World War III now, or what?"

"Your guess is as good as mine," Wren replied. "Nancie is unpredictable."

"Kinda like this weather," Mike remarked as thunder rumbled. It was loud enough to be audible in the gym. Moments later, the lights flickered.

Risa held her tongue. She would have liked to comment on Nancie Nickelson's "stormy" personality, but figured she'd done enough damage for one night.

"Want to get going?" Wren asked her.

She nodded, but sensed it was really his wish.

"Hey, nice to meet you, Risa," Mike called as she departed with Wren and Alexa.

"Back at you," she replied over her shoulder.

Silence filled the car on the way back to Wren's place. Risa thought about apologizing again, but figured it wouldn't do any good. What was done was done.

When they arrived at his duplex, Wren killed the engine. Tossing the keys into the backseat where Alexa caught them, he instructed his daughter to go into the house ahead of him. He'd be there shortly. Once the child was safely inside, Risa figured she was about to get a good lecture—or a sermon. Either way, she probably deserved it. Ruefully, she stared straight ahead at the rain streaming down the windshield. Wren did the same, and for a long while, neither uttered a sound.

Finally, Risa cracked.

"Okay. Go ahead. Yell at me. Tell me what a horrible person I am for telling your ex-wife just exactly what I think of her. Just say something, Wren."

"That's just it. I don't know what to say, except I feel like we should talk."

"You're angry with me."

"Not at all." He turned and looked at her with those deep brown eyes of his and Risa's heart melted. "I'm just worried about you."

"Me?" She had to laugh. "What are you worried about?"

"I think you're taking our relationship too seriously."

"What, you never went to bat for a friend before, Wren?" she questioned. "You never stuck your neck out for someone you cared about?"

"Sure, I've done that."

"I know you have." Risa touched the back of his hand, then slipped her fingers in between his. Wren didn't pull away. "But you're right. I do take our relationship seriously." She paused. "The truth is, I'm in love with you. I can't help it."

Beneath the glow of the streetlights outside the car, she saw him wince. Then he withdrew his hand.

"I know what you're going to say," she continued. "You're about to tell me that you don't feel the same way I do. But Wren. . .can't you at least give me a chance?"

"I probably would if it weren't for my faith," he said, both hands gripping the steering wheel, his gaze set dead ahead.

"What do you mean?"

"We don't share the same beliefs, Risa. I'm a born-again Christian. You're not. Besides, I'm convinced that God only gave me one shot at marriage."

"Some God you have. Doesn't He want you to be happy?"

"Yes. But He wants me to be happy with the woman He ordained to be my wife before the beginning of time."

"Her? Your ex-wife?"

Wren nodded.

"Like I said. . .some God you have. That woman is mean and selfish and brings you nothing but misery. Remember the night we stopped for coffee after class and you described your marriage? It didn't sound like 'happily ever after' to me. You said you tried to please Nancie, but she was never satisfied. You bought her a house in Shorewood, but it wasn't prestigious enough. She wanted Whitefish Bay. You work hard and earn a decent living, but that wasn't good enough for her either. Then she divorced you and took everything. She still gets a chunk of your salary and then she makes you pay for child care, among other things. Now she drives a cute foreign sports car and you drive this old thing."

"I know, it doesn't seem fair." Wren sighed. "But the fact is, our failed marriage is as much my fault as Nancie's."

"Whatever." Irritated and feeling more than a little hurt, Risa opened the door and climbed out. Cold raindrops pelted her, but she didn't care.

"Risa, wait."

She ignored Wren's request and strode purposely for her car, parked across the quiet street. Pulling her keys out of her purse, she unlocked the door.

Wren caught her elbow. "Please, Risa, will you let me explain all this? Can I show you from the Bible what God told me? I'd like to hear what you have to say after reading the passages."

She looked up into his beseeching eyes. Rain dripped from his hair, nose, and chin. In just those few moments, they'd both been soaked to the skin.

"Well, I suppose I could come in for a while," she said before giving him a seductive smile. She stepped closer. "Maybe I should get out of these wet clothes. Got something black and slinky?"

"I've got some black sweats. I don't know how 'slinky' they'll be, though."

Risa shook her head. "Sweats aren't what I had in mind, Wren."

"Yeah, I know." He cleared his throat. "Come on. Let's get out of this rain."

She followed him up to the porch and into the house, deciding that if she wanted to spend time with Wren, she'd have to do it on his terms. . .for now. At least he wasn't completely brushing her off.

True to his word, he provided her with a pair of clean sweatpants and a sweatshirt. He even found a pair of thick white athletic socks for her feet. He threw her wet things into the dryer. Then, while Alexa pored over her math book at the dining room table, Wren opened his Bible in the living room. Risa did her best to cozy up beside him on the couch, but had a feeling he didn't even notice.

"First things first," he said, flipping through the pages reverently. "I want to show you some verses in the book of Romans. Do you know who the apostle Paul was?"

Risa nodded. "I was raised Catholic."

"Okay. Then you're familiar with him and the Bible." He looked at her askance. "Do you believe this Book?"

She shrugged. "I pretty much gave up religion altogether after what my stepfather did to me. He used to attend mass every day, but I can tell you there was nothing holy about that guy—or his disgusting friends!"

"Risa, anyone can attend any kind of church and still be as lost as an atheist. Church doesn't save one's soul—Jesus Christ does. Here, look. . . ."

Wren pointed to a verse and read, " 'For all have sinned and fall short of the glory of God.' " He turned a couple of pages and read aloud another verse. " 'For the wages of sin is death, but the gift of God is eternal life in Christ Jesus our Lord.' " He lifted his gaze to hers. "See, none of us is good enough to get to heaven on our own. All of us fall short of God's glory. We all deserve eternal punishment in hell. That's what the Bible is saying here. But if we want eternal life, there is a way to get it. God provided the way. All we have to do is accept His free gift of salvation."

"Okay," Risa said a bit hesitantly, "and what is that 'gift'?"

"God's Son, Jesus Christ."

"He died on the cross for the whole world."

"Right, but His sacrifice was not a generic one-size-fits-all deal. He's a personal Savior, and Christ died for your sins and mine. We sent Him to the cross, Risa."

Shifting uncomfortably, she didn't particularly care for the idea that she was a "sinner," except she knew she wasn't perfect either. She'd made her share of mistakes. "All right. I agree. I've sinned. So how do I 'accept' Jesus Christ? Go to mass, confession, pray on my rosary five times a day?"

Wren shook his head and grinned. "All you do is confess to God that you're a sinner in need of salvation. God's salvation, not the ones created by man. Then invite Jesus into your heart. Ask Him to share your life. He will."

Risa dropped her head back and laughed. "That's it? Give me a break!"

"That's it. Salvation is a simple thing—so simple, it confounds the wisest of men."

Risa still wasn't convinced, so Wren turned a few more pages of his Bible and pointed out yet another verse. " 'Everyone who calls on the name of the Lord will be saved.' "

"And then what happens? Will I have to do what God wants instead of what I want?"

Wren shook his dark brown head. It still looked damp from the rain. "You don't have to do anything, Risa. But you'll want to please God. He changes His children from the inside out, not the other way around."

"What if God doesn't want me to get married?"

"If you want to get married someday," Wren replied, smiling slightly, "then my guess is God put that desire in your heart. But you've got to be open to His choice of a husband. The man you select might not be the best one for you."

Risa nodded knowingly. They'd come full circle. "You're telling me that you aren't the man God wants for me, right? But how do you know?"

"Good question." Once more, Wren skipped over several more pages in his Bible. The next passage he showed her was highlighted with a yellow marker. "This verse is found in the book of 1 Corinthians, chapter seven. It also was written by the apostle Paul. It says, 'A wife must not separate from her husband. But if she does, she must remain unmarried or else be reconciled to her husband. And a husband must not divorce his wife.' "

"You didn't divorce your ex-wife," Risa argued. "She divorced you."

"Right. But look at this. . . ." Wren had to search out the next set of verses which, moments later, he found in the gospel of Luke. Again he'd highlighted a portion of the text in yellow. "This is what the Savior said, 'Anyone who divorces his wife and marries another woman commits adultery, and the man who marries a divorced woman commits adultery.' "

"But, Wren, I'm not a divorcée!" Risa exclaimed, unable to understand.

"But I am," he replied softly. "You can't marry me. Besides, Nancie might have taken the initiative, but I agreed to the divorce. For all intents and purposes, I divorced her, too.

"Look," he added patiently, "I know there are a lot of Christians who've been through the whole process. I have friends who have been divorced and are now happily remarried. I in no way stand in judgment of them. All I know is, it wouldn't be right for me to remarry. God used this verse in Scripture to tell me that."

Tears of discouragement filled Risa's eyes. She looked away.

"You're a puzzle, Wren Nickelson."

"To a lot of people I am, that's true." He closed his Bible. "And now I'll really blow you away by admitting that I'm still in love with my wife."

"Ex-wife," Risa reminded him. "And I'm not the least surprised to hear it either. But you're too good for her."

In the dining room, Alexa had twisted around in her chair and now sat watching on curiously. Risa felt all the more frustrated. She'd forgotten the girl was nearby.

Wren obviously had forgotten, too. "Lex, are you done with your homework?"

She nodded.

"Then get yourself ready for bed."

Disappointment crossed her small face, but she did as her father instructed.

"I'd better get going," Risa said, rising from the couch. "Can I return your clothes tomorrow at work?"

"Sure. Let me go downstairs and get yours out of the dryer."

"Forget it, Wren. Just bring them with you in the morning."

He nodded agreeably and stood by while she removed the thick socks she'd borrowed and stepped into her leather flats.

"I won't make the cover of *Vanity Fair* in this outfit," she quipped, feeling self-conscious now on top of all her other tumultuous emotions.

He just smiled and politely saw her to the door.

With one hand on the knob, she turned to face him again. "I'm still not giving up on you—us." She saw his gaze soften, and she loved him all the more for it. "You're the most wonderful man I've ever met."

"There's a slew of guys better than me out there, Risa. But your first love needs to be the Lord Jesus Christ before you'll ever find a man here on earth who will make you happy."

She didn't believe him. She didn't understand. Pulling open the door, she turned and walked into the drenching, bitter rain.

∽

Nancie had almost secured a date for Saturday night. Deciding that the redheaded hussy had been right when she'd said Nancie should get out of Wren's life forever, she strove to make new friends at work and build a future of her own. She'd gone so far as to request that Wren leave

Laura at the Bairds' instead of taking her to his place every day after work. He complied and, as a result, Nancie hadn't seen him in more than a week. She didn't stay with the girls on Monday night so that he could attend his writing class, and she'd all but convinced herself that she couldn't care less about Wren's goofy novel.

With that said and done, she'd set her sights on Pete Larsen. Ironically, he, too, was a redhead, although his shade was darker than Risa's, more auburn than carrot orange. Nancie could tell he'd been attracted to her since his first day on the job—the day after Nancie was mugged. Pete had even pursued her after his colleagues had dubbed her a "blond broomstick rider" in the cafeteria. However, once he learned she had children, his interest evaporated.

"It's not like the girls have to come with us," Nancie had stated in her own defense. "They stay with their father on weekends. And this is only a date, for pity's sake!"

"I know," Pete replied. "But I don't want to get tangled up with a woman who has kids."

"You don't like kids?"

"Yeah, I do. . .just not some other guy's kids. Been there, done that, Nancie. Your daughters would most likely hate me because they're devoted to their dad, and it ultimately would affect our relationship, so let's not even go there."

"Fine." She tried to hide her hurt feelings and disappointment as she left the office and walked to the rapidly emptying parking lot.

Driving home Friday evening, the beginning of Memorial Day weekend, Nancie felt more discouraged than ever, although she had to admit Pete had a point. Alexa would hate him for sure.

She arrived at her apartment complex and parked her car. Then while she entered the building and collected her mail, she mentally listed friends she could phone and make plans with for the weekend. But after she'd placed several calls, she realized no one she knew was going to be available. They either had families or "significant others" to whom they were committed. And Wren had the girls. . .and Risa.

Once again, Nancie found herself totally alone.

Chapter 11

"Hi, Ruth. Sorry to bother you. Any idea where Wren and the girls might be?"

Standing at her front door with a baby's arms wrapped around her knees, Ruth Baird smiled a greeting. "No bother. Come on in."

Nancie followed her into the house and decided that Ruth looked attractively disheveled tonight. Strands of her light brown hair had escaped their clip and fell loosely around her face. She wore a denim jumper over a red T-shirt, and on her feet were blue leather clogs.

"I suppose you have plans tonight," Nancie began once Ruth had guided her into the living room.

"No. Actually, I'm not sure what's going on. I'm waiting for Max to get home and tell me." She laughed. "We like to spend as much time as we can at the marina, but it looks like rain again, and I heard a news report say we're going to have bad weather all weekend."

"That figures."

Ruth sent her a sympathetic grin. "Hey, I just made a pot of flavored coffee. It's decaffeinated. Like a cup?"

"Sure."

Shooing her children into the basement playroom, Ruth made her way into the kitchen. She reappeared minutes later with two cups of steaming coffee that smelled distinctly of cinnamon.

"It's cinnamon hazelnut," Ruth affirmed.

"Thanks." Nancie took the proffered mug and brought it to her lips. "Mmm. . .delicious."

Smiling, Ruth sat down in the burgundy upholstered armchair. "You asked if I knew where Wren and the girls were, and I think I might. He picked them up at noon, since school let out early today, and mentioned planning to spend the weekend at a cabin up north. He said it was an annual thing."

"That's right. . . ." Nancie took another sip of her coffee, wondering how she could have forgotten. "Wren meets his brother up there. He's got two girls about the same ages as Alexa and Laura. And Steve is divorced, too, so both men have something in common. Two daughters and mean ex-wives."

"Oh Nancie," Ruth stated, casting her a look of admonition, "I don't think you're mean." She took another swallow of coffee. "Is it imperative that you get ahold of Wren?"

"No. I just wanted to ask him if we could share the girls this weekend." She paused before adding, "My plans sort of fell through."

"What a shame."

Nancie shrugged.

"Well, Wren's plans almost came to an abrupt halt, too. He's had a chest cold that turned into bronchitis. From the way he was hacking, I was sure the poor guy had pneumonia. Finally, his station manager convinced him to see a doctor and he got some medicine."

Nancie raised an eyebrow. "Are you aware of who his station manager is?"

Ruth shook her head.

"Her name is Risa, and she's got designs on Wren. Big time."

"Really?"

Nancie nodded.

"Oh boy. . ." Ruth's shapely brown brows furrowed with concern. "He said this week had been a real trial for him, and he asked me to keep him in prayer. Wren told me that his station manager had removed him from his route until he felt better and had put him in a position as her assistant. I just assumed he was struggling with the job change."

"He probably was."

"No, there was more to it. I realize that now. Wren's difficulties had to do with that woman. . . . What did you say her name is? Risa?"

Nancie nodded, but refused to probe further. She could only guess what had happened this week. Lucia had suddenly become the heroine in Wren's novel.

∽

"Women. Can't live with 'em, can't live without 'em."

"I'll say." Wren grinned at his brother's cliché, then proceeded to cough his fool head off.

"Man, are you sure you should be out here fishing in the rain with your cold?"

"No," Wren wheezed in reply, "I shouldn't be. And if I don't get better, Risa won't let me return to my route next week."

"So?"

"So, if I don't return to my route, I'll go crazy."

"Hmm. . .Risa's your boss?"

"Yep, but she wants to be something else."

"No kidding?" His brother raised curious brows.

"No kidding." Wren sighed and coughed again. "Steve," he confessed, "falling in love with her would be so easy."

"So what?"

"So. . .she's not a Christian, for one thing."

His older brother grunted out a disappointed reply, and Wren felt grateful that at least he understood that much, being a believer himself.

"Risa's got this way about her," he continued. "She makes me feel ten feet tall, she's caring, sweet, and she's a knockout. I've tried very hard not to notice her appearance, but she flaunts it, and she's starting to get to me."

"God doesn't tempt us beyond what we can bear. And He is faithful."

"I know, I know. . . ." Wren peered down at the lake, feeling as though he were drowning spiritually. "Nancie and I were getting along really well for a while. I had hoped we'd reconcile. But then I wrecked everything by kissing her one night. Alexa caught us, and Nancie hasn't spoken to me since."

Steve shot him a dubious glance. "Forget Nancie, will you? She did you a favor by divorcing you."

"I can't forget her. She's my daughters' mother." He paused, considering his brother through the hazy rain. "Can you forget Jean?"

"Yep."

Wren knew he'd come to their conversation's fork in the road, the point at which he and his brother no longer saw eye-to-eye. Steve harbored deep resentment against his ex-wife and Nancie, and he had no convictions about remarriage. It did no use to try and persuade him either.

Wren was about to change the subject, when another coughing spell hit. "I think I'd better go back to the cabin and vegetate by the fire."

"Good idea. I'll vegetate with you so you won't have to swim to shore."

They shared a laugh.

∞

Nancie paced her bedroom, debating whether to drive up north and crash Wren's weekend at the cabin. He wouldn't care if she did, but Steve was likely to throttle her.

"Okay," she said, stopping in front of the telephone, "this will be my sign. If I call up there and anyone but Wren answers, I'll hang up and forget this whole idea."

Lifting the portable phone, she punched in the number from memory. She almost sighed with relief when she heard Wren's voice at the other end.

"Hi. It's Nancie, but don't let your brother know it's me!"

"Um. . .no, we didn't order any pizza."

Nancie grinned. "Quick thinking, Wren."

He rasped out a chuckle. "Not really. Nobody else is around. Steve took all the girls roller skating in town and left me home so I can get rid of a cold."

"Ruth told me you were sick. Bronchitis, isn't it?"

"Yeah."

Nancie slowly lowered herself onto the edge of the bed. "Wren, I need a huge favor. I'm almost ashamed to even ask this of you, but. . ."

"But what?"

She swallowed down an odd sense of trepidation. Nancie hadn't ever been a coward. What was becoming of her? She shook her head. She needed to get some professional counseling.

But in the meantime, a couple of days up north might clear her head.

"Wren, as you know, I'm having a hard time with life in general," she began, "and I wondered if I could drive up and spend the weekend with you and the girls."

The long pause that met her question caused Nancie's heart to sink.

"Steve's up here with us," Wren finally said.

"I know."

Another pause.

"I don't think it's a good idea, Nancie."

"I realize I haven't given you much reason to want me around," she persisted, "but I promise I won't ruin your weekend. I'll be nice. I haven't forgotten how." She'd added the latter for a bit of levity, but didn't hear so much as a snicker issue from the receiver. "Please, Wren," she stated earnestly. "Please let me spend the weekend with you. There's plenty of room in the cabin, and I'll stay out of Steve's way." She momentarily fretted over her lower lip, then said, "Yours, too."

"I'm not worried about me. It's Steve. . . ." She heard him cover the receiver and cough for several long seconds. He didn't sound good. Not good at all.

"Wren, are you okay?"

He cleared his throat. "Yeah, I'll be fine."

"Well, look, I can help entertain the four girls if I come up, and that'll take some of the responsibility off your shoulders so you can rest. Tell Steve I'll cook and clean up the dishes so he won't have to lift a finger."

"You must be desperate," Wren quipped.

"I am," Nancie confessed in all seriousness. She expelled a heavy sigh. "I wish I could explain what I'm going through in a way that you'd understand, but I honestly don't know how to verbalize everything I'm feeling. I had even thought dating a guy at work would be a welcome distraction, but that never materialized—and it sure didn't help me sleep any better this past week."

"Have you seen a doctor?"

"That's my next step. But nothing's open this weekend."

"Wanna know what I think?"

"Hmm?" Nancie grimaced, sensing Wren was about to let her have it. But to her amazement, he did no such thing.

"Nancie," he began in such a soft tone that it brought tears to her eyes, "I think you've been wound so tight for so long that you don't know how to relax anymore. Sure, come on up. But I honestly believe you need more rest than I do."

Her voice caught in her throat. "Thanks, Wren."

"You bet. What time should we expect you?"

"I can be there by noon tomorrow."

"See you then."

Nancie clicked off the portable phone, closed her eyes, and dropped her head back in relief. Wren was going to let her come to the cabin. *Maybe there is a God in heaven who loves me after all.*

Chapter 12

Nancie thought the drive out of Milwaukee County and into Northern Wisconsin's wide-open spaces was therapy enough for her weary mind. Once she'd completed the four-and-a-half-hour road trip, she felt physically tired but emotionally uplifted from cruising through one pastoral scene after another.

Now all she needed was some sunshine on this gloomy day.

Opening the trunk of her car, Nancie pulled out her overnight bag and headed toward the cabin. She stopped abruptly, however, when her former brother-in-law blocked her entry.

"Hi, Steve," she said carefully. "Did Wren tell you I was coming?"

"Yeah, he told me. I'm not too happy about it though."

He let the screen door slam shut behind him and stepped forward. Nancie squared her shoulders, anticipating trouble.

"But as long as you're here, I'm going to tell you just what I think of you." Steve wagged an accusatory finger at her. "You're a bloodsucker. You suck the life out of people in order to get what you want, and then you dump them by the wayside. You don't care who you hurt as long as you get your way. You're no good, Nancie."

She opened her mouth to hurl back a retort, but closed it again, remembering her promise to Wren. She'd have to buck up and take the insults. . .this time.

"I suppose you're sorry you didn't get this place from Wren when you took him to the cleaners for everything else!"

Nancie didn't reply, but slowly set down her bag on the pavement.

"Well, I made sure you couldn't touch it." Steve raised his voice. "This cabin has been in our family for generations."

"I never wanted the cabin," she told him tersely.

"Good. Because you won't get your hooks into this property like you did the house in Shorewood. You sold that one right out from under my brother and didn't give a whit about him or the girls."

"Steve, that's enough," Wren called through the door. The next instant, he was outside on the walkway, standing between her and his brother.

"Whatever problems you've got right now, Nancie," Steve shouted around Wren, "you deserve 'em. Every last one."

The barb met its mark and she winced, although she somehow managed to hold her tongue and keep her word to Wren. But, oh, how she itched to put Steve in his place! She had enough dirt on him to do her own share of mudslinging. And he called himself a Christian? Right. That's not what she'd heard from his ex-wife.

"And another thing," Steve began. However, before he could get another word formed, Wren grabbed hold of the front of his green sweatshirt and brought him up short.

"I said that's enough," he told his brother, a muscle working in his jaw.

Steve glared at him, then pushed him away, and stalked back into the cabin.

After watching him go, Wren turned to Nancie with a look of apology. "That wasn't supposed to happen. Steve and I talked about this last night."

"Don't worry about it," she said flatly. "He obviously had some venting to do." Whether from containing her anger all this time or feeling wounded after the verbal assault, tears pooled in Nancie's eyes. She blinked and glanced away so Wren wouldn't see her cry. "I guess I shouldn't have come."

"Well, you're here now, so let's make the most of it." Wren coughed hard before stooping to pick up her bag. "Steve won't bother you again."

She nodded subtly and looked on as Wren disappeared into the cabin. She didn't follow him. She couldn't. Not yet. She needed to regain her composure.

Turning, she surveyed the landscape. Not much had changed since she'd been here last. Towering pine trees still loomed overhead, while beyond them the grassy knoll grew lush and green from all the rain. And the same dirt path wound its way down the hill to the lake.

The screen door slammed and Nancie assumed it was Wren. But then she heard the soft, questioning voice come from behind her.

"Aunt Nancie?"

She swung around and peered at her niece, who stared back at her curiously. Nancie decided the girl resembled the Nickelsons with her dark brown hair and dark eyes, and she looked as though she could be Alexa's sister.

"Heather." Nancie smiled warmly. "My goodness, you're so grown up."

"I'm thirteen now."

"You look sixteen."

The girl beamed, obviously pleased by the comment. But then her smile faded. "Don't mind my dad," she said in a hushed tone. "He yells all the time."

Before Nancie could reply, the door banged again and Alexa stepped out of the house.

"Hi," Nancie said, unsure of what her daughter's reaction might be. Would it mirror Steve's?

Much to her surprise, Alexa closed the distance between them and slipped her arms around Nancie's waist. "Hi, Mom," she said, laying her head on Nancie's shoulder. "Uncle Steve shouldn't have said those mean things to you."

Nancie sucked in a breath. It was the first display of affection Nancie had received from her oldest daughter in a long, long while. Reveling in it, she stroked Alexa's hair and kissed the top of her head. "Thanks, sweetie."

"Hey Lex, maybe your mom will take us to see that movie!"

Alexa pulled back and gazed up into Nancie's face. "Will you?"

"What movie are we talking about?"

The two girls immediately began to chatter about the story line and the actor in the leading role. Obviously he was the latest teenage heartthrob.

Alexa still had her arms around Nancie, so she could hardly refuse the request. Besides, it gave her the purpose for coming up here that she'd so desperately needed. "Sure, I'd be happy to take you guys to a movie."

"And maybe we could go shopping, too," Heather added.

"Dad and Uncle Steve hate shopping. Besides, Dad's sick."

"Oh you poor girls," Nancie crooned jokingly. "You've suffered such hardships."

Alexa smirked.

"Well, let's go find out when the movie starts and plan our afternoon."

"Mandi and Laura will have to tag along," Heather said as they strolled to the cabin.

"That's all right." With her arms around both girls' shoulders, Nancie ushered them inside.

She walked up the few steps from the mudroom, deciding this place hadn't changed; and it smelled just as musty as she remembered. One great room had long ago been divided into a kitchen and living room, marked off by the sink and wooden cupboards arranged in a half-wall design on one side and more cabinets on the other. This allowed someone cooking or washing dishes to see everything that was going on at the other end of the dwelling. Doorways leading into the three bedrooms and one bathroom were accessible to the left, and to the right, a large addition ran the entire length of the cabin—it included a sunporch on the living room side and a spacious dining area off the kitchen.

"Aunt Nancie is taking us into town," Heather blurted.

Standing close together near the fireplace, Wren and Steve ceased their conversation at once. Nancie could only guess what—make that whom—they were discussing.

In that moment, she realized Steve's hostility wouldn't have fazed her a month ago. But combined with the mugging incident, the gossip at work, Risa's remarks, and her own depressed mood, his animosity seemed to suddenly crush her into a hopeless mass.

"Can we go, Dad?" Alexa asked Wren.

He glanced Nancie's way and smiled, although it looked forced. "Sure. It's fine by me." He looked back at his brother. "What do you think, Steve?"

"I'm for anything that'll get *her* out of here."

"Sweet!" Heather cried excitedly. She seemed oblivious to her father's insult of Nancie. "C'mon, Lex. Let's get ready." The two older girls dashed off into one of the bedrooms with the younger ones in tow.

"Steve. . ." Wren frowned a warning at his brother.

"I can't help it." With that, he stomped out onto the sunporch.

Wren turned to Nancie again and gave her a rueful shrug. "Again, I'm sorry." He lowered himself into a nearby armchair. Placing his elbows on his knees, he rubbed his hands over his face in a weary gesture before lifting his gaze to hers once more. "I had really hoped to avoid any confrontations. Last night Steve told me he disliked the idea of your visit, but he didn't object to it. I would have phoned you and told you not to come if I'd known how he would be."

"Sounds to me like Steve had a good twelve hours to gear up so he could blast me when I arrived."

"I suppose so. . . ." Wren shook his head. "But I do appreciate the way you didn't blast him back."

Nancie narrowed her gaze. "I wanted to, believe me."

He grinned. "I'm sure. And I'm amazed at your self-control."

She lifted her shoulders, feigning indifference. "I promised I'd be nice and it was never my intention to ruin anyone's weekend, although it seems I've done exactly that just by showing up."

Wren scratched his jaw thoughtfully with his left hand, and Nancie noticed he'd taken off his wedding ring. She stared at his bare finger, wondering what to make of it. However, before she could ask, the girls swarmed her.

"Can I sit in the front seat on the way there?" Heather asked.

"Can we buy ice cream?" her younger sister followed up.

Laura tugged on the hem of Nancie's oversized shirt. "Can I sit in the front seat on the way home?"

"Are we going shopping first?" Alexa wanted to know.

"Have fun," Wren called over the din, looking amused.

"Oh, we will," Nancie replied. "This beats sitting home alone any day. But can I borrow your minivan? I don't have enough seat belts in mine."

Wren nodded and pulled the keys out of his pants pocket. Alexa snatched them and ran outside, declaring that she was going to start up her dad's vehicle. The other children darted after her.

Nancie tossed her keys to Wren. "Feel free to use my car while I'm gone if you need to." On that note, Nancie exited the cabin and joined the girls.

So far, so good, Wren thought as he reclined comfortably in the corner of the living room. He covered himself with a thick blanket and basked in the heat radiating from the blazing fireplace. A fever he could live with; contention between his brother and ex-wife, he couldn't. But in the time since Nancie had returned with the girls, bearing two large pizzas as peace offerings, no arguments had erupted.

Steve suddenly entered the kitchen, dumped his plate in the sink, and walked toward him, chewing the last of his crusty supper. "Okay, maybe she is trying to be nice," he whispered. "My question is, why? What does she want?"

"Nothing. It's like I said. She's burned out from school and work and she needs to relax. This is a great place to do exactly that, don't you think?"

A dubious expression crossed his face. "I don't know. . . ."

"Did you apologize for going ballistic earlier?"

"Nope, and I don't intend to either."

"Steve, I thought we agreed. Your Christian testimony is at stake here. How's Nancie ever going to come to know the Lord if she doesn't see Him in us?"

"If she hasn't been converted by now, she never will be."

"You don't know that!"

Just then Nancie walked into the kitchen and cast a wary glance their way. "Are you feeling any better, Wren?"

"Like she really cares," Steve retorted under his breath.

Wren widened his gaze beseechingly before looking toward the sink, which Nancie had begun to fill with soap and water. "I'm fine," he replied.

One by one, the girls brought in their supper dishes. Before washing them, Nancie wiped down the dining table so the four cousins could play a board game. When she returned to the sink and stuck her hands in the bubbly water, Steve set down the newspaper he'd been reading and sauntered over to her side. Wren rose slowly, praying that his brother would mind his manners.

He didn't. He tore into Nancie shamelessly. Wren wanted to intervene, but he couldn't seem to muster the energy to referee. He felt like a feeble observer.

After Steve had had his say, Nancie opened her mouth to have hers. . .and Wren held his breath. This was going to get ugly. He knew his ex-wife was capable of shredding a guy, and he ought to know, having been the recipient of many a vicious tongue-lashing. While Steve might deserve it, Wren didn't think he could watch. His brother had no idea what he was in for.

And he certainly didn't want the kids to overhear!

Quickly making his way to the other end of the kitchen, Wren closed the double doors to the dining area. Pivoting, he leaned against them. To his astonishment, Nancie had gone back to washing dishes without uttering a syllable. Her blond hair partially covered her face, but Wren still saw the tears slipping down her cheeks as she kept her gaze fastened to the soapsuds. His heart went out to her.

He looked over at his brother then and suddenly felt like knocking his block off!

Steve met his stare. "Even when we were teens, you always fell for the bad girls."

"Will you quit already?"

"Nope. I'm not done yet. I've figured out what she's up to. Nancie's no fool, and she knows how much you'd like to get your family back together. So she's playing with you, Wren. That's right. She's up here for the sole purpose of destroying your chance at happiness with that woman you're in love with. . .Risa."

Wren's heart just about leapt into his throat. His brother had no right to divulge such information—and it wasn't even true. Sure he had feelings for Risa, feelings he wasn't about to deny. But he wasn't certain they could be labeled "love." Besides, he had yet to earnestly seek God's face in the matter.

Nevertheless, he gauged Nancie's reaction. He'd suspected that she was jealous of his relationship with Risa. But would she really go to such lengths to keep them apart?

Nancie shook the soap off her hands, wiped away her errant tears, then grabbed the dish towel. Facing Wren, she tipped her head. "Well, now I know why you suddenly removed your wedding band."

"See, I told you!" Steve exclaimed, giving Wren's shoulder a shove.

"You wanna get lost for a while?" he replied irritably.

"Sure. I'll go play that Barbie board game with the girls." Looking smug, Steve left them alone.

Wren resumed his inquisitive regard of Nancie while she fidgeted with the dish towel. At last, she set it down.

"Look, Wren," she said in a straightforward manner, "I'm not going to stand in the way of your newfound happiness with Risa. Okay, so I'm envious. Fine. I'll admit it. But I'm hardly the villain your brother described."

Tapering his gaze, Wren inched his way forward. "I'm just curious. Who are you envious of—Risa. . .or me?"

"What?" Nancie frowned, obviously confused.

"Well, if you're envious of me, then I'd say it's because you've been looking for Mr. Right and haven't found him. But if you're envious of Risa, then I'd be inclined to wonder if maybe somewhere in the back of your mind you're harboring hopes of reconciliation."

Nancie smiled, and it was the first time Wren had seen her look even remotely cheerful all day. "I think I'll plead the Fifth on that one," she said, folding her arms in front of her. She looked more like the Nancie he knew. . .and, yes, loved.

"If you don't answer my question," Wren persisted, trying to conceal a grin, "I'll be forced to draw my own conclusions."

"All right, I'll answer it. But I'll have to think about it first." Her smile faded. "I honestly don't know what I'm feeling these days, Wren. My life is in a tangled knot that I'm trying desperately to untie. Before it's too late."

"What does that mean, 'before it's too late'?"

"I don't know," she whispered, turning back to the sinkful of dishes. "That's what frightens me. I just don't know."

Chapter 13

Wren sipped his coffee as he stood at the picture window in the dining area; he was watching Nancie, who was down by the lake. He knew she hadn't slept much last night, because he hadn't either. Between his coughing fits and her insomnia, they'd ended up sitting in the living room together. Then he'd pulled out the medical thriller he was reading. It had been written by a Christian couple, and as usual, Wren quickly became absorbed in the plot. Nancie soon asked if he had something she could read, so he'd directed her to a shelf of inspirational romances. He explained that his mother had grown fond of the sleek little novels. Nancie elected to give one a try, and before either of them knew it, dawn had brightened the eastern sky.

"Hey, what are you looking at out there?" Steve peered over his shoulder and groaned loudly. "Oh. It's *her*."

"And 'her' is making me very nervous."

"How come?"

Wren glanced at his brother. "Nancie can't swim and it looks like she's standing on the very edge of the dock."

He set down his mug, unable to stand there another moment worrying about her. Without a word to Steve, he made for the door and headed down the winding path, trying to make some noise as he went so he wouldn't startle her. He even coughed for several long moments before reaching the water.

"Hey Nancie," he called, stepping out on the dock. He paused by one of the large wooden supports. "Looks like the sky is clearing."

When she didn't respond, he moved closer.

"Whatcha doing?"

"Thinking," she finally replied, her gaze lingering on the murky water.

"Well. . ." Wren grabbed hold of her waist and pulled her back several feet. "I'd prefer that you do your thinking away from the edge of the dock, thank you very much."

She turned and looked up at him as a slow smile spread across her face. "Wren, the most incredible thing just happened."

He raised his brows expectantly.

"It started earlier this morning. I was remembering everything your brother said, and it really upset me. Mostly because I realized a lot of it is true." Nancie faced the lake again, folding her arms over her thick, multicolored cotton sweater. "I came down here feeling utterly hopeless, believing I was unlovable. And like Steve said, I deserved it. I felt like it wouldn't have mattered if I lived or died."

"Nancie. . ."

"I actually contemplated suicide, Wren," she continued. "I don't know if I would have gone that far, but I shudder to think that the idea even crossed my mind."

A tiny grin curved her lips. "But then this slim ray of sunshine broke through the clouds. It was there and then gone again in a matter of moments, but I saw it." Closing her eyes briefly, she shook her head. "Wren, I know that was God. He showed me something similar on Friday night, too. That shaft of light was another sign from Him, letting me know He really exists."

The nervous swell in Wren's chest began to subside. He'd been ready to check Nancie into the nearest hospital, but suddenly he got the feeling that wouldn't be necessary.

Her grin broadened. "I got that much settled anyway. There's really a God up there, just like you've been telling me for years. But, unfortunately, the realization didn't make my depression magically vanish, so I asked Him if anybody on earth still cared about me." She paused and laughed before pushing her windblown blond hair out of her face. "And then you came coughing your way down from the cabin." Her eyes grew misty, but she blinked away the tears and gazed off in the distance.

"You know I care about you, Nancie. I've never stopped caring about you."

"I know." She sounded contrite.

"And Alexa and Laura love you."

"I know that, too. I'm a very fortunate woman."

"Yes, you are."

"But I've taken a lot of things—a lot of people—for granted, haven't I?"

"Ah well, I guess I can't argue with you there."

She peered at him from beneath an arched brow and smiled. Tipping her head to one side, she considered him with longing in her eyes that Wren hadn't seen in years.

"Will you kiss me?" she asked almost meekly.

The request took him by surprise; however, he was more than happy to oblige.

Stepping forward, he slipped his arms around her waist and pulled her to him. Then he slowly lowered his mouth to hers, drinking in its softness. They shared a breath and something more—something akin to the oneness Wren had never experienced with any other woman, or ever would. He knew that now. They were made for each other.

Drawing his head back, Wren searched her face. Her eyelids fluttered open and she regarded him dreamily.

"I forgot what a good kisser you are," she murmured, her arms still wrapped around his neck.

"You're not so bad yourself."

"Kind of out of practice."

Wren smiled. "Glad to hear it."

She gave him a look of chagrin.

Suddenly a bronchospasm erupted, extinguishing the heat of the moment.

"Sorry, Nancie," he sputtered. "I totally forgot I was sick when I kissed you."

"I totally forgot myself." She laughed softly. "Oh well, too late to worry about that now," she said, looping her arm around his elbow. "But maybe we'd better get you back inside the cabin. This damp air can't be good for you."

Wren allowed her to lead him up the path. He thought things seemed so perfect between them now—just like when, years ago, their marriage had been sailing on smoothly and they'd loved each other with an unbridled passion and steadfast devotion. But then a wedge had come between them—a wedge that existed to this day and always would, unless Nancie came to Christ.

But Wren sensed she was close. So close. . .

Nancie decided to accompany Wren, Steve, and the girls to church. The message was one she'd heard before—nothing new. Over the years she'd gone to church with Wren quite often, especially after his conversion experience, but then she'd enrolled in school and had better things to do on Sunday morning. And once the service ended this morning, she had to admit that the idea of biblical Christianity being the only right and true religion irked her just as much as it ever had. Oh, she might have changed her view of God—He existed and there was a heaven—but wasn't He the same God the Buddhists and other religions prayed to? As long as a person believed in God, wasn't that enough?

She verbalized her opinions to Wren on the way back to the cabin. But it was Alexa who spoke up.

"The devil believes in God and Jesus, too, Mom," she said from the backseat. "But he's not going to be in heaven."

Sitting in the driver's seat of Nancie's car, Wren glanced at his daughter in the rearview mirror and grinned. "That's right, Lex."

"The devil believes?" Nancie shook her head. "Okay, now I'm totally confused. But forget it. I don't want to talk about this anymore. Let's change the subject."

Turning her head, she watched the scenery whiz by as they rode through town.

Finally Wren drove up the gravel road, and Steve's vehicle came into view. Obviously he and his girls had beaten them home. Nancie crawled out of the passenger side of the car, and Wren tossed her the keys over the roof.

"It's a fun little car to drive," he said, "but it's definitely too small for me."

"It's perfect for me in the city. I can find a parking space almost anywhere."

"I believe it."

Alexa and Laura led the way into the cabin. Their cousins were in the process of changing from their Sunday dresses into play clothes. In the kitchen, Steve had set a package of ground beef on the counter.

"I thought we'd barbecue this afternoon," he said, emerging from one of the bedrooms in shorts and a T-shirt. "It turned out to be a pretty nice day."

Nancie nodded, thinking that was about the only thing she and her former brother-in-law agreed on—the weather.

In the room she shared with Alexa and Heather, Nancie changed her clothes, too, pulling on jeans and a cranberry-colored, short-sleeved cotton blouse. When she finished, she realized the cabin was silent. Peering out the dining-area window, she saw that everyone else was down at the lake. Steve and Wren were in the boat, starting the engine. All six wore fluorescent orange life jackets. She watched, but didn't feel left out at all. Boat rides had never been her idea of a good time. She had always preferred dry land.

Leaving the window, she made another pot of coffee in the kitchen. It didn't feel all that warm outside to her. The sun shone brightly, but the temperature felt all of seventy-five degrees. Once she'd filled a mug with the steaming brew, she traipsed down the pathway to the lake, intending to sit on the dock and observe the activities from there. Much to her delight and surprise, Heather was up on the water skis—shorts, T-shirt, life jacket, and all—while her father manned the motorboat and her cousins cheered her on.

In no time, other boats were on the small lake, whirring noisily past the dock. Nancie watched as Alexa tried to water-ski, but each time she stood, she fell into the water. Even so, Nancie enjoyed the spectacle without a single worry. Unlike herself, her daughters had learned to swim at an early age.

While Wren pulled Alexa into the boat, Nancie let her gaze wander to the other side of the lake. She spied a small rowboat gliding across the water, doing its best to stay out of the way of the more powerful, motorized crafts. As she looked on, she saw the man with the oars row and row, while a towheaded toddler—a little boy, perhaps—stood atop one of the benches, pointing to something on the shore.

That kid is going to fall in, Nancie thought, wishing the adult would make the baby sit down. And no life jacket? Nancie shook her head in dismay.

Just then, exactly as she predicted, the child toppled overboard. She stood up and jogged to the end of the dock, thinking she would soon see the man dive in after him, but all he did was stand up in his rowboat and begin calling for help.

What an idiot! She cupped her hands and hollered to Wren and Steve. After gaining their attention, she pointed across the lake. Steve revved the motor, and the entire crew was there in no time. Seconds later, Wren and Steve both dove into the lake while Nancie stood and watched in horror.

Suddenly Nancie realized this wasn't just a little accident anymore, it was a full-blown emergency. Racing to the cabin, she grabbed her cell phone and called 911. She gave the operator the appropriate information, and then, her phone still in hand, she returned to the dock. She got there just in time to see Steve handing the man in the rowboat the child's lifeless form. Unfortunately, the guy didn't know what to do next, so Steve catapulted himself over the side of the boat and attempted to resuscitate the boy.

Finally the rescue squad appeared and stood beside Nancie on the dock. All three called to Wren. "Bring the child here! Bring the child here!"

In a flash, Steve handed over the little one, from rowboat to motor boat, and Wren sped across the water. As the paramedics labored over the little boy right there on the dock, Nancie helped the girls out of the boat. All four wore anxious expressions, yet none of them had panicked during the ordeal, and Nancie marveled at their courage. She herself was quaking inside.

Once the child was immobilized and intubated, he was carried to the awaiting ambulance and rushed to the hospital.

"I hope he makes it," Nancie said in a shaky voice.

Wren shook his head sadly. "I'm afraid he's already dead."

"But those emergency technicians, they—"

"Nancie, they have to do all that. Now it's up to the doctors at the hospital. And yeah, by some miracle, I hope he makes it, too. But Steve couldn't get him breathing."

Tears started streaming down Heather's small face. Soon they all wept, and Nancie gathered as many girls in her arms as she could hold.

Across the lake, Steve was assisting the man in the rowboat to shore.

"Is that the child's father?" Nancie asked in between sobs.

Wren shook his head. "It's his uncle or cousin or something. I'm not quite sure. Apparently he was babysitting."

"Oh no. . ." Nancie's heart seemed to plunge to her toes, and her tears flowed all the harder. Wren put a comforting arm around her, and she buried her face in his shoulder. "S–somewhere," she stuttered sorrowfully, "there's a mother out there who has no idea she just lost her precious little boy forever."

Chapter 14

The afternoon had passed in a repressed silence, a consequence of the tragedy on the lake only hours earlier. Wren, Steve, and the girls had said prayers for the child, and Nancie had added her own silent plea. But at around suppertime the police arrived, asking questions for their report. They divulged the news that the little boy, whose name was Nathan, had indeed died at the hospital.

"Man, if we'd only found him in time," Steve muttered after the police had gone and they all sat around the dining table. "But that lake was so dark and murky from all the rain, I couldn't see my hand in front of my face underwater, let alone a drowning kid."

"You did what you could, Steve," Nancie told him. "Don't torture yourself."

He shook his head in sad reply, then sipped his coffee.

"The water was so cold," Alexa added, "that it took my breath away when I first jumped in to try water-skiing. That's probably what happened to little Nathan. He probably gulped water right into his lungs and sank to the bottom."

"Oh man, if we'd just found him sooner," Steve murmured again.

Nancie exchanged concerned glances with Wren.

"Steve, that boy died despite our efforts," Wren stated emphatically, "not because of them. Let it go."

"Yeah, Uncle Steve," Laura said with a caring note in her sweet voice, "we can at least be happy that Nathan is in heaven with Jesus right now."

A hint of a grin tugged at the corners of Steve's mouth.

Nancie cleared her throat. "Laura honey, we don't know if little Nathan is in heaven." She peered over her youngest's blond head at the two men. "Come on, guys, let's not heap deception onto our grief. I mean, we don't know what kind of family Nathan had. What if his parents don't even believe in God?"

"Nancie, salvation is a decision," Steve informed her as he gazed into his mug. "Doesn't matter what someone's parents believe. A person has to be able to understand what sin is, realize his need for the Savior, and then make the decision to get saved. Babies can't do that. . .that's what God's grace is for."

Wren agreed. "I think of King David in the Bible, when he was mourning the death of his infant son—the one Bathsheba gave him. He said something like, 'I will go to him, but he won't return to me.' The implication is that David knew he'd see the baby in heaven someday."

"See, Aunt Nancie?" Heather said. "Little Nathan's in heaven."

"That's quite the Bible lesson," she replied sarcastically. But, noting all the responsive faces staring at her, she knew she was outnumbered in this debate.

Changing the subject altogether, she glanced at her wristwatch. "It's almost seven. I think we should all eat something." She stood, suddenly thunderstruck. "Good grief, I sound like my mother." Looking over at Wren and Steve, she added, "I sound like *your* mother!"

Wren hooted before lapsing into one of his coughing fits, and for the first time in hours, Steve cracked a full-fledged smile.

∞

Wren sneezed and pulled the thick blanket around him before moving the recliner closer to the fire. His body ached from the hair follicles on his head to his toenails. "I think that swim in the lake this afternoon did me in," he told his brother, who sat across the room on the couch.

"I'll bet it did."

A girlish shrill wafted in from the sunporch, and Steve glanced in that direction.

"Sounds like they're having fun," Wren remarked, situating himself in the chair before bringing his feet up. He sighed. Much better. Now if only that cold medicine would kick in.

"Our daughters were discussing hairstyles and makeup, last I heard."

Wren smiled. "See? It's a good thing Nancie came up this weekend. She's kept all four girls busy since supper."

Steve sat forward. "As long as you brought up the subject. . ."

Wren groaned. "Don't start, Steve."

He ignored the request. "Listen, I saw you and Nancie out on the dock this morning. I had to keep the kids away from the window, 'cause I couldn't decide if it was PG-13 or not."

Wren closed his eyes. "I kissed my ex-wife. Big deal."

"It was the way you kissed her that I'm talking about. You're going to get hurt all over again. May I remind you that I'm the guy whose shoulder you cried on after Nancie threw you out of the house and said she didn't love you anymore?"

Wren opened his eyes and saw his brother toss a thumb toward the porch.

"That's the same woman."

"People change."

"Not her. She's got an agenda, and she's using you to accomplish whatever it is she wants now."

"That's not true. Nancie's burned out, and I honestly think God is working through these circumstances to reach her heart. In fact, I have an inkling Nancie wants to reconcile. After all, she knows how I feel about her and she's done nothing but encourage me this weekend."

"It's a game with her, Wren."

He shook his head. No. This time it was for real. . .for keeps.

"Whatever." Steve held a section of the newspaper over his face. The conversation had ended.

Feeling drowsy, Wren closed his eyes and slept.

Sometime later, he awoke to find Nancie sitting where Steve had been. She was eyeing him speculatively, so Wren sat up a little straighter.

"What are you staring at? Was I drooling?" He wiped his mouth and chin self-consciously.

"No, you weren't drooling," she replied with a soft laugh. "I was just watching you sleep and thinking about everything that happened today—mostly your heroics in trying to save little Nathan." Holding up the novel in her hand, she added, "I must be enjoying these romances too much."

Grinning, Wren resumed his comfy position on the recliner. His eyelids felt heavy, so he closed them.

"Have you ever thought seriously about writing a book?"

"Sure I have. I think anyone who enjoys writing dreams of authoring a bestseller."

"Will yours be a romance?"

He couldn't help smiling as he thought about his characters. Pretty soon George and Nan would discover the hidden treasure within the castle walls. Then Lucia was going to show up and wreak havoc between them.

"I guess I like more of a mystery," he finally replied. "But the romance will be part of the plot because that's what sells. . .or so I've been told."

"You're going to try and sell your book?"

Wren peered at Nancie through one eye. She sounded alarmed for some odd reason. "Well, if I ever get a whole book written, I might submit it to a publisher. But I'm an amateur. Right now I write for fun, and that's it."

"Oh. Well, that's good."

Wren closed his eyes again.

"If you ever need any help writing the romance angle, feel free to ask me."

Both eyes snapped opened and regarded her this time.

Nancie's soft brown eyes twinkled mischievously before she resumed her reading.

Wren thought up a reply, but coughed instead of speaking, then moaned as the pain in his chest spread like fire.

"You're not feeling any better, are you?"

"Oh, I'll be fine."

"Sure you will."

"What about you?" he countered. "Aren't you going to try to get some sleep?"

"Yes, but I'm waiting for Alexa and Heather to quit chatting before I go to bed. I'm all talked out for one day." Nancie sighed. "Those girls never run out of things to say!"

Wren smiled before drifting off to sleep once again.

Memorial Day dawned bright and sunny. Steve took Nancie and the girls to a parade in town while Wren continued his convalescence at the cabin. All seemed well, until they returned around noon. Nancie looked upset, and Steve was furious. Wren didn't even have to ask what had happened. He knew.

"The Wicked Witch of the West pales in comparison to your ex-wife," Steve said, poking his index finger into Wren's chest.

"Now what did you do?"

"Me?"

From over Steve's shoulder, Wren saw Nancie carrying out her overnight bag. Shouldering his brother out of his way, he started after her.

"Let her go," Steve said, catching his arm. "She doesn't love you. I asked her point-blank. She's using you, just as I thought."

"Aw, Steve," Wren moaned, "why couldn't you have minded your own business?"

"Because you're my brother and I don't want you to get hurt again." Steve gave him a pitiful look. "Fine. Don't believe me. Go ask her. Hear it for yourself."

Wren strode purposely from the cabin, half wishing Nancie would drive off before they could talk. *Lord, help me handle the truth,* he prayed, *whatever it is.*

Nancie was standing near her car, telling the girls good-bye, when he reached her.

"Hey, let's go fishing one last time before we head home," Steve called, and the kids went running off in the direction of the lake, squealing merrily. Wren felt grateful to his brother for coming up with the quick diversion, although it might not have been necessary had Steve kept his mouth shut.

"Nancie?"

She refused to look at him at first, and Wren wasn't sure how to begin the conversation, so they stood on the gravel drive in strained silence for what seemed like a millennium.

Finally, she whirled around angrily. "He pushed my buttons, Wren, and I lost it. I couldn't help it. I tried to put up and shut up all weekend, but your brother crossed the line this morning."

"Were the girls around?"

"No. They were in the stands, watching the parade. I was on my way back from the concession stand when Steve cornered me. He insulted me again and I threw my lemonade in his face. Then I told him off."

"Oh boy. . ." Wren looked heavenward. He could well imagine the scene.

"Want to hear more?"

"No." He scratched his jaw thoughtfully, then dropped his hand to his side. "But. . .Steve told me you said some things. Things about you and me. Would you mind repeating them?"

Leaning up against her car, Nancie stared straight ahead into the woods. Her arms were folded tightly over her light blue, long-sleeved T-shirt. With her blond hair pulled back into a loose ponytail, she made a fetching sight in spite of the circumstances.

"Nancie, will you tell me? Please?"

A muscle worked in her cheek before she answered. "He pushed me to my limit, Wren."

"Okay. So you lost your temper. What did you say? Did you mean it?"

She turned and faced him, lifting an obstinate chin. "Yeah, I guess I meant it. I said it. I said I didn't love you. You've heard that before, right?" She produced a curt laugh. "Steve also accused me of using you this weekend, and maybe I did. I was hurting and I needed someone. I knew you'd be there for me, so. . ." She swallowed hard. "So I used you. Fine. I admit it."

Gazing deeply into her amber eyes, Wren didn't believe a word of it. Oh, she might have said those things in the heat of a rage, but she hadn't meant them. At the moment, she looked as sorry as a little girl who was about to lose her best friend.

"Well Nancie," he replied at last, "if you used me, I can't say I didn't enjoy every minute of it."

She blinked incredulously, and Wren almost laughed out loud at her expression.

She shook her head as if to clear it. "You should hate me. Scream. Yell. Call me every rotten name you can think of."

"And what would that prove? That I'm no better than my brother? No, I think not. Steve's a bitter man. He's got so much animosity inside him stemming from his own divorce that I've actually begun to worry about him."

Nancie's features softened, but she still seemed perplexed by his composure.

He looked at his wristwatch. "I'm probably going to leave here in a couple of hours, or whenever the girls are done fishing," he said, changing the subject. "Will you be home if I drop Laura off later this evening?"

She nodded, then opened her car door. "Thanks, Wren," she murmured before scooting in behind the wheel.

Within minutes, she accelerated down the road.

He whispered a prayer as he watched her go. "Lord, thank You for Your infinite grace. I'd be a leveled man right now without it."

Chapter 15

All day Tuesday, Nancie tried to concentrate on her work at the office, but her efforts were in vain. She couldn't stop thinking of Wren and the way he had stood there calmly when she'd said she didn't love him. He hadn't even flinched. Of course, she'd told him that a hundred times if she'd told him once.

Except this time, it just wasn't true.

In her heart of hearts, Nancie acknowledged that something had happened to her over the weekend—something indefinable yet life-changing. Her very thought process wasn't the same. Suddenly her views on God, family, and death were very different. She now realized that the realm of humanism was flanked by an isolation she couldn't tolerate. In tailoring herself for the world of success, her values had gotten skewed. Now she had to reprioritize and reclaim what was once hers.

But did she really want to? And was it too late?

Perhaps.

Steve had said Wren was in love with Risa. Nancie decided it might be true, and she wondered if the fiery redhead was the reason why Wren hadn't buckled under her false admission yesterday afternoon. At the same time, she couldn't be sure. The way Wren had kissed her Sunday morning communicated quite the opposite. Did he kiss Risa the same way?

Nancie expelled a wondering sigh.

And then there was the memory of Nathan's drowning fresh in her mind. She had contemplated dying that same day and in the same way. But ironically, it was a small child who'd lost his life in the lake, not her.

Life was so fragile, Nancie realized, and she felt as though hers lay in pieces. A broken marriage, broken relationships. . .and her children were products of a broken home. It was all her doing, and now she could add a broken heart to the list.

∞

When Wren saw the showers early Tuesday morning, he knew Risa would never let him walk his mail route. He also realized he couldn't work alongside her inside the station again. He didn't think he felt strong enough to work, period, so he decided to do something he'd never done in all his years at the post office. . . . He called in sick.

Next he made another appointment with his doctor, who gave him a stronger antibiotic and cough syrup, in addition to a work excuse for the rest of the week. Wren protested. One day off was all he needed. But after the physician threatened hospitalization, explaining that Wren was on the brink of developing pneumonia, he promised to comply.

Once back home, Wren gave himself permission to be totally lazy. Sprawled on the couch, he watched television. Soon his mind wandered, and he thought about Risa. He thought about Nancie. One woman said she loved him, the other said she didn't. Unfortunately, the one who didn't was the one he still dreamed about at night, and just thinking of the triangular mess caused an empty pang in Wren's heart. He needed someone to love him and, likewise, he longed for someone to love. Was he wasting his time pining for Nancie and a reconciliation that would never be?

Suddenly Wren curtailed his wayward thoughts. He had no business considering a romantic relationship with either woman. They didn't share his faith.

Forgive me, Lord. You know what I want, what I need. Help me to wait patiently for You to give it to me.

∞

Risa felt so bad when she heard Wren was even more ill than he'd been the previous week, that she phoned her Nana Mandelini and asked her to cook up a batch of her famous chicken noodle soup.

"Are you sick?" came the worried reply with a hint of an accent from the "old country."

"No, no. The soup's for a friend. He's got a bad case of bronchitis."

"He? Tell me about this 'he.'"

Risa grinned. Her grandmother had been trying to marry her off since she was sixteen. "Oh, there's not much to tell yet."

"I hope he's Italian."

"Ah. . .no, he's not."

A pause. "Well maybe I'll like him anyhow."

Risa laughed softly. "You'll like him a lot, if you ever get to meet him. He's polite and kind and goes to church, but he's. . .well. . .we're just friends right now."

The older woman muttered something in Italian that Risa interpreted to mean, "A man and a woman can never be just friends."

She grinned. That's what she was counting on!

"Can you make the soup, Nana?"

"Yah, yah, I'll maka the soup."

"Great. I'll pick it up after work—about five-thirty. Is that okay?"

"Yah, okay."

Risa gave her grandmother a smooch through the phone line. "You're the best, Nana. Ciao."

∽

"What do you mean, Wren called in sick?" Nancie couldn't believe what Ruth was telling her. "He's never called in sick. He must be dying!"

Ruth lifted her hands helplessly. "He phoned me this morning and said he'd drive Alexa to school, but asked if I'd pick her up since he didn't know when he'd get an appointment at the clinic. That's when he told me he'd called into work, and I haven't heard from him since."

Nancie glanced at her watch. She'd worked late this evening in an effort to make up for her daydreaming, and now it was after six. She looked at Alexa and Laura, noting their troubled expressions.

"Come on, girls," she said. "Let's go see what's up."

They clambered into the car, and Nancie drove to Wren's place. She parked, and they made their way up the wooden front porch stairs. Surprising them all, he met them at the door, swinging it wide, and beckoned them into the house.

"I thought you were dying," Nancie said somewhat facetiously as she walked in.

"Yeah, Dad, are you okay?" Alexa asked. "You didn't pick me up at Mrs. Baird's today."

"I know. I slept all afternoon and didn't wake up until I heard Risa at the door. She brought over some chicken soup. She said her Italian grandmother made it and that it's a sure cure for my chest cold."

"Is Risa here?" Nancie questioned softly yet warily. "Maybe I'd better go."

"No, it's all right. I wouldn't let Risa in because I don't want her to get sick." He reached over Nancie's shoulder and pushed the front door shut. "But since you've already been contaminated, you might as well come in and stay for supper."

"Very funny, Wren."

He smirked.

"I'm starved," Alexa said.

"Me, too, Daddy."

"Then come on in and sit down at the table," Wren invited.

"You sure?" Nancie hedged. "I hate to eat the meal Risa intended for you."

"I'll eat, too. . .and there's plenty." As they stepped into the dining room, Wren indicated the large red enamel tureen in the center of the table. "This would likely feed an army, wouldn't you say?"

Nancie took in the sight, observing the crusty Italian bread beside the pot of soup, and was suddenly reminded of the old adage about reaching a man's heart through his stomach. Risa certainly knew what she was doing.

The girls sat down at the table, and Wren headed for the kitchen to fetch some bowls and utensils. Nancie followed him.

"Here, let me do that. You're sick."

"I'm not that sick," Wren protested.

"Sick enough to miss work, and I don't think you've ever done that before."

"Yeah, well, there's a first time for everything, right?"

Nancie didn't reply, but studied her ex-husband thoughtfully. His complexion looked pasty.

"What did the doctor say?" she inquired further, pulling two glasses out of the cupboard.

"He said I have to rest all week, and he gave me a work excuse."

"Hmmm. . ." Nancie filled the glasses with milk before following Wren into the dining room.

He lifted the lid off the kettle, and the appetizing aroma from the soup filled the room. With everyone at the table, Wren prayed over the food before they began to eat. Nancie felt a bit guilty partaking of the meal, knowing Risa would doubtlessly like to see her choke on every last bite. But she quietly ate anyway, since she had to wait for Laura to finish supper before they could leave for home. Besides, she felt concerned for Wren. She wanted to help him out if she could; however, snippets of her last conversation with Risa flitted through her mind. *I wish you'd get out of Wren's life forever.*

Guardedly, she looked over at Wren. Did he wish the same? Was he only being polite for the girls' sake?

Suddenly he pushed aside his half-empty bowl, plucked a paper napkin from its plastic holder, and wiped his mouth.

"You can't be full already," Nancie said.

He shrugged. "Guess I'm not as hungry as I thought." He looked miserable.

"Wren, go to bed. I'll stay with the girls tonight. We'll clean up the dishes and I'll help Alexa with her homework."

"Aw, Nancie, I can't ask you to do that."

"Then it's a good thing you didn't ask," she replied tartly, although she hoped the sweet smile she threw his way would communicate her earnestness to help him out.

Rising from the chair, she collected dishes and strode into the kitchen. As she rinsed their bowls, she heard him question the girls about school. They'd soon be out for the summer, and both Alexa and Laura were looking forward to a break from homework. Minutes later, Wren sauntered in.

"You really don't have to do this, you know," he said, coming to stand next to her at the sink.

"I know."

"But you're trying to even the score, right?"

Nancie shut off the faucet and looked at him. "What are you talking about?"

"I let you come up to the cabin last weekend, so now you feel obligated to wash my supper dishes."

"Is that what you think?" Nancie asked defensively. Then she quickly changed her tone. "Oh, I suppose I deserve it."

Wren didn't reply, but took hold of his pill bottle and shook out a capsule. He swallowed it down with cough syrup.

Nancie gaped at him. "I don't believe it."

"What?"

"What you just did. The Wren Nickelson I know would have accurately measured that medicine before taking it."

"I guess I feel too lousy to measure."

A sarcastic quip almost escaped her lips before Nancie thought better of it. Wren wasn't one of those guys who whined and complained. He didn't act like an invalid when he caught a common cold or the flu, and he abhorred being coddled. The fact that he admitted to feeling "lousy" spoke volumes.

"Look, I can stay with the girls for a while tonight if that will make things easier on you. Otherwise, I'll go home and scrub my kitchen floor."

An amused expression spread across his features. "Your life sounds as exciting as mine."

"Yeah, well, I'm working on it."

"Me, too."

Nancie took his arm and propelled him toward his room, but she couldn't squelch her sudden curiosity. "How are you working at it?"

"Praying about some things," he answered vaguely.

"About you and Risa?" she prodded.

He gave her a sideways glance and grinned meaningfully. "I'm pleading the Fifth on that one."

"You're cute, Wren," she shot back at him.

"And you never answered my question."

"I know," she replied sincerely. "Maybe when you're feeling better, we'll talk."

"It's a deal. So, are you sticking around awhile?" he asked at his bedroom door.

"I said I would."

"Good," Wren stated in a weary-sounding sigh. "I don't think I can stand another minute." He stumbled to his bed and crawled beneath the covers.

Nancie frowned after him, feeling more than a tad concerned. Following him into the room, she laid her palm on his forehead. "You're burning up. When did you take something for your fever?"

"After I got back from the doctor's office."

With a shake of her head, she walked to the bathroom. Opening the mirrored medicine cabinet, she pulled down a bottle of tablets. Then she filled a glass with cold water from the kitchen tap and returned to Wren. She had to wake him in order to feed him the pills.

"Thanks," he murmured.

"Sure."

After studying him for several long moments, Nancie decided he would be all right. She made her way back to the dining room, where she cleared the rest of the dishes off the table.

"Is Dad going to be okay?" Alexa called from the living room, where she and Laura sat watching television.

"I think so. If he rests he should be fine in no time."

"I'm going to make him something," Laura said, bouncing off the couch and breezing past Nancie. Reaching the wooden hutch, she opened one of the long bottom drawers and pulled out several sheets of construction paper and a narrow container of watercolors. "Dad always feels better when I paint him a picture."

Nancie smiled and reentered the kitchen. She washed the dishes and wiped down the counters. Having accomplished that task, she returned to the dining room, where Alexa sat at the table, math book open, and across from her Laura continued to create her masterpiece.

"Want some help?"

Alexa peered up at Nancie and shook her head. "I think I'm getting the hang of it."

"Good." Nancie watched as her daughter resumed her homework, marveling at the fact that Alexa didn't have to be threatened into completing it. An argument between them had frequently erupted over the topic of her school assignments.

"You know, Alexa," Nancie began carefully, "you and I have been getting along well lately."

"Yeah." She brought her gaze up, wearing a tentative smile. "But I still want to live with Dad, okay?"

Nancie swallowed her disappointment. "Sure. . .except I hardly get to see you these days."

"You saw me this weekend."

"Yes. But I only saw you a couple of times last week. I think we should make plans to spend time together. Maybe you can stay overnight with me on Saturday nights."

Alexa shook her head. "I have to help Dad and get ready for church on Sunday."

"You could get ready at my apartment."

She shrugged and looked back at her arithmetic book, and Nancie sensed a barrier starting to build between them. She'd have to discuss this matter with Wren. Obviously he carried more clout with their oldest daughter than she did.

"All right, Alexa. Let's just forget it for now."

"Hey, I gotta idea," Laura piped in. "Lex can stay with you on Saturdays, Mumma, and Risa can help Dad."

"I don't think so, Laura," the eleven-year-old shot back emphatically.

"Why not?"

"Because."

Nancie pursed her lips and observed the exchange curiously.

" 'Cause why, Lex?"

" 'Cause Risa isn't a Christian so Dad can't date her, and that's what Risa wants. She wants to go out with Dad. Like any moron can tell!"

"I'm not a moron." Laura looked at Nancie. "Mumma, Lex just called me a moron."

"No, she didn't. Alexa was simply making a general statement." She gave the older girl a pointed look. "I hope that's what you were doing. A good Christian doesn't call her little sister names."

"Sorry, Laura," she muttered, lowering her eyes to the math book once more.

"I forgive you," came the priestly reply.

For a while each child concentrated on the task before her. Then Laura looked up from her picture. "Mumma, do you like Risa?"

Nancie raised surprised brows. "Um. . .well, I don't know her," she said diplomatically, "so I guess I don't know."

"I think she's nice," Laura said, dabbing her paintbrush in the glass of murky water. "And sometimes. . .well, I wonder if she's going to be our new mom."

"Didn't you just hear what I said?" Alexa shouted at her. "Risa can't be our new mom if she's not Christian!"

"She might become a Christian, and then she could," Laura hollered right back.

"Shut up!"

"That's enough, girls." Nancie put a stifling hand on Alexa's shoulder. "I think it's time to change the subject." Regardless of the words tumbling from her lips, Nancie's insides were churning. She glanced at Laura in disbelief. "But before we do, I want you both to understand that no matter what happens, I will always be your mother. Got it? There will never be a 'new mom' as long as I'm around."

"Does that mean you and Dad are getting back together?" Alexa asked. Hope pooled in her soft brown eyes, rendering Nancie momentarily speechless. "Mom?"

"I don't know what's going to happen," she finally replied in a whispered voice.

Alexa was thoughtful, then squirmed in her chair. "Mom? If you and Dad did get back together, would you have to get married all over again?"

Nancie frowned, thinking about it. Then she wagged her head, trying to clear it. She was actually thinking about it!

"Um, yeah, I guess we would," she mumbled.

"Well, if you did get married all over again," Alexa persisted, turning sideways in her chair so that her knees bumped against Nancie's, "could I be in the wedding?"

Nancie's jaw dropped.

"Me, too. I want to be in the wedding!"

Nancie started laughing. She couldn't help it. How in the world had she gotten herself embroiled in this silly conversation?

The girls began to giggle because she was laughing so hard.

"I think that's a 'yes,' " Laura teased.

"You girls are too much," Nancie told them.

"Is it a yes, Mom?" Alexa wanted to know, looking earnest again.

Nancie sighed. "Okay, yes. If the impossible should ever occur, then you and Laura can stand up in the wedding. How's that?"

Laura cheered and Alexa smirked.

"Guess what my Bible verse is this week, Mom?" she asked.

"What?"

"Matthew nineteen, verse twenty-six: 'Jesus looked at them and said, "With man this is impossible, but with God all things are possible." ' "

"Mmm. . ."

"See, Mumma? It's not impossible," Laura said, her small face brightening.

"But there is one other thing," Alexa added.

Nancie lifted expectant brows. "What's that?"

"Just like Risa, you gotta get saved."

"Well, I've got news for you," Nancie said, wondering why her heart was suddenly hammering. Was she really that excited to share the news? "I think I am saved. It happened this weekend—actually, yesterday on the ride home. I talked to God the whole way, and I know He heard me."

Alexa let the pencil fall from her fingers and stared at her in disbelief.

"It's true," Nancie said warmly. "For years I heard your father tell me about becoming a Christian, but I never saw my need for it. . .until this weekend."

"Cool," Laura said. "I'm saved, too. Now we'll both go to heaven."

Nancie smiled at her youngest, but felt a bit concerned for Alexa. She seemed to have gone into shock.

"Alexa?"

"Dad!" she shrieked, causing Nancie to startle. "Dad!" Jumping to her feet, she bolted for Wren's bedroom.

"Alexa, stop." Nancie ran after her, wondering what happened, what had gone wrong. "Alexa, don't wake him up!"

Too late.

"What's going on?" Wren's voice sounded foggy.

"Mom said she got saved!"

"Alexa, will you please calm down?" Nancie grabbed her arm in irritation. "Leave your father alone. He's sick."

"What?" Wren reached for the lamp on the nightstand and turned the switch. Squinting from the sudden brightness, he glanced at the two of them.

"Mom said she got saved!" Alexa said again.

Wren's gaze shifted to Nancie for confirmation.

She nodded, then shrugged. Now she wasn't sure what took place. Perhaps she'd been mistaken. . . .

Wren sat up a little straighter. "Tell me all about it."

"When you're better," she said, feeling oddly embarrassed. "And

Alexa is going to finish her homework before she gets punished."

"Yes, Mom," she said obediently. She bounced from the bedroom, laughing.

"I can tell she's just terrified of me," Nancie murmured. She rolled her eyes and looked back at Wren. "What are you grinning at?"

"You. Did you really get born again, Nancie?"

"I don't know," she said honestly. "I guess so."

Wren threw off the covers and got up. He was still in his clothes—jeans and a sweatshirt, rumpled as they were. "I feel much better."

"Fibber."

He grinned and took Nancie's elbow. "Let's go into the living room and you can fill me in on the details."

Chapter 16

Wren's thoughts were spinning—and it wasn't from the cough medicine. Two days had passed since Nancie announced her conversion to Christ, and Wren still couldn't get over it. He felt certain it was a sincere decision on her part, too, even though Nancie hadn't known quite how to articulate it.

He shook his head as the noonday sun streamed down on him where he sat out on the front porch of the duplex. After all those years of praying for her, Nancie had finally become a Christian. And to think that he'd almost given up hope.

Two of the upstairs neighbors came out their front door and bid Wren a "nice day." Then they walked in the direction of the bus stop. Wren decided he missed not walking his route when the weather was so good. A sure sign he was on the road to recovery. Well, tomorrow was Friday, and he would see the doctor again. No doubt he'd get the "all clear" and go back to work Monday.

Just then Risa pulled up in her car. After parking alongside the curb, she got out, waved, and headed for Wren. He almost felt like he had conjured her up, what with the way his thoughts had been rambling.

"Hi," she said, taking a seat beside him on the porch step. She was dressed in her post office blues and had her sunglasses perched on top of her head. "You look better."

"I feel better." Wren smiled. "What are you doing here?"

"Lunch break."

"Ah."

"I wanted to come over and check on you. I've tried calling the past two nights, but only got your voice mail. I was worried."

"Nancie's been staying with the girls in the evening so I can rest, and she won't answer my phone. The girls are almost as bad. Each one thinks the other's going to get it."

Risa shook her head. "Just my luck."

The wind caught her long red curls, and Wren felt her hair brush against his shoulder before she pushed it back off her face. He discretely shifted his position and inched away.

"Risa, I've appreciated your friendship for the last six months more than I'll ever be able to express."

"Uh-oh, I can hear a 'but' coming."

He grinned at her remark and continued. "But things have changed between Nancie and me, and it really looks like we'll get back together."

Risa fell silent, staring out across the avenue. Finally, she looked at him without a trace of sadness in her eyes, only concern. "If that's how you feel, okay. I respect your decision. But I hope you're not making a mistake." Her gaze narrowed in all seriousness. "Wren, did you ever think Nancie might want you back because she's jealous of my interest in you?"

"I've considered the possibility, yes."

"Consider it again. Once Nancie's got you, she'll hurt you a second time. She wants you wrapped around her little finger so you'll be available to bail her out of any inconvenience. I mean, look, Wren, something goes wrong in her life and she runs to you."

He shook his head. "That's not the case."

"Oh yeah? Well, when I called you chivalrous, she said that was 'boring.' When I cheered you on at the basketball game, she reprimanded me, saying I was inflating your ego."

"You do have that effect on me," Wren teased.

He laughed.

She didn't.

"Nancie doesn't say a nice word about you, Wren."

He cleared his throat. "Like I said, things have changed."

"You defend her. . . ." Risa expelled an exasperated breath. Then she sat back, casually resting her elbows on the next step up. "I can't believe it."

Wren thoughtfully considered his hands, dangling between his knees. "You know, Risa, I believe in second chances. Second and third and fourth and fifth chances even. I believe we ought to forgive someone four hundred and ninety times, and that's just for the same offense."

"Your ex-wife has surely surpassed that number."

"I'm not keeping score. And that's my point."

She leaned forward. "You're such a special guy, and Nancie knows it. That's why she's determined to keep you—except she wants to keep you on a leash."

"I think I'm smart enough to sense it if that were really the case. No, Nancie is slowly changing her mind about a lot of things, and I'm one of them. She's a Christian now. She came out and told me so Monday night."

"Oh, right." Risa laughed sardonically. "Your ex must be desperate! But I've got to admit, she knows where to throw her punch. I mean, I could lie and say I'd had some terrific religious experience and that I'm a Christian, too. I know your faith is important to you, Wren. But I'd never use it as a means to further our relationship."

"I'm glad to hear it, but that's not what Nancie's doing either."

Risa lifted her palms in surrender. "Okay, I give up." She turned to Wren, placing a hand on his shoulder and looking him squarely in the eye. "But when she hurts you again, I'll be waiting with open arms."

With that, she stood and bounded down the steps, making her way to her car.

Wren let her go.

☙❧

Risa considered herself a professional woman, so she pushed aside her troubled thoughts of Wren and his ex-wife and conducted business as usual. But as she left work, she noticed dark clouds gathering in the west, and they seemed to mirror her frustrations.

If he could only see what that scheming woman is up to, she thought.

She drove to her home, located in the lower east side of the city, parked her car on the street, then walked to the building. The smell of precipitation hung in the air. More rain was coming, and, inevitably, more tears.

Inside her apartment, she set down her work bag and strode to her bedroom, where she changed clothes. Once she'd pulled on her jeans and a T-shirt, she heard the deep rumble of thunder and decided to watch the approaching storm from her living room balcony.

I ought to talk to Wren's pastor, she brooded. *Maybe he could straighten Wren out. Counsel him. Perhaps the good reverend might even absolve Wren's marriage and convince him that God wants us all to be happy, not martyrs.*

After a moment's deliberation, she stepped back into the apartment. Yes, that's what she'd do. She'd drive over to Wren's church and see if the pastor was there. Last Thursday night, the guy was playing basketball with the other men. There was a chance he'd be there tonight.

Grabbing her purse off the glass-topped table, Risa hurried to her car. She climbed in only seconds before the sky opened and released its pent-up fury.

Was it some sort of sign from heaven?

When Risa was a child, she might have thought so. She used to believe God's emotions were synonymous with the weather reports. When He was angry, there would be thunder and lightning. If God was happy, the sun shone brightly. During the winter months, except at Christmastime, of course, God deserted all of Wisconsin and the temperature plummeted.

Risa smiled inwardly as she drove slowly through the storm. How utterly silly. Obviously, God left human beings to their own devices. If He really cared what happened here on earth, He would have intervened on her behalf years ago. A loving, caring God would have sent a bolt out of the blue to strike her stepfather dead for all the physical and verbal abuse she'd suffered by his alcoholic hand.

Reaching the church, Risa shook off the shadows from her past and made a run for the side door. It was open, so she slipped inside. Finding herself in a hallway, she silently walked past the gymnasium. The lights were off. She wondered if she were the only one in the building, and it gave her an eerie feeling to think that might be the case.

Wandering down one corridor, then another, she found a row of offices. All but one was locked up tight. Seeing two men and a woman huddled around a copy machine, she cleared her throat.

" 'Scuse me."

They all turned her way and smiled a greeting.

"I'm looking for the pastor of this church."

"He's out of town until late Saturday," replied the petite woman. Her hair was a sandy brown and she wore a simple light blue skirt and white blouse.

"Okay. Thanks anyway," Risa replied, spinning on her heel.

"Hey, wait. Don't I know you?"

Chuckles emanated from the group.

"You know everyone, Mike," someone quipped.

With her hand on the doorknob, Risa glanced back and saw the familiar face of Wren's friend, Mike Gerardi.

Slowly she faced him and he stepped toward her.

"Risa, isn't it?"

"Yes." She tipped her head in polite regard. He sure wasn't dressed for a basketball game, what with his french blue dress shirt and neatly pleated khakis.

"Is there anything I can help you with?" he asked. "I'm one of the associate pastors here."

"You?" Risa was hard-pressed not to gape at the man. He didn't look like a pastor. He looked like an ordinary guy. But then again, the pastor had looked just like everyone else out on the court last week, shooting hoops with the best of them. Odd how she had always thought clergy should be garbed in white robes and black collars—or was it the other way around? "Well, um. . ."

"We could go get some coffee and talk. Have you eaten dinner?" Mike snapped his fingers before Risa could utter a reply. "I got it, we can go to my cousin's place. Best Sicilian food in town. We can talk there."

Typical Italian man, she thought as he ushered her from the office. And she supposed that if she didn't mention any names and voiced her concerns in a hypothetical manner, it might be all right. On the other hand, if Mike was indeed one of Wren's buddies, perhaps he'd be the perfect candidate to talk some sense into him.

They strode through the hallway side by side.

"Are you married?" she asked. She always asked.

Mike stopped short. "Are you kidding? I wouldn't be taking you to dinner if I was married."

"Sorry. It's happened before."

An understanding expression flittered across his dark features.

"I'm not married either," she said.

"I know." Mike resumed their stroll to the parking lot. "Wren told me."

This time Risa braked. "He did?" She eyed him suspiciously. "What else did he say?"

Mike grinned. "What, you expect me to talk on an empty stomach?"

With a sigh of mild annoyance, Risa allowed him to take her elbow and escort her out of the building. They jogged through the rain to his car, where an almost startling notion entered her mind. . . .

Nana would adore Mike Gerardi.

Chapter 17

The storm passed and now a light drizzle fell beyond the kitchen window as Nancie helped Wren clean up the supper dishes. She washed; he dried and put them away. Since it was after nine, both girls were in bed, sleeping. Laura had begged to stay overnight, so Nancie acquiesced. Wren was feeling much better, and the task of getting both his daughters up, fed, and off to school wouldn't be a strain.

Nancie smiled coyly. "Do any writing with all your time off this week?" she asked. "I mean, now that you're up and around. . . ."

He grinned back at her. "As I matter of fact, I puttered around a little this afternoon."

She rinsed a glass and set it in the drainer. She couldn't wait to read it. Maybe she should confess to peeking at his manuscript. . . .

"Say, Nancie, I've been meaning to bring up this subject for a while," Wren began, changing the direction of her thoughts.

"What subject?"

"You and me."

"Oh."

Lifting his brows, Wren regarded her speculatively. "Oh?"

Nancie laughed softly. "I guess I've been expecting it."

He nodded thoughtfully. "So what do you think?"

"I think," she hedged, shutting the faucet off and turning to face him, "that part of me wants very much to reconcile, but the other part is scared silly."

Wren smiled patiently. "I think that's normal, don't you?"

"I suppose."

He flipped the dish towel over his shoulder and his expression became one of earnestness. "What frightens you about our getting back together?"

Nancie knew the answer. She'd lain awake several nights this week, contemplating this very topic. "I'm afraid that we might find out nothing has really changed between us."

"But it already has."

"Somewhat. But, to be totally truthful, I'm afraid you're going to hold me back."

"In what way?" he asked, wearing a puzzled frown.

"In my career, my education."

Wren inhaled deeply, and Nancie wondered if he were trying to keep his temper in check. Now that the religious barrier between them had toppled, this was the great divide that still existed. "Have I ever stood in your way, Nancie?"

"Not physically, no. But you have emotionally. Throughout our marriage, you wanted me to be someone I'm not. You wanted me to be a Ruth Baird. . .not that there's anything wrong with her. But that's not me."

"Excuse me, Nancie, but I distinctly recall a reversed scenario. You're the one who wasn't satisfied with me or anything I gave you. You wanted some Fortune 500 executive and I'm just a plain ol' mail carrier."

She held up a forestalling hand. "I know, I know. That's true. And I'm sorry I hurt you. I'm sorry for the awful things I said and did."

Wren reached out and stroked her cheek compassionately. "Forget it."

"But you were just as awful."

He dropped his hand and sighed. "I failed as a husband. Okay. I admit it."

"But you've got to understand why you failed, Wren, or else it's going to happen again."

"I failed because I couldn't afford a BMW and vacations to Paris."

"Wrong. You failed because you could never accept me for who I was, faults and all. After Alexa was born, you wanted me home— cooking, cleaning, changing diapers—but I wanted a part-time job to stimulate my mind."

"And you got it."

"But not without a fight and a host of complaints. Then, after Laura came along, you pressured me to become a Christian, emphasizing that the Bible says women should be kept at home."

He frowned. "The Bible doesn't say that."

She pointed an accusatory finger at him. "You showed me the very passage."

Wren shook his head. "You misinterpreted it, Nancie. The Bible doesn't mean women should be physically kept at home, like some prisoner. It refers to an attitude. And can I help it if I want a home complete with wife and kids? I think that's a basic need, not some lofty expectation."

Nancie folded her arms and raised a stubborn chin. "I'm not giving up my career."

"And I don't want you to. I'm simply asking that you love me, the girls, and our home more than your career and education."

"But I do. I always did."

Wren shook his head. "No, career and education took first place in your heart, Nancie, to the point where you were frantic about finding someone to stay with our children when they had chicken pox instead of caring for them yourself. They were sick. They needed their mother. But instead, you paid a stranger to come into our home and babysit."

"She was very qualified."

"Doesn't matter." Wren irritably raked his fingers through his hair. "As a wife and mother your family takes precedence over your job or anything else."

"See, there you go," Nancie retorted. "You think you're putting me in my place by using that bossy, arrogant tone of yours. Listen, Wren, when it comes to sick kids, you can take off your share of work to stay home and babysit, too."

He shook his head. "As a mother, that's your responsibility."

Nancie lifted a brow. "Not when I earn more money than you do."

The verbal blow hit its mark; she could tell from Wren's wounded expression. Instantly she felt bad for hurling the fact in his face.

He pulled the dish towel off his shoulder and gazed out the window above the sink. "This isn't going to work. I can tell already."

"Maybe if you'd compromise, it could."

Wren shook his head ruefully. "That's not it." He glanced at her briefly before looking back at the rain-splattered pane. "You'll cringe when I say this, but a man's home is his castle."

Nancie groaned and, yes, cringed.

"Look, as dumb as it sounds, it's true. I've got to lead my family, Nancie. I can't surrender my God-given responsibility to you."

"Why do you have to surrender? Why do you have to be king? Can't we have a democracy?"

Wren glanced at her once more, obviously considering the questions.

"There's got to be some way we can work this out," she said. "I'm willing, if you are. But you can't be so dogmatic about traditional family roles. Times have changed."

"God hasn't. He's the same yesterday, today, and forever."

Nancie threw her hands in the air. "Here we go again."

"And for your information," Wren continued, "I've done all the compromising I can ever do. As my spouse, you can work and go to school, but you have to be a wife and mother first."

"That's a male chauvinistic view if I ever heard one."

"Whatever. That's my final offer. Take it or leave it."

"Offer?" Nancie laughed bitterly. "You can take that offer and stuff it in your ear, Wren Nickelson!"

She turned on her heel and stomped to the living room, where she grabbed her purse. Nearing the front door, she picked up her coat and umbrella before storming out of the house.

∽

Wren felt horrible for losing his patience with Nancie. She was a new babe in Christ, but he'd acted as though God's standards should automatically make perfect sense to her. Why couldn't he have lovingly, calmly vowed to work things out and then let the Lord nurture Nancie so she'd form her own convictions about her role as a wife and mother?

He knew the answer. Pride. And pain. Nancie had hurt him with her salary barb, and he'd reacted. Just like always.

The phone jangled and Wren scurried to find the cordless receiver, hoping the caller was Nancie.

To his disappointment and delight, it was his mother.

"Hi, Mom, how are you today?"

"Well, my arthritis flared up with all this rain, but otherwise, I'm fine."

"Good." Wren collapsed onto the couch and put his feet on the coffee table.

"What about you? That chest cold clear up?"

"Just about."

"Good. Well, I won't keep you. I'm just calling because I was talking to Ron Dempsey this morning. He's a friend of Dad's and is going to be retiring soon. He's in charge of the mail room at that company. . .oh, I forget its name, but it's the one that practically owns the whole town. The printing company up here in Neenah."

"American Printworks."

"That's the one!" his mother declared. "Ron told me they've been interviewing for his replacement, but can't seem to find the right person. I mentioned that you've worked for the United States Postal Service for over ten years, and Ron said you should apply."

"Why?" Wren asked, unsure of where his mother was going with this idea.

"Why? Well, because. . .you'd be closer to us."

He chuckled.

"The cost of living is lower up here, Wren. And the air is cleaner. Besides, Ron said this job would probably pay more than what you're making as a mailman, and the company offers excellent benefits."

"Hmm. . ." Wren thought it over, then shrugged. He wasn't looking to change jobs. "Thanks for thinking of me, Mom, but—"

"I told Ron that you've been sick all week but felt better now, except you still had the day off. He wanted me to tell you to call him and he'd fit you in for an interview this afternoon."

Wren started to protest, then realized this could be an answer to his prayers. He had already decided it wasn't smart to work at the postal station with Risa. Wren knew he had to transfer, for her sake as much as his own. There could never be anything between them. As for a wage increase, that would please Nancie; however, he wondered what she'd say about moving up north. An instant later, Wren knew she'd refuse to leave her career for him.

If she really loves you, she'll follow you anywhere, his heart of hearts seemed to say.

But that's exactly what he was afraid of—that Nancie didn't love him quite that much.

Then perhaps it's time I found out.

"Wren?"

He snapped from his soul-searching. "Sure, Mom, give me that phone number. I'll call right away."

Chapter 18

Wren steered his way through rush-hour traffic, glad that he didn't have to do it every day. Between all the construction and the road rage, it was a harrowing business just trying to change lanes.

Nevertheless, the trip to Neenah had been worth it. He'd filled out an application in the human resources department, had an interview an hour later, had gone to his folks' place for a while, then returned to American Printworks for a second interview with Ron Dempsey, the current manager of the mail room and distribution center. Wren had the feeling he would be offered the position. Of course, company officials wanted to verify employment and check references; however, they said they'd get back to him Monday morning. Everyone involved had seemed pleased and optimistic.

Now if only Nancie would see his possible job change as a blessing—that is, assuming she hadn't entirely changed her mind after last night.

He continued along the highway, mulling over every detail of his life these past few weeks. The miraculous had occurred; Nancie had become a Christian and was considering a reconciliation. It still seemed so impossible—but that was God, accomplishing the improbable, the incomprehensible. Nancie's salvation had definitely strengthened Wren's faith. And each evening this past week, he'd had a small taste of what it would be like to have his family back together. He wanted it so badly, but realized now he couldn't push or run ahead of the Lord. On the other hand, it was sheer torture to be so close to the very thing he had hoped and prayed for, yet he was still so distant. However, he had a hunch this employment development would be the deciding factor. Wren had been praying earnestly since his mother's phone call this morning and felt strongly that if offered the manager position, he would accept it.

Whether Nancie liked it or not.

The traffic inched its way along the interstate, and Wren realized that he typically made decisions in an effort to please Nancie, not God, and certainly not himself. He wanted her love and would do just about anything to get it. Certainly there wasn't much give and take, although Wren saw changes. But would they last?

They will if I start behaving like more of a man and less of a wimp. Wren had to chuckle. George was definitely beginning to rub off on him.

∽

Risa wrapped up some last-minute end-of-day details before gathering her belongings.

"Whatcha doing this weekend, Risa?" a coworker asked, closing the customer window before balancing her drawer.

"Not sure yet."

"No hot dates?"

Risa gave the brunette a hooded glance. "Yeah, right." In truth, she wished she did have a "hot date." She wished Wren would forget his ex-wife. . . . She wished so many things. Unfortunately, her dreams weren't likely to materialize. She'd heard much the same thing about religion, the Bible, and God's expectations from Mike Gerardi as she did from Wren. Since the two men were friends, they were obviously in cahoots. But who would have ever guessed Mike was a pastor? Not Risa, that's for sure. And as much as she hated to admit it, he'd shown her a nice time last night.

My family would drop over dead if they knew I'd gone to dinner with a pastor, she thought amusedly. Except it probably wouldn't happen again.

Bidding her subordinates a good weekend, Risa locked up the postal station and walked to her car. She had hoped Wren would be back at work today, but he'd called late this morning to say his doctor's appointment had been changed to Monday morning. Deciding to take a bit of a detour on the way home, she stopped at his place to say hello. Maybe they could order a pizza and rent a movie. Wren's kids would like that. And if that witch of an ex-wife was there. . .

Risa shoved the idea aside. She didn't want to think about it.

She pressed on the doorbell, peeking through the front door window. The flat appeared deserted. . .sounded deserted, too. She rang the bell once again. Nothing.

Disappointed, Risa turned, stepped off the porch, and made her way home.

∽

Nancie looked at her watch when the phone rang. Lifting the portable off the coffee table, she checked the caller ID. "It's about time, Wren," she answered. "It's almost seven o'clock."

"Hi. Yeah, sorry." He coughed, but it sounded one hundred times better than five days ago. "Ruth said you've got the girls."

"They're here. Where have you been?"

"In Neenah."

Nancie frowned. "Visiting your parents?"

"I did that, too," he said, sounding irritatingly vague.

"What else did you do?" she probed, unable to keep the trace of sarcasm from her voice.

"I had a job interview."

Sitting up quickly, Nancie almost dropped the phone. "A what?"

"An interview. At American Printworks."

"I see. . . ." Nancie chewed the corner of her lower lip, wondering why he didn't say something about an interview before now.

"It was an impromptu thing," he stated, as if divining her thoughts. "How come you picked up the girls at four o'clock?"

"I left work early and stopped by your duplex. I wanted to talk to you. When I didn't find you home, I went to Ruth's. That's when she told me you were going to be late, so I figured I might as well take the girls to my place and feed them."

"Thanks."

"Did you pay Ruth?"

A pause. "Yep."

"Good." Nancie reclined on the couch again. "The girls are at the playground with their bikes. Alexa's girlfriend is with them."

"Okay. Well, when should I pick them up?"

"Can you come right now, Wren, so we can talk while they're gone?"

"Sure. I'll be right over."

Nancie clicked off the phone. She didn't think Wren sounded like himself. He sounded stiff, unemotional. Oh well, he either wasn't feeling well or he probably thought she was still angry about last night—and she had been. But she'd gotten over it. And she knew Wren didn't stay mad for long. Must be the job interview thing causing him to act guarded.

American Printworks. Nancie knew of the company. Who didn't? It was a large, prestigious firm, one that touted its small express airline that only the elite could afford. Moreover, rumor had it that in order to get hired at AP, one had to "know" someone, another employee. But of course, that wouldn't be ethical, let alone legal. However, she believed there was some truth to the report.

So whom did Wren know? And why had he applied there? What if he got the job? Would he move up north or commute an hour and a half each way to and from Milwaukee? A job up in Neenah? What's he thinking?

Ten minutes later her intercom alerted her to Wren's visit. Her questions were about to be answered. She buzzed him up and met him at the doorway of her apartment.

"Tell me about this job interview," she said, beckoning him inside. As he walked in, she gave his attire a once-over, noticing Wren still wore navy dress pants, a crisp, light blue cotton shirt, and coordinating but loosened necktie.

"First things first," Wren replied. He regarded her with a soft, rueful expression. "Sorry about last night."

"Apology accepted."

He nodded a reply, but Nancie sensed he still felt troubled.

"I'm sorry, too," she stated out of obligation more than anything else.

A hint of a smile curved Wren's mouth. "I think you were right to admit being afraid last night. It'd be horrible to wind up divorcing a second time. The girls would be devastated."

Nancie folded her arms and looked at him askance. "What's your point, Wren?" she asked tartly. "Have you suddenly changed your mind?"

"No. . .no, I haven't. But we've got a ways to go yet, don't we?"

She felt confused. "Is that why you're considering a job transfer to Neenah?"

"Partly."

She shook her head. "How's that going to mend things between us?"

"Well, for one, the position is a step up and I'd get a wage increase. . . ."

Nancie immediately understood. "You're still upset with me because I threw in the remark about making more money."

"I'm not upset, but yeah, it bothers me."

She shook her blond head. "Look, Wren, get out of the dark ages. Women in today's society can be the primary breadwinners."

"Maybe so. But not in my family."

Nancie brought her chin back up and glared at him. But to her amazement, he didn't back down. He stared right back. Finally, it was she who tore her gaze from his.

Walking to a livingroom window, she looked out over the housetops. She could see the playground in the distance and recognized her daughters' colorful T-shirts near the large wooden gym set. She glanced at her watch. The girls still had twenty minutes before they were supposed to be home. Nancie had given them a curfew of eight o'clock, since it stayed light outside until about eight thirty.

Satisfied that Alexa and Laura were safe, she turned back to Wren. He'd taken a seat on the couch, and Nancie saw the weary etchings around his eyes. No doubt today had exhausted him since he hadn't yet completely recovered from his bout of bronchitis. He should have stayed home and rested instead of traipsing up north.

"Okay, so let's pretend you get this job," Nancie began. "Then what? Are you planning to commute?"

"No, I'd have to find a place up there."

She nibbled her lip in contemplation. "So, I'd have the kids during the week and you'd come down on Friday night, pick them up, and take them back to Neenah with you for the weekend?"

He sort of nodded and shrugged simultaneously. "We'd work something out."

Sure we would, she thought sarcastically. She could well imagine the fight Alexa was going to put up. She'd want to live in Neenah with Wren. Nancie would never see her. And what about day care arrangements when she had to travel?

"Wren, if you're so far away, what am I supposed to do if I have an out-of-town conference or meeting to attend?"

"You'd have to see if Ruth can watch the girls overnight, I imagine."

"And you'll pick up the tab for that?"

Wren shook his head. "No. In fact, I decided that I'm not forking out money for day care expenses anymore."

"Excuse me? I thought you said you'd be making more money."

"I did, and I would. But then you'd get more support out of my paycheck, so you can pay the babysitter."

"Oh, no, that's your responsibility."

"No, it's not. Check our divorce decree, Nancie. I'm required to pay you a percentage of my income. It's says nothing about day care costs."

Nancie narrowed her gaze at him, realizing what he was up to. "You're trying to back me into a corner and force me to conform to some simpering wifely role, aren't you? Well, forget it. It won't work. Fine. I'll pay the day-care fees."

"Good. You can start next week."

She glowered at him. "You're despicable. I can't believe I considered remarrying you." She put her hand across her forehead, feeling a throbbing headache coming on. "It's all coming back to me now—the whole reason I divorced you in the first place."

Wren stood, his shoulders slumped slightly forward as if a tremendous load bore down on them. Still Nancie refused to feel guilty for hurting him. He was hurting her right back.

"I want a wife and a mother for my daughters," he said so quietly that she had to strain to hear him. "I don't care if she works outside the home or goes to school as long as the girls and I are always more important than her career and her education. And, Nancie, if you're not willing to leave a job for me, that tells me I'm not as important."

"Oh Wren, give me a break." She felt like a lead weight was lodged in her chest. "You might give a girl a little forewarning, you know. You might ask and not dictate."

"Would you?" he questioned, appearing almost hopeful. He closed the distance between them and slipped his arms around her waist. "Would you leave your position at a prominent firm to be my wife and live two hours north of here? We could buy a cute little home in the country...."

Nancie felt sick. This past week she'd concluded that she would never in her life find a man who loved her as much as Wren did. But was love enough to compensate for the sacrifices he was demanding of her?

He kissed the side of her head and folded her into a snug embrace. She hated to admit she needed him, but, weakness in her character that it was, she did. She was the kite flying gloriously in the air. He was the one down below, holding onto the string. If he let go, she would twirl uncontrollably and crash to earth. But now he was reeling her in!

Loosening his embrace, he took a small step backward. He searched her face. "I'm sorry about playing hardball here tonight. I'm not trying to trap you into a decision or force you into doing anything you don't want to do. But I wanted to be sure you understood my feelings because, as you said, you might not be able to live with them."

Nancie felt like crying, but pride held her tears in check. "I guess I have a lot of thinking to do," she replied more confidently than she really felt.

Wren nodded before leaning forward and placing a light kiss on her lips. Then he smiled into her eyes, although it was the saddest smile Nancie had ever seen.

"I'll pick up the girls at the playground," he announced, making his way to the door. "Have a good weekend."

"Thanks. Same to you."

They sounded all too formal.

She watched him go and, after the silence in the lonely apartment filled her ears, a sort of numbness filled her heart. Had Wren just let go of the kite string?

Chapter 19

Nancie slept fitfully and awoke early on Sunday. It seemed as if her internal alarm clock refused to let her snooze past seven no matter how much or how little sleep she'd gotten the night before. Rising and making a pot of coffee, Nancie actually considered attending a worship service; however, she didn't have the nerve to walk into Wren's church. She'd snubbed members of that congregation for years, and she didn't see how she could show up unannounced. They'd probably stone her.

Retrieving the fat newspaper from the hallway, Nancie sat down on the couch, coffee in hand, and picked through each section disinterestedly. Finally her conscience was so riddled with guilt that she closed her eyes in prayer.

"God," she murmured, "I'm sorry I was rude to those people. I said terrible things to them in the past, and if I ever get an opportunity, I'll apologize. I promise."

Feeling somewhat better, she drew her attention back to the newspaper. However, try as she might, she couldn't concentrate on a single article. Instead, she became preoccupied with memories, flitting unbidden through her mind. And for some odd reason, she recalled every unkind thing she'd ever said to Wren.

"God, it's me again," Nancie whispered, gazing at the stark white ceiling in her living room. "Okay, I'll admit it. I have a problem of foaming at the mouth when I get angry. I say things I don't mean. I've hurt Wren in the past, too, but he's not exactly perfect either, You know."

With an exasperated sigh, Nancie pushed the newspaper off her lap. With all this confessing, she might as well go to church.

But she wouldn't. She couldn't. Unless. . .

Getting up from the couch, she found the cordless phone and dialed Wren's number. No answer. She glanced at the clock on the wall. Surely he hadn't left for church already. Chewing her lip in thought, she wondered if he'd taken the girls up north to visit his folks. With all this new job business on his mind, Nancie had a hunch that was the case.

"God, please don't let Wren get this job," she pleaded, squeezing her eyes shut. "How are we supposed to renew our relationship if he moves out of town?"

She plunked down in a nearby armchair, frustrated, agitated. She'd gotten in on the ground floor of a career with endless possibilities. Once she completed college, she was practically guaranteed a promotion. And Wren expected her to walk away from such an opportunity?

It was then that she heard God speaking to her. Not in an audible voice; rather, it was more an impression on her heart, like an inscribing in stone. *You wanted to reprioritize. Here's your chance.*

Immediately Nancie recalled how last Tuesday she had mourned the direction of her life. She had all but convinced herself that Wren was in love with Risa, but such wasn't the case. Then all week long, she'd felt married to Wren in all but the physical sense. It had been like a delightful game of playing house.

But could she really find happiness in a "wifely" role for the rest of her life?

Ruth Baird came to mind, so Nancie decided to call her. It was an impulse, no doubt about it. However, she knew Ruth and her husband attended another church in town. Perhaps she'd sit in on its pastor's sermon this morning.

"Oh sure," Ruth said cheerfully after Nancie explained the situation. "We'd love for you to join us this morning."

Ruth listed the address and time of service.

"Great. I'll see you soon."

Nancie hung up the phone, then hurried off to shower and dress.

∞

Risa placed one wary foot in front of the other and stepped into the sanctuary of the modest little church. She hadn't been to mass in years and hadn't ever gone to a Protestant "worship service" as Mike called it. Slipping into one of the back pews, Risa still couldn't believe the guy was a pastor—and a most convincing one at that. Even Wren hadn't been able to get her out to church.

Wren. Her heart still ached miserably just thinking about him, although she knew it was her own fault. He never led her on, but she'd forged ahead anyway. She was only too glad that he wasn't here today. She didn't want Wren to think she'd begun stalking him, for pity's sake! But Mike had assured her Wren was out of town for the weekend. Several unanswered telephone calls seemed to confirm it.

At last the service started, and the congregation was asked to open their hymnals. Organ and piano music filled the small church, and soon the singing matched it in a joyous sound. Next came some announcements, followed by the offering, and then the pastor stood at the pulpit and began his message. At the end of the service, she went away thinking about what she'd just heard. It was much the same thing Wren had showed her from the Bible the night of the rainstorm.

As she made her way into the throng heading out of the sanctuary, Mike approached her and pulled her aside. "So what did you think?" he asked.

She smiled tersely. "I think this religion stuff isn't for me."

His dark brows furrowed in concern. "Well, let's talk about it. My sister, Patti, wanted me to invite you for a noon dinner. She's a great cook and—"

"No thanks," Risa cut in. She couldn't be certain of the good pastor's intentions. Was he after another convert or looking for romance? In either case, she wasn't interested. "Have a nice life, Mike."

With that, Risa left the church, fully expecting never to set foot inside the place again.

∞

Nancie felt a little guilty watching Ruth load her dishwasher and straighten up the kitchen while she just sat there doing nothing. "Are you sure I can't help you?"

"Positive."

"Well, I appreciate you inviting me over for lunch."

"It was fun."

Nancie smiled, although it was bittersweet. "All the commotion around the table made me miss my girls."

"Oh, I'm sorry," Ruth said in a sympathetic tone. "It's got to be hard being away from them every weekend."

Nancie nodded. "And it's getting harder."

Ruth turned and leaned her backside against the counter. Tipping her light brown head to one side, she gave Nancie a thoughtful look. "What do you want most in your life right now?" she asked. "If you could have anything in the world—any one thing—what would it be?"

Nancie couldn't help showing a little smirk. "A million dollars and my fam—"

"Ah!" Ruth held up a forestalling hand. "I said any one thing. You said money."

"Oh, now wait a minute. Before you think I'm a 'material girl,' you need to know I was only kidding around."

"Were you?"

"Of course."

"Jesus said, 'The mouth speaks what the heart is full of.' "

Nancie merely smiled at the comment, but inwardly she bristled and hoped she wasn't about to hear a second sermon today.

"You know, my sister has a great job. I used to be so envious of her. All I could see was that she got to drop off her kids at day care and then go to her challenging work while I was stuck at home changing diapers and listening to whining, bickering children all day."

Nancie gave her a curious look. "You? You felt that way?"

"Uh-huh."

"That's how I felt. Exactly."

"Well, then my sister's six-month-old daughter died of SIDS— sudden infant death syndrome. She'd been napping at the sitter's house at the time. It wasn't anyone's fault, of course, but my sister blamed herself—still does."

"How tragic."

Ruth agreed. "But through that misfortune, I realized how precious every day is with my kids. I vowed never to take them, my husband, or my home for granted again." She chuckled. "God supplied my heart with an abundance of love and then He blessed me with my own business—a day care."

While Ruth turned back to the sink and finished cleaning up, Nancie thought about little Nathan's drowning on Memorial Day. Yes, life was precious. And yes, Nancie had taken her family for granted, too. However, she wanted to make things right. But how could she accomplish it if Wren moved out of town?

He just can't get that job, she thought with an edge of determination.

Sometime later, she left the Bairds' home and drove back to her apartment where she changed clothes. Then she lay down in her bedroom and took a short rest. All the while she pleaded with God to foil Wren's possible employment with American Printworks. She found it ironic, too, that she was actually praying he wouldn't make the move, take the step up. Years ago she would have been rejoicing. Then again, years ago she didn't have her career in the sales department to be concerned with.

Why do I have to be the one to make the sacrifice? she wondered. *That's not fair.*

But soon Nancie pushed aside the question and prayed once more that she wouldn't be forced to give up anything—because Wren wasn't going to get that job!

∽

It was seven o'clock when Wren finally phoned Nancie and let her know he and the girls were back in town. He offered to drive Laura to her place, but Nancie said she'd pick her up instead.

On the drive over, Nancie rehearsed what she wanted to tell Wren. She wanted to say she loved him and that somehow, some way, they'd work everything out.

Nancie parked her car and walked to the house. Crossing the porch, she pressed the bell switch. Alexa appeared and threw open the door, mumbling a brief, "Hi, Mom," before dashing off to whatever she had been doing. Nancie let herself in and, as she shrugged out of her spring jacket, she saw the girls were involved in some electronic table tennis game that they were playing using the television and two hand-held controls.

"Where's your dad?"

"In the kitchen," Alexa replied, "with Risa."

Nancie's heart stalled. "Oh really?"

142

At the sound of her sharp tone, both girls glanced at her. She gave them each a tight smile, then proceeded to the kitchen. She could hear Wren talking, although she couldn't make out what he was saying. But it didn't matter. That woman had to go.

Pausing in the dining room, Nancie collected her wits. She took a deep breath and tried to remember her new resolution to watch her words, to hold her tongue.

Then she walked in.

"Hi." She looked at Risa, then Wren, noting his mild look of surprise.

"Did you just get here?" he asked.

"Just now. I rang the doorbell and everything."

Wren momentarily pursed his lips in thought. "Oh," he said as realization struck, "I was in the basement."

Nancie shifted her gaze to Risa, who glared back at her. Nancie couldn't deny that the redhead made a fetching sight in her fitted jeans and white cotton top. Her curly hair hung around her face and shoulders attractively, and it caused a painful swell of jealousy in Nancie's chest.

"What are you doing here?"

A sad but smug grin tugged at Risa's glossy mouth. "I came to say hello to a good friend and make sure he's feeling better."

"And she's just leaving," Wren cut in before Nancie could utter a reply.

He ushered Risa toward the door, and Nancie watched until the woman was gone.

"I suppose you're in your prime having two women fighting over you," she shot out as Wren strode toward her.

He stopped short under the wide wooden doorframe between the living and dining rooms. Nancie sensed a battle brewing between them.

"Mom, don't be mad," Alexa said, dropping the game control and bolting up off the floor. "I let Risa in while Dad was in the basement doing laundry." She looked from one parent to the other. "I didn't really think about it. I just let her in. Sorry."

Wren's features softened. "It's okay, sweetheart," he told her. Looking back at Nancie, he pointed to the kitchen, where they could verbally tear each other to pieces without the girls overhearing.

Spinning on her heel, Nancie marched into the other room. She chose a place to stand, then turned to face Wren and folded her arms in front of her. She hated feeling so jealous and suspicious; however, Alexa's admission had alleviated much of it.

"Do you see why I can't stay in my present job situation much longer?" Wren began.

"Risa's that much of a temptation, huh?"

"You'd better believe it."

"Wren, that's so weak. Can't you stand up to her? Tell her to get lost!"

He shook his head and lifted his gaze as if to say she didn't understand. And she didn't.

"Nancie, I care about Risa. That's the truth. . .and the problem. She was a good friend to me when I needed one. But she knows I want to reconcile with you and she's hurt by it. I always made it clear to Risa that ours was a platonic relationship, but, regrettably, things between us somehow developed more than I should have allowed."

Nancie tipped her head. "What does that mean?"

Wren sniffed and gazed at the linoleum flooring. "It means I used Risa for months the same way you used me on Memorial Day weekend. I say that to my shame." His gaze came back to hers. "But she filled a void."

"Okay. . ." Nancie's anger dissipated. "That's understandable."

"It's unfortunate."

"But now it's over, right?"

Wren shook his head. "It'll never be over, Nancie, as long as Risa makes herself available to me."

"Because you care about her?" Nancie questioned carefully.

Wren nodded.

"Are you telling me you're in love with her?" Fingers of apprehension climbed her spine as she waited for the reply.

"No, I'm not telling you that." He rubbed the back of his neck wearily.

She narrowed her gaze in disappointment. "But you're not denying it."

Wren dropped his hands and gave her a level look. "No, I guess I'm not completely denying it either, although I don't know what it is I actually feel for Risa. I know it's not a relationship God would want me to pursue, but these feelings are real and they're there and I don't know what to do with them."

Nancie mulled it over. "Well, at least you're honest."

Without a reply, Wren exited the kitchen and Nancie listened as he instructed Alexa to get ready for bed. When the girl reached the hallway, Nancie watched her do a silly jig while singing about her last two and a half days of school.

Wren reentered the kitchen minutes later, and out of the corner of her eye, Nancie saw Laura scoot to her bedroom.

"Laura wants to sleep over," Wren informed her, "and I thought that might be okay. When the girls go to bed, we can talk some more."

Nancie nodded, seeing the wisdom in that. "Can I make a pot of coffee?"

"Go for it."

Stepping to the cupboard, she pulled out the coffee can and began preparing the brew. She marveled at Wren's predicament, yet understood very well how it had come about. He was handsome and sensitive to a fault. The all-around nice guy. And yet if he hadn't been so "nice," Nancie might still be wallowing in that horrid depression. . .or worse, she might be dead.

One at a time, the girls came out to say good night and kiss their mother. Again, that feeling of playing house enveloped her, and she noticed Alexa and Laura were cherishing each and every aspect of the game.

But was it just pretend? Nancie had to decide. Could she give Wren what he wanted in life and still be happy, or was he better off with Risa?

No way! her heart protested. *She can't have him.* Nancie grinned. That answered that.

Once the coffee finished brewing, Nancie poured a cup and headed for the living room. She discovered Wren sitting on the couch, hunched forward, his hands folded and suspended between his knees. She thought he looked discouraged.

Compassion filled her being and she sat down beside him. Setting her mug on the coffee table, she slipped her arm across his shoulders. "I love you," she whispered. "I'm not just saying that either."

She watched him grin, although his gaze remained fixed on his hands.

"The truth is," she continued, "I never stopped loving you, Wren. But for years, I loved myself more."

Taking a deep breath, he sat back and Nancie let her arm fall away.

"I love you, too. I know that's for sure."

Smiling, she reached for her coffee and tucked her legs under her before she curled up beside him. Wren brought his arm around her.

"I'll make you forget all about Risa," she promised. "Everything will work out."

"You think so?" There was a challenging glint in his eyes that Nancie found irresistible.

"I know so." She kissed him to emphasize her point.

"Mmm. . .maybe you're right."

She laughed. "And I didn't even spill my coffee."

His grin broadened. But after several moments, his somber look returned. He searched her face. "Do you love me enough to follow me anywhere, Nancie?"

She knew he was referring to his possible job offer with American Printworks. "I love you enough to discuss it if it comes down to that."

But it wouldn't, she thought. *It just couldn't!*

Chapter 20

It was ten o'clock in the morning, and Nancie felt as though she were walking on air, above the clouds. Her boss had named her to head up their department's next big project. At last she could prove herself and earn the respect of the company's top executives. What a way to start a Monday!

The rest of the day continued in much the same vein. Over and over again Nancie thanked the Lord for her good fortune, certain that this was God's way of letting her know Wren hadn't gotten the job and that she wouldn't have to ditch her career. They could still re-marry and begin anew—Wren need only transfer to a different postal station.

Around four thirty that afternoon Nancie phoned him, knowing he would likely be home. As it rang, she wondered if he was feeling bummed out; she warned herself to be sensitive.

Then he answered.

"Hi. Did you just walk in?" she asked.

"About twenty minutes ago. I've got Laura with me."

"Okay." A nervous swell rose in the pit of her stomach. "So, what's the verdict?"

A pause. "I got the job. You're talking to the new manager of American

Printworks' mail room and distribution center. I handed in my resignation today."

Nancie could scarcely believe it. She had prayed so hard. . .how could God have allowed this to happen?

"Nancie? You still there?"

"Yes, I'm here." She swallowed hard. "I've got good news, too," she said, although the glory of it had suddenly vanished. "I'm in charge of the sales department's next project. It's a big one."

"Congratulations." He sounded sincere.

"Yeah, same to you," she felt obligated to reply.

"Should we celebrate? Name the restaurant."

She was so overcome with disappointment, she could barely croak out an answer. Finally she told him to choose the restaurant.

"Okay. I'm sure the girls and I can think up a place to go."

"Do they know?"

"About my job change?"

"Yes."

"I just finished telling them before you called, but they've got a lot of questions. Maybe we can field them together at dinner."

"Sure," she said. "Sure, that'll be fine."

With that, she hung up the telephone and felt her heart sink.

∞

Wren could tell Nancie wasn't happy about his new position. He knew she wouldn't be. But he had to hand it to her, she was doing a great job in keeping her displeasure from the girls.

"So are you guys getting married?" Alexa wanted to know.

Wren forked a piece of steak into his mouth, leaving Nancie to answer that one. She appeared quite dignified, sitting across the table from him. Her hair was pinned up in a professional manner, and the beige-and-navy plaid suit she wore incorporated tiny gold stripes that enhanced her elegance.

Nancie caught his gaze and held it. "I don't know. We're trying to work things out."

Wren decided that's the best reply he could hope for at this point.

"Until you do," Alexa said, "can I live with Dad?"

Wren turned his attention to his baked potato. He wanted to let Nancie respond to as many of the girls' questions as possible, since they were the same ones he'd been pondering all weekend. When he had tried to discuss them with her before, she had changed the subject each time he brought it up.

"If you live with your father," Nancie replied, "I'll never get to see you."

"Yeah. And besides, it's not fair," Laura interjected, "because I wanna live with Dad, too."

He tried not to wince, although he had a feeling that was coming.

"Wren?" He looked up, noting Nancie's pained expression. "Any suggestions?"

He set down his fork. "Well, perhaps for the summer the girls can live with me during the week. Mom said she'd babysit for free. On Friday nights I can drive them to your place."

Nancie drove her knife into her veal with a bit more force than necessary. "See, girls? Your dad has it all figured out." She shot him a look that could have withered a cactus.

"Are you mad, Mom?" Alexa asked perceptively.

"Not at you, sweetheart," Nancie crooned.

"At me?" Laura wondered with a worried frown.

"No, honey."

The girls turned wide eyes toward Wren.

"Your mom doesn't like it that I have to move so far away for my new job," he tried to explain.

Alexa smiled impishly and looked at Nancie. "Are you going to miss him?"

"Incredibly."

Wren had to grin at Nancie's underlying sarcasm. But later, it wouldn't be so funny. He had a feeling he was in for it.

Alexa didn't pick up on the quip, however. "Well that's dumb, Mom. Why don't you just marry Dad and move, too? Then we'll be all together and no one will have to miss anyone."

"Sounds like a plan to me," Wren said. As long as he was in trouble, he might as well dig himself in deep.

"I think I'm ready for dessert," Nancie announced in a velveteen voice as she pushed her plate aside. "And I'm in the mood for a huge hot fudge sundae."

Alexa and Laura were in immediate agreement, and Wren said nothing. He knew better than to interfere with women and their chocolate.

∞

Risa managed to avoid Wren for an entire week and a half. He had candidly informed her that he loved his ex-wife and planned to re-marry her, so Risa stayed out of his way. When their paths did happen to cross, she was polite, friendly, and unemotional. She gave him her best supervisor smiles and words of encouragement, but never let on how badly her heart ached. Never once. For such a performance, Risa decided she ought to get nominated for an Academy Award. However, on this particular Wednesday afternoon, she couldn't seem to mind her own business. She'd been secretly observing him all along and recognized misery when she saw it.

She sneaked up on him as he prepared to leave for the day. "Excuse me."

He whirled around. "Hey Risa," he said casually.

"Hey." She leaned up against the wall and folded her arms. "Pardon me for noticing, but in spite of your exciting new job and wedding plans, you don't seem very happy."

"Yeah, well, Nancie and I are barely speaking to each other." He caught himself and shook his head. "Never mind. Forget I said that."

"Too late, it's already said." He made like he didn't hear her, so Risa shrugged. "Okay. Well, you know my phone number if you ever feel like talking."

"I almost called a couple of times," he confessed in hushed tones. "But I can hardly go running to you every time my wife gets mad at me."

"Ex-wife," she corrected him. "And this only goes to show that you'd be wise not to make the same mistake twice."

Wren expelled a weary-sounding breath and, as usual, Risa's heart went out to him.

"So what are you two sparring about now?"

"Nancie can't bring herself to leave her career in order to marry me and move to Neenah."

"Surprise, surprise."

Wren lifted a brow, indicating his displeasure at the cynicism.

"Sorry. But if the man I loved asked me to leave my job and marry him, I'd have my written notice on the boss's desk in five minutes." Risa shoved her hands into her uniform pants pockets and stared down the corridor. "True love is hard to find."

He didn't reply.

"Want to go find something to eat after work and talk?"

"No, but thanks for the offer." He gave her a grateful smile.

She shrugged again. "Okay. Guess I'll see you tomorrow."

"Yeah—see you tomorrow, Risa."

She walked away, amazed at Wren's faithfulness to a woman who deserved nothing but his condemnation. *Why can't it be me?* she wondered ruefully. *Why can't it be me?* She had a hunch it never would be her, either, because she'd never again in her life meet another Wren Nickelson.

∽

Nancie felt sick to her stomach as she and the girls carried boxes out to the rented truck. He was really doing this, the scoundrel. He was forcing her to choose between him and her career. Well, despite what he wanted, namely, a conversation on the subject, Nancie refused and kept a tight lid on her emotions. No doubt that's what was really getting to Wren. Her silence was killing him. However, she took no delight in the revelation. It was killing her, too.

"Hi, Nancie. Nice to see you again."

She gave the dark-haired man standing on the porch beside Wren a perfunctory smile. He looked vaguely familiar.

"This is Pastor Mike Gerardi from church," Wren informed her.

"Oh, right. Hello." She walked past him and suddenly remembered her promise to God. Hadn't she said she'd apologize for her rudeness in the years gone by if she ever got the chance?

Yes, she had, and now it was time to make good on that vow. God was the only one she shared her heart with lately. But for days she had felt like the Lord had let her down, had abandoned her. Then last week, clearly out of the blue, Ruth Baird made a comment, likening God to any good parent. "He doesn't give us everything we want just because we ask for it." Nancie had understood the parallel at once, but it still didn't make her decision any easier.

"Um, Mike? Can I have a word with you?"

He looked surprised, but nodded.

Nancie ignored the curious frown on Wren's face and waved the pastor into the rapidly emptying dining room.

"What can I do for you?" he asked.

She inhaled deeply, gathering her resolve. Apologies didn't come easily. "I just wanted to tell you how sorry I am for being rude in the past. I know you and other members of your congregation only had my best interests in mind whenever you came calling, but I didn't see it that way."

He smiled. "All's forgiven."

"Thanks."

Nancie returned to the girls' bedroom and began packing another box.

It was around the dinner hour when Nancie decided to take a break and sit on the covered porch. The four guys from church who had come to help with the furniture had long since gone home, while Wren and the girls went to pick up a pizza.

Lowering her bone-tired body onto a step, she surveyed the discarded junk, piled along the curb. A light drizzle had begun, and if it wasn't trash before, it would be soon. Strangely enough, she felt remorse at the sight of the worn couch and matching armchair, the scuffed-up side tables, coffee table, and boxes of chipped dishes and cracked goblets that Wren said he no longer wanted. Completely understandable, and yet those were the same things, in the same sorry shape, that he insisted upon salvaging when Nancie had filed for divorce almost two years ago.

Wren had changed.

With elbows on knees, Nancie rested her head in her hands. And that's when she saw it. His obsolete computer. It was protruding at an odd angle from one of the cardboard boxes near the street. Inexorably, she felt drawn to it. She walked off the porch and into the light rain, wondering why Wren had pitched his computer. Didn't he need it until he bought a newer computer?

Nancie lifted the machine from the box and, to her horror, she found scraps of Wren's novel, wet and crumpled yet recognizable, lying beneath it.

"But you can't throw it away," she murmured. "You haven't finished the story."

Her heart dropped as she considered the implication. Because of her, Wren's dreams were all but dashed at the roadside. She stood there for a moment, feeling like she couldn't breathe.

Then suddenly she knew what she had to do. Lowering the computer back into the box, she dragged it across the street and stowed it in the trunk of her car. When at last the deed was done, Nancie rubbed her palms together and made her way back to the duplex.

Chapter 21

Warm, early-morning sunshine spilled down on Nancie as she sat on Wren's front porch. Make that Wren's former front porch. He had left Saturday night in the rented moving truck filled with his belongings. Alexa and Laura had gone with him, and all three were now temporarily staying with Wren's folks. Since he was to start in his new position next week, Wren had informed Nancie that he planned to use these next few days to clean up the old place and get his security deposit back, then find an apartment in or around Neenah. Nancie had taken it upon herself to help Wren with both projects, and now she sat awaiting his arrival.

She smiled, anticipating his expression. He would wonder why she wasn't at work; after all, it was Monday. And then she'd tell him.

Carefully, Nancie pulled the folded piece of paper out of her blue jeans pocket and stared at the information. She'd been busy yesterday, and she'd been a real estate agent's nightmare. Without Wren knowing, she had driven up north, bought a local paper, and spent all afternoon scouting through homes that were listed on the market. She knew exactly what she wanted, and she was stubborn enough not to settle for anything less, in spite of the best sales tactics. But she might have found it—their castle in the clouds. She and Wren had an appointment to tour the home this afternoon. From what the real estate agent said, it sounded perfect.

Now all she had to do was tell Wren about it—about everything.

Tucking the note back into her pocket, Nancie waited another half-hour before Wren finally showed up. As she had expected, he was surprised to see her.

"What are you doing here?" he asked, stepping slowly to the porch. He wore an old blue T-shirt and worn-out, paint-splattered jeans; he carried a plastic bucket in his left hand.

"I thought I'd help you clean the flat."

He raised curious brows. "Well, thanks. Did you take the day off or something?"

Nancie nodded.

"That's nice of you."

She followed him into the empty, hardwood-floor echo chamber of a house. "Actually, Wren. . .I resigned this morning. I gave my boss a two-week notice and then I took today off."

He turned around slowly and faced her. If he'd been surprised before, he was dumbfounded now. His dark brown gaze fastened to hers, as if trying to read into her heart, to guess her motives.

But that wasn't necessary. Not anymore. From now on, she'd be transparent with Wren.

"I love you," she stated simply. "I can't live without you. I mean, even after the divorce, when I thought I was independent and on my own, I still relied on you for a lot of things. But you were kind enough to be there for me despite the way I hurt you." She smiled, though tears filled her eyes. "Sorry, buster, but I know a good thing when I see it." She strode forward, pointing her index finger at him. "You're not getting away from me, and I'm never going to let another woman come between us. Got it?"

He nodded and slipped his arms around her waist. "You're the one I love, Nancie. Always have, always will."

"I know," she said in complete honesty. "And I love you that much more for it."

He pressed a tender kiss against her lips, sealing their precious new commitment. Then he held her against him, and Nancie lay her cheek against his shoulder.

"I'll never hurt you again," she promised.

He kissed her forehead in reply.

She lifted her head. "No more arguing, fussing, fighting. . .none of it. We're going to live happily ever after."

Wren smiled into her eyes, before releasing her almost abruptly. "That's music to my ears, Nancie, but first things first and that means a wedding."

"I promised the girls they could be in it."

Wren gaped at her for a moment. "When did you do that?"

"A couple of weeks ago."

"Was someone planning to inform the groom of these plans?"

Nancie laughed. "Eventually. But you've got it easy. All you have to do is show up in a tux."

Wren pursed his lips agreeably. "I think I can handle that."

"And. . .you might have to pay for the reception," she added on a note of chagrin.

"I can handle that, too, as long as you don't rent the Taj Mahal or something."

Smiling, she leaned forward and grabbed the handle of the wash bucket. "It's a deal. But in the meantime, we've got a busy day ahead of us. We have to get this place cleaned up in time to make a three o'clock appointment."

"What appointment?"

Nancie nibbled her lower lip somewhat nervously. "I can't tell you just yet. Is that all right?"

After a brief deliberation and a curious, if not doubtful, look, he nodded.

By eleven-thirty the place was spotless. By noon the landlord showed up, inspected it, and wrote Wren a check for his security deposit. Next, Nancie followed Wren in her car as they drove to his parents' house, where they changed clothes. His parents, along with Alexa and Laura, were full of questions. Wren and Nancie promised to answer them after they returned.

Hand in hand, they walked to the driveway.

"I'll drive," Nancie said, "seeing as I have a vague idea of where I'm going."

"A vague idea?"

She had to laugh at Wren's concerned expression; however, her insides were trembling. This was going to be the tough part. But restoring dreams usually wasn't easy.

She pulled the slip of paper from her pocket and reread the directions. "I did a bit of homework yesterday," she began, "and I might have found us a place to live."

"That's the big secret?"

"It's part of it."

For once in her life Nancie felt grateful that Wren was a patient man. He didn't drill her or quiz her, but sat quietly in the passenger seat, awaiting his fate.

Finally, she realized they were nearing the house, so she pulled off onto the shoulder of the road. They got out of the car and started walking. To their right, a brown, wood-plank fence marked off the property.

"I haven't seen this place yet, but from the description I was given, it sounds like what I want."

Wren inclined his head somewhat hesitantly.

And then they came upon it—a two-story brick house on a hill. In the front, off to one side, was a miniature turret that gave the place a castlelike appearance.

Nancie laughed. "It's perfect!"

Wren put his arms on the fence and stared at the structure.

She cleared her throat. "A man's home is his castle."

He glanced at her with amusement in his eyes.

"A castle in the clouds," she added.

Wren didn't respond to the use of his novel's title. Then again, Nancie wasn't supposed to know the name of it.

"Can't you just see George and Nan trying to redecorate this place without killing each other?"

That did it.

Slowly he turned, one hand on his hip, the other on the fence. He gave her an incredulous look. "How do you know about George and Nan and the castle?"

Nancie swallowed and did her best to appear contrite. "I found your book."

"Found?"

"Accidentally on purpose. You see, it was at about the time I felt sure you were trying to get custody of the girls, so when I saw you stuff some papers in the buffet drawer and lock it, I got suspicious. I thought they were legal documents. I also watched where you put the key. After you left for your writing class, I peeked in the drawer...and found your story."

He said nothing, but his dark eyes and stony expression spoke volumes.

"Don't be angry with me, Wren," she pleaded. "I like your book. You're a wonderful writer."

He shook his head and turned away, gazing in the direction of the house again. "I never intended for anyone else to see that story. I'm so embarrassed."

"Don't be. I'm the only other person who knows about it. And I'm not going to push the issue, but I hope you're going to continue writing your book."

"Hadn't planned on it."

"But I have to know how it ends."

"Happily ever after," he quipped.

Nancie backed up to the low fence and rested her elbows on it. "Well, I certainly hope George told Lucia to take a swim in the moat with the alligators."

Wren chuckled and moaned simultaneously. "Oh Nancie, I can't believe you read that piece of tripe!"

"Don't call it that." She shrugged, unable to fully explain how she felt. "Your story affected me...and I think it affected you, too."

"It was good therapy for me to write those scenes," he admitted. "They saw me through a lonely, discouraged time in my life. But I'm not really a writer."

"Yes, you are. Okay, so you're not exactly Faulkner or Hemingway. Not yet, anyway. But you've got a special way of conveying a meaningful message...and it changed my life."

"Well, that just proves God can use anything."

She smiled and let the subject go. Then she nodded toward the house. "What do you think?"

"I think we can't afford it, by the looks of it. What's the asking price?" When she told him, his tone changed. "That's more than reasonable—it's downright inexpensive. What's the catch?"

"The owner got transferred out of state and wants a quick sale. What's more, it's an older home, kind of in the middle of nowhere, and it's not part of the fashionable subdivision we passed, so it's not as desirable as some of the other homes on the market."

Wren seemed contemplative.

"Should we at least take a look?" she prodded.

"Sure, why not?"

They walked up the inclined driveway and met the real estate agent in the yard. After briefing them on several particulars, he led them into the vacant house.

They toured the first floor—living room with a fireplace and sunroom, formal dining room, spacious kitchen, family room with patio doors leading outside to a deck. Upstairs there were three spacious bedrooms and one smaller room that the agent said had been a sewing room.

Nancie nudged Wren with her elbow. "This can be your writing room."

"Yeah, right."

"Well, feel free to wander," the agent said. "I'll be downstairs. When you're through with your inspection, we can talk."

"So, what's your opinion of the place?" she asked, once the real estate agent was out of earshot.

He gazed out the window. "It's a pretty small castle and not half as spooky as the one in Saxony."

Nancie smiled.

"It's also more costly than the half-dollar George had to pay."

"I'm glad you mentioned money," she said, coming to stand beside him. She looped her arm around his. "I have a certificate of deposit that I bought after I sold our house in Shorewood. I planned to pay for my education with it, but I'd rather we use it for a down payment instead."

Wren turned from the window and eyed her speculatively. "You sure about that?"

"Positive."

"That's quite a sacrifice."

"Not really. Not when I consider the whole picture of our lives together with our daughters." She smiled up at Wren, knowing she meant every word.

He stared back at her thoughtfully. "We need to pray about buying this house, Nancie."

"All right," she replied easily, although there was a time when that directive would have irked her to no end.

"But I like it." His gaze went back to the window and beyond. "I like it a lot. I guess we can at least put an offer in on it."

Nancie's spirit soared. "And this will be your writing room? And you'll finish the rest of the story?"

"Yes, I'll finish it." Wren looked back at her, smiling broadly. Then he gathered Nancie in his arms. "But you know, we really don't need fairy tales in order to live happily ever after. We've got the Lord, each other, and two beautiful daughters. That's enough."

He kissed her then, and Nancie knew without a shadow of a doubt that what he said was true.

Epilogue

Wren never thought he'd see the day. Today marked his first book signing, and he felt almost as nervous as when he and Nancie remarried.

With his wife at his side, he sat in front of a rectangular table draped with a charcoal gray cloth. It matched the cover of his book, *Castle in the Clouds*, and the manager of this particular Christian bookstore had been kind enough to host Wren's first autograph session.

Now, if only a few readers would show up. . .

"Don't be nervous," Nancie said, deciphering his thoughts. She sat calmly beside him in her denim jumper, looking every bit of eight months pregnant. Still, she gave him a reassuring smile. "It's a good book. It's going to be a bestseller."

Wren had his doubts. However, the fact that his novel had even been published was triumph enough for him. And he couldn't have done it without Nancie.

One by one, readers straggled to the table, looked over Wren's novel, and chatted a bit. Occasionally someone actually bought his book and returned for an autograph.

"This isn't exactly the kind of book signing I imagined," he confided to Nancie. "I envisioned a line extending out the door and into the mall—and writer's cramp. But it's eleven-thirty, and we've sold all of three or four copies."

"That's because your book is so new. It takes time to build a readership."

Wren sighed. "I'm glad you're my PR person. And I'm doubly glad you work for free!"

Nancie's amber brown eyes twinkled with amusement. But then a little frown began to mar her brows.

"What's the matter?" Wren followed her line of vision and saw a woman with a headful of tangerine curls peering thoughtfully at a shelf in the store's Christian Living section. Tucked in the crook of her arm was Wren's book, and he didn't have to see her face to know the woman was none other than Risa Vitalis.

He glanced back at Nancie, deciding she ought to feel secure enough in their relationship not to be jealous or threatened by Risa's presence.

Her next words confirmed his hunch.

"I've been thinking about her lately," Nancie said of Risa. "I've been praying for her." She met his gaze. "I hope that, like your character Lucia, she finds the Lord."

Wren nodded. The more the plot had thickened in his novel, the less he had liked the idea of killing off that particular antagonist. Besides, his research had shown that probably wouldn't have been well-received in the Christian marketplace.

"Here she comes," Nancie whispered.

Wren turned and watched Risa's approach. She smiled a greeting before handing him his book.

"I heard about your book signing from Mike Gerardi. Congratulations. . ."—she glanced from Wren to Nancie—". . .both of you."

"Thanks," Wren said, picking up his pen. He felt flattered that Risa would make the ninety-minute drive to Appleton from Milwaukee in order to support his latest endeavor.

"How have you been?" Nancie asked.

"All right. I see you're expecting child number three."

Wren looked at Nancie in time to see her lovingly pat her protruding belly in affirmation. Feeling like the proud papa that he was, he grinned and handed the book to Risa.

"I'm glad to see you guys are doing okay," she said with a light of sincerity in her eyes. She looked at Wren. "Good-bye."

It sounded final. It looked final.

Risa swung around and left the bookstore.

"I hope *she's* doing okay," Nancie murmured, her voice tinged with concern.

Wren expelled a slow breath. "If Pastor Mike is keeping in touch with her, I'm sure she's just fine."

Nancie smirked. "Now wouldn't that be a story?"

"What, Risa and Mike?"

She nodded, raising a conspiratorial brow. "Definite possibilities, wouldn't you say?"

He shrugged; he hadn't really thought about it, although they did seem an unlikely pair. "Well, one thing I've learned over the course of the past eighteen months is that all things are possible with God."

"Amen to that!"

Wren and Nancie shared a chuckle, and then another reader stepped up to the table. A smile lingering on his face, Wren reached for the book the man held out to him. *Amen to that,* Wren silently agreed as his smile widened to an ear-to-ear grin.

Andrea Boeshaar has been married for nearly forty years. She and her husband have 3 wonderful sons, 1 beautiful daughter-in-law, and 5 precious grandchildren. Andrea's publishing career began in 1994. Since then, 30 of her books have gone to press. Additionally, Andrea cofounded ACFW (American Christian Fiction Writers) and served on its Advisory Board. In 2007, Andrea earned her certification in Christian life coaching and is currently the purveyor of The Writer's ER, a coaching & editing service for writers. For more information, log onto Andrea's website at: www.andreaboeshaar.com. Follow her on Twitter: @AndreaBoeshaar, and find her on Facebook: Andrea Boeshaar Author.

Familiar Strangers

by Gina Fields

Chapter 1

"Mama, are you going to marry Jeff?"

Sara Jennings tucked the pillow-soft comforter around her daughter's small body. "I don't know. Maybe someday."

Chloe promptly wormed her arms from beneath the binding cover. Like her mother, she didn't like feeling confined.

"That's what you always say," the four year old said.

Sara eased down to sit on the edge of the bed. "I know it is, but I haven't made my mind up yet." She scooped up a one-eyed giraffe from the foot of the bed and nestled the tired-looking toy into her daughter's waiting arms. *Poor George,* Sara thought. She really should find a button and replace his missing eye.

"But if you marry Jeff," Chloe persisted, "then I would have a daddy, like Missy and April."

Sara sighed. How did one explain to a child so young why she didn't have a daddy when her two best friends from her Sunday school class did?

The same way she always did, Sara decided, wondering how much longer she could get away with the same answer. "Sweetie, do you re-member what I told you the other day about some boys and girls having two parents and some having only one?"

Chloe gave a doleful nod.

"It doesn't mean you're any less special than the children who have both a mommy and a daddy. It just means I get to love you twice as much."

Chloe dropped her gaze to the spiked hair atop the giraffe's head. "I know," she responded in an I've-heard-it-all-before tone. "But I still want a daddy."

Sara's shoulders rose and fell in dejection. Ever since Jeff Chandler, the widowed director of a Chicago homeless shelter, had asked Sara to marry him six weeks ago, she and Chloe had had this same conversation several times over. And Chloe's answer was always the same. *"I want a daddy."* Not *"I want Jeff to be my daddy."*

Chloe's vague answer left Sara wondering if Chloe wanted Jeff, in particular, for a father or if she simply wanted *"a daddy."*

Since the marriage proposal, Sara had watched closely for signs of a developing parent-child relationship between Jeff and Chloe, but so far she'd seen little evidence of any. Sure, Jeff and Chloe were close, in an uncle-niece sort of way. But that special bond, like Jeff shared with his own two adolescent children, simply wasn't there.

And that alone gave Sara pause in making her decision.

If and when she ever decided to marry, the prospective husband would have to acknowledge and accept he was getting a package deal—a wife and daughter. Sara would rather die an old maid than have Chloe feel inferior to stepsiblings. Or anyone else, for that matter.

Sara leaned over, and Chloe rubbed noses with her mother. "Good night. Sleep tight," Sara chimed. "And don't let the bed bugs bite!" they finished together.

Giggling, Chloe reached up and rewarded her mother with a hug and a butterfly kiss on the cheek. Then, turning to her side, she snuggled George the Giraffe to her chest and closed her eyes.

Sara reached over to turn off the lamp, but then she paused to study her daughter. Chloe's long, tawny lashes curled against rosy cheeks, and her hair had grown so that it flowed like silk around her shoulders. Hard to believe they'd already celebrated her fourth birthday. Where was the baby that had nuzzled at her breast, cuddled on her shoulder, offered her toothless grins? Where had the last four years gone?

Into one mindless day after another, Sara silently answered her own question. A cycle of perpetual routine she had come to accept as her destiny.

And today had been no different.

She had gotten up at 6:00 A.M., showered and dressed for work, and had breakfast with Chloe and Evelyn Porter, the regal, elderly lady from whom Sara rented two rooms. Then Sara had bundled up Chloe in a thick sweater and warm toboggan—because, even in late May, Illinois mornings could be brisk—and together they had walked to one of the four houses Sara cleaned weekly in the upscale Chicago suburb where they lived.

While Sara scrubbed toilets, dusted furniture, and battled cobwebs, Chloe, as usual, had been content watching one of her favorite cartoon videos or playing with one of the games Sara brought along. But as always, guilt had pricked Sara's conscience at least twice that day because her daughter spent so much time entertaining herself.

As a single mom, Sara found meager comfort knowing she was doing the best she could do. After all, any plans she had made, any goals she had set for herself, had been ripped from her grasp five years ago. Now her plans and goals all centered on Chloe.

When Sara had finished her household tasks, she and Chloe walked back to Mrs. Porter's, where Sara helped her landlady prepare supper. Then, after the three shared the evening meal and the kitchen was put back in order, had come Sara's favorite time of day, when she tucked Chloe into bed with a hug and a prayer.

Another ordinary day. A day like any other. Nothing grand or spectacular about it.

In fact, Sara knew of only one truly grand and spectacular day since she'd come to live with Mrs. Porter almost five years ago. That was the day Chloe had been born. That day, that hour, that single moment had marked a new beginning for Sara. The instant she looked into her daughter's eyes, she knew God was giving her a second chance at life. She could either take it or throw it back in His face and continue mourning the life she had lost.

Sara had decided to take it.

And now, looking down at her daughter's face, she didn't have one single shred of regret. Reaching over, she brushed a strand of hair from Chloe's cheek and she was reminded, not for the first time, how different she and her daughter were. Chloe had straight blond hair and huge sapphire-blue eyes, while Sara had corkscrew curly brown hair and light brown eyes. Except for their slight frames, Sara couldn't find a single physical similarity between her and her child.

Did Chloe favor her father?

Only God knew.

Pulling the comforter up a few more inches on Chloe's shoulders, Sara shook off the melancholy spirit stealing over her. She would not waste time feeling sorry for herself; she had too much to be thankful for: a man who loved her enough to want to spend the rest of his life with her; a friend in Evelyn Porter, who had offered Sara a home when she was homeless; and a perfectly healthy daughter who gave her a reason to face one tedious day after another. A surge of love rose in Sara's chest and almost overflowed in the form of tears. All things considered, she was pretty well blessed.

She leaned down and planted a soft kiss on her daughter's cheek. Chloe's eyes fluttered open, then slowly drifted down again as the child slipped from twilight sleep into dreamland. Sara switched off the lamp and crept from the room.

Stifling a yawn, she went down the red-carpeted steps leading to the first floor. There was still plenty she needed to do: fold the laundry, unload the dishwasher. But those things could wait until morning. This had been a long day, and Mrs. Porter's chamomile tea smelled too delicious. All Sara wanted to do was pour herself a cup of the pungent brew and curl up with the suspense novel her landlady had brought home from the library that day.

Massaging her nape, Sara padded in socked feet across the marble foyer floor into a kitchen dimly lit by a single twenty-five-watt bulb that glowed from the range hood. Sara smiled as she ambled to the stove. Mrs. Porter might be "financially secure," as the refined lady so modestly put it, but when it came to cutting monetary corners, she was downright miserly.

Sara, on the other hand, was frugal because she had to be. She reached into the cabinet for a cup and saucer. Someday, when she saved enough money to buy herself and Chloe a home of their own, light would be an item on which she would not scrimp. Not only on the inside of the house, but on the outside as well. Abundant sunlight and wide-open spaces. One day, she and Chloe would have both—if Sara had to scrub a dozen toilets a day to get them.

"Sara?"

She was stirring a teaspoon of honey into her tea when Mrs.

Porter's genteel, high-pitched voice filtered into the kitchen from the adjoining room.

"I'll be right there." Sara put her spoon in the sink.

"You may want to hurry!"

Frowning, Sara glanced over her shoulder at the open doorway leading to the adjoining family room. Were her ears deceiving her, or was that a note of urgency she'd heard in Mrs. Porter's voice?

"Please," Mrs. Porter added in what sounded like an afterthought, as though she'd suddenly realized she had stepped out of character by using a tone other than her usually calm and proper one.

Gingerly balancing her cup on her saucer, Sara headed for the door.

Her landlady sat in a plush recliner, her eyes riveted on the television screen. The glow from a nearby floor lamp's low-wattage bulb reflected off her short white hair like a silver halo.

"Is something wrong, Mrs. Porter?" Sara asked.

Her gaze fixed on the screen, Mrs. Porter said, "I think you'll want to see this."

When Sara glanced toward the TV, she thought she knew why Mrs. Porter had called to her. On the screen was one of the most peaceful coastal scenes Sara had ever seen. Foamy waves lapped lazily over cream-colored sand, then slipped quietly, almost reluctantly, it seemed, back out to sea. Vigilant seagulls sailed over the water, and restless palm leaves danced in the wind.

Mrs. Porter knew Sara loved the ocean, knew she dreamed of seeing it one day for herself. Every time she saw a picture of the rocky cliffs bordering the Pacific or read about the mysteries of the blue Atlantic, longing filled her heart. But only in her imagination could she walk the endless stretches of beach, revel in cool water tugging at her ankles, lift her face to the wind's salty kiss.

Her shoulders rose and fell as a wistful sigh escaped her chest. *Someday*, she told herself. *Someday*. . .

A suave-looking gentleman appeared on the screen. The wind kicked up the front of his well-groomed gray hair as he strolled up the beach. "We come to you tonight from the tranquil beaches of Quinn Island, South Carolina," he said. "A place where southern hospitality is in abundant supply, and residents of this small, close-knit community pride themselves on maintaining one of the lowest crime rates in the Southeast."

He stopped and squared off to face the camera. "But almost five years ago, on the night of August eighth, tragedy struck Quinn Island with as much force as the battering winds of a class five hurricane, when one of their own, Lydia Anne Quinn, disappeared *without a trace*." The face of an attractive young woman, smiling like she held the world by its reins, flashed on the screen.

Sara stared at the screen for a moment in stunned silence. Then she blinked, and her world tilted, teetered on its side for a few precarious seconds, then tumbled from its axis, sending her stomach into a wild tailspin. She felt the blood drain from her face, and the cup and saucer slipped from her limp fingers. She was vaguely aware of searing liquid scalding her denim-clad right knee and seeping through the wool of her socks.

This can't be happening, she told herself, thinking any second now she'd wake up. When a sharp edge of broken china penetrated her sock and bit into her heel, she realized she was not dreaming. The day she had both longed for and feared had finally arrived. And life as she knew it was about to change. *Forever.*

Because the face on the TV screen. . .was hers.

∞

Still strong and agile at seventy-two, Mrs. Porter had helped Sara to the sofa before the younger woman completely collapsed, then fetched a Band-Aid for Sara's bleeding heel. The two women now sat side by side, holding hands, as they watched bits and pieces of Sara's life—the one she'd lived before waking up in a Chicago hospital five years ago.

Once Sara had watched every missing-person show televised in the Chicago area, thinking maybe, just maybe, a story would evolve that would lead to her identity. Even if she didn't have a family looking for her, she figured, surely *someone* would have noticed her absence—a boss, a coworker, a friend.

But, after a while, when episode after episode passed without re-vealing anything that might be of consequence to her past life, she grew weary of the waiting, the anticipation, and then the letdown. So she'd stopped watching, stopped waiting for someone to find her, and she accepted that whoever might have known her in her past life had either given up searching—or hadn't cared enough to ever begin to search. Now, here she was, on national TV. Someone *had* cared enough. Enough that they had never given up looking for her.

Aside from the throbbing of her now-bandaged heel, she was too shocked to feel anything but numb.

"Lydia Anne Quinn led a charmed and privileged life," came the skilled voice of the screen host. "She was born twenty-nine years ago on April second, the oldest daughter of William Quinn, the partner in a successful charter fishing business, and his wife, Margaret Quinn, a former teacher who left the classroom to become a full-time mom after Lydia was born."

"I'm twenty-nine years old," Sara whispered in awe. Her doctor had estimated her age, and every year Mrs. Porter insisted Sara celebrate her birthday with Chloe. Just last month, Sara had celebrated her twenty-seventh.

But she wasn't twenty-seven—she was twenty-nine. And her birthday wasn't April twenty-sixth, like Chloe's—it was April second.

After five years in ageless limbo, she finally had a beginning.

A portrait of herself and three other people, obviously her family, flashed on the screen. Her father appeared to be only a couple inches taller than her mother. He had the same curly brown hair and light brown eyes as Sara. Her sister, a tall, willowy blond, favored her mother.

Sara studied the portrait intently to see if something in one of the faces would kindle a spark of recognition, a sense of connection. But she felt nothing. They were all total strangers to her.

"Lydia was a high achiever," the host continued. "A straight-A student, head cheerleader, and homecoming queen her senior year in high school. She graduated summa cum laude from South Carolina State University. At the time of her disappearance, she owned and operated Lydia's Boutique, a prosperous dress shop located on Quinn Island's mainland. And she was planning to marry this man"—the scene changed to a handsome young man—"Attorney Daniel Matthews, who was the last person known to have talked to Lydia the night of her disappearance."

Sara's breath caught in her throat. She had been engaged. . .to an attorney. . .and he was *beautiful*. He wore his dark brown hair cut short on the sides, a little longer on top, and combed back in a side part— with the exception of one rakish lock that dipped toward her right brow. His wedge-shaped jaw, olive complexion, and prominent cheekbones hinted at an ancestry other than pure Anglo. Native American, maybe? His brown eyes held a touch of sadness that made Sara's pounding heart roll over.

"Lydia was on her way home from New York," the young attorney explained to the off-camera interviewer. "She'd driven up three days before to attend some fashion shows and order new designs for her dress shop. Normally, she would have flown, but she'd just purchased a new car the week before and wanted to drive it."

His educated southern drawl had a smooth, velvet-edged quality that captivated Sara. Without thought, she pulled her hands free from Mrs. Porter's and leaned forward a couple of inches, her own hands clasped tightly in her lap. Daniel Matthews was seated, she noticed, on a sofa in someone's living room. Whose home was he in? His? Hers? Her parents'?

"Her mother usually took these trips with her," he went on, "but Mrs. Quinn had undergone hip surgery a few days before, and she wasn't able to go along. Her sister Jennifer stayed behind to run the shop. So this was a solo trip for Lydia. Her first."

An indefinable emotion clouded his features. He paused, dropping his gaze to some point below the camera lens. Seconds hung in suspension while he appeared to struggle with his private thoughts. Then he raised his head and lifted his shoulders a few inches, as though summoning the fortitude to plow ahead. "Before she left, I bought her a cellular phone so she could check in with her parents or me while she was on the road, or call someone if her car broke down.

"The night she was expected home, she phoned me around eleven o'clock. She had crossed the South Carolina state line, but she had run into a traffic jam. She said she was going to get off the expressway somewhere above Darlington and try to work her way around it.

"I knew some of those rural roads could be deserted, especially so late at night, so I tried to talk her into staying on the interstate. But she told me not to worry, that she had a map."

He closed his eyes, and a raw grief flickered across his face. He swallowed hard, then wet his lips. Somehow, Sara sensed he was steeling himself against his next words.

Finally, he opened haunted eyes. "The last words she said to me were, 'I'll call you when I get home. I love you. Good-bye.' " His voice, as he delivered his final statement, was raspy with emotion.

Sara took a deep shuddery breath and pressed a trembling hand to her chest. Unexpected tears warmed her eyes. This man had loved her. Deeply. She could see it in his grieving expression, hear it in his tortured voice. And she had loved him, had told him so just before something dark and horrible had taken away what might have been a precious memory.

The scene switched to a foreign-made sports car sitting alongside a dark, deserted stretch of highway. The driver's door stood open. The host stepped into view on the right side of the screen.

"But Lydia didn't make it home that night," he said. "Instead, Daniel answered a knock on his door three hours later to find the Quinn Island sheriff and a deputy standing on his doorstep. The news they had to deliver was not good. They had received a call from the Darlington Police Department. Lydia's car had been found, abandoned, alongside a sparsely populated stretch of highway outside the Darlington city limits."

As the host spoke, a patrol car pulled up and stopped behind the sports coupe. Two actors portraying police officers got out and approached the abandoned vehicle cautiously. They continued playing their role while the host resumed the story.

"The driver's door was standing open, and Lydia's purse and cellular phone were found on the front passenger seat. Next to the flat rear tire on the passenger's side, a crowbar with traces of hair and blood was found."

Sara's hand rose and touched the jagged scar on her left temple, the one doctors had said probably robbed her of her memory. Had the crowbar delivered the blow? What about the four-inch laceration on the back of her head and the one over her right ear, the bruises and broken bones...?

Like hot water breaking into a boil, anger exploded in Sara's chest. The crowbar had not delivered the damaging blows to her defenseless body, the hands that held it had.

The doctors had told her she'd been brought into the hospital in the wee hours of August twelfth. According to the story unfolding on the TV screen, that had been a little more than two days after her disappearance. For forty-eight hours she must have been in the hands of her assailants. During that time, she had been stripped of all she was, all she had been, all she had loved.

A raw ache rose in her throat. Closing her eyes, she wrapped her arms around her waist and bit down hard on her lower lip. Faceless demons still haunted her. Demons that had robbed her of her memory, her past. The results of their actions, however, had left an irrevocable mark upon her life.

She squeezed her eyes shut tighter and started rocking, trying to shut out the harsh reality that wrapped around her like a fog. She had a family who loved her. . .and a fiancé who was still searching for her.

After almost five years of struggling to put some sort of life together for herself and her daughter, she had been found. She knew with certainty she was going home, but she also knew that things would never be as they once were. Not for her. Not for her family. Not for a man named Daniel Matthews. Because she was not the same woman who had left them half a decade ago. A sob tore from her throat. Could her parents, her sister, her fiancé accept the woman she had become—and the horrible things that had happened to her?

She felt Mrs. Porter's arms slip around her shoulders, and she turned her face into the crook of the older woman's neck. She was going home to a place she knew nothing about, a family of strangers, and a man she had promised to marry. What kind of homecoming would it be?

And what would they think about Chloe?

Chapter 2

At a television station in Manhattan, Daniel Matthews stood in the *Without a Trace* studio room, his gaze on a big-screen television boxed inside a pewter-gray wall. Arms crossed and feet braced shoulders' width apart, he watched as the story of his fiancée's disappearance unfolded. Behind him, eight telephone operators, stationed in two rows of four each, sat at individual computer terminals, headsets in place, waiting for the first call to come in.

Odd, Daniel thought as Lydia's picture gave way to a portrait of her and her family, *how losing someone you love can make time stand still.* He still looked for her face in every crowd and around every corner. Still surfed the net for countless hours in hopes of finding a clue to what had happened to her. Still waited each night for the phone to ring, for her to tell him she had made it home safely after all. At least once each day, he relived that fateful night when she'd been abducted from her car on a deserted stretch of highway north of Darlington.

He scrubbed a weary hand down his face, his mind buzzing through the brutal days that had followed. After six months of relentless searching proved futile, the sheriff had tried to convince Daniel the worst had happened. That Lydia had been killed and whatever was left of her would probably never be found. But Daniel refused to believe that.

Only when a body was discovered and positively identified would he accept that she was gone from him forever.

"How're you holding up?"

Daniel looked to his right, wondering how long Bob Siler, the head producer of *Without a Trace*, had been standing next to him. "I'm okay," Daniel answered, massaging the back of his neck.

"Really? You don't look okay."

A grin pulled at one corner of Daniel's mouth. He knew Bob's words were spoken out of concern and not criticism. Their frequent communications over the last few months had led to an amicable friendship.

"It's just the anticipation," Daniel said. "You'd think after five years I'd be used to it."

But he wasn't, and he doubted he ever would be. Every time a clue trickled in, hinting at what might have happened to Lydia, his reaction was always the same. Sweaty palms, a stiff neck, and a heart that pounded so hard his ears burned.

Then would come the letdown, a gut-wrenching twist to his insides that left his chest feeling hollow when the clue led to another dead-end.

"Daniel, you know what the chances are," Bob said as though reading Daniel's mind.

"Yeah, I know," Daniel replied. *Slim to none.* That's what everyone, including Bob, had told Daniel. In fact, from the start, Bob had been so negative about a program segment on Lydia's abduction, Daniel had been shocked when the producer had called two months ago to tell him the network had decided to air the story.

Of course, six months' worth of weekly calls from Daniel to the station might have had something to do with the decision. The show's producers had eventually figured out the persistent attorney wasn't going to give up until the story of his fiancé's disappearance was told. Since all else had failed, Daniel figured getting her picture on national TV was his best chance of finding her—maybe his last chance.

"I just want you to be prepared," Bob said.

Daniel chose not to respond. How did one prepare himself for the unknown? He jammed his fists into his pockets to keep from drying his damp palms on his dark dress slacks. "How long does it usually take before the calls start coming in?"

"It varies. Sometimes immediately. Sometimes a couple of hours. We've even had a few come in several days after a program aired."

A picture of Lydia's dress shop flashed on the screen, and a painful knot rose in Daniel's throat. The wedding gown she'd planned to wear less than a month after the date of her disappearance still hung in the back of that shop. Would he ever see her march down the aisle in it?

A buzzer indicated an incoming call. Pinpricks of anticipation raced up the back of Daniel's neck. Both men turned, but only Bob hurried to the operator who had answered the call. Daniel stood waiting, praying, his head throbbing from a sudden rush of blood.

Then Bob looked Daniel's way and motioned him over. Daniel sprinted across the room to join Bob, who was huddled over the operator as she transferred information onto the computer.

"What did you say your name was, ma'am?" the operator asked, then typed in *Elizabeth Bradford.*

"And you're calling from where?"

"Riverbend, Illinois."

"I know that area," Bob mused. "It's a ritzy suburb north of Chicago."

Ritzy, Daniel repeated to himself. Lydia would like ritzy. He held his breath.

"You said Ms. Quinn looks like someone you know?" the operator continued.

"Yes."

Daniel clenched a fist, ready to punch the air with glee.

"She looks like Sara Jennings, my cleaning lady."

Daniel's mounting hopes dissipated like a warm vapor in a cold wind. The last thing Lydia would be was a cleaning lady. She hated housework. In fact, before her disappearance, she had paid someone else to clean her one-bedroom apartment once a week to keep from having to do it herself.

The sudden drop from elation to disappointment left Daniel shaky. He ran trembling fingers through his hair.

Bob glanced back over his shoulder. "You don't think it's worth following up?"

Daniel released his pent-up breath with force. "No. The last thing you'd find Lydia doing for a living is cleaning houses."

"Anything's possible," Bob said. "I think we should at least look into it."

"Sure." Daniel hunched his shoulders. "Why not? Like you said, 'Anything's possible.'"

But Lydia? A cleaning lady? He didn't think so.

Spirits weighed down, he lumbered back across the room and re-sumed his vigil in front of the large-screen television and waited for the next call to come in.

∞

Daniel closed the lid on his suitcase. Last night, he'd waited at the stu-dio for two hours after the show ended. Aside from the strange call from the lady in Riverbend, Illinois, there had been no other calls. Bob had told him not to lose hope so soon, but the sympathy in the produc-er's eyes had belied his true thoughts. *Lydia's gone,* his expression had said. *Time to move on.*

Daniel ran a weary hand over his face. Maybe Bob was right. Maybe it was time to move on. Daniel just didn't know how without Lydia.

A knock sounded on his motel room door. He opened it to find the bellhop, standing at attention, his uniform as fresh and crisp as a navy captain's.

"Your cab is ready, sir."

"Thank you." Daniel turned to retrieve his suitcase.

"I'll get that, sir." In the blink of an eye, the bellhop slipped past Dan-iel and claimed the luggage.

Unaccustomed to being waited on, Daniel checked various pockets for his keys, wallet, and plane ticket to keep from cracking his knuckles, a nervous habit he'd picked up shortly after Lydia's disappearance. Be-fore stepping outside into the hallway, he slung his navy blazer over his shoulder and turned one last time to scan the opulent suite the *With-out a Trace* network had provided for him. Lydia would have loved the room. The blue velvet window dressings, the mottled marble fireplace, the plush white carpet. She was a woman at home in elegance.

In his mind's eye he saw her pirouetting in delight around the room like a gypsy, a long red dress swirling around her slim ankles and her shiny highlighted hair flowing about her pale shoulders. When she was in a good mood, her laughter and energy were contagious.

"Did I forget something, sir?"

Reluctantly, Daniel turned his attention back to the bellhop stand-ing a few feet down the hall. "No. I was just double-checking, but I think we got everything."

When he looked back into the room, his dancing gypsy was gone.

He pulled a deep breath into his tightening chest, then slowly released a long sigh. "Good-bye, my love," he whispered.

As he closed the door, an eerie sense of finality swept through him. And as he walked away, the words *Move on, Daniel. Time to move on,* seemed to follow him down the hall.

He pressed a generous tip into the bellhop's hand and slid into the car. "Kennedy Airport," he told the cabby. The driver eased his car out into the noisy New York traffic.

They had barely traveled a mile when Daniel's cell phone rang. He dug it out of his blazer pocket and flipped it open. "Hello?"

Silence filled his ear.

"Hello?" he repeated after five seconds.

Silence still, but he thought he heard someone breathing on the other end of the line.

"This is Daniel Matthews. May I help you?"

The line went dead.

Frowning, he pulled the phone away from his ear and pressed the caller ID button. He didn't recognize the number, but the area code triggered something in his memory. After a moment of thought, he realized it was the same area code as the woman who had called the studio the night before. But Daniel wasn't sure about the rest of the number. Could it be the same woman? If so, why was she calling him and not the TV station? And how did she get his number?

Only one way to find out. He hit the button that dialed the number on the display screen.

"Hello." The voice sounded like that of an elderly woman.

"Hello," he returned. "This is Daniel Matthews."

"Yes, Mr. Matthews," came a cheerful reply. "My name is Evelyn Porter. It's so good to finally speak to you."

"Thank you," he said, totally confused. "How did you get this number?"

"Directory assistance."

"Of course," he said, remembering he was having his home calls forwarded to his cellular phone. "What can I do for you?"

"Nothing, really."

Daniel clenched his teeth. Was this someone's idea of a joke? If so, he was in no mood. Tempering the rising anger in his voice, he said, "Then why did you call?"

"I didn't."

"Then who did?"

"The young lady who lives with me."

"And that would be. . . ?"

A slight pause, then, "Why don't I just let you talk to her."

Daniel waited while a muffled, inaudible conversation took place on the other end, then a faint click sparked a distant but distinct memory.

An earring. Lydia's earring always clicked on the receiver when she answered the phone. He sat up straighter in the seat.

"Hello?"

His lungs shut down and his heart slammed against his chest. The voice was hers.

"Hello," she repeated a little louder. "Is. . .anyone there?"

"Lydia? Is that you?"

"I. . .think so."

I think so? What kind of answer was that?

The pressure against his ribs reminded him he wasn't breathing. Slowly, he exhaled. "I don't understand."

"It's a bit complicated, Mr. Matthews. I'd rather not get into it over the phone."

Conflicting emotions tumbled through him. She'd called him *Mr. Matthews*. So formal. So impersonal. Was this another false alarm? Someone looking for a generous handout or public attention? He'd had enough of those in the past five years to last a dozen lifetimes.

"Mr. Matthews?"

But the voice. It was a bit timid and cautious sounding for Lydia, and the southern accent had a slight northern clip. But the sweet-as-honey intonation and the soft-as-silk inflection were definitely hers.

"Are you still there, Mr. Matthews?"

"Yes. Yes, I'm still here. I'm just. . .a little confused." *Make that a lot confused,* he added to himself.

"I'm sorry. I guess I do need to explain a little."

"Please."

He heard a slow, steady intake of breath. "Almost five years ago, sixteen days after Lydia Quinn's disappearance, I woke up in a Chicago hospital. I had been in a coma at least two weeks."

"Why? What happened?"

"I don't know. . .exactly. I couldn't remember." At least four seconds drifted by. "I still can't."

"*Still* can't?"

"That's right."

Daniel searched his mind and came up with only one possible answer. "Amnesia?"

"Yes."

His eyes slid shut. That explained everything. Why she hadn't come home. Why she hadn't called. She hadn't known *where* to come or *who* to call.

Opening his eyes, he pulled a pen from his shirt pocket and his plane ticket from the inside pouch of his blazer. "How do I get there?"

"Before I tell you, Mr. Matthews—"

"Daniel, please," he said with a grimace. If he didn't know better, he'd think he was talking to a stranger. He paused in the midst of balancing the plane ticket on his knee as reality sank in. They *were* strangers. At least he was to her. Right now, she didn't know him from anyone else she might pass on the street. How long before she regained her memory? *Would* she ever regain her memory?

"Okay. Daniel." Her wary voice interrupted his disturbing thoughts. "I think you and I should meet first and make absolutely certain I am Lydia before we get anyone's hopes up."

Get anyone's hopes up? She had to be kidding. His were already flying way above reach. But she had the right idea. Why get her parents' and sister's hopes up until he was absolutely certain she was Lydia? And when he saw her, he would be.

"I agree," he said.

"And would you please not notify *Without a Trace* yet?"

Her request struck him as odd. She had never been one to shun attention. She would have wanted the whole world to know she'd been found. But now was not the time to ponder her reasons for wanting secrecy. He'd agree to anything to get her to tell him where she was. "Okay. If that's what you want."

"It is."

He trapped the ticket between his knee and the heel of his hand, ready to write down her address.

"I have my reasons," she added, as though she owed him some sort of explanation.

A chilly finger of foreboding slid up Daniel's spine. What had happened to her in the last five years? What had she done with herself?

What kind of life had she led?

"This is where I live," came the mysterious yet oh-so- familiar voice.

Daniel snapped to attention and started writing down the information.

∞

Sara hung up the phone softly. She couldn't believe it. She had actually talked to someone from her past. Last night, after the show had ended, she had phoned directory assistance and gotten Daniel Matthews's telephone number, but she had waited until the morning to call. She'd needed time to think, time to figure out the terms on which she would meet him. After all, she had more to think about than herself. She had Chloe.

"Well," Mrs. Porter said from where she sat beside Sara on the family room sofa, "when do we get to meet Mr. Matthews?"

"Soon, I imagine. He's on his way to Kennedy Airport right now. He was in New York for the premier show last night and was on his way to catch his flight back to Quinn Island this morning. But now he's changing his plans. He's going to take the first flight he can get to Chicago. He could be here as early as this afternoon."

Rising, Sara crossed her arms and wandered to the tall window beside the stone fireplace. Sweeping aside the sheers that hung beneath tapered blue damask draperies, she looked out at the small oasis of flowers she had planted. The miniature roses climbing a cast-iron fence were just beginning to burst open in brilliant shades of pink. The red azaleas lining the edge of the yard were in full bloom, and the blossoming impatiens in the small flower bed surrounding a cedar bird feeder nodded lazily in the crisp morning breeze.

In her other life had she loved the feel of the earth sifting through her hands? Had she found one of the most amazing things in the world planting a seed and watching it grow?

Had she believed in God?

Does Daniel?

So many questions to be answered. So much territory to be rediscovered. Sara had always thought if this moment ever came, she'd be ready. Now that it had, she wasn't so sure.

Mrs. Porter touched Sara's shoulder. Sara turned to face the closest thing to a family she and her daughter knew. With wise eyes full of understanding, the older woman clasped Sara's hands. "Sara dear, I know you're scared. But remember, God sees the big picture. This will all unfold according to His plan."

"I know," Sara said past the mixed emotions that clogged her throat. God had brought her through too much over the past five years for her not to realize He had a hand in her being found. She squeezed Mrs. Porter's soft hands. "It's going to be hard leaving you."

Mrs. Porter's eyes grew misty. "I know. But you'll soon meet a man who loves you so much he's never stopped searching for you. You have a family who's grieved for you for almost five years. Just think of the joy you'll bring them all when you return to them. And you know I'll always be here for you and Chloe, no matter what. I hope you'll remember that."

Sara's own eyes teared. "You can count on it."

The two women embraced in a hug that Sara knew marked the ending of one era of her life and the beginning of another. This heartfelt gesture was a symbol of time shared, joy experienced, and blessings both great and small, they had brought to one another. The next would be to say good-bye.

Chapter 3

"Here we are," Daniel told the Chicago taxi driver.

The cabbie shot him an I-think-I-know-where-I'm-going look in the rearview mirror as he turned into the entrance of Twin Oaks subdivision in Riverbend, Chicago.

Unperturbed by the driver's obvious irritation, Daniel grasped the back of the front passenger seat and slid forward, reading the house numbers. After his phone conversation with Lydia that morning, he had managed to secure a flight to Chicago almost immediately. Now, here he was, four hours later, on the brink of a long-awaited reunion with her.

The empty years of searching were almost over.

He craned his neck to read a number partially hidden by a tall flowering bush. Nothing about the affluent neighborhood surprised him. Class suited Lydia, and everything about the stately homes lining the well-kept street bespoke class. He was sure she had fit in well here.

"There it is," he said, pointing to the third house up the street. "Fourteen-oh-one."

The driver swerved up to the curb in front of the colonial-style brick home. Passing the cabbie a generous bill, Daniel said, "Keep the change," and vaulted from the car, hauling his overnight bag behind him.

He strode up the sidewalk and hurdled the two steps leading to the front stoop in one smooth motion. Without pause, he rang the doorbell. Impatiently, he straightened his blazer and finger-combed his hair. When the doorknob rattled, every muscle in his body tensed.

But the woman who opened the door wasn't Lydia. She was an elderly lady with a short crop of silvery-white hair, immaculately applied makeup, and an out-of-style but elegant dark green polyester dress. Pearl-studded earrings as big around as quarters hung from her earlobes, and a generous row of pearls circled her aged neck.

He raised his brows. "Mrs. Porter?"

As she inclined her regal head, a welcoming smile brought a youthful sparkle to her light blue eyes. "So nice to meet you, Mr. Matthews." Her gaze swept down his body and back up again, making him feel like a ten-year-old under wash-up inspection before Sunday dinner.

When her eyes once again met his, one appraising brow inched up her forehead. "I must say, the television cameras didn't do you justice."

Daniel appreciated the woman's attempt at friendly banter, but at the moment he didn't want to waste precious minutes on idle small talk. "Thank you. Is Lydia here?"

"Yes. She's upstairs." Mrs. Porter stepped back, and Daniel entered the foyer. A crystal chandelier hung from a high ceiling, and the walls were dressed in burnished gold wallpaper. The mottled marble floor and the stairway's heavy wooden railing were polished to a glossy sheen. The faint scent of lemon oil and potpourri hung in the air. Obviously someone, perhaps the maid, had recently been cleaning.

Mrs. Porter closed the door and stepped around him. "I'll show you to the living room," she said, then led him toward double doors at the end of the foyer. Glancing back over her shoulder, she added, "Better known in my day as the courting parlor," and sent him a saucy wink.

Daniel couldn't help grinning. He had a feeling he was going to like this woman. The engaging way she combined flippant flirtation with elegant sophistication settled one or two of the butterflies swarming around in his stomach.

She swept open the mahogany doors and he followed her into a spacious, richly adorned room. In the center of the room, two Queen Anne sofas dressed in silken ivory faced each other over an ornately carved coffee table. On one side of the sofas, a mahogany baby grand stood in the slanted light of two tall-paned windows dressed in red velvet. On the other side, floor-to-ceiling shelves offered a versatile library of books.

"I'll go get Sa—" She paused an instant. "Excuse me, *Lydia.*" With that, she turned and left the room.

Daniel drew in a deep breath and released it through pursed lips. The moment he'd hoped, longed, and prayed for over the past five years was finally within his grasp.

He paced the floor for a couple of minutes, glancing at the open doorway every ten seconds or so. Then he wandered to one of the tall windows next to the piano. To his far right, he noticed a well-tended flower garden. A hungry bird, pecking away at lunch, perched on the lip of a cedar bird feeder that served as a centerpiece for a circle of impatiens. Bits and pieces of seed husks drifted down like snowflakes to the colorful blossoms below.

One corner of Daniel's mouth tipped upward. Lydia liked flowers—the ones with long stems or in vases, the kind he used to send her in celebration of a special day.

All at once, gooseflesh raced across the back of his neck. Slowly, expectantly, he turned, and the vision before him stole his breath.

Her free-flowing brown curls fell in a soft cloud around her face and shoulders. Her delicate skin glowed with candescent purity. Her amber eyes captured his soul.

Was this really Lydia?

Her heart-shaped face and petite build matched that of his beloved, but that's where the likeness ended. All the classic professionalism that represented Lydia's ambitious character—highlighted hair blown and gelled straight and turned under at the shoulders, enough makeup to camouflage what she considered every minor flaw, a form-fitting business suit and matching pumps—were all gone.

This woman was dressed in a simple salmon pink dress that molded her tiny waist, then blossomed into a full skirt of countless crinkling folds that flowed freely over her slim hips and swirled around her tiny ankles, exposing only her small, ivory-slippered feet. No long, polished fingernails. No jewelry, except a basic gold-tone watch with a white leather band. Her earrings, if she wore any, were hidden by her hair.

While Daniel thought this sprite of a woman charming, he knew, beyond a fraction of a doubt, Lydia would never dress in such a down-to-earth and casual way.

Had he been wrong? Had he come here with high hopes only to find the wrong woman?

He knew exactly how to find out. He took a guarded step forward.

❧

As he came nearer, Sara clasped her hands tighter to keep them from shaking. Since last night, she had imagined what this moment would be like at least a hundred times. But not even in her most vivid dreams had she captured the reality.

His mere presence was overpowering; it wrapped around her like a warm blanket after a long, cold walk in the rain. His hopeful expression drew her. His seeking brown eyes mesmerized her.

How did I survive these last five years without you?

The thought stole into her mind, scattering her rehearsed reserve. When he stopped with a meager foot between them, she had to remind herself to breathe. He said nothing, just stood staring at her. When the weight of his perusal became more than she could bear, she bit her lower lip and ducked her head.

She watched his right hand rise slowly, felt his forefinger curl beneath her chin. He lifted her head until she once again looked into those penetrating dark eyes.

"Smile for me," he said.

His voice tremored, and her heart contracted. But his request baffled her. She searched his face, then opened her mouth to ask *Why?*

"Please," he said, intercepting her intended question. "I just. . . need. . .to see you smile."

Her forehead creased. How could she smile on command?

Then she thought of the thing most precious to her, her daughter, and her lips curved of their own volition.

His gaze dropped to her chin, then slipped up to a spot an inch below the right corner of her mouth. She knew what had drawn his attention—a misplaced dimple, a unique oddity she never thought about until someone mentioned it. When he lifted his gaze back to hers, the tears in his eyes rocked her.

"Lydia," he whispered on a breath of wonderment. "It *is* you."

In less than a heartbeat, she found herself enveloped in his arms.

His warm, male scent wrapped around her. She turned her head so that the side of her face rested on his chest. His racing heart kept pace with her own.

Her arms, with a sudden will of their own, rose and slipped beneath his blazer and around his waist. Her hands spread over the smooth material of the polo shirt that covered his muscular back. He buried his face in her hair and cupped the back of her head with one hand. A sob escaped his throat, shuddered through his body. . .and into hers.

Tears pushed against the back of her eyes as something strange, something wonderful flowed through her. Not a spark of recognition or even a trace of familiarity. Instead, she felt a long-awaited sense of belonging.

But her sanguine thoughts were shattered when he eased back, braced her head with his hands, and hungrily covered her mouth with his own.

∞

She pushed so hard against his chest, he stumbled backward. The outward curve of the baby grand bit into his hip, saving him from falling, and the wide-eyed terror on her face and the trembling hand pressed against her chest brought him reeling back to his senses.

"I'm sorry," he said. "I shouldn't have done that."

She didn't move, didn't speak. Just stared at him in stunned silence. Reaching out a hand, he took one cautious step forward.

She took a defensive step back, halting his advance.

He let his hand fall limply to his side. "I truly am sorry. It's just that the shock of seeing you again overwhelmed me."

"It's okay," she said, although her shaky voice betrayed her wariness. "It's just that. . .I don't know you."

The meaning of her words slammed into him, clipping the wings of hope that had carried him since that morning, when he'd first heard her voice on his cell phone. She did not know him; therefore, she did not love him anymore. Some of his most treasured remembrances were of her—but her memories of him, of what they once had. . .were gone.

He'd shared her past, but what about her future?

∞

With one shaky hand pressed against her stomach and the other against her chest, she willed her racing heart to slow down. She wasn't sure what shocked her most, being kissed by a man she'd met less than ten minutes ago, or her reaction to it. The second his lips had touched hers she'd been swept away by a heady sensation. She wasn't some wanton strumpet ready to fall into the arms of the nearest handsome man. At least, she didn't think she was.

When she felt she could speak again without stuttering, she swallowed and wet her tingling lips. "Why don't we sit down?"

He nodded, then waited while she perched on one end of the sofa like a nervous bird ready to take flight. He eased down next to her, settling back and crossing an ankle over the opposite knee.

How did he manage to look so composed after what had just happened between them? Had the kiss not shaken him as it had her? Apparently not, if appearances were anything to go by.

For a few tense seconds, she studied the hands she'd clasped in her lap; then she lifted her gaze to find his intense brown eyes on her. Releasing a shuddery breath, she raised her hand and tucked a curl behind her ear, then dropped her hand back to her lap. "I think we've just established that this is going to be a challenge for us."

A rakish grin pulled at one corner of his mouth. "Like starting over."

He said the very words circling in her mind. But she wasn't ready to broach the details of their relationship just yet. She wanted to start with something safe, something still detached from her addled emotions.

"Tell me about Quinn Island," she said. "And my family."

Lacing his hands over his stomach, he stared into space for a few seconds, apparently trying to decide where to begin. "Quinn Island consists of one small barrier island and about twenty-five thousand acres inland," he said at last. "It was named for its founder, Samuel Quinn. Actually, you're a direct descendent. He was your grandfather—ten greats back, I think—but I tend to lose count on about the fourth great."

She found herself smiling at his wit.

"He and his family sailed to the East Coast from Ireland early in the eighteenth century," he added.

"You mean my family has lived there almost three hundred years?"

"That's right. Although the only true Quinns living among the island residents now are your father's and his brother's families."

"Why's that?"

"The town lost many residents to malaria during the 1700s, when the rice crops were so prosperous. Then many more moved away when the

Civil War and a series of hurricanes halted rice production in the late nineteenth century. But time passed, newcomers moved in, and now Quinn Island is a thriving little town by the sea."

As he continued telling her about her heritage, her home, and her family, his smooth southern drawl served as an antidote to the anxiety that had been growing inside her since the night before. She found herself relaxing, settling back at an angle to face him, one arm folded across the top of the sofa and one leg curled beneath her.

When he described the barrier island, she grew a little breathless. She could almost feel the cool damp sand beneath her feet, smell the salt in the air, feel the breeze tug at her hair. Almost picture herself there. Almost, but not quite.

"It sounds so beautiful," she said when he finally paused.

"It is." His grin sent a flutter through her stomach. "Actually, you own a beach house on the island."

"I do?"

He nodded. "Your late Grandfather Quinn left it to you seven years ago."

"And I lived there?"

His smile waned. "No. You preferred living inland. You rented a town house apartment in town, near your shop."

That bit of information surprised her. For the last five years, she'd lived with the dream of living on a beach. As he talked more, she worried her lower lip with her teeth and focused blankly on the space beyond his right shoulder. Apparently, a lot had changed, but the biggest truth staring her in the face was how much *she* had changed. Had she really been the sophisticated southern belle Daniel spoke of with such affection?

"Lydia?"

His soft voice penetrated her thoughts. "Yes," she responded hesitantly. Answering to "Lydia" made her feel uneasy, like she was infringing on someone else's identity.

Twin lines creased his forehead. "You don't have to talk about it now, if you don't want to, but I was wondering. . ." He swallowed, as if the rest of the sentence was lodged in the back of his throat.

She thought she knew what he wanted to ask. "You want to know what happened that night."

He answered with a somber nod.

"I really don't know. All I can tell you is what the doctors and police told me."

He reached over and wrapped his hand around one of hers, caressing her knuckles with his thumb. "Lydia, you don't have to—"

"No. It's okay. You need to know."

Daniel's chest tightened with anticipation. He waited in silence for her to continue.

Finally, she pulled in a deep breath. "My first memory is of a faint beeping sound, which I later learned was a heart monitor. Then pain. Deep, heavy pain all over my body and inside my head."

He tightened his hold on her hand, but she didn't seem to notice.

"When the doctor managed to get some of the pain under control, I realized I was in a hospital. I asked him what I was doing there. He told me I had suffered severe trauma as the result of a physical assault. He asked if I remembered what happened to me. Of course, I didn't.

"Then he asked my name, and I couldn't tell him that either." She pursed her lips. "That was the most frightening thing of all, not knowing who I was, where I came from, how I had gotten there. . ." She sighed. "It still frightens me sometimes."

Her lips drew downward in a thoughtful frown. "When the doctor realized I couldn't remember anything, he explained I had been brought into the hospital two weeks earlier, unconscious and barely alive. I had been beaten and apparently left for dead."

"Who brought you into the hospital?"

"A truck driver, a man named Peter Maulding from Mobile, Alabama, found me at a rest stop just outside Chicago. He'd stopped to stretch his legs, and when he went to throw a coffee cup away, he noticed a bloody blanket rolled up around a large bundle inside the dumpster. When he looked closer, he saw a lock of my hair sticking out of one end. He called for help on his truck radio. The ambulance and police came and took me to the hospital."

Chewing on her lower lip, she glanced away. "The nurses said Mr. Maulding called every day to check on me. I finally got to talk to him a week after I regained consciousness. I thanked him for saving me. He simply said 'God be with you, ma'am,' and hung up. He never called back after that."

Daniel made a mental note to locate Peter Maulding and send the truck-driving angel of mercy his own personal thanks.

"It took thirty-two stitches here," she continued, cupping the back of her head with her free hand. "And fifty-three here." Twisting around, she pushed back her thick curls, offering him a view of her left temple, where a jagged scar fanned out in several directions, like a web spun by a drunken spider. One rough side of the scar disappeared into her hairline.

She pulled her hair back over her temple, expertly concealing the blemish; a move, Daniel suspected, she'd practiced a million times over.

"There were other injuries. A lot of bruises, broken ribs, a broken shoulder, a collapsed lung. . ."

The more she told him about what some demented monster had done to her, the less he wanted to hear. When he felt he could bear no more, he searched his mind for a way to steer the conversation in another direction.

"How did you come to live with Mrs. Porter?" he asked when she paused to take a breath.

A smile touched her lips. "She was an auxiliary volunteer at the hospital. Still is. She visited me every day from the start. The nurses said she would talk to me, just like I was alert and could hear her, and she read passages to me from her Bible. They also said she prayed for me, for my healing.

"The visits continued after I woke, even though I was bitter and angry and not very pleasant company at first. I was so mad at God for allowing me to lose everything, even though I didn't know what it was I'd lost, I wanted no part of hearing that He loved me." A soft sigh drifted from her. "But Mrs. Porter was a stickler. She would say, 'Don't you worry, my dear. God and I are going to love that hate right out of you heart.'"

"And did they?"

Her delicate features softened even more. "Yes, they did. And when I was ready to leave the hospital and had no place to go, Mrs. Porter brought me here and nursed me back to health. When I got my strength back, she helped me find work."

"What kind of work?"

"Housework. I clean houses around the neighborhood four days a week. Fridays, I work here."

Daniel wouldn't have believed it if the words hadn't come from Lydia's own mouth. He couldn't think of an immediate response, so he simply stared at her.

She tipped her head to one side. "You look surprised."

"I am," he blurted, then shook his head to clear the fog that had gathered there. "I mean, someone called in during the program last night and said you looked like her cleaning lady, but I thought surely she was mistaken."

"Who was it?"

"A woman name Elizabeth Bradford."

"Yes." Lydia nodded. "I clean her house on Wednesdays. She lost her husband last year and she's having a hard time adjusting."

"Then you really do clean houses for a living?"

"Yes, I do."

He must have looked as dumbfounded as he felt, because after studying his face a couple of seconds, she said, "Why does that shock you so?"

"Because you hate housework. You used to hire someone to clean your shop and apartment once a week so you wouldn't have to do it yourself."

"Maybe I just didn't know how good I was at it."

"Are you saying you like it?"

She shrugged. "I can't complain. It keeps food on the table and a roof over our heads."

Another jolt of surprise pushed his eyebrows halfway up his forehead. "Our? You mean you keep up this entire house and feed yourself and Mrs. Porter on what you make cleaning houses?"

Her eyes widened and her mouth fell open.

Daniel's trained lawyer's eye read the expression. She'd let something slip unintentionally. He waited to see if she would explain.

She blinked, which seemed to snap her out of her stupefaction. "No. Mrs. Porter is financially secure. I merely rent two rooms from her for me and someone else."

A sharp, foreboding fear shot through Daniel. Was there another man? He'd never even considered the possibility.

Pulling her hand free from his, she leaned forward and opened a small coffee table drawer. Daniel held his breath. He felt like a loaded gun was pointed at his chest—and Lydia's finger was on the trigger.

She withdrew a picture in a gilded frame. Closing the drawer, she held the photo out to him. "This is Chloe."

With an unsteady hand, he reached for the frame. He found himself looking down at the image of a blond-haired, blue-eyed little girl with the face and smile of an angel. He felt his lips curve. "She's beautiful."

"She's my daughter."

His gaze snapped up to Lydia's. "Yours?"

She inclined her head. "She was born almost eight months after I was brought into the hospital. The doctors estimated she was one month premature."

Daniel tried to recover from the blow she had just delivered. She had a child. A daughter. How could that be?

She dropped her gaze to her lap and fidgeted with the creases in her skirt. "Daniel, ever since last night, I've wondered. . ." She pursed her lips, wet them, then swallowed. "I, ah, need to know. . ." Raising her lashes, she searched his face with beseeching brown eyes. "Could she be yours?"

Her question took him aback—and wounded his pride. "How could you even ask such a thing?"

She flinched like he'd raised a hand to strike her, and he would have given anything to take his sharp retort back.

"Lydia, I'm sorry." He reached for her hands. "For a second there, I forgot you couldn't remember."

"It's okay." She tugged one hand free from his and dabbed at a tear in the corner of her eye. "I just. . .needed to know for sure."

"No," he rasped, "she can't be mine. We were. . .are both Christians who had decided—well, we were going to wait until we married."

She bit her lower lip. A teardrop escaped, rolled down her cheek, and splattered his hand.

Cruel fingers of dread cut off the air in his lungs. *No, God, no! Please! Not Lydia!* A sick feeling churned in his stomach and burned his chest. He squeezed his eyelids shut. "You were. . ."

"Raped," she said in not much more than a whisper, supplying the word he couldn't speak. She followed up with an even softer "Yes."

Over the past five years, he had considered the possibility of a sexual assault. But since that morning, he had been so caught up in the joy of finding her. . .

The pain sweeping though him was more, much more than he'd

ever imagined. If only he had been there. . . An almost unbearable weight bore down on his chest. He *should* have been there.

He felt her slim hand slide over his. "I'm sorry, Daniel. I just needed to know."

The coolness of her touch, like an early summer rain, and the sincerity in her voice, as though she owed him an apology, jerked him back from the dark hole into which he was slipping. He opened his eyes and looked into her solemn face. *Lord, if there is ever a time You're going to give me strength, please let it be now.*

He cradled her wet cheek in his palm. "No, Lydia. I'm the one who's sorry." He enfolded her in his arms. "This should not have happened to you."

If she wondered why, she didn't ask. She just slipped her arms up around his neck.

Cupping the back of her head with one hand, he buried his face in her sweet-smelling hair and began to rock her. "I am so, so sorry," he repeated.

But his words did nothing to ease the self-condemnation he felt. All the "I'm sorry's" in the world could never undo what he had let happen to her.

Chapter 4

*L*ydia reined in her raw emotions. What was she doing, falling to pieces all over Daniel this way? Hadn't she known, deep down, that he wasn't Chloe's father? If the timing of her daughter's birth hadn't been enough to convince her, the sharp contrast between Chloe's fair complexion and Daniel's dark one should have been.

Still, since learning she had been engaged to him, a small part of her had hoped Chloe could be his, had yearned to know her child had been conceived in love and not violence. On the other hand, another part of her had feared if he were Chloe's biological father, the relationship could complicate things in the long run. She certainly didn't want Chloe trapped in the middle of a custody battle between an amnesiac mother and a father she didn't know.

Lydia released a shuddery sigh. At least she could find one consolation in confirming her daughter wasn't Daniel's child: She had been a woman of moral character, engaged to a man of honor. A deep sense of loss for what might have been, what would never be, washed over her.

Realizing she needed distance in order to regain her equilibrium, she forced her silent tears to ebb as she pushed away from him. She brushed at the shoulder of his sports coat as though the busy friction of her fingers would dry the dampness there. "I'm sorry. I didn't mean to cry all over you."

He captured a lingering tear with his thumb. A small gesture, but it almost unraveled her barely garnered emotions all over again.

"It's okay," he said. "It's turning out to be quite an eventful day for you. I think you're entitled."

Eventful didn't touch it. Spectacular. Out of the ordinary. All the things she thought she'd missed over the past five years rolled into one single day. How could she have ever thought she'd be ready for this moment? For facing her past? For a man like Daniel?

"Is she here?"

Daniel's question seemed misplaced, like he'd pulled it out of a trivia hat.

"Who?" Lydia asked, trying to think past the fog swimming around her brain.

"Chloe. I'd like to meet her."

"Oh."

Snapping back to reality, she stepped away, forcing Daniel to drop his hand from her face. She combed nervous fingers through her thick mane. "She's upstairs with Mrs. Porter. I'll go get her."

As soon as she was out of his sight, she once again pressed a hand to her quivering stomach. She couldn't believe the effect meeting him was having on her. The moment she had walked into the living room and he turned, looking at her with those dark eyes, she had felt a connection. Was it possible some dormant emotion from her past had been rekindled, even though she couldn't remember him? Or was she simply feeling the need to fill the unsatisfied longing that had grown over the last five years, the need to belong somewhere, to someone?

She hadn't known Daniel Matthews long enough for it to be anything more.

She found Chloe rocking in Evelyn Porter's lap, listening to a story.

" 'The sky is falling! The sky is falling!' " Mrs. Porter's voice hip-hopped through the air.

Henny Penny doesn't have a thing on me, Lydia thought, stepping farther into the room. Her world couldn't be any more precarious right now if the sky really was falling.

"Chloe, are you ready to go meet Mr. Matthews?"

"Yes!" Chloe pushed aside the book and scrambled down from Mrs.

Porter's lap, the ever-present George the Giraffe tucked under her arm. Ever since Lydia had talked to her daughter that morning about Daniel, the curious tyke couldn't wait to meet "a man Mommy knew before moving to Chicago."

Lydia straightened Chloe's hair bow while she delivered a lecture on the appropriate times to say "please" and "thank you." Then, after a quick inspection to see if the child's green empire-waist dress, white tights, and black patent leather slippers were still clean and intact, she grasped her daughter's hand and headed for the door.

As they descended the steps, the flutter in Lydia's stomach increased. What would Daniel think of Chloe? Could he learn to love this innocent child created out of an act of black rage? Or would he ultimately reject her?

Lydia paused outside the living room, looked down at her daughter, and gave the tiny hand inside hers a reassuring squeeze. Then, squaring her shoulders, she opened the door.

Daniel stood waiting for them beside the sofa, his hands tucked casually inside his pockets. His gaze met Lydia's briefly, then dropped to Chloe.

Lydia felt an insistent tug on her hand. At her daughter's silent prompting, she stopped just a few feet inside the door. The next move would have to be Daniel's.

He came forward slowly, his attention fixed on Chloe.

The child rarely met anyone outside her sheltered world. What would she do? Hide behind her mother's skirt? Run? To Lydia's amazement, Chloe stood statue still, her huge blue eyes gauging Daniel's every move.

He got down on one knee and looked into her eyes. "You must be Chloe."

Still clutching George beneath her arm, Chloe gave an emphatic nod.

"Your mom's been telling me about you. I'm Daniel."

"My mama said your name was 'Mr. Matthews.' "

Lydia's lips twitched, and a chuckle escaped Daniel's throat.

Resting his forearm across his raised knee, he said, "Only to people who aren't my friends. But I can already tell you and I are going to be very good friends, which means you can call me 'Daniel.' What do you think?"

Like a rehearsed act, both faces tilted upward and two beseeching gazes locked on Lydia's.

She was a stickler for manners and respect, and she didn't want Chloe to get in the habit of calling her elders by their first names. But with the pair looking up at her like two kids campaigning for an ice cream cone, she felt her resistance slip away. "Sure." She knew when she was defeated.

Chloe gave Daniel her most charming smile. "She says I can call you 'Daniel.' " In the same breath, she added, "Will you come play in my sandbox with me?"

Before Lydia could protest, Daniel was standing and lifting Chloe to his hip. "Sure, I will." He passed George to Lydia.

She stood, mouth agape, the giraffe with a bad hairdo dangling from her hand. She wanted to remind Chloe that she had on her best Sunday dress, and Daniel that he had on a pair of professionally creased Docker pants and what looked to her like an expensive pair of loafers. But the words froze in her muddled brain.

She wasn't so surprised at Daniel being enamored with Chloe. Once the child warmed up to someone—and she had warmed up to Daniel in record time—she had a charming personality that drew people to her.

But what was it about Daniel that had allowed him to slip so easily past Chloe's usual reserve? He'd waltzed right up to the child and, in the space of a minute, maybe two, swept the little girl off her feet.

Like mother, like daughter. The old cliché popped into Lydia's head, poking fun at her usual levelheadedness.

But Lydia and Chloe weren't the only ones who had fallen prey to Daniel's magnetic charm. Mrs. Porter had raved about him, too. She had said, *"He's got to be one of the most engaging young men I've ever met,"* when she came upstairs to fetch Lydia after showing him in.

First Mrs. Porter, then Lydia, now Chloe. Did the man affect the entire female population this way?

He stopped before opening the door Chloe had pointed him to and turned. "Coming, Mom?"

Realizing her mouth still hung open, she snapped it shut. "Ah, yes. I'm coming." George in tow, she hurried to catch up with them.

Thirty minutes later, she sat on the steps of the patio, chin in hand, her long skirt draped over her feet and legs, watching Daniel and Chloe. At first, Lydia had contemplated joining them, then decided the four-by-four sandbox made of scrap lumber she'd salvaged during a neighbor's renovation was barely big enough for two playmates, especially when one was a guesstimated six-foot-two man.

Daniel and Chloe shoveled sand and built imaginary houses where imaginary stick people lived. They laughed and giggled. The well-dressed attorney who had stepped into hers and Chloe's lives less than two hours ago didn't seem to mind one bit that the seat of his pants and the soles of his polished cordovan shoes were nestled in gritty, clingy sand.

He had shucked off his blazer and tossed it over a nearby swing seat, revealing lean, muscled forearms beneath the sleeves of his white polo shirt. Whenever he tilted his head a certain way, the afternoon sun lit the chestnut highlights in his dark hair. Every once in a while, his laughter floated through the air, each time touching a place inside her she hadn't even known existed. He looked like a man in his element, a man carved by God's own hand for fatherhood.

Lydia realized where her thoughts were drifting, and she mentally rebuked her wandering mind. She could chase dreams of Chloe being Daniel's daughter until the sun set in the east. The truth remained that Daniel was not, and never would be, Chloe's biological father. Considering the circumstances of Chloe's conception, it would take a mighty big man to overcome that obstacle and accept the child as his own.

And this early in the game, Lydia didn't know if Daniel was quite big enough.

∽

An hour later, after tucking Chloe in for her afternoon nap, Lydia stepped outside her daughter's room ahead of Daniel. With little effort, Chloe had talked him into picking up where Mrs. Porter had left off reading *Henny Penny*. Then she had fallen asleep in his lap.

Lydia waited for the faint click of the closing door. "Chloe's quite taken with you," she said.

He grinned. "I'm quite taken with her."

Trapping her lower lip between her teeth, she looked down the hallway at nothing in particular. They had so many things to discuss. So many circumstances to consider. "You understand now why I didn't want any attention drawn to your finding me."

"To protect Chloe?" he guessed correctly.

Nodding, she turned her attention back to him. "I know the chances are slim, but if one of the men who attacked me—"

His eyebrows shot up. "Men? You mean there was more than one?"

Lydia closed her eyes ruefully and pressed a cool palm to her forehead. She kept letting things slip before she was ready to talk about them. Was she losing her mind now along with her identity?

Dropping her hand, she lowered her gaze to the base of his neck exposed by the V-opening of his collar. "Yes. The doctors said there were at least two." When she raised her lashes, he looked away, but not before she caught the pain in his eyes.

She knew, in many ways, his grief cut deeper than hers. He had lost someone very dear to him the night of her abduction. But she had no memory of the attack. When she talked about it, she felt as though she were talking about someone else, someone she'd read about in the newspaper or seen on the evening news but never met. She couldn't feel the fear, the horror, the pain she must have felt that night. Besides the physical scars her body carried, the only evidence left that such a violent act had been committed against her was something very dear to her—her daughter.

"Would you like some tea?" she suggested. She and Daniel could both use a break, take some time to calm their frazzled nerves before talking about the next step they should take.

Daniel nodded, then followed her downstairs and into the kitchen.

∞

Fury almost choked him. He wanted revenge on the demons who had violated Lydia. Even as his inner voice told him his thoughts were immoral, he envisioned himself torturing the life out of each faceless monster.

She refused his offer of help, so he pulled out a chair, sat down, and watched her flutter around the kitchen like an energetic butterfly. She filled a teakettle with water and placed it on the stove, then reached into the cupboard and pulled out two ceramic cups.

"We have chamomile and regular," she said. "Which would you like?"

Since he didn't know what chamomile was, he decided to play it safe. "Regular."

"Cold or hot?"

"Cold." Five years ago, she had known that.

"Sweetened? Unsweetened? Cream? Lemon?"

She threw the single-word questions at him like he was a dartboard, and he felt himself smile. She looked so captivating, standing there holding the cups against her chest like two cuddly kittens, her amber eyes wide in anticipation of his answer.

"Sweet," he said, referring to more than the tea. "No cream or lemon."

She had also known he didn't take cream or lemon in his tea five years ago, a little irritating voice inside reminded him, tempering the joy he felt at simply watching her putter around the kitchen. How was it that practically everything she did reminded him she couldn't remember him or what they had once shared, yet at the same time, charmed him so? In some ways, he felt like he was experiencing the rapture of falling in love all over again. In other ways, he felt as though he were groping in the dark, wondering which way to turn, what to reach for.

She set his iced tea in front of him, then returned to the counter where she added a teaspoon of honey and a tea bag to a cup of boiling water. Balancing the cup over a saucer, she padded to the table. "Would you like something to eat? I can fix you a sandwich."

He'd missed lunch, but the way he felt right now, his appetite might not ever return. "No, thank you. Tea's fine."

He waited until she sat down, then lifted his drink in a mock salute before taking a long, cool sip. When he set his dewy glass back down, he watched as she dipped her tea bag in and out of the steaming liquid in her cup. The water, he noticed, was turning a color that reminded him of stagnant pond water. Finally, she laid the bag on the edge of the saucer and took a careful sip of the pungent-smelling brew.

"What kind of tea did you say that was?" he asked as she settled the cup back in its saucer.

"Chamomile. It's supposed to have a calming effect." She shrugged one shoulder. "Most of the time it works."

Maybe that's what he should have had. He studied the fog rising from the cup, debating on changing his mind—until he caught another whiff of the acrid-smelling liquid. *Nope,* he decided without further contemplation. That chamomile stuff reminded him of the rabbit tobacco he and his cousins used to sneak to their grandpa's woodshed to chew during their rambunctious adolescent years. The aftermath was never worth the effort. Retching had never been fun.

Besides, the only thing he drank hot was coffee.

The contrary little beast inside him nudged him again, pointing out that Lydia had never cared for hot tea either. Water and diet soda had been the only liquid she'd ever let pass through her painted lips.

His gaze slid to her mouth. Those lips weren't painted at all right now, just barely moistened by a trace of the sheer gloss she'd been wearing when he first arrived. He had to admit, he liked them that way.

He took another long drink of tea, then studied the dew beading on his glass while he tried to collect his scattered senses. How could one experience so many conflicting emotions at once? Joy and sorrow. Pleasure and pain. Courage and fear.

So far, he'd found only a remnant of what he'd lost five years ago, and he didn't know if that was good. . .or bad.

∞

Lydia set her teacup in its saucer and studied Daniel. He looked so sad with his head bowed and his gaze fixed on his half-empty glass. What was he thinking? After learning all that had happened to her, was he sorry he'd found her? Was he tormented by what the attack had cost her? Cost him?

He'd said they were both Christians and had decided to wait until their wedding night to claim each other as one. He had been a man of honor about to marry a woman of purity. Lydia suspected he was still a man of honor, but she was no longer a woman of purity. And that was only one cold, harsh fact wedged between them. There would, she suspected, be many, many more.

Above all, there was Chloe. Right now, Daniel was caught up in the thrill of finding *Lydia*. But what about later, when the excitement of new beginnings died and the dust of celebration settled? Would he be reminded of how Chloe had been conceived every time he looked at her?

Was finding out worth the risk?

Lydia reached over and laid her palm on Daniel's forearm. When he looked up, the anguish in his eyes almost made her look away. Almost. But she somehow hung on to her resolve and pushed forward. "Daniel, I truly am sorry."

He frowned. "What for?"

"For all the terrible things you're finding out about me. That I'm not the same woman I was five years ago."

Abruptly, he stood. Caught off guard by the sudden action, she flinched. The heavy oak chair upset by the impact of the back of his knees teetered on its hind legs for a few precarious seconds, then settled with a dull thud on all fours.

Before Lydia could react, he captured her upper arms in his firm yet tender grip and lifted her. The space between their bodies vanished as she gaped up at him in surprise. He looked down at her with a turbulent expression in his eyes she couldn't define. Each of his breaths brushed her face like a swiftly passing storm.

"Lydia, what happened to you was not your fault!" he said through clenched teeth. "Do you hear me? It was *not…your…fault.*" He punctuated each of his last three words with a gentle shake.

Then, as swiftly as the storm came, it dissipated. His features softened and his eyes filled with…compassion, sorrow, remorse? She wasn't sure. She just knew the entire atmosphere changed from turbulent to tender in less than a second.

"It's not your fault," he repeated, each breath now touching her face as soft as a whisper. "And it doesn't change the person you are." He shook his head, gazing down at her in a way that made her feel like she had just stepped into a beautiful dream. "It doesn't change a thing, Lydia. Especially the way I feel about you."

He gathered her in his arms, cupped the back of her head with one hand, nestled her cheek against his chest. "I love you, Lydia. I always have. I always will."

She knew he meant it, just as sure as she knew the arms holding her were sincere, and the hands caressing her would never harm her. Regardless of what had happened, he still loved her and was willing to go the distance.

But was she?

She didn't know. She was afraid of getting hurt, of hurting Chloe…of hurting him.

She slipped her arms around his waist and allowed his strength to surround her. Each rise and fall of his chest, every heartbeat, seemed to mirror her own. Her resistance was gone, had vanished like a bad dream at dawn the moment he said, "I love you." What in the world was she going to do?

She released a shuddery sigh. "I can't pick up where we left off," she heard herself say. "You know that, don't you, Daniel?"

"I know." He drew back and braced her face with hands neither too big nor too small, neither too rough nor too smooth. "We'll start over, and take it slow." He caressed her cheek with his thumb. "You're my destiny, Lydia. We were meant to be together."

A look of deep longing rose in his eyes, igniting inside her a desire to fulfill his dreams. The atmosphere grew still, and for a moment they did nothing but stare at each other. Then his gaze dropped to her mouth. Her heartbeat accelerated in anticipation of his kiss—and the knowledge that when it came, she'd be powerless to resist.

But it never came. Instead, he simply slipped his arms around her again and held her. She marveled at the incredible feeling of being embraced by a man who loved her enough to remain loyal through five long years of separation.

But would that love survive the future? He'd said nothing had changed, but she knew it had. And he knew it, too, even if he wasn't yet ready to admit it. A chilly finger of foreboding brushed her spine, intruding on her moment of bliss, reminding her of the stark reality anchored to their reunion.

He remembered the woman she was.

She knew only the woman she'd become.

What they once had was gone.

Once Daniel figured that out, would he still think of her as his destiny?

Chapter 5

Much later that evening, Daniel all but collapsed when he sat down on the freshly made brass bed. When he'd earlier mentioned finding a motel room, Mrs. Porter had insisted he stay in one of the two empty bedrooms upstairs. He hadn't put up an argument—he wanted to stay as close to Lydia as possible.

He massaged the back of his neck where fibers of tension had gathered. He knew the night would bring little sleep, but he did need to get what rest he could. He hoped to get Lydia home by day after tomorrow, which meant tomorrow would be filled with hasty preparation.

But there was one task he couldn't postpone until morning. He fished his cell phone out of his blazer pocket and dialed. The phone on the other end rang once.

"Hello?" came the anxious voice of Margaret Quinn. "Daniel, is that you?"

"Yes, Margaret, it's me."

"Where on earth are you?" Lydia's mother wanted to know. "We called your office this afternoon and your secretary said there'd been a change in your plans. Did the television station receive any more calls after we spoke with you last night?"

Daniel decided to get right to the point. Lydia's parents had waited long enough for this call. "I'm in Riverbend, Illinois—"

"Illinois? Wha—"

"I've found Lydia."

Silence filled his ear, then a breathless, "Oh dear heavenly Father," slipped from her lips. "Bill! Bill! Come quickly! Daniel's found Lydia! Where is she?" Margaret asked Daniel next in the same breath. "Can I speak to her?"

"I'd rather you wait until tomorrow to do that."

"Tomorrow!" Her voice was appalled. "You can't be serious. Tell me how to get there. We'll take the first flight out."

"Before you do anything, Margaret, I need to tell you a few things."

Daniel heard a faint click. "Daniel?" came the slightly out-of-breath voice of Bill Quinn. "Is it true? Have you really found her?"

"Yes, Bill, it's true."

"Oh, thank God." The older man released a sob.

Bill's reaction played havoc with Daniel's overwrought emotions, which he'd barely managed to temper before making the call. He squeezed his burning eyes shut. He had to get this out. He had to somehow tell them about Lydia without breaking down again himself. *Help me, Lord,* he silently prayed, and a fragile but definite sense of calm stole over him.

"There are some things you need to know before you talk to her," he finally managed to say, and without hesitation he plowed ahead, telling them about her waking up in a Chicago hospital sixteen days after her disappearance, her amnesia, and how she came to live with Mrs. Porter. He finished with "She has a daughter...as a result of the ra—" he closed his eyes, forcing down a sudden wave of nausea, "—as a result of the attack."

"Oh, my baby," Margaret said in a raspy, choking voice. "My poor, poor baby."

"The little girl," Daniel added, barely holding onto his brittle composure. "Her name is Chloe."

"Chloe," Margaret repeated.

"That's right."

For five full seconds, Margaret Quinn said nothing, as though she were giving the child's name a chance to take root somewhere. Daniel prayed it would be in her heart.

"What does she look like?" she finally asked, unable to disguise her concern and curiosity.

Daniel's anger at the torture Lydia had suffered returned, dropping on his chest like an exploding bomb that spread into each limb. "Not like Lydia." *And not me. She'll never look like me.* "But she's the most beautiful child I've ever seen," he added, and meant it.

Three seconds ticked away. "I'm sure she is, Daniel." The woman's timorous laugh brushed Daniel's ear. "What about that, Bill? We're grandparents."

Daniel breathed a sigh of relief. He couldn't help worrying about how Mrs. Quinn would take the news of Chloe. Margaret Quinn always had her family's best interest at heart, even when she was overbearing. But she sometimes focused too much on image and appearance, especially where her daughters were concerned.

"How is she, Daniel?" Bill cut in. "Is she there with you? When can we talk to her?"

"Physically, she's fine. Emotionally? I don't know. She seems to be okay, but quite honestly, it's too early for me to tell what kind of impact her memory loss has had on her. That's why I wanted to prepare you before you speak with her. She doesn't remember anything or anyone from her past before the abduction, so, please, don't expect more from her than she's able to give right now. I know you're both anxious to see her, but I think it'd be best to wait until we get home."

"When will that be?" Margaret asked.

"Hopefully, in a couple of days. Another thing, she wants to return quietly. No hoopla and fanfare." This he said more to Lydia's mother than her unassuming father.

"But so many of her friends will want to welcome her home," Margaret argued, as Daniel had expected her to. She probably had half the homecoming party planned by now.

"In time, they can," he responded, unbending. "But it will have to be when Lydia's ready. Remember, she's coming back to a place and people she doesn't remember. That's overwhelming enough in itself."

"I think Daniel's right, Margaret," Bill injected, and Daniel silently thanked the older man. "Let's keep the homecoming limited to family for now."

"Okay," Margaret relented, albeit reluctantly. "If you think that's best, Daniel."

"I do." He raked his hair away from his forehead. A rebellious lock flopped back down over his left brow. "Listen, I'd better go. I'll call back first thing in the morning. If she's up to it, you can talk to her then."

After hanging up, Daniel sat for a long time with his elbows on his knees and his hands clasped in front of him, staring at the darkness beyond the bedroom window. For some reason, the words of an old song he associated with funerals came to mind.

Precious memories, unseen angels,
Sent from somewhere to my soul;
How they linger, ever near me,
And the sacred past unfold.

As he sat there, with the lines of that old hymn floating through his head, the past did unfold, memory by precious memory, starting with the first time Daniel noticed Lydia as more than another kid in the neighborhood. He'd been home on Thanksgiving break his fourth year in college and had attended a high school football game with a friend. Lydia had been seventeen then, captain of the cheerleading squad, and to Daniel, the most beautiful thing he'd ever seen.

At least a hundred more memories played themselves out in his mind: her college graduation, the day she opened her dress shop, the evening he proposed. Right up until the day she'd left for the fateful New York trip, pouting in that pretty way of hers because he wouldn't postpone his first solo court case to go with her.

When the reflections came to a haunting end, he dropped his forehead to his hands. A harrowing question preyed on his mind: Would things between him and Lydia ever be as they once were? An even more frightening question followed, casting shadows of doubt over the first: Did he even want to return to the life they'd once shared?

He gave his head a disparaging shake. He didn't know. He truly didn't know. He never imagined finding her would bring so much confusion. . .and pain. "Oh God, help me," he pleaded. "Please, please help me."

Daniel didn't know exactly what he was asking for. Only that he would need guidance in the days to come from One much stronger than he.

When he finished praying, he closed his eyes and wept.

∞

Lydia Quinn, she said to herself for about the hundredth time in half as many hours. She tossed a pair of socks in the open suitcase on her bed. *Lydia Anne Quinn. Ms. Lydia Quinn.*

No matter how she rehearsed the name in her mind, it still sounded as foreign to her as the first time she'd heard it. She paused in packing and stepped in front of her dresser mirror, trying to picture herself as a sophisticated southern belle. Like the dozen or so other times she'd stood there since the day before yesterday, all she saw was "Sara," mother of Chloe, close friend and companion to Evelyn Porter.

Shaking her head, she went back to packing. How was she ever going to step back into her old shoes? This wasn't some fairy tale where the peasant heroine slipped on the glass slipper and found a perfect fit. This was her own life, and she had a feeling her shoe size had changed dramatically over the past five years.

When she closed the case, the latch caught with an amplified click of finality. Her life here was coming to an end. In less than an hour, she, Chloe, Mrs. Porter, and Daniel would leave for the airport. In less than two, they'd be on a flight to Quinn Island—her home. She was so glad Daniel had invited Mrs. Porter to come along and stay for a few weeks. At least Lydia would have a confidant while she reacquainted herself with her family.

As she turned to her dresser and started tossing her meager toiletries into a makeup bag, her mind drifted back over the hours since Daniel had walked into her life. Yesterday had started out like a whirlwind. She had been moved by the conversations with her parents and sister over the telephone. Hearing the weepy joy in their voices was enough to toy with her own emotions. But that was it. She hadn't even been able to work up a tear at the prospect of returning home to these three people who obviously loved and missed her very much. A sigh escaped her lips. Surely, that would all change once she got to know them.

After the phone call, Lydia had made rounds in the neighborhood, saying good-bye and letting the families she worked for know Mrs. Porter's great-niece, a college student on summer break, would soon be taking over her cleaning jobs. By the time she returned, Daniel had booked a flight to Myrtle Beach International Airport, arranged to have a shuttle pick them up this morning and take them to O'Hare, and made plans to have Lydia's and Chloe's few material possessions—aside from their clothes—shipped to her parents' house.

Lydia wasn't quite sure how she felt about his assertive efforts. In some ways, she was grateful he was a take-action sort of guy. He had taken care of a dozen little details that would have been a bit over-whelming for her. After all, she was acquainted with very little of the world outside the subdivision she'd lived in for the past five years.

Even so, Daniel could have kept her better informed. Other than wanting to know how soon she could be ready to go home, he hadn't asked her opinion about anything. And that pricked an irritating little nerve in Lydia. She might have lost her memory, but she hadn't lost her mind. She still had the ability to think and make decisions for herself and her daughter.

She sensed another's presence and paused short of dropping her tube of lip gloss in the makeup bag. Even before looking toward the open doorway, she knew who she would find there. Deliberately, she set the lip gloss back on the dresser and closed her eyes, stealing a deep breath of fortitude. This was going to be the hardest good-bye of all.

Opening her eyes, she turned slowly to face the sad green eyes of her best friend. "Jeff," she whispered, and a lump lodged in her throat.

He stood with his hands shoved into the pockets of his khaki pants, his shoulders hunched forward. When their gazes met, he pursed his lips, and his chin quivered. Behind the lenses of his wire-rimmed glasses, his eyes grew misty. His desolate expression reflected the feeling rising in Lydia's chest. They had been through so much together, from the premature birth of her daughter, to the untimely death of his wife. And she would miss him—a lot.

But Lydia knew, as did he, things had changed. The love he had hoped would one day blossom between them would never come to pass.

"I'm going to miss you, kid," he said, his voice heavy with sorrow.

Three steps each and they were in each other's arms. "I'm going to miss you, too," she said.

"I love you. You know that, don't you?"

"I know. I love you, too."

But theirs was not the kind of love that made two people one—the kind he and his deceased wife had shared. And deep down, Lydia was sure he knew that, too.

∞

"I love you. You know that, don't you?"

"I know. I love you, too."

Daniel stopped short of stepping up to the open doorway of Lydia's room. What was this? Lydia proclaiming her love to another man?

He leaned against the wall for support. Why hadn't she told him this before now?

A brief silence followed, leaving Daniel to wonder what was happening between them. Were they holding each other? Kissing each other? The image of Lydia locked in another man's arms lent new strength to Daniel's limbs. He'd just found her, and he had no intentions of losing her—again. He pushed away from the wall and stepped up to the open doorway, bracing himself for the scene he expected to find.

Lydia apparently caught his movement out of the corner of her eye and stepped away from the strange man. When she turned to face Daniel, he expected a look of guilt or embarrassment, an expression that said *"I wish the floor would open up and swallow me."* Instead, she greeted him with an innocent smile.

She tucked her hand into the crook of the stranger's arm, and together they stepped forward. "Daniel, I'd like you to meet a very dear friend of mine."

The man stretched out his right hand. "Jeff Chandler. It's nice to meet you."

Yeah, right, thought Daniel, as he returned the handshake. Either the man really was just a friend or he was an idiot. If he felt for Lydia half of what Daniel did, he'd be bracing himself for a battle, not shaking the enemy's hand.

With a curt nod, Daniel pumped the man's hand, once. "Daniel Matthews. Likewise."

"Yes, I saw you on *Without a Trace* the other night." Jeff pushed his glasses up the bridge of his nose, then stuffed his fists into his pockets. "Sara's waited a long time for this day. I know you're happy she's going home."

Lydia. Her name is Lydia. He slipped a possessive arm around her, urging her to step away from Jeff. Daniel feared she'd stiffen, pull away, send some sort of silent signal that she didn't want him showing such an open gesture of affection in front of her "dear friend."

But she didn't. In fact, he thought he felt her lean into him a little.

"Words can't express how happy I am," Daniel said. "Her parents and sister, too."

Jeff's gaze held Daniel's for a moment, and Daniel got the peculiar sensation that the man was trying to convey some sort of silent message. Then a look of sad resignation rose in Jeff's eyes, and, in spite of himself, Daniel felt a thread of sympathy for Lydia's friend.

"You're a fortunate man," Jeff said. He turned his attention to Lydia, and his features softened even more. "I'm going to go say good-bye to Chloe now." He leaned over, kissed Lydia's cheek, and squeezed her hand. "Take care, kid. You know where I am if you ever need me."

Lydia nodded, and even though she smiled, Daniel noticed tears gathering in her eyes.

Jeff turned and walked away, and for a moment, Daniel looked after him. What did the man really mean to Lydia?

She stepped away from him, taking her comforting warmth with her. When he focused his attention back on her, she was standing with her arms crossed, glowering at him like a first-grade teacher ready to go head-to-head with a willful student.

"How much of that conversation did you hear?" she asked.

He decided to play innocent, see how much information she would volunteer about her relationship with Jeff. "What do you mean?"

"I mean, you came in here like a man on a mission. And I'd like to know how much of my conversation with Jeff you listened in on."

He took a few seconds to size her up. In the past, she'd never been so direct. . .or insightful. He rubbed his jaw. The determination and challenge in her demeanor told him there was no point in trying to continue with his charade. She'd already seen through it.

"I heard him tell you he loves you," he admitted. And with that admission came a feeling Daniel hadn't experienced in a very long time. A slip in control. It felt strange. . .like a shoe on the wrong foot.

"Then you heard me tell him I love him, too."

He inclined his head.

"I do," she said.

Hearing her confess her love for another man while she was staring him down had more impact on him than when he was standing outside her door. He thought he'd suffocate right there on the spot.

"But I'm not in love with him," she added.

He arched an inquisitive brow. "Meaning. . . ?"

She glanced away, a frown pinching her forehead. After a long, thoughtful moment, she looked back at him. "I met Jeff when I was in the hospital. His wife Caroline was one of my nurses."

Daniel perked up. Jeff had a wife. That was good.

"I don't know why they and Mrs. Porter chose to befriend me, but they did," Lydia continued. "They supported me emotionally while my body healed physically. They stood beside me during my pregnancy and Chloe's premature birth. They were, I suppose, a substitute family to me and Chloe."

An expression of deep pain clouded her delicate features. "Then the unthinkable happened and Caroline was diagnosed with Lou Gehrig's disease. I was with her and Jeff when she died eighteen months ago."

Now Daniel felt like a heel. The man had lost, big-time. A loss that, in many ways, Daniel could relate to.

Lydia drew in a deep breath, released it slowly. "After her death, I tried to help Jeff out with his kids when the burden of single fatherhood overwhelmed him. I tried to listen when he got so lonely for Caroline he thought he was going to die. I tried to be there for him, like he had been there for me.

"The kind of love Jeff and I share is the kind between two friends who have been to hell and back with each other." Her light brown eyes sought for understanding. "Haven't you ever had a friend like that?"

A picture of Lydia's sister Jen floated across his mind. They had gone through the heartbreak of Lydia's disappearance together, had grown closer through it. He had to admit he understood exactly what Lydia was trying to say.

"Yes, I have," he said, pulling her into his arms. Resting his chin on the top of her head, he added, "I'm sorry I jumped to the wrong conclusion."

"You don't owe me an apology, Daniel. Considering you didn't know the circumstances, I'm sure what you heard sounded suspicious."

"Still, I shouldn't have barreled in here like 'a man on a mission.' "

She drew back, smiling up at him. "I don't know. I found it kind of flattering, myself."

A pleased grin lifted one corner of his mouth. "You did?"

"Yes. I did."

Like a warm cloak in a chilly wind, the air grew heavy with

enthralling tension. Slowly, their smiles faded. She wet her lips. Her involuntary movement drew his gaze to her mouth, and a shudder of longing shook him. He became aware of her every breath.

He lifted his eyes back to hers. "I guess you know I want to kiss you."

Releasing a pent-up breath, she pushed away. "Please don't. Thinking about going to Quinn Island and meeting my family has me addlepated enough as it is."

Addlepated. Now there was a word he'd never heard her use before. But he thought he knew what she meant.

Patting her chest like she was trying to calm an unsteady palpitation, she turned to her dresser. She dropped a tube of lip gloss into a makeup bag, zipped it, and tossed the bag into a small open suitcase on the bed. After securing the luggage, she straightened and turned back around to face him. "There's one other thing I need to tell you—"

Outside, a vehicle horn blared.

A rueful smile tipped her lips. "I guess it can wait. There's our ride to the airport."

She slipped the thin strap of her purse over her shoulder and reached for the luggage lying on the bed, but Daniel was one step ahead of her.

"I can at least carry the small one," she said.

"I've got it."

She nodded, offering no further argument.

Standing in the middle of the room, she took one last lingering look at her surroundings. Then, drawing back her shoulders, she lifted her chin a determined inch, forcing more courage into her actions than her anxious eyes reflected.

"Well," she said, "I guess it's time to go home."

Chapter 6

"How many times have I done this before?" Lydia asked Daniel as she fastened her airplane seat belt with slightly shaky hands. A jittery knot bounced in her stomach.

"Five or six," Daniel answered, making sure Chloe was safely secured in her seat.

Daniel had been fortunate enough to reserve adjoining seats in the same row for him, Chloe, and Lydia. He—at Lydia's insistence—had taken the window seat, Chloe sat in the middle, and Lydia sat next to the aisle. She really wasn't interested in seeing how high the plane could fly.

Mrs. Porter sat in the aisle seat one row up.

Lydia rechecked Chloe's restraint. She knew Daniel had aptly secured the belt, but fidgeting gave her something to do with her hands besides wringing them in her lap. "Was I always this nervous?"

"A little the first time. But after that you always looked forward to the flight."

Mild turbulence during takeoff had Lydia clinging to her armrests; Chloe reached for Lydia. But once Daniel explained an airplane penetrating air pockets was like a pin popping balloons, Chloe found the occasional bump-bang rather amusing and began to giggle.

Lydia's uneasiness, however, didn't calm until the plane leveled off and the flight became smooth. Then, she realized, she didn't mind flying at all. She reminded herself of what Daniel had said about her enjoying flying in the past after she'd conquered her first-flight jitters. Maybe she had finally found something she had in common with her old self.

Her fit of anxiety returned full force when the pilot announced they were approaching Myrtle Beach International Airport. Meeting people who knew more about her past than she did weakened her fortitude, made her feel as though the thin shell of her self-composure might break under the mildest look of criticism.

"Are you okay?" Daniel asked as the plane rolled to a stop.

Lydia met his gaze of concern. "A little nervous," she admitted. "I never realized meeting my own family would be so. . ."

"Scary?"

She forced a smile. "Yeah." Looking down at her daughter, she pasted on a cheery expression. "Are you ready to meet Grandma and Grandpa Quinn and your aunt Jennifer?"

With a sparkle in her eyes, Chloe bobbed her head and raised her arms so Daniel could unfasten her seat belt. They fell in line and shuffled down the aisle. Daniel, with Chloe perched on his hip, led the way since he was the only one familiar with the airport and its unloading routine. Lydia followed Daniel, and Mrs. Porter fell in behind.

Lydia forced herself not to withdraw while people of all shapes, sizes, and ages craned their necks in search of their loved ones. She scanned the colossal wall of faces, hoping to locate those waiting for her. Seeing them first would at least give her a chance to brace for their reaction.

A man in a dark suit, carrying a briefcase in one hand and holding a cellular phone to his ear with the other, breezed by, bumping Lydia's shoulder and, for an instant, he drew her attention away from the crowd.

"Hey, do you know how to say 'Excuse me'?" she heard Daniel say.

The busy man just shot Daniel a flippant glance and kept on going.

Lydia's lips pinched together. Sure, the man had been rude, but that was no reason to solicit a brawl in the middle of an international airport. She was going to have to talk to Daniel about his impetuous overprotection.

"There they are!" A female voice rose above the crowd. "Lydia! Lydia!"

Before Lydia could lock onto the source of the voice, she found herself clenched in a fierce embrace. A blanket of blond hair brushed her face. Her nostrils filled with the sweet fragrance of expensive perfume. She tilted her head so her chin could rest atop the woman's shoulder and reminded herself to hug this still unknown member of her family.

Just as quickly as she'd grabbed Lydia, the woman set her back, keeping a hold on her upper arms. Lydia found herself looking into the misty blue eyes of a slim young woman at least six inches taller than herself.

Jennifer. Her sister. Lydia recognized the sibling from *Without a Trace*.

"Oh Lydia." Tears streaming, Jennifer lifted her hands to frame Lydia's face. "Look at you. You look wonderful."

Jennifer's gaze zipped to the area beyond Lydia's left shoulder. "And this must be Chloe."

As Jennifer stepped aside and flitted toward her niece, Lydia saw the couple who had been standing a few feet behind her sister. The woman leaned on a cane; the man held a protective arm around her. They were looking at Lydia like a young mother and father admiring their newborn for the first time after a long, complicated pregnancy.

"Mom? Dad?" Her voice was as small as a frightened child's. Lydia stepped forward at the same time they did, and they all came together in a fervent embrace.

Almost immediately, a warm feeling of acceptance stole over Lydia. She might not know these two people yet. Their faces might not be familiar to her as they once were, and their names might still sound strange and foreign. But one thing she did know—they loved her, as parents love their children. She could hear it in the tremble of their voices when they spoke to her, feel it in the strength of their arms as they held her.

Maybe she'd arrived "home" after all.

∽

They claimed their luggage, then made their way out to the parking area where Daniel had left his sleek white sedan—a lawyer's car, for sure. They fastened Chloe's seat belt and then Daniel, Lydia, and Mrs. Porter got in his car with the child, while Bill, Margaret, and Jennifer left to retrieve Jennifer's car from another lot.

An hour later, Daniel turned onto a road marked Plantation Lane.

He threw up his hand at the fourth deputy sitting in the fourth patrol car Lydia had noticed parked alongside the road since they'd entered the Quinn Island city limits ten minutes ago.

"Daniel," she queried, "are all these deputies for my benefit? Or is Quinn Island just well blessed with lawmen?"

"They're for your benefit and Chloe's. I called the sheriff yesterday and asked him to keep an eye out in case someone learned of your return. When the news starts spreading, it will draw a lot of attention. I didn't want you having to deal with that today."

"I appreciate that," she said. And she did appreciate his foresight— but not that he'd failed to inform her of his contact with the sheriff. She chewed her lower lip in frustration. What else had he failed to tell her?

"Also, Lydia," Daniel added, "I had to inform the sheriff you'd been found. Remember, you were the victim of a crime. There are going to be a lot of questions. . .interrogations in the days to come. I want you to be prepared for that." He glanced her way. "I'll be there with you through the whole thing. You'll not have to go through it alone."

Like ice cream in the summer sun, her irritation melted. She couldn't stay annoyed at him—he wouldn't let her. He was too gentle. Too kind. Too doggedly determined to look out for her and Chloe.

"Thank you," she told him. "That means a lot."

He turned his attention back to the road, and she turned hers to the roadside, where oleanders, palm trees, and other foliage that looked native to a tropical island lined the street. She made a mental note to ask Daniel the names of the plants she wasn't familiar with—and to buy a pair of dark sunglasses. The midafternoon sun seemed so much brighter here than in Chicago.

After they'd traveled about half a mile, Daniel turned the car onto a paved drive and stopped in front of a gate. When he pressed a button on a small box clipped to his sun visor, the black iron doors swung open. He maneuvered the vehicle through the gate, while Jennifer, Margaret, and Bill followed in Jennifer's car.

The narrow road was banked on each side by huge oaks. The branches of the mammoth trees, dripping with Spanish moss, offered a patchy overhead canopy that sprinkled the pavement with mottled shadows and sunshine.

They rounded a bend, and Lydia gasped in awe. The two-story brick house, a renovated and updated remnant of rice plantation days, with four heavy white columns and four second-story dormer windows, was like a regal queen on her throne. The house sat in the midst of acres of green lawn sparsely dotted with more oaks and native trees she couldn't yet name.

The house itself, with its tall bay windows and steep roof, was impressive enough. But the vast, wide-open space surrounding the building was breathtaking. A person could look out any given window and see nothing but nature, Lydia surmised. She had a feeling Chloe was going to love it here.

The rest of the afternoon Lydia spent getting acquainted with her family and her new surroundings. She toured the house, got familiar with the rooms she, Chloe, and Mrs. Porter would occupy, and looked at photo albums. She learned she had once taken ballet, voice, and violin lessons, and she wondered if she would still be able to dance, sing, or play the violin if she tried.

A stark reminder of what had been taken from her came when Jennifer pulled out Lydia's scrapbook of wedding plans. Everything had been organized with precision—bridesmaids' dresses, groomsmen's tuxedos, types of flowers—right down to how much each item would cost. The prices astounded Lydia.

How did I do it? she wondered. She could put a house in order faster than Mr. Clean, but thoughts of keeping books and organizing big events terrified her. From the looks of her wedding planner, her wedding was to have been a *big* event.

The final page included the wedding announcement that had been published in the local newspaper. She and Daniel had planned to marry in the First Community Church of Quinn Island, because, Jennifer said, it was the only local church big enough for the wedding party and anticipated crowd. Then, after a Paris honeymoon, they were going to live in Daniel's house while they built another.

Lydia closed the planner with a dismal sigh. What a charmed life she must have led. Too bad she couldn't remember any of it.

Daniel's parents arrived for supper. His father was also an attorney and shared his partnership with his son. Mrs. Matthews worked diligently in the Quinn Island Historical Society, the woman's club, and an organization that housed foster children until suitable homes could be found. They both greeted Lydia in a way that made her feel just as loved as her own parents had, then oohed and ahhed over

Chloe like true doting grandparents.

Time passed. Mr. and Mrs. Matthews left. Chloe, who had missed her afternoon nap, and Mrs. Porter, who'd also missed hers, wore down and went to bed. Then a somnolent quietness fell over the five remaining adults, as though they were all tired and weary, with nothing noteworthy left to say. Eventually, Bill and Margaret retired, and Jennifer soon followed; she rented a town apartment, but she had decided to spend the night at her parents' home in celebration of Lydia's return.

Daniel remained until shortly before midnight, then stood from where he sat next to Lydia on the sofa and held out his hand. "Walk me out?"

When they stepped out onto the wide front porch, she turned around to face him. He captured both of her hands in his, and for a moment he simply looked down at her. She wished she could see his eyes, read what was in them. But the overhead light threw dark shadows over the deeper planes of his handsome face, concealing whatever silent message he held there.

"I'm going to miss you tomorrow," he finally said.

A thump of fear hit Lydia in the chest. Her eyes stretched wide. "Miss me? You mean, I won't see you tomorrow?"

A pleased grin pulled at the corner of his mouth. "Do you want to?"

Realizing how childish she'd sounded, she ducked her head.

He released one of her hands and curled his forefinger beneath her chin, lifting her head so that she was again looking at him. "I want to see you, too, but I thought your parents and Jennifer would want to spend some time with you and Chloe tomorrow."

Of course, he was right. But thoughts of being away from him for the first time since meeting him three days ago triggered a strange and inexplicable uneasiness inside her. But what could she do about it? Fall down on her knees and beg him not to leave her alone at the mercies of her new and unfamiliar world?

She thought not.

"You're right," she said, forcing so much bravery into her voice, she sounded like an amateur actor in an unrehearsed play. "I do need to spend tomorrow with my family."

What about the next day? she wanted to ask. After all, it was Saturday. Would he want to see her then? And why did she so desperately want him to want to?

"How about dinner tomorrow night?" He moved his hand from beneath her chin and brushed the backs of his fingers across her cheek. His gaze left hers and traveled over her face, like he was trying to carve her into his memory.

Her stomach fluttered. How was she supposed to focus on what he was saying when he touched her that way? "Dinner?" she finally managed to squeak.

He nodded. "We can call it the first official date of our new beginning."

"Okay," she agreed, her voice sounding small and faraway. Then her maternal instincts jabbed at her moonstruck conscience, reminding her she had one small priority. "What about Chloe?"

"I've already got that covered. She said she'd be ready at seven."

Lydia blinked. "You mean, you don't mind taking her along?" Jeff had often wanted to leave her behind.

He tugged on her hand, urging her to inch forward into his open arms. "Now, why would any man mind being the escort of the two most beautiful girls in the world?"

Lydia knew he was exaggerating, at least where she was concerned. But who was she to argue? He wanted to take Chloe along, and, whatever his reasons, that thrilled Lydia beyond description. She slipped her arms around his waist and rested her cheek against his chest. "Thank you, Daniel."

"For what?"

"For not leaving Chloe out."

"I like having her around."

Lydia closed her eyes. *So far, so good,* she thought with a contented sigh. *So far, so good.*

Chapter 7

The next morning, Lydia stood on the sidewalk outside Lydia's Boutique, perusing the dress shop with her mother, her sister, her daughter, and Mrs. Porter. When Margaret had asked Lydia what she wanted to do that day, Lydia had told her mother she'd like to see the shop. She was curious to see the place that was once so much a part of her life, see if she could envision herself working there. So far, she couldn't.

"It's hard to believe I actually own this place," she mused out loud.

"Trust me, you do," her mother said. "Jennifer has done a wonderful job keeping it open and profitable while you've been away, but it was your dream."

Lydia squinted through the bright morning sun as she studied the calligraphic lettering on the windowpane and the decorative trim on the eave spanning the front of the white-frame building. Then she scanned her mother's and sister's faces, noticing their proud expressions. *Whose dream is it now?* she had to wonder.

She couldn't picture it as hers. In fact, she didn't think she had much fashion sense at all. She wasn't even fond of shopping. Of course, her life in Chicago hadn't offered her the opportunity to shop often. When she did, her purchases were always based on affordability.

Mrs. Porter had surprised her sometimes with an outfit beyond her own means, usually on a birthday or Christmas. But, generally, once Lydia got back on her feet after her long trek to recovery, her friend and former landlady had respected her desire to provide for herself and daughter.

Lydia noticed Margaret leaning heavily on her cane, and she took the weary woman's arm. "Let's go inside so you can rest a little while."

Margaret gave her daughter a grateful smile, and the four women and Chloe went through the door.

Lydia had learned her mother's limp was a result of the surgery she'd had prior to Lydia's disappearance. Margaret had never fully recovered from the hip replacement, and Lydia couldn't help wondering what part grief over her abduction had played in her mother's incomplete recovery.

As she helped her mother negotiate the steps, a sad and discouraging thought filtered through her. She would never be able to replace all that was taken away that fateful night on a deserted highway. But she would do her best. She owed this woman, her sister, her father, and Daniel that much.

When Lydia stepped into the shop, she stepped out of her comfort zone. She glanced around in awe at rows and rows of stylish clothing, both women's and children's, hanging from wall racks and circular supports placed expertly across a polished hardwood floor. Lacy lingerie lined the shelves and supports at the back of the store. Two crystal chandeliers hung from a dazzlingly white ceiling, and soft classical music seemed to float through the walls. The two store clerks, one at the counter and one organizing a sales rack, both looked as though they had just stepped off the set of a classy New York fashion shoot.

Feeling a bit overwhelmed, Lydia drew in a deep breath, only to wish she hadn't. Even the air in the store smelled expensive.

"Mama, is this really your store?" Chloe asked, gaining her mother's attention.

Instinctively, Lydia lifted her daughter to her hip. She didn't want to be responsible for anything that might get broken by the curious four-year-old. "That's what they say, sweetheart."

"Can I have a new dress?"

"Of course you can, angel," a beaming Margaret answered. "In fact, you can have all the new dresses you want."

"Maybe one," Lydia injected, intentionally keeping her gaze averted from her mother's. At some point, Lydia suspected she was going to have to talk to Margaret about who was mother to whom.

The salesclerk at the counter noticed the women and made her way to the front of the store, her gait reminding Lydia of a sleek, pampered house cat. "Hi, Jennifer," she said in a cultured voice that matched her cultured smile. "I thought you were taking the day off."

"I am. We just dropped by for a visit."

The two women engaged in what Lydia thought was an incomplete hug—they daintily grasped hands and merely touched cheeks together.

As they parted, the clerk, with her shiny black hair pulled back in a slick French chignon, fleetingly scanned each face as she turned to Margaret. Then her gaze snapped back to Lydia like a yo-yo on the rebound. After about two seconds of shocked paralysis, the elegant woman's painted mouth dropped open as though she'd just seen Lazarus raised from the dead.

Lydia forced herself not to withdraw. She figured she'd see many similar reactions in the next few days. She might as well start getting used to it.

Jennifer touched Lydia's arm. "Lydia, this is Jaime. She's the assistant manager of the store."

Lydia shifted Chloe to her left hip and extended her right hand. "Hi, Jaime. It's nice to meet you."

Jaime blinked like she'd been slapped. "Meet me? We went to school together. I was going to be in your wedding."

Lydia tried to muster up a smile but failed pitifully. "I'm sorry. I don't remember you. I have amnesia."

"Amnesia?" The clerk's voice rose and fell in a wave of shock.

"Yes." Lydia knew the woman deserved an explanation. But Lydia wouldn't go into the details of her abduction in front of Chloe.

As though sensing her sister's distress, Jennifer shuffled toward the door and hooked her manicured hand in the crook of Jaime's arm. "Come in back with me for a minute. There's something I need to show you." With that, she led Jaime away.

Lydia breathed an inward sigh of relief, making a mental note to thank her younger sister later.

"Now," said Margaret, hobbling to a dress rack and flipping through the dresses there, "let's see what we can do about getting you started on a new wardrobe."

New wardrobe? Lydia blinked. She already had a wardrobe. She looked down at her ribbed pink shell, full-length denim skirt, and navy sandals. Of course, her closet wasn't stocked with stylish designer classics, like her mother and Jennifer wore. One couldn't find many of those in discount stores and thrift shops. But her meager collection served its purpose.

"Chloe and I really need only one dress each, to wear on our dinner date tonight with Daniel."

Her mother didn't seem to hear her.

Lydia sent Mrs. Porter a what-should-I-do? look. The older woman lifted her shoulders in a don't-ask-me gesture, then turned and started flipping through some dresses on a sale rack.

"What about this?" Margaret turned to display a red dress designed to mold a curvy body.

Lydia didn't think she had many curves to mold. Even if she did, they weren't for anyone's eyes but her own and, maybe someday, a husband's. She shook her head. "It isn't me."

Puzzlement pinched Margaret's forehead. "You don't like it?"

"It's okay. It's just not something I would wear."

"Why don't you try it on and then decide?"

Lydia held up a hand. "Really, there's no need."

An injured look fell over Margaret's face as she turned and hung the dress back on the rack. She hobbled to a chair next to the dressing area and sat down.

Oh, great, Lydia thought. *Now I've hurt my mother's feelings.*

She set Chloe down and searched another rack, pulling out the first dress she came across in her size and style. Holding the garment up in front of her, she stepped up to her mother. "What do you think about this?"

Margaret critically eyed the dress, then lifted her gaze to her daughter's. "Do you want the truth, dear?"

The smile Lydia had pasted on for her mother's benefit wavered. "Of course."

"It doesn't suit you."

Well, touché, thought Lydia. She supposed one turn deserved another. Although she really hadn't meant to offend Margaret by rejecting the dress she'd chosen. Lydia was just stating a fact, her opinion, which, she'd noticed, didn't always set well with her mother.

"What are we looking for?" Jennifer asked, rejoining the group.

"Chloe and I need something to wear tonight. We have a dinner date with Daniel."

Jennifer's eyes lit up like a sunbeam. "Let me see what I can find." Like a kid on a treasure hunt, she scampered away and started digging through the racks.

Lydia's lips curved as she watched her sister retreat. Jennifer seemed so well suited for the affluent dress shop's environment. Much more so than Lydia herself did.

Margaret spurned Lydia's invitation to join her and Jennifer in their search, claiming she needed awhile longer to rest her leg. So Lydia left the pouting woman and returned the dress she held to the rack. As she reached to hang up the garment, she caught a glimpse of the price tag and realized her mistake. The one hundred dollars she had removed from her savings pouch and tucked into her billfold before leaving the house was barely enough to buy Chloe an outfit, much less purchase one for herself.

She turned to Jennifer and Mrs. Porter, who both seemed intent on finding her the perfect garment for her evening out with Daniel. "You know what?" she said. "I think I may have something to wear back at the house, after all. Why don't we just concentrate on finding something for Chloe today?"

"Oh, come on, sis," Jennifer said, inspecting a short, black, sequined dress that sparkled like a blanket of black diamonds under the chandeliers. "What's one more outfit?"

About two hundred bucks, Lydia was tempted to say, but she decided to keep the quick retort to herself. Aloud she said, "One more than I really need."

Jennifer gave Lydia a baffled look. "That never stopped you before."

Lydia sent the baffled look right back. "It didn't?"

"Of course not." Jennifer held the dress up to Lydia. "Your philosophy was always that a woman couldn't have too many clothes. Your closet was the envy of every female in Quinn Island."

Perplexity creased Lydia's forehead. She knew Jennifer hadn't meant to be critical. She'd simply blurted out a statement of fact from one sister to another. Still, Lydia couldn't help feeling a little offended. She was also a bit unsettled by what this particular revelation about herself revealed. Had she really been so self-absorbed and frivolous with her money when so many people in the world were cold, hungry, and homeless?

Still trying to digest the information, she looked down at the dress Jennifer held up before her. Embarrassment crept up her neck just looking at the garment. She had T-shirts that were longer.

"Where are my old clothes?" she asked, figuring she might find something among her pre-amnesia wardrobe to wear for her date.

"We had everything put into storage when the lease on your apartment ran out. All that stuff is at least five years old. Why don't you try this on? I think it'll look great on you."

As gently as possible, Lydia pushed the dress away. "I don't think so. But thanks anyway."

Mrs. Porter, who'd been flipping through the sale rack all along, turned with a knowing grin and held up a dress that halted Lydia's ready protest. The younger woman stood dazed for a moment, admiring the sleeveless garment with its modest scooped cowl neck, trim waistline, and long skirt that graced yards and yards of silky beige material she knew would feel like luxury floating around her ankles.

She reached out and turned over the tag. Just as she feared. Even with the discount, she didn't have enough to buy a dress for both her and Chloe. And Chloe's needs came first.

She dropped the tag, brushing her fingers across the smooth material as she pulled her hand away. "It's a lovely dress, Mrs. Porter. But, really, I'd rather concentrate on getting Chloe one today."

Jennifer touched Lydia's arm. "Liddi, what is it?"

"Nothing," she answered, feeling the weight of her sister's perusal bearing down on her.

"Is it money you're worried about?"

"No," she lied. "I just didn't bring enough along today to pay for two dresses. I'll get Chloe one today, and come back and get mine later."

Understanding curved Jennifer's lips. "Lydia, that isn't necessary."

"Of course it is."

"Lydia," Mrs. Porter spoke up, "I think what your sister is trying to say is that you own the shop. The dresses won't cost you anything."

But Lydia had already thought about that. She gave the dress a palms-out gesture. "That dress cost this shop something. It's not right for me to just take it."

"Lydia—" Jennifer started, then stopped and rubbed her fingertips across her forehead, as though she were having second thoughts about what she'd intended to say.

"What?"

The younger sibling shook her head. "Nothing." She turned and motioned to Jaime, then reached for the dress in Mrs. Porter's hand. As the clerk stepped up to them, Jennifer said, "Jaime, go figure our cost on this dress and let me know what it is, please."

Jaime nodded and walked away. When the clerk was out of earshot, Jennifer turned back to Lydia. "Lydia, you have money. Since Daniel's the family attorney, we turned your finances over to him to take care of while you were away. I'm sure he'll go over everything with you when he has a chance." She squeezed Lydia's hand. "I just thought you'd want to know that."

Jennifer knelt in front of Chloe. "Now, let's go see what we can find you to wear, princess, while your mother tries on her dress."

Margaret decided she wanted to be a part of finding her granddaughter a frock. With the enthusiasm of two fairy godmothers contemplating a peasant maiden's costume for a ball, she and Mrs. Porter followed Jennifer and Chloe to the children's section of the shop, leaving Lydia to try on her dress alone. And to think.

So, I have money, she mused as she stepped into a fitting room. How much money? Enough to buy her and Chloe a small place of their own? Enough to help fund the new homeless shelter for which Jeff was trying to raise money? What about the missing persons' organization her mother had founded in her honor? Would a few extra funds help find another lost loved one?

She unzipped the dress and slid it from its hanger. What would it feel like having enough money to grocery shop without having to check the prices of every item on her list? Put more than a widow's mite in the offering plate on Sunday? Buy Chloe that one special dress?

Mentally, she pulled back the reins of her elaborate thoughts and slipped the dress over her head. She'd better wait and talk to Daniel about her net worth before making plans to build houses or fund homeless shelters.

As she twirled in front of the mirror, inspecting the most beautiful garment she ever remembered seeing, her thoughts turned to her and Chloe's dinner date with Daniel. With very little deliberation, she decided to buy the dress.

Chloe chose a purple frock with a high waistline and white lace trim, which didn't surprise Lydia. Purple was her daughter's favorite color.

With the outfits hanging from fancy silk-covered hangers and protected with long garment bags bearing the store emblem, Lydia left the shop with just over fifteen dollars in her purse. Hopefully, the White Seagull, her sister's restaurant of choice for lunch, would be easy on the pocket.

Fortunately, it was. Lydia breathed a sigh of relief as she glanced at the menu posted outside the café entrance. The quaint little establishment had outdoor seating with a view of the marsh channel that separated the island from the mainland. The table umbrellas flapped occasionally in a breeze brisk enough to offer comfort to the patrons but tame enough that it didn't send the eating utensils flying.

As soon as they all settled around the table, Margaret leaned on her forearms and looked at Lydia. "Sweetheart, why don't I call Judy Spivey, your old hairdresser, and see if she can work you and Chloe in this afternoon?"

The question—which sounded more like the follow-up statement to a decision that had already been made—caught Lydia off guard. She couldn't think of an immediate response.

"She always did such a good job with your hair before," her mother added. "And don't you think Chloe's hair would look better in a chin-length bob?"

Self-consciously, Lydia raised a hand to her thick, wind-tossed tresses. She was rather fond of her hair just the way it was, even if her corkscrew curls did usually have a stubborn will of their own. As for Chloe, well, she'd been a bald newborn and a fuzzy toddler. It had taken four years for her hair to reach shoulder length. No way was anyone going to lay scissors to those light blond locks just yet.

Silently praying she wouldn't offend her mother again, Lydia reached over and covered the woman's hand with her own. "Give us a few days to get settled in, then we'll see about making an appointment with the hairdresser."

"But what about your date tonight?"

Lydia squeezed her mother's hand. "We'll get by," she said with an appeasing smile, then gratefully reached for the menu the waitress had just laid on the table.

Thankfully, Margaret let the matter drop, but Lydia had a feeling it would be picked up again later.

Lydia had helped Chloe with the child's menu and was trying to decide between the homemade vegetable soup and the chef's salad for herself when she heard Chloe giggle. Curious, Lydia cut her daughter a sidelong glance to find the child cupping a hand over her mouth, trying to stifle laughter. Lydia shifted her gaze to the other women at the table. They were all looking at her with amusement in their expressions, like some sort of conspiracy was under way.

Then everything turned black.

Chapter 8

Smiling, Lydia raised her hands to the fingers covering her eyes. She'd known those hands only four days, but would recognize them anywhere—even if she went another five years without feeling their touch.

An unexpected yearning wove through her, and for the first time since seeing her face on *Without a Trace*, she felt grievously cheated. Half a decade ago, she had not only been robbed of her past life, but of her precious memories of Daniel.

She pulled his hands away from her eyes and twisted her head around, looking up into his handsome face. His muscular forearms were exposed by dress shirtsleeves rolled up to his elbows, and beneath the unbuttoned top button of his shirt, his tie hung loose like he'd pulled at the knot with his forefinger. The wind pushed his dark hair flat against his forehead. His smell, all man heightened by a faint scent of spicy cologne, wrapped around her senses like a silk thread.

He captured one of her hands before she could drop it back to the table. "Fancy meeting you here," he said. "I knew there was a reason I was craving one of the 'Gull's subs today. My guardian angel was sitting on my shoulder, pointing me in your direction."

He leaned down and kissed her forehead, and Lydia released an inward sigh of contentment. He seemed to know just what to say and do to make her feel cherished.

Before letting go of her hand, he gave her fingers a gentle squeeze. Then he turned to Chloe, lifting the eager four-year-old out of her chair and up over his head. "And what about you, angel face? Have you been keeping these ladies straight?"

Chloe's answer was an attack of giggles.

A stranger looking on would think he had made the move a thousand times. Was he this way with all kids? Or did he see something special in Chloe?

Or was Lydia engaging in wishful thinking?

"Me and Mama bought pretty dresses for our date with you tonight," Chloe said as Daniel lowered her to his hip.

Daniel flashed Lydia a pleased smile, then turned his attention back to Chloe. "You did?"

"Uh-huh." Chloe gave her head an emphatic nod. "Mine's purple."

"Purple? I like purple. You'll make all the other girls very jealous."

He tickled Chloe's stomach, sending her off in another fit of giggles, before setting her back in her seat.

"Why don't you join us, Daniel?" Margaret suggested.

"I believe I will. Let me go wash up and I'll be right back." With that, he headed for the indoor area of the restaurant.

Lydia returned to her menu and had just about decided on the soup when a hand holding a small tape recorder appeared in front of her face, blocking her view.

"Miss Quinn," an unfamiliar male voice said, "could you answer a few questions about your abduction and the five years you were away from Quinn Island?"

She tipped up her head and looked into the eager face of a young man in a crumpled gray suit with press credentials clipped to the jacket pocket. A thirty-five millimeter camera dangled around his neck, and the end of his tie lay across the top of his shoulder, like he'd been running.

Lydia blinked. "I. . .ah. . ." Words failed her. She stared up at the man, unable to react.

"I understand you have a young daughter. Is this her? Is she a result of the assault, or do you know who the father is?"

Seconds passed like long minutes. Lydia became aware that everyone in the busy eating area was staring at her. The invisible walls of the outdoor café started closing in on her, trapping her. Still, she couldn't react, couldn't speak.

Out of the corner of her eye, she saw her mother and Mrs. Porter start to rise; then, for some reason, both ladies sat back down.

That "some reason" appeared instantly at her side in the form of Daniel. He clamped his hand over the microphone end of the recorder. "No, Mark, Miss Quinn will not answer any questions."

The man swung toward Daniel. "As a member of the media, I've got rights—"

"So has Miss Quinn." Daniel's voice was calm.

"But—"

"I can go talk to the judge." Daniel's tone remained low and steady, but Lydia could see a vein throbbing beneath his ear, and she sensed the fury caged just beneath the surface of his dark eyes. "I'm sure he'll have no problem issuing a restraining order to anyone who comes within a hundred feet of Miss Quinn with the intention of invading her privacy."

Lydia thought surely the reporter would back down. Amazingly, the smaller man persisted. "Come on, Daniel. The people of Quinn Island have a right to hear her story."

Daniel pulled his hand away from the tape recorder. "Then there's always harassment. Did you get that on record, Mark?"

The reporter snapped off the recorder and crammed it in his jacket pocket. "I'll get my story," he sneered. "I have another source, you know." With that, the irate man turned and stalked away.

Lydia propped her elbows on the table, dropped her forehead to her hands, and started shaking.

Daniel slid a chair against hers and sat down, slipping his arm around her shoulders. "Lydia, are you okay?"

The words on the menu blurred. Her world tilted. Someone touched her arm.

"Lydia," came her mother's concerned voice, "can I get you something? A glass of water?"

She heard everyone calling to her, but the darkness closing in around her was stronger. She couldn't pull herself back from it. The menu started to fade.

"Mommy!"

That did it. The alarm in Chloe's voice jerked her up straight. She focused on her child, and the concern and confusion in her small face bruised Lydia's heart. "Mommy's fine, sweetheart." They reached for each other at the same time. Lydia shifted her daughter to her lap. With arms and legs, Chloe clamped onto her mother's neck and waist and laid her head on her mother's shoulder.

"Did that man hurt you?" the little girl wanted to know.

"No, sweetie. He didn't hurt me."

"Then why did Daniel make him go away?"

In her peripheral vision, Lydia saw Daniel open his mouth to answer. She held up a hand to stop him. When she felt assured of his silence, she took the same hand and rubbed her daughter's back. "Because the man was asking about things I didn't want to talk about."

"What kind of things?"

Lydia pursed her lips, thinking. "Private things."

"Like my private places, where no one's s'pose to touch me."

"Yes. Something like that." Lydia felt her face warm, but she was awed by how closely her daughter's comparison paralleled her own feelings. Chloe was a private part of Lydia she had always been able to protect from evil and harmful things. At least, she had until today.

Chloe planted her small hands on her mother's shoulders and pushed back. "We need to pray for him." She bobbed her head with each word for emphasis. "Like Moses prayed for his people."

Lydia tucked a wisp of stray hair behind her daughter's ear. "You're right. We should." But she wasn't quite ready to forgive the stranger who had so rudely intruded on her and her daughter's life.

The waitress appeared at the table and Lydia asked Chloe if she was ready to order.

Wrinkling her nose, the little girl shook her head. "I'm not hungry anymore."

"Me either." Lydia glanced around the table. "I think Chloe and I will just wait in the car."

Daniel stood, reaching for the back of her chair. "Come on. I'll take you back to the house."

She looked up at him. "But don't you have to get back to the office? And what about lunch?"

"We'll fix us something there." He captured her upper arm and helped her stand.

"But I don't want to be an imposition."

He trapped her chin beneath his thumb and curled forefinger. "You, my dear, could never be an imposition."

Lydia had no more energy to argue. She turned to her longtime friend. "Mrs. Porter—"

Mrs. Porter waved a hand through the air, shooing Lydia, Chloe, and Daniel away. "You run along, dear. I'll come with Margaret and Jennifer."

With Chloe perched on her hip, Lydia left the restaurant under the security of Daniel's protective arm. But inside she felt like she was dangling from a faulty trapeze swing with no safety net beneath her. What had just happened back there with that reporter? When he had asked about Chloe, she couldn't move, couldn't speak, couldn't react. All she could do was sit there and stare at him.

Then there was Daniel, like her own guardian angel, putting the reporter in his place, taking care of her. . .and Chloe. What would she have done today if he hadn't been there?

Daniel took the initiative and fastened Chloe's seat belt, then opened the door for Lydia. She climbed in like a battery-operated doll with a weak battery. As she watched Daniel circle the front of the car on his way to the driver's side, the layers of numbness began to peel away from her brain, leaving her mind exposed to the stark reality of her situation.

She needed him.

She felt a crack in her wall of independence, a small piece chip away. She needed Daniel, but God knew she didn't want to.

Ever since the day she had recovered from the assault and started making her own way, she had been determined not to need anyone. Not Jeff. Not even Mrs. Porter.

Not anyone.

Because she knew too well that fate could deal a person a cruel blow—and he or she could find themselves alone, like she had five years ago. During her recovery—when someone else had held the soupspoon to her mouth, bore her weight every time she went to the bathroom, provided her with a roof over her head—she had discovered that dependence was not the kind of existence she wanted for herself. And when she rose above it, she vowed she'd never go back.

She might one day fall in love with Daniel, marry him, share his home and children. But she *did not* want to depend on him for survival. Because if she did, and then something happened one day to take him away from her, she feared she might curl up into a ball and die, like she'd tried to do before she had Chloe. She didn't want to risk going back to that terrible feeling of helplessness. She didn't want to care about anyone that much. But she had a sinking feeling it was too late—and an even deeper fear that her dependence on Daniel went beyond basic need. Far beyond.

He had stepped into her life, swept her off her feet, carried her over the rough places, and, so far, had refused to put her down. What would happen if he decided to? Would her heart survive it?

The leather seat of the car creaked a little under Daniel's weight, and he touched her face. She closed her eyes and tilted her head so that her cheek rested in his palm.

Heaven help her, she needed him.

∞

"What was the reporter talking about when he said he had another source of information on me?" Lydia asked while she and Daniel prepared two ham and cheese sandwiches. Chloe, who sat at the table engrossed in a coloring book and crayons, preferred plain cheese.

Since Friday was the maid's shopping day, Lydia, Daniel, and Chloe had the house to themselves during lunch, which suited Lydia just fine. Something about spreading her own mayonnaise and slicing her own tomatoes helped her corral her scattered nerves and made her feel more at home in the spotless plantation house kitchen.

"Mark dates Jaime," Daniel answered as he slapped two slices of ham on his sandwich. He started to follow suit with Lydia's, but she fanned away the second piece of meat with an inward shudder. Where did he put all the food he consumed? Certainly not on that lean, muscular frame of his.

She added the cheese. "You mean the clerk at the dress shop? The one who told me she was supposed to have had a part in our wedding?"

He added slices of tomato. "That's the one."

On went blankets of lettuce. "So, that's how he found out I was going to be at the White Seagull. We were talking about it at the shop when we checked out."

The top layer of bread fell into place. "I would say so."

The phone rang, and Lydia almost jumped out of her slippers. With one hand over her racing heart, she turned to pick up the wall receiver.

Daniel abandoned the glass he was filling with ice and grabbed her wrist. "Don't answer that."

She frowned up at him. "Why? It could be Jennifer or Mother. Or Mrs. Porter."

"Let me." He squeezed between her and the wall and picked up the receiver. "Hello."

Almost immediately, he scowled. "No, Miss Quinn will not be available to answer any questions this evening." A short pause, then, "No, she won't be available tomorrow either." His scowl deepened. "Not then either. She's not interested in talking to the press, period." His hand, which still circled her wrist, inched down to grasp her hand. "Not that it's any of your business, but I'm her attorney, and, no, I'm not interested in talking to the press either. Thank you, and have a good day."

With that, he hung up and turned to her. He raked his free hand through his hair. A rebellious lock dipped toward his left brow. "Lydia, I don't think it would be a good idea for you to answer the phone for the next few weeks."

She didn't have to guess at the meaning of his words. "Daniel, exactly how many people do you think know I'm back by now?"

He pursed his lips, glancing into the distance over her left shoulder as though mentally stacking numbers, "Oh"—he cut his gaze back to hers—"I'd say about half the town."

Chewing her lower lip, she pulled her hands from his and turned, taking a few steps away from him. "Goodness, news travels fast here, doesn't it?"

"News like this does."

His hands cupped her shoulders. Drawn by his magnetic touch, she leaned back into him. His strong, comforting arms enveloped her shoulders. She raised her hands to his forearms and laid her head back against his chest. He rested his chin on top of her head and, ever-so-gently, began to sway from side to side. She closed her eyes and floated with him, feeling as though they moved as one, like ice dancers skating to a love song.

"I know your amnesia puts you at a disadvantage, love," he said. "Everyone here knows you. You don't remember anyone. But we'll get through this together, you and I."

She released a rueful sigh. "Seems like, Mr. Matthews, I've become somewhat a burden for you."

"On the contrary, Miss Quinn. You've given me back my reason for living."

A hand came up and brushed the hair away from her temple. His soft lips touched the jagged scar there. She felt the sting of tears behind her closed eyelids, and an overwhelming need to say "I love you." But the words tripped over the lump of emotion lodged in her throat.

He slid his palms up her arms, stopping when he reached her shoulders. Slowly, he turned her around. She knew he was going to kiss her and that she was going to kiss him back. A dizzy current raced through her as she floated toward him.

But ten small fingers crawling up her leg shattered her cloud of ecstasy in a million tiny pieces.

She pushed away from Daniel and looked down. What on earth had she been thinking? A trembling hand rose to her fluttering stomach. Obviously, she hadn't been thinking. Otherwise, she wouldn't have forgotten her daughter was sitting at the table less than six feet away.

She kneeled down in front of Chloe and grasped her daughter's hands. "What is it, sweetheart?"

Chloe tilted her head to one side, pushed out her lower lip in an artful pout, and looked at her mother with eyes that reminded Lydia of a wounded puppy. "I want you to hold me, Mommy."

Chloe only used "Mommy" when she really needed, or just plain wanted, her mother's attention. This was one of those "just plain wanted" times. But Lydia couldn't fault the timing. Had it not been for her daughter's interruption, she would have been engaged in the kind of scene she censored when Chloe watched TV. Lydia even blushed when she saw a man and woman locked in a passionate kiss on the television screen. That kind of intimacy, in her opinion, belonged to the privacy of the two consenting adults. Anything more belonged within the sanctity of marriage.

"Now Chloe," Lydia said, "I think you're big enough to walk. Besides, if I hold you, who's going to carry our food to the table?"

Chloe turned huge accusing eyes on Daniel.

In answer to her daughter's silent message, Lydia said, "I was hoping we could eat out on the terrace"—she really needed the fresh air—"and I don't think it's fair to ask Daniel to carry all the food out there by himself. Do you?"

Chloe ducked her head and shook it.

When Lydia stood, she noticed a look of sincere remorse on Daniel's face.

"I'm so—"

She cut off his apology with an upheld hand. "It wasn't your fault." Scooping up hers and Chloe's plates, she headed for the terrace, knowing without looking that her daughter followed close behind.

"I'll be out in a minute," she heard Daniel say, but she never looked back, never broke her stride.

She didn't blame him for their momentary loss of self-control. He was a man. A passionate man who had, from day one, been honest and open about his feelings for her. She, on the other hand, was the mother of an impressionable four-year-old who had been sitting right there in the kitchen with her and Daniel when she had so willingly fell into his arms.

How could she have been so stupid?

∞

How could he have been so stupid?

Daniel berated himself while he stood, hands stuffed in his pockets, watching the two most important people in his life disappear through the kitchen door. In a moment of passion, he'd forgotten all about Chloe—and his vow to let Lydia make the first move.

She was so vulnerable right now, trying to find her place in a world she knew nothing about, live among people who unknowingly placed high demands on her. He didn't want to be one of those people. In fact, "those people," as well meaning as some might be, were exactly what he wanted to protect her from. Now, here he had gone and almost given in to his increasing desire to hold and kiss her. He would have if Chloe hadn't intervened.

He leaned back against the cabinet and scrubbed a shaky hand down his face. He needed to get out to the terrace and figure out how to worm his way back into Chloe's good graces. But he couldn't. Not right this minute. His insides were still quivering.

∞

Some two minutes later, when Daniel felt his emotions were under control, he carried his sandwich and the drinks—purple Kool-Aid per Chloe's request—outside on a tray. He cautiously sat down in the vacant seat next to Chloe, positioning himself on the side of the child that was opposite her mother.

The first five minutes, he got nowhere. He talked and asked questions he thought four-year-olds might be interested in answering. Chloe chewed on her plain cheese sandwich, sipped her purple drink, and pointedly ignored him. The heel of her tennis shoe tapped out a steady *thump, thump, thump* on the chair leg as she swung her short leg back and forth.

He looked to Lydia for help. She merely gazed back at him with a twinkle in her eyes, then glanced away and took a dainty sip of drink, trying, he could tell, not to laugh.

She was enjoying seeing him squirm. *Spiteful woman,* he thought with affection, then almost grinned himself. Guess it served him right for losing his head and crawling all over her in the kitchen in front of her daughter.

He heaved a sigh and went back to Chloe. He'd interrogated hardcore criminals who had been easier to crack than this kid. "You know what, Chloe? I know where there's an ice cream parlor that serves purple ice cream."

Her leg stopped swinging. She stopped chewing.

Daniel waited a few seconds, then added, "Do you like purple ice cream?"

One, two, three seconds passed before Chloe nodded, once, without looking at him, then went back to chewing. Her leg went back to swinging.

At last, they were getting somewhere. Daniel felt like raising his hands and physically praising the Lord.

After fifteen minutes and a promise of a purple ice cream cone the very next day, Daniel felt confident all was forgiven. Chloe was talking and smiling again at his corny jokes, and the untimely kitchen incident seemed to be fading quickly from her young mind.

At least he thought so until she twisted her head around, peered up at him, and said, "Are you going to marry my mama?"

Daniel blinked. Now, how was he supposed to answer that? He glanced at Lydia, who looked the other way. No help there.

He folded his arms on the table and looked down at Chloe. Wanting to stay on good terms with the child, he gave an answer he felt was both unassuming and honest. "Maybe. Someday."

"That's what she says about Jeff."

Lydia swung her head around, gaping at Chloe like the child had just revealed a well-guarded secret.

Daniel almost choked on the last bite he'd taken of his sandwich. "She...says...what...about Jeff?"

"Whenever I ask my mama if she's going to marry Jeff, she always says 'Maybe someday,' " The singsong innocence of Chloe's voice did nothing to calm the spasms inside Daniel's chest.

Seemingly oblivious to the earthquake about to explode in the man beside her, the child turned her attention back to the sandwich she held in one hand and took another bite.

Daniel lifted a sharp, questioning gaze to Lydia.

"I'll explain later," she said with a nonchalant shrug.

Had she lied to him in Chicago when she told him she and Jeff were just friends?

She started stacking plates on the tray, and he followed suit with the glasses. She could count on explaining about Jeff. *Soon*. Like, within the next hour. No way was he going to spend the rest of the day wondering how she felt about this other man. And if she had any intentions of "maybe someday" marrying him, Daniel would simply have to change her way of thinking.

Because he had no intentions of her marrying anybody...except him.

Chapter 9

"I'm not sure going out tonight is such a good idea," Lydia told Daniel as she set the dishes in the sink.

Daniel understood her reservations, and he had already come up with a solution. Stepping up beside her, he slid his hands into his pockets so he wouldn't follow his instinct to touch her. "What if I were to take the afternoon off and take you and Chloe to a place where your privacy will be respected and no reporters will harass you?"

She shifted to face him. "I can't let you do that. You've already missed four days of work this week. You must have tons to do."

A sharp pang of regret jabbed at his chest. Once he had put his work before her, and his decision had cost them both—dearly. He would not make that mistake again.

"Only half a ton," he said, forcing a chipper note into his voice. "Which is nothing out of the ordinary. Besides, when I found you in Chicago on Tuesday, I went ahead and cancelled all my appointments for the week. The only thing waiting back at the office for me is a stack of paperwork, which isn't nearly as appealing as spending an afternoon on the island with you and Chloe."

Her eyes lit up with a childlike exuberance. "The island?"

He nodded.

Even as she shook her head, he could see her struggling to contain her enthusiasm. "Seriously, Daniel. I don't want you to feel you have to entertain us."

Chloe was back at the table engrossed in her coloring, but Daniel suspected she was keeping a keen eye on him and her mother. He resisted the urge to reach for Lydia's waist and risked capturing her hands instead. "The only reason I went into work this morning was because if I hadn't, I would have been on your parents' doorstep at dawn wanting to see you, and I really felt your family needed a little time with you."

A well of emotion still too raw to be contained rose in his chest, as did the conviction in his voice. "Lydia, I have waited for this day for so long that I live in fear I'll wake up and find it's all been just a dream." He squeezed her fingers. "There's nothing at work that can't wait until Monday. But there's something here I've wanted for five years. I'd like to spend every minute with you that I can. That is, if you have no objections."

"I don't," she responded, her voice sounding small and breathless. "We'd love to go to the island with you."

A small degree of satisfaction settled over Daniel. Maybe, just maybe, she was beginning to feel for him just a little of what he felt for her. "Great. Let me make a phone call, and in about thirty minutes, we'll be set to go."

"Do Chloe and I need to change?"

He considered Chloe's shorts and Lydia's casual skirt and top. "No. You're both perfect just the way you are."

He placed his call, making arrangements to borrow a car since his was too easily recognized. In addition to the vehicle, he requested hats and sunglasses for himself, Lydia, and Chloe so they could leave the grounds in disguise.

When he hung up the phone, he turned around and squared off to face Lydia, who stood about three feet away, her hands laced in front of her. For a fleeting moment, he lost sight of his purpose. Did she realize what a captivating picture she made, standing there mesmerizing him with those soft brown eyes of hers? Somehow, he didn't think so.

Mentally, he shook his head, reminding himself of his intention. "Now, I'm ready to hear about Jeff," he said.

She shrugged. "There really isn't much to tell."

"Then it shouldn't take you very long."

She glanced pointedly at Chloe, then looked back at him, clearly expecting him to relent and wait until later to hear what she had to say about Jeff.

Daniel merely leaned back against the counter, crossed his arms and ankles, and waited.

She studied him a moment, apparently contemplating what to do, then rolled her eyes and threw up her hands in defeat. "Come on, Chloe. Let's go see what's on PBS."

Chloe shot Daniel a wary look, and at first he feared she'd refuse to go.

Lydia held out her hand. "Come on, Chloe," she repeated with a mild note of firmness. "Daniel and I need to talk about something, then we're going to ride out to the island with him and see the ocean."

Chloe lit up like a sunbeam. "We are?"

Daniel sauntered to the table "That's right. We might even round up a bucket so we can play in the sand."

The child jumped down from her chair and, ignoring her mother's hand, dove for Daniel, wrapping her arms around his knees.

He peeled her arms from his legs and kneeled down in front of her. When she reached around his neck and planted a butterfly kiss on his cheek, his chest tightened. The sting of unexpected tears nipped at his eyes. He quickly blinked them away. The little girl's charms were as potent as her mother's, but in a totally different way.

Chloe followed her mother out of the kitchen with a jaunty bounce in her step and her ponytail swinging from side to side behind her. As soon as the door closed behind them, Daniel placed another quick call, adding a sand bucket, shovel, and a beach blanket to his earlier request.

When he hung up, he leaned back against the counter once again and tried to prepare himself for Lydia's return. What would he do if she told him she was in love with Jeff and was thinking about marrying him? He forced a deep breath into his lungs. He wasn't sure what he'd do. But, if he were a betting person, he'd wager he'd lay down and die, right there on the spot.

When she stepped back through the door, every muscle in his body tensed like a rope engaged in a tug-of-war game.

She stopped about three feet in front of him and crossed her arms. "You're buying her affection, you know."

One corner of his mouth tipped. "It's worth it."

Their eyes locked, igniting a bolt of electricity that crackled over several seconds of silence. Then she blinked, and he felt her pull herself back, as though she'd suddenly realized she was standing too close to a cliff ledge.

Shifting her weight to one foot, she said, "So, you want to know about Jeff."

He nodded, once. That was all the knot in his throat would allow.

"About two months ago he asked me to marry him."

He slowly arched an inquisitive brow. "And you were considering it?"

"I was. . .waiting."

"Waiting for what?"

"To see if something more than friendship would develop between us, or if a parental bond would develop between him and Chloe."

"And was anything developing?"

A soft smile curved her lips. "No. I realize now that Jeff and I are simply good friends. That's all we'll ever be. He knows that, too."

He heaved a deep sigh of relief. When he exhaled, his muscles turned to pulp as the tension drained from his body. He scrubbed a hand down his face. "I lost you once. I don't want to lose you again. To anything, or anybody."

They both grew still and very quiet, and Daniel saw a tenderness in her eyes he knew he'd never seen before. And in that single defining moment, he realized she cared about him. *Really* cared about him. About his thoughts, his feelings, and what he had suffered. Even after all she'd been through, she still found room in her heart to care about what her disappearance five years ago had done to him.

He was overcome with. . .something. He wasn't sure what. It was a feeling he'd never, until that moment, experienced. But whatever it was, it moved him. And humbled him.

"I was going to tell you about Jeff's proposal," she said, answering a question he'd asked himself at least a dozen times since Chloe had made her little earth-jarring statement awhile ago. "Yesterday, before we left for the airport, I started to tell you, but the shuttle arrived and there wasn't enough time. Since then, I really haven't thought about it."

Daniel nodded, satisfied he knew all he needed to know. There was no one else, and she had planned to tell him about the proposal.

He eased away from the counter. "You know," he said, "I'd really like to hug you before we go, but I'm afraid to." Afraid Chloe would walk in. Afraid he couldn't let go.

Suddenly, she had the brown eyes of a minx and the mischievous grin of an imp. Strolling forward, she raised her hands to his waist. His throat went a little dry.

"Just don't forget my daughter's in the very next room," she said.

Daniel would have laughed out loud, but he didn't want to draw the protective four-year-old's attention just yet. Slipping his arms around Lydia, he said, "I think, *maybe,* I can manage that."

Her arms circled his waist and she laid her cheek against his chest. Feeling more contented than he had in a very long time, he rested his jaw on top of her head. My but she was full of surprises. Why hadn't he ever noticed that about her before?

"Mama, are we goin' in that?" Chloe said from where she stood on the top step next to her mother.

The old SUV sitting in the circular drive had an unpainted front fender and a creased back bumper. Under a multitude of dings, dents, and scratches, lay a dull coat of yellow paint. Daniel had borrowed the eccentric-looking vehicle from his eccentric-looking cousin named Steve.

Pasting on a bright smile, Lydia peered down at her child, who now wore a floppy straw hat and a child-size pair of oval-lens sunglasses. "We sure are, honey. Wasn't it nice of Steve to let us borrow it?"

Chloe scrutinized the vehicle, but she made no further comment. She might not have been showered with many luxuries outside their basic needs, but she was accustomed to riding in Mrs. Porter's and now Daniel's comfortable, well-kept sedans.

Lydia donned her straw hat and sunglasses, and Daniel jammed a white baseball cap, bill turned backward, over his dark hair. He had also changed clothes and now wore an olive green polo shirt, a pair of faded jeans, and a well-worn pair of running shoes.

He fastened Chloe in her seat and opened the door for Lydia. Amazingly, the inside of the car was as neat and clean as a king's castle and smelled as fresh as the morning sunshine. When Daniel fired the engine, it purred like a well-fed kitten.

Steve had left in Daniel's car about five minutes earlier, hoping to draw away any media or overzealous well-wishers who might be stationed at the front gate. Even so, as Daniel approached the entrance to the drive, unease stirred up a swarm of butterflies in Lydia's stomach. When the gate clanged shut behind them, she felt as though she'd been locked out of her house in the middle of a cold, dark night.

"Are you sure no one will bother us on the island?" she asked as Daniel eased out onto the highway.

He'd noticed how the knuckles of her clasped hands had turned white when he drove through the gate. Reaching over, he pried her hands apart and laced his fingers through hers. Her fingertips felt like icicles pressed against the back of his hand, but he wasn't surprised. Her hands had always gotten cold when she was nervous. Today, they had been cold a lot.

"If anyone sees you and recognizes you," he explained, "they may stop and say hello and tell you they're glad you made it home, but they won't bother you. Not like the people on the mainland who know you so well."

"Oh Daniel, the people haven't bothered me so much, other than that nosy reporter." The last phrase she added as though she'd just tasted something sour. "It's just that everyone seems so thrilled to see me. Since I can't remember any of them, I can't empathize with their experience, because mine's a totally different one." She shook her head and turned her attention to the view outside the passenger window. "I don't mean to sound cold, but it's just going to take some time to recapture what I once felt for everyone."

Just like it'll take time to recapture what you once felt for me, Daniel thought. Something heavy settled on his chest. He shifted gears in the old five-speed. "You don't sound *cold*, sweetheart. I know it's going to take time."

And when she learned that five years ago a self-serving decision on his part had ultimately put her in the situation she was now in, would she even want to love him at all?

Chapter 10

$\mathcal{F}$ifteen minutes later, Daniel drove over the bridge spanning the channel that separated the island from the mainland. About a quarter-mile after crossing the bridge, he veered to the right and drove down a street sparsely lined with houses shrouded by verdant trees and lush landscaping.

Lydia eyed each home on the island with curiosity, noticing they were all modestly built, but well-kept and welcoming. When Daniel passed the first four without stopping, she said, "Which one belonged to my grandfather?" She simply couldn't see herself as the owner of one of these charming little cottages by the sea.

"You'll see," was Daniel's answer.

They passed a female jogger accompanied by a gorgeous collie on a leash. The runner gave the SUV a critical glower, but she showed no interest in the occupants.

A smile settled on Lydia's lips. So that was why Daniel had chosen such a deprived-looking vehicle for their outing. Onlookers paid more attention to the automobile than to who was inside.

"Mama, where's the ocean?"

Smiling, Lydia peeked around the bucket seat at her daughter, then looked to Daniel for the answer.

"It's on the other side of the houses, Chloe," he explained. "All those plants and trees around and between the houses were placed there on purpose, to make a shield between the road and the ocean."

"But when do *we* get to see it?" Chloe persisted.

He glanced at Chloe via the rearview mirror. "Soon, angel. We're just about there."

A kneeling elderly woman tending her flower bed raised her garden trowel in greeting. Returning the affable gesture, Lydia asked, "Are the people who live on the island friendly?"

"Very. They keep an eye out for one another, occasionally get together for things like barbeques and birthday parties. At the same time, they respect each other's privacy."

The small, wood-frame island church, supported by partially submerged stone pillars, appeared to be floating on top of the marsh. Daniel had told her the aged building had encountered at least a dozen major storms since it had been built over 120 years ago. Somehow, the old house of worship had withstood them all and was still standing.

As they drove past the church, Lydia decided Daniel was right when he had told her the island was like a world within itself. Strictly residential, no nightclubs, no bars, no social clubs that labeled one class or another. Just a safe haven for people who wanted to escape the madness of a harsh, demanding world and live in quiet tranquility.

A place for people like her. . .and Chloe.

The tension tugging at Lydia's nape began to ebb, heightening her awareness of Daniel's thumb caressing the back of her hand.

The road ended where someone's driveway began. Instead of stopping, Daniel pulled into the private road that was flanked on each side of the entrance by a replica of a ship's helm wheel. He navigated a ninety-degree curve to the left and continued up a gently sloping hill, then stopped in front of a charming two-story cottage with a wraparound porch. The gray paint appeared fresh and unweathered, but the shrubs and flowers could have used the tender hand of a good gardener. The poor bushes either reached across the stone walkway like long, gnarly fingers or drooped in haggard disarray outside their intended boundaries. Lydia's hands itched to start pruning. The wide stone walkway that led up to matching front-porch steps added a pleasing touch of traditional grace and dignity to the quaint appeal of the structure.

Lydia studied the house and its surroundings with keen interest. It was the last building on the island, so there could be only one reason Daniel would stop here. "This. . .belongs to me?" Her disbelief spilled over into her voice.

"Yes. The cottage and the entire southern tip of the island is the property your grandfather left you seven years ago."

She shifted her gaze to his. She could tell from the expectancy in his expression he was waiting for her reaction.

So was she.

She studied the cottage once again. A lazy white cloud drifted behind the gabled wood-shingled roof. The sun, blazing high in the western sky, bathed the gray, trimmed-in-white house and its fertile surroundings in a soft blanket of white light, making it look almost ethereal. The fat leaves of two tall palm trees, one flanking each front corner of the house, swayed back and forth in a temperate breeze, as though beckoning her to step out of the car and come.

But something held her back. The excitement, thrill, and exhilaration she had expected to feel upon arriving at her island retreat had dwindled, leaving in their wake an odd sense of hesitation. How did she accept such a generous gift from someone long gone, someone she didn't even know?

A bump on her left elbow drew her attention. She swiveled her head around to find Chloe had unfastened her seat belt and scrambled to the space between the front bucket seats. Blue eyes wide, she gaped at the cottage "Is this our house, Mama?"

"Yes. I suppose it is." But it didn't seem real. In fact, nothing had seemed real since she left Chicago. Except Daniel. And, sometimes, she feared he was too good to be true.

"Are we gonna live here?" Chloe wanted to know.

"I don't know, honey. We'll just have to wait and see."

Lydia raised her eyes to Daniel's. The warmth in his smile eased some of her trepidation.

"Would you like to have a look inside?" he asked.

"Isn't it locked?"

A grin curved his lips. "Yes, but I have a key."

One corner of her mouth quirked in amusement. "Why doesn't that surprise me?"

When she stepped out of the SUV, she drew in a deep breath. The balmy air smelled faintly of the flowering shrubs huddled around the house and something else. The salt and sea, maybe?

Lydia was anxious to see the beach. She wanted to see if the earth merging with an endless plane of water was really as awe-inspiring as she thought it would be, and to discover why the ocean had been so alluring to her in her second life—the one she'd lived as Sara.

"I'm sorry the yards have been neglected," Daniel said as they approached the stone front porch steps. "The landscaper I was using moved away from Quinn Island. What with getting ready for the *Without a Trace* show and all, I haven't had a chance to replace him. I'll get on it first thing Monday though."

"You'll do no such thing," Lydia said.

He stopped short on the second step, prompting her to glance back over her shoulder at him as she stepped onto the porch. He was staring at her with a strange, somewhat stunned, expression. She shifted around to face him. "What is it?"

"Why don't you want me to hire another landscaper?"

"Because I want to do it myself."

"Really, Lydia, it's no trouble. In fact, I already have one in mind."

"I'm not talking about hiring a landscaper, silly. I'm talking about doing the landscaping myself. I love yard work."

He blinked. "Are you serious?"

"Of course I am."

He continued staring at her as though she'd just dropped in from outer space.

"I have a feeling I just said something out of character here," she said.

He took the final two steps, forcing her to tilt her head in order to maintain eye contact. He stared down at her. "You used to hate yard work."

"I did?" She found that a little hard to believe.

"Yes, you did." He grasped her fingers and lifted her hand. Dropping his gaze to their point of contact, he added, "You didn't like messing up your hands." His thumb traced the irregular plane across her knuckles. "You have the most beautiful hands." A wistful smile tugged at the corner of his mouth. "You loved having your nails done."

She pulled her hand free of his and curled her fist in the folds of her skirt. Obviously, Daniel had taken a left turn down memory lane, because she didn't have beautiful hands anymore. While living in Chicago, she'd barely had time to file her nails once a week. She certainly hadn't had the time—or money—for something so frivolous as a professional manicure. And four years of cleaning had left her skin rough and dry despite the hand creams she used daily.

Still, given the choice of an hour at a manicurist's table and one planting and pruning the neglected foliage around the beach cottage, she'd choose the latter.

How would Daniel feel about that? Sorely disappointed, Lydia suspected.

"Mama, when we gonna get to see the water?"

"In just another minute or two," Daniel answered, pulling a set of keys from his pocket.

Grateful for the timely interruption, Lydia kneeled in front of her daughter. "I'm proud of you for being so patient, Chloe. Sometimes, when grown-ups get to talking, we get sidetracked."

"What's sidetracked?"

"It means sometimes we forget what we're supposed to be doing." It seemed she'd been doing that a lot over the past four days.

Daniel pushed the door open and stepped back. "Well, ladies, here we are."

Reaching for Chloe's hand, Lydia rose and stepped cautiously across the threshold. Entering the house felt eerie, like entering a vacated office building long after business hours. Her sandals echoed with a dull, hollow-sounding thud against the hardwood floor. White sheets draped over furniture cast ghostly impressions around the large, dusky room beyond the foyer. Dust fairies, awakened by human presence, danced in the sunlight that sliced through the open door behind them.

Chloe pressed her small body against her mother's thigh. Laying her hand on her daughter's shoulder, Lydia stopped short of stepping beyond the foyer. "It's okay, honey. Those are just bedsheets, spread over the furniture to keep it from getting dirty."

Daniel stepped up beside them, flipped a wall switch, and the bright overhead lights chased the spooky shadows into cheery pale yellow walls. A painting of a sailboat in a heavy gilded frame hung over what Lydia guessed was the living room sofa.

She noticed immediately the absence of cobwebs and dust buildup. The house might not have been lived in for seven years, but it certainly hadn't been neglected.

She cut Daniel a sidelong glance. "Let me guess. You've looked after this place for the last five years."

He shrugged. "I've tried. I have someone come in and clean occasionally, and I try to get out here once every month or so to see that everything's okay."

Scanning the room, she heaved a deep breath. "I don't know how I'm ever going to repay you for all you've done while I've been away."

He caught her chin between his thumb and forefinger, tilting her face toward his. "Love is free."

The room swayed, and Lydia wondered if a wave had slipped beneath the house and carried them out to sea.

"Mama, look."

Lydia hadn't even noticed that Chloe had left her side. A wing of panic fluttered in her chest when she didn't immediately see her daughter. Then she noticed the backs of two tiny pink tennis shoes planted beneath a child-shaped lump under the curtain hanging over the back door.

Daniel led Lydia across the room and pulled back the curtain. There stood Chloe, her little nose pressed against the full-length pane of a French door, a ring of fog where her breath fanned the glass. Beyond the window was the site Lydia felt she'd waited an entire lifetime—at least, the only life she could remember—to see. White crested waves rolled into shore, spreading a soft sheet of foam over bright pale sand, then languidly drifted back out to sea. A sailboat bobbed up and down amid a rippled blanket of diamonds tossed by the sun across the blue-green water. Two silver seagulls rode the wind.

Both Chloe and Lydia gasped and jumped back when three large pelicans dipped in front of the door window.

"It's even more beautiful than I imagined," Lydia said.

Daniel reached around her and unlocked the door. "I'm glad you like it."

Like it? She had a feeling she was going to love it.

Daniel opened the door and the wind rushed in, catching her and Chloe both off guard as it pushed them backward. The breeze grabbed their hats and tossed them across the room at the same time Daniel reached out to support mother and daughter. His body was a sustaining wall that kept them from falling.

When Lydia and Chloe were both steady, Lydia said, "Wow, I never realized the wind would be so strong." Fortunately, she had pulled her hair back in a loose ponytail at the nape of her neck. She could just imagine what her stubborn curls would look like after an hour's tryst with this breeze.

"We're supposed to have some rain showers coming in this afternoon, so it's a little more brisk today than usual. Even so, it should be a little calmer down on the beach. Up here on the knoll, you get the full brunt of the breeze coming in off the ocean."

"Good, because I know a little girl who's going to be very disappointed if she can't at least get her feet wet." She knew a big girl who would be, too.

"Do you want me to get the stuff out of the car now or later?"

"Later," she said. Grasping his hand, she pulled him out the door behind her.

Hand in hand, with Chloe in the middle, they descended the stairway leading down to the sand. When they were two steps from the bottom, Lydia stopped, halting Chloe and Daniel in the process. "Is it okay if we take off our shoes?"

"Sure, if you want to."

She glanced down at Chloe, who peered back up at her through the sunglasses that were a small replica of her own. "What do you say, Chloe? Do we want to take our shoes off?"

"Will the beach hurt my feet?"

Daniel kneeled down next to Chloe. "No, sweetheart. The beach won't hurt your feet as long as you don't step on the sharp shells."

"Then we want to."

Side by side, she and Chloe sat down on the steps and removed their shoes, Chloe tucking her white socks neatly inside her sneakers before setting them next to her mother's sandals.

"Aren't you going to take yours off?" Lydia asked Daniel.

He took off his hat, turned it around so the bill was in its proper position, and jammed it back down on his head. "Maybe later."

She guessed he had his reasons. At the moment, she felt too happy and carefree to stand around and contemplate what they were. "Okay." She shrugged, then looked down at Chloe. "Ready?"

Chloe gave an emphatic nod.

Instead of taking off in an eager run, like she was tempted to do, Lydia took the first step slowly, relishing the feel of the warm, dry sand beneath her feet. She didn't want to miss a thing.

She took a few more steps, then crouched down, encouraging Chloe to squat next to her. Lydia scooped up a handful of the soft ivory earth and let the granules sift through her fingers. Chloe mimicked her mother.

Lydia watched her daughter concentrate on the sand leaving her small hand to be carried by the wind to another resting place a short distance away. "Doesn't that feel nice, Chloe?"

With all the seriousness of a scientist on the brink of a discovery, Chloe bobbed her head.

They rose and traveled the short distance to a ribbon of shells that had been washed ashore and deserted by the previous high tide. Lydia and Chloe knelt to examine the abandoned treasures, testing the shape and texture of several in their hands. Chloe chose two that particularly struck her fancy and shoved them into her shorts pocket, along with a handful of sand.

When they were satisfied they had, for the time being, viewed enough of the sea jewels, Daniel lifted Chloe over the crusty string of shells, then insisted on doing the same for Lydia.

Here, the sand was harder, cooler, packed by the countless waves that washed over it in the course of a day. Daniel bent down, slipped off his shoes and socks, and set them aside. When he straightened, Lydia quirked a quizzical brow.

He simply shrugged. " 'If you can't beat 'em. . .' "

Once again, they linked hands, this time with Lydia taking the middle position. It seemed appropriate, somehow, that she be linked to both her daughter and the man beside her—the man who had become such an integral part of her life in such a very short time—when she stepped out into the water for the very first time. Together, they walked to the line in the sand the last wave had made, then ambled a few steps further.

The next surge rolled in and surrounded their feet and ankles with a cold rush of water. Lydia and Chloe gasped. Chloe retreated a few inches, but made no effort to crawl up her mother's leg for protection, as Lydia had expected the child to do.

Then the wave rolled back out, and Lydia gasped again, instinctively tightening her hold on her daughter's hand. "Oh my," she said. Something had slipped ashore and was pulling the sand out from under her feet.

In less than a heartbeat, Daniel's arm was around her. When the earth stopped shifting, she looked down to find a seemingly unperturbed Chloe watching the retreating water and grinning like she had just taken her first ride on a carousel and was awaiting her next. Had Lydia been the only one who had felt it?

She swiveled her head around and looked up at Daniel, whose face beamed with amusement. "I should have warned you," he said, without the slightest hint of remorse. "When the water goes out, it takes some of the sand with it. Makes you think the earth's opening up to swallow you."

She blinked. "Right. I suppose I should have figured that out." Somehow, the side of his shirt had gotten bunched up in her fist. She let go, cringing at the wrinkles she'd made.

Just as the next wave rolled in, Chloe pulled free. Lydia turned and started to reach for her daughter, but Daniel stopped Lydia with his hands on her waist.

"She's fine," he said.

Hesitantly, Lydia watched while Chloe started skipping in circles, giggling as the foamy water rolled in and swam around her feet, then eased back out to sea.

Lydia felt Daniel tug on her waist, urging her to lean back against him. A willing recipient of his support, she relented.

Once, Chloe glanced up at them and Lydia stiffened, remembering how her daughter had reacted the last time she was in Daniel's arms. But this time Chloe merely grinned at Lydia and Daniel, paying no mind to the cozy position they were in. "Look at me, Mama," she said. "I'm a mermaid." Then she went right on dancing with the sea, the sand, and the sun.

When Daniel chuckled, the muscles of his chest rippled across Lydia's back. After watching her daughter a long moment, a smile tipped Lydia's lips. She had never seen her usually reserved daughter so buoyant and deliriously happy. Lydia herself had never felt so buoyant and happy. So free.

Capturing the wind-tossed strand of hair that had escaped her ponytail, she looked out over the water. The sailboat was long gone, and now a fishing barge crawled across the horizon at a snail's pace. Overhead, in a sky blue canopy blotted with clouds of cotton, a plane puttered by, towing a banner advertising where to get the cheapest beach towels and suntan lotion. Below, the cool water continued to tug around their ankles, shifting the sand beneath her feet.

Lydia rested her head back against Daniel's chest. He laid his jaw against her temple and started swaying from side to side in that steady, rhythmic way of his that made her feel they moved together as one. Closing her eyes, Lydia opened her heart and accepted the gift that her grandfather had so generously given. Contentment filtered in and filled a place inside her that for five long years had been empty. For the first time in her life that she could remember, she knew where she belonged.

Chapter 11

$\mathcal{D}$aniel laid Chloe on a freshly made bed in the cottage. Since the child was accustomed to an afternoon nap, she had worn down two hours into their beach excursion.

Instead of returning to the Quinns' so soon, Daniel had suggested they make one of the beds in the cottage for Chloe. He was thankful when Lydia agreed. Since their reunion, he hadn't had a chance to really talk to her, learn much about her life between Quinn Island and Chicago, simply be with her.

He pulled a thin cover up over Chloe's shoulders and kissed her soft, round cheek, lingering a few seconds. Beneath the sunscreen he'd insisted she and her mother apply while on the beach were several other refreshing scents: little girl, baby shampoo, and sunshine.

A longing so deep it hurt fisted inside Daniel's chest. In the short course of four days, he had come to realize he wanted to be this child's father. He wanted to be there to tuck her in every night, see her when she woke each morning, see her off on her first day of school, hear her excitement when she lost her first tooth. And he wanted to marry her mother. Wanted it so badly, his arms ached when he crawled into bed each night, alone.

What sometimes puzzled him, though, was that his feelings for

Lydia seemed even stronger than they were before. How could that be?

He straightened the covers around Chloe's shoulders once more, even though they didn't need it. Maybe the old adage really did ring true. Maybe he simply hadn't known what he'd had until he'd lost it.

As he straightened, Lydia leaned over to kiss her daughter's cheek; then they crept from the bedroom and into the living room. He followed Lydia's lead as she wandered to one of the double windows overlooking the beach. Together, they opened the shutters. Dark, smoky-gray clouds were gathering on the horizon, and the waves breaking close to shore had grown more violent. The rain would be here soon.

Sliding his fists into his pockets, he shifted so that he faced her profile. In the silence that had fallen over the room, he watched as she stood, arms crossed, gazing out at the aggressive hands of Mother Nature.

He'd been doing that a lot today. Just watching her. At times, while they were on the beach, he'd wished he could see the world through her eyes. To her, every experience had been an adventure, every discovery a secret waiting to be revealed. Even though the light of eager excitement had shone in her lovely face as she canvassed the seashore, she had been a patient explorer, as though to hurry would be to miss something miraculous and spectacular. And her gentle endurance as she answered her daughter's one million and one questions had merely strengthened his growing need to become a father and a husband. Chloe's father. Lydia's husband.

His gaze slid to the view beyond the window. All ships and wildlife had run for cover in anticipation of the upcoming storm, leaving behind only the sand, the darkening sky, and the roiling waters. Daniel loved these waters. In fact, he jogged the island shores three times a week. Sometimes, more than that. Over the past five years, when the weight of the world, of losing Lydia, had become almost more than he could bear, he'd often found himself out there during the most desolate hours of the night. Something about feeling the damp, salt-laced wind whisper across his skin, watching the white-crested waves, like ghosts rising from the ocean, crash against the jetties, hearing the lone call of a night bird, left him with a sense of sanity he couldn't find anywhere else.

"Why me, Daniel?"

Lydia's soft voice penetrated his weighty thoughts. "Why you what?"

She angled her head and looked at him. "Why did my grandfather leave all this to me? Why not Jennifer, or my father?"

A smile of understanding tipped his lips. Her grandfather had once told him that when Lydia was a child, she would spend hours scavenging the beach with her grandmother, or digging up treasures in the sand, or simply watching the ocean. Even though that had changed as Lydia had gotten older, the late Otis Quinn had always felt she would one day return to the first place that had captured her heart—the island. That was why he'd left his beach cottage to her.

But Daniel knew that wasn't the answer she was looking for. "Your grandfather," he explained, "through inheritance and hard work of his own, obtained a substantial field of assets during his lifetime. Trust me, Lydia, everyone else got their fair share."

Shaking her head, she turned her attention back to the world beyond the window. "I wish he were here so I could thank him personally. This place feels like paradise to me."

"Me, too," he admitted.

A paradise that, five years ago, she had hated. The quiet seclusion, the boring neighbors, the remote solitude that Daniel found so calming. He studied her expression, fascinated at how she now looked at the capping waters through eyes of awe and wonderment. How long would it be before she remembered she wasn't interested in "living at the end of the earth"?

Daniel's last thought led to an even more perplexing question, one he was eager to have answered. "Lydia?"

"Hmm?" she muttered without looking at him, as though she were in a daydream and had no desire to leave.

"Will you ever regain your memory?"

She blinked, and that faraway expression of awe faded from her face. Slowly, she turned her head and looked at him with a mixture of trepidation and uncertainty, like a novice swimmer about to tread unknown waters. "We haven't had a chance to talk about that yet, have we?"

Cupping her shoulders, he urged her to face him, then grasped her hands. The forlorn look in her eyes tore at his insides. He didn't want to force her to talk about anything that might upset her. But her memory loss was an issue they couldn't evade. It was there, staring them both in the face, every minute of every day. They needed to deal with it. . .so they could move on.

"No," he said, "we haven't. But we need to. Don't you think?"

"Yes." Her shoulder dropped an inch in resignation. "We do." Her gaze skimmed the room, settling on the sofa. "Let's sit down."

He helped her remove and fold the sheet covering the sofa, then tossed it over the arm of a linen-covered chair.

They settled on the couch facing each other: she with her hands clasped in her lap, one leg tucked beneath her; he with one arm folded over the back of the sofa, a leg bent and resting on the cushion between them.

After only a slight hesitation, she began. "After a battery of tests and a failed attempt at hypnosis, the doctors determined my memory loss was permanent."

He took a moment to digest the information. She would never regain her memory. Her past—and her memory of theirs together—was gone. Forever. What did that mean? For her? For him? For them?

"Are they certain?" he asked, grabbing at a straw he saw slipping far beyond his reach.

She nodded. "The tests were actually just protocol. Their final diagnosis was based on the type of head injuries I sustained."

He'd half expected, half anticipated this. But the reality still hit him full force, like an unforeseen sucker punch to the chest.

She ducked her head and studied her hands. "Daniel, I know you had hoped my memory would return. . ." Pausing, she pursed her lips, then lifted a misty gaze back to his. He could see she was fighting tears. "I'm sorry," she added, as though that was the only thing left to say.

Seeing her struggle overrode his own confusion and pain, giving him the strength to offer her the comfort she needed. The comfort he owed her.

He cupped her cheek with his hand. "Lydia, you don't owe anyone an apology for what happened to you. Especially me." Forcing nonchalance into his voice, he added, "So, your memory will never return. We'll deal with it. The important thing is, it doesn't change the way I feel about you." He took a few heartbeats to scan her face, giving himself enough time to steel the courage to seek his next answer. "I guess the next thing we need to figure out is how you feel about me."

She raised a cool palm and covered the hand pressed against her face. "Oh Daniel, I know I have feelings for you, and that those feelings run deeper than anything my limited memory has ever known." She gave her head a slow, regretful shake. "But right now, I have no idea who Lydia Quinn really is. Who *I* am." A long second drifted by. "I'm going to do my best to figure that out, but it's going to take time. How long? I don't know." Her eyes pleaded with his for understanding. "Are you willing to wait?"

"Of course, I'll wait," he said without hesitation. He'd waited five years to find her. He'd wait five more to win back her love if he had to. "I wasn't planning on going anywhere anyway," he added.

A garbled sound—half laughter, half sob—escaped her throat. Her arms reached out to circle his neck.

With a sigh of acceptance, Daniel enfolded her in his embrace. She had feelings for him. *Deep* feelings, she had said. He closed his eyes. He wanted more. So much more. But he knew what she was offering today was all she could give. For now, that would have to be enough.

Her sweet scent made him long to claim her lips, taste the sweetness in her kiss. But he quelled the urge to do more than simply hold her. He would wait. Because he knew, when he finally earned her love, that the wait, no matter how long, would be well worth it.

Chapter 12

"What do you think about this?" Lydia held up the dark pantsuit for her customer's approval.

With a disapproving frown, Mrs. Pratt shook her head. "I don't know about the navy, dear. Do you have something a little more colorful?"

Lydia managed to hold onto her smile. "I think so." She hung up the pantsuit and for the third time searched the garment rack in an attempt to find the mayor's wife a suitable outfit to wear to an upcoming Fourth of July celebration.

Lydia had been back in Quinn Island for a month, back working in the shop for three weeks. And for two weeks and six days, she had hated her job. Hated it. . .with a passion.

She hated trying to figure out which garments suited the tastes of Quinn Island's finest. And she hated it when, nine times out of ten, her patrons looked down their nose at her selection.

She hated wearing ridiculously expensive, and usually uncomfortable, clothes in order to blend in with the atmosphere of the store. And she hated that the mother in an average-to-low income household couldn't come into the shop and purchase a simple Sunday dress for her daughter without spending an entire week's wages.

But the thing she hated most about being the sole owner of an affluent dress shop was leaving Chloe behind in the mornings.

In Chicago, Lydia had been able to take her daughter with her on her housecleaning jobs. Determined to follow the same pattern here, she had set up a children's entertainment center in one corner of the store equipped with television, VCR, toys, and books. The play area helped in occupying young children brought into the store by their parents for short periods of time. But, halfway through Lydia's first day on the job, Chloe had gotten bored and restless. She didn't like being restricted to the four waist-high walls designed to look like a playhouse. And Lydia would often dash back to check on her daughter while waiting on a customer—which didn't set too well with her clientele.

She'd finally relented and taken her parents up on their offer to watch over her daughter during shop hours. To Lydia's dismay Chloe was thrilled. Lydia's parents—especially her mother—were constantly showering their granddaughter with gifts, taking her to fun places, doing things with her that had always been beyond Lydia's means.

Lydia paused, considering a flamingo-colored pantsuit. Deciding Mrs. Pratt wouldn't look good in pink, she moved on.

So far, Chloe's daily adventures with her grandparents didn't seem to be spoiling her. But Lydia feared it was just a matter of time. Oh, she had told her parents they were indulging their granddaughter too much, and her father seemed to take her concerns to heart most of the time. But her mother *never* listened to, or else she simply chose to ignore, Lydia's requests. And Lydia hadn't quite figured out what to do about it yet.

Turning, she held up a red outfit for Mrs. Pratt's approval. The woman, whose patience seemed to be wearing thin, shook her haughty head again.

Lydia gritted her teeth, biting back a sharp retort. She thought the pleasingly plump woman with the peaches-and-cream complexion would look good in the red.

Pivoting back to the rack, Lydia continued with her search. Why did the women who visited the shop feel she or Jennifer or one of the clerks had to help them make their selections anyway? Didn't anyone in this town have a mind of her own? On a whim, she whipped out the flamingo pantsuit she'd passed up a minute ago. Mrs. Pratt had already snubbed three of Lydia's choices. What was one more?

To Lydia's surprise, the woman's eyes lit up like headlights on high beam. "That's it." She grabbed the matching garments from Lydia's hand. "Wait right here and you can tell me how it looks after I try it on." With that, she did an about-face and shuffled to the dressing room.

Lydia gave serious thought to hiding beneath the garments hanging on the rack. She didn't want to give her opinion on the pink pantsuit, because she'd have to lie in order not to offend Quinn Island's first lady.

Like a perceptive angel of mercy, Jennifer appeared at Lydia's side. "You have a phone call, sis."

Lydia looked heavenward and mouthed, "Thank You, God. Thank You." Then she faced her sister with an elated smile. "You don't mind finishing up with Mrs. Pratt, do you?"

The corners of Jennifer's lips turned down. "I knew I should have taken a message."

Lydia made her escape as Mrs. Pratt came out of the dressing room. "Oh Jennifer dear," Lydia heard the mayor's wife say. "If I had known you were here..."

With a subtle grin, Lydia circled the counter. Couldn't Jennifer see that *her* name belonged on the deed and ownership papers of the shop? Not Lydia's?

Sitting down on a stool behind the counter, she kicked off her four-inch heels. As she reached for the receiver, she crossed her legs and massaged one foot with her free hand. She had yet to figure out the reason for wearing pinching shoes for the sake of style.

"Hello. This is Sa—Lydia Quinn." How many more times was she going to do that? "May I help you?"

"Miss Quinn, this is Andy Kelley at Kelley's Used Cars. I'm just calling to let you know your car's been serviced and is ready for pick up."

Excitement kicked up a little dance beneath Lydia's ribs. Her car. *Her* car. The sweet little white number she'd closed the deal on last Friday was ready to pick up. Come tomorrow, she'd no longer have to depend on everyone else for transportation. She could chart her own course.

"Thank you, Mr. Kelley. I'll be there first thing in the morning to pick it up."

She hung up the phone, only vaguely still aware of her hurting feet. The timing was perfect. Tomorrow was her Wednesday off. And Daniel, who had just finished a time-consuming court case, was taking half the day off to spend with her and Chloe. Since they had made no definite plans, Lydia could pick him up and they could drive to the island for a picnic. Wouldn't he be surprised? She couldn't wait to see the look on his face when he saw what she had done.

The front door chimed, and Lydia glanced toward the entrance to see that another patron had arrived. She jumped off the stool and was halfway around the counter when she realized she could feel the coolness of the hardwood floors beneath her feet. She ran back behind the counter, slipped her shoes on, then headed for the front of the store, greeting her next customer with an enthusiastic smile.

∞

"Thanks, Dad. For everything," Lydia told her father the next morning as she stepped up to her new used car. Last week, he had helped her pick out, test-drive, and examine the midsize SUV for operating efficiency. Today, he had driven her to the dealer to pick up the car.

She always had such fun with him. He was easygoing, sometimes funny, and would always share his knowledge when asked for advice. But he never insinuated he knew what she should like or what was best for her.

Like Mrs. Porter had always done, he simply let her be.

"Anytime, sweetheart. All you have to do is ask whenever you need me."

She kissed his cheek, then looked down at Chloe, who stood beside her granddad, holding onto his forefinger while nestling George the Giraffe under one arm. "Are you ready to go?"

Chloe cocked her head and peered at her mother through the sunglasses Daniel had given her the first day they had gone to the island. "Are you sure you know how to drive?"

Chloe had never seen her mother drive. In order to obtain a driver's license, one had to have proof of existence—a birth certificate, a social security card. Lydia had none of those things in Chicago.

But she had remedied that just last week. Plopping her fists on her hips, she leaned over so that she was practically nose-to-nose with her daughter. "I passed the driver's exam and got my license back, didn't I?"

Chloe pushed her glasses up on her nose and readjusted George. "Yes," she said, but her expression still looked a little wary around the edges.

After fastening Chloe in the car, Lydia kissed her father's cheek again and climbed in. Heat and humidity were already beginning to weigh down the late June morning. But when Lydia switched on the engine, instead of reaching for the air conditioner button, she pressed the control that zipped down the window. She wanted to feel and smell the fresh air as she drove *her* car for the first time.

At the beginning of her search for an automobile to suit hers and Chloe's needs, Lydia and her father had scavenged the new-car lots. But she had soon concluded it was senseless to pay high five figures for a car that would depreciate several thousand dollars the minute she drove it off the lot. So she had settled for a two-year-old, average-sized, aver-aged-priced, SUV with a gray cloth interior and bright, white exterior. A car that had Sara Jennings's name written all over it.

No, she retracted her thoughts with a mental shake of her head. The car had *Lydia Quinn*'s name written all over it.

She shifted into Drive. No matter how hard she tried, she still sometimes had trouble thinking of herself as *Lydia*, Quinn Island's for-mer prom queen, instead of *Sara*, Chicago's plain Jane Doe.

When she first pulled out onto the highway, her pulse quickened. But a couple miles into the trip, she was navigating the steering wheel like driving was second nature.

She stopped at the supermarket deli and picked up a lunch of fried chicken, fries, slaw, and banana pudding. On the way to the checkout, she grabbed a six-pack of soft drinks and some eating utensils. The reporters had finally stopped hounding her, and the townspeople had all gotten used to the news of her return, so she got in and out of the store with just a few polite greetings and inquiries as to how she and Chloe were doing. But, even if she had had to sidestep a member of the news media, the feeling of freedom would have been worth it.

At precisely twelve thirty, Lydia pulled into the driveway of Dan-iel's one-level brick home. When she saw his car still sitting beneath the carport, she knew she had timed her arrival just right. She'd given him enough time to get home from his office and change clothes, but had caught him before he left to come and pick up her and Chloe.

As she and Chloe climbed out of the car, he ambled out of the front door, letting the screen door slap closed behind him. He approached with slow, curious steps. Lydia stopped beside Chloe's door, took off her sunglasses, and just watched him. The blazing midday sun lit chestnut highlights in his dark hair. His yellow polo shirt molded his sinewy shoulders, and his faded jeans could have been tailor-made to fit his slim waist and thighs.

Instead of stopping where she and Chloe stood, he continued on, strolling around the car with his hands in his pockets. A guarded look of bewilderment settled over his face.

When he had made a complete circle, he stopped in front of her. "What is this?"

Feeling about as proud of herself as a peacock, Lydia stuffed her fists in her overall pockets and rocked back on her heels. "It's my new car. Ya like it?"

Daniel scratched his forehead with his thumb. "Ah, when did you get it?"

She noticed he had evaded her question, which knocked her elation down a couple of notches. "Bought it last week. Picked it up this morning."

"All by yourself?"

She feigned offense. "What? You don't think I know cars? This baby has a V-6 engine, automatic transmission with automatic overdrive, antilock front and rear disk brakes, and gets twenty-nine miles to the gallon on the highway." She shuffled from one end of the car to the other like a seasoned salesperson while she shot off the list she had practiced with her father. And when she stopped, pivoted, and beamed at Daniel, she was pleased with the results.

His mouth dropped open like a trapdoor with a broken hinge. "Where did you learn all that?"

"From Grandpa."

Lydia's smugness fizzled like a drop of water hitting a hot skillet. She glowered down at her daughter. "Thank you, Chloe. I was really anxious to let Daniel know that."

Unperturbed, the informative four-year-old simply pushed her glasses back up on her nose.

Reluctantly, Lydia lifted her gaze to Daniel's face. Just as she expected, he was smirking.

"Your dad helped you pick out the car."

She lifted her nose an impertinent inch. "We picked it out together."

He scanned the vehicle again, front to back. "Why didn't you tell me you were buying a car?"

"I wanted to surprise you." And, even though she loved him—and she did love him, with every fiber of her being—she didn't want to be influenced by his sometimes aggressive decisiveness.

He scratched his forehead with his thumb again. "You surprised me all right."

Like a factory inspector, he ambled around to the driver's side, opened the door, checked the mileage and all the control gadgets—half of which Lydia still hadn't figured out. He requested the keys, then switched on the engine, and revved the motor. While the car was running, he checked the heat, the air conditioner, and the radio. Switching off the engine, he pulled a lever that popped open the hood, then got out and scrutinized the conglomeration of metal called a motor. Seemingly satisfied with what he saw, he closed the hood and got down on his hands and knees, looking underneath the car.

All the things her father had done when she'd expressed an interest in the vehicle.

Standing, he brushed off his knees and then his hands. "Nice car. Been well taken care of," he said, but it was what he didn't say that bugged her.

Crossing her arms, she shifted her weight to one leg. "What is it, Daniel?"

"Nothing," he said with all the innocence of a car thief.

She had learned enough about him to know when he was holding back on her. Tilting her head to one side, she leveled him with an unbending glare.

He opened his mouth to speak.

She pursed her lips.

His shoulders dropped in resignation. "I like the car, Lydia, I really do. It's just that—"

She held up a hand. "Wait a minute. Don't tell me it's not me. If I hear one more person say something's not me, I'll scream."

With a spark of amusement in his eyes, he grinned. "We wouldn't want you to do that, now, would we?"

She found herself smiling in return. "No. I don't think we would."

He crouched down to give Chloe his usual hug and nuzzle on the cheek. Sometimes, Lydia envied that little affectionate greeting from Daniel that belonged only to her daughter. All she ever got was his hand on hers or an arm slipped casually around her.

She appreciated Daniel's modest patience in courting her, but, good

FAMILIAR STRANGERS

grief, didn't the twentieth date or so warrant at least a good-night kiss?

"I smelled food in the car," he said as he stood. "Does that mean we're going on a picnic?"

"How does an afternoon on the island sound?"

"Sounds like my kind of date."

While he helped Chloe with her seat, Lydia skirted the front of the car and slid into the driver's seat.

Daniel opened the passenger door and poked his head inside. Arching his brows, he said, "You mean you're not going to let me drive?"

Caressing the steering wheel, she shook her head. "Not just yet. I feel like I've just gotten my first set of wings and I still want to fly."

She noticed a subtle change in his expression; the slightest hint of sadness rose in his eyes. "As long as you always let me fly with you." He folded himself into the passenger seat and closed the door.

Despite the elevated temperature, a chill raced down her spine. Something was wrong. She sensed it.

When he grasped her chin between his thumb and forefinger, leaned over, and pressed the softest of kisses to her forehead, she pushed her misgivings to a remote corner of her mind. *We're okay,* she told herself with forced conviction. *We're still okay.*

On the drive to the island, he started snooping, poking around in her dash pocket, thumbing through the owner's manual, studying the service record left by the last owner. But, Lydia noticed, he was quiet. Too quiet. And somber.

"Daniel, what is it about my getting this car that bothers you so?"

∽

He kept his gaze focused on the owner's manual he held open in his hands. He knew it was petty, a grown man getting his feelings hurt because the woman he loved hadn't told him she was buying a car. But he couldn't seem to help it. She had once made him a part of her every decision. Lately, though, she was making more and more choices without consulting him. Sometimes, like right now, an ornery little monster would rear its ugly little head and set him to wondering if she'd eventually get to where she didn't need him at all.

"Daniel?" she gently prodded when he didn't answer.

He certainly wasn't going to tell her he was sitting there licking his wounds, so to speak. But he could ask her one thing. He returned the owner's manual to the dash pocket and closed it. All he'd really wanted to do anyway was make sure she hadn't forgotten proof of insurance. "I was just wondering why you bought this particular car?"

"It's practical for me and Chloe. It's in good running condition. It was reasonably priced."

It was practical for *her* and *Chloe*. Did he not fit into her picture anywhere? "But you could have bought any car you wanted."

"And I did."

He considered her answer. Before, she would never have settled for a used car, or one that she'd considered so "average." He raked his hair away from his forehead and heaved a sigh. That didn't seem to be the case anymore.

He studied her hauntingly familiar, yet somehow new, profile. Since her return, she was always doing things that sometimes surprised him, sometimes shocked him, and many times delighted him. Her former tastes for expensive toys had never really bothered him before, not much, anyway. After all, they both came from old money and had profitable jobs. They could afford it. But her more recent tastes for practical, more functional essentials with reasonable price tags charmed him—and paralleled his own way of thinking.

"What are you going to do with your other car?" he asked, referring to the sports coupe she'd been driving the night of her abduction. Right now, it was in her uncle's basement garage, where it had been towed after the initial police investigation.

"I'm going to sell it and give the proceeds to the missing persons' organization my mother founded." She shrugged a shoulder. "Who knows? Maybe the money will help locate another lost loved one."

His level of respect for her increased twofold. Reaching over, he laced his fingers through hers, leaving her with only one hand to drive. "Since when did you get to be so amazing?"

She didn't have an immediate comeback, and he couldn't help grinning. The way she now blushed at compliments was so appealing.

"Maybe. . .since I met you," she finally said, and started working her fingers free from his. "Now, give me back my hand before I run off the road."

Chapter 13

"Mr. Matthews, you have magic hands."

Daniel smiled at the woman lying back against the settee arm, her eyes closed, looking thoroughly satisfied with the foot rub she was getting. "And you, Miss Quinn, have beautiful feet." Small and dainty. They fit perfectly in his hands.

"Mmm," was her only response.

Feeling quite relaxed himself, he settled further down on the sofa and propped his bare feet on an ottoman.

The afternoon had been glorious. They had eaten out on the back lawn, then taken a quick swim to combat the scorching temperatures. When Chloe had worn down, they had returned to the cottage, changed from swimsuits back to their street clothes, and tucked the little girl into the same bed she'd slept in the first time Daniel had brought her and Lydia to the island.

Laying his head back, Daniel scanned the living room of the cottage, which was beginning to look and feel more like a home than a house that had been forsaken for seven years. They had removed the linens from the furniture on their second visit and spruced up the yards on their third. Last week, Lydia had added a few personal touches—scented candles to the coffee table, a ginger jar to the mantle, and a silk flower arrangement to the dining room table. Today, she had brought a crocheted afghan and thrown it across the wicker rocking chair that sat next to the fireplace.

Little things that make a house a home, Daniel thought. And with just a little nudge to his imagination, he could picture this house as a home: his, Lydia's, and Chloe's.

With a circling thumb, he started working his way up from Lydia's heel. She shifted and gave a contented purr. He loved pleasing her, and since she'd returned to Quinn Island, that had been amazingly easy to do. The simplest things—a walk on the beach, a single red rose, an unexpected foot rub—brought her pleasure now.

His smile mellowed. She had been so flabbergasted, and so appealingly embarrassed, the first time he'd pulled her feet into his lap, slipped off her shoes, and started massaging. And so appreciative afterward. He couldn't have been more shocked than when she pulled his feet into her lap and returned the favor.

Mentally, he shook his head. That had been a first. But then, there had been a lot of firsts since her return. Some pleased him. But some he didn't quite know what to do with, like her showing up at his house today with a car she'd picked out and purchased without his knowledge.

He pushed the nagging thought to the back of his mind. Wasn't it enough to simply be with her like this? Something stirred inside him—a deeper longing, a stronger need. He struggled against the desire to move his hands to her slim ankles, to lean over her and satisfy his hunger with one sweet kiss.

She had given him no indication she was ready to move their relationship forward. What they presently had would have to be enough. . .for now.

She flinched when he hit a particularly sensitive spot in the middle of her foot. "Hey, no tickling," she chided, opening her eyes to level him with a halfhearted glare.

Just to see her eyes dance with laughter and feel her small toes curl beneath his fingers, he kept circling the end of his thumb in the center of her foot. Just before she reached the point of squirming, she jerked her feet away.

"You don't play fair."

He helped her sit up. "I couldn't resist," he said.

"No. You just wanted your own feet rubbed." Facing him, she

scooted back, folded one leg in front of her, and patted her thigh.

Who was he to argue? Taking her cue, he propped one foot on her bent knee. She set to kneading, her smooth brow pinched in concentration.

He watched in fascination. He would have never thought that a woman rubbing a man's feet could be so enthralling. Of course, this wasn't just any woman. This was Lydia, and she was what made this simple act of altruism so attractive. He relaxed back against the sofa arm.

"Daniel," Lydia said as she started working on his other foot, "if this house were yours, would you move into it?"

"In a heartbeat," he answered without hesitation.

Her frown of concentration melted into a warm smile. "Good."

His brow dipped in befuddlement. "Why?"

She glanced up at him, her amber eyes all aglow. "Because I've decided to move out here."

Her answer brought him up short. He pulled his feet away from her hands and slid forward, his knee bumping lightly against hers as he draped his arm over the back of the couch. "Are you serious?"

Annoyance wilted her shoulders. "Daniel."

"I know. I know. If you hear 'Are you serious?' one more time, you're going to scream. But...are you serious?" His voice squeaked with surprise.

She shook her head like he was a hopeless cause. "Yes, I am. Why does that surprise you so?"

"I don't know." But really he did. She had been totally against living on the island in the past. She hated the feel of salt on her skin, the wind in her hair, and the quiet seclusion. "I guess because you liked living in town so much before. You were a people person."

She took a moment to consider his answer. "Well, I've changed my mind." From the tilt of her lips, she apparently found his stunned expression amusing. "That is a woman's prerogative, isn't it?"

"I suppose, but. . ."

"But?"

"You'll be so far away from everything."

"Just three miles from town."

"And it's so secluded out here. Suppose there's a break-in?"

"You said the island was the safest place on the coast."

"Well, yeah, but...what if Chloe gets sick?"

"I have a car. I know how to use the phone."

He opened his mouth, but, for the life of him, couldn't think of another justifiable argument.

She grinned in victory.

He scowled in defeat.

He knew he had a tendency to be overprotective, as she had so gently pointed out on several different occasions. But he couldn't help it. The thought of her being out here alone gripped his stomach with fear. What if something happened to her or Chloe? He couldn't go through losing Lydia again. And with Chloe in the picture, the stakes were now twice as high.

She bracketed his head with her hands and leaned forward until her face was only a breath away from his. "Daniel, I'm not a child. I'm a grown woman, with a child of my own."

He couldn't argue with that. Still, he had his reservations. "I know. It's just the thoughts of you and Chloe being out here all by yourself. . ." An old familiar weight bore down on his chest. "Sometimes, things can happen. . .*fast*. When you least expect them to. I'm entitled to be concerned."

Understanding softened her features. "I know. But you can't live in fear that something bad is going to happen every time I get out of your sight. And you can't put me and Chloe in a bubble and shield us from the world. Now, I can promise you I will do everything possible to ensure my and Chloe's safety." A knowing glint of laughter flickered across her lips. "And, I'm sure you will, too." Then the laughter was gone. She spread her fingers, as though trying to encompass his mind and conquer his fears. "The rest we have to leave up to God."

He closed his eyes, his insides quaking with the struggle between past demons and present rationality. Somehow, rationality won. "You're right," he begrudgingly admitted as he opened his eyes. "I can't lock you and Chloe away, and I can't be with you every minute of every day. But. . ." He scrubbed a defeated hand down his face, then desperately grabbed at one last straw. "How would you feel about me parking a camper in your backyard?"

She threw her head back and laughed. The infectious sound managed to calm, to a small degree, his inner turmoil.

He offered her a sheepish grin. He knew parking a camper in her backyard wasn't reasonable. But he'd do it, if she'd let him.

Following instinct, he pulled her close and wrapped his arms around her. She slipped hers around his neck. He could live to be a hundred and never get tired of the feel of her body in his arms.

She raised a hand, combed her fingers through the back of his hair. Jolted by a strong need for more, he closed his eyes. Why didn't he just go ahead and kiss her? The worst thing that could happen would be for her to push him away, like she did that first day in Chicago.

He drew back, cupped the side of her face with his hand, and before he even had a chance to act upon his thoughts, she pushed him away.

"Oh Daniel. Look!" She jumped up and breezed past him.

It took him a few seconds to adjust to the change in atmosphere. When he did, he twisted around to find she had opened the back door and was kneeling down to pick up something, her abundant curls fluttering in the breeze. She stood, and when she turned around, she was holding a kitten—if you could call it that. The neglected little thing looked more like two huge yellow eyes sewn into a scraggly coat of matted gray fur.

As though pleading for mercy, the haggard feline looked at him and released a weak "Meow."

"Poor baby." Lydia cradled the kitten against her chest as gently as a mother would a newborn. "She's scared to death and starving."

Standing, Daniel rubbed the back of his forefinger beneath the kitten's chin. The kitten turned her head and flattened her ear against his hand, touching a soft spot inside him. "I think Chloe had some milk left over from lunch. I'll go see if I can dig up a pan and warm it up."

While they waited in the kitchen for the milk to heat, Daniel watched Lydia lavish the kitten with attention. She set the scrawny thing down on the bar, then plopped her chin on folded hands so that she and the animal were eye level to each other. The cat arched her bony body along Lydia's face, then it sniffed at Lydia's hair and was knocked backwards by a sneeze. Laughing out loud, Lydia picked up the stunned kitten and rubbed her cheek against the top of its fuzzy head.

Daniel stood awestruck. Lydia had apparently forgotten she hated cats. She didn't like animals, period. She detested getting fur on her clothes. Bemusement tugging at the corner of his mouth, he turned back to the stove and poured the milk into a bowl. He certainly wasn't going to be the one to remind her of that fact.

Five minutes later, they sat side by side on the floor, their legs crisscrossed, watching the kitten devour the warm milk.

"Where do you think she came from?" Lydia wondered out loud.

"My guess is some heartless jerk set her out thinking somebody here on the island would take her in. . .or that she'd starve to death."

The light in Lydia's eyes grew dim. "Poor thing." Reaching out with a forefinger, she ruffled the fur on the kitten's back. "Lost, alone, no place to call home." A brief silence filled with heavy thoughts passed. "I know exactly how you feel."

Daniel curled a finger beneath Lydia's chin and urged her to look at him. "You're not lost anymore."

Bitter tears stung her eyes. "Sometimes, I wonder. . ." The second the words were out, she drew back and swiped a hand across her face. She hadn't gotten through the last five years by crying on someone else's shoulder or playing off another's sympathy. And she certainly wasn't going to start now. "Sorry. I didn't mean to whine."

Apparently undeterred, Daniel grasped her chin and forced her to look at him again. "Lydia, why don't you let me in? Let me help you carry some of that burden while you're trying to figure everything out."

"I'm not a baby, Daniel." Pushing his hand away, she vaulted up off the floor and strolled to the window over the sink. Crossing her arms, she looked out at the waters battering the island's southern shore.

She was angry with herself. In a weak moment of self-pity, she had opened a door she had meant to keep closed. The past, the only one she could remember, was gone. She was no longer Sara Jennings. She was Lydia Quinn. She was *born* Lydia Quinn and, somehow, she had to accept that. She just never realized it would be so hard.

Daniel's hands, so understanding and tender, cupped her shoulders. Following his gentle bidding, she relaxed back against him. His strong arms enfolded her shoulders. She raised her hands to his forearms, laid her head back against his chest. Balmy scents of warm milk, saltwater, and the most intoxicating one of all that belonged only to him drifted through her head, filling her with a selfish yearning. Sometimes she wished she could shut out the world and create one of her own that included only her, Daniel, and Chloe.

But even as the thought flitted through her mind, her pragmatic side reminded her that kind of thinking was unreasonable. She had responsibilities, people who depended on her, more demands than she could ever possibly meet. And she owed it to her loved ones to try to meet those demands.

Daniel's warm lips touched her temple. "I love you, Lydia. That's one thing you'll never have to try to figure out."

She turned in his arms, letting her palms rest against his chest. "How, Daniel? How can you love some crazy, confused woman who's nothing like the one you fell in love with years ago?"

He touched her nose. "First of all, you're not crazy. Secondly, who can explain love?" He shrugged. "I certainly can't. All I know is that it's still there, stronger than ever. I don't question it; I just accept it."

If he didn't question it, then why should she? Focusing on her hands, she fiddled with a button on his shirt. "Then why don't you ever kiss me?"

He tipped her chin. "Because you asked me to wait."

Her brow dipped in befuddlement. "I did?"

"Uh-huh." He nodded. "Remember the first day we came to the cottage? You asked me to wait until you figured everything out."

Closing her eyes, she pinched the bridge of her nose. "Daniel, I was talking about renewing our engagement. I figured, in the meantime, we would date and. . .you know. . .let our relationship follow the natural course of things."

He grasped the fingers she held to her face and kissed the back of her hand. "Why didn't you say something? Or at least give me a sign?"

She tried to focus more on what he was saying than the chill bumps racing up her arm. "Because I'm a woman," she answered, thinking surely that would explain it all.

Apparently, it didn't. "Yes," he said, his dark eyes roaming her face with a mixture of amusement and appreciation. "I'm well aware of that." He started rocking, carrying her with him in that gentle sway of his that kept time with a song only he and she could hear.

"The man is supposed to make the first move, not the woman."

The rocking stopped, and surprise lifted his brows. "You never felt that way before."

Her eyes opened wide. *"What!"*

"Nothing," he quickly injected, then closed his eyes, giving his head a quick shake like he was trying to clear it of a distraction. When he met her gaze again, he added, "Forget I said that." He let go of her hand and captured her wrists, urging her to put her arms around his neck. She didn't resist.

"Now, about this kissing thing." He slipped his arms around her waist. "Seems like I was waiting on you. You were waiting on me."

Biting her lower lip, she nodded. She didn't have enough air to speak.

He pulled her closer. "What are we going to do about it?"

"I guess. . .this."

Following her heart, she rose on tiptoe and lifted her face up to his.

"Mama!"

Chloe's voice coming from the hallway shattered Lydia's moment of rapture. She squeezed her eyes shut against the impact as her emotions slammed back to earth. Then, lowering her heels to the floor, she opened her eyes and pressed a forefinger to Daniel's lips. "Hold that thought. Okay?"

He kissed her fingertip. "Got it."

They parted just before Chloe turned the corner coming into the kitchen, her small hands circling the ribs of the kitten Lydia had long forgotten. The neglected cat looked like she was frozen in a permanent state of shock, but she didn't seem to be in any pain.

Lydia rushed across the room to show her daughter how to hold the kitten properly. Chloe held up the furry, yellow-eyed skeleton and said, "Look what I found, Mama. A kitty cat."

∽

Daniel was still holding onto Lydia's thought when she later drove him home so he could pick up his car and follow her back to her parents' house.

While swapping secretive little glances with Lydia, he suffered through a preplanned dinner at the Quinn's dining room table. Then he sat through an hour of some insipid game show Margaret insisted they watch, her idea of a family thing. Then came Chloe's story time and bedtime which he breezed through with utmost patience.

But after he and Lydia had tucked her daughter in, with kitten Mittens—named for her white front paws—in a basket beside the bed, and closed the bedroom door, he grabbed Lydia's hand, and together they rushed down the stairs like two kids on Christmas morning. They hit the foyer running, but Daniel stopped short when Margaret stepped from the living room into their path. Lydia, who was one step behind him, apparently didn't see the older woman and smacked into his back, almost catapulting him forward to the floor at her mother's feet.

He reached back with his free hand to steady her. "Mrs. Quinn!"

Uh-oh. He'd called her "Mrs. Quinn" instead of "Margaret." He hadn't done that in years. He sounded just like a kid caught sneaking a cookie before lunch.

Out of the corner of his eye, he saw Lydia peek out from behind his shoulder. "Hi, Mom." Unfortunately, she sounded just as guilty as he.

With a quizzical frown puckering her forehead, Margaret Quinn looked from Daniel to Lydia, then back to Daniel. "Where on earth are you kids going in such a hurry?"

Daniel opened his mouth, but all that came out was a caught-in-the-act-sounding "Ahh." And Lydia was no help. She just stayed under cover behind him.

Then, like a perceptive guardian angel, Lydia's father appeared. "Come on, Margaret," he said, grasping her hand. "There's something on TV I want you to see." Sending Daniel a conspiratorial wink, the older man pulled his thoroughly perplexed wife back into the living room.

The instant they were out of sight, Daniel and Lydia scrambled for the door.

They sprinted toward the side of the wraparound porch, startling the night creatures into silence. When they rounded the corner, where they knew they would be safe from windows and prying eyes, Daniel leaned back against the wall.

Slightly out of breath, he slid his back down the smooth plank wall far enough to compensate for their height differences. "Now, there's this matter of a—"

She grabbed his head and kissed him.

Daniel couldn't move. Couldn't breathe. Couldn't think. All he could do was stand there and receive what she was offering. Her love, without reservation. No, she hadn't actually said the words. But it was there. He could feel her pouring it into him, washing him clean, like the purest of streams running down from the highest of mountains.

Fireworks exploded in his chest. The doors to his heart, soul, and mind—places that had been only half open before—swung wide open, the emotions flowing out of them. His throat ached.

And when she finally pulled back, looking at him like he was her lifeline, he saw her in a completely new light. He couldn't explain it; he didn't even know if he wanted to. He just knew that things were different. A lot different than they were before. What he felt for her was deeper and more far-reaching than anything he had ever known.

And as new as the first rose in spring.

"Well," she said, her voice filtering into his awestruck thoughts, "aren't you going to say anything?"

"I'm. . .speechless."

She brushed her thumb across his lower lip. He felt the tingle all the way to his fingertips.

"There's something I need to tell you," she said. Dropping her hands to his chest, she raised her lashes and looked so deep into his eyes, he could feel her gaze touching his soul. "I may not have myself figured out yet, but I do know how I feel about you."

"I'm listening."

"I love you, Daniel. I love you with all my heart."

He cradled her face in his hands. He couldn't hold back the tears; he didn't even want to try. "Lydia. My precious, precious Lydia, you don't know how I've longed to hear you say that."

Her lips curved. "Well, get used to it, because I have a feeling you're going to be hearing it a lot in the future."

"Good, because I love you." He lowered his head to hers. "I love you," he repeated in a whisper against her mouth before he claimed her lips.

This time, it was he who gave. He willingly laid every fiber of his being in the palm of her hand, holding back nothing for himself.

And when she reached out with her heart to accept his gift, he knew, for the first time in his life, what it felt like to give freely and love without condition.

∞

Much later that evening, Lydia walked hand in hand with Daniel to his car. "I can't wait until Chloe and I get moved into the cottage," she mused out loud.

"Me either. That way, we won't risk running into your parents when we're headed out to the front porch to neck."

"*Daniel!*" She smacked his shoulder with her free hand. "We did not neck."

Well, no, really, they hadn't. They'd just kissed, held hands, and each other. But he sure did love making her blush, even if he couldn't quite see the rosy color rising in her cheeks with nothing but stars and a half-moon for light. He knew it was there.

"Besides," she added, "we'll have an inquisitive four-year-old dogging our every step out at the cottage."

"She goes to bed early."

Lydia shook her head. "You're crazy."

"About you."

Her soft chuckle floated through the air. "I give up."

Her mention of moving to the island reminded him of something he had been curious about since early evening. Stopping next to his car, he urged her to face him and grasped both of her hands. "Tell me something, Lydia. When we were out at the island this afternoon, why did you ask me if I'd move into the cottage if it were mine?"

"Because, if you and I do make it to the wedding altar, I didn't want Chloe and me to move out there, fall more in love with the place than we already are, then have to pull up stakes and move again. Before I made my decision, I needed to know it was a place where you would want to live, too."

"You mean, you didn't make your final decision until you had my answer?"

"No."

Was it possible to love her more? He tugged her into his arms. "Thanks for thinking about me."

"That seems to be about all I do lately."

"Good."

He lingered over a kiss, then held her for a tranquil moment with her head resting against his chest, his cheek resting on the top of her head.

"We're going to make it, Daniel," she said with a sigh. "I have a feeling."

Daniel released a slow breath full of contentment. He had a feeling, too. And it was awesome.

Chapter 14

"Thanks for allowing me to come in during my lunch break, Daniel. It's Lydia's Wednesday off, and that leaves us a little shorthanded."

"No problem," Daniel said, reaching for the sales contract on a piece of investment property Jennifer had recently acquired. "I should get this wrapped up with the sellers this afternoon. I'll give you a call as soon as everything's finalized."

Nodding, Jennifer stood.

Daniel slipped the contract into her file and reached for the phone, intending to call Lydia to see if she could meet him for lunch. She'd told him she was going to hang new curtains in the cottage today, but surely she could take a break.

But Jennifer lingered, so he stopped short of picking up the receiver and peered up at her. From the worry lines marring her pretty forehead, he could tell something weighed heavily on her mind.

He pulled his hand away from the phone, leaned back in his swivel chair, and laced his hands over his abdomen. "Wanna talk about it?"

"If you've got time."

He really didn't. Allowing her to come in and sign her contract on the spur of the moment hadn't left him much time for lunch, and he really did want to see Lydia. But Jennifer had been there for him so many times over the past five years, he felt he owed her a sympathetic ear whenever she needed one.

He motioned to the chair she had just vacated, and she sat back down. Leaning on her forearms, she focused on her fidgeting red-tipped fingers while she apparently weighed out whatever it was she needed to say.

As patiently as possible, Daniel waited.

Finally, she looked up at him. "Daniel, I was just wondering what you think of Lydia?"

He approached her question with a lawyer's analytical caution. "I'm not sure I understand what you're asking."

"What I'm asking is, what do you think about the way she is now?"

"I still love her, Jen. That's not changed." *And that,* he thought, *explained it all.*

"I know, but. . ." She chewed her thumbnail for a long, thoughtful moment before adding, "Does Lydia sometimes do or say things that totally confuse you or catch you off guard?"

His lips curved in a slow grin. "All the time. I mean, sometimes when I'm with her I think I'm looking at Lydia, then she'll do or say something totally out of character, and I feel like I'm seeing someone else." He shook his head, slipping into a daydream filled with visions from the evening before. "When I hold her now, it even feels different."

∞

Lydia pulled into the parking lot of Matthews and Matthews, Attorneys-at-Law. Since Daniel was working on a property dispute set to go to trial tomorrow, she knew he might not take time for lunch. So, in an impetuous moment, she had decided to lay aside the curtains she was hanging, pick up some takeout, drop by his office, and have lunch with him. Granted, the local burger express didn't specialize in the healthiest food in the world, but at least she would know he'd eaten something to tide him over until their dinner date tonight.

As she parked her station wagon, she noticed Jennifer's car sitting a few spaces away. Her sister was probably there going over paperwork on some new investment. The shrewd businesswoman was always looking for a profitable deal.

Oh well, Lydia thought as she grabbed the bags from the passenger seat, if Jennifer hadn't eaten, they could all have lunch together. Even though she and Jennifer were as different as night and day, Lydia thoroughly enjoyed her sister's company.

Lydia stepped out of her car, inhaling the boggy, grassy scent of the saltwater marsh across the street. Would she ever come back down to feeling normal again? Not if the last two weeks were any indication of what the future had in store for her. Life had never been so near perfect. She and Chloe had gotten settled into their new home on the island, she was head over heels in love with the most wonderful man in the world, and, for the first time she could remember, she was looking forward to the rest of her life with childlike excitement.

Yes, she thought as she closed the car door, *things are about as perfect as perfect could be.*

As she reached for the entrance door with one hand, she reached for a small part of her that was missing with the other. She felt a little lost not having her daughter along, but the child's grandparents had confiscated her for an afternoon at the park. Since Lydia had planned a day of much work and little play, she had conceded to the outing.

The desk with a missing secretary gave the reception area a lulling out-to-lunch feel. Scanning the doors flanking each side of the workstation, Lydia noted the senior Matthews's door was closed. But Daniel's was standing wide open, which, she knew, meant "Come on in."

Catching her breath in anticipation, she tiptoed across the room.

"Does Lydia sometimes do or say things that totally confuse you or catch you off guard?"

Jennifer's voice, and the mention of her own name, stopped Lydia before she stepped into view of the doorway.

"All the time," came Daniel's answer. "I mean, sometimes when I'm with her I think I'm looking at Lydia, then she'll do or say something totally out of character, and I feel like I'm seeing someone else." A brief pause, then, "When I hold her now, it even feels different."

Nothing could have prepared Lydia for the forceful blow that knocked her cloud of joy out from under her or for the feeling of her newfound elation hitting the floor with such rock-solid impact. Before her weakening limbs could collapse beneath her, she turned. As quickly and quietly as possible, she left the office.

∽

"But, you do think she's all right, don't you?" Jennifer said, continuing her conversation with Daniel. "I mean, you don't think there are any mental repercussions from the attack, do you?"

Daniel noticed that the lines of worry in Jennifer's forehead had deepened. She *really* needed assurance that her sister was going to be all right.

"No, Jen," he said. "With Lydia's permission, I spoke with her doctor and reviewed her medical file. There is no permanent damage other than the memory loss."

Jen's troubled eyes filled with tears. "But she's so different now."

Daniel retrieved a box of tissues from his credenza and offered it to Jennifer, then he leaned forward and folded his arms on his desk. "Jennifer, I don't think anyone can go through what Lydia went though and not be changed. I mean, think about it. She not only lost her memory that night, she lost me, you, your mother and father. Everything that made her what she was, including herself. When she woke up sixteen days later, her entire past, up until that moment, was gone.

"Then, out of sheer survival instinct, I think, she was forced to live as a woman named Sara Jennings for five years. Now, here she is, back on Quinn Island, trying to readjust to the life that really belongs to her. She's been jerked around a bit, to say the least, but she's trying hard to adapt, and every day she makes progress." He reached over and patted Jennifer's hand. "She's going to be fine, Jen. She just needs a little more time to figure everything out. That's all."

Jennifer sniffed, dabbing at her eyes with a tissue. "Do you think she'll ever go back to the way she used to be?"

As always, whenever he stopped to ask himself exactly the same question, a niggling fear wormed through him. "I honestly don't know." And he honestly didn't know if he wanted her to.

Pursing her lips, she lowered her gaze. "Can I make a small confession?"

"Attorney-client privilege. Your secret's safe with me."

"There are some things. . .many, really. . .about this new Lydia that I like better."

Me, too, Daniel said to himself. But out of loyalty to the Lydia of his past, he kept the admission to himself. "Lydia will be fine, Jen," he repeated. "You'll see. Just fine."

When Jennifer turned to leave, Daniel checked his watch, then combed a harried hand through his hair. No point in calling Lydia now.

His lunch hour was almost over.

❧

After dropping her keys twice, she finally managed to unlock the door. Tears streaming, she flew through the house, out the back, stumbled down the steps, and fell to her knees on the beach.

"When I hold her now, it even feels different."

The cold, cruel reality in those words almost choked her. She curled her fingers into the gritty sand. Daniel wasn't in love with her. He was in love with a memory.

She looked up to the heavens through bitter tears. The salty breeze stung her wet cheeks. An errant strand of wind-tossed hair plastered her cheek, clung to her mouth. This hurt. Hurt. . .worse than anything.

A sob tore through her body. "Oh God, help me! *Please*, help me! I don't know who I am anymore."

Burying her face in her gritty hands, she bowed her head to the sand and continued to weep. . .and to pray.

❧

By the time she returned to the house an hour later, she'd cried so many tears, her entire body felt dehydrated. And the back of her neck, she could tell, was sunburned. She pushed her mangled curls away from her face. Maybe she should have just stayed down there and withered away in the sun. It wouldn't have been nearly as painful as facing the brutal reality in Daniel's words less than two hours ago.

She opened the door to a ringing cell phone. She saw the call was from David, and she wasn't ready to talk to him yet.

The phone stopped ringing; She waited for the voicemail notification, then checked the message. "Hi, hon. I just had a minute and thought I'd call. It's been a few hours since I talked to you."

She could hear the grin in his voice. She closed her eyes against the ache in her throat. He had called that morning before he left for work, and everything had been so wonderful then. If she could just roll back the hands of time for a few short hours.

No! She opened her eyes and brought herself up straight. Going back wouldn't do any good. She'd merely be looking at the world through the rose-colored glasses of blind love, and Daniel's heart would still belong to another.

"I guess you decided to go shopping for the cottage after all. If I don't hear from you in an hour or so, I'll ring you back. And, no, I'm not being overprotective and checking up on you. I simply called because I love you."

Anger shot through her like a hurtling arrow, and she shivered. "Liar!" she sneered as the phone line went dead, then immediately wanted to recant the sharp retort. Why should she be mad at Daniel? He couldn't help how he felt. He didn't even realize yet he wasn't in love with her.

Like a back draft, another realization hit her. "Oh God," she whispered through her fingers, "this is going to hurt him. Just as much as it's hurting me." Her pain heightened. Legs giving way, she crumbled to her knees. The flood of tears started all over again. "Oh God, what am I going to do?" Wrapping her arms around herself, she began rocking back and forth. "*Please* show me what to do."

Miraculously, she found a small calm in the midst of her storm. And in that silence, a still, small voice spoke to her and told her what to do. Wearily, she picked herself up off the floor, scooping up Mittens as she did so.

A zombielike walk down the hall took Lydia to her bedroom, where an unhung curtain still lay draped over the ironing board. Setting Mittens on the seafoam green-and-rose spread that covered her iron bed, she opened her nightstand drawer and withdrew a clothbound book. Testing the feel of its satiny ivory-colored cover, she sat down on the bed. Mittens poked her curious nose over Lydia's arm to see what was so interesting.

Lydia had found the journal among her old belongings when she had taken them out of storage. At the time, she had been surrounded by her family and Daniel, so she'd tucked the book away to read at a more opportune time. She settled back into the mountain of pillows propped against the headrail. Guess this was that time.

Two-and-one-half hours, 177 handwritten pages, and one cup of chamomile tea later, she knew exactly who Lydia was—someone that she herself would never be.

She closed the journal and stared unseeingly at the waves crashing against the jetty beyond her window. "Sara," she whispered.

From beneath the pain of a broken heart, a tiny spark of peace winked at her. Then the window of her soul opened up and revealed the truth to her. *Sara*. That was it. That's who she was.

Not the owner of an elegant dress shop. Not a sophisticated southern belle. Not Quinn Island's golden girl. She was not the woman Daniel Matthews fell in love with all those years ago. She was Sara. Just plain Sara. And for her, that was enough.

She drew in a shuddery breath. She'd finally figured it out. The sigh that followed was painful. Now, all she had to do was tell Daniel.

Then, she would crawl to some private corner of the world, curl up, and die for a while.

∞

Daniel stood at Lydia's front door, waiting for her to answer the doorbell. He hadn't even gone home to change after work. When she had called thirty minutes ago and said she needed to postpone their dinner date because she wasn't feeling well, he had made a quick trip to the grocery store. He'd picked up soup, saltines, and soft drinks—all those things his mother used to push down his throat whenever he was sick— then driven straight to the cottage.

He shifted the grocery bag from one arm to the other. A full minute had passed. He pushed the doorbell again, shrugging off the uneasiness crawling up his back. Maybe she was in the shower, or maybe she was too sick to get out of bed and answer the door.

He was reaching in his pocket for his key when he heard the shuffle of her small feet.

"Daniel, you shouldn't have come," came her weary-sounding voice through the closed door. "I told you I wasn't feeling well."

"I just wanted to check on you, see if you needed anything."

"No. I don't! I just need to be left alone."

He flinched at her sharp tone. Something was wrong. *Very* wrong. And he wasn't going anywhere until he found out what.

"Daniel," she pleaded, her voice now sounding weak and defeated. "Please. . .just go home."

Didn't she know him better than that? "Lydia, I'm not leaving until you open the door and let me see for myself how you are."

Silence stretched tauter than a harp string.

"I have a key," he reminded her, and he was about to use it when he heard the latch give from the other side. Slowly, she opened the door, and what he saw almost bowled him over. Her hair was a mess, and she was dressed in a long, white, terry robe and fuzzy pink slippers. And she had been crying—hard. "Lydia. What's wrong?"

She stood, one hand still on the doorknob, the other fisted tightly at her side. Was that fury smoldering in her eyes? "I. . .told. . .you. . . I'm. . .not. . .feeling. . .well," she ground out through clenched teeth.

"I'd say that's an understatement." He pushed his way inside, almost tripping over Mittens. Closing the door, he set his loaded grocery bag on the floor and captured Lydia's forearms. His gut twisted at the sight of her tear-swollen eyes. "Talk to me."

She pulled away, as though his touch had burned her. Cupping her elbows, she took several backward steps. As she did so, Daniel sensed her erecting some sort of wall between them. But why?

Something dark and foreboding swept over him, leaving him chilled to the core. Cautiously, he took a step forward.

She took another back. Sorrowfully shaking her head, she said, "I don't want to do this tonight, Daniel. I'm not prepared."

He lifted his hands in a helpless gesture. "Do what, Lydia? For heaven's sake, tell me what's going on!"

A tremor shuddered through her body. Biting down hard on her lower lip, she closed her eyes.

He longed to reach for her, comfort her. But he sensed, somehow, if he did, she'd just slip farther away, farther behind whatever impenetrable wall she was building between them.

When her trembling ceased, she opened her eyes, turned, and wandered to a double window overlooking the sea. Slowly, he followed, stopping an arm's span behind her.

Seconds passed like hours. Daniel fought the choking hand of dread reaching for his throat. His hands sweat; his lungs burned; his head hurt. He didn't know what was coming, only that it was bad.

Finally, she said, "I've finally figured out who Lydia is."

In light of the uneasy currents ricocheting around them, he knew better than to say *That's good*. He somehow swallowed around the sticky dryness in his throat. "And?"

"It's not me."

He willed her to look at him, but he got no results. "What do you mean, it's not you?"

"Just exactly what I said. I'm not now, nor will I ever be, Lydia."

He trapped his temples between his thumb and second finger, trying to keep his reeling mind from crashing. "This doesn't make sense."

"It makes perfect sense if you stop to think about it. I don't act like

Lydia; I don't think like Lydia; I don't like the same things Lydia liked." Her face was void of emotion and her body as rigid as a mannequin. It was clear she was trying not to feel. *Forcing* herself not to feel.

"I don't want to be a shop owner," she droned on like a robot. "I want to be an advocate for missing and abused children. I don't want someone telling me how I should dress or wear my hair; I want to decide those things for myself. I don't want to have to recoil every time I have something to say; I want to speak my mind without worrying that I'm going to offend someone every time I do so. I don't want to live in a town house; I want to live right here on the island for the rest of my life."

She finally stopped to take a breath.

"Do you think any of that matters to me?" he ground out.

"It should. It should matter a great deal to you." Her stoic features softened and her rigid shoulders dropped slightly. But she still refused to look at him. "Daniel," she said in a voice now laced with compassion, "five years ago, on that deserted Darlington highway, Lydia died. Sixteen days later, Sara was born. You didn't ask for it, and neither did I, but that's the way it is." Finally, she turned her head and looked at him, and the depth of pain in her eyes almost ripped him in two. "Lydia's gone, Daniel. I can't replace her. I've accepted that. Now you have to."

He shook his head in denial. "No way. This isn't right."

"Don't you see, Daniel? It's the only thing that is right. Everything else has been wrong up until now."

Fear as quick and sharp as a two-edged sword sliced through him. He pulled a face in disbelief. "What are you saying, Lydia? That you really don't love me?"

No, she wasn't saying that. She would never be able to say that. But she couldn't let him know it.

She turned back to the window. She was dying inside, and she needed to get him away from her. "I'm saying you need to go home and mourn Lydia, Daniel. Go home, and mourn the woman you really love."

He raised his hand.

She closed her eyes. "Please don't touch me," she said quickly, before he had a chance to. Because if he did, she'd shatter into a million pieces around his feet. Then she'd allow him to pick her up and put her back together again, regardless of the cost to her and to him.

When she mentally felt him withdraw his hand, she opened her eyes and continued staring out the window. But out of the corner of her eye, she could see his chest rising and falling with emotion. It took every ounce of willpower she possessed to hold back the tears filling her eyes.

"Okay," he said, then paused to take two more heavy breaths, like he needed them to replenish his strength. "You want me to go; I'll go. For now. But as soon as I figure out what happened between now and this morning, I'll be back. You can count on that, Lydia."

"Sara. My name is Sara."

He just stood there, chest heaving, hands clenching and unclenching, staring at her like he didn't know what to do with himself.

She had to get him out. Now, before she broke. "You may hate me for this now, Daniel," she said softly. "But someday you'll thank me. Now, *please*. Go."

He captured her chin and forced her to look at him. What she saw in his eyes was both frightening and promising. Anger, confusion, and pain were mixed together with love and determination.

"Hate you?" he said, his voice full of harsh incredulity. "Sweetheart, I will *never* hate you. You can call yourself Sara, Jane, Polly, Sue. Pick one; I don't care." His grip on her chin tightened, stopping short of the point of pain. "I'm not in love with your name; I'm in love with you."

She almost reached out and grabbed the fragile thread of hope he was dangling in front of her. Almost. But just in time he dropped his hand, leaving her weak and incredibly weary.

"Now, I'm going to leave," he added, his hand now clenched back at his side. "Because I'm afraid if I don't, I'm going to knock a hole in your wall. But I'll be back. *Soon*. And that, my dear Sara Jane Polly Sue, is a promise." With that, he turned and stalked away.

She stood by the window and waited until she heard him drive away, then waited a few minutes more. When she was certain he wasn't coming back, certain he wouldn't come in and see her, she buried her face in her hands and crumpled to the floor.

∞

One-and-one-half hours later, Daniel walked out of the Quinns' home, climbed into his car, and headed home. Maybe he should feel guilty that he had just conspired with Lydia's entire family to find out what was going on with her, but he didn't.

He was a desperate man.

Chapter 15

"Hi, Bill. Come on in." Daniel stepped back to allow the older man entry. "Have you talked to Lydia today?"

Bill shook his head. "Not today. I drove out to see her last night, but she's still not talking."

Daniel's stomach churned with disappointment. It had been three days since his and Lydia's perplexing parting. So far, no one had been able to get her to open up about what had happened that day to make her suddenly turn around and head in the other direction. She would open her door to her family, but not her heart. To Daniel, she would open neither, and it was driving him crazy. He was on the verge of claiming insanity and camping out on her doorstep.

"I did receive a call from Chicago this morning though," Bill added.

Daniel arched his brows. "Mrs. Porter?" Lydia's friend had gone home several weeks ago; why hadn't he thought of her? If anyone could get through to Lydia, it was her former landlady. "Has Lydia talked to her?"

Bill nodded. "Mrs. Porter called her yesterday, just to see how she was doing."

"And?"

Bill grinned. "Why don't you ask me to sit down? Then I'll tell you what she said."

Chagrined at his lapse in manners, Daniel muttered, "Sorry," and led the way to the den. He'd been doing a lot of peculiar things over the past three days.

Bill settled on a forest green leather sofa, and Daniel perched on the edge of a matching recliner seat, elbows on knees, hands clasped in front of him.

"Seems like. . .*Sara* overheard a conversation between you and Jennifer on Wednesday that made her feel you were disappointed in the woman she'd become since her abduction."

Daniel's brow creased in concentration. He had to jiggle his memory in order to recall his Wednesday meeting with Jennifer. "Jennifer came into the office that day to sign some papers. We did talk a bit about Lydia, but Lydia wasn't there."

"Yes, she was. Standing right outside your door."

"Eavesdropping?" Daniel couldn't believe it.

"No. At least not intentionally. She'd come to bring you lunch, but when she heard her sister ask you if she ever did things to confuse you, and you told Jen 'yes,' that even holding her was different now, she left."

"I also told Jen that my love for Lydia hasn't changed. Didn't she hear that, too?"

"Guess not."

Daniel flopped back in his chair. "So that's what this is all about. A simple misunderstanding."

Bill shook his head. "I'm not sure it's all that simple."

"Sure, it is. As soon as I explain to her that she didn't hear the whole conversation, she'll realize she jumped to the wrong conclusion, and we'll probably have a good laugh over it." After he kissed her until their breath was gone. But he didn't think her father would be interested in hearing about that.

Bill leveled Daniel with a somber look. "Did she jump to the wrong conclusion, Daniel?"

"Of course she did. What else could it be?"

"Perception. Insight. The sudden realization and acceptance of how things really are."

Daniel frowned. "What are you saying, Bill?"

"That maybe Lydia, as we knew her, really is gone, and we need to stop looking for her to come back to us."

Daniel shook his head in denial.

"Think about it, Daniel. She's known us only six weeks. *Six weeks.* She's like a child who was stolen from her home in infancy and not returned until adulthood, or someone who's just moved here from out of town. We can't expect her to come back and step into the life that we all had planned for her." Tears brought a sad sparkle to the older man's eyes. "I know she's tried. She's given her best shot at giving us back what we lost, but for whose sake? Hers or ours?"

Propping his elbow on the chair arm, Daniel massaged his throbbing temple. He didn't want to accept what Bill was saying. Didn't want to accept that Lydia was really gone. Even though, deep down, he suspected he had known it for some time. "So what are you saying?" he repeated. "That we should just forget about the past? Pretend it never happened?"

Bill gave his head a solemn shake. "I don't think any of us could do that, or that anyone, including *Sara*, would expect us to. I'm just saying that maybe it's time we stopped trying to hold onto it, and accept the gift that we've been given in return." His gaze bore into Daniel's for a wise and perceptive moment. "A good place to start would be by letting go of all that guilt you've been toting around for the last five years."

Daniel shifted his gaze to the cold, empty fireplace. He still found it amazing that Bill Quinn had never blamed him for his daughter's disappearance, for not taking that trip with her.

"Fate dealt us all a bitter blow that night, Daniel," Bill continued. "There wasn't one of us who didn't stop and ask ourselves if there was something we could have done." Voice mellowing, he added, "No one blames you, son. Don't you think it's time you stopped blaming yourself?"

Daniel continued to massage his temple, continued staring unseeingly at the fireplace. He didn't know how to respond to all that Bill had said. Daniel needed time to think, weigh everything out, and pray.

As though sensing Daniel's need for solitude, Bill stood. Daniel started to follow suit, but the older man stopped him with an understanding hand on his shoulder. "Don't get up. I'll see myself out."

Daniel nodded and settled back in his chair. Would he ever muddle through all the confusion? With a sigh, he raised his hand and started kneading his temple again. Was anything in life ever certain? At the moment, he could think of only one thing.

"Bill?" Daniel called just before the man exited from the room.

In the open doorway, Bill turned back.

"This whole Lydia being Sara thing may still have me a bit addled," Daniel said. "But there is one thing I'm not confused about. I love your daughter. Of that, I'm certain."

A knowing gleam warmed the older man's eyes. "I know you do, Daniel. If I didn't, I wouldn't be here."

Bill started through the door again, then apparently struck by another thought, he stopped and turned around. "One more thing. You told Jen that your love for Lydia hasn't changed. Are you sure about that?"

"If anything, I love her more."

"More? Or different?"

Both came to mind so quickly that Daniel blinked in surprise. He did love her more, stronger, deeper than before. And that love was different, because *she* was different.

Daniel gave the man standing at the doorway a blank look of dawning enlightenment. Why, he'd gone and fallen in love all over again, with a woman named Sara.

Bill simply smiled. "That's what I thought. Now, all you have to do is convince my daughter."

⚭

Dear Diary

Sara pulled her hand away from her new journal and studied the words she'd just written. For some reason, they didn't feel right. She drew in a deep breath and released it through pursed lips. Why did she feel a need to start a journal anyway? What benefit was there in telling your innermost secrets to a book?

"Mama, can me an' Mittens go climb on the rocks?"

Holding a strand of windblown hair away from her face, Sara looked up at the child standing beside her in a neon pink bathing suit. A gray ball of fur swarmed around her ankles, sniffing at a bottle of sunscreen lying on the beach blanket where Sara sat. For some reason known only to a child's mind, Chloe was fascinated with the mountain of huge rocks that was an extension of the jetty at the end of the island.

"No, you may not," Sara answered, adjusting the strap that had slid off her daughter's shoulder. "You might fall and get hurt or slip and get your foot trapped between the rocks." She pushed Chloe's sunglasses up her nose. "Besides, the tide's coming in and you might get washed away.

Then what would I do without my little girl?"

"You'd cry and cry, just like you do for Daniel."

Sara blinked back the stinging onslaught of tears. Why did the child have to be so perceptive?

Chloe tilted her head, the end of her ponytail brushing one shoulder. "Is he ever coming back to see us?"

Chloe had questioned Daniel's absence several times over the past four days, but Sara didn't have the strength yet to explain to her child that he would no longer be a constant part of their lives. She wanted to wait until she got past the stage of sporadic weeping that often hit her unawares at any given time of the day. "Honey, Daniel is your very good friend, and he loves you very much. I'm sure he'll find a way to see you soon."

"But don't he want to be your friend anymore?"

Probably not. But she couldn't tell Chloe that. "Daniel is everybody's friend," she said, hoping the answer would satisfy her daughter. Before the child could come up with a response, Sara added, "Now, you and Mittens go on and finish your sand castle. We only have a few more minutes before we have to go in."

Chloe and Mittens scampered a few feet away to a lumpy mound of sand that looked more like a range of bald mountains than a castle. The calming call of a seagull harmonized with the voice of the waves crashing against the jetty. While Sara listened to the beauty of the sea song, she watched her daughter and reminded herself that she was a woman truly blessed. She had a God who would never forsake her. A child who was healthy and happy. A family who loved her and—although they were still a bit taken aback—supported her desire to legally change her name to Sara Lydia Quinn. Oh, yes, and she had Mittens. The cat had promptly become a comforting, permanent member of hers and Chloe's family.

The only thing missing was Daniel.

She forced a breath past the catch in her throat. *Four out of five isn't bad,* she reminded herself. One couldn't have it all.

With a fingertip, she caught a tear trying to escape the corner of her eye. " 'For I know the thoughts that I think toward you, saith the Lord,' " she whispered to herself, " 'thoughts of peace, and not of evil, to give you an expected end.' "

The verse had given her a sense of peace in the midst of every storm she had ridden over the past five years, and it gave peace now. She had to be thankful she'd found out Daniel's true feelings for her before one day he woke up next to her and realize he'd married a stranger.

But peace did not take away the pain. At least, not yet anyway. She pressed a palm against the weight on her chest. Even when her heart was once again able to reach beyond pain to sweet remembrance, things would never be the same. There would never be another Daniel.

She turned her attention back to the book and poised her pen over the paper. *Dear Diary,* she read, then realized what was wrong. With one quick stoke, she marked through *Dear Diary* and wrote *Dear God.*

This would be her prayer journal. The place she went to daily to talk to God and thank Him for all the goodness and blessings He had brought to her life, a place to pray for others and ask for strength. Especially in the days of loneliness ahead.

She wrote nonstop for ten minutes, finishing her first entry with:

God, please help Daniel understand why I had to let him go. Help him get through the pain, for I know, right now, he is hurting. He's lost so much. Help him find the woman who is right for him. I know there's one out there somewhere. Someone who will make him happy. Someone as true and kind and as generous as he. He has too much love to offer not to share his life with someone like that. And I promise, when that time comes, I will be happy for him.

Love,
Sara

She blotted the teardrops from the page with the end of a beach towel and closed the journal. Then she wiped the moisture from her face with her hands. She'd get through this. Somehow, by the grace of God, she would survive.

She glanced up to check on Chloe. Her bucket lay overturned in the midst of the lumpy sand castle, and her blue shovel was stuck up in the sand. But Chloe and Mittens were gone.

"Chloe?" Her pulse quickened as she searched the shrinking beach, then surged with alarm when she located her daughter trying to climb up the jetty rocks. "Chloe!" She threw the book aside and vaulted up in a run. "Chloe! Wait!"

Thank God, Chloe complied.

Sara ran out into knee-deep water and scooped up her daughter off the rocks. She trudged back to dry land and set the child down on solid ground. Then, kneeling, she clasped Chloe's upper arms. "Chloe, what has gotten into you?" The child rarely disobeyed a request. "I told you not to climb on the rocks. You could get hurt!"

Sunglasses now gone, Chloe looked up at her mother through worried blue eyes. Her small chin quivered. "But I have to get Mittens. She's gone after the fish."

"What fish?"

Chloe pointed toward the water. Sara's line of vision followed her daughter's pointing finger, and sure enough, there was Mittens halfway out the jetty, slapping at small fish jumping out of the swirling waves. *"Mittens,"* Sara chided under her breath. Didn't the crazy cat realize her legs were three inches—not three feet—long?

"We have to get her, Mommy," came Chloe's small, panic-stricken voice. "Or she'll wash away."

Sara turned back to her daughter. "Okay, Chloe. I want you to go sit on the steps and don't move. No matter what."

"What are you going to do?"

"I'm going after Mittens."

"But what if you get washed away?"

"I won't," she said, hoping she was right. "I'll be very careful. But, if something does happen, and I can't get back, then you go to the house and call 911. Okay?"

"Okay."

"Now, go sit down, and stay there until I get back."

With bare feet, Sara gingerly negotiated the jagged rocks until the wind caught her off guard, making her lose her footing and scrape an ankle. She picked her way over the rest of the rubble on hands and knees, clenching her teeth a little harder every time Mittens ignored her summons.

"I'm going to wring your skinny little neck when I get you back to shore," she ground out as she crawled up onto the six-inch wide jetty platform. Her hand slipped and snagged a small splinter. Wiping the blood that seeped from her palm on the seat of her cutoffs, she added, "If you don't make me shark bait first."

∞

Cradling a small bouquet of mixed flowers in one arm, Daniel climbed the front steps of the cottage. He had no idea what he was going to say to her when she opened the door—and she would open it, even if he had to use his key first. He just knew that somehow he had to convince her he loved the woman she was now—not the woman she used to be. That was a love whose time was past. Like Bill had said, it was time to let it go. Accept what God had given him in return—and Daniel was wholeheartedly ready to do that. Now, if he could only persuade her to accept him.

He stepped up to the door, his stomach a knot of nerves and anticipation. He'd do whatever it took to plead his case. After all, it was a matter of life and death. *His.*

With a deep, bracing breath, he rang the doorbell. What should he say to get her to hear him out before slamming the door in his face? Maybe he could start with something like, *Hi. My name is Daniel. What's yours?*

Almost immediately, he shook his head. Too corny sounding. And she'd probably never fall for it, anyway. He glanced down at the flowers resting in the crook of his arm. He had chosen a mixture of painted daisies, sweet-smelling lavender, morning glories, and several other species he couldn't name, all nestled in a bed of pink baby's breath. They reminded him of a field of wildflowers, and he had known the minute he saw them in the florist's window that Sara would love them, a lot more than she would a box of long-stem roses.

He looked back at the door. Where was she? He'd expected to hear some activity from her or Chloe by now. He knew they were home; her car was in the garage area beneath the house.

He rang the doorbell again, waited about half-a-minute, then bounded down the steps and headed for the narrow path carved through the thick island flora that led to the back of the house. Maybe she and Chloe were on the beach, which would be even better. That way, she couldn't slam the door in his face.

When he broke through the thick cloud of plant life, he scanned the beach area. He found only an abandoned beach blanket and sand bucket. One corner of his mouth tipped. She and Chloe were probably exploring. His gaze drifted a little farther down the beach to the jetty, and his steps faltered. Sara was crawling out on the narrow platform, about to be swallowed up by the roiling waves of the incoming high tide.

Terror slammed into him at the same time adrenaline kicked in, and he didn't stop to think. Taking off in a dead run, he screamed, *"Saaaaraaaa!"*

∞

The waves slapped at Sara's hands and knees, but she was almost there. Only a couple more feet and she would have Mittens, who had realized the error of her ways and had climbed up onto the top of one of the poles anchoring the jetty.

Sara paused, listening. Had someone called her name? Her instant of distraction left her unprepared for the next wave that sloshed over the jetty, and her left knee slipped off the platform. A jolt of alarm quickened her pulse and she steadied herself. Best keep her mind on what she was doing.

She hooked her hand around the quivering cat; as she pulled the kitten to her chest, she hesitated again. Someone had called her name, and it sounded like Daniel.

Twisting her head around, she found him sprinting down the beach toward her, waving his arms over his head and yelling, "Sara! Wait! I'm coming!"

Something cold and powerful hit her on her blind side, and the next thing she knew, she was being swallowed by the churning dark waters of the Atlantic.

∞

"Sara? Sara? Can you hear me?"

There it was again. Daniel calling her name. Calling her up out of the darkness. She must be dreaming.

Something cold and wet covered her mouth and forced air into her lungs. Her body convulsed. She coughed as air rushed from her chest, then her body settled back down.

"That's it, baby," came that beautiful voice again. "Come on back to me."

Slowly, she opened her eyes, and there he was, kneeling over her, nursing the back of her head with one hand, his wet hair dripping on her face. Oh, but he was beautiful.

"Oh thank God." He buried his face against her shoulder. "Thank God, you're alive. I thought I had lost you."

Instinctively, she raised her hand to the back of his head and held it there. As the fog evaporated from her mind, she struggled to sit up. "Chloe?"

He drew back, cradling her face with his palm. "She's fine. She's sitting on the steps with one of the neighbors."

"Mittens?"

"She's fine, too. You were still holding onto her when I got to you."

Assured her family was safe, she reached up and laid her hand against his cool, damp cheek. "Sara." It wasn't a question, but a statement of awe and wonder.

His eyes crinkled. "Yes, sweetheart. You're fine, too."

"No, you. You called me 'Sara.' When I was out on the jetty, and you were running toward me, without stopping or thinking or. . .anything, you called me Sara."

His brow furrowed in thought, then smoothed. "Yes, I guess I did."

The center of her being flooded with joy that extended to every fiber in her body. "Thank you, Daniel. You saved my life today, in more ways than one."

∽

"We're going to keep you overnight, just for observation."

Sara let her head flop back on the pillow. "Is that really necessary, Dr. Bayne?"

He shifted his gaze from the chart he was writing, peering at her over his reading glasses. "Probably not, but I'd rather be safe—"

"I know. I know. You'd rather be safe than sorry."

"That's right." He patted her knee. "Now, there are some very anxious people outside waiting to see you. I think I'd better let them in before they knock down the door."

Her father and Chloe came in first. After greeting them both with a hug and kiss, she settled Chloe on the bed next to her. "Where are the others?" she asked her father.

"They're outside. The doctor said we could come in only two at a time. Hospital rules." He eased himself down on the edge of the bed and picked up her hand. "Jen and Margaret will come in next, then your mother and I will take Chloe home with us for the night. Since Daniel's going to stay the night, he decided he'd take his turn last."

Her eyes widened. "Daniel's spending the night?"

Her father sent her a teasing wink. "I gave my permission, as long as he keeps himself in the guest cot."

A bit discomfited, she ducked her head. He lifted it back up with a finger beneath her chin. "I don't think we could run him out of this place tonight with a shotgun. That young man loves you, Sara. *You.* I hope you've figured that out by now."

"I have, Dad. And I love him, too."

"An' me, too," Chloe chimed in, and a round of laughter followed.

Her mother and Jennifer kept their visit short, then Mr. and Mrs. Matthews stuck their heads in to express their happiness that she'd survived her cat-rescuing venture unharmed.

The second Daniel's parent's left, Sara adjusted the pillows supporting her back and combed her fingers through her tangled hair. She'd give a week's wages for a mirror and brush right now. She had to be a mess. Wetting her lips, she straightened her covers and clasped her hands in her lap. She hadn't been this nervous the first time she had met Daniel, six weeks ago in Chicago.

He hesitated in the doorway, a dream in the shadows, then strolled into the glow of the overhead lights, her knight who had come to carry her away to happily ever after. A leather overnight bag dangled from one hand. Someone, his parents probably, had apparently brought him some fresh clothes, but he hadn't taken the time to change yet. His navy slacks and yellow pullover shirt were both pretty much a mess, and he hadn't even combed his hair. But he was the most beautiful sight she had ever seen.

He stopped a few feet inside the door and tossed the overnight bag to a nearby chair. "Hi," he said, dazzling her with a sheepish grin.

If she didn't know better, she'd say he sounded shy. "Hi, yourself."

"My name's Daniel. What's yours?"

A silent message passed between them. The promise of a new beginning was sealed. Anticipation and excitement danced across her skin. "Sara. My name is Sara."

"Sara," he mused, as though testing the flavor of the word on his tongue. Slowly and deliberately, he ambled forward. "I like that name," he added as though he approved of the taste.

The fluttering butterflies in her stomach veered off course, darting around in a dozen different directions, bumping into each other. "Thanks. Daniel's nice, too."

"You think so?"

"Yeah. I think so."

He eased down on the edge of the bed, captured her hands in his.

His tender gaze consumed her. "So, Sara. What are you doing tonight? And tomorrow night? And for the rest of your life?"

She shrugged a shoulder. "I dunno. Wanna get married?" It was bold, it was forward, and it was cheeky. But it was right. She *knew* it was right.

A spark of surprise and delight widened his eyes. Then, almost as quickly as his elation had come, it faded. He released one of her hands and pressed his forefinger to her lips. "Hold that thought."

She kissed his fingertip. "Got it."

Just before he dropped his gaze, she caught a glimpse of pain. A pain, she sensed, he had carried too long. She wanted to lift her arms and embrace him, comfort him. But something told her to wait. To let him explain.

He recaptured both of her hands, caressing the backs of her fingers with his thumbs. "There's something I need to tell you about the trip to New York."

"Okay."

Lifting his lids, he met her unwavering gaze. He could live an eternity drowning in those eyes, eyes that showered him with love and devotion. A quick wave of apprehension clenched his stomach. After he told her why she took that New York trip alone, would she still look at him like he hung the moon?

He wasn't sure he wanted to find out, but he knew she deserved to know the truth. "I was supposed to go with you on that trip, Sara. I had my room reservations made and my bags packed, but I backed out at the last minute because a court case got pushed up a week on the trial schedule."

She waited a moment, as though she expected him to say more. When he didn't right away, she gave a nonchalant shrug. "So? You're an attorney, Daniel. I was a dress shop owner. We were both doing our jobs."

"Yes, but I could have let my dad handle the case. I could have talked to the judge, told him I couldn't change my plans. I could have done a number of things, but I didn't." Shame pressed down upon him, almost choking him. "I chose my work over you, Sara, and because I did, you suffered a brutal attack and lost your memory. Can you ever forgive me for that?"

"There's nothing to forgive, Daniel," she said without hesitation.

Her lack of pause told him she meant it. She did not blame him for her abduction. But that didn't change the fact that it had happened, that because of his self-serving attitude, she had been alone that night.

"Daniel, do you ever ask yourself 'What if?'" she added after a prolonged moment of silence.

He studied her face, the wisdom in her expression, and found there a deep well of understanding. "Yes," he admitted. "All the time."

"I've done that a lot myself over the past six weeks. What if I hadn't taken that exit? What if I had stayed on the interstate? What if I had been a few minutes earlier and been involved in the accident that caused the traffic delay?" She pulled her hands free of his and framed her face with his palms. "What if you *had* been with me that night, and you, too, had fallen prey to the men who attacked me?" Her features softened. Her eyes grew misty. "If that had happened, I suppose I would have a pretty tough time forgiving myself, too."

He shook his head. "But it wouldn't have been your fault."

"Exactly."

She gave him a moment to consider her words. "Oh Daniel, you're such a wonderful protector. You take such good care of me and Chloe, and I know you took good care of Lydia, too. That's one of the reasons you're finding it so hard to forgive yourself.

"But it wasn't your fault. God was in control of our lives, and *no one* is to blame. And no one is holding you accountable except yourself." He felt her fingers spread over his head, as though she were trying to encompass his mind with assurance. "Let it go, Daniel. I know for an honorable heart like yours, that's easier said than done. But you can do it. With God's help, you can do anything."

Daniel knew he was looking into the face of a woman who knew what she was talking about. A woman who had awakened one day wounded, pregnant, and alone. A woman who hadn't known who she was or where she came from. A woman who had crawled up from the pits of hell and learned to stand on her own.

A woman who had taught him how to give freely and love without condition.

Looking deep into her eyes at that moment, he knew nothing from the past would ever come between them. A shadow receded from his heart, and a burden he had carried for five long years grew lighter. She was right. With God's help and her love, he could do anything. Even, one day, forgive himself.

He felt a touch of God's grace flow through him, and a surge of love flooded his soul as the last chain of bondage fell from his heart. He shifted his head and kissed her palm. "You're something else. You know that?"

"I know," she said without a single shred of vanity. Then, with a minxish grin, she grasped the front of his shirt and pulled him forward. "Now, there's this matter of a thought. . ."

He stopped with his mouth less than a breath away from hers. "Oh yeah, as I was saying. What are you doing tonight?" He brushed her lips with his. "And tomorrow night?" He brushed her lips again. "And for the rest of your life?"

"I dunno. Wanna get married?"

"Yes, Sara. Yes I do."

The silence that followed was filled with faith, hope, and love. All three. But the greatest of these was love.

And in the midst of that love was forgiveness.

Gina Fields is a lifelong native of northeast Georgia. She is married to Terry and they have two very active, young sons. When Gina is not writing, singing, or playing piano, or doing one of a hundred homemaking activities, she enjoys volunteering for Special Olympics.

One Last Christmas

by Joyce Livingston

Chapter 1

Sylvia Benson hid behind the potted palm and tried to remain calm. Her intense gaze riveted on the man and woman seated at a table for two in the far corner of Dallas's trendy Fountain Place Avanti Restaurant. Hadn't her husband told her he would be having lunch with one of his key advertisers today? *That's no advertising client! That's Chatalaine Vicker, the woman who writes the society column for his newspaper. I'd recognize that gorgeous face and body anywhere. What is he doing here with her?*

"More coffee, ladies?"

Caught up in staring at the blond beauty seated across from her husband, Sylvia hadn't even noticed the waiter standing by their table, coffeepot in hand. She flinched, then covered her cup. "None for me, thanks."

The other women at the table, all friends from her church, bobbed their heads at the man without even a pause in their conversation.

Still trying to remain inconspicuous, Sylvia shifted her position slightly. Making sure the potted palm shielded her, she took another look at the pair in the corner. Surely, Randy hadn't lied to her. Not her Randy. Although he *had* been spending more time than usual at the *Dallas Times* office, occasionally even working weekends. *Come on,*

Sylvia, give that husband of yours the benefit of the doubt, she told herself as she stared at them. *Maybe his client had to cancel their luncheon appointment at the last minute.* But even if that were true, what would Randy be doing with Chatalaine? And why hadn't he told her he would be free for lunch? After all, she was his wife. If he had wanted someone to go to lunch with him, she could have cancelled her luncheon appointment with her friends.

She leaned back in her chair and tried to shake off her suspicions. *It's probably all perfectly innocent, and I'm making something out of nothing. Business associates have lunch together all the time. Maybe they're discussing Chatalaine's column. After all, Randy* is *the* Times's *managing editor.*

"What *are* you looking at, Sylvia?"

Sylvia turned quickly toward the question and found her friend Sally, staring at her. "Ah, nothing. Just thought I recognized someone."

Sally rose, placed her napkin on the table, and picked up her purse. "I'm going to the ladies' room. Anyone want to go with me?"

Without missing a beat in their conversation, Denise and Martha rose and headed for the ladies' room, still talking.

Sally gave a slight giggle. "You're not coming?"

"No, I'll wait here. You go on."

"Don't let that waiter get away if he comes with the dessert cart while we're gone," Sally said with a mischievous lilt. "I need chocolate."

Sylvia snickered. "You're terrible!"

She waited until her friends were out of sight, then turned and tipped her head slightly, parting the palm fronds again and peering through them. What she observed went a long way toward fueling her suspicions. The two were talking and giggling like two teenagers. *If this is supposed to be a business luncheon, those two are enjoying themselves entirely too much! Maybe I should just march right over there and confront them, ask them what they're doing together, and see what kind of an explanation I get.*

However, she didn't. Her pride would not allow it. Instead, she decided to wait until later, when she and Randy were alone. She sat there quietly, her nerves French-braiding themselves while all sorts of scenarios played themselves out in her mind. She flinched when the waiter filled her water glass, his close proximity pulling her out of her thoughts.

"Would you like to see the dessert cart, ma'am?"

"Ah—in a minute maybe." She motioned toward the hallway off to the left. "As soon as my friends come back from the ladies' room."

When he nodded and moved away, Sylvia twisted in the chair, unable to resist another peek. Randy was standing beside Chatalaine now, extending his hand to assist her as she rose. How long had it been since he had done that for her? Things were not looking good.

From behind her potted palm camouflage, she watched the attractive couple move across the restaurant toward the exit. After giving them enough time to reach the parking lot, she signaled the waiter and asked for her check.

I wonder how long this has been going on? She drummed her fingers on the table. *You're making too much of this, Sylvia. There's probably a perfectly reasonable explanation as to why your Randy and that woman had lunch together.* She dabbed at her misty eyes with a tissue. *If you confront Randy about this now, you may be sorry. Tomorrow is Thanksgiving, and the children will all be home. You don't want to ruin Thanksgiving for your family with your unconfirmed suspicions, do you? At least wait until DeeDee and Aaron go back to college. Then, if you still think there may be something going on between your husband and that woman, you can ask him.*

The plan sounded logical. But, at this minute, she felt anything *but* logical. Both she and Randy were Christians. Randy would never go against the commitments they had both made to God on their wedding day. Or would he? Had his faith slipped, and she had been so busy, she hadn't even realized it?

"He hasn't brought the dessert cart yet?" Sally slipped into the chair, eyeing Sylvia with a grin.

Sylvia scooted her chair back and placed her napkin on the table. "I—I really need to go home."

Sally's brow creased. "Go? You and I haven't even had time for a little girl talk. What's your rush? I thought you said you didn't have any plans for this afternoon."

Sylvia reached for her purse, pulled out a couple of dollar bills, and dropped them on the table beside her plate. "I'm sorry, Sally. We'll talk more next time we have lunch. I've developed a splitting headache."

Sally gave her a slight giggle. "Hey, that's the line we use with our husbands, not our girlfriends."

Sylvia frowned as her hand rose to finger her temple. "I'm really sorry, Sally. I hate to duck out on you like this, but I need to get home, take something for this headache, and lie down. Please tell Denise and Martha good-bye for me." She didn't have a headache before seeing

Randy with that woman, but witnessing them together—after he had told her he was meeting with a client—had brought on a doozy.

Sally's face sobered. "Oh sweetie, I'm sorry, I was only kidding. Do you feel like driving home by yourself?"

"Sure, I'll be fine. Don't worry about me." *Actually, I'm miserable!* Though Sally was one of her best friends, she simply could not reveal her unproven suspicions about her husband.

When he came home from his office, it was all Sylvia could do to keep from screaming out at Randy and asking him about his lunch with Chatalaine. But for the sake of the twins, DeeDee and Aaron, who had arrived home from college that afternoon, she kept quiet, pasting on a smile and brooding within herself. She had a difficult time even looking at Randy.

She waited expectantly at bedtime, hoping he would mention it. But he didn't. Even when she asked him how his day went, he simply replied, "Fine. Routine, just like any other day." Then he crawled into bed and turned away from her.

Okay, if that's the way you want it! Don't tell me. She yanked the quilt up over her head and gritted her teeth to keep from screaming at him, telling him she had seen the two of them having a cozy lunch together.

After a sleepless night, she crawled out of bed earlier than she'd intended and began to go mechanically through the tasks of baking the turkey and preparing the rest of their very traditional meal. Her mind still on the events of yesterday, she took out her anger and frustration on the celery stalks and onions as she mercilessly chopped them up on the cutting block.

Randy came into the kitchen about eight, his usual pleasant self. He rousted Aaron and DeeDee and even teased Sylvia about the bag of giblets she'd left in the turkey she'd prepared for their first Thanksgiving together as husband and wife. About eleven o'clock, their oldest son, Buck, and his wife, Shonna, arrived, bringing two beautiful pecan pies Shonna had baked. Randy greeted them warmly, then dragged both Buck and Aaron into the den to watch a football game while the three women finished setting the table.

"Is something wrong?" Shonna stared at her mother-in-law while removing the gravy boat from the china cabinet. "You're pretty quiet this morning."

DeeDee nodded her head in agreement. "Yeah, Mom, I noticed that, too."

Is it that obvious? "I'm fine. Just had a hard time getting to sleep last night." Sylvia forced a smile. It was nice having Shonna and DeeDee there to help her. "Maybe we'd better use that big serving bowl, DeeDee. Hand it to me, would you, please?"

By one o'clock, the Benson family gathered around the lovely table for their Thanksgiving feast. With everyone holding hands, Randy led in prayer. As he did at every Thanksgiving, he thanked God for their food, for the willing hands that prepared it, and for their family seated at the table. Sylvia found it difficult to keep her mind on his words. All she could think about was her husband having lunch with that gorgeous blond. Was this all for show? Inside, was Randy wishing he could be spending Thanksgiving Day with Chatalaine?

After he had consumed the last crumb of pie on his overloaded dessert plate, Randy pushed back from the table and linked his fingers over his abdomen. "Great Thanksgiving dinner, hon. The turkey was nice and moist, just the way I like it. As usual, you've outdone yourself." With a tilt of his head, he gave her a slightly twisted smile. "If my mother was alive, she would agree, and you know how picky she was."

"Thanks. That's quite a compliment." Sylvia nervously shifted the salt and pepper shakers, finally placing them on either side of the antique sugar bowl, a prize possession that had belonged to her mother-in-law. *Oh Randy, how I hope I'm wrong! I know we haven't had much to do with each other these past few years, but surely that didn't drive you into another woman's arms.*

"Sorry, Mom. DeeDee and I have to go." Aaron tossed his napkin onto the table and nodded to his sister.

"You *have* to go this early?" Sylvia dabbed at her mouth with her napkin. "You just got here yesterday."

The good-looking young man, who looked so much like his father, gave her a quick, affectionate peck on the cheek. "I know. But you knew we'd planned to get back to school right after our meal. DeeDee and I promised we'd help our youth director with the lock-in tonight, and we've got a ton of stuff to do to get the fellowship hall ready before the kids get there."

"Great dinner, Mom." DeeDee pushed back from the table. "I hate to run and leave you and Shonna with the dishes, but if we don't leave now, we won't make it."

Sylvia rose and walked to the door with her children, with Randy following close behind. "I'm glad you're both active in the church you attend, but isn't there someone else who could—"

"Hey, DeeDee and I are the lucky ones. Most college students don't live within driving distance of their homes. Besides, we have to get back to our jobs." Aaron threw a playful punch at his father's stomach. "Maybe this old man'll help you with the dishes."

Randy let out an exaggerated "ugh" before wrapping his arm around his son's shoulders and pulling him close. "I'm counting on the two of you taking care of each other."

Buck shook hands with his brother, then kissed his little sister's cheek. "Yeah, Aaron, watch after this cute freshman. I know how those college boys can be. I was one of them once," he added with a chuckle. "Come to think of it, maybe I'd better have DeeDee keep an eye on you since you're a freshman, too."

Both Aaron and DeeDee kissed Shonna, then picked up their backpacks from the hall bench and headed for the door.

Sylvia followed them, then kissed each one on the cheek, giving them a hug as she struggled to hold back her tears. "I really hate to see you leave, but I'm so thankful the two of you get home as often as you do. It's just that—"

Grinning, Aaron tapped the tip of his mother's nose. "I know. You love us."

"We love you, too, Mom." DeeDee nudged her father with her hip. "You, too, Dad."

The two stood in the open doorway waving as their two precious children crawled into Aaron's beat-up old van. "Promise you'll drive carefully!" Sylvia called after them before its door slid closed.

"We gotta go, too, Mom." Buck motioned his wife toward the door. "Shonna's parents are expecting us. Can you believe we're gonna eat two Thanksgiving dinners today, and her mom's nearly as good a cook as you?"

Shonna rolled her eyes and pelted her husband with a pillow from the sofa. "Don't let my mom hear you say that, if you expect to win brownie points with her."

Randy and Sylvia watched until Buck's car was out of sight before shutting the door. For the first time since the restaurant incident, she was alone with her husband, and she felt as nervous as a tightrope walker wearing hiking boots.

Randy moved through the family room after grabbing the heavy Thanksgiving edition of the newspaper that lay on the hall table. "I wish the kids hadn't had to rush off. I really miss them and all the noise they make when they're here."

Sylvia followed, scooping up the pillow Shonna had tossed at Buck. With an audible sigh, she placed it back in its proper place on the sofa. "I like the kind of Thanksgivings we used to have, before they grew up. Thanksgivings where we spent the entire day together, just enjoying one another's company." She allowed the corners of her mouth to curl up slightly and managed a nervous chuckle. "I didn't even mind you and the boys spending most of the afternoon in front of the TV watching football."

He gave her another twisted smile; this one she did not understand. Was his demeanor sending up bells of alarm? Signals he hoped she would catch? He seemed nervous, too. Ill at ease. Was he going to tell her that he, also, had to rush off? Was he planning to spend the rest of the day with his girlfriend, now that their children had gone? *Girlfriend?* That word struck horror in her heart and made her lightheaded.

"Those were good days, weren't they?" Randy pulled the newspaper from its bright orange plastic wrapper, tossed it into his recliner chair, then moved into the dining room. As he stared at the table, almost robotically he reached for the salt and pepper shakers and placed them on a tray. "But things change, Syl. People change. Life changes."

What does that mean? She began adding cups and saucers to the tray, eyeing him suspiciously. "My, but you're philosophical today."

Randy nodded but did not comment and continued to add things to the tray. His silence made her edgy. She wanted to reach out and shake him. *Say something. Tell me about your lunch with Chatalaine! Give me some excuse I can believe!* "Would you like another sliver of pumpkin pie?" she asked, biting her tongue to keep from saying something she might later regret. *What is it the scripture says? A tiny spark can ignite a forest fire?*

"No, thanks. It was great, but I'm full." He picked up the tray and headed for the kitchen.

"More coffee? I think there's still some left in the pot." She quickly gathered up the remaining silverware and followed.

"I've had plenty." He placed the tray on the counter, then sat down at the table. "Want me to help you with the dishes?"

Sylvia glanced up at the big, round clock on the kitchen wall. The one Randy had given her for Christmas two years ago. An artist friend of his had painted the words, SYLVIA'S KITCHEN, across the face in bold letters and had even added a tiny picture of her where the twelve should've been. She had cried with joy at the thoughtful gift. Even now, with the tenseness she felt between them, just looking at the clock brought a warm feeling to her heart. "No football on TV?"

He shrugged. "I don't want to watch TV."

She pasted on a smile and counted his options on her fingers. "You don't want pie. You don't want coffee. You don't want to watch the game. But you want to help me with the dishes?"

Randy straightened in his chair and placed both palms flat on the table in front of him, his gaze locking with hers. "What I really want—" He paused and swallowed hard. "Is—is a divorce!"

Chapter 2

Sylvia's breath caught in her throat. All she could do was stare at him in disbelief. Her heart raced and thundered against her chest. *This can't be happening! Please, God, tell me I'm dreaming!*

"I—I didn't want to hurt you, Syl. But I couldn't think of another way to tell you other than just blurting it out like that. I've been trying to tell you for weeks."

He reached for her hand, but she quickly withdrew it and linked her fingers together, dipping her head and turning away from him. She could not bring herself to look at him. Not the way she was feeling. Her legs wobbled beneath her and, afraid they might not hold her up a second longer, she clutched onto the cabinet. *So, what I witnessed in the restaurant and hoped was an innocent lunch was exactly what I suspected? You do have a girlfriend!*

She found herself anchored to the spot—speechless. She had been concerned there was something going on between Randy and Chatalaine. But had it gone this far? *No! Please, God. No!*

"Say something, Syl. Don't just stand there. I hate myself for telling you like this—"

"*You* hate yourself?" She sank onto the kitchen stool and looked up slowly, her shock turning to anger as her heart pounded wildly and her stomach began to lurch. "You can't begin to imagine the feelings of hurt and resentment welling up inside me! Why, Randy? Why? Has our married life been that bad?"

He stood awkwardly and began pacing about the room, his fingers combing through his distinguished-looking graying temples. "Like I said, Syl. Life changes. We change."

Sylvia spun around on the seat. Fear, anger, betrayal bit at her heart, and it felt like a wad in her chest. Her fingers clutched the stool's high back for both support and stability. "Of course things change! The raising of our three children has taken most of my time, while you've been building your career at the newspaper! But our kids are gone now. Out on their own. We finally have the time for ourselves we've always talked about! It's our time now! Yours and mine! Why would you even think about a divorce?" *Say it, Randy. Be a big enough man to tell me you're leaving me for a younger woman!*

He stopped pacing and stood directly in front of her. The pale blue eyes she had always loved, now a cold, icy gray—eyes she barely recognized. He hesitated for what seemed an eternity, then turned away as if to avoid the sight of her. "Our marriage died a long time ago. Have you been so blind you haven't noticed?"

"Have *I* been so blind? Don't try to blame this on me, Randy Benson!" Sylvia felt like she had been sucker punched in the stomach as his words assaulted her and threshed away at her brain. "How stupid do you think I am? You're leaving me for that Chatalaine woman, aren't you?"

He flinched, and she could see he was startled by her mention of the woman's name. "Chatalaine? What made you say that?"

"I—I saw the two of you together." Why couldn't she cry? She wanted to cry, but the tears would not come. It almost seemed as if she were standing outside her body, watching this dreadful scene happen to someone else. "Yo—you've been having an—"

"Me? Having an affair?" He turned and grabbed onto the back of her chair. "I resent that accusation, Syl! How dare you even consider such a thing?"

She leaped to her feet and stood toe-to-toe with him. She wanted him to look at her when he told her his dirty little secrets. "Come on, Randy. Tell me. Admit to your little trysts!"

"Are you crazy? I have no idea what you're talking about."

She felt him cringe as her hands cupped his biceps and her fingers dug into his flesh. "You're a Christian, Randy! How could you?"

"Look, Syl, I'm sure you don't want to hear this, but the two of us—you and I alone—are responsible for the breakup of this marriage. I should have put my foot down—"

She felt the hair stand up on her arms. "Put your foot down? Exactly what do you mean by that?"

He stared at the floor. "Perhaps that was a poor choice of words. What I meant was—" He stopped, as if wanting to make sure his words came out right this time. "I—I should have complained more, instead of holding things back. Keeping things inside."

"Things? What kind of things?"

He gave a defeated shrug. "You were so busy with the kids, you never had time for me. I needed you, Syl, but you shut me out."

"I didn't shut you out, Randy. You were never here long enough to be shut out, or have you forgotten all the days, nights, and weekends you spent at the newspaper? What about the times *I* needed *you*?" she shot back defensively.

"I'd much rather have been at home like you, but as the breadwinner of this family, I didn't have that luxury."

"Oh, and I did have that luxury? Staying home with crying babies, doing a myriad of laundry each week, cooking countless meals, cleaning the house so things would look nice for you when you came home?" She could not remember the last time she had been so angry.

"I didn't want things to turn out like this. I—"

"Don't tell me the devil made you do it!" she shot out at him, suddenly wanting to hurt him as he was hurting her. He tried to back away, but she clung tightly to his arms and would not allow it.

"Syl, don't. You're only making this harder for both of us."

"Don't what? Cry? Scream? Get mad? You don't think you deserve to be screamed at? After what you've just said?" She continued to hold onto him, wanting him to feel her anger and frustration, to see it on her face. She wanted him to sense her fury. To feel her angst. What do you say to a man who just asked you for a divorce, when all this time you've had no idea he's been cheating on you?

He gave her a disgruntled snort. "If I didn't know better, I'd say you were jealous, but I don't think you care enough to be jealous."

She jammed her hand onto her hip. "Oh? Does that question mean I have a reason to be jealous?"

"Of course not. I was referring to your attitude."

She continued to hold tightly to his arms, sure that if she ever let him go, it would be for good. She could not bear the idea of life without him. She inhaled a deep breath and let it out slowly, begging God to give her the right words to say and the right way to react, to make her beloved husband come to his senses. Why didn't he come right out and tell her about Chatalaine? That she was the real reason he wanted out?

After an interminable silence, she willed herself to calm down and said, trying to mask her disillusionment, "We can't do this, Randy. Divorce is not an option. We've both invested way too much in this marriage to give up on it now. Please, don't do anything you'll regret later. Have you prayed about this?"

He gently pried her fingers from his arm and walked away, turning when he reached the door to the hallway. "My mind is made up, Syl. For weeks, I have been trying to muster up the courage to do this. Now that I have finally said it, I am going to go through with it. You'll survive. I will continue to provide for you. I—I just want out."

"Would you pray with me about it?" she asked in desperation.

He shook his head. "No."

"Is Chatalaine married?"

"What's she got to do with this?"

His puzzled look infuriated her.

"You thought I didn't know your dirty little secret, didn't you?" she spat back, glowering at him.

"What secret?"

She felt her nostrils flare and her heart palpitate. "Come on, Randy, tell me about your lunch with your *client*! The one with the bleached blond hair and long, shapely legs that go up to her armpits. Did you make a sale? Is your social columnist going to purchase advertising with your precious newspaper because of your charms and your flawless sales pitch?"

He crossed the room quickly and grabbed onto her wrist, his nose close to hers. "Look, Syl. I have no idea what you're talking about. Yes, I had lunch with Chatalaine. A perfectly innocent lunch. The client called on my cell phone just before I reached the restaurant and said he couldn't make it. Since her column runs on the front page of that section and I was planning to pitch a succession of ads in the "Dallas Life" section, I thought it would be helpful to have Chatalaine there." He turned loose and stepped back with a shake of his head. "You're barking up the wrong tree if you're trying to accuse me of being unfaithful."

Like she always did when she was upset, Sylvia gnawed nervously on her lower lip, biting back words she knew she would be sorry for later if they escaped. *Is it possible I could have been wrong? Was it an innocent lunch like he said?*

"Face it, Syl. Another woman didn't break up our marriage. It's been dying for years, and we've both contributed to its death by ignoring it. I've realized it for some time. Maybe, if you were honest with yourself, you'd admit it, too. All we've been doing is marking time."

Divorce? That meant Randy would be leaving. She gasped at the paralyzing thought. "You're—you're not moving out, are you? Christmas is coming and the whole family will be—"

"There'll never be a good time. If there was, I'd have left months ago." He backed toward the hall again, as if wanting to put distance between the two of them, to pull away from her and all she represented.

This may be your only chance to try to save your marriage, she cautioned herself as she stared at the only man she'd ever loved. *Be careful what you say. Words, once said, can never be taken back.* "Please, Randy," she began, trying to add a softness to her voice when, inside, a storm was raging. "Give our marriage another chance. Just tell me what I'm doing wrong, and I'll change. I don't want you to leave. I—I love you!"

He did not look up. "I've worked long, hard hours for this family; now it's time for me. I'm going to get out and enjoy myself. Do some things I've put off for way too long."

His indifference broke her heart. "You could still do those things—"

"No." Keeping his gaze away from her face, he frowned and pursed his lips. "It's too late, Syl. I'm moving out. I packed up most of my personal things this morning while you were in the kitchen. I'll come back for the rest later."

Heaviness pressed against her heart and made it difficult to speak. "Yo–you're moving in with that woman?"

He gave her a look of annoyance. "No! Haven't you heard a word I've said?"

She rushed toward him and grabbed onto his arm, her fingernails nearly piercing the flesh. "You can't go! I won't let you!"

He pulled her hand away and rubbed at the red marks on his arm. "Hurting you is the last thing I wanted to do, Syl, but I can't keep living like this. The only fair way was to tell you this so we could both get on with our lives."

"Get *on* with our lives? How can I live without you, Randy? You expect me to believe you're not leaving me for another woman? Not for Chatalaine?"

His doubled up fist hit the palm of his other hand as his face filled with anger. "How many times do I have to tell you, Syl? There *is* no other woman! My lunch with Chatalaine was a legitimate, business-related luncheon, and I resent the idea that you would even think I'm cheating on you! Whatever happened to trust?"

"Trust? You ask *me* about trust?" Seeing the strange look in his eyes made her wonder at his words. Was that look guilt? Was he using anger and indignation to cover up his philandering? "Can you look me in the eye, Randy, and tell me this was the first time you and that woman have had lunch together?"

He did not have to answer. His face told it all.

"We've had lunch a few times but only to discuss her column—and those were on days you cancelled on me at the last minute because you were called to serve on some committee at the church or had to take a casserole to a sick person. You were always doing something for someone else when I needed you. Don't try to blame this on Chatalaine and a few business lunches."

Why hadn't she kept her mouth shut? "You're—you're really going through with this? Couldn't we maybe just have a separation for a while, so you can make sure you really want this before you take legal action?"

He gave her a flip of his hand. "A separation? Why? We've been living separate lives for years. I can't even remember the last time we—" He stopped midsentence.

His words hurt, and as badly as she hated to admit it, he was right. They'd both been so busy; they'd either been dead tired at the end of the day, she'd had one of her migraine headaches, or one of them had gone to bed early. But weren't there other ways of expressing your love other than physical? She had always thought taking good care of their children had been an act of love toward Randy. Keeping his house in perfect order and making sure his shirts were starched and ironed the way he liked them, to her, spoke of her love and adoration. Having good, nourishing meals on the table—sometimes having to reheat them because he got home late—all of those things and dozens of others were ways of saying *I love you*, weren't they?

"The children will have to be told," he said so matter-of-factly it only added to her already frazzled nerves.

She stepped back and crossed her arms over her chest, staring at him and seeing a stranger. "This is your party, Randy. Are you going to do the gentlemanly thing and tell them, or are you going to wait and let them find out for themselves? They'll hate you, you know."

"I'm hoping they won't hate me."

"They will. Our sons have always looked up to you as their role model. You've certainly fallen off that pedestal."

"I'll tell them," he murmured softly.

Sylvia pushed past him, rushed into the family room, afraid if she stood on her feet another minute she'd collapse.

Randy followed.

She shrugged and released a hefty sigh. "They say the wife is always the last to know. I guess that's because loving wives like me trust their husbands." She sat down quickly on the cushy green leather sofa, the one the two of them had selected together to commemorate their twentieth anniversary, and rubbed her hands over its smooth surface. "You certainly had me fooled. I thought we were getting along fine. I loved our life together."

He moved to the matching recliner, the roomier one they had specialty-ordered as his chair. But Sylvia reached out her hand and hollered, "Stop!"

He abruptly stepped to one side, giving her a puzzled look. "Stop what?"

She blinked her tear-filled eyes and pointed her finger at him defiantly. "Don't you dare sit in that chair! That chair is reserved for the head of this house. That wonderful, godly man I married. That description no longer fits you!"

Randy scooted over to a small, upholstered chair. "How about here?"

She nodded, feeling a bit chagrined, but he had to face reality. The breaking up of their marriage was something *he* wanted, not her.

Neither spoke for several minutes.

"I do love you, you know," she said finally, the tears now beginning to flow down her cheeks unashamedly. "I've always loved you. There's never been anyone else. Only you. Even if I haven't shown it much."

Randy hung his head and smoothed at the arm cover on the club chair. "I loved you, too, but—"

"But you no longer love me? Is that it?"

"I guess."

She glared at him, his answers not at all what she wanted to hear. "For a man who just asked his wife of twenty-five years for a divorce, you sure do a lot of guessing! Tell me outright, Randy. Do you or do you not love me?"

"I love you as the mother of my children," he said weakly, "and I care about you."

She bit at her lip until it hurt. "But you no longer love me as your wife? Your soul mate? Your lover? Is that the reason you never hug me anymore? Or touch me like you used to? Is that what you're saying?"

"I gu—yes."

"When did you make this amazing discovery? Before or after that woman came into your life?" She rose slowly, crossed the room, and knelt beside him. She had to find a way to make him change his mind. "Look into my eyes, Randy. See the pain I'm feeling. Think about the times we've shared together over the past twenty-five years—times both good and bad. Think about the struggles we've gone through together. And, yes, think about the times we've expressed our love for one another, though they may have been few lately. Then tell me. Tell me you don't love me anymore. Say the words. Convince me."

His gaze went to his lap, and for long moments, he stared at his hands, methodically checking one fingernail at a time before he looked up at her. "I think whatever love I felt for you is gone, Syl, and has been for some time."

Those words cut so deeply, Sylvia was sure they had actually punctured her flesh and her blood was pouring from the cuts they had inflicted. Slowly, she stood and pulled herself up tall. She had to be strong even though her heart was breaking. Strong for herself and strong for her family, what there was left of it.

"If you're sure that's the way you feel and you're not willing to give our marriage another chance, then go, Randy. Go now. Give up the life the two of us made together. Give up your children, your home. Just remember, it was you who broke up this family. I have God to turn to, but I doubt very seriously He'll want to hear from you, unless it's to ask His forgiveness for what you're doing." She moved quickly to the double glass doors leading onto the patio, sliding one side open before she turned to face him again, her lips trembling. "It's your decision."

Without a word, Randy stood, started to say something but didn't, then hesitantly moved through the door and onto the porch.

Sylvia slid the door closed behind him and twisted the lock, shutting it on twenty-five years of marriage.

Chapter 3

Sylvia rushed to the narrow window beside the front door and pulled back the drapery just far enough to be able to watch Randy as he walked to his car, climbed in, started the engine, and drove away without even a backward glance. It was as though her very life ended with his departure. She wanted to pray, to ask God to bring her husband back to her, but the words would not come. It seemed even God had walked out on her. How could He have let this happen to their marriage?

Now what? Should she cry? No, she was too mad to cry. Throw things? Call the pastor? Go to bed and pull the covers over her head?

In robotic fashion, too numb to do anything, she moved to his recliner where the holiday edition of the *Dallas Times* still lay unrolled. How many times had she actually read the society column in the "Dallas Life" section? Probably not more than a dozen in all the years Randy had worked for the newspaper. Although her husband was constantly involved with community activities since he had been appointed managing editor, they rarely attended social functions together.

Maybe we should have, she told herself numbly as she lugged the heavy newspaper into the kitchen and poured herself that last cup of coffee before unplugging the pot. *Maybe that's one of the areas of Randy's life where I should have been more involved.* She tried to remember. *Did he ever ask me to go to one of those functions and I refused? Unfortunately, now that I think about it, he did. A number of times. But I had no interest in such things, and he never pressed the issue when I said no. If he felt they were important, he should have mentioned it instead of going on alone.* Her cup hit the table with a loud clunk, spattering coffee over the gingham placemat. *He went on without me!* That realization made her insides quiver. *I should have been with him! I should have bought that new dress he suggested and gone along, despite my lack of interest! For Randy's sake! Have I actually taken him for granted all these years, like he said? Is it my fault he's turned to someone else?*

She grabbed the dishrag from the sink and dabbed at the spilled coffee before settling down in the chair with the newspaper. Before she had seen her with Randy, she had never given much thought to Chatalaine. To her, the woman was just one of the many employees who worked for him. A columnist. Nothing more.

Until now.

Now, she was reasonably sure Chatalaine Vicker was the reason their marriage was about to end.

Sylvia thumbed through the paper, discarding section after section, until she came to the one marked "Dallas Life." There, glaring out at her with what she now perceived as a smirk instead of a smile, was the lovely, young face of Chatalaine Vicker, her nemesis.

Suddenly, feelings and emotions hitherto foreign to Sylvia came racing to the surface, and she wanted to go to that woman and scratch her eyes out. The woman who apparently wanted her husband and was more than likely willing to do whatever it took to get him. Did Randy really expect her to believe he wanted to leave her simply to find himself?

Blinking hard and trying to focus her eyes through the tears and terror she felt, she looked at the photograph again. She had to admit the woman was beautiful. The colorful picture, taking up a good portion of the first two columns, showed a full-length, enticingly posed view of Chatalaine's gorgeous, willowy figure as she stood leaning against a wall, her long arms crossed over her chest, a captivating smile adorning her perfectly made-up face. Even her name looked captivating, spread across the top of the page in an elegant, sprawling script. *What woman has a name like Chatalaine?*

Sylvia looked from the picture, to the half-empty cup of coffee, back to the picture, and back to the cup again. "Here's to you, you home wrecker!" she told the print version of her adversary as she slowly poured the remaining hot, black coffee over Chatalaine's face and body. "You wanted him. It looks like you got him! And I never even knew we were competing."

The ringing of the phone startled her, and the cup fell from her hands as she leaped to answer it, spilling the last few drops of coffee onto the floor. *Oh dear God, let it be Randy calling to tell me it was all a joke!* "Hello!" she said eagerly into the phone, smiling and brushing away a tear.

"Hi. Just wanted to wish you a happy Thanksgiving."

She recognized the voice immediately. It was their pastor's wife, who was also her best friend. Sylvia's heart sank. "Hi, Jen."

"Hey, you don't sound so good. Are you coming down with a cold? Your voice sounds husky."

I can't tell her. Not yet. Not until I've had a chance to think this through. Do I want my church friends to know my husband has just asked me for a divorce? "May—maybe I am. I'm really not feeling up to par." She struggled to keep her words even, free of the raging emotions whirling inside her, when what she really wanted to do was cry out for sympathy. If she felt she could tell anyone, it would be Jen. But not now. Not yet.

"So? Is your family gathered around the TV set watching the game like my family is?"

Sylvia swallowed at the lump in her throat that nearly gagged her. Oh, how she wished they were in front of the TV. "No, DeeDee and Aaron both had to go back to college, to help out with the youth lock-in, and Buck and Shonna are spending the rest of the day with her parents."

"I'll bet Randy is glued to the set. I think the teams are tied. There's so much whooping and hollering going on in the other room, I can barely hear you."

"Ah—no. Randy isn't here. He—he had to—ah to go down to the newspaper office." Although Sylvia had worked hard all her life at either telling the truth or just remaining silent, she felt she had to lie to protect Randy, still hoping he would change his mind and come home.

"On a holiday? Isn't that asking a bit much of the guy?"

"Ah—that's what happens—when you're the managing editor, I guess."

"Poor boy. His body may be at the paper, but I'll bet his mind is wishing he was there with you."

"I hope so." This time Sylvia's words were honest. She did hope he was wishing he was there with her, but after his dogged determination to get away from her, she doubted it.

"Well, that's all I called you for. To wish you a happy Thanksgiving and tell you that we love the two of you. So many folks in our congregation are experiencing marital troubles. It's refreshing to talk to someone who has accomplished twenty-five years of marital bliss. You two are a real inspiration to the rest of us."

Sylvia felt sick to her stomach as she clung to the phone with clammy hands, feeling like an imposter. "Ha–happy Thanksgiving to you, too, Jen. Thanks for calling."

After pressing the OFF button and placing the phone back on the table, she sat staring at it with unseeing eyes. *Marital bliss? That's what I'd thought it was, too, but apparently, Randy thought otherwise.*

She glanced around the room, noting the stacks of dirty dishes still waiting to be loaded into the dishwasher, the roaster with the remnants of her famous pepper gravy clinging to its sides, and the pile of silverware she'd set aside to be washed by hand—the silverware she only used for special occasions. As she idly picked up a serving spoon, she had to laugh, despite her feelings of loneliness and despair. *Special occasions? Your husband asking you for a divorce is definitely a special occasion—one in which you never expect to be a participant.*

Placing her flattened palms onto the tabletop for support, she stood with agonizing stiffness, propelled herself one laborious step at a time across the spacious kitchen to the sink, and began to rinse the plates and place them in the dishwasher. Doing it the same way she had done hundreds of times before, but, this time, her mind was far from what she was doing.

Where is Randy this very moment? With that woman?

The question made bile rise in her throat. She picked up one of the delicate crystal goblets Randy had given her on their twentieth anniversary and flung it against the stone fireplace in the corner of the room. The glass shattered, sending shiny shards across the highly polished tile floor. Those glasses had been her prized possession, and she had always washed and dried them by hand to make sure none were ever broken. But today, somehow, the sound of breaking glass felt like a balm poured over her tormented soul.

Is he holding her hand?

A second glass hit the fireplace.

Is he holding Chatalaine in his arms?

The third glass missed its mark and broke against the wall, but she did not care. It was the sound she needed to hear.

Is he kissing that woman?

The fourth and fifth glasses broke simultaneously as she hurled one from each hand toward the fireplace. Sylvia jumped up and down, clapping her hands and laughing hysterically, relieving some of her pent-up tension in this unorthodox manner.

The last two glasses soon joined the others, and they all lay broken on the tile floor, their fragile beauty forever destroyed.

She stood for a long time, mesmerized as she stared at the broken pieces. Somehow, they symbolized the end of her marriage. Her dream. Her life. She wanted to turn and flee from the house she loved. The walls were permeated with memories. Memories she cherished. But today those memories seemed to haunt her, to ridicule her. To tell her she was a fool and a failure. If she had been the wife Randy had wanted, would he have been so easily lured away by that beautiful woman? It was a question she knew she would ask herself time and time again in the weeks to come. *I didn't have a chance,* she reasoned, looking for any excuse to absolve herself and her part in the failure of their marriage. *What woman wouldn't be attracted to Randy? He's not only handsome, he's witty, charming, and highly successful.*

Her thoughts went to Chatalaine and how beautiful she had looked at the restaurant. Her gorgeous blond hair falling softly over her shoulders, her designer suit fitting her like wallpaper, displaying her perfect figure to the fullest advantage, her long slender legs, and fashionable high heels. The striking woman was a walking, talking, real-live Barbie doll.

Finally, willing herself to move, she pulled the dustpan and broom from the pantry, trudged across the kitchen floor, and began to sweep up the mess. Her body became as still as a mannequin when she heard the front door open and close. *Randy?*

"Mom, what happened?"

Disappointed it was not Randy, she turned to face her oldest son, sure that, after what she had been through, she must look like a mess. Even without checking the mirror, she knew her dampened mascara must have left dark streaks down her cheeks, her eyes had to be swollen from crying, and probably her nose was red from rubbing it across her sleeve.

Before she could stop them, two words escaped her lips. "Dad's gone!" She ran to Buck and buried her face in his chest, sudden sobs racking at her body, causing short gasps for air. Everything she had been holding back came gushing forth.

"Gone? What do you mean—*gone*? Is he hurt? Is he at the hospital? Did he have a wreck?" He grabbed onto her arms and pushed her away, staring into her face. "Mom! Tell me! What?"

Sucking in a deep breath, she blurted out, "He—he wants a divorce!"

"What?" Buck began to shake his head. "No, not my dad! He'd never do anything like that. Why are you saying this, Mom? Why?"

"He *is* doing it, Buck. I tried to talk him out of it, but—"

Buck doubled up a fist and plowed it into the palm of his other hand, looking eerily like his father. "It's another woman, isn't it?"

Sylvia nodded as she lowered her head and worked at keeping fresh tears at bay. "He says it isn't."

"That woman at the paper?"

Her eyes widened with surprise. "How did you know she was the one?"

Buck moved to the counter and checked the coffeepot. Finding it empty, he crossed to the cabinet, took out a glass, filled it with water, and took a long, slow drink before setting the empty glass in the sink. "I saw them together," he said, his back still to his mother.

She ran to him and circled her arms around his waist, pressing her face into his strong back. "Oh Buck, no. You didn't."

He pulled her arms from about him and slowly turned to face her. "It seemed perfectly innocent at the time. I was having lunch with a friend at a little restaurant over in Arlington, and who walks in? Dad, with some woman."

"Did he know you were there?" she asked cautiously, wishing her son had not been forced to become a part of this fiasco.

"Yeah. I waited until they were seated and walked over to them. He introduced her as one of his employees—Catherine, Katrina—something like that. He said they had driven to Arlington to meet with some advertisers, and since it was lunchtime, they decided to have a bite to eat before driving back into Dallas. I believed him then, but now—with Dad talking about divorce, well, I just don't know."

Sylvia covered her face with her hands and tried to control her rekindled rage. "Oh Buck. Why didn't you tell me? Give me a warning."

He patted her shoulder. "I tried not to give it a second thought. I wanted to believe him and his explanation seemed logical, the way women hold so many managerial positions nowadays."

She examined her heart. "I probably wouldn't have believed you even if you'd brought me back a Polaroid shot of him kissing her. I would've figured out a way to explain it. I trusted him."

"I—I asked Dad later if that was the real reason he was with her."

"You did? What did he say?" Did she really want to hear his answer?

"He really blew up at me. He told me I was a young punk with wild ideas, and he was insulted that I would even consider him being unfaithful to you. I felt like a jerk. He is my dad. The one I've looked up to all my life!"

"He says I should have seen it coming. That I'm to blame in all of this as much as he is." She slipped an arm around her son and hugged him tight. "I guess, if I'd had my eyes open, I should've seen it coming. He's been different for the past few months. Quiet and reserved sometimes, even spacey. Sometimes he was here—yet he wasn't. I should have read the signs. If only I'd—"

"Don't let him do that to you, Mom. Face it. Dad might be a Christian, but he's still a man. A mere mortal. We're all at risk for doing things we know we shouldn't." He gave her a smile that warmed her cold heart and began to melt some of the ice that had begun to form there. "You've been a terrific mom and, from my vantage point, the perfect wife. I can't imagine any woman being able to take your place."

Take my place? Oh Lord—please—no! She mustered up a smile in return, not wanting him to know how much that phrase upset her. She was grateful for his words of consolation and encouragement, but his last words had pierced her soul. "Thanks, sweetie, but you've seen her. You know how beautiful she is. And young! I can't compete with Chatalaine Vicker."

"Hey Mom, don't talk that way. You're a real knockout." He gave her chin a playful jab. "Get yourself a bottle of bleach and turn that brown hair of yours into a ditzy blond, take off a few pounds here and there, hit the makeup counters, add a couple of sexy, low-cut dresses and a pair of spike-heeled shoes, and she wouldn't have a chance at taking Dad away from you."

His humor cut through some of the insecurities she was feeling, and she laughed. But her laughter was soon overshadowed by the continual ache in her heart. "I wish I could convince myself it was merely her good looks that drew him to her, but I'm afraid it's much more than that."

Buck frowned, causing deep wrinkles in his forehead. "You—you don't think they're having—"

She reached up and quickly put her hand over his mouth. "Shh, don't even think it."

Buck gently pulled her hand away. "Would you take him back? After the way he's hurt you?"

"Of course I would," she answered without hesitation. "On our wedding day, I promised before God that I was marrying your father for life, and I meant it. We both said, 'For better and for worse.' God never promised marriage would be easy, Buck."

Buck gave her that shy grin again. "But you had no idea how much worse, *worse* could be or that Dad would do something this bizarre. I'm going to ask Shonna to lock me in the closet if I ever start showing signs of a midlife crisis."

"Buck!" She giggled at his inane comment. "No, I never thought we'd have a problem like this, but I knew I'd have God by my side to help me work out the rough spots. I may have been young, but I wasn't stupid," she added through fresh tears. "I knew what I was vowing. I thought your father did, too."

He grinned a silly little grin. "You do know you look like a raccoon, don't you, Mom?"

She hurried to the little mirror on the back of the pantry door and gazed at her ridiculous reflection, summoning up a smile for his benefit. "I knew I looked bad, but not this bad! Why didn't you tell me?"

"I think you're kinda cute."

She grabbed a dishrag from the drawer, dampened it at the faucet, and began rubbing at the black circles and streaks around her eyes and down her cheeks. "What are you doing here anyway? I thought you and Shonna were spending the rest of the day at her parents' house."

"We are. I left my billfold in the bathroom after that fabulous Thanksgiving dinner you cooked. I came back to get it."

She patted his arm affectionately. "I'm glad you did. I needed someone to talk to. It seems God isn't listening to me."

"Come on, Mom, you know that's not true."

"If He is, why isn't He making your dad come back home where he belongs?"

"Who says He's not trying to convince him to do just that?"

She gestured around the room with a broad sweep of her hand. "Do you see your father here?"

He grabbed it and linked his fingers with hers. "You don't believe

God is dealing with Dad? Think about it, Mom. Our father is giving up everything. You know he's got to realize, eventually, he's making a stupid mistake. You have to turn this over to God. Hasn't He promised He'd never leave you or forsake you?"

She pulled her hand free and cradled his chin. "My wonderful, well-grounded son. God does answer prayer. He already has."

He frowned. "What do you mean?"

"He made you leave your billfold in the bathroom, otherwise, why would you have come back here—just when I needed you?"

"See? I told you God answers prayer."

She had to smile at the silly expression on his face. What a joy Buck had been to her since the day he was born. "Yes, He does."

"What now, Mom? Are you going to tell DeeDee and Aaron?"

She crossed the kitchen, seated herself at the table, and began fumbling with the colorful basket of silk flowers she had put together in a craft class at the church. "Not yet. I don't want your brother and sister to know until it's absolutely necessary. And, please, don't tell anyone else about this—except Shonna of course. I don't want there to be any secrets between the two of you, but ask her to keep this to herself until I'm ready to let everyone know. I want your father to have plenty of time to change his mind. If everyone knows, he'll be embarrassed, and I can't let that happen. Let's give him some time, okay?"

Buck planted a kiss on his mother's cheek. "My faithful, forgiving mother. What a treasure you are. I only hope Dad comes to his senses and realizes it before it's too late."

"Your father needs your prayers, Buck. So do I."

He kissed the tip of her nose. "You got them, both of you."

"Now," she said, trying to put up a brave front and pointing toward the door. "Go to your wife and enjoy what's left of your Thanksgiving Day."

"You gonna be all right? I can stay with you. Shonna will understand."

"I'm going to be fine. I'll call if I need you."

He pulled his cell phone from his belt and held it toward her. "You've got my number?"

She stood on tiptoe and kissed her son's chin. "Yes, I have your number. Go."

As he strode out the door, Sylvia kept the smile on her face, but the minute the door closed behind him, it disappeared, and the feelings of misery and betrayal she had endeavored to squash down deep inside rose to the surface. *Oh dear God—what a mess we've made of our lives. Only You can straighten this out.*

After sweeping up the broken glass, she took a long, leisurely shower and let the hot water run over her face and body, washing away her tears, until she could stand it no longer. She toweled off and slipped into her pajamas, then dried her hair with the blow dryer and stared into the mirror. Though she fit nicely into a size twelve, her proportions were nothing like Chatalaine's. Giving birth and nursing her children had seen to that. Everything had gone south. She glanced at her reflection and the worn flannel pajamas—the comfortable ones she wore more often than any of her others—and thought about the three delicate, lacy nightgowns she had in her bureau drawer. The ones Randy had bought for her the past three Valentine's Days. Two of them still had the tags on them. The third had only been laundered twice. Why hadn't she worn them? Hadn't Randy told her he had bought them for her because he thought she would look beautiful in them?

Finding it difficult to pray and wondering how God could have let this happen to her, she muttered a few thank-yous, asked God to send Randy home where he belonged, and added a quick, "Amen." Many of the things Randy had mentioned, things that took her away from him, were things she had done at the church. For God. Is this the way He was rewarding her for her labors? By allowing her husband to walk out of her life?

As though God Himself were speaking to her, in her heart she heard, *"It wasn't Me that let him go, My child. You turned your back on him and let other things take over your life and become more important than the relationship between the two of you."*

"But God," she cried out. "Everything I've done has been for a good cause. The church activities. The children. Their school functions. Teaching my Sunday school class. Leading the women's prayer group. Heading up the Care and Share pantry. I did all of those things for You!"

"None of it for your own glory? None of it when you should have been with your husband, being a helpmeet to him? When you made those vows before Me, you promised to do many things. Have you honored all of those promises, My daughter?"

Sylvia stared at the Bible on her nightstand, remembering their wedding and the way the two of them had placed their hands on a Bible when they had made those vows. "But Lord, Randy made those same vows. He's the one who is breaking them, not me! It's not fair that he's expecting me to take part of the blame."

"Examine your own heart, daughter. Examine your own heart."

After turning out the light, she lay in the darkness, thinking. Pondering the words God had spoken to her. How many times in the past five years had her husband seemed aloof? Distant. Sometimes acting as if he had no interest in her *or* the children. Had an affair been going on right under her nose, and she had been so absorbed with her life she hadn't noticed? Looking back, the signs had been there. She just had not seen them—or cared enough to see them. The late nights at the office. Sudden trips to the newspaper on weekends to take care of some insignificant problem that cropped up. Calling at the last minute to say he couldn't attend one of the children's school functions. He claimed he was doing those things because of increased competition from both his competitors and the way more people were watching television news to keep them informed rather than the newspapers. Even on the few nights he was home, he would hole up in the den most of the evening and work at the computer. At least, she had *thought* he was working on the computer. Perhaps, instead, he had been talking to Chatalaine on that online Instant Message thing.

Had those excuses been simply that? Excuses to find a way to get out of the house? Away from her? Maybe to meet Chatalaine?

She flipped over onto her side with a groan, her tears flowing again. This would be Randy's first night of staying away from home. Was he having feelings of exhilaration? Or was he, too, feeling pangs of loneliness? She shuddered at how awful it felt being in bed alone. Surely, he was telling her the truth. That nothing was going on between him and that woman. *God, please keep him pure. Don't let him succumb to fleshly desires.*

Without Randy by her side, the bed seemed big. Overpowering. Like an angry giant. She closed her eyes and flattened her hand on his pillow, trying to convince herself that he would be there when she opened them.

He wasn't.

She tugged his pillow to her, drinking in the lingering fragrance of his aftershave and relishing its scent, draping her arm over it much as she did over Randy each night after they turned out the lights. *Oh Randy. I love you so much. How will I ever live without you? You're my very life!*

Chapter 4

The last time Sylvia remembered looking at the clock on her nightstand, it was 5:00 a.m. She awakened at eight, feeling like she'd not slept at all, with the sheets askew, and the lovely old nine-patch quilt half off on the floor.

Randy!

She flipped over, her hand quickly moving to his pillow.

But Randy wasn't there.

It hadn't been a bad dream.

He had really left her.

Laboriously, she made the bed, dragging herself from side to side, though why, she didn't know. An unmade bed was the least of her worries. She brushed her teeth and ran a comb through her hair out of habit, not really caring how she looked. Visions of the long-legged blond on the front of the "Dallas Life" section of the newspaper blurred her brain and made her woozy. Her three children had left home. Buck to get married, and Aaron and DeeDee to attend college. Now Randy, her life's mate, was gone, too, and for the first time ever—she was alone. Really alone. Since she and Randy had married so young, she had gone directly from her parents' home to their little apartment, with no stops in between.

She stood at the window for a long time, gazing into the backyard. With all her busyness, she had even neglected the flowerbeds she had at one time loved. When was the last time she had weeded and fertilized them? Even the perennials had quit blooming. If it weren't for the faithful geraniums, there would be no blooming flowers at all. Thanks to them and their endurance, every few feet a tiny blast of red spotted the otherwise colorless flowerbeds. She winced at the thought. Was her marriage like those flowerbeds? Had she let other things, like the weeds growing so prevalently, go unattended, get in the way, and crowd out the important things of her life until they had withered and died? At the thought, her stomach again turned nauseous, and for a moment, she reeled, clutching the windowsill for support. *Oh Randy. How could I have taken our life for granted? How could I have taken you for granted? Did I really drive you into that woman's arms?*

Moving slowly into their walk-in closet to pull out her favorite pair of jeans, she froze. Except for a few garments he never wore, Randy's side of the closet was empty. Even the hangers were gone. Shoeboxes no longer filled the long shelves above the rods. No more beautiful designer ties hung from his tie racks. Even the prized rifle his father had given him when he was sixteen no longer stood in the corner behind the clothing where he had kept it so it would be out of sight of the children. Standing on tiptoe, she reached up and ran her hand along the top shelf, in search of the little .25 caliber pistol he always kept there in case an intruder entered their home.

It, too, was gone!

Randy was gone!

Everything was gone!

Her heart thudded to a sudden stop. Surely, he wouldn't do anything foolish! Not her levelheaded Randy!

But the Randy who had told her he was leaving wasn't her levelheaded Randy. He was a stranger wearing Randy's body. She only thought she had known him. This new Randy was an unknown entity, and she had no idea what he might be capable of doing. *Oh Randy, Randy! If only you would've told me a long time ago how unhappy you were with our marriage, maybe—* She banged her head against the window jamb, but it was too numb even to feel the pain. *If I'd been any kind of attentive wife to you, I should've known. Looking back now, I can see the signs. I'd attributed your silence to you having things on your mind about the paper. All those times when you seemed aloof, I'd thought you were tired. The many times you sat staring at the walls, I assumed you were too physically and mentally exhausted to talk. Were you deliberately ignoring me because you simply no longer wanted to be around me? How could I have been so blind? Why didn't I ask you if something was wrong? Were you seeing Chatalaine even then?*

The image of the elegant woman popped into her mind, uninvited, when she moved toward the bed, pausing at the full-length mirror on the way. Her breath caught and nearly gagged her as she stared at her reflection. *Can this be me? Where is that young woman my husband used to admire? The one whose hair was brown and shiny, instead of dull and graying? The one who was twenty pounds lighter and cared about her figure? Who always put her makeup on first thing in the morning and went out of her way to kiss her husband good-bye when he left for work? The one who hung on his every word, making sure she was there whenever he needed her?* She glanced down at her faded jeans and the well-worn T-shirt that had become the *uniform* she crawled into when she came home from one of her functions, eager to make herself comfortable. *When did I decide it was no longer necessary to look my best at the end of the day when Randy came home from work? When did I become so careless?*

Grabbing her robe from the chair where she had left it, she draped it over the mirror, shutting out the image that threatened to destroy what little self-esteem she had left. But it didn't help. The reflection remained etched on her memory, and she did not like the feeling.

She had to talk to Randy. To beg him to come back home where he belonged.

"Good morning. *Dallas Times*. If you know your party's extension, you may enter it now, otherwise listen to the complete list of options before making your selection," the canned recording said when she dialed the phone. She punched in the numbers by rote and waited for him to answer.

"Good morning. Randy Benson's office. This is Carol. May I ask who's calling?"

Instantly, Sylvia realized she had dialed the extension for Randy's office and not his direct line. "Ah—Carol—this is Sylvia. May I speak to Randy?"

"I'm sorry, Sylvia. He isn't in. He's in meetings over in Arlington most of the day. I don't expect him back until late this afternoon."

A meeting in Arlington or another one of his rendezvous?

"When he's out of the office, he usually checks in with me several times a day. Would you like me to have him phone home?"

"Yes, would you, please? I'll—I'll be here all day. I really need to talk to him."

"Would you like me to try and reach him?"

"No, just tell him when you hear from him." She thanked the woman, then hit the OFF button, and placed the phone back onto the charger, disappointed.

She had no more than lifted her hand from it, when it rang. She snatched it up, both hoping it was Randy, yet not sure what she would say if he did call. "Hello."

"Hi, Mom. I've been concerned about you. Are you okay? Do you want me to come over?"

As much as she loved hearing her oldest son's voice, she was filled with disappointment. "No, honey, I'm—I'm okay. Just depressed."

"I love you, Mom. You know I'll come if you need me."

She smiled into the phone. At least her son still loved her. "No, I don't want you taking off work. Don't worry about me, sweetie. I'm still hoping, praying, somehow this will all work out."

"I still want to call Dad."

"I know, but please don't. Let's make it as easy as possible for your father to come back home, and I don't want there to be any rifts between the two of you."

"Okay, but if you—"

"I know, and thanks, Buck. Get back to your job. Your mother will survive."

"Survive?" she repeated aloud when she hung up the phone. "I'm not so sure I *will* survive or even want to if Randy doesn't come back home."

She busied herself doing several loads of laundry, weeping when she pulled a couple of Randy's favorite shirts from the hamper. Her tears fell softly onto the fabric when she cradled them close, the faint aroma of his aftershave tantalizing her nostrils. When the last piece had been pulled from the dryer and folded, she closed the laundry room door and made her way into the kitchen, checking the clock as she moved to the refrigerator and pulled out a bottle of cranberry juice. It was nearly noon, and she hadn't eaten a bite of breakfast or even had a glass of water.

Why hasn't he called? Surely, Carol has heard from him by now.

She jumped for the phone when it rang about three, but it was not Randy calling; it was Buck, checking on her again.

An hour later, a telemarketer called, offering to give her an estimate on siding. Normally, she listened courteously to their spiel before saying, "No thank you," and hanging up, but not this time. This time his call infuriated her, and she cut him off right after his "Are you the home-owner?" question.

For the next hour, she sat staring at the phone.

But it didn't ring.

Nor did it ring at six, or seven, eight, nine, ten, or eleven, other than two more calls from Buck.

When the doorbell rang at half past eight the next morning, she rushed to answer it, stubbing her toe on the ottoman on the way, but it was the UPS man bringing a package. Something Randy had ordered from a computer supply company.

Other than Buck's regular concerned calls, the phone did not ring a single time on Saturday, and Sylvia found herself in a deep pit of de-pression with the walls closing in on her. Why didn't Randy call? If only he had left the phone number where he would be staying. She was tempted to look up Chatalaine Vicker's number in the phonebook but decided against it. Whether Randy was at her place or not, he would be furious with her for checking up on him. She tried watching TV to keep her mind off him, but that didn't work. Next, she pulled out the quilt she had started when their children were small and had never finished. Maybe the rhythm of working the needle would help sooth her jagged nerves, but she found she had misplaced her thimble, so she returned it to its box in the family room closet. The novel in her bedside chest held no more interest than it had a day or two before and ended up back in the drawer.

In desperation, she turned to her Bible for solace, but even it did not help. A bookmark fell out onto the bed as she closed its cover. Her gaze locked on the quotation printed there in a beautiful script. Its message ripped her heart to shreds. "*Love thrives in the face of all life's hazards, ex-cept one.*" *Neglect.* The words ricocheted through her being, replaying over and over, bathing her heart with guilt. She *had* neglected Randy! *Oh dear Lord, what have I done? Help me, I pray! Help me put our marriage back together!*

At seven the next morning, after another sleepless night, she phoned

Jen, her pastor's wife and best friend. "I won't be able to teach my class today," she told her, trying to make her voice sound raspy, as if she were coming down with something. She knew if she ran into any of her friends, her face would immediately tell them she had a problem without a word being spoken. Her swollen eyes and reddened cheeks, too, would be a dead giveaway, even if she could keep her tears in check, which she knew would be impossible.

"I'm sure Randy is taking good care of you, Sylvia, but if there's anything I can do—" Jen laughed. "Like open a can of chicken noodle soup, heat it in my microwave, and bring it over to you, I'd—"

"I know," Sylvia answered, interrupting, but the last thing she needed was to have to explain her appearance to someone. "There's really nothing you can do, but thanks, I appreciate the offer. I—I think I'll just rest and take it easy."

She stayed in her pajamas and robe all morning, mostly just sitting in Randy's recliner, rubbing her hands over the armrests, and staring out the pair of sliding glass doors, watching the birds feed at the birdfeeder he'd built for her for Mother's Day four or five years ago. She had spent many happy hours watching the cardinals and blue jays sort through the seeds, picking out the kinds they liked best.

Buck stopped by about one o'clock, bringing her cartons of sweet and sour chicken, fried rice, and crab Rangoon from her favorite Chinese restaurant. Although she appreciated his efforts and concern and thanked him with an enthusiasm she did not feel, the food was tasteless and held no appeal. He took out the trash before leaving, telling her he'd be back the next day, but to call if she needed anything in the meantime. He explained Shonna had wanted to come with him, but he'd told her it might be best if she waited until Sylvia was feeling up to seeing her. She thanked him, saying she would phone Shonna in a day or two. Maybe then she would feel more like talking about things.

After sleeping most of the afternoon, she ate a bit more of the rice about seven and crawled into bed at eight, facing another sleepless night without her husband by her side.

She phoned Randy's office again on Monday, this time punching in the numbers to his direct line. It rang four times before Carol picked up in the outer office.

"I'm sorry, Sylvia. He is in a staff meeting. I am afraid it is going to be a lengthy one. He has already asked me to call the deli and have box lunches delivered. But I'll tell him you called."

Sylvia let her head drop to her chest with an, "Oh. Of course. I forgot. He always has staff meetings on Monday."

Seeming to sense a problem, Carol offered, "If it's important, maybe I can interrupt."

"No! Don't do that. Just ask him to call, please."

She stayed by the phone the rest of the day, watching the hours tick by, waiting for his call.

But it never came.

When the phone rang Tuesday morning, she grabbed it up on the first ring.

"Mrs. Benson. This is Hank from Hawkins Flowers. Could you please tell Mr. Benson we were able to get the apricot roses after all? He seemed so disappointed when he ordered and had to settle for pink roses. I knew he'd want to know."

"Apricot roses?"

"Yes, and tell him we delivered them with his note attached, just as he'd asked. My driver said the lady was thrilled with them. Whoops, the other line is ringing. Thank you for conveying my message. Mr. Benson is a good customer, and we appreciate his business."

Sylvia stood with her mouth hanging open as the broken connection clicked in her ear. When the man had called, she had hoped the flowers were for her, and her heart had soared. Then he had said they had already been delivered. To whom had he sent flowers? Certainly not her! There seemed to be only one answer.

Chatalaine.

Why else would he go to all the trouble to make sure he was able to get roses of a certain color?

She staggered her way across the family room and plunked herself into Randy's recliner. When was the last time he had sent flowers to her? Her birthday? No, he had taken the whole family out to celebrate, but there had been no flowers for her. Usually, he sent her a gigantic poinsettia for Christmas, but this past year, he did not even do that. Mother's Day last year? No, Buck and his wife had given her a beautiful white orchid corsage, but Randy had barely told her, "Happy Mother's Day." She cupped her head in her hands, her fingers rubbing at her eyes wearily as the song "You Don't Bring Me Flowers Anymore" resonated through her head. No, her beloved husband did not bring her flowers anymore. Apparently, his flowers were going to someone else now. Someone who paid more attention to him and met his needs more adequately than she did.

As Sylvia lay in bed that night, she came to a decision. If Randy would not return her calls, she would go see him at his office. Yes, that is exactly what she would do.

By nine the next morning, her hair swept up in a twist, her makeup meticulously applied, and decked out in the dress she'd bought on impulse several weeks earlier, Sylvia was in the elevator on her way up to Randy's fourth-floor office. She had decided it was a bit too tight for her and a bit too short and had almost returned it to the store. Now she was glad she hadn't. She had purposely worn the necklace and matching earrings he had given her several Christmases ago, although she doubted he would remember. Normally, she wore shoes with less than two-inch heels, but this morning she was wearing the pair of strappy, spike-heeled sandals she'd purchased to wear to one of Randy's award banquets. She had ended up not going and staying home because DeeDee complained of a sore throat. She had never worn the shoes long enough to break them in, and her feet were killing her. However, if it meant catching her husband's attention, the pain would be worth it.

"My, you look nice," Carol said as Sylvia exited the elevator, "but I'm sorry. You just missed him. He hasn't been gone five minutes."

Sylvia wanted to cry. And nearly did. But knowing her tears would only upset Carol, she reined them in and forced a casual smile. "He didn't know I was coming. I thought I'd surprise him." Her heart broken and tears threatening to erupt despite her tight hold on them, she said a quick good-bye to Carol and stepped back into the waiting elevator. She had so hoped to see Randy and talk to him. Maybe then she could convince him to swallow his pride and admit he wanted to come home.

She exited the elevator and hurried out the front door toward the *Dallas Times*'s public parking garage to the left of the big building. But as she approached the entrance, a white minivan exited through the gate not thirty feet in front of her, her husband at the wheel and a gorgeous blond in the passenger seat.

Devastated by the sight, Sylvia leaned against the building for support, both hurt and angry. *He doesn't have time to return my calls, but he sure has time for his little cutie!* Lifting first one foot, then the other, she snatched off the offensive sandals from her aching feet and ran the rest of the way to her car in her stockings, not caring if anyone saw her or if she got runs in her new pantyhose. All she wanted to do was get home where she could hide out and unleash her overwhelming rage. *How dare he?*

Finally, she reached the house, not even sure which route she had taken. She flung herself across the bed and screamed out to God, asking what she had done in her life that was so bad she would deserve this kind of treatment.

When the doorbell sounded at four, she couldn't decide if she should answer it or not. It might be Randy, and at this point, she was not sure she even wanted to talk to him. If she told him she had seen him with Chatalaine, he would probably make up some ridiculous excuse. Or maybe he would just admit it, and she wasn't sure she was ready to hear those words from his lips.

The doorbell rang a second time. She stood pressed against the wall, weighing her options.

Whoever was there began pounding on the door. Since she had not changed the locks, she knew if it were Randy, he would just use his key. So rather than explain to whomever might be there, she opened the door.

"I knew you were here. Your car is in the driveway, and your keys are hanging in the front door. You'd better be more careful."

Chapter 5

Jen!" Sylvia quickly wiped at her eyes with her sleeve. "I—I didn't know it was you!"

Jen moved inside and stood glaring at her, her face filled with concern. "Aw, sweetie, what's wrong? You look awful!"

Sylvia turned and led the way into the living room. "I—I'd rather not talk about it."

Jen took her hand and tugged her toward the flowery chintz sofa. "Look, Sylvia, you're my best friend. If you think I'm going to walk out that door before I find out what's bothering you, you're crazy. Now, sit down here beside me and tell me about it, or I'm going to call Randy's office and ask him." Giving her a quick once-over, she continued. "You're all dressed up. Were you on your way out?" Spotting her stocking'd feet, she raised her brows and gave her a smile. "You forgot your shoes."

Sylvia leaned back against the sofa's soft cushions and closed her eyes. She needed to talk to someone. She hated to confide in Buck. After all, Randy was his dad, but she had to open up her injured heart to someone. The silence was driving her wild.

"Okay, out with it. What's wrong? You know you can trust me, don't you?" Jen placed her hand softly on Sylvia's arm. "You're doubly safe talking to me. As your best friend, I'd never betray your confidence, and as the wife of your pastor, I'm bound by God to keep my mouth shut."

Sylvia opened her eyes and stared at the ceiling. "I don't know who I can trust, Jen."

"Out with it, Sylvia. It'll make you feel better to talk about it. Are you sick? Has one of the kids gotten into trouble?"

"Worse than that."

Jen paused. "How much worse?"

Sylvia turned to her friend. She could be trusted, and she would never do or say anything that would harm either her or Randy. "Randy—he—"

Jen let out a gasp. "Oh, no! Is there something wrong with Randy? Harrison and I were just saying the other day, that man is the picture of health."

"No, he's fine. Healthwise."

Jen looked at her impatiently. "Then what about Randy?"

"He wants a di–divorce."

Her friend just stared at her in disbelief, as if words failed her. Finally, she slipped her arm about Sylvia and pulled her close. "I'm so sorry, Sylvia."

Sylvia gulped hard, then for the next half hour, she related the entire story about Randy's leaving and her suspicion he'd left her for another woman, even though he'd denied it. She was careful not to mention Chatalaine's name. "I'm at my wit's end. I've about decided to give up and let him have the divorce without contesting it."

When she finished, Jen asked, "You, Sylvia Benson, are going to give up? Without a fight? That is not like you. If you still love this man and want him back, you are going to have to slug it out for him. This pity party you're having isn't going to cut it. It only makes you look weak, and from my vantage point as a pastor's wife with experience in dealing with broken marriages, weak is never appealing or convincing to the spouse who walked out on the marriage. Especially if there is another woman involved. She's usually pulling out all the stops to get the man to leave his wife and marry her. It's her mission in life, her goal, and she won't quit until she gets him."

Sylvia looked at her with wide eyes, surprised by Jen's direct words. "If that's true, how do you expect me to compete?"

"That, friend of mine, is for you to figure out! But if it were me, and I loved my husband as much as I thought you loved Randy, I'd fight for him with every ounce of my being."

Sylvia pulled away from her and lowered herself into Randy's recliner. "I wouldn't begin to know how to fight. She—she's—" She selected her words carefully, even though she knew, as a pastor's wife, her friend would never go about telling tales and break a confidence. "She's beautiful, Jen."

Jen did a double take. "You've seen her?"

Sylvia nodded. "It's that society columnist from Randy's paper."

"Chatalaine Vicker?"

"Yes."

"Wow. You are right. She is beautiful!"

"Now you see why I said I couldn't compete with her."

Jen shook her head sadly. "I always thought, as happily married as the two of you seemed, Randy would be the last man to succumb to infidelity, but no man is safe. Or woman, for that matter. Many women leave their husbands and kids for so-called *greener pastures*, only to find they weren't as green as they'd expected." Jen seated herself on the sofa and leaned back into the cushions. "He sure wouldn't be the first Christian man his age to let his head be turned by a pretty woman. Is he wearing gold chains, leaving his top three buttons unbuttoned on his shirt so his chest hair will show, and talking about buying a motorcycle?"

Sylvia smiled through her tears. "Not that I've seen."

"Then there may be hope for him."

"You think he may be going through a midlife crisis?"

Jen shrugged. "Who knows? We women have menopause—men have a midlife crisis. We get grouchy. They get childish. All of a sudden, they need their space. We've seen it over and over again during our years in the ministry. I can't begin to tell you how many times my husband has had to counsel couples in this very situation. Usually, if both partners love the Lord, the husband comes to his senses before anything stupid happens, and if each person wants to revive the marriage and is willing to compromise and do their part, their relationship can be salvaged."

Sylvia sniffled as she reached for a tissue. "Salvaged? You make it sound like a battleship that went down at sea, was found, and pulled up later— battered and covered with barnacles."

"In some ways, that's what a broken marriage is like. But unlike the battleship, it sinks slowly—with the husband and wife barely noticing the leak that will eventually destroy it. Funny, you mentioned barnacles. I've heard my husband use those very words when he's been counseling a couple. He often likens them to wounds that married folks inflict on each other over time—like hastily said words, forgetting birthdays and anniversaries, neglecting to say I love you, taking each other for granted, not spending time together, and on and on and on."

Jen reached across and squeezed her hand. "The wounds are tiny at first, barely noticeable, but then infection sets in, and the wounds fester and grow until they actually threaten life if left unattended. Placing a Band-Aid over them merely covers them, but underneath the wounds remain infected, spreading wider and wider until they demand attention. At that point, drastic measures have to be taken. Though the wounds can probably be treated successfully with time and attention, many folks prefer immediate surgery. Cut it off and get rid of it."

"Divorce."

Jen nodded. "Yes, divorce. Sometimes those hurts go way deeper than we can possibly imagine."

The two women sat silently staring at one another. Finally, Sylvia spoke. "I–I've neglected Randy, Jen. I've put everything ahead of him and his needs. I realize that now."

"I'm afraid, as women and mothers, we all have a tendency to do that very thing. And for worthwhile causes. But that doesn't make it right." Jen confessed. "I have to admit, sometimes I feel neglected. Being married to a pastor doesn't mean everything is hunky-dory at all times. We get calls all hours of the day and night from people who need him. I've cooked many a supper only to have him call and say he won't make it home because someone is having trouble and needs him. As the pastor's family, the children and I always take the backseat in any situation. Harrison and I have our moments of conflict, too. We have the same pressures and problems our church members have; only we're expected to be perfect. The power of darkness would like nothing more than to see trouble in the pastor's home, and the enemy works 24/7 to make it happen."

Sylvia stared at her friend. "You and Harrison? But—you two are perfect. I've never once heard you say a cross word to each other!"

"That's because we keep our best face forward and do our arguing within the four walls of our home." Jen leaned forward, bracing her hands on her knees, her face serious. "Look, Sylvia, no one is perfect. Not you. Not Randy. Not Harrison and certainly not me. Marriages are fragile things. We can't let them go unattended or take them for granted. I know Harrison and I have to work at it constantly. Several years ago, we realized, due to the demands of life, we were drifting apart and decided to do something about it. That's why Friday night is our night. Unless an emergency happens, which it does quite often, from five o'clock until midnight every Friday night, the two of us are together. Alone. No kids. No in-laws. No parishioners. Just my husband and me. One week I plan the evening. The next week, Harrison plans it. It's always a surprise. It may be as simple as hamburgers at McDonald's and a movie or a picnic in the park. Other times it's as complex as a dinner theater. But it's our time together. We've even sneaked out of town a few times and spent the night at a motel." Jen's eyes sparkled as she talked.

"I wish Randy and I had done something like that." Sylvia leaned back in Randy's recliner and stared at the ceiling, trying to remember the last time she and her husband had spent the entire evening together, just the two of them. "Maybe if we had, he'd still be here."

"Men try to act real tough, put on a facade. Rarely do they admit they're hurting. They pretend they have tough skin, but they're as vulnerable as we are, honey. If someone had asked me which man in our church would be least likely to do something like this, I would have said Harrison first, with Randy running a very close second."

Sylvia blinked back tears. "Me, too. I never dreamed—"

"That's the problem, Sylvia. Most of us don't even suspect a problem until it rears its ugly head. We're too caught up with life to see what's right under our nose."

"Do—do you think it's too late to fix it?"

"Let me ask *you* a question. Do you think God wants the two of you together?"

Without hesitation, Sylvia answered, "Yes! Of course He does."

"Then fight, Sylvia! Fight with all you're worth. If you must go down, go down swinging."

"Fight?"

Jen doubled up her fist and punched at the air. "Yes, fight. Fight for your marriage."

Sylvia let out a sigh. "But I'm not a fighter. I wouldn't know how to begin."

"You? Not a fighter? I've always thought of you as a fighter. Aren't you the woman who went to bat with the city council over the zoning for the church's youth building annex and won? I was amazed the day you spoke at that council meeting. I never knew you had it in you. You were so passionate and articulate, they had no choice but to grant the zoning to you. I can't think of anyone who could have done a better job."

Sylvia smiled a small victorious smile. "I really wanted the youth of our church to have that annex."

"And you did all you could to make it happen, didn't you? You moved way out of your comfort zone. You have to do the same thing now if you want to win." Jen scooted to the edge of the sofa. "If you want to revive this marriage, you're going to have to face up to your part in its failure and do something about it."

"Like what? What can I do?"

"That question, my friend, is one you'll have to answer." Jen pulled her car keys from her pocket and rose to her feet. "I hate to leave you like this, but I have to pick up one of the children, and I'm already late. I will give you this bit of advice though. Like you, I'm sure God wants the two of you together, so why don't you let Him help you with the answer? Pray about it, Sylvia. Listen to God. Read His Word. If your heart is open and you're willing to do whatever He asks, He'll tell you how."

Sylvia pushed herself out of the recliner and stood, her heart overflowing with love and appreciation for this godly woman. "I'm glad you came, Jen."

"Me, too, even though I had to pound on the door to get you to let me in." Jen gave her arm an affectionate pinch. "I'll be praying for you, you know that."

"I'm counting on it."

Sylvia stood in the doorway, waving at her friend and confidante as she drove off. God had sent her at just the right time. With renewed hope in her heart, she closed the door.

Reading her Bible that night, Jen's words kept coming back to her. *"If you want to revive this marriage, you are going to have to face up to your part in its failure and do something about it."*

"But what, Lord? What can I do?" Sylvia cried out after she dropped to her knees beside her bed. "I've left messages nearly every day, and Randy hasn't returned any of my calls. I've gone to his office only to find he left with that woman. I don't know what to do. Jen says I have to fight for him, but how? How do I fight? Show me what to do. Surely, You want Randy and me together. Help me, God! Give me wisdom. Give me guidance!"

No flash appeared.

No revelation from heaven.

As she lay there in the darkened room, Sylvia continued to pray, quoting every scripture verse she had memorized about God answering prayer. Eventually, she fell asleep, the pillow wet with her tears.

∽

It was after midnight when Randy crawled into bed in his new fifth-floor, high-rise apartment. Why hadn't he noticed the noise from the nearby set of elevators when he had leased it? And who could be going up and down in it this time of night, anyway? How did they expect a guy to sleep with all that racket?

He flipped onto his side and pulled the sheet over his head. Morning would arrive soon enough, and he needed to be at the office early to prepare for a meeting with one of his key advertisers. Unable to fall asleep, he ran the meeting's agenda over in his head, hoping to come up with a few more reasons why the client should up his advertising budget for the coming year. Circulation was down as more and more people turned to TV for their daily news. And with the cost of production going up every day, it was becoming harder and harder to meet the anticipated yearly profit margin. Maybe he should have gone with CNN when they had given him the chance. They'd made him a good offer, but that would have meant moving to Atlanta.

Though he'd known she really didn't want to, Sylvia had even said she was willing to make the move.

Sylvia! Why did his thoughts on any subject seem to end up with Sylvia, when he had finally gotten up the courage to move out of the house and put an end to their stagnant marriage? Now that he was going to be free to do whatever he chose, maybe he should contact CNN again and see if they were still interested in his joining their staff. The kids were grown. He could always hop on a plane and come back to visit them whenever he wanted, and he could send them tickets to come and visit him. Atlanta was an exciting city, with lots of things to see and do. Sylvia would love the Antebellum Plantation and shopping at the trendy Lenox Square Mall.

Sylvia! There I go again!

He kicked off the covers and rolled onto his back, staring at the tiny slivers of light creeping in around the edges of the Venetian blind. *I wonder how she's doing? I guess it was pretty lousy of me to tell her I wanted a divorce on Thanksgiving Day, but I've tried several times to tell her, and there never seemed to be a right time. She'll get used to me being gone. No more picking up after me, doing my laundry, cooking my meals.*

His thoughts went to the pile of dirty shirts, underwear, and socks piled up on the chair. He would have to take care of them this weekend. The apartment manager had told him there was a coin-operated laundry room on the basement level. Maybe he would just wash them himself. How hard could it be? Toss them in, add the soap, and pop in a few quarters. In all the years they had been married, he had never once done a single load of laundry. Sylvia had always done it. His clean clothes were always either hung in his closet or folded neatly in his bureau. He had never even taken his suits to the cleaners. She had done that, too. Had he ever thanked her? Surely, he had. No, come to think of it, he hadn't. Doing laundry had been part of her job, just as getting to the newspaper office by seven had been his. Had *she* ever thanked him for bringing home *his* paycheck?

As he lay there, other things Sylvia had done over the years played out in his mind. The house had always been clean, with things put in their proper places even though, at times, she'd had a sick child to tend to or felt ill herself, but she'd done them without complaining or asking for credit. The meals appeared on the table as if by magic. He'd never given a second thought to when she'd had time to do the shopping. Not once had he stopped to calculate the time she'd spend in the kitchen peeling vegetables, browning meat, preparing casseroles, baking pies and cakes, or trying out new recipes she thought he'd enjoy.

She had become quite handy around the house at doing repairs, too. She'd even asked for a cordless drill and screwdriver for Christmas a few years ago so she could put a decorative molding up in their bedroom and a chair rail on the dining room wall. At the time, he had laughed, then humored her by buying them for her. Why hadn't he put those things up for her himself? Didn't she have enough to do? Well, he was busy, too. Working ten-hour days took its toll on a man. *Come on, Randy, be honest with yourself. You could have done those things for her, but you'd rather play racquetball with a client or watch a football game on TV. You weren't exactly a model husband.*

He rammed a fist into the empty pillow beside him, then flipped over onto his stomach. *Enough! I've got to get some z's! I've made my decision, and there's no turning back. I waited way too long as it is. It's my time now, and Sylvia is just going to have to learn to live with it!*

☙

The ringing of the phone brought Sylvia out of a fitful sleep.

Chapter 6

She dove to answer it, hoping it was Randy.

"Good morning, Betty," the voice on the other end said cheerily. "This is your wake-up call."

Quickly sitting up on the side of the bed, Sylvia stared at the red numbers on the clock. Five a.m. "What? Who did you want? Betty? There's no Betty here."

"Whoops, sorry," a male voice said apologetically. "I must've dialed the wrong number. I promised my girlfriend I'd call at five. She has a plane to catch at seven. I hope I didn't wake you."

"It's okay," she mumbled before dropping the phone back into its cradle. After blinking several times, she stared at the clock, then lay back on the bed, snuggling under the covers and into the twisted nest of sheets and blankets she'd created by her night of tossing and turning.

"Okay, God. It's You and me here, and I need help. What can I do? I need a plan." As she lay there, praying and waiting on the Lord, she began to, once again, go over the scripture verses she had learned as a child and in her adult Sunday school classes. At one time, she had even enrolled in the Navigator's Scripture Memory Course.

"All things work together for good to them that love God. . . ."

"Trust in the Lord with all thine heart; and lean not unto thine own understanding. . . ."

"Now abideth faith, hope, charity, these three; but the greatest of these is charity. . . ."

"Who can find a virtuous woman? for her price is far above rubies. The heart of her husband doth safely trust in her, so that he shall have no need of spoil. . . ."

"Spoil," she said aloud. "Could that mean another woman? Umm, let me see. What else does the thirty-first chapter of Proverbs have to say about the perfect marriage?"

"She will do him good and not evil all the days of her life."

"Haven't I done that for Randy?"

Delving into the recesses of her memory, she continued into the chapter and quoted each scripture as she'd learned it from the King James Version of the Bible.

"Her children arise up, and call her blessed; her husband also, and he praiseth her. Many daughters have done virtuously, but thou excellest them all."

Not me, Father God. I put everyone else's needs above those of my husband.

"Favour is deceitful, and beauty is vain: but a woman that feareth the Lord, she shall be praised. Give her of the fruit of her hands; and let her own works praise her in the gates."

She tried to go on to other scriptures she had learned, but the last verse of Proverbs thirty-one kept ringing in her heart, and she began to repeat it over and over. *"Give her of the fruit of her hands; and let her own works praise her in the gates. Give her of the fruit of her hands; and let her own works praise her in the gates."* "What are You trying to tell me, Lord? What am I missing here?"

"Give her of the fruit of her hands; and let her own works praise her in the gates." Why was He impressing this verse upon her?

Suddenly, it came to her. The plan she needed. Of course! It was perfect. She and Randy needed to go back to where they started. Learn to love each other all over again. Learn to appreciate one another and what they had each contributed to their marriage! Let their own works praise them in the gates!

Randy sat behind his big desk and stared at the business plan he had spent hours preparing for his key client. Well, things happened. It wasn't the man's fault his wife had to be rushed to the hospital with a drop in her sodium levels. He glanced at the open book on his desk. His next appointment wasn't until one o'clock, which gave him time to work on several other pressing things he had put aside in order to work on the business plan.

"Mr. Benson." His name crackled over the intercom on his desk.

"Yes, Carol, what is it?"

"Your wife is here."

Randy frowned at the intercom. Sylvia was in the outer office? He had refrained from returning her calls, unable to face the crying scene he knew would come if he talked to her. "Ah—" he said slowly, trying to think quickly of an excuse to turn her away.

"I told her your nine o'clock appointment cancelled."

Carol! You shouldn't have done that. Now I don't have an excuse for not seeing her. "I'll—I'll be right out." *Maybe she won't cause a scene if I talk to her in the outer office,* he reasoned as he rose and headed toward the door.

He was not prepared for the sight that greeted him.

Sylvia tugged at her skirt, then smoothed her jacket. *Why didn't I wear the taupe pantyhose instead of this black pair? I wonder if my hair looks okay? Should I have put on more lipstick? Is the neckline on this blouse too low cut? Why didn't I check myself out in the mirror in the ladies' room before coming up here? Oh my, I'm a nervous wreck!*

Her heart was pounding way beyond the speed limit as the door to her husband's office opened and he stepped out, dressed in his black Armani suit, starched white shirt, and the black-and-white polka dot tie she had given him for Christmas. He badly needed a haircut, making the long silver streaks combed back from his temples even more attractive. "Hi, Randy," she said, conjuring up the sweetest voice and smile possible and holding up a white bag with the words Moon Doggie's Bakery emblazoned on it in big red letters. "I hope you've got time for a coffee break. I've brought your favorites. Chocolate éclairs from Moon Doggie's!"

"Well, lucky you," Carol told her boss with a smile, "to have such a thoughtful wife."

Right away, Sylvia knew Randy hadn't told anyone at the office about their breakup, unless he had told Chatalaine. Without waiting for him to invite her in, she brushed past him and into his office, going to the little counter where Carol kept his coffeepot turned on all day. "Sit down," she said, grinning at him. "I'll put these on one of your paper plates and pour us each a cup of coffee." She could feel Randy's eyes boring into her.

"What are you doing, Syl?"

She turned slowly and gave him a coquettish grin and a tilt of her head. "Pouring my husband a cup of coffee."

"You know what I mean. Why are you here?"

Placing their cups on the desk, she scurried back to the counter for their plates and napkins. "Can't a wife surprise her husband once in a while?"

"Don't you think that it's a bit late for games? We are not teenagers."

His retort was cool, but she ignored it and continued to smile as she pulled a chair up close to the desk and settled herself into it. Her feet were killing her in the spike heels, but she kept smiling anyway, ignoring the pain. "Napkin?" she asked, reaching one out to him.

"I don't get it." He took a swig of coffee after blowing into his cup, and all the while, he stared at her. "I've never seen you like this. You're so—dressed up—for nine o'clock in the morning. Is that a new dress?"

Yes, it's a new dress. I bought it several weeks ago, because I knew it was your favorite color, to wear to the awards banquet you wanted me to attend with you. But instead, I ended up going to the hospital with old Mrs. Taylor when she had her heart attack, and you went on alone. "It's pretty new. I haven't had it very long." She stood and, smiling, did a pirouette. "You like it?"

His eyes widened, and he continued to stare at her. "Yeah, I like it. As a matter of fact, you look terrific."

Good, that's what I wanted you to think. Otherwise, I wouldn't have worn these ridiculous shoes. "It's a bit more youthful than I usually wear, but hey, I'm still young!" she said, adding a merry chuckle. "I have years ahead of me."

"We both do." His tone seemed a bit melancholy to her, or was she imagining it and hoping he was as miserable without her as she was without him?

"I'd like for us to spend those years together, Randy."

He cleared his throat loudly, then rose from his chair. "My mind is made up, Syl. If you've come here thinking you'll change it with a bag of éclairs, you're wrong."

"Sit down, Randy, please. I haven't come here to make a scene. I'm not planning on having a shouting session, unless that's what you want. Your news hit me hard, I'll admit that, but I now realize many of your reasons for wanting to end our marriage were valid. Neither of us has been doing our part to make this relationship succeed." *But at least I don't have a boyfriend waiting in the wings!*

He slumped back in his chair with a look of defeat. "So what do you want, Syl? I told you I still planned to take care of you and the kids."

"I'm not concerned about that, Randy." She reached across the desk and covered his hand with hers, relieved when he made no attempt to pull it away. "I—I love you. I always have. I always will, even if you go through with the divorce."

"I've already talked to my attorney, Syl. He's drawing up the papers."

"Randy, I've thought over the things you said, and looking back, although my heart was in the right place, my body wasn't. I should have been there for you. Instead, I've put the needs of others, the children, and the church ahead of you and your needs. But you were always so self-sufficient and didn't seem to need me. I just assumed you didn't mind when you had to go places and do things alone. You never complained. Not really. And *you* served on the church board. That took you away many evenings while I sat at home alone. Was that so different from what I was doing? We both accepted Jesus as our Savior, and we both love the Lord and want to serve Him—sometimes His work takes us away when we'd like to spend the evening at home."

"I'm going to resign from the church board, Syl," he admitted in an almost whisper. "When the word gets out we're getting a divorce, I doubt Harrison or any of the members of the church will want me serving as their deacon."

Especially not if you're leaving me for another woman! It hurt her that he avoided her gaze.

"I—I haven't told anyone here at the office or at the church yet—about us, but I suppose you've told Jen, since she is your best friend."

She wanted to lie, but she couldn't, not if she expected him to be truthful with her. "Yes, I told her, but I'm sure it will go no further than Harrison."

"You're probably right. They're good people."

"People who have the same problems as anyone else."

He nodded as he fidgeted with the handle on his cup. "I guess. They're human, too."

"I've come here today, Randy, prepared to make you a deal."

He raised his head and stared wide-eyed at her. "Short of saying yes to a divorce, I don't know what kind of a deal you can offer."

"Like I said, I still love you and don't want our marriage to end. So—here is the deal. I'll give you your divorce, uncontested, if you'll do one thing for me."

The look of relief in his eyes nearly made her cry. "What?"

"I want us to have one last Christmas together."

He shook his head slowly. "You mean you want me to move back in until after Christmas? No way! Leaving this time was hard enough. I'll not do it a second time!" He rose and moved around the desk toward the door.

"Your call, Randy. Do you want me to make a scene here in your office?"

He turned back to her. "Of course not!"

"Then sit down and listen to me."

∽

Randy did as he was told and settled back into his chair, staring at his wife of twenty-five years. He had never seen her like this, and her demeanor confused him. This wasn't the Sylvia he knew, the one who always walked away from him rather than have a confrontation, the woman who could never refuse anyone who asked for help.

And what was she doing dressed like this? She rarely wore short skirts that revealed her knees. And she was right. It was much more youthful than she usually wore, but in all the right places. She looked like she had just stepped out of the beauty shop. Every hair was perfect. Her makeup, which she rarely wore, made her skin look—oh, he couldn't think of a word to describe it, but she looked good. Really good.

"Before we shut the door on our marriage and we each go our separate ways, I want us to spend the week of Christmas together."

"Impossible. Christmas is a busy time here at the—"

"You haven't taken a day's vacation yet this year, Randy, and I know you have at least three weeks coming. Surely, if you want a divorce as badly as you say you do, you can manage a week off." She stood and stared at him, waiting for his answer.

"I—I suppose, if I wanted to—"

"Then want to. If you'll spend from December the nineteenth to midnight, December the twenty-fifth, with me, doing whatever I ask of you, and you still want the divorce, I'll give it to you, uncontested."

"Like—do what?"

"Like I said—whatever I ask. That should be simple enough, and re-member, your children will be with you some of that time. If you go ahead with the divorce proceedings now, you know they won't have a thing at all to do with you over the holidays. This way, you'll be able to have a lovely Christmas with them, then file for divorce after Christmas is over." *That also means you won't be able to see your little cutie during that time, but I'm not going to mention that now and start another argument. I want you home for Christmas.*

"The children still don't know?"

She shook her head. "Only Buck. He came back about an hour after you left me on Thanksgiving Day. He'd left his wallet in the bathroom. I'm afraid I was in pretty bad shape. I had to tell him, but I made him promise not to say anything to anyone other than Shonna. I'm sure he's kept that promise. He's not happy about this, Randy, but for DeeDee and Aaron's sake, I'm sure he'll treat you civilly. At least until December the twenty-sixth."

"You're making this really tough, Syl." Randy leaned back in his chair, locking his hands behind his head and closing his eyes.

She knew her offer had come as a shock. "I don't plan to place all the blame on you when the kids are told. I'm sure I had a part in the failure of our marriage, too. I—I may not have been the wife you wanted me to be, but I did try."

"This is the craziest idea I've ever heard! I will *not* move back home, even for a single night!"

She worked hard at maintaining her cool. He had to say yes. She was counting on it. *Don't blow it now!* "It'd be a way to avoid a knock-down, drag-out in court."

"If you kept your end of the bargain."

"I guess you'll have to trust me," she answered, willing her voice to remain calm, at least on the surface. "Randy? What do you say? If you want this divorce, you'd better make up your mind real fast. Once I walk out that door, you can consider this offer withdrawn, and our lawyers can handle everything. Take it or leave it."

He inhaled a couple of quick breaths.

"Make up your mind, Randy. Think how nice it'd be to have at least one more peaceful Christmas with the kids."

"But what good would spending another week under the same roof accomplish?"

She glanced at her watch. "Time's a wasting."

Looking pressured, he leaned forward and folded his hands on the desktop. "You know this is only going to prolong things."

"Perhaps."

"And I'm supposed to move back into the house during that time?"

"Yes. I want your undivided attention every minute of those seven days. It's a small sacrifice if you want to avoid a nasty divorce court battle."

"You're leaving me no choice, you know."

"That was my intent."

Agitated, he rose and began to pace about the room, frantically running his fingers through his hair. Finally coming to a stop in front of her, he leaned toward her, his voice shaking with emotion. "Look, Sylvia, we've been living separate lives for years. The only thing we haven't done is the paperwork making it official. This whole thing seems a bit silly to me."

She wanted to shout at him, but she held her peace, pulling out the one last card left in her deck. Moving to the other side of the desk, she gave him a smile as she shrugged, slung the strap of her purse over her shoulder, and headed for the door. "Okay. If you'd rather do things your way, I'll see you in court."

She had only taken a few steps when Randy grabbed her arm and spun her around.

"All right, you win. I'll do it, but I'm not happy about it."

She pulled her arm from his grasp. "Sorry, that's one of the conditions of the deal. You at least have to act as if you're happy about it. I won't have you sulking around our house like a spoiled child who didn't get his way. Christmas is a happy time, Randy. The celebration of the birth of our Savior, Jesus Christ. I won't have you ruining it with a downtrodden face and a smart mouth."

He lifted both palms with a look of defeat. "Okay, okay. We'll do it your way."

Her heart did a flip-flop. Randy was going to agree! "You'll at least act like you're enjoying being home for Christmas?"

"Yeah, if you're a good sport about this, I guess I need to be one, too."

She had to get out of there before she shouted *Hallelujah!* "Good, I'll expect you in time for supper on December the nineteenth, and don't be late. No excuses, Randy, or the deal's off. Have everything taken care of at the office by the nineteenth. No running to the paper. No meeting with clients. None of that. Because if that happens, like I said, I'll see you in court, and I can assure you it won't be a pretty sight. I'll take you for everything I can get!"

He gave her a guarded smile. "You drive a hard bargain. I didn't know you had it in you."

She grabbed hold of the doorknob and smiled over her shoulder. "Only when my marriage is at stake, then I can be a wildcat!" She did an exaggerated "Meee–ooow," showed her claws, then moved out and closed the door behind her.

"I'm so glad you came, Mrs. Benson," Carol told her from her place at her desk. "Mr. Benson has seemed a little down the past few days. I'm sure your surprise visit cheered him up."

"I—I hope so." Sylvia had to smile. *If you only knew, Carol.*

∞

For the next couple of weeks, Sylvia rushed about like a mad woman on a mission, cleaning the house until it sparkled, readying their bedroom for Randy's return, shopping for Christmas presents, and a to-do list full of other things. She was busy from early morning until late at night, and for the first time in days—happy. She'd even printed out a small banner on her computer's printer saying, "Give Her of the Fruit of Her Hands; and Let Her Own Works Praise Her in the Gates," and taped it on the mirror in her bathroom as a reminder, claiming that verse as her own, confident God had given it to her. She made out a carefully choreographed schedule for each day Randy would be with her and planned the important activities they would do together. Just knowing Randy was going to be back home with her, even for a few days, made her feel giddy and young again. How long had it been since she had planned something special for just the two of them? Too long!

Each night as she knelt beside her bed and prayed in Jesus' name, she asked God to give her wisdom and guidance and for the strength to keep her mouth shut when the need arose. It would be so easy to tear into her husband about Chatalaine, but now that she was convinced that her own negligence and not just Chatalaine's youth and good looks threatened to end her marriage, she found it easier to put the woman out of her mind. She needed to concentrate on herself and the devotion and dedication she had pledged to Randy on their wedding day.

Other than talking to Jen and Buck, she kept things to herself. At first, Buck was skeptical of her plan. He felt she was getting her hopes up and did not want to see her hurt anymore than she'd already been hurt. But at her request, he and Shonna agreed to go along with her plan and to treat his father as if nothing had happened.

Finally, December the nineteenth arrived. Sylvia spent part of the morning at the beauty shop having her long hair cut into a pixie style with wisps of hair feathering her face. "You look years younger," the beauty operator had told her as she gave her the hand mirror and swung her chair around. "I left a few wisps along your neckline, too. I think you'll like it that way."

Sylvia had gazed into the mirror and had to agree. The style did make her look several years younger. She was sure Randy would like it.

She was too excited to eat lunch and opted for a banana and a glass of cranberry juice. By two o'clock, she had baked a lemon meringue pie, piling the heavily beaten egg whites high and creating curly mounds just like Randy liked them. She hadn't baked a lemon meringue pie since she'd made one for the Fourth of July picnic at the church, although Randy had always claimed it was his favorite dessert. When she pulled the pie from the oven and placed it on the counter to cool, she looked at the deliciously browned meringue and experienced terrible pangs of guilt. Why hadn't she baked more of those pies for Randy? The children loved them, too. They took no time at all. She had baked several of them to take to the church bake sales, but had not made a single one for him in years.

By four, the table was set with the stoneware she usually reserved for company. The few freshly cut flowers she'd purchased at the market had been arranged in a colorful vase as a centerpiece, the crab casserole he liked was in the oven baking, and everything was in readiness. All she had to do was take her shower and get dressed.

When the phone rang a few minutes later, she cringed. *Randy, if that's you calling to say you're going to be late or that you can't make it, I'm going to be furious.*

"Hello."

"Hi," Jen said on the other end. "I just want you to know I've been praying for you all day, and I'm going to keep praying right on through Christmas Day."

Sylvia's heart soared. With a praying friend like Jen, how could things not go right? "Thanks, Jen. You don't know how much that means to me. I'm as nervous as I was on our first date."

"You'll do fine, honey. Just be your natural sweet self."

Sylvia huffed. "You wouldn't have thought I was sweet if you'd heard me threatening Randy in his office that day. I wasn't about to take no for an answer. Jen, I know God gave me that verse."

"I know it, too, and I think your plan is marvelous. If Randy doesn't see what he's giving up by the time Christmas Day arrives, I'll be mighty surprised."

"I'm counting on that. I don't even want to think about failing."

"You won't fail. Not with both of us praying about it. God knows your heart, Sylvia, and He knows the two of you belong together."

Sylvia thanked her for praying, said good-bye, and rushed up the stairs to take her shower.

∽

Randy stared into the mirror at the stubble on his cheeks and chin. Like his father, he had been blessed with a head of thick hair, but with it came the proverbial five o'clock shadow.

What a week he'd had. It seemed everything that could go wrong—did. Two of his key employees quit to go to work for the state government, where they would get better benefits. One of the main presses broke down as they were running the "Dallas Life" section for the Sunday paper, and Carol had tripped on the stairs and broken her arm. To top it all off, his rechargeable razor had quit on him when he had started to shave, and now he was going to have to use the emergency disposable razor he kept in his shaving kit. The way things were going, he would probably cut himself.

Well, trouble or not, he had taken off a bit early to get ready to move back into the house for the next week, and he was committed to going through with it. The paper would have to get along without him for a while. The only good thing going for him was his assistant manager, a young man who showed great promise. Randy had spent most of the day going over last-minute details with him, and, hopefully, the guy would be able to handle any crisis that might develop in his absence. Sylvia had made it perfectly clear she wasn't about to accept any excuses that would take him away from her for the next week, and he certainly did not want to end up in an expensive court battle if he could avoid it.

It was hard to believe she hadn't made any attempt to contact him since that day she'd appeared in his office, other than to send him a short handwritten note reminding him she'd be looking for him at six that evening. He had expected her to call him at the office continually, bemoaning the fact that he had asked for the divorce, but she had not, and he appreciated it. Maybe they *could* get through this divorce without all the hullabaloo he had expected, after all. He should be so lucky.

He jumped when his cell phone rang, almost afraid to answer it for fear there had been another fiasco at the newspaper.

"Hi, Randy," a male voice on the other end said pleasantly. "I have a favor to ask."

Randy recognized the man's voice immediately. It was Bill Regier, a fellow deacon.

"I know you've been so busy at the newspaper you haven't been able to attend church the past few Sundays, but my wife is insisting we go visit her folks over New Year's, and I wondered if I could talk you into teaching my junior high Sunday school class? They're a great bunch of kids, and I know they'll like you."

Teach Sunday school? Me? When I've just asked my wife for a divorce? Randy rubbed his free hand up the stubble on his jaw. "I—I don't think so, Bill. I've been kinda out of the loop lately—you know—with too many things going on in my life. It's a busy time of year, and—"

"Hey, this isn't rocket science. It won't take that much preparation. You can just tell the kids how you came to Christ. You know, when you accepted Jesus and what's happened in your life since. It'll be an inspiration for them. These kids need role models in their lives. Some of them are from the bus ministry and come from broken homes. They need to see what a real man is like. A man like you—with values and principles."

Randy was glad their conversation was on the phone so the man couldn't see his face—a face he was sure betrayed his guilt. "I—I'd like to help you out, Bill, but—but I'm afraid I can't do it this time. Year-end stuff, you know?"

There was a pause on the other end, then, "Well, okay, but it's these kids' loss. Maybe another time, when you're not so busy, huh?"

"Yeah—maybe another time." Randy tapped the OFF button, but continued to stare at the receiver. *Role model, Bill? You won't think so when you hear about the divorce.*

∞

Sylvia opened the Dillard's shopping bag and dumped the assortment of new cosmetics she had purchased several days ago onto the dresser. She'd never worn much makeup, never thought she'd need to, but after seeing the beautiful Chatalaine in the restaurant that day, she'd felt dowdy and washed out. Colorless. The woman at the department store's makeup counter had been extremely helpful and had given her all kinds of tips on applying moisturizer, foundation, blusher, eyeliner, mascara, and even lip-liner. Now, if she could just remember all she had learned. "*Beauty is only skin-deep,*" the old saying her mother used to quote, popped into her mind as she gazed at herself in the mirror. She let out an audible giggle as a second quote came to mind. This one she had heard while playing one of Billy Graham's videotapes. "*Every old barn can use a little paint now and then!*"

"Well, this old barn certainly can!" she chided as she picked up the bottle of moisturizer. She began to apply it freely to her scrubbed-clean skin. After smoothing on the foundation and blusher, she picked up the eyeliner pencil and, using a finger to pull each eyelid tautly to one side, she carefully made a narrow line, one above and one below her lashes on each eye. *Umm, not bad for a beginner!* Next came the mascara, something she rarely used. "*One light coat, let it dry a few seconds, then apply a second coat more freely,*" the woman had said. Once that was done, she reached for one of the new lip liner pencils she'd purchased and chose one in a deep mauve shade. "*Frame your mouth, staying right on the very edge of the lip line,*" she could almost hear the beauty consultant say as she applied it. She had never used lip liner before, but she had to admit, it did define her lips. Next, she reached for the mauve lipstick, in a shade a bit lighter than the liner. Sylvia applied it generously, then blotted it carefully on a tissue before looking back into the mirror. The woman who smiled back at her looked nothing like the woman who'd faced her in that same mirror the day before. What an improvement!

"*Man looketh on the outward appearance, but the Lord looketh on the heart.*" The words she had committed to memory so many years ago echoed in her heart. *I haven't forgotten that, God, but I want to look my very best for Randy. I want to knock his socks off!*

She spritzed her hair with the setting mist and used her fingers to lift and separate the wisps, pulling a few of them toward her face, just like the beautician had shown her when she'd cut her hair. A few puffs of hair spray, the addition of her new gold hoop earrings and a fine gold chain about her neck, and she was ready to slip into the gorgeous, rose-printed silk caftan she'd bought for their first evening together. She had already done her fingernails and toenails in the same rosy-mauve color. She gave herself a quick spray of the perfume Randy had given her for Christmas two years ago—the one she'd never even bothered to open. Then she slipped into her gold, heelless sandals, took one last glimpse at the mirror, and headed downstairs. She felt giddy, almost like a fairy princess on her way to the ball. Now if only Randy would behave as she imagined Prince Charming would behave. She laughed aloud as she whirled her way into the kitchen for a few last-minute preparations, visualizing Randy appearing at her door dressed in all white with gold braid at his shoulders and astride a fine white horse.

She turned on the coffeepot, checked the oven, gave the salad another toss, shifted the fresh flower vase a half inch to make sure it was centered just right, then moved into the living room to await his arrival.

At exactly six, the doorbell rang. She straightened, her heart pounding. If it was Randy, why didn't he simply use his key? After all, this *was* his home.

Chapter 7

Randy stared at the door, suitcase and garment bag in hand. Maybe he should have just used his key and gone in rather than ringing the doorbell like a visitor. But he *was* a visitor! He had moved out of this home he had known and loved. He glanced toward the west, to the three-bedroom addition they had added nearly twenty years ago, after DeeDee and Aaron became toddlers. He looked to the east at the big bay windows of the family room where the garage used to be. How they had needed that extra space when the kids started school and began bringing their friends over. Fortunately, their house had been on a corner lot, making it possible for them to expand the kitchen and build a nice attached three-car garage onto the backside of the house.

He remembered when they had nearly sold this home and simply bought a larger one in another neighborhood, but both Sylvia and the kids had wanted to stay where they were, near all the friends they had made and their church. As the managing editor of the newspaper, he could well afford to buy a bigger house now, but this home had always filled their needs. It was warm and comfortable, thanks to Sylvia and her decorating talents.

Realization smacked him between the eyes as the door opened and

Sylvia appeared. He no longer lived here. He *was* a visitor!

∞

"Hi," Sylvia said, her voice cracking slightly with pent-up emotion. "Come on in." She watched Randy move through the door and place his things in the hall. It was obvious he was feeling every bit as awkward as she was.

He gazed at her, looking first at her hair, then her face, then the new caftan she was wearing. She liked the look she saw in his eyes. Though she felt herself trembling, she willed her voice to remain pleasant and calm. "Supper is nearly ready. Would you like a glass of iced tea or maybe a cup of coffee?"

"Ah—no. Nothing, thanks."

She laughed within herself as she gave him a purposely demure smile. He was wearing a burgundy knit polo shirt that nearly matched the dark burgundy lines surrounding the huge mauve roses in the print of her caftan.

"You've cut your hair," he said, his eyes still focused on her. "I like it."

A flash of warmth rushed to her cheeks at his compliment. "Thank you. I like it, too. The hairdresser said it made me look years younger." *That was a stupid thing to say!*

"It does."

But not as young as your precious Chatalaine?

She gestured toward the living room and his recliner. "Would you like to sit down? I put a couple of your favorite CDs on to play." *Christian CDs. Or don't you like that kind anymore?*

"Sure. I guess."

He followed her into the living room and sat down in what used to be his chair. "Pretty dress. I guess you'd call it a dress. Looks good on you."

She lowered herself gracefully onto the chintz sofa and smoothed at the long caftan. "Thank you."

"It's new? I've never seen it before."

"Yes, new." *I bought it to impress you, hoping you'd like it.*

"How are the kids? I haven't heard from any of them."

"They're fine. DeeDee and Aaron are working hard on finals. Buck and Shonna are busy getting ready for Christmas. He's working lots of overtime." *Buck is furious with you! And DeeDee and Aaron will be, too, when they hear you're deserting your family for that woman!*

"I guess—you're doing okay. You look wonderful."

Doing okay? No, I'm not doing okay! I'm awful! I can't sleep, can't eat, cry all day and all night. I'm miserable without you! "I'm—managing. Thank you for the compliment. How are you doing?"

"Okay. Busy. At the office, you know. Busy time of the year."

"Yes, I remember," she said, fully aware of his rigid position. *He must be feeling as awkward in my presence as I feel in his. Two strangers, instead of a man and woman who've been married for twenty-five years and have three grown children.* "How is your apartment working out?"

"Other than hearing the elevator go up and down all night, it's working out fine. I need to get some furniture. The place is still pretty empty."

"Is it near your office?" She had wondered where he had moved, but he had never even given her a hint, let alone the address.

"About a mile. I could walk it, I guess. On nice days."

They sat in silence, listening to a gospel medley about God's love, each avoiding the other's eyes.

"I—I think the casserole should be done by now," Sylvia said, rising. "It's your favorite."

"Not the crab casserole you used to bake for me?"

The enthusiasm on his face made her smile. "Yes. The crab casserole."

He rose and rubbed his hands together briskly. "Sounds like I'm in for a treat!"

She crooked a finger at him, adding the demure smile once again, and headed for the kitchen, knowing he was following at her heels.

"Umm, does that smell good." He made an exaggerated sniff at the air. "I can't remember the last time you made that casserole."

"Far too long ago." *I'm ashamed to admit.*

He moved into his usual chair as she pulled the casserole from the oven and placed it on the iron trivet on the table. "Need any help?"

She shook her head. "No, I just need to get our salad bowls from the refrigerator, and we'll be ready to eat." Once the salad bowls were set in place, she lowered herself into her chair and bowed her head. Normally, Randy prayed at suppertime, but after a few moments of silence, she prayed aloud, a simple prayer thanking God for their food and asking Him to be with their family. She wanted to thank God audibly for bringing Randy back home, but felt it better left unsaid. At least aloud. The last thing she wanted to do was make him feel uncomfortable. She wanted to "let her works praise her in the gates"—her own home.

When she lifted her eyes, she found Randy staring at her. Was it a look of admiration, or resentment, or even tolerance? She couldn't tell. All she could do was her very best to make him see what he was giving up by moving out. One last look at the life they had shared. *Oh God, make him want to come home for good! Please make him want to come home.*

She offered him the serving spoon. "Go ahead and help yourself while I get the rolls from the oven."

"This looks wonderful," he told her, scooping a huge serving from the casserole dish. "I wasn't sure you even remembered it was my favorite."

I remembered, Randy, I just didn't care, I guess. I always fixed the things the kids liked, putting your wants and needs aside. You never complained. I just figured it wasn't important. "I remembered."

He took the first bite and chewed it slowly, appearing to savor it by the looks of his contented smile. "I know the kids never liked crab. I sure couldn't have expected you to go to all the trouble to fix the crab casserole for me. You had enough to do."

"I like it, too. I wish now I *had* fixed it for you."

He looked up, his dark eyes fixed on her. "I do, too, Sylvia."

"Have a roll. They're nice and hot," she said quickly, needing to change the subject.

"Thanks."

"Are you ready for coffee?"

He sent a gentle smile her way and pointed to her still empty plate. "Eat, Sylvia, while everything is hot. I can wait on the coffee. The water is fine."

They finished their supper in near silence, their only conversation forced. Sylvia tried to relax, but it was hard. She wanted to throw herself into Randy's arms and beg him to come back to her.

When they had finished and nearly all the casserole was gone, Randy leaned back in the chair with a satisfied sigh, linking his fingers across his chest. "That's the best meal I've had in a long time. Thanks, Sylvia."

"You're welcome." She gave him an impish grin. "If you had your choice of desserts, what would it be?"

"Lemon meringue pie of course," he answered without hesitation. "Don't tell me—"

"Yes," she said smiling with pride as she rose and pulled her beautiful pie from the cabinet. "Lemon meringue pie." For a moment, she thought Randy was going to cry. The look he gave her was one she had not seen in a long time, and it tugged at her heartstrings.

"I know you're doing all these nice things in hope I'll change my mind—about the divorce—but, Sylvia, I am going to go through with it. I don't want you to get the idea that things are going to change just because you've fixed my favorite foods."

Now *she* wanted to cry, but instead, she pasted on a smile. "Let's not discuss the divorce. For this week, that word is off-limits. We made a deal, remember? And I plan to honor my end of the bargain. Give me this one week, Randy, as you've promised. This one last Christmas together, okay?"

He nodded, and she could tell his smile was as false as hers.

"Good, let's enjoy our pie." She cut generous wedges for each of them, then filled their coffee cups.

"Oh babe, that's good," Randy said, taking his first bite. Then he seemed embarrassed that he had called her *babe*, the pet name he had used the first few years of their marriage.

She ignored his embarrassment as she forked up her own bite of the delicious pie. She had to admit it was one of the best lemon meringue pies she had ever baked. She hadn't lost her touch. "I'm glad you're enjoying it, Randy. I'd hoped you would."

"I guess I should offer to help load the dishwasher," he said, placing his fork on his plate and folding up his napkin.

"I'd like that." Normally, before she had gone off to college, DeeDee helped her mother with the clearing of the table and the dishwasher loading. To her recollection, Randy had never helped with the dishes. He had been too busy with his studies the first four years of their marriage. After he graduated, he had worked at two jobs to make ends meet so she could quit work and stay home to raise their family. Since that time, she had always been a stay-at-home mom, and he had never needed to take part in household chores.

Maybe he should have! Then he'd have a better idea of what I've been doing for this family all these years. Things, apparently, he's taken for granted.

He gave her an I-really-didn't-mean-it smile, stood, and began stacking up their plates and silverware. "You'll have to show me how to do it."

"It's quite simple." She took the plates and silverware from him and rinsed them off under the faucet before handing them back to him. "Plates stand on end in those little slots on the bottom shelf. Silverware goes in the basket. Glasses and cups upside-down on the top shelf, saucers same place as the plates."

She watched him awkwardly place the dishes where she had told him. "One capful of dish soap goes in the dispenser, then swing the lid closed, shut the door, and latch it."

Once the dishwasher was in operation and the rest of the table cleared, with things put where they belonged in the cabinets and refrigerator, she shook the tablecloth, stuffed it into the laundry basket in the utility room, and placed the colorful basket of silk flowers back on the table. "That's that! Let's go into the family room. A letter came in today's mail from DeeDee addressed to both of us. I haven't opened it yet."

He followed her, heading for the cushy green leather recliner—his recliner. But he stopped midroom as if remembering the last time he had tried to sit in that chair and she had chastised him, saying he no longer belonged in it.

"Go ahead," she said, trying to sound unconcerned, but remembering that same incident as vividly as if it had happened that very evening. "We bought it especially for you. Remember?"

He moved into the chair cautiously, settling himself down and propping up the footrest.

Sylvia watched with great interest, wishing she had a camera to capture his picture. He belonged in that chair, in this house, not in some high-rise apartment. She pulled a footstool up close to his chair and opened the note from their daughter, reading it aloud.

> "Dear Mom and Dad.
>
> I was sitting here in my room, listening to my roommate complain about her parents, and I suddenly realized how lucky I am to have been born to the two of you. Mom, you're the greatest. You always put your kids' needs ahead of your own and were always there for us, doing the little things that made our childhood so happy and carefree."

Sylvia's heart swelled with happiness at her daughter's words. She went on without so much as a sideways glance at Randy. She knew one look in his direction and she'd lose it.

> *Dad, you work too hard. I wish you hadn't had to spend
> so much time at the newspaper, and I know I used to gripe
> about it all the time, especially when you had to miss my
> volleyball and basketball games. But now that I am older,
> I realize you did it because you loved me, and you wanted
> to provide all the things for us kids that you never had and
> to be able to send Buck and Aaron and me to college.*

Sylvia was sure she heard a distinct sigh coming from the cushy green leather chair, but she read on, sure their daughter's words were affecting him as much as they were her.

> *I've never thanked you two properly, but I want you to
> know I love you both and appreciate you and everything
> you've done for me. If my life ever amounts to anything,
> it'll be because of the two of you and the way you love the
> Lord and the witness you have been to me. Maybe now
> that Aaron and I are gone, you two can do some of the
> things you've put on hold while we were growing up. I
> pray for you every day, asking God to protect you and keep
> you both well. I'll see you December twenty-fourth.
> With love, Your daughter, DeeDee.*

When she finished, she folded the note and slipped it back into its envelope, not sure what to say or if she should just remain quiet. When Randy didn't speak, she rose, crossed the room, and placed the envelope on the coffee table.

"She's—she's a great kid, isn't she?" he finally asked, after clearing his throat.

"Yes, she is. All three of our kids are great kids."

"You've done a good job with them. I'm—I'm afraid I can't take much of the credit."

She moved back to the footstool and seated herself, smiling up at him, ignoring the ache in her heart. "I wouldn't have been able to be a stay-at-home mom if you hadn't worked so hard to provide for us."

"But it took me away from home. I missed the kids' games, their school activities, so many things."

She gave his arm a tender pat. "But you were at church with us most Sundays, and you've served faithfully on the church board all these years."

"You—you still haven't told them—about—"

"No, I haven't, and I'm sure Buck hasn't either, and I don't intend to, Randy. When and if the time comes, you'll have to be the one to do it."

He leaned his head against the headrest and stared off in space. "It is going to happen, Sylvia. I've been thinking about this for a long time. I nearly asked you for a divorce last summer, before you and the kids went to Colorado to attend that Christian camp, but I thought it might be easier on everyone if I waited until DeeDee and Aaron went off to college."

"Easier on them? Or easier on you?" she prodded gently, wishing right away she had kept her question to herself. "Don't answer that," she added quickly. "We're putting all that behind us now. I had no business even asking."

He gave her a faint smile, then closed his eyes. "This chair is comfortable. Feels like it was made for me."

She reached out and pulled his shoe off, and when he didn't protest, she pulled the other one off and placed them on the floor beside the chair. "I know."

"The music's nice."

"I thought you'd like it."

For the next few hours, they sat listening to the stack of CDs she had put on the player. Randy in his recliner, Sylvia stretched out on the chintz sofa. As the last song played and the room became silent, Sylvia heard a faint snore coming from the recliner. Randy was fast asleep.

She tiptoed into the hall, quietly picked up his suitcase and garment bag, and carried them up the stairs and into their room. She hung his garments in his nearly empty closet, then placed his suitcase on the bench at the end of the bed. She nearly unpacked it for him—and would have before their separation. But now it seemed like an invasion of his privacy, and she did not want to upset him by doing something that might offend him.

After washing her face and reapplying a faint trace of the rose-colored lipstick, she rubbed a sweet-smelling body lotion on her face and arms and slipped into the pink, lacy gown she had bought when she had been shopping for the other items she planned to wear during their week together. Before she left the room, she fell to her knees by the bed and asked God to be with the two of them and to give her the grace to be patient, loving, and kind. Lastly, she asked Him to keep her from saying things she shouldn't and to bring Randy back home for good—home where he belonged.

He was still sleeping in the chair when she came back into the family room, his head twisted to one side, his arms resting on the armrests. He looked like a little boy, and she wanted to kiss his sweet face. She could not remember the last time he had fallen asleep in that chair.

"Randy," she said softly, giving his shoulder an easy shake. "It's nearly eleven. Time to go to bed."

He sat up with a start, blinking as if he had to get his bearings. "How—how long have I been asleep?"

She reached out and gave his hand a tug. "Probably an hour."

He lowered the footrest and allowed her to pull him to his feet. "I–I'll get my things," he said, heading toward the front hall.

"They're already in our room."

He gave her a wild stare. "I—I was planning on sleeping in the guest room."

"This is still your home, Randy, at least until midnight Christmas Day. You'll be sleeping in our bed tonight, where you belong."

Chapter 8

He backed away from her, holding his palms up between them. "I—I don't think so."

She stepped toward him, determined to make her plans work out as she had envisioned them. "We *do* have a king-sized bed. There's plenty of room for both of us. I'll sleep on my side. You sleep on yours."

When he did not respond with more than a doubtful grunt, she added, trying to keep her voice sweet and on an even keel, "You do plan to keep your part of the bargain, don't you?"

He gave a defeated shrug and headed for the stairs without answering. As soon as he reached their room, he unzipped his suitcase and pulled out what looked to be a brand-new pair of pajamas, still bearing the creases from their packaging. Sylvia muffled a laugh. Although she'd bought him a number of pairs of nice men's pajamas during the years they'd been married, he'd always refused to wear them, opting for a T-shirt and boxers, saying only old men in hospitals or care homes wore pajamas.

She waited patiently, sitting on her side of the bed while he showered, using the time to read her Bible. Minutes later he emerged, his curly hair damp, and wearing the new pajamas. "Shower feel good?"

He nodded. "Yeah, I've always loved that big showerhead. Makes a guy feel really clean."

Is that a faint tinge of aftershave I smell? Did he put that on just for me?
"I like that showerhead, too, especially when I rinse my hair," she added,
closing her Bible. "I put a glass of water on your nightstand."

He glanced toward the glass. "Thanks."

"I'm not going to bite, Randy," she told him, giving him a raise of
her brow.

"I—I know, I just feel—awkward, that's all, now that things are—
different—between us."

"I still love you," she reminded him gently, not wanting to add to his
discomfort.

He took a swig of the water, set the glass back in the coaster, and
lowered himself onto his side of the bed, keeping his back toward her.

Sylvia quickly scooted across the bed on her knees and cupped her
hands on his shoulders. Although he flinched and gave her a what-are-
you-doing look, he did not move away. "You've been working too hard.
Let me rub your shoulders."

"You don't have—"

"I know I don't have to—I want to. Now sit still." She began gently
kneading his deltoid muscles, letting her fingers perform their magic.

"Umm, that feels so good."

"You're way too tense, Randy. Come on, relax."

"I don't want you to tire yourself."

"I'll quit when I get tired. Now let me work those neck muscles."

He bowed his head low and, oohing and aahing with each stroke, he
let her fingertips press into his strong neck.

"I used to do this when we were first married, when you came home
from your classes, remember?" she asked, leaning against him.

He nodded. "Yeah, I remember. Knowing you'd be waiting for me at
the end of a hard day at college, ready to massage my weariness away, was
what kept me going those last few hours."

Finally, he reached up and took hold of her hand. "Stop. That's
enough. As much as I'm enjoying it, I don't want you to get hand cramps."

She leaned over his back and planted a kiss on his cheek before
scooting back over onto her side of the bed and slipping under the quilt.
As he turned to look at her, she flipped back his side of the covers, then
turned her back to him. "Good night, Randy."

She felt the bed move slightly as he crawled in, pulled up the covers, and turned out the light on his nightstand. "Good night, Syl."

Sylvia arose early the next morning and carefully slipped out from under the covers, leaving Randy sprawled on his side of the bed, tangled up in the sheet and quilt. She had to smile. Parts of his thick hair stood in mounds where he had gone to sleep with it wet from his shower.

She wiggled into the new pair of jeans she had bought and topped them with a bright fuchsia T-shirt, a color she never wore. Most of her life, she had opted for beige, white, or soft pastel colors, never gaudy ones. But this week called for extreme measures, so many of the new things she'd bought were way out of her usual color realm, colors more like what she thought Chatalaine would wear.

Chatalaine.

She was glad Randy had not mentioned that woman's name. She did not plan to either. The less he thought about Chatalaine, the better, as far as she was concerned. She had him on her turf now, and she planned to keep him there all week.

After spritzing her newly cut hair and finger combing it as the beautician had shown her, she painstakingly applied her new makeup and added another dash of Randy's perfume. By the time he arrived in the kitchen, also dressed in jeans and a T-shirt, the table had been set and she had breakfast well underway. "Good morning," she called out cheerily. "I hope you slept well."

He ran his fingers through the hair at his temples. "Extremely well. I like that mattress. The one I have at the—"

She put a finger to his lips on her way to the refrigerator, silencing him. "We're not going to talk about your apartment this week," she said as she pulled the bottle of cranberry juice from the fridge and filled their glasses. "The bacon is ready, and I'll put the eggs-in-a-basket on a platter as soon as we've prayed, so they'll be good and hot. Would you pour the coffee?"

He moved to the coffeemaker, lifted the pot, and filled their cups. "Umm, that smells good. New jeans?"

She froze. She had bought the faded ones purposely so he would not think they were brand new. "I haven't had them very long."

"Nice T-shirt."

"I've decided I like bright colors."

"Looks good on you."

Sylvia smiled, then bowed her head and prayed. Though he usually prayed at breakfast, she knew he must feel awkward doing it under the circumstances, and she wanted him to be at ease.

"I thought we'd take a walk after breakfast," she said lightly as she placed her napkin in her lap.

He picked up his fork with a quizzical look. "Oh? Where to?"

She grinned. "You'll see."

"Ah, Syl?"

"Yes?"

"Could—could I have a piece of that pie for breakfast before we leave?"

They finished their breakfast, pulled on their jackets, and headed out the kitchen door and through the garage. Randy seemed surprised when Sylvia stopped and opened her car door.

"I thought you said we were going for a walk."

She motioned him inside, crawled in herself, and hit the button on the garage door opener. "Too boring to walk around here. I thought we'd walk around the Lakeside Park area. It's pretty over there."

He closed the door and buckled his seatbelt. "I haven't been to that area in years."

"I know."

It was a beautiful day. The sun was shining, and there were just enough breezes to make the leaves on the trees sway gently. Sylvia parked the car along the curb, and they set out walking.

"You don't have your cell phone on your belt," she said almost jubilantly.

"I didn't think you wanted me getting any calls."

She grinned. "I don't, but I don't want you to cut yourself off totally, in case there is an emergency at the newspaper."

"I think things will be all right. That young man I told you about should be able to—"

"You never told me about any young man."

His pace slowed and his brows rose. "I didn't?"

"No, you didn't, but I'm glad you have someone to help you at the paper. You've needed a dependable assistant for a long time."

"I hate turning things over to someone else."

"I know."

"Did I tell you Carol broke her arm?"

She stopped walking as her jaw dropped. "No! When did that happen?"

"Yesterday. About noon. I had to take her to the hospital. It happened right after they called and told me one of our big presses went down."

Guilt hit her like a Mack truck. "Oh Randy, I'm so sorry to hear that. What a day you must've had. Is she okay? Did you get the presses rolling?"

"I guess she'll be all right when the swelling goes down. She'll be off at least until after New Year's, but she still won't be able to type when she comes back. I'll have to hire a temp to help her. And no, the presses were still down when I left the office, but two guys from the company that sold it to us are flying down from Cincinnati to help get it back in operation." He took a few more steps, then turned to her again. "I guess I didn't tell you two of my key men in the newsroom quit this week. They got jobs with the State Department. They gave them much better benefits than I could offer. I don't blame them, but it sure left me high and dry. They were good men."

Her eyes widened. "No, you didn't tell me about them. Oh Randy, I had no idea how hard it was for you to take this entire week off. If you need to call the office—"

He placed his hand on her arm. "No, they aren't expecting a call from me. I've told everyone *not* to call me, short of a real emergency. I've put the newspaper first in my life for way too long. From now on, I'm looking out for Number One. Me. I'm going to do the things I've always wanted to and never had the time or the money."

Like buy a motorcycle and wear gold chains around your neck?

"I may even take up golf, or fishing, maybe even hunting. I haven't decided yet. I might even do some traveling."

Alone? Please don't tell me you plan to take Chatalaine with you!

"I've even considering taking flying lessons; maybe buy myself a small plane."

"My, you do have plans. I hadn't realized you were interested in any of those things."

"Most of them were only pipe dreams—things I wanted to do when I retired, but too many men I know—guys my age—have been dropping like flies. Never even making it into their sixties. I don't want to be one of them."

Is that what this is all about? Your mortality?

"My dad died just a few months before his sixtieth birthday, his dad in his late fifties. I want to do things while I'm in good enough health to enjoy them, and I figure now's as good a time as any. From what my older acquaintances tell me, it ain't gonna get any better."

You are *in a midlife crisis!* "But your grandfather on your mother's side is still alive, and he's in his eighties!" she countered. "That's in your favor."

"But my body is much more like my father's side of the family."

Sylvia grabbed his hand and tugged him toward a nearby park bench. She sat and pulled him down beside her. "No one is invincible, Randy. Only God knows when He's going to call us home."

Randy ignored her comment as he looked around, taking in the park, the chip-lined walking path, and the park bench itself. "Hey, this is all beginning to look very familiar," he said, eyeing her with a laugh. "We didn't just happen to stumble onto this particular bench, did we?"

Her heart rose like a kite caught in an updraft. "You remembered!"

"I proposed to you in this very spot nearly twenty-six years ago."

"Yes, you did. And I gladly accepted your proposal, Randy. You're the only man I've ever loved. That little diamond you placed on my finger that day was the most beautiful ring I had ever seen. I'll never forget how excited I was. I was going to be Mrs. Randy Benson!"

"Boy, were we naive. A couple of kids who had no idea what we were doing or what the future held for us."

She cupped her hand on his shoulder and smiled into his deep blue eyes. "A couple of kids in love who were willing to face anything to be together."

"Your parents weren't too happy when they saw that ring on your finger as I recall."

"No, they much preferred that I attend college and get a degree in nursing, but marrying you was all I wanted out of life. Once they realized that, they accepted it." She scooted a tad closer to him. "Our life and our marriage may not have been perfect, but I never wanted it to end."

He stood quickly and glanced at his watch. "Hey, it's nearly noon. I'm hungry; how about you?"

"Sounds good to me, and I know just the place to have lunch."

She took his hand and led him across the street and down two blocks, to the little all-night diner where they used to eat hotdogs when they could afford to splurge and eat out.

Randy opened the door and stood back to allow her entrance. "Boy, I didn't even know this place was still in business."

"Then you do remember coming here?"

He nodded, stepping inside. "Yeah, I remember. You were pregnant with Buck, and you continually seemed to have a craving for foot-long hotdogs with pickle relish and loads of mustard. I wonder if they still have them on their menu."

They crowded into the only booth that was available, a small single-sided bench in the far corner.

"Yep, they're still on the menu! You up to it?" Randy asked when the waitress brought their water glasses.

Sylvia smiled back at him. "You bet!"

They giggled through lunch like two junior high kids, consuming their hotdogs and even ordering chocolate shakes to go with them.

"I'm stuffed," Randy said on their way back to where they had parked the car. "Why didn't you tell me to stop when I ordered that second hotdog?"

"Would you have listened?" she answered, slipping her hand into his as they walked along.

He gave it a slight squeeze, but did not pull away. "Probably not!"

When they reached the car, Sylvia handed Randy her keys. "You drive."

He opened her door and waited until she was safely inside before jogging around to the driver's side. "Where to, lady?"

She could not hold back a smile. "How about our home?"

When they reached the house, the answering machine was blinking. Sylvia rushed to it and punched the button. A man from a florist shop was calling, and he sounded very much like the man who had called before, about the apricot roses. "Just wanted you to know, Mr. Benson, the lady loved the red roses. She said to tell you they were so beautiful they made her cry!"

Sylvia's blood ran cold. Randy may not have mentioned Chatalaine's name, but he was making sure she received flowers from him while he was away from her.

"Wow, am I ever glad to hear that," Randy said, moving up beside her. "I wanted those flowers to get to her as soon as possible. She needed to know someone cared about her."

Sylvia wanted to reach out and slap him. Hard. How dare he? When he had promised the week was to be hers?

"Poor Carol. I know she's hurting. No one ever sends her flowers. I hope those roses make her feel better."

Carol? He sent those flowers to Carol? Of course he did! She's been his secretary for years. Sylvia nibbled on her lower lip, glad she had not blurted out something she would have regretted later. Feeling riddled with guilt, she picked up the phone and held it out to him. "You want to call the office? See how things are going?"

He took it from her and placed it back in its cradle. "I'm sure things are fine." He looked about the room, his gaze fixing on the Venetian blind. "While I'm here, you want me to fix that window blind? I know it's been driving you crazy. I'm—I'm sorry I haven't gotten around to repairing it for you."

She nodded, grateful for his offer. The blind had been driving her nuts. Something in the mechanism was broken, and she had not been able to lower it to block out the late afternoon sun. "If you're sure you want to."

"Looks like I've got the time," he said with a grin, heading toward the garage, where he kept his tools.

She watched from her place on the sofa as he unfolded the stepladder and strapped on his tool belt, amazed at how handsome he was. "*Women age. Men mature.*" Where had she heard that silly saying? But it was true. Randy had matured, and on him, it looked good. No wonder that society columnist had gone after him.

"There you go. Good as new!" Randy crawled down and folded the ladder. "Go ahead. Give it a try."

Sylvia quickly moved to the window and gave a slight tug on the cords. As smooth as glass, the shade lowered into place. "Hey thanks, that's great. Now the sofa won't fade."

"You're welcome. I'm just sorry I haven't done it before now. Got anything else that needs to be fixed?"

"The drain thingy in the lavatory in the half bath off the kitchen won't lock down."

He gave her a mock salute before heading toward the little bathroom. "Tool-time Randy and his trusty tool belt are on their way!"

In ten minutes, he was back. "Why don't I check that filter in the furnace while I'm at it?"

For the rest of the afternoon, Randy made the rounds of each room in the house, replacing lightbulbs, tightening screws, checking cabinet hinges and knobs, all sorts of manly me-fix-it projects. What impressed Sylvia most was the joy he seemed to get out of doing those things, the very things she had been at him for months to take care of.

By the time he finished, she had supper on the table.

"I knew it!" he said, coming into the kitchen after a quick shower. "Broccoli soup with garlic toast! I could smell it clear up in our bedroom!"

"I was hoping you'd be pleased." She checked the pot on the stove one more time and made sure the soup was not sticking to the bottom of the pan. "It's ready."

Randy rubbed his hands together. "Umm. Let me at it."

"You're not too full from those two hotdogs?"

He grinned. "What hotdogs?"

Again, Randy helped her clear the table and load the dishwasher when they had finished supper. Sylvia could not believe he had actually eaten two big bowls full of the broccoli soup and consumed four pieces of toast.

"What now?" he asked as they turned off the kitchen light and headed for the family room.

"I thought we'd watch a movie."

He wrinkled up his face. "Not a chick flick."

He headed for his recliner. She shook her head and pointed to the empty spot beside her on the green leather sofa. "Not there. Here."

He gave her a shy grin and settled himself down beside her while she punched the PLAY button on the remote control.

The tape began to roll, and Randy leaned forward, his eyes narrowed. "Naw, it can't be! An action movie? Surely not!"

Sylvia quirked a smile. "Don't tell me you've seen this one!"

He leaned back with a satisfied look. "Nope. I didn't even know it had been released to the video stores yet. I've been wanting to see it but—"

She rolled her eyes. "I know—you've been too busy."

"Exactly. But no more. From now on—I'm going to—"

"Take care of Number One," she inserted quickly, though it broke her heart to say it.

"Right! I didn't think you liked action movies," he said as the credits finished and the story started.

I hate them! "They're okay. Some of them have good story lines." *If you can weed them out from all the car chases and noise!*

Before long, Randy was so into the movie, he barely seemed to notice she was sitting beside him. *Will this thing ever end?*

When the movie ended, Randy took her hand in his and looked

into her eyes. She held her breath; sure he was going to say something romantic.

"Is there any lemon meringue pie left?"

Men! She wanted to pick up one of the sofa pillows and pelt him like she had seen Shonna do to Buck, but instead she smiled sweetly. *Maybe the way to a man's heart is through his stomach after all. Hopefully, Chatalaine is a lousy cook!* "Sure. I'll cut you a piece."

Randy finished his piece of pie with an appreciative sigh. "That's the best pie I've ever tasted."

"Think you can sleep on a full stomach?" she asked him as she pointed to the clock on the fireplace. "It's after eleven."

He let out a big yawn, stretching his arms first one way, then the other. "Oh yeah. I'm so tired I could sleep standing up. I can't believe how far we walked this morning."

They turned out the lights and made their way up the stairs to their room. This time, Randy did not question their sleeping arrangements. By the time Sylvia had washed her face and slipped into her gown, he was already sitting on his side of the bed in his pajamas. "Is that a new gown?"

She nodded. "Yes. Do you like it?" *I had it on last night. Were you so worried about sharing the bed with me you didn't even notice?*

"Yeah, I like. What happened to those—"

"'Granny gowns', as you used to call them? They're in the back of my closet. I'm thinking of giving them to Goodwill. They're all cotton and would make wonderful rags," she added with a chuckle. "I'm making some changes in my life, too, Randy. Getting rid of my granny gowns and fuzzy slippers is one of them."

He gave her a quick once-over. "Well, you're a knockout in that gown. You should wear that color more often."

She moved across the bed on her knees and began her massage routine. Again, Randy did not protest. He just leaned over and let her willing fingers work on him again. "This has been a good day," he finally said when she moved back to her side of the bed. "Thank you for it."

"You're welcome." Giving him a playful grin, she slid under the covers and flipped onto her side, facing away from him, praising the Lord. Randy seemed mystified by her calmness, which is exactly what she wanted. "Good night, Randy."

"Good night, Syl."

Chapter 9

They awoke the next morning to another perfect Dallas day. After a hardy breakfast, they loaded into the car and headed for the zoo.

"Do you have any idea when I last visited a zoo?" Randy asked when they stopped at the gorilla section.

"I remember exactly. You were pushing DeeDee in her stroller, so I'd say that was about seventeen years ago. As I recall, you tilted that stroller up onto its rear wheels and jogged around the alligator pit, making motor sounds while she giggled and clapped her hands."

"Then, when she fell asleep, I carried Aaron on my shoulders while you pushed the stroller."

She threw her head back with a raucous laugh. "Poor little Buck! We made him wear that harness thing your mother bought so he wouldn't get lost. Remember how he hated that thing?"

"Do I! I finally had to take it off him. I couldn't stand his crying. Then he complained because we held onto both his hands."

"I guess—sometimes—we were overprotective."

"Hey, you!" Randy made a face at one of the gorillas, sticking his thumbs in his ears and wiggling his fingers at the animal.

Sylvia tugged on his arm. "Randy, people are staring at you!"

He shrugged complacently. "Who cares? Remember, I've turned over a new leaf! No more inhibitions!"

She eyed him with a shake of her head. *Turned over a new leaf? Sounds to me like the whole tree has fallen on your head!* "Oh, yeah. For a minute there, I forgot." She pointed to an area past the gorilla section. "Look, there's the duck pond."

Randy bought a bag of feed from the little vending machine, and they sat down on a nearby bench, tossing the feed to the many ducks that gathered. "We sure had three cute kids, didn't we? It seems like only yesterday little DeeDee was letting the ducks eat out of her hand. Those were good times, Syl."

"Yes, they were. We didn't have much in the way of worldly goods, and at that time, neither of us knew Jesus, but we had each other and nothing else mattered." She let out a deep sigh. "How I wish we could go back to those sweet times."

Randy threw the remaining feed onto the ground, watching a dozen ducks scramble to snatch it up before the others got it. "But we can't, Syl. What's done is done, and there's no undoing it."

It could be undone, if you were willing to give it a try!

Randy suggested they stop by the sandwich shop near their house for lunch since Buck and Shonna would be coming for dinner in a few hours. By three, they were back home, with Sylvia tying an apron about Randy's waist so he could help her prepare dinner.

The minute Buck came through the door, Sylvia rushed into the living room and pulled him to one side, warning him to behave and not mention one word about the divorce or seeing his father with Chatalaine.

"How's it going?" Buck asked in a whisper.

"I'm not sure, but we've been getting along extremely well. He may be humoring me, but at least I'm having a chance to spend time with him—just the two of us—which we haven't done in a long time."

He doubled his fist and gave a playful blow to her chin. "Hang tough, Mom. Shonna and I are praying for you and Dad."

She stood on tiptoe and kissed his cheek. "I know, Buck. God is able. I'm counting on Him answering our prayers."

Randy came into the room, pulling off his apron. He cautiously extended his hand toward his son. With a huge grin, Buck took his hand and shook it heartily as his mother breathed a sigh of relief. The last thing she wanted was for her husband and son to have harsh words.

After greetings all around, the four moved into the dining room, where the candles were already burning brightly, to share the dinner Randy and Sylvia had prepared. The dinner conversation was light and cheery, with both Randy and Sylvia relating their experiences of the past two days. Everyone laughed when Sylvia told them about Randy making faces at the gorilla.

"You're lucky they didn't stick you in the cage with him," Shonna said with a giggle. "After a trick like that."

By ten, the couple left after much hugging and kissing. Randy lingered at the door until Buck's taillights disappeared into the darkness. "What a good guy our son has turned out to be."

"We can be very proud of our kids," Sylvia said, gathering up the empty glasses that had accumulated in the room and carrying them to the kitchen.

"So, what's on the agenda tomorrow? A trip to the local museum?" Randy asked as they climbed the stairs. "Are we going to check out the mummies or look at abstract paintings?"

"Neither. Tomorrow morning, I thought we'd stay home, but I have something planned for the afternoon."

Randy stopped on the landing. "The whole morning at home? That sounds nice."

"But you have to make me a promise." She could see by his face that he expected a caveat. "I want you to call the office and make sure everything is going well."

He tilted his head quizzically. "You sure you want me to call? That wasn't part of the deal."

"It's my deal, which means I have the right to change the rules anytime I like," she said, pinching his arm playfully before turning and scurrying off to their room.

When she came out of the bathroom wearing another new nightgown, Randy noticed immediately and gave her a "Wow!" She did a quick turn around, twirling the long flowing skirt like DeeDee always did when she was a child playing dress-up in her mother's clothes.

Randy let out a long, low whistle. "I'd say getting rid of those granny gowns was a vast improvement!"

"You—you don't think it's too low cut? Too sheer?"

"No ma'am. Not one bit!"

She crawled up onto the bed and pulled her Bible from the drawer. "If you don't mind, I thought I'd read a couple of chapters before going to bed."

He propped his pillow against the headboard and leaned against it. "Fine with me."

"That is, unless you're ready to go to sleep. I don't want the light to keep you awake." She gave him a coquettish smile again. "If you don't mind waiting a bit, I'll massage your neck muscles again. I noticed you rubbing at them when we were all sitting in the family room. Has your neck been bothering you, Randy?"

His hand rose and stroked at his neck. "Some. I asked a doctor about it. He said it was tension."

She put her Bible aside and crawled across the bed, moving up beside him, her hands kneading into the tight muscles. "You poor baby. Why didn't you tell me?"

"Nothing you could do about it. He said the only thing that would help was getting rid of some of the stress in my life, and that's not an easy thing to do."

Is that why you're trying to make such radical changes in your life? Because the doctor advised it? I'll bet he didn't tell you to get rid of your wife of twenty-five years. Did you tell him you had a girlfriend? "I'm sure it's not easy, with the job you hold at the paper."

"He said I'd better start getting more exercise, too. That long walk you and I took yesterday was just what the doctor ordered."

She worked his deltoids until her fingers began to cramp. After bending to kiss his cheek, she moved to her side of the bed and crawled under the quilt. "I'm really tired, and I know you are, too. Maybe we'd better put off reading the Bible until morning. Let's get some sleep. We have lots of work to do tomorrow."

Randy crawled into his side of the bed, propping himself up on his elbow. "Work? What kind of work?"

"You'll see." She gave him her sweetest smile before scooting to the edge of her side of the bed. "Good night, Randy."

"Good night, Syl." A second later, she heard the snap of the light switch, and the room fell into utter darkness.

"Syl?"

"Yes."

"Thanks for the neck rub."

"You're welcome."

"Syl?"

"Yes."

"Thanks for another great day."

"It was great, wasn't it?"

"Yeah. It was."

∞

Randy's eyes opened wide when the alarm sounded. Surely, it was not morning yet. He flinched! *Oh, oh! What am I doing?* His arm draped over Sylvia's shoulder, he was on her half of the bed. He froze when she moaned and reached toward her nightstand to turn off the alarm. He quickly withdrew his arm and scooted to his side, sitting up with a loud, exaggerated yawn. "What time is it?"

"Seven," she droned sleepily.

"Seven? I'm usually wide awake at five. You realize this week is going to throw my entire routine off whack, don't you?" He watched as she stood, reached her hands toward the ceiling with an all-out stretch, then headed toward the bathroom. *Boy, did I goof. I can't believe I was on her side of the bed after making such a big deal about sleeping in the guest room. But, wow! She looked so cute with that new haircut and wearing that fancy, low-cut red nightgown.* He shook his head to clear it. "Wanna tell me about today's project?" he called out to her.

She appeared in the bathroom doorway. "Not yet, but it'll be fun."

As he sat on his edge of the bed, waiting for her to return, his gaze fell to the Bible on her nightstand. How long had it been since he'd read his Bible? He shut his eyes tightly, trying to block out its vision. A shudder coursed through his body. *"Are you sure you want to leave your wife?"* a small voice seemed to ask from within his heart.

"I don't love her like I used to," he answered in a whisper.

"You don't love her like you used to? Or are you turning your back on that love, trying to block it out to excuse your childish behavior?"

Randy crossed his arms over his chest defiantly. "I've made up my mind. It is time for me now. For the past twenty-five years, I have sacrificed for my family, putting their needs first. I've worked round the clock to attain the position I have at the paper, spent every free hour I could find serving on the church board, and where has it all gotten me?"

"*You are in reasonably good health. You have a beautiful, loving wife, terrific kids, a great home, more than adequate income, and you are a born-again Christian. What more could you ask?*"

"Time for me! Time to do the things I'm interested in, before I either die or simply cannot do them because of poor health or because I'm too old. There's so much I haven't experienced. When I come to the end of my life, I don't want to have regrets for the things I never did. Why can't people understand that?"

"Randy?"

His wife's voice brought him back to reality as she came out of the bathroom.

"Were you talking to someone? I heard voices."

"No, just talking out loud. Bad habit I seem to have picked up lately." He gave her a smile he hoped she did not perceive as guilt. "Among my other bad habits."

"See you downstairs," she said with a grin. "Gonna be a simple, quick breakfast this morning—juice, coffee, and cold cereal. We have things to do. Wear your jeans and a T-shirt."

Sylvia was already sitting at the kitchen table, sipping her juice when Randy arrived—showered, shaved, and ready for the day. Once the dishes had been loaded into the dishwasher, she reached for the two clean aprons hanging on a hook on the back of the pantry door. "One for me," she said, tying it about her waist, "and one for you."

"An apron? What's this for?"

"We're going to bake Christmas cookies!"

He gave her a skeptical stare, then allowed her to tie his apron about his waist. "This should be an experience!"

"It'll be fun, and remember, our kids will be home in a few days, and they'll be expecting homemade cookies. Think how proud you'll be when you tell them you helped me bake them!" She gave him a gentle swat on his seat. "Now go wash your hands. I'll get my cookbook."

He did as he was told, and by the time he was finished, Sylvia was already beginning to assemble the things they would need. "What kind are we going to make?"

She gave him a mischievous smile. "Actually, we're going to make three kinds. Chocolate chip, of course, since all the kids—and you—love them. My famous spritz cookies run through the cookie press and decorated, and lastly, it wouldn't seem like Christmas without sugar cookies cut into all those wonderful shapes and sprinkled with red and green sugar crystals. So we'll have to make those, too."

"Wow, we are going to be busy." He rubbed his hands together briskly. Just hearing the names of the cookies made his mouth water. "What do you want me to do?"

She handed him a tall canister from the counter. "Take that big bowl and measure me out six cups of flour."

He placed the canister on the island, pulled a clean coffee cup from the cabinet, and began to measure out the flour. "Like this?"

Her eyes widened. "No, you can't use a coffee cup! You have to use a measuring cup!"

He gave her a shrug. "Why? A cup is a cup!"

"Oh my, I can see I'm going to have to watch your every move."

Using the proper measuring cup, Randy began again to spoon out the flour. "Here you go," he said, trying to conceal a grin as he pushed the bowl toward her. "I lost count, but I think there are six cups in there."

Again her eyes widened.

"Just kidding, Syl, just kidding. There *are* six cups of flour in there. Honest."

She took the bowl from his hands and placed it on the counter next to the mixer. "I doubt it. It looks as though some of it went onto the floor, and you have to have at least a fourth of a cup on your apron!"

He looked quickly down at his apron, and she giggled aloud. "Just kidding, Randy. Gotcha!"

"What do you want me to do next?"

She motioned toward the kitchen wall phone. "Call your office."

He eyed her with a questioning smile. "Only if you want me to."

Fortunately, there were no major catastrophes going on at the office. A few minor ones, but the man he had left in charge was doing an admirable job of handling them. Randy was glad she had insisted he call. It set his mind at ease and made him realize it was only reasonable that he turn some of his responsibilities over to someone else. There was no way he could do it all.

They laughed their way through the three kinds of cookies, and by the time the last cookie sheet went into the oven, the kitchen was an absolute mess. Chocolate chips, red and green sugar sprinkles, and several colors of icing adorned the counters, the floor, and even the two cookie bakers, but the cookies looked beautiful spread out across the dining room table.

"I did it! I actually made cookies!" Randy said proudly as he stood beside Sylvia surveying their handiwork. He slipped an arm about her waist. "But I have to admit, babe, I never realized how much time and work you put into making all those Christmas cookies that seemed to appear by magic on Christmas Day. I don't think I ever thanked you."

∞

Sylvia blinked hard to hold back tears of gratitude as God's Word filled her heart, giving her renewed hope. *"Favour is deceitful, and beauty is vain: but a woman that feareth the Lord, she shall be praised. Give her of the fruit of her hands; and let her own works praise her in the gates."*

"Syl? Did you hear me?" Randy asked, giving her a slight squeeze.

"I—I heard you, Randy, but I want you to know—I never expected any thanks. They were my gift to my beloved family. Yes, they took time and work, but I loved every minute of it. I made those cookies because I knew you and the children would enjoy them."

They had a quick bite of lunch, then worked side by side cleaning up the kitchen until it once again sparkled.

"You still haven't told me what we're going to do with the rest of the afternoon."

She tapped the tip of his nose with her finger. "You and I are going shopping!"

He responded with an unenthusiastic groan. "I hate shopping, you know that."

"You'll like this shopping. We're going to buy a Christmas tree!"

By the time they reached the third Christmas tree lot, Randy was a basket case, ready to accept any old tree, but Sylvia insisted they had to find just the right one.

"I know exactly what you want," the elderly man at the YMCA Christmas tree lot told them as she described the tree she had in mind.

Randy's excitement revived when he saw the tree the man selected for them. "It's perfect, Syl. It'll look great in the family room!"

She had to agree, it was perfect. The right kind, the right height, the branches were densely filled with needles, and the color was an exquisite, healthy dark green.

"We'll take it," Randy said enthusiastically, almost snatching the tree from the man's hands.

"Don't you want to ask how much it is first?" the ever-frugal Sylvia asked.

Randy shook his head vigorously. "I don't care what it costs. It's exactly what we were looking for!"

It was nearly four o'clock by the time they got the tree mounted in the tree stand and placed in its majestic position in the corner of the family room. His hands on his hips, Randy stood back to admire it.

"Guess what you get to do!"

He turned to her with a frown. "Not the lights!"

She nodded. "Yes, the lights. Like you did on our first Christmas."

Together, they made several trips to the attic, bringing down all sorts of boxes and bags, until the entire family room floor was cluttered with decorations. As soon as they located the big box containing the lights, Randy began winding them around the tree, with Sylvia sorting out the various strings and handing them to him. Once the last string was connected and the extension cord in place, Randy proudly placed the plug in the wall and the beautiful tree came to life, with hundreds of tiny twinkling lights sparkling and blinking.

"Oh Randy. It's beautiful! I've never seen a prettier tree. You did a great job with the lights."

His eyes surveyed the tree from top to bottom. "I kinda messed up there at the top. I should've put more lights up there."

She gazed at the tree, not caring if the lights were even. Randy had put those lights up—willingly. That is all that mattered. "I think it's perfect," she said dreamily.

He bent and kissed the top of her head. "You're biased."

For the next hour, they opened boxes, pulled out ornaments, and hung them on the tree. As they worked, they reminisced over each one, remembering where and when they had purchased them or who had given them to them as a gift. Some the children had made. Some Sylvia had made. Some others had made, but each one had its own special story.

"Remember when you bought me this one?" Sylvia asked, pulling a fragile, clear-glass angel from its fitted Styrofoam box.

He carefully took the ornament from her hand and stared at it. "Our tenth Christmas together?"

She nodded, surprised that he remembered. "Yes. You—you told me—"

"I—I told you that you were my angel. I bought it in the hotel gift shop when I was on a business trip to New York City. That face reminded me of you. You were supposed to come with me, but both DeeDee and Aaron came down with the chicken pox at the same time, and you had to stay home."

She felt her eyes grow misty. "I—I should've left them with my mother and gone with you. They would probably have been fine without me. Just like your office is getting along fine without you." She moved toward him, her hand cupping his arm. "Why didn't we find time for each other, Randy?"

He swallowed hard, then placed his free hand over hers. "I don't know. Life's demands, I guess."

Suddenly, he pulled away, and she was sure he did it to change the subject and break this melancholy mood they both seemed to be in. "Are—are you hungry?" she asked, wanting to put him back at ease. "I've got a pot of chili simmering on the stove."

His smile returned. "With grated fresh onion, cheese, and chips?"

"Just like you like it, and apple crisp for dessert."

After supper, when the kitchen had been restored to order, Sylvia led Randy back into the family room. "Tired?"

"A little. Stringing lights is hard work." He moved into his recliner and propped up the footrest, then sat staring at the tree. "Pretty, isn't it?"

"Absolutely beautiful! I've never seen a prettier tree." Sylvia punched the PLAY button on the CD player, and Christmas music filled the room.

"Me either. It's nice just sitting here, watching the lights, listening to Christmas carols, and relaxing. Surely you don't have a project for tonight."

She smiled and shook her head. "Not really. I've already wrapped all the Christmas presents. I want to put them under the tree, that's all. You sit right there and watch me."

"You work too hard, Syl. I never realized how hard."

"Give her of the fruit of her hands; and let her own works praise her in the gates." "What I do isn't work, Randy. It's a labor of love." She bustled about the room and, after spreading around the base of the tree the Christmas skirt she had made several years ago, she pulled dozens of beautifully wrapped presents from the closet and arranged them on top of it. "There. All done."

He stared at the vast array of gifts. "When did you do all of that?"

"I started the week after Thanksgiving. Shopping for our family was like a—therapy—for me. It kept my mind off—things."

"I get the message," he said, leaning his head against the headrest. "I'm sorry, Syl, but there wasn't an easier way or a better time to tell you that I—"

She quickly pressed her fingers to his lips. "Shh. We're not going to talk about that this week. That was our agreement."

"I—I just don't want you to get your hopes up."

Though Sylvia remained silent, her mind was racing. *My hopes are up, Randy! I can't help it. However, I can see, if I am going to win you back, I'm going to have to give it everything I've got. Hopefully, what I have planned for tomorrow will bring you to your senses!*

Chapter 10

By the time Randy crawled out of bed the next morning, Sylvia had strung a long evergreen garland along the top of the mirror over the fireplace, arranged the fragile Nativity set on the dining room buffet, and placed dozens of Christmas decorations and Christmas candles all over the house. Many of them were things she herself had made over the years.

"Hey, why didn't you wake me up?" he asked, looking from one decoration to another. "I would've helped you."

She pointed to the empty boxes standing in the hall. "You can carry those boxes back up to the attic, if you want to help."

He grinned as he shoved up the short sleeve of his T-shirt and flexed his bicep. "Glad to. Easy task."

By ten, Sylvia was instructing Randy to pull the car into the parking lot of Dallas Memorial Hospital.

"Why here? I'm not sick, and you haven't mentioned feeling bad."

She smiled as she pushed her door open and climbed out. "Indulge me."

Once inside, they walked to the bank of elevators opposite the reception desk. As they entered the open one, Sylvia punched the button marked FIVE. She could feel Randy's eyes on her as the elevator ascended. She led him down a hall to a long set of plate glass windows with a sign above them that read NEWBORN NURSERY. "This look familiar?" The look on his face told her he well remembered the place.

༄

Randy pressed his cheek against the cool glass as memories flooded his mind. "Oh yes," he answered in a voice that sounded raspy, even to him. "Especially that little bed over there in the far corner. I thought we were going to lose him, Syl, and we nearly did." He felt her move up close to him and lean her head against his shoulder. "I'd never been so scared in all my life."

"The birth of a child is truly a miracle. God took the love of two young people who thought they had the world by the tail and, through their love, created a tiny image of the two of them and breathed the breath of life into him. Our little boy. Our precious first child. Our Buck."

Randy closed his eyes, his head touching hers, and tried to shut out the memory of the tiny baby as he had gasped for life with each tiny, laborious breath. "He—he was so small. So helpless. I could've held him in my palm."

"But God intervened and strengthened his little lungs. Our baby lived, and look at him now. Buck is tall, straight, and healthy. A real answer to prayer." She slipped her hand into the crook of his arm. "I can remember us both begging God to spare our child, making Him all sorts of promises. That was an emotional time for us, Randy, one I'll never forget. But there were happier times right here in this nursery, too. Remember when the twins were born?"

He rubbed at his eyes with his sleeve. "Do I ever! I was so afraid of losing you, I must've driven the doctors and nurses crazy. After the trouble we'd had with Buck, I couldn't imagine you giving birth to two babies!"

She snickered. "I was so worried about you, I had trouble concentrating on my breathing. I was afraid you were going to faint on me."

He wrapped his arm about her waist. "And I did! I was never so embarrassed in my life."

"You were only out a few seconds. Good thing that male nurse caught you, or you might've ended up on the floor having to have stitches in your head."

"I'll never forget the experience of seeing our children born. How did you ever go through it, Syl? The pain must've been excruciating."

She leaned into him and gazed at the newborn in the little bed nearest the window. "Our babies were worth it." Watery eyes lifted to his. "They were *our* babies, Randy. Yours and mine. I loved them. I loved you."

For long moments, neither of them said a word, just continued to stare through the glass. Finally, Sylvia took his hand and silently led him back to the elevators. "There are several other things I want to show you," she said in a mere whisper as the elevator doors opened.

When they reached the corner of Fourth Avenue and Bogart, Sylvia instructed Randy to turn left.

"This looks very familiar. I think I know where we're headed. Are you sure this is a good idea, Syl?"

"Humor me, Randy, okay?"

He pulled through the cemetery gates, made a quick right turn, then a left, and parked at the side of the road. "Wanna reconsider?" he asked as she pushed open her door and made her way between the gravestones.

By the time she reached her destination, Randy was at her side. She knelt beside the tiny grave marked ANGELA RENAE BENSON and bowed her head. Seconds later, she felt Randy kneel beside her.

Sylvia tried to be brave, to keep her emotions under control, but she could not, and she began to weep.

"I'm sorry, Randy. Maybe you're right. Maybe coming here wasn't a good idea, but I wanted you to remember all the things we've gone through together. All the love and the joys and the heartaches we've shared."

"I—I do remember, Syl. I tried to be strong—for you—when we lost our little Angela, but inside I didn't feel strong. I felt like a failure. I wasn't even there for you when she was born. I was—too busy—at the newspaper, tending to some unimportant problem when you called and said your mother was taking you to the hospital. I should've dropped everything and rushed to your side, but I didn't."

She leaned against him, needing his strength. "It—it wasn't your fault, Randy. We would've lost her whether you made it or not."

"I—I wonder if she would've looked like DeeDee? With lots of dark curly hair and that cute little button nose?" He leaned forward and traced their baby's name with the tip of his finger.

"Angela was a product of our love, Randy, just like Buck and DeeDee and Aaron. She—she would've been ten years old in February."

"Let's go, Syl," he said tenderly as he rose and offered her his hand. She stood slowly, giving the tiny grave one last look. Then she leaned into Randy as his arm encircled her, and they walked back to her car.

"Now where? Home?"

She pulled a tissue from her purse, blotted her eyes, then blew her nose loudly. "Not yet. Head on down Fourth Avenue and turn onto Lane Boulevard."

They rode silently for several miles, when suddenly Sylvia grabbed onto his arm and said, "Pull over."

"Oh, Syl. Not here!"

When he braked, she crawled out of the car and motioned for him to follow, carefully moving down a slight embankment toward a grove of trees. When she reached her destination, she stopped and turned to him. "I nearly lost you here, Randy. I'll never forget that day."

He reached out and ran his fingers across a long diagonal scar on the nearest tree's trunk. "I thought for sure I was a goner when that drunk ran me off the road. It felt like I was doing ninety miles an hour when I left the boulevard, but I was only doing around forty according to the witnesses." He bent and rubbed at his knee. "I wasn't sure I was ever going to walk again."

"You could've been killed."

"I know."

"It was a miracle you lived. God spared you, Randy. He had a purpose for your life."

"I may never have walked again if it hadn't been for you and all those months of physical therapy you helped me with. How could you do it, Syl? With everything else you had to do, you put aside two hours a day to help me work my leg."

"Give her of the fruit of her hands; and let her own works praise her in the gates." "I wanted to do it, Randy. I loved you."

He took a couple of steps back, stuffing his hands into his pockets. "If you're trying to make me feel bad, you're succeeding."

"Making you feel bad is not my purpose, Randy. I just want you to remember the things that make up a marriage. Both good and bad."

He extended his hand, and they climbed back up the embankment. This time, Sylvia moved into the driver's seat.

They crossed town to an area near the college where Randy had attended school and obtained his degree in journalism. Sylvia brought the car to a stop in front of a rundown old tenement building.

Randy shielded his eyes from the sun as he stared at the place they had once lived, pointing up to the third floor with his free hand. "That was our apartment right up there. I can remember you standing in that very window, smiling and waving at me when I came home from class every afternoon."

"Seeing you coming up that sidewalk was the highlight of my day. What fun we had," Sylvia said, waxing nostalgic. "Remember those old wooden crates you got out of the dumpster at some warehouse. We used those for end tables and a coffee table and thought they were grand. I don't remember who gave us that old brown frieze sofa bed, but it did the job. I loved that apartment. Our very first home. I was so proud of it."

He laughed, and his laughter made her smile. "You were easy to please." His smile disappeared. "I always hated it that you had to work nights to put me through school. As I sat in that apartment each night, studying, I kept thinking about you waiting tables in that all-night restaurant and the creeps that must've come in there. I should never have let you support me like that, and you sacrificed your own education to make sure I got mine."

"But you sacrificed, too! You cared for Buck while you were studying. Otherwise, I couldn't have worked. We sure couldn't afford a babysitter, and neither of us wanted to leave him with one anyway." She gave his arm a reassuring pat. "I didn't mind. Honest."

His fist pounded into the palm of his other hand. "That place was a dump! I can't believe we lived there."

"That *dump* was an answer to prayer, Randy. Remember how excited we were when we finally found something we could afford?"

"I remember promising you we'd be out of there and in a better place in a year. We ended up staying there nearly all four years!"

"Just knowing you wanted a better place for us and were working to get your education so we could eventually have one was enough for me." She grabbed onto his hand and tugged him to the little drugstore on the corner. Once inside, she went to the soda fountain and ordered two root beers, a delicacy they had only been able to afford when she had worked a little overtime at the restaurant or some customer had left an overly generous tip. They sat side by side on the tall soda fountain stools and sipped their drinks the way they had done it nearly twenty-five years ago. On the way out, Sylvia bought a bag of red licorice, the long, stringy kind, another delicacy they had indulged in from time to time. She opened the bag and handed several strings to Randy.

He bit off a long piece, then winced. "We actually liked this stuff?"

She gave him a wink. "Come on—you loved it and you know it!"

He grinned. "Yeah, I guess I did."

"Beat you to the car," she hollered over her shoulder as she took off down the block. He did not catch up with her until she had reached the car.

He threw his arms around her as they both stood leaning against the car, panting and breathless. "What are you trying to do, lady? Throw me into a heart attack? I haven't run like that since—since—"

She chucked him under the chin with a giggle. "Oh? It's been so long you can't even remember when?"

"Maybe!" He pulled open the passenger door. "Who's driving? Me or you?"

"I'll drive." She crawled in, started the car, and waited until he had his seatbelt fastened. "One more stop, then we can go home."

She only had to drive a few blocks to reach their final destination for the day—a little red brick church on a crowded lot, surrounded by a tall wrought iron fence. She expected Randy to protest, but when he did not, she opened the door and climbed out. As she had hoped, the big wooden doors were standing open. Slowly, she walked inside, hoping Randy would follow.

An elderly woman who was waxing the pews smiled up at her as she entered. Without a look back to see if Randy was behind her, she moved slowly to the altar and knelt on the worn kneeling pads, folding her hands in prayer.

When she finished praying and looked up, she found Randy kneeling beside her. "This is the exact spot where we gave our hearts to the Lord, Randy. Do you remember?" she whispered.

He nodded.

"Though we used to attend church here occasionally, until that morning, neither of us had much interest in the things of the Lord, but when the pastor brought that message—"

"About engraving us on the palms of His hands and how God has a plan for each of us, a plan to prosper us and not harm us?"

Sylvia turned to him in amazement. "You do remember!"

"Isaiah 49:16 and Jeremiah 29:11. I'll never forget those verses. They've helped me through some hard times."

Tears pooled in her eyes, making it difficult to see his face. "Hard times, like now?"

Randy stared into her eyes for a moment, and though she could not be sure, she almost thought she saw traces of remorse. But he turned away and walked back up the aisle, leaving her alone at the altar. She quickly bowed her head once more and poured out her heart to God. "Lord Jesus, only You can put this family back together again. Please soften Randy's heart, and God, make me be the kind of wife You would have me be. I so want to serve You. I want to know that perfect plan You have for me and for Randy. Forgive me for the many times I've sinned against You. Only now, since Randy has been back home and I've examined my own life, have I seen how I, too, have been responsible for the problems we're facing. Help me to do Your will. Please, God, please!"

They stopped at Randy's favorite steak house for dinner and, although steak was not Sylvia's favorite, she ordered the same thing Randy ordered and willed herself to enjoy it. When Randy excused himself to go to the men's room, Sylvia held her breath, hoping he was not going to phone Chatalaine. Funny he had not mentioned her name, not once since he had arrived on the nineteenth. But why should he? No doubt he knew even the mention of her name would start an argument. No, Randy was too savvy for that. As long as she did not mention the woman's name, she was sure he would not either. However, he was back in no time. No way would he have had time to phone the woman.

When they reached home, Randy plugged in the Christmas lights while Sylvia cued up another Christmas CD. They stayed up long enough to watch the nightly news and one of the late night talk shows before heading upstairs.

"Big day tomorrow," she told him as she climbed into bed. "The kids will be here for Christmas Eve, and we—you and I—have gobs of food to prepare. DeeDee and Aaron promised to be home by four, and Buck and Shonna are coming as soon as he gets off work."

Randy set the alarm on his side of the bed and flipped off the light before sliding under the covers. "Syl?"

"Yes."

"I can't say I exactly enjoyed today, but I have to admit it was an eye-opener."

"Oh?"

"I mean—I'd almost forgotten some of the things you and I have gone through together. I guess I—put them out of my mind."

"That's understandable. I wanted to forget some of them, too."

"Syl?"

"Yes."

"I don't want you to get the idea that I'm hard-hearted, but at the same time, I don't want you to get your hopes up. I'm still planning on going through with the divorce."

"Good night, Randy. I love you."

Silence.

Suddenly, she felt Randy's weight shift in the bed, then his warm body snuggle up next to hers, his arm draping over her. "Good night, Syl."

Her heart pounded so furiously, she was sure he could feel the vibration. "Good night, Randy. Sleep tight."

∽

Sylvia jerked out of Randy's arms and sat up with a jolt as his alarm sounded at seven. *Today is December the twenty-fourth! I have less than forty-eight hours to convince Randy to forget about the divorce and move back home where he belongs! Help, Lord!*

"Why don't I fix breakfast today?" Randy asked as he crawled out from under the covers and stretched his long arms.

Sylvia glanced at the Bible on her nightstand. "You sure you don't mind?"

"Not a bit! I'll come back up and take a shower later. Just don't expect anything too fancy."

She waited until she heard him go down the stairs, then picked up her Bible and began to read. *I'm sorry, Lord. Although it seems I keep shooting prayers up at You continually, I've neglected my Bible reading since Randy has come back home.* She turned to one of her favorite chapters, Psalm 139, and began to read. " 'O lord, thou hast searched me, and known me. Thou knowest my downsitting and mine uprising, thou understandest my thought afar off.'" She read through the few verses silently until she came to the twenty-third verse. " 'Search me, O God, and know my heart: try me, and know my thoughts: And see if there be any wicked way in me, and lead me in the way everlasting.'" *That's my prayer, Lord. Please, show me how to make these last few hours count. I can't lose my husband!*

As Sylvia reached for her jeans, she thought she heard the front door close. But deciding the noise must have been Randy working down in the kitchen, she went into the bathroom to put on her makeup and fix her hair. By the time she reached the kitchen twenty minutes later, he was sitting at the table waiting for her, a large white sack resting in the center.

"How does an Egg McMuffin sound?"

"Wonderful," she responded happily, meaning it, as she sat down beside him and reached for the sack.

∽

The strains of "Silent Night" filled the house as the six members of the Benson family gathered around the dining room table. Randy, Sylvia, Buck, Shonna, DeeDee, and Aaron. Sylvia's heart was so filled with gratefulness that they were all together like this—this one more time—she thought it would burst. Her wonderful son, knowing the secret their parents were carrying and apparently wanting to take the strain off his father and mother, offered to say the blessing on their food. Sylvia had hoped Randy would insist on doing it. However, when he kept his silence, she gave Buck an appreciative smile and a nod, and they all reached for one another's hands, forming a circle. Buck's prayer was brief but sincere, as he asked God to bless the food and the hands that prepared it and to bless each one assembled, especially his mom and dad.

"Your dad has been helping me all day," Sylvia told her family as she passed the carving knife to her husband.

Aaron gave a teasing snort. "Hey Dad, why've you been hiding your culinary talents all these years? This stuff looks pretty good!"

DeeDee slapped playfully at her twin brother. "Be quiet, Aaron, or he may never do it again."

"Tell me what you fixed, Dad, so I can avoid it," Aaron added, backing away from DeeDee as she swung at him again.

"I'm not telling," Randy said with a chuckle as he began to slice off thick wedges of the roasted turkey. "You'll either have to take your chances or starve. Your choice."

Aaron cocked his head as he weighed his options. "You win. I'll take my chances. Pass the mashed potatoes."

"I think everything looks wonderful, Father Benson," Shonna said as she held out her plate. "You and Mother Benson make a great team."

Sylvia gave her an exaggerated bow. "Thanks, Shonna. It's nice to be appreciated."

"We all appreciate you, Mom," Buck interjected with a quick sideways glance toward his father. "Don't we, Dad?"

"We sure do. I'm just beginning to realize all your mother does for this family. Giving us great meals like this is just a small part of it."

Sylvia's heart pounded erratically. "Thank you, Randy. It was—was sweet of you to say that." *"Give her of the fruit of her hands; and let her own works praise her in the gates."*

"Hey, are you going to give me a piece of that turkey, Dad," Aaron asked with a playful frown, "or am I going to have to arm wrestle you for it?"

The meal continued pleasantly with good-humored bantering going on between Randy and his sons.

After the last bite had been consumed and everyone's napkin returned to the table, Shonna and DeeDee volunteered to clear the table and help Sylvia clean up the kitchen, suggesting the men go into the family room and relax. Once everything was back in shape and the dishwasher humming away, the women joined them. Buck was already at the piano playing a Christmas carol.

"Hey, all of you," he told the gang, gesturing for them to join him, "it's time for the Benson family sing-along."

The five gathered around him and joined in as he led off with "O Holy Night." Sylvia's breath caught in her throat as Randy moved next to her, harmonizing with her as they had done so many times before. They sang three more carols, then Aaron suggested it was time for their annual reading of the Christmas story from the second chapter of Luke before they turned to the opening of the presents.

"Why don't you read this year, Buck?" Randy said, reaching for the big family Bible on the bookshelf. "My throat is a bit husky."

As her son gave his father a frown, Sylvia felt her mouth go dry. *Don't say anything you'll be sorry for, Buck. Please!*

Buck reached out and took the Bible from his hands without comment and opened it to Luke 2 and, after allowing everyone time to be seated, began to read.

"I love that chapter," DeeDee said as her older brother closed the Bible and returned it to its place. "You helped me memorize it when I was a kid, Dad. Remember? The first year I was on the church quiz team."

All eyes went to Randy. "Yeah, I guess I did. You were a quick learner, as I recall."

"Just think," Aaron said, dropping down on the floor near the tree and drawing his knees up to his chest, circling them with his arms, "God sent His only Son to earth as a baby, knowing He would die on the cross to save us from our sins. Isn't that an awesome thought?"

Sylvia moved to the leather sofa and settled herself beside her daughter-in-law. "It's hard to fathom He could love us that much, when we're so unworthy."

"What do you think of the tree your mother and I picked out and decorated?"

All eyes turned to Randy as he abruptly changed the subject. "Pretty, huh? I put the lights on."

"It's beautiful, Daddy," DeeDee said, leaning over her father to kiss his cheek. "You did a good job."

"I didn't know the old man had it in him," Aaron chimed in with a wink. "How come Mom's had to decorate the tree by herself all these years?"

"I—I like decorating the tree," Sylvia inserted quickly, not wanting Randy to have to explain himself. "But it was nice to have your dad do it for a change."

"Whose turn is it to distribute the presents this year?" Aaron picked up the gift nearest him and gave it a shake. "Looks like the man in the red suit has already been here and gone."

Sylvia leaned forward and swatted at him. "Don't talk that way, Aaron. I've always thought talking about Santa and pretending he's the one who brings the presents takes the glory away from Jesus and the real meaning of Christmas."

Aaron did an exaggerated double take. "You mean there really isn't a Santa Claus?"

"Just for that remark, young man, you can pass out the gifts," Sylvia said, hoping this wouldn't be the last Christmas her family would all be gathered like this. She could not imagine Christmas without Randy sitting in his chair.

"Okay, if you insist." Aaron began picking up the presents, reading the name on each tag out loud, shaking the package, and predicting what he thought might be inside before handing it to the person for whom it was intended.

"Here you go, DeeDee. I'm guessing Buck and Shonna are giving you—a Barbie doll!"

He turned to his older brother. "Buck, inside this present DeeDee is giving to you, I predict you have a—a—a teddy bear!"

Randy's present came next. "Wow, Dad, what do you suppose is in this little box from Mom? Maybe that new set of golf clubs you told me you wanted?"

Sylvia watched with expectation as Randy opened her present.

"Oh Syl," he said as he tore the last bit of paper off and opened the box. "You shouldn't have."

"What is it, Dad?" DeeDee asked, sliding closer to his chair.

"It's—it's the palm-sized video camera I've been wanting. How did you know—"

Sylvia grinned. "Buck told me you'd mentioned it to him. I hope I got the right one. You can exchange it if—"

"It's exactly the one I wanted. Thanks, Syl. Now I can take pictures of this motley crew as they open the rest of their presents."

Sylvia breathed a contented sigh. He liked her gift.

On and on and on it went, with each of Aaron's gift predictions sending the group into fits of laughter. Sylvia wanted to remember those sounds forever. As she glanced at the clock, she felt panic set in. Only twenty-eight hours to go, and although she and Randy had experienced some wonderful times since he'd arrived on the nineteenth, he seemed no closer to changing his mind about staying than when he'd arrived.

"And this last one is for Dad," Aaron said as he stood and hand delivered it to his father. "Another one from Mom. How many does that make? Looks like you came out better than the rest of us this year."

"That's not true. Each of you—"

Aaron held up a finger and waggled it at his mother. "Just kidding, Mom. Don't get bent out of shape. After all, that old man is your husband. He'll be around long after us kids move out for good."

Randy sent her a quick glance that chilled her bones.

"Well, that's it!" Aaron reached for the big trash bag Sylvia had brought in to hold all the torn wrapping paper and ribbons.

She looked down at the presents piled on the coffee table in front of her. Each of the children had given her wonderful gifts, and she was grateful for each one of them, but none of the gifts had been from Randy, and she wanted to break down in tears.

"Actually," Buck said, rising and taking Shonna's hand in his, "there's another present coming, but it won't be delivered for some time. Shonna and I are going to have a baby! In July!"

Sylvia's heart leaped for joy. How she had longed to have a grandchild to cuddle and care for. She was going to be a grandmother! Her gaze went to Randy, who was just sitting there, as if in a stupor.

"Hey, old man!" Aaron said, punching his father in the arm. "You're gonna be a grandpa!"

Randy donned a quick grin and stood as both Buck and Shonna hurried to his side. "Congratulations, son. You, too, Shonna. That's gonna be one lucky baby. You two will make great parents."

"Aw, they won't be half as good as you and Mom," Aaron said, hugging his mother's neck.

"Who wants dessert?" Randy asked as he surveyed the group. "Your mom and I made her famous Millionaire Pie."

Buck raised his hand. "I'll take a very small piece. I'm stuffed with those fabulous Christmas cookies you and Mom baked. Those things are good!"

"Thank you, thank you, thank you!" Randy bowed low, then asked, "Small pieces of pie for everyone?"

The entire group shouted yes in unison.

"I'll help Dad," Buck said, motioning Sylvia to remain seated.

A cry choked in her throat. *Buck, no! Please don't say anything to your dad about Chatalaine or the divorce. Or about him not giving me a gift. Please!* She watched in fear as the two men headed for the kitchen.

Seeming to sense her fear, Shonna slid over on the sofa and wrapped her arm about Sylvia's shoulder. "It'll be okay. Buck won't say anything," she whispered so only her mother-in-law could hear.

A few minutes later, Buck and Randy came back into the room carrying six plates with small wedges of pie on them. Buck passed out the plates while Randy handed each person a fork and napkin.

As Sylvia started to rise again, Buck shook his head. "I'll get the coffee and cups, Mom. You eat your pie."

She gave him a slight grin, thankful for his thoughtfulness.

"Buck and I had quite a talk in the kitchen," Randy told everyone as he forked up his first bite of pie.

Sylvia nearly choked.

"He tells me he's thinking about going back to college for his master's."

"I think he should," Aaron said, nodding. "He's a smart guy."

They continued with good conversation until, eventually, the pie was gone. "I have to get up early, Mother Benson, so we'd better be going. We're due at my parents' house at ten, and I still have to make two pies tonight."

"You are going to be here for breakfast, aren't you?" Sylvia asked quickly.

Buck bent and kissed his mother's cheek. "Sure, Mom. We'll be here by eight. We wouldn't miss your famous cinnamon rolls."

Aaron rose and tugged his sister to her feet. "We'd better get to work, too, little sister."

"Work? You two?" Buck asked with a teasing smile.

Aaron nodded. "Yep. Our friends are picking me and DeeDee up at ten for our ten-day skiing trip to Colorado, and we haven't even started packing our gear."

DeeDee took her mother's hand and patted it with concern. "You and Dad going to be okay? Being here by yourselves on Christmas Day?"

Sylvia nodded. "We'll be fine, honey. Just enjoy yourselves. I know you two have been looking forward to this ski trip since last year. Just promise me you'll be careful."

Everyone walked Buck and Shonna to the door. After hugs all around and more congratulations to the expectant parents, the couple left, and Randy closed the door.

Aaron and DeeDee each kissed their parents, thanked them for a wonderful Christmas, and headed up the stairs to their rooms.

"I—I think I'll go to bed, too," Sylvia said, as she gathered up her gifts. With a heavy heart, she climbed the stairs, leaving Randy to turn off the lights and check the doors, a job she had taken over in his absence.

I have to forget my husband didn't even give me a present. I can't let him see me sulking like this. Maybe, since he's spent the week with me, he simply didn't have a chance to do any shopping. I have to stop feeling sorry for myself. Deciding a quick shower might lift her spirits, she gathered up her gown and slippers and moved into the bathroom. When she came back out fifteen minutes later, Randy was sitting on the side of the bed in his pajamas, reading the instructions for his new video camera.

Sylvia pasted on her cheeriest smile as she sashayed across the room toward him. *If Randy does leave, I want him to remember me smiling and looking radiant and more like the woman he married twenty-five years ago.*

He looked up with a broad smile, as if nothing whatsoever was wrong. "Hey, another new gown? I really like this one! Even better than the red one."

She twirled around, holding her hands out daintily like a ballerina, and ended up sitting on the bed beside him.

"Oh, I like that perfume!"

She lifted her head, offering her neck to him. He bent and took in an exaggerated whiff. "Zowie! Now that's what I call a perfume!"

She gave him a coy smile. "You bought it for me for Christmas two years ago."

"Do I have good taste, or what?"

"Thanks for another wonderful day, Randy," she said as she crawled onto the bed beside him, her fingers cupping his neck. "I think the kids had a good time tonight. I know I did." She began to knead his muscles as he tilted his head to one side. "That was some present Buck and Shonna gave all of us. Can you believe we're going to be grandparents?"

"I always wondered what it would be like to hold my first grandchild in my arms. I guess we'll find out in July."

She loved touching his skin, wafting in his manly scent, feeling his hot breath on her hands. She longed to leap into his lap and smother him with kisses, but if she did, she knew he'd probably run for the door, and she wouldn't have that one last day with him, so she restrained herself.

"There, does that feel better?" She scooted off the bed and bent to kiss his cheek. Suddenly, Randy grabbed her and pulled her to him, kissing her more passionately than he had done in years. Although surprised by his sudden action, she melted into his arms, fully participating in their kiss.

"You are so beautiful," Randy whispered in her ear as he held her close and nuzzled his face in her hair. "I've missed the closeness we used to share." He kissed her again, holding her in his arms tighter than ever.

"I've missed it, too," she whimpered breathlessly against his lips.

"This has been one of the best weeks of my life, Syl. I'll never forget it."

She clung to him, wishing this moment could last forever, but just as quickly as he had pulled her to him, he pushed her away.

"Hold me, Randy! Please! I love you!"

"I—I can't! Don't you see? I'll be leaving tomorrow night! Holding you and kissing you like this—well, it isn't fair to either of us. Our marriage is over, Syl! It died a long time ago! What we're having this week is make-believe."

She could not believe what she was hearing! She had been so sure God was answering prayer. "But Randy, you said this was one of the most wonderful weeks of your life! We've had a great time together! We're going to be grandparents!"

"You don't get it, do you, Syl? Just because we've both been bitten by the festivities and hoopla of Christmas doesn't mean things won't return to what they were before when we get back to normal. We've both been like Ken and Barbie this past week! On our best behavior. Working to please each other and avoiding having words. We've been blinded by the joys and frivolity of the Christmas season. Bright lights, candles, ornaments, music. What happens when Christmas is over and the lights and ornaments are put back in their cardboard boxes and returned to that drab attic? I can't take that chance. It took me nearly two years to get up the courage to tell you how I really felt—how unhappy I've been. I can't go through it again!"

She wanted to slap him, scream, hit a door, something, anything to wake him up. "Can't you see I love you, Randy? This hasn't all been your fault. I see that now! However, we can both change. We can work out our problems and differences if we really want to do it. We can't throw this marriage away like last week's copy of your newspaper. Our marriage is a living and growing thing!"

"A living thing that has been dying a slow death, Syl. It's time for the burial." He snatched up his pajamas and headed toward the bathroom, closing the door behind him.

Sylvia had never felt so hurt and rejected. Why hadn't she seen this coming? How blind and stupid could she have been? With tears flowing, she climbed into bed and pulled the sheet over her head. She heard Randy come out of the bathroom, felt him crawl into bed, and heard the click of the lamp.

Twenty-four hours. If I can't convince Randy to stay by then, it's all over. I promised I'd let him have the divorce, and I have to keep my word. Father God, are You listening, or are You forsaking me, too?

"Syl?"

She wanted to pretend she was asleep, but she could not. "Yes."

"Good night."

"Good night, Randy."

Sylvia lay awake until the red numbers on the clock showed 3:00 a.m. From the even rhythm of Randy's breathing, she was sure he was asleep, though she herself had barely closed her eyes. She crawled carefully out of bed and padded gently down the stairs, mumbling to herself. "Someone has to put the stockings up and fill them with little gifts and candy. Since Santa isn't real, I guess I'll have to do it."

"Give her of the fruit of her hands; and let her own works praise her in the gates."

Chapter 11

December 25 dawned even more beautiful than any other day in the week they had been together. Although Sylvia was dead tired from lack of sleep, she jumped out of bed with a smile. *This is your last chance, girl. Make the most of it!*

Randy turned over with a frown. "You're chipper this morning."

"Why shouldn't I be? It's Christmas morning, and my family will all be gathered around the table for breakfast." She snapped her fingers, then yanked the cover off him. "Rise and shine, Grandpa!"

He covered his face with his hands. "Grandpa? That term sounded nice last night, but this morning, just the mention of it makes me feel old."

She crossed the room and opened the blinds, letting the room fill with sunshine. "Not me! It makes me feel young. I can hardly wait for the patter of little feet in this house again."

He pulled himself to a sitting position and ran his fingers through his hair. "Are you forgetting dirty diapers?"

"I don't even mind those." She poked him in the ribs with the tips of her finger. "Hustle, hustle! Buck and Shonna will be here soon. You don't want them to see you in those hideous pajamas, do you?"

He looked down at his pajamas. "What's wrong with them?"

"The colors are nice, but have you looked closely at the pattern?"

He raised an arm and squinted at the sleeve. "No."

"Randy! Those yellow dots are little ducks!"

"Ducks? I thought they were polka dots. Why didn't you tell me? I was in such a hurry when I bought them, I guess I never really looked at them."

"No, I'm sorry to tell you, but those are not polka dots; those are ducks. Cute little yellow duckies." She hurried to the door. "The kids will be here in ten minutes. If you don't want them to tease you about your ducks, you'd better get dressed."

"Is that another new T-shirt?" he called after her. "Looks good on you. I like purple!"

She had to smile. "Yes," she called back over her shoulder. "I bought it because I thought you'd like it!"

By the time she had filled the coffeepot and put the rolls in the oven, the front door opened and Buck and Shonna came bustling in. Within seconds, DeeDee and Aaron came down the stairs, with Randy two steps behind them. "Well," she said with a joy that overwhelmed her sorrow, "looks like the gang's all here. Anyone want to check their stockings?"

Buck, Shonna, DeeDee, Aaron, and even Randy, all made a mad dash to the family room, pulling their stockings from the fireplace and rummaging through their contents, pulling out the little wrapped gifts, whistles, paper hats, balloons, bubblegum, trinkets, and candy canes. Randy put on his paper hat, looped two candy canes over his ears, and paraded through the room loudly blowing his whistle while the whole family laughed hysterically. Buck soon joined him, followed by Shonna, DeeDee, and Aaron. Sylvia could stand it no longer, pulled on her hat, draped her candy canes over her ears, and stuck a whistle in her mouth, too. Following Randy's lead, the little battalion made their way through the house, traipsing through nearly every room, until they were all too weak with laughter to keep it up any longer.

"Now that we've made complete fools of ourselves," Sylvia said, pulling the candy canes from her ears, "does anyone want breakfast?"

The Benson family laughed their way through breakfast, enjoying the huge platter of homemade cinnamon rolls Sylvia had baked, along with juice, coffee, and the large slices of the country ham she'd put in a slow oven when she'd gotten up to fill the stockings.

Buck and Shonna left at nine thirty to go to her parents' house. At ten, DeeDee and Aaron kissed their parents goodbye and joined the group of eager skiers honking in their driveway. Sylvia cast a cautious glance at the clock. *Fourteen hours to go.*

As soon as the door closed behind them, Randy tugged on her hand. "Come on, Grandma. I'll help you clean up the breakfast mess."

Putting on the best smile she could muster, she followed him into the kitchen and began gathering the dirty dishes and carrying them to the sink while he put things in the refrigerator. *I've got to stop counting the hours!*

"You outdid yourself again. These cinnamon rolls are the best you've ever made." He unwound a rounded section of the last roll on the plate, broke it off, and popped it into his mouth.

"Thanks. I'm glad you enjoyed them."

"So, what's the plan for today?" He slipped the empty plate into the dishwasher, then placed a hand on her wrist with a winning smile. "By the way, Merry Christmas."

She reached up and planted a quick kiss on his cheek. "Merry Christmas to you, too, Grandpa." *Why didn't you get me a present, Randy? Am I that unimportant to you? Do you hate me that much? I'll bet you got your little cutie a wonderful present!* "And by the way, we're staying home. All day."

"I was hoping you'd say that."

Once the kitchen was cleaned up, Sylvia pulled a covered dish from the freezer and left it on the counter to thaw for lunch. Then the two of them headed for the family room. To her surprise, Randy plunked himself down on the sofa instead of moving to his recliner. She picked up the copy of the *Dallas Times* that Buck had brought in when he and Shonna had come for breakfast and sat down beside Randy. "I put on a fresh pot of coffee," she said trying to sound casual as she pulled the oversized Christmas Day paper from its wrapper. She shuffled through the various sections, finally coming to the sports section, which she handed to Randy. As soon as his attention was focused on it, she quickly pulled out the "Dallas Life" section, bearing that spectacular picture of Chatalaine and her willowy figure and Cheshire cat smile, folded it, and placed it on the lamp table on her side of the sofa, face down. Compared to that woman, Sylvia felt dowdy, rumpled, and old. As soon as she had a chance, she planned on putting it in the trash container. No need for Randy to be reminded of his paramour on this, her final day with him.

Randy scanned through the sports section, then placed it on the cof-fee table. "Not much sports news today." He gazed at her for a moment, then cautiously slipped an arm about her shoulders and pulled her close. "I want you to know, Syl, how much I appreciate everything you've done to make this Christmas special for all of us. The kids, me." He hesitated as he raised a dark brow. "I—I hope we can always remain friends—for our children's sake."

Her heart dropped to the pit of her stomach, and she swallowed both her pride and a hasty reply. *Hold your anger! You have less than thir-teen hours left. Don't blow it! Make every minute count. This may be your last chance to woo him back.* Instead of snapping his head off, which was what she would have liked to do, she smiled up at him, cradling his freshly shaven cheek with her hand. "Can we put this conversation off until later? I don't want to even think about it now."

He gave her a puzzled look, apparently caught off guard by her un-expected response. "Ah—yeah—I just wanted to make sure you—"

Deciding to make her move, since she really had nothing more to lose, she whirled about and climbed onto his lap and began to stroke his hair, her face mere inches from his. Though he eyed her suspiciously, he did not move. After giving him an adoring smile, she tenderly kissed first one eyelid, then the other. One cheek, then the other cheek. Slowly, she let her lips move to his mouth, his closeness playing havoc with her senses. "I love you, Randy. You may leave me, but you'll never be able to forget me," she murmured softly as her mouth sought his again. She nearly screamed out as his arms circled her, pulling her against him. *Please, Randy, say you love me, too!*

When their kiss ended, she rested her forehead against his, her fin-gers twined about his neck. "Don't do it, sweetheart, don't leave me. We have so much for which to be thankful. Some of our best years are yet to come. Don't let them get away from us."

As if her words suddenly brought him back to reality, back to his unshakable resolve, he pushed her away and turned his head. "Don't, Syl, don't do this!" Literally picking her up and setting her off his lap onto the sofa, he stood to his feet, clenching and unclenching his fists at his sides.

Tears of humiliation and hurt stung at her eyes as she struggled to meet his icy glare. "But Randy—"

"Is there any coffee left? I need a cup."

She drew a quick breath through chalky lips. Brushing her tears aside, she stood, her heart thundering, and hurried toward the kitchen. "I think we both could use a good, strong cup of coffee. I'll get it."

Once in the kitchen, she worked frantically to pull herself together, dabbing at her eyes with a dish towel and mulling over what had just happened. *Come on, Sylvia, get hold of yourself. Maybe you moved too fast, too aggressively; after all, that's not your style. You probably frightened him.* She gave a snort. *And that Chatalaine woman wasn't aggressive? If not, how did she manage to snare my husband away from me so easily and so quickly? She was probably all over him. Telling him how handsome he was. How smart. How successful—batting her baby blues at him.* She filled their coffee mugs, lifted her chin, and moved back into the family room, determined to keep Randy from seeing how badly his words had hurt her. "Here ya go! Strong, just like you requested."

She watched as Randy took the cup and seated himself on the floor in front of the sofa, sticking his long legs out in front of him. "Mind if I sit down beside you?"

"Of course not."

She sat down, crossing her legs at the ankles and took a long, slow sip of her coffee, hoping the tension between them was surmountable. Suddenly, she noticed a Christmas CD was playing. Randy must have turned it on while she was in the kitchen. "I love that CD."

He leaned back against the sofa and tilted his head as if listening to the song with rapt attention. "Folks should play Christmas carols all year. Seems a shame to play them only in December."

"I think I could sit here forever, watching the lights blink on the tree and listening to that music." She made a nervous gesture to brush her hair away from her face.

They sat silently until the CD finished playing, then picking up their empty mugs, Sylvia rose. "I—I guess I'd better get us some lunch."

"Need any help?"

She shook her head. "Thanks, but no. I'll bring our trays in here." Fifteen minutes later, she returned, handing Randy his tray as he moved up onto the sofa.

"Umm, your barbecue ribs? I hoped that was what I smelled."

"And the mustard potato salad you always liked to go with the ribs." She started the CD player again before sitting down with her tray in her lap, hoping the lovely Christmas music with its message of God's love would calm their spirits. They ate in silence as the music played. When they finished eating, Sylvia carried the trays back into the kitchen.

"Good lunch. Thanks. No special projects for this afternoon?"

She caused a smile to dance at her lips. "Of course I have a project! A relaxing one I think you'll enjoy. On and off this past year, I've been working on our family scrapbooks, mounting many of those pictures we've been tossing into that big drawer all these years. I thought you might like to take a look at them." She was pleased when he gave her an enthusiastic smile. After taking three scrapbooks from the shelf and placing them on the coffee table, she sat down by Randy and opened the one on top. "This first one starts the year we began dating. Look at this funny picture of the two of us on that parade float. Can you believe we ever agreed to wear those silly costumes?"

He leaned in for a better look. "You were a real looker. No wonder I fell for you."

"Well, you were quite handsome yourself. All the girls thought so."

He flipped the page and pointed to a photo in the top corner. "I'd nearly forgotten about that old bicycle. I wonder what ever happened to it."

She leaned into him with a giggle. "Remember how you used to ride it backwards? I could never figure out how you did that."

"Oh, look, here's a picture of my mom in that old car my dad had."

"And here's another one of the two of us paddling that old canoe we rented at the boathouse."

Randy let out a raucous laugh. "As I recall, you lost hold of your paddle and turned us over when you tried to reach for it."

She punched his shoulder playfully. "Me? I wasn't the one who lost that paddle; it was you, Randy Benson! You turned us over!"

"Oh, there's a picture of Buddy Gilbert. Remember him? He spent more time in the principal's office than he did in the classroom. That kid was always in trouble."

She flipped over several pages and pointed to a full-page picture of the two of them, taken after their wedding by the photographer. "We made a handsome couple, didn't we? Look how happy we were. I was so excited about being Mrs. Randy Benson, I couldn't get the smile off my face. I felt like a fairy princess in that dress. And look at that flashy tuxedo you were wearing. What a handsome groom you were."

"I'll never forget how beautiful you looked in that dress."

Her pulse quickened. "I—I don't want you to forget, Randy."

The lines bracketing his mouth tightened, and she wondered if, once again, she had gone too far. "Do you have any of Buck's baby pictures in here?"

She flipped a couple more pages, then pointed to the picture of a preemie wearing the funny little hat they put on tiny newborns. "He's only a few hours old in that picture. Can you believe that tiny baby is now over six feet tall and extremely healthy? God did a miracle in his life."

Randy gazed at the picture, touching it with his fingertips. "I was so scared, Syl. I was so afraid we'd lose him."

She carefully leaned her head onto his shoulder, hoping and praying he would not push her away. "Me, too. I knew how much you wanted a son."

"And now we have two sons."

"And DeeDee." She sat up and flipped another page. "Look, there's a picture of our twins. So many of the nurses remarked how cute they were. Nothing skinny about those two."

"I expected you to have a hard delivery when the doctor told us how big they were. Look at Aaron's fist! That boy came out ready to do battle."

"Aaron has always reminded me more of you than Buck. He and DeeDee both have your coloring and your dark, curly hair. Buck is more like me."

Randy took her hand and gave it a pat. "He not only looks more like you, he has your same patience and disposition. Lucky kid!"

"Here, I want you to see the pictures we took that time we all went on vacation to Branson, Missouri." She flipped a few more pages.

"What a trip that was. Why did we ever decide to camp out in that big tent rather than stay at a motel? It rained every day we were there."

She let out a giggle at the thought. "Everything we owned was drenched. As I remember, that tent molded before it dried out, and we had to throw it away. Your idea of camping out wasn't such a good idea after all, but the kids had fun."

He reared back. "My idea of camping? It was your idea."

"But you're the one who always talked about the fun you had camping out when you were a boy!"

"In the backyard! If it rained, all I had to do was grab my pillow and blanket and go in the house."

Sylvia planted her hands on her hips. "I never wanted to camp out. I only suggested it because you had talked about it so much. I never realized you'd only done it in your backyard!"

"I guess the joke was on both of us."

They went through all three albums, reminiscing with each page, laughing, sometimes crying, sometimes just remaining silent, and enjoying their memories. So many times, Sylvia thought Randy was on the brink of saying something, especially when she could see tears in his eyes. Sometimes she thought she saw a flicker of love, but he remained silent. Close to her at times. Withdrawn at other times.

"Our twenty-five years might not have been perfect, Randy, but they were ours. Yours and mine. We created a life together because we loved one another and wanted to spend our years together. I've never once been sorry I said 'I do,' and I've never stopped loving you, and I never will, no matter what happens."

"Syl—"

"Don't say it, sweetheart. I know you don't want to hear that right now, but I have to let you know how I feel." She motioned toward his recliner. "Why don't you take a little nap while I fix dinner? I'll wake you when we're ready to eat."

"I can help—"

Deciding her emotions had already been yanked around enough for one day and needing a few private minutes to herself, she held up a palm. "Not this time, Randy. Rest."

"But—"

"Please. Let's do this my way, okay?"

She hurried into the kitchen and checked the oven. The beef roast she had put in to bake that morning was just right. She scurried into the dining room, put her lace tablecloth on the table, and set it with her most delicate china and silverware. In the center of the table, she put a candle ring of fresh greenery, the one she and Randy had purchased at the YMCA lot when they had bought their Christmas tree, and added a big, fat red candle in the center. She lit the candle and stood back, admiring its beauty, then lit the candelabras on the highly polished buffet, giving the entire room a soft, romantic glow.

Once the gravy was made, the potatoes and carrots put into their serving bowls, squares of homemade cranberry salad placed on lettuce leaves, and the corn bread browned just right and everything placed on the table, she removed her apron, checked her appearance in the pantry mirror, and went into the family room to awaken her husband.

"I couldn't sleep," he told her as she came into the room. "I've been thinking about all those pictures you've put in those albums. It must've taken you weeks to arrange them like that and add all those notes under each photograph."

"Give her of the fruit of her hands; and let her own works praise her in the gates." She grabbed his hand and tugged him to his feet with an inward smile as she remembered the verse the Lord had given her. "Like most of the things I do, Randy, it was a labor of love. Come on. Dinner's ready."

He stopped at the archway leading into the dining room, his eyes wide. "Wow, you're going all out. Is that round thing what we bought when we got the Christmas tree? That thing around the candle?"

She moved to her place at the table, pleased that he noticed it. "Yes, do you like it? It smells wonderful. It's bayberry."

He hurried around the table and pushed her chair in as she sat down, then moved to his own seat. "Umm, brown gravy."

"I—I thought maybe—rather than having one of us pray—we might recite the Lord's Prayer together."

"If you want to."

She bowed her head and closed her eyes, folding her hands in her lap. " 'Our Father which art in heaven.' " She paused, but not hearing Randy, went on. Eventually, he joined in with her, but she could tell there was no enthusiasm in his tone, and she almost wished she had not suggested it. " 'For thine is the kingdom, and the power, and the glory, for ever. Amen.' "

"This is nice, the two of us eating in the dining room like this." He heaped a huge helping of mashed potatoes on his plate, then reached for the gravy boat. "We should've done this more often."

"I tried a number of times, even had the table set and a special meal fixed, but then something would happen at the newspaper, a press would quit working, a paper delivery didn't show up on time, or some other catastrophe would happen, and you'd call and say you weren't going to make it home for dinner."

His face grew serious. "I'm sorry, Syl, I didn't know. You never complained about it."

"I didn't want to add to your problems. You had enough to take care of."

"Guess you haven't been too happy these past few years either."

She shook her head vigorously. She had to make him understand. "That's not true! I *have* been happy. However, I would have been happier if you and I could've had more time together; but I understood, sweetheart. Honest, I did! I knew you would've preferred being home with your family—" She drew in a deep breath as visions of Randy asking her for a divorce on Thanksgiving Day came back to haunt her. "Or—or at least I thought you would."

"I—I used to want that, but I never realized you did, too. You seemed to have more interest in the family cat than you did me. I've felt like an outsider in my own home for more times than I can remember, Syl. You shut me out. You *and* the kids. Sometimes I felt like none of you cared if I lived or died, as long as the paycheck continued."

She bristled. "That's a rotten thing to say, Randy Benson! I'm just glad the children aren't here to hear you make such a ridiculous statement! Do you have any idea how that makes me feel? Or do you even care about my feelings?" She swallowed hard and let out a long, low breath of air as she glanced at her watch. "We have to stop this. We only have three hours until midnight. I want those three hours to be pleasant, not a shouting match."

He nodded but did not look at her, just moved his carrots around on his plate.

"How's the roast?"

He raised his head slightly and gave her a weak smile. "Perfect. Best I've ever had. You're a terrific cook."

"Thank you." Sylvia tried to appear calm on the outside, but inside she was seething. *Why did I let him bait me like that? I wanted this evening to be perfect, one that would make Randy see what he was giving up if he left me, and what did I do? Nagged at him like some cartoon figure! Three hours! Lord, what shall I do? I'm all out of ideas. I felt sure that once Randy spent this week in our home, being reminded of the vows we took and the lives we've lived for the past twenty-five years, he'd want to come home. But now—I'm wondering if he, too, is counting the minutes until midnight—so he can get out of here, away from me!* She could not stop them. Tears flooded down her cheeks like a sudden rainstorm on a spring day.

Randy noticed and, hurrying around the table, put his arm about her. "Syl, are you okay? Aren't you feeling well?"

She turned away from him and got up from her chair. "I'm sorry,

Randy. I never meant to spoil our evening. Give me a few minutes, okay? I'll be fine. Finish your dinner." With that, she rushed from the room and up the stairs, seeking the solitude of their bedroom.

∞

Randy stood by, helplessly watching her leave the room. *"Randy, old boy, that was some smooth move. Are you so concerned about how you feel that you've forgotten other people have feelings, too?"*

He sat back down and tried to eat, but the guilt he felt for mouthing off made the food wad up in his stomach. Sylvia had been nothing but kind to him all week, going out of her way to prepare the foods she knew he liked, taking him to places he hadn't been in years, and doing so many other things.

He placed his fork on his plate and leaned back in the chair, staring into the flame of the candle. She didn't deserve this kind of treatment, yet what else could he do? It was not fair to get her hopes up. Their marriage was over. Had been for years, as far as he was concerned. She did not care about him. Not really. Otherwise, she would have realized how he felt long ago. She would have changed and done something about it.

"She would have changed? She would have done something about it?" That still, small voice said from deep within his heart. *"What about you? Did you make any attempt to change into the man she wanted you to be? Did you once even consider her happiness, as well as your own? Don't let these last three hours slip by. This is Christmas Day, Randy. You're not a selfish man. Surely, one day of the year you can put Sylvia first and forget about yourself."*

"I'm sorry, Randy. Please forgive me."

He turned to see Sylvia standing in the archway, and she was smiling. "Nothing to forgive, Syl. I was as much to blame as you, maybe more."

She reached out her hand as she moved toward him. "Can we start the evening over?"

He took her hand, lifted it to his lips, and kissed it. "I'd like that."

Once they were seated, Sylvia picked up the platter of corn bread and passed it to him. "It's kinda cold now. I could heat it for you."

He took it from her hands with a genuine smile. "It's fine, Syl, just like it is."

The rest of the meal was pleasant as each of the Bensons went out of their way to avoid confrontation or any mention of the divorce. "Would you like to wait a bit before having dessert?" she asked him when they had finished. "Later, in the family room with another cup of coffee?"

"Sounds good to me." He rose quickly. "Let me help you with the cleanup."

"I don't want to waste a minute of the few hours we have left," she told him as she picked up the roast platter. "I'm going to put things in the refrigerator and leave the dishes until later." They carried things to the kitchen, placing the dirty dishes in the sink, then headed back to the family room.

∽

"Sit by me, Randy." Sylvia patted the sofa cushion beside her.

He glanced at his watch, then stood gazing at her for a few moments before moving to her side and resting his head on the sofa's high back. "Sure hope the kids made it to Colorado okay."

Scooting a tad closer to him, she leaned her head on his shoulder, taking in his nearness, the smell of him, and the slight sound of his breathing. No matter what the future held, she wanted to capture this moment forever in her memory. She and her beloved, sitting close to one another, watching the lights twinkle merrily on the tree, listening to Christmas music extolling their Savior's birth. Would there be more nights like this, or would this be the last one?

Taking her hand in his, he caressed it with his thumb, causing her heart to do a flip-flop. Even after all these years, just his touch made her tremble.

"Are you cold?" Randy slipped an arm about her shoulders and pulled her to him. "That better?"

She nodded and snuggled up close. She wanted so much to tell him how she loved him, how much she wanted him to stay, but the words would not come. "*Maybe you've said too much already, My child.*" She flinched as the still, small voice spoke from deep within her heart.

But God, I have so little time left! I have to make Randy see how important it is that we stay together as husband and wife!

"*Perhaps, if you'd worked as hard at trying to please Randy these past few years as you have this week, he wouldn't have considered leaving you,*" the voice answered in a kind way. '*Yes, raising your children was important; it was a job I called you to do. And all the things you did for other people, to please and serve Me, were important, too, but not at the cost of putting your husband last.*"

I—I never meant to put him last, and part of it was his fault. He was always so busy—

"And you weren't?" the small voice asked.

Yes, I was busy. Too busy. However, I can't take the whole blame. What about that woman? That Chatalaine person?

"Syl, are you sure you're not coming down with a cold or something?" Randy asked.

His voice pulled her from her thoughts. "A cold? No, I—I don't think so, I'm just—just, well, you know. It's nearly midnight."

He checked his watch again. "I know."

Pressing back tears, she forced a smile and jumped to her feet. "Why don't I fix us some hot cocoa? Doesn't that sound good? With marshmallows on top like we used to fix for the kids."

He gave her the sideways grin she always loved. "Only if we can have some of those cookies we baked to go with it."

"You got it!" She gave him her sweetest smile and hurried into the kitchen, hoping to regain her composure. A few minutes later, she was back with the tray, setting it on the coffee table in front of them.

"Here ya go!"

They enjoyed their treat while talking about their children and Christmases past. Though Sylvia chattered on happily, panic was clutching its fingers tightly about her throat, and a jagged piece of her heart was breaking off with each stroke of the second hand on the clock. There was nothing in Randy's speech or demeanor that gave even the slightest indication he planned to stay beyond midnight. *Is he wondering about Chatalaine? Where she is and what she is doing? Oh God, please, no! Don't let that woman break up our marriage! I love him so! I need him! My family needs him!*

Finally, Randy stood and walked to the hall closet, pulling something from his coat pocket. "I have something for you." He lowered himself back down beside her, holding a small, beautifully wrapped package in his hand. "It's actually my Christmas present to you, but I felt funny giving it to you Christmas Eve with everyone there. I—I decided I'd rather give it to you in private."

Feelings of joy and happiness flooded over Sylvia as he placed the package in her lap. Halting a compelling urge to weep, she carefully pulled off the paper, making sure not to tear it, revealing a square white box. She smiled up at Randy, both pleased and relieved he had actually bought a gift for her. It did not matter what it was. She would have been happy with the empty box, just knowing he had not forgotten her after all.

"Open it." He took the wrappings from her hand and placed them on the table.

Inside, was a deep blue velvet box. Her hands shook as she lifted the lid and gasped. "Oh Randy!"

"It's the diamond heart necklace I always said I'd buy you but couldn't afford. Like the one we saw in the jewelry store window, remember? The store where I bought your gold wedding band." He lowered his head sheepishly. "I—I should have bought it for you years ago."

Sylvia was so deeply touched, she could barely breathe as she stared at the spectacular necklace. They had joked about it for years, but she had never actually expected him to buy it for her. "Oh Randy, I love it. It's so—so beautiful! Are you sure—"

He took the box from her hands, removed the necklace from its bed of white velvet, and opened the clasp. "Here, turn a bit and let me fasten it on you."

As she turned, she heard the clock on the fireplace chime a single chime. *Eleven thirty!*

"There!" Randy said, leaning forward to admire the necklace. "You look as beautiful in it as I knew you would."

"Does—does—" She lifted watery eyes to his, her voice raw and shaky with emotion as she fingered the necklace. "Does this mean you're staying?"

Randy looked into her eyes for some time before he answered. "No, Syl, that necklace is not only a Christmas present; it's my going-away gift." He glanced quickly at his watch, then said without preamble, "I—I'll be leaving at midnight."

Sylvia grabbed onto his arm, tears of humiliation and hurt blurring her vision. "No, Randy, no!"

His hand covered hers as her world tilted off its axis. "This week has been wonderful—I won't deny it, but there's no going back, Syl. I think we both know that. Our marriage has been on the skids for a long time. One week together, taking a walk down memory lane, could not resurrect it. Let's face it. It's dead and ready to be buried."

"But Randy, there's more at stake here than you and me! What about our children?"

He blinked hard, then looked away, as if he didn't want her to see how this thing, this giant that was tearing them apart, was affecting him more than he'd admit. "They'll recover."

"They won't, Randy," she said, sounding stronger and more rational than she had dreamed possible. "Don't expect them to understand, because they won't."

"I'll—I'll have to deal with that. Try to make them understand. We're not the first couple to divorce. Over 50 percent—"

"Don't try to excuse this by quoting statistics! Do you think God will accept your statistics as an excuse when you stand before Him?" She grabbed onto his chin, forcing him to look at her. "You're a Christian, Randy! You know this is displeasing to God!"

He shrugged but did not pull away. "Lots of things are displeasing to God, Syl. Not just divorce."

She tried to find a snappy retort, some scripture she could quote to him to prove he was in the wrong, but her mind went blank.

Randy reached up and slowly pulled her hands from his face. "I'm sorry, Syl. Honest, I am. I've struggled with this thing for the past two years; now it's time for action. I have to try my wings. I know it'll take time, but I'm hoping, eventually, we can at least be civil to one another—for our children's sake. After all, we managed to spend this week together."

"Only because I thought there was hope for us." Sylvia shot a quick glance at the clock. One minute to midnight.

"You promised, Syl. One week with you, and if I still felt the same way, you would give me the divorce—uncontested. You are going to keep your word, aren't you?" he asked softly, as if he expected her to go into a rage and back out on her deal, maybe even take a swing at him.

She had no choice. She'd done her best to try to get Randy to change his mind, and despite the many times she thought he was being swayed during their week together, he was as determined as ever to go through with the divorce. To go back on her word now would only make her look foolish and like a liar. Stunned and shaken and assailed with emotion, she stood to her feet. "I won't back out. I did give you my word, but I want you to remember one thing. I never wanted our marriage to end this way. I love you, Randy. I'll always love you."

He took her hand and held onto it tightly for a moment, then backed away.

"Not so fast. I still have fifteen seconds. I have one more request."

His brows rose in question.

"Hold me, Randy. Kiss me good-bye like you used to when we were young and so much in love nothing else mattered."

"But—"

"Time is getting away—"

He stepped forward awkwardly and pulled her into his embrace, his lips seeking hers. To her surprise, his kiss was warm, passionate, and lingering as he pulled her so close it took her breath away and their kiss deepened.

As the clock chimed midnight, he pulled away and walked out of her life.

Sylvia watched him go through that door and close it on twenty-five years of marriage. She wanted to die.

Chapter 12

The next few days were the saddest days Sylvia had ever spent as she closed herself up in the house, keeping the shades drawn to shut out the sunlight.

DeeDee and Aaron were still gone. Buck and Shonna had visiting relatives at their house and were only able to spend a little time with her. They had invited her to come to their home, but she did not feel up to it and certainly not up to putting on a happy face and visiting with strangers.

And, worst of all, the God she loved and trusted had not answered her prayers. He, too, had forsaken her, just like Randy. She had never felt so all alone. In less than two days, she devoured the two-pound box of chocolates Buck and Shonna had given her for Christmas. Good, nourishing food remained in the refrigerator. She had no interest in it whatsoever. Chocolate was the only thing that seemed to satisfy. She did not want to talk to anyone, not even Jen, and especially not God!

Television held no interest, not even the Sky Angel Christian channel with its twenty-four hours of music, preaching, and talk shows.

She leaped to the window at the sound of every car going down the street, sure it was Randy coming back to tell her the whole thing had been a mistake or a bad joke that went too far.

She grabbed up the phone each time it rang, hoping to hear his voice. But it was never Randy. She even screamed into the phone at the next telemarketer who called, threatening to report him if he ever called her again, which was definitely not her true nature.

Each day, she rushed to the mailbox hoping to find a letter from Randy or a card, even a simple note, but none ever came.

She wanted desperately to call him, to beg him to come back to her, to give her another chance to show him how much she loved him and wanted their marriage to succeed. She wanted to tell him she was even willing to forgive his infidelity and would never mention it to him again. But then, just the thought of Randy and that woman together made her want to throw up, and she knew how hard it would be to keep that promise.

But what if Randy had been telling her the truth about Chatalaine? That there really hadn't been anything between them? As far as she knew, he had not made a single attempt to call the woman during the entire week. How would she have felt if Randy had falsely accused her of cheating on him, and she had been innocent? The thought struck horror to her heart. Could Randy have been telling the truth all along? Had he really simply been tired of being married to her as he had said? And wanted out? And there had never even been a relationship with Chatalaine?

No, she could not call him, not even to tell him she forgave him. A call from her, after he had finally made his move and walked out on her, would only anger him, especially if Chatalaine was there at the office with him. She glanced at the phone. It was so tempting to call, but she turned away.

Jen phoned several times, but Sylvia always ended their conversation as quickly as possible without being rude, leaving her friend to wonder how she really was. She had even refused Jen's offer to pray for her. Why should anyone pray for her? God did not care about her. If He had, He would have brought Randy to his senses and healed their marriage. *No, prayer doesn't change anything,* she told herself as she shoved her Bible into the drawer with plans to leave it there. *No more daily Bible reading—no more praying for me. If God were real, He would have shown Himself and kept Randy here where he belonged.*

Late the afternoon of the thirtieth of December, the doorbell rang, and Sylvia rushed to answer it.

"Are you Sylvia Benson?" the man standing at the door asked.

She nodded. "Yes, that's me."

"This is for you." He handed her a plain-looking envelope and, without another word, hurried to his car and drove off.

She carried it into the house, tearing it open on the way. As she pulled the paper aside, she let out a loud gasp and collapsed onto the sofa, one hand resting on her forehead, her heart beating fitfully. *These are the divorce papers Randy had said would be coming!* After taking several restorative breaths to calm herself, she lifted the pack of papers and read the first few lines. "Oh Randy, how could you? I never thought you would actually go through with it, especially this soon. Not until you'd had a chance to tell the children!" She tossed the papers aside, too weak and too wounded to read another word. "God," she called out shaking her trembling fist. "Why—why have You forsaken me?"

She wandered about the house aimlessly, not knowing what to do or where to turn. Should she call Buck? Tell him about the divorce papers? What good would it do? There was nothing he could do to help her other than hold her hand to console her. He and Shonna had a house full of relatives. It would not be fair to her son and his wife to upset them at a time like this. Especially since Shonna was pregnant. She could just imagine the happiness and festivities going on at Buck's house as he and Shonna shared their good news with her parents and aunts and uncles. No, she could not do anything to take away from their joy.

She skipped supper, barely remembering she should eat, and went to bed early, pulling the covers over her head, touching the pillow where, only a few days ago, Randy had laid his head. Just the thought of his never being there again sent her into wild hysterics of crying until her eyes were so red and swollen, she could barely open them.

The next morning, Jen phoned again, this time trying to talk Sylvia into coming to the New Year's Eve service at the church. "You can't lock yourself away like this, Sylvia. It's not good for you."

"Not good for me, Jen? What *is* good for me?" she spat into the phone. "I don't think any of my church friends want me crying on their shoulders—the poor little woman whose husband left her for another woman because he didn't want to be married to her anymore."

"That's not true, sweetie. Your church family cares about you. You are not the first person whose marriage ended in this way. You didn't want your marriage to break up. You were the innocent partner."

Sylvia grasped onto the phone tightly, her knuckles turning white. "You're wrong about that, Jen. There was nothing innocent about me. Stupid, maybe, but not innocent. I see that now. Even if that woman hadn't come along, our marriage wouldn't have lasted. I—I put Randy last in my life. Behind our children, the church, my activities. I was never there when he needed me. It took our week together for me to realize that. If only I could go back and do things over."

"Well," Jen drawled out, as if not knowing what else to say, "I'm praying that you'll come tonight. I'm sure you need God and the church more than you're admitting. We all need Him, Sylvia. If you don't want to have to talk to anyone, sneak in after the service starts and sit in back. You can even leave a few minutes before midnight, if you want. Just come though. Start the New Year out right."

"Don't waste your time watching for me, because I probably won't be there."

As Sylvia hung up the phone and gazed about the room, Jen's words drilled into her heart. *I'm sure you need God and the church more than you're admitting.* She shrugged as she pulled her robe tighter about her and settled down in Randy's chair to finish her cup of cold coffee, idly picking up the remote and hitting the ON button.

"You may think no one loves you, no one cares what happens to you, but God cares," a gray-haired man with a kind face was saying as the Sky Angel channel lit up the screen. "Oh, He isn't some magical genie who snaps into being when you summon Him, eager to grant your every wish. However, He has a plan for you. A plan to prosper you and not harm you."

Her ears perked up, and she began to listen in earnest. *That's the very verse Randy quoted!*

"God has engraved you on the palms of His hands. His plan for you is perfect. Oh, at times it may seem like He's not listening when you call out to Him. Even as a born-again Christian, you may feel praying is a useless thing. Sometimes, you may have doubts about His existence and even wonder if there is a God. Satan puts those doubts in your mind. You must not let him have the victory."

Sylvia leaned forward with rapt attention.

"We who are Christians and claim His name must always remember," the preacher continued, "God has His own timing for everything.

Only in His appointed time will He bring things to pass. All we can do is wait upon Him, pray, and seek His will. If you are listening to my voice right now and you feel God has forsaken you, it's time to give up your pity party and start living again. Seek God's face. Confess your sins. Turn to Him. Trust Him. His plan is always best for you."

Sylvia stared at the screen. It was as though the man was speaking directly to her. *I have been having a pity party! It's time I faced up to the fact that I have done everything I could to save our marriage and I failed. It's time I turned it all over to God. My life. Randy's life. If God cannot put things back together, no one can!*

She glanced about the darkened room. Dozens of the little fluted white papers that separated the chocolates she had consumed lay scattered about the floor. Empty coffee cups adorned the coffee table. Tissues she had used to wipe at her eyes and blot her nose were strewn everywhere. Two days! She had two days to get things back in order before DeeDee and Aaron came back from their skiing trip. She could not let them come home to the house in such disarray. It was going to be bad enough to learn their father had left their mother and had served her with divorce papers.

Putting her sorrow and heartache aside, she flung open the drapes, lifted the blinds, gathered up the trash, cups, and dishes, putting them in their proper places. The kitchen was still a mess from the dirty dishes, pots, and pans she had left on the cabinet and in the sink the night Randy had left. Rolling up the sleeves on her robe, she dove into the mess with zest and soon had the kitchen looking the way she usually kept it—spotless. She ran the sweeper in the family room, leaving the tree standing in the corner, waiting for either Buck or Aaron to help her get it out of its stand and to the curb where the trash man would pick it up. She dusted and waxed until the whole downstairs shone.

Next, she hurried upstairs, changed the sheets on the bed in their bedroom, even scooting the bed to a different wall to give the room a renewed look.

By eight o'clock, after eating a bowl of soup, she was in the shower with plans to attend the New Year's Eve service. The cool water falling onto her face from the showerhead was invigorating, and she knew, though life was going to be hard in the coming days, she would make it. She still had her health, a beautiful home, a terrific bunch of kids, her church friends, and, most importantly, God. Granted, she and God's relationship was a bit strained, but in time, she knew He would soften her heart and the two of them would be on good terms again. She knew now—she had left God—He had not left her.

She slipped into the service shortly after ten o'clock, just after the song service had begun, and took a seat way in the back in an empty area under the balcony. Thankfully, the lights in the sanctuary were turned low since candles burned in the candelabra on either side of the pulpit. Her gaze went to the third row from the front on the left side of the sanctuary, the row where she and Randy sat when he wasn't too busy at the paper to attend church. She would have to find another pew to sit in on Sunday mornings. That one held too many memories. Maybe she would just sit with Jen from now on. She always sat alone or with one of the widow women since her husband was always up on the platform preaching.

The song service was wonderful, as was the special music. It was as though all the worship team's songs had been chosen with her and her needs in mind. When the pastor asked for those who wanted to give a testimony of what God had done for them this past year, at least a dozen people responded. As Sylvia listened to their words, her own problems seemed to fade. With some, the Lord had brought them through a life-threatening disease. With others, an injury—one that had robbed them of a way to support their families, but God had been faithful and supplied their needs. With one family, it was the loss of a child through an accident. One couple's marriage had been ripped apart by infidelity. However, through confession of sin, apologies, forgiveness, and God's grace, the family had been reunited and was happier than ever. Each story was different, yet each ended with victory through the Lord Jesus Christ.

Sylvia didn't even try to keep the tears from flowing as she listened. Their stories were like a soothing salve on her troubled mind. If they could make it, surely she could.

The pastor's New Year's message was exactly what she needed to hear as he spoke about putting old things aside and beginning things anew. He talked about restoration with God and renewing your joy in Jesus. He even encouraged making New Year's resolutions, not in the way the world makes them, but as goals we should set to make us the people God would have us to be. Goals like daily Bible reading and prayer and serving Him.

A few minutes before midnight, the pastor invited anyone who wanted to pray the New Year in to come forward and kneel at the altar. Sylvia watched as a number of parishioners stood and moved forward. This was the time she had planned to duck out and leave. However, as she stood, to her surprise and dismay, her feet led her forward, and she found herself walking toward the altar. She no longer cared if anyone saw her tears or realized she would soon join the ranks of the divorced people who attended the church. All she had on her mind was getting to that altar, kneeling, asking God's forgiveness for ever doubting Him, and turning her life over to Him.

When she reached the front, she immediately dropped to her knees, folding her hands and resting them on the curtained railing. With a broken and contrite heart, she began to pray silently, talking to God, spilling out her heart to Him in Jesus' name.

As she prayed, she felt a hand on her shoulder. Without even needing to glance back, she knew it was Jen. She continued to pray, thankful for such a good friend. Remembering the pastor's challenge, she let her tears of surrender flow down her cheeks, her heart filled with gratitude to God for the many blessings He'd given her throughout her life and for the blessings He'd promised in His Word to continue to pour upon her. *I am not much, Father, and I have made so many mistakes, but take me, use me, mold me into whatever You want me to be.*

"I love you," a male voice whispered softly in her ear.

Startled, since she had assumed it was Jen who had kneeled beside her, she turned quickly toward the voice. "Ra–Randy? What are you doing here?"

His cheeks stained with tears, he warily slipped an arm about her, whispering, "Although you and I have grown apart over the past few years, Sylvia, I want you to know there has never been anyone in my life but you. I have so missed the closeness we used to have. You were always so wrapped up in our children's lives—I guess I was jealous of the time you spent with them."

She rubbed at her eyes with her sleeve. "Jealous of our children?"

He nodded, wiping at his own eyes. "I—I was so busy at the newspaper, we never had time for each other. I have acted like the typical midlife-crisis male and let my ego cloud my judgment. I responded like the old fool that I am, wanting to move out and find myself. I knew better, Sylvia. I knew I was going against God's will. Looking back, I cannot imagine how I ever let myself try to put the blame for our failed marriage on you. But thanks to you and our one last Christmas together, I now see what a fool I have been. I didn't fully realize what a mistake I was making until I got back to my apartment after leaving you that last night we had together. I have been miserable ever since. Spending the week with you and realizing what I was about to give up made me see things in a new light, but I was too proud to admit it."

"But—but the divorce papers! They were delivered to me just yesterday."

He scrunched up his face and drew in a deep breath. "I didn't know my attorney was going to have them delivered that soon. I was sick about it when he told me. What that must have done to you! I'm so sorry, Syl."

"But—but what about Chatalaine? What are you going to do about her?"

"I—I know you don't believe me about Chatalaine, but sweetheart, honest, there never has been anything going on between us. You can talk to her if you want and ask her yourself. We're both invited to her wedding next week."

Sylvia's jaw dropped. "Chatalaine is getting married?"

"Yes. She's been engaged for nearly a year and madly in love with the man she's going to marry, almost as madly in love as I was with you when we were young—and as I am now." He dipped his head shyly. "You're the only woman I've ever loved, Syl. I've asked God's forgiveness for my stupidity."

"But the apricot roses? I thought they were for her. When the florist called—"

"He called you?"

She nodded. "Yes, and he said you'd made a big deal about making sure they were apricot roses when you'd ordered them."

Randy let out a slight chuckle. "And you thought they were for Chatalaine?"

"Who—who else would they be for?"

"Syl, do you remember when we attended old Nick Bodine's funeral last summer?"

"Yes, but what has—"

"I spoke to his wife after the service, and she mentioned Nick had sent her apricot roses on her birthday every year since they'd been married and how much she was going to miss receiving them on her next birthday. I asked her when that was, then wrote it down in my appointment book."

"You sent the apricot roses to Mrs. Bodine?"

"Yes, I always liked Nick. He was a good worker and always had a kind word for everyone. I sent them to her on her birthday, with a note telling her to pretend Nick had sent them to her and to have a happy birthday."

Fingering the heart-shaped necklace, she leaned into him, overcome with his thoughtfulness. "Oh, Randy, that was so sweet of you. No wonder you insisted they be apricot roses. I'm sure she loved them."

He slipped his finger beneath her chin and lifted her face to his. "Syl, do—do you think you can ever forgive me for walking out on you like that?" He hugged her tightly to him.

She smiled through tears of happiness and caressed his face with her fingertips as she rested her forehead against his. "Oh yes, my beloved husband. I can forgive you, even as God has forgiven both of us. Despite everything that has happened between us, I have never stopped loving you. I, too, had my priorities all mixed up. While I loved our children and wanted them to have the best lives possible, they were a *product* of our love and not a *substitute* for it. God never meant for them and all the other things in our lives to become a wedge between us. I'm the one who let that happen, and I'm sorry. So sorry I ever doubted you."

After falling on each other in a loving embrace, they suddenly realized, except for Harrison and Jen, who were sitting on the front pew smiling with happiness, the church was empty. Everyone else had gone. They had been so caught up with each other and their love for one another, they hadn't even noticed.

"You have no idea how excited and happy we are to see the two of you together again," Jen said, her eyes clouded with tears as she hugged both Randy and Sylvia. "We've been praying for you, asking God to bring the two of you back together where you belong."

Randy kept one arm about Sylvia but extended his free hand toward his pastor. "I—I'd like to keep serving on the church board, if you think it'd be okay. That is, if my wife agrees. I'm going to make many changes in my life, but leaving my wife isn't going to be one of them."

He turned to Sylvia, squeezing her hand between the two of his, his eyes filled with tears, his voice cracking with emotion as he spoke.

"Would you—could you even consider taking me back? Let me move back home—after what I've done to you?"

Sylvia, too, succumbed to the tears that pleaded to be released. Though he spoke the words she had longed to hear, prayed to hear, she found it difficult to speak. Each heartbeat told her she could trust him. He would never leave her again. "Oh Randy, of—of course, I'll take you back," she said between sobs of joy. "Spending my life with you is all I've ever wanted." She grabbed onto his shirt collar with both hands and drew him to her, placing a tender, loving kiss on his lips. "Come home with me, darling, where you belong. Where I want you. Where God wants you."

"That's exactly where I want to be."

Sylvia leaned into her husband as Randy kissed her again.

"Hey you two, break it up," Jen said, rubbing at her eyes and reaching to touch Sylvia's arm. "You're making Harrison and me cry, too."

"Yeah," Harrison added, circling his arm about his wife's waist. "We tough guys aren't supposed to cry."

Randy planted one more quick kiss on Sylvia's lips, then wiped his sleeve across his face. "From now on, I'm setting limits on the time I spend at the newspaper. It's time I get my ducks in a row."

Sylvia let out a giggle at the word *ducks*, as Randy sent her a smile at the little joke only the two of them understood—about his pajamas.

"Of course, we still want you on the board, Randy. You have always been an important part of this church. You're a great asset to us—and to God."

Randy nodded toward their friends. "Well, I'd better get my wife home before she changes her mind. Thanks for caring about us, you two, and for praying for us."

Harrison reached out and gave Randy's hand a hearty shake. "Our pleasure. It's always nice to see God answer prayer and bring a couple back together. Guess I'll see you two sitting in the third row next Sunday morning?"

Randy nodded. "You bet. Right where we belong."

As Randy turned his key in the lock when they reached home, he leaned over and kissed his wife. "Until I spent that week with you, babe, I never realized all the things you did to make our house a home."

"I loved every minute of it." The scripture God had given her the night she had prayed and asked God Himself to give her a plan flooded her memory and gave her cause to thank Him. *"Favour is deceitful, and beauty is vain: but a woman that feareth the Lord, she shall be praised. Give her of the fruit of her hands; and let her own works praise her in the gates."*

Once inside, they walked hand in hand up the stairway and into their bedroom. Randy paused in the doorway, his eyes scanning the area. "You've moved the furniture! I like it this way."

"Moving the furniture is only one of the many changes I plan to make, Randy. Remember what Aaron said Christmas Eve when he was passing out the gifts?"

Randy frowned, as if he was not sure what she meant.

"When he saw the various presents I had given you and acted as though he was upset because he didn't get as many, he said, 'It's okay, Mom. After all, that old man is your husband. He'll be around long after us kids move out for good.' He was right, Randy. It's time you and I began to think of the two of us as a couple and not only as a family. We need to concentrate on us and our needs, as well as those of our children. I want us to do things together, sweetheart. To grow old together."

He gave her a toothy grin. "Will you still love me when we're in a care home and I'm wearing my yellow ducky pajamas?"

"Even then!" She wrapped her arms about his neck and planted a kiss on his lips. "Will you love me when I'm wrinkled and my breasts droop to my waist?"

He laughed, then returned her kiss. "I'll probably be so senile by that time, I won't even notice!"

She tangled her fingers in his hair, much like she'd done when they'd first begun to date. "I hope God grants us many more years together, Randy. We've lost so much time. I want us to make up for it."

"We will, dearest. We've been given a second chance. I want to make the most of it, too."

She leaned into him, enjoying their intimacy. This was where she belonged. In the arms of the man she loved. How close she'd come to losing him—losing everything she held near and dear.

"Syl," he said, his voice taking on a low, throaty, tender quality as he lovingly gazed into her eyes. "Thanks to you and your love and patience with me, this didn't turn out to be our one last Christmas together. I love you, babe."

"I love you, too, Randy."

Joyce Livingston has done many things in her life (in addition to being a wife, mother of six, and grandmother to oodles of grandkids, all of whom she loves dearly), from being a television broadcaster for eighteen years, to lecturing and teaching on quilting and sewing, to writing magazine articles on a variety of subjects. She's danced with Lawrence Welk, ice-skated with a chimpanzee, had bottles broken over her head by stuntmen, interviewed hundreds of celebrities and controversial figures, and done many other interesting and unusual things. But now, when she isn't off traveling to wonderful and exotic places as a part-time tour escort, her days are spent sitting in front of her computer, creating stories. She feels her writing is a ministry and a calling from God, and she hopes readers will be touched and uplifted by what she writes.

A Wedding Renewal
in Sweetwater, Texas

by Kim O'Brien

Dedication

For my family with love and thanks
for all the support and encouragement.

Chapter 1

The phone rang Friday morning at 7:45 a.m.

"Help!"

Sylvia Baxter squeezed the phone between her shoulder and ear as she filled two cereal bowls with Froot Loops. "Eat," she whispered to her sons who were shooting a Matchbox car down the center of the table.

"Eat?" Rema repeated. "I call on the verge of collapse and all you can say is 'eat'? What kind of help is that?"

"Oh Rema, I was talking to the boys." Sylvia deftly steadied the gallon jug of milk before Tucker accidentally dumped its entire contents on his cereal. "What's the matter?"

"I'm married to the world's biggest jerk, that's what." Rema's voice drilled into Sylvia's ear. Her best friend had a flair for the dramatic, which made it hard at times to accurately judge the true depth of the crisis. "You aren't going to believe what he did this time."

"Tell me."

"It's a long story. Honestly, Sylvia, every time I think that guy has lost the power to hurt me, he proves how wrong I am."

Sylvia sighed sympathetically. Rema sounded genuinely distressed. She glanced at the clock. This morning she was dressing up as Mr. Slice at the boys' school in order to boost sales for the weekly pizza fund-raiser. She also had to go to the craft store, grocery shop, unclog the bathroom sink, and run a couple loads of laundry.

Calculating quickly, Sylvia figured if she skipped breakfast, ignored the house, and made all the green lights on the way to the elementary school, she'd have an extra hour.

"Don't worry." Sylvia spotted one of Tucker's sneakers beneath the table. Where was the other? "Whatever it is, we'll fix it. Come on over. After I get the boys off to school, we'll hop in the spa and have a soda. You can tell me all about it."

∽

By the time Sylvia returned from taking the boys to school, Rema had arrived. She'd let herself in through the back gate and was sitting on one of the deck chairs, staring into the turquoise depths of the pool. Waving, Sylvia opened the back door. "Let me change into my suit and I'll be right out. Why don't you get the sodas?"

"Okay." Rema's kitten heels clicked on the tile as she followed Sylvia into the coolness of the air-conditioned kitchen. Opening the refrigerator door, she reached for the drawer Sylvia kept stocked with sodas. "I might need something stronger than soda. My head feels squeezed, like I have a migraine coming."

"Don't worry." Sylvia peeled off her jeans and slipped into a well-worn one-piece bathing suit, purchased because it advertised the kindest cut on the market. "I have a whole new bottle of Excedrin."

Stepping back outside, Sylvia tossed her towel on the back of a lounge chair, considered going back in the house for sunglasses, and then decided against it. The March sunlight was bright, but it was impossible to have a good conversation with someone without seeing his or her eyes.

At eight thirty, sunlight already bathed the kidney-shaped pool. The temperature was in the low eighties and promised to get even warmer. It never failed to amaze Sylvia, who had grown up in Ohio, how fast summer came to Texas. The water felt cool at first, and then deliciously silken as she settled herself into the spa.

"So what did Skiezer do this time?"

Rema handed her a soda and popped the other open. "Family game night strikes again."

"Uh-oh." Sylvia set her soda can on top of the stone rim around the hot tub and leaned back against the jets.

"Our game of Sorry turned nasty. Skiezer tried to get the boys to gang up on me." Rema frowned. "Talk about low. Who tries to convince a five-year-old and a nine-year-old that their mother is mean and deserves to lose?"

"He probably was only teasing you," Sylvia suggested hopefully.

The topic of marriage was as familiar as the taste of soda on Sylvia's tongue. How many hours had they sat in this same spot and swapped confidences? Ever since she and Rema had met at the Methodist church's preschool, they had been fast friends. She studied the lines of worry in Rema's face. Beneath the artfully applied makeup, Rema looked truly discouraged. Her heart ached in sympathy.

"What happened next?"

"I called him a big, fat cheater then stormed out of the room. I had to sit for thirty minutes in my closet just to calm down."

Sylvia laughed. "Thank heaven for closets."

"What is it about men?" Rema sank to chin level in the water. "Just for once, I want to be with someone who stares into my eyes and isn't about to accuse me of something."

"I know what you mean." Sylvia also sank deeper so she was eye level with her friend. "I love Wilson and all, but sometimes I read these romances and my heart just aches. The guys in those books never spend their evenings doing e-mail."

"Or inspecting the walls to see if any of the kids have left fingerprints." Rema's gaze turned thoughtful. "Or snapping their fingers when they're on the phone to get your attention."

Rema fired off a series of finger snaps, rolled her eyes, and jerked her head around as if she were having some sort of seizure. Sylvia laughed so hard she almost swallowed a mouthful of water.

"Let's face it," Rema said, a grin replacing her earlier worry lines. "Our husbands are never going to star in a best-selling romance." She snorted. "If Skiezer's going to star in a book, it'd definitely have to be something by Stephen King."

"Wilson would be perfect for *The Invisible Man*," Sylvia confessed. "I never see him anymore." She shook her head a little sadly. "He used to be romantic, but now all he does is work, work, work."

"Skiezer, too. His Bluetooth is permanently attached to his left ear."

"Rema, don't you wish, just for once, that somebody would come crashing through your front door and sweep you up in his arms and carry you off somewhere really romantic?"

"I'd settle for someone who greeted me when he came home from work as warmly as he did the dog." Rema's thin, arched eyebrows drew together. "Sylvia, I don't understand why Skiezer has to be so—so controlling."

"Maybe because he feels insecure."

Rema seemed to mull this over for a moment. "So insecure that he wanted to annihilate me over a game of Sorry?"

"Did you beat him last time?"

"I don't remember. Maybe." A pause. "Yeah. By a mile."

Sylvia waited.

"So what do I do? Throw the next game? Because if I have to let him win at everything, what kind of marriage is that?"

"I don't know," Sylvia said. "Maybe you should talk to him. Tell him how you feel."

"Talk about feelings?" Rema snorted. "He'd rather undergo a root canal."

"You could explain that women need to feel cherished by their husbands." Sylvia looked off into the privacy fence that surrounded their small backyard. She found herself more than a little bit relating to Rema's problem. "We want our men to be strong enough to sweep us off our feet and gentle enough never to hurt us with an unkind word. And we want them to spend even more time during the day thinking about us than we do about them."

Rema groaned. "Oh Sylvia, you've been reading those romance novels again. There's a reason they call that stuff fiction."

"I don't care," Sylvia stated, no longer sure if they were discussing Rema's situation or her own. "What's the saying? That art imitates life, or something like that."

"Only if it's good Chick Lit."

Chuckling, Sylvia craned her neck for a peek at the kitchen clock. "Oh darn it," she said. "I've got to get to the school. Do my Mr. Slice thing."

"How come they don't call you Mrs. Slice?"

"I'm not sure," Sylvia admitted, "maybe because pizzas aren't supposed to have breasts?"

Rema laughed. "I don't think pizzas are supposed to have arms and legs—or other parts either."

"Well, I may be Mr. Slice, but it's the moms who are buying the pizza." She rose dripping from the spa. "I've got to go. You going to be okay?"

"Yeah, I knew this wasn't a crisis, but it just helps to talk sometimes."

Sylvia smiled and wrapped herself in a towel. "Yeah, I know what you mean. I still think you should talk to Skiezer about opening up more, but if that isn't going to work, maybe you should try family movie night."

"Yeah," Rema agreed. "I will. Now you get going. I've made you late enough as it is."

Later, dressed in black leggings and the foam pizza costume, Sylvia peered at the world through strategically placed slits in the pepperoni. The air smelled old and stale, and a trickle of sweat rolled down her chest. *It's all for a good cause,* she reminded herself as she walked down the kindergarten hallway. The school would receive money from every pizza sold that evening.

"Hello, Mr. Slice," a little boy with a crew cut and chunky black-rimmed glasses called out.

"Hello there!" Sylvia replied, trying to sound like the world's friendliest pizza. "Are you going to see me in the box tonight?"

"You bet." The little boy grinned. His eyes grew round with wonder, and his voice assumed a deferential tone as if he were in the presence of royalty. "You're really cool."

"Well thank you." Sylvia grinned back, although she knew the boy couldn't see her face.

As she reached the first classroom, she paused. Apparently she made a pretty cool slice of pizza—but what about herself as a woman? Reaching for the doorknob with her pepperoni hands, she thought how easy it was to get lost in a marriage, to become a mom and wife and lose that piece of herself that had nothing to do with fixing healthy meals, doing the laundry, or shuttling the kids around. Not that there was anything wrong with those things, she assured herself.

It was just, well, lately it felt like she and Wilson were more roommates than soul mates. Just this morning, hadn't he called her *Mom,* as in, *"Hey Mom, have you seen the power cord to my PC?"*

Her advice to Rema rang in her ears with alarming clarity. If she wanted something more from Wilson, she'd have to do more than just wish for it. She needed to take action.

Chapter 2

Three days later, Sylvia leaned over the bathroom sink to study herself in the mirror. Her brunette hair, freshly cut and colored, now had highlights and lowlights. She turned her head and admired the caramel-colored streaks that had taken three hours at the beauty salon to put there. She liked the way the layers framed her face, maybe even took off a year or two. She couldn't wait to show Wilson. Hopefully he'd like it and not ask how much it had cost.

The chirp of the door alarm announced Wilson's arrival. Smoothing her fingers over her new black capri pants, she took one last deep breath for courage. *Okay,* she thought. *Here we go.*

As she stepped into the kitchen, the first thing she saw was Wilson holding Tucker upside down by the legs. The little boy's fingertips just touched the tile floor, and he was yelling, "I am Upside-Down Man." Simon was clinging to Wilson's back like a small monkey. All three Baxter men were grinning from ear to ear.

"Wilson, put Tucker down," Sylvia ordered. "He just ate spaghetti about ten minutes ago. Do you want him to throw it all up?"

Wilson lowered Tucker and shot her an apologetic glance. When his gaze lingered on her, Sylvia felt a rush of pleasure. She could almost see the wheels in his brain turning as he struggled to figure out why she looked so great.

"Sorry." Wilson, still staring at her, gave Tucker a pat on the head. "I was hoping I'd gotten home in time to eat with you all tonight."

"You never get home in time to eat with us," Simon said.

"You dad works hard." Sylvia automatically defended Wilson. Besides, she didn't want the conversation going in that direction. She touched her hair in a hint that Wilson was supposed to say something nice about it.

Simon, however, beat him to it. "Mom got her hair cut."

"It looks very nice," Wilson said, but he looked more worried than impressed. This was okay with Sylvia. He was probably trying to figure out if he had forgotten an important date. They used to celebrate all kinds of things—like the anniversary of the first time he asked her out, and the day he had proposed to her.

"You sure you like it?" Sylvia casually combed her fingers through the new layers.

"Yes, but I liked the way you looked before just as much," Wilson said.

"I liked her hair better before," Tucker stated with as much importance as he could muster in his five-year-old body.

"Tucker, your mother looks beautiful no matter how she wears her hair."

Sylvia beamed. "Thank you." She almost, but not quite, missed the wink he exchanged with Tucker.

Simon frowned. Behind his glasses, his eyes blinked furiously as his seven-year-old brain focused its considerable horsepower on her hair. "How do they make it change color? Do they use paint? Does it wash out?"

"We'll ask Marie the next time I have it done," Sylvia promised. She pointed her finger in the direction of the upstairs game room. "Now scoot. *Bobsled Billy* is on TV. Do you want to go and watch?"

Usually she limited the amount of time she let the kids watch television, but tonight she was relenting in order to give herself and Wilson a little private time.

She turned in time to catch Wilson staring at her new black capri pants. Another thrill worked its way through her body, and suddenly she was very glad that she'd bought a size smaller than usual. So what if she could never wash these pants and zip them again. She purposely crossed the room to give him a view of the way the material clung to her body.

Reaching the refrigerator, she turned around, half-hoping to see that look on Wilson's face—the unblinking, hungry-for-love man gaze. However, he wasn't even looking at her. All three Baxter men had their heads bent closely together. Simon had his half-assembled balsa racer clutched in his small hand.

"You've done a good job sanding this, Simon." Wilson examined the car's triangular shape. "This is really good. I'm not just saying that either."

"How about mine?" Tucker stuck his race car so close to Wilson's face it nearly hit him in the nose. "Look at mine."

"It's incredible," Wilson assured him. "You two are going to be the hotshots at the Pinewood Derby."

"Daddy! Daddy!" Tucker shouted. "Are you going to come to the race?"

"Wouldn't miss it."

Racer derby? Balsa cars? Sylvia shut the refrigerator, forgetting why she'd opened it in the first place. *This is even worse than I thought.*

Didn't he see that she'd bought a new outfit, put on makeup, and set the table with candles? She ran her fingers through her hair and felt, well, as if she were a car and someone had let the air out of her tires. Her moment was over. Not only that, but she feared that Wilson privately agreed with the boys and liked the way she used to look much better.

Watching Wilson with the boys, she realized she didn't have the heart to send Tucker and Simon upstairs. Clearly Wilson was enjoying being with them. Her hopes of a romantic evening died. *We're a family,* she thought, *and this is how it is supposed to be.*

Yet, was that true? What about herself and Wilson as a couple? They loved each other. He told her so every night right before he fell asleep—that is, if he wasn't in his office working. Maybe though, it wasn't the kind of love she wanted from him. Maybe she was just a package deal—someone who came with the kids.

Frowning, she tried to remember a conversation with Wilson that hadn't involved the coordination of schedules, the boys, or some item of Wilson's that needed to be found.

When he'd married her nearly ten years ago, he'd promised to love and cherish her until death do us part. She still wanted that, she realized—that crazy, romantic kind of love.

It was time to stop fooling around. New hair and tight pants obviously weren't going to cut it. She needed something stronger. She wrinkled her brow, thinking hard. A complaint session in the spa with Rema would be fun, but she didn't want fun—she wanted a plan.

Tonight, when Wilson buried himself in e-mail, she would hit the phone and call an emergency meeting.

Chapter 3

On Wednesday evening, four women gathered around Sylvia's kitchen table. Placing the bowl of potato chips next to the onion dip and the platter of double fudge brownies, Sylvia checked to make sure everyone had a drink before settling into her seat.

The minute she sat, the kitchen became utterly silent. Sylvia hesitated, straining for any noise that might indicate that Wilson wasn't safely enclosed in his study or the boys weren't asleep. This was *woman* business.

Finally satisfied, she popped the top of a diet soda. No matter what this session yielded, she was convinced it would include an edict to lose five pounds. Therefore, regular soda, which she preferred, was out of the question. Unfortunately so were the chips and brownies.

"I like your hair," Susan commented, breaking the expectant silence. "It flatters your complexion."

Sylvia patted her hair, aware that Susan could simply be being nice. With her kind blue eyes and graying blond hair, Susan was probably the least appearance-conscious person in their group. "Thanks," she said.

"The cut is terrific," Andrea Burns added, crossing one leg of an expensively cut trouser over the other. "I like the layers." Andrea's own dark hair was cut short and edgy. As a corporate lawyer, Andrea wanted to present a no-nonsense exterior, a look she had perfected down to the point of her high-heeled executive pumps.

"Are you sure the highlights aren't too red?" Sylvia asked a tad self-consciously.

"No, they're perfect." Kelly, a fragile-looking platinum blond, sipped from a stainless steel canister that contained a lime green concoction that Kelly had been trying to get Sylvia to try. "But I don't think we're here to talk about hair color. You said it was serious. How can we help?"

Sylvia looked away from Kelly's forest green eyes. She could see the doctor in Kelly getting ready to focus on whatever symptoms Sylvia presented, and then prescribe a solution. As if it would be that simple.

It suddenly seemed impossible to blurt out that Wilson had lost interest in her. Mortifying, really, to admit she needed help. And yet, a voice in her brain said very clearly, "*If you feel this way about your marriage now, what do you think you're going to feel like five years from now?*"

Taking a deep breath, Sylvia reminded herself that these were her closest friends. They would help her. She leaned forward and spoke very quietly. "Two days ago I had my hair done and wore tight capri pants, and Wilson was more interested in the boys' Pinewood Derby racers."

A chorus of sympathetic clucking noises resounded around the table. "It's like I'm not even there anymore," Sylvia continued, gaining speed. "He comes home from work, eats dinner while I put the kids to bed, and then he settles in front of his computer while I watch TV by myself." She searched the faces around her. "I know Wilson loves me, but it's so *lonely*."

Rema squeezed her arm sympathetically. "Marriage can be a lonely place, Syl."

"But it shouldn't have to be," Sylvia argued. "That's why I've called all of you here tonight. You all are my closest friends. With our combined years of experience in marriage, I was hoping we could come up with a solution."

"If we could," Andrea said, "we'd be millionaires."

Susan placed warm fingers on top of Sylvia's cold ones. "Wilson adores you. I've seen the way he looks at you."

"He'd be lost without you," Kelly added. "Seriously, Sylvia, I've always admired your relationship with Wilson."

"That's awfully nice, Kelly," Sylvia mused, "but my marriage is far from perfect."

"Everyone struggles." Susan's round face reflected supportive concern.

Sylvia sighed. "I know that—and it's not like anything is really wrong. I mean, we don't fight or anything. And I still love him." She glanced around the faces of her friends and took heart in the sympathetic expressions. "It's more like there're two worlds—my world, which is the house and the kids; and his world, which is work. I feel like there isn't a lot of overlap."

Andrea pulled a legal pad out of her briefcase and uncapped an expensive-looking gold pen. She wrote the date then the number one. "This could be a tough one," she said after a moment.

"So what do I do?" Sylvia's brow wrinkled. "Just accept the fact that once the romance is gone, it's gone?" She reached for a handful of potato chips, momentarily forgetting her need to lose five pounds. Unhappily, she stuffed them in her mouth.

"How about marriage counseling?" Susan suggested. "Our church has several Christian counselors. Maybe you and Wilson need to talk to a professional."

"Wilson's too smart for that," Sylvia said. "He'd not only answer the questions correctly, but also throw in free financial investment advice. The counselor would end up on Wilson's side, and I'd end up looking like an idiot."

Heads nodded around the table. "But I'll keep it in mind," Sylvia added, not wanting Susan to think she didn't appreciate the advice.

Kelly's pencil-thin eyebrows rose. "Why not just talk to Wilson and tell him how you feel?"

"He'd listen," Sylvia said, "and he'd say he would do better, but I don't think he'd change." She grabbed some more chips and wondered if gathering the group had been a mistake. So far no one had a solution, and she felt worse than ever.

"Face it, ladies," Rema broke in, "if sensitivity was a required course in school, most men would fail it."

Susan set her teacup on the table. "You know, I did this study once on the book of Proverbs, which talks about how a woman can have an incredible marriage. A lot of the women in our group had doubts going in, but all of them ended up saying it was one of the best studies they'd ever done."

Sylvia sat up a little straighter. "An incredible marriage?"

" 'She rises and her husband and children call her blessed,' or something close to that," Susan quoted.

"Well, when I rise, I don't want to tell you what my husband and kids call me," Rema joked.

"Blessed," Sylvia repeated. This sounded awfully close to *treasured*, which was what lacked in her marriage. "What else do you remember?"

"Something about her good deeds bringing her recognition from even the leaders of nations."

Sylvia narrowed her eyes. She didn't want recognition from the leaders of nations. She wanted Wilson to love her. However, maybe she had been looking at the problem from the wrong angle. She couldn't change Wilson, but maybe she could change herself. Standing, Sylvia smiled down at them. "Ladies, we're on to something. I'm going to get my Bible."

Sylvia retrieved her Bible from its spot beneath a stack of romance novels on her bedside table. She sent a small prayer of apology to God for not thinking of this sooner.

Returning to the kitchen, she handed the heavy book over to Susan. "You're a genius for coming up with this."

Susan put on her reading glasses and flipped through the pages. "Here it is, Proverbs 31, 'A Wife of Noble Character'."

The room became so absolutely silent that Sylvia swore she could hear Wilson's fingers clicking on the keyboard upstairs. A chill of excitement ran down her arms. *This is it,* she thought, *the answer to my prayers.* "Read," she urged her friend.

Susan cleared her throat. " 'A wife of noble character who can find? She is worth far more than rubies. Her husband has full confidence in her and lacks nothing of value. She brings him good, not harm, all the days of her life. She selects wool and flax and works with eager hands.'"

"Hold on." Sylvia held up her hand. "We have a problem here. Spin wool and flax? I have trouble threading a needle."

Susan shook her head. "You're being too literal. Remember, this was written ages ago. We have to focus on the idea and *modernize* it."

"You mean she should hit Saks?" Rema leaned forward eagerly. "Syl, I'll go with you. We'll open you a charge card and buy the best wool and flax on the market."

"That's absolutely not what it means," Susan said sternly. "It's talking about character. It's saying that we should be trustworthy and think of the needs of others more than ourselves."

"Sylvia already has a great character," Rema said loyally. "She's the most giving person I know."

To the kids maybe, Sylvia thought, but what about what she gave to Wilson? Didn't he get whatever was left of her after she put the kids to bed? Maybe she was as much at fault as he was. "Thanks, Rema, but there's room for improvement. Trust me." She turned to Susan. "Do you remember enough of the study to take me through it?"

She shook her silvery blond head. "Not off the top of my head, but I could go home and try to find my notes. Basically, we looked at each verse and talked about it and how we could apply it to our marriages."

"We can do that," Andrea stated. "Give me the first verse and I'll write it down."

" 'A wife of noble character who can find?' " Susan read, " 'She is worth far more than rubies. Her husband has full confidence in her and lacks nothing of value.' "

"Well," Rema said after a moment of silence. "We all know Sylvia is completely trustworthy, which means we should focus on the 'satisfying his needs' part of the phrase." A wicked glint came into her dark eyes. "I'm thinking that maybe Sylvia needs to buy some new lingerie."

There was some laughter. Sylvia felt herself blush. "I thought we were going to talk about character."

"Sylvia's right," Susan said.

"Okay then, the key word is *needs.*" Kelly looked straight into Sylvia's eyes. "What does Wilson need more than anything?"

Fighting the nervous giggle that had worked its way up her throat, Sylvia felt the intensity of four women staring at her. "He needs to lose five pounds," she blurted out. "And stick to an exercise program."

They both did, Sylvia admitted to herself. For years exercise and diet had topped their New Year's resolution list. In fact, they'd justified the additional expense of the swimming pool for this very reason. However, although the kids swam like small dolphins up and down the pool, she and Wilson rarely did anything but relax in the hot tub. They hadn't done a lot of that lately either, she realized.

"An exercise program," Kelly repeated thoughtfully. "Excellent. You need to get those endorphins flowing."

Excellent? Sylvia searched her thoughts for something else that Wilson needed. Something less strenuous. She liked Rema's shopping suggestion, but considering how vehemently it'd been discarded, didn't have the courage to suggest it.

"Was there something the two of you used to do together before you had the boys?" Kelly moved the bowl of chips just as Sylvia's fingers reached for another handful. "Keith and I love to go jogging together."

"Well, we used to do a lot of things," Sylvia said. She smiled as she remembered a particularly enjoyable date when they had hiked around Mystic Lake and then climbed hundreds of rickety stairs for a picnic lunch on the platform of an observation tower.

"We used to go for hikes," she admitted.

"Perfect," Susan exclaimed. "Don't you see? If you two start doing the things you used to do before you had kids, you'll not only get the exercise you need, but also rediscover how much fun you used to have together."

Heads nodded agreement around the table. Sylvia stared hopefully at Rema, as if her closest friend could be counted on to come up with an eleventh-hour rescue. However, Rema nodded enthusiastically. "You can start Saturday," she said. "I'll watch the boys for you."

Sylvia tried to imagine herself and Wilson hiking. At first all she could envision was two middle-aged, slightly overweight people pretending to have a good time as they dripped sweat and slapped mosquitoes. However, the more she thought about it, the more potential she saw. First, there would be no power outlet so Wilson would have to leave his computer at home. Second, they might see some kind of wildlife, preferably small, which might spark Wilson's primal instincts, and he might put his arm around her protectively. Third, if nothing else, she'd burn calories and therefore be able to wash those new capri pants and still fit into them.

"Okay, guys," Sylvia said at last. "I'll start Operation Proverbs 31 on Saturday, as planned. Pray for me, okay?"

"We will, *and*, we'll pray for you right now," Susan said.

All the women joined hands. Sylvia bowed her head and closed her eyes. She took a deep breath as Susan began.

"Heavenly Father, we ask that You be with Sylvia this week as she struggles to integrate the principles You've outlined in Proverbs

31 into her life. Please help her understand Your words, and give her the strength to do whatever she needs to do in order to strengthen her marriage. We know all things are possible through You. It is in Jesus' name we ask. Amen."

"We will," Susan agreed. "Let's meet again, next Tuesday. You can tell us how it's going."

"Agreed." Sylvia sank back in her seat. "Thanks, everyone. I don't know what I'd do without you."

Four faces grinned back at her. Sylvia sighed, feeling better already. Something wonderful was about to happen in her life. She knew it. She could hardly wait to begin the Proverbs Plan.

Chapter 4

As Wilson lifted the mountain bikes from the roof of the minivan, Sylvia watched the muscles in his arms flex. For a forty-two-year-old man, actually for an any-aged man, she corrected herself, her husband looked pretty good. She'd always been attracted to his height and solid build. The few extra pounds he'd gained over the years only added to his masculinity.

"I pumped your tires up." Wilson wheeled her bike over to her, squeezing the front tire to confirm his words. "Here, feel how tight they are."

Sylvia squeezed the front tire and managed a grateful smile. Although she appreciated the concern, she hoped Wilson wouldn't get sidetracked. He loved bikes. Loved looking at them, loved talking about them, and most of all, making sure their bikes were in tip-top condition before he let anyone ride one. The last time they'd gone for a family ride it had taken over an hour just to get out of the driveway, and by then the boys had been tired and cranky and ready to come home.

Maybe she should have stuck to the original plan and gone hiking. However, walking had seemed too middle-aged, too complacent. Not only that, she admitted to herself, she'd been afraid Wilson would turn her down.

Wilson lifted the back tire and spun it with his finger. He stood transfixed, watching the wheel rotate between the brake pads. If it wasn't perfect, she knew he'd pull out his tools and get to work. They could stand there for at least an hour. She resolved to get the date back on track.

Sylvia cupped her hand to her ear. "The mountain paths are calling. Let's get going."

Wilson frowned. "Your back tire needs truing. I'm not a 100 percent sure, but it looks like your derailer is bent." His eyebrows drew together. "How could that have happened?"

Probably when she'd driven the minivan too deeply into the garage and smashed the bike against the back wall. She buckled her helmet. "I'm sure it'll be fine. Come on, honey."

Giving her bike's rear tire one last frown, Wilson reached for his mountain bike. For a moment, he held it at arm's length, smiling and looking at it admiringly. Sylvia sighed. Why couldn't he look at *her* that way?

However, as soon as they started down the grassy path, some of the tension eased between her shoulder blades. The sun warmed her back even as a breeze cooled her cheeks. Around her, wildflowers grew chest high. Their fluttering leaves seemed like applause as they pedaled past. *This is great,* Sylvia thought. *How beautiful God's world really is. How thankful I am to be a part of it.*

"I can't believe we're here." Wilson pedaled easily at her side. "You and me and a gorgeous day at Lotoka Park."

Sylvia shot him a sideways glance. He looked so pleased that a rush of warmth spread through her body. "It's like we have the whole park to ourselves."

"All one hundred acres of preserve, twenty-five miles of dirt paths."

"We'll have a picnic lunch by the water," Sylvia added. "I made a special lunch."

She didn't add that she'd spent hours consulting countless books and magazines, searching for new recipes which would be both delicious and nutritious. She intended to follow the instructions in Proverbs 31 to the letter.

They passed smoothly through the meadow, picking up speed as the land dipped slightly. The wide tires on her bike cushioned the uneven earth. Strapped to her bike rack, their picnic lunch rode like a silent passenger behind her. She could practically feel the years slipping away. When had she last felt so young and free? Usually the boys would have been with them, and she would have been worrying about Simon, who wasn't very athletic and would be devastated if his younger brother sailed past him.

Sylvia stopped herself. This was the problem. The boys always found their way to the top of her thoughts. Today it was going to be all about Wilson.

"The trail is narrowing," Wilson pointed out. "You can go ahead of me."

Rushing toward them with alarming speed, the trail did indeed narrow. Sylvia hesitated and braked slightly. Although she felt fairly certain that from the side, her black Lycra shorts were flattering, she held no illusions about the view from the rear. She didn't want him to think that her butt was the size of Texas.

"Oh no, no," she protested. "You go first."

"Ladies first."

"Wilson, you know I have no sense of direction."

"It's okay," he replied. "I've studied the trail maps. Basically, all the paths lead to the lake. It'll be more of an adventure if you lead the way."

Sylvia swallowed her protest. The last thing she wanted was to waste precious time arguing. Besides, she had to stop worrying so much about how she looked. The important thing was to have fun together. She pedaled faster and pulled ahead of Wilson just as the meadow ended and the forest of pine trees began.

Almost immediately, the trail changed. Tree roots bulged through the earth, making her bike jostle and bump. She heard the food rattling in their soft-sided cooler and tried not to imagine her carefully prepared salads being pulverized in their containers.

After ten more minutes of this, she decided it didn't matter. By the time they arrived at the lake, her butt was going to be so sore that she wasn't going to be able to sit and would have to eat standing up. She had pictured a much, much smoother path.

"Unweight the front tire when you hit a big root," Wilson shouted from behind. "You won't get bounced around so much."

Unweight the front tire? "What do you mean?" Sylvia clenched her jaw as the bike hit a lump the size of a speed bump. No amount of padding in her bike shorts would ever make up for the amount of jostling her body was taking. She didn't even want to think about what the bike helmet was doing to her hair.

She hit another tree root and heard the cooler give an alarming thump behind her then Wilson's shout, "Pull up on the handle bars before you hit the root," he instructed. "And lift your rear out of the seat until you land."

I'm too old for this, she thought in despair. Too old to be jumping tree roots on a mountain bike, too old to change anything about herself, much less her marriage. What was she doing?

Her despair deepened as the trail became even narrower and steeper. Thick, scabby trunks of the pines pressed closely on either side of her, and she kept pedaling unexpectedly into cobwebs.

When the path forked, she chose the one on the right because it appeared slightly less rocky. However, she'd barely gone twenty yards when the ground changed, becoming overgrown with grass. The ribbon of trail disappeared completely. "I think we've gone off-road," she shouted.

"We're fine," Wilson called back. "Isn't this great?"

Sylvia bit her tongue and kept pedaling. She tried not to think of snakes slithering in the grass or how many mosquito bites she was getting. *You're having fun,* she ordered herself. *Don't be whiney.*

"Shouldn't we be at the lake yet, Wilson?"

"Any minute," Wilson agreed, heartedly. Too heartedly.

"Are you sure?" They came to another meadow. She slowed but didn't stop. The grass tickled her leg. If the path became any more overgrown, they'd need a scythe to get through. A chorus of buzzing noises increased in volume on either side of her head as if the crickets were coordinating their plan of attack.

"Of course I'm sure." She heard Wilson smack his leg. "Ouch! Darn bugs. How come they don't go after you?"

"Because I'm coated with spider webs from blazing the trail."

"Well, why don't you brush them off?"

"If I take one hand off the handlebars, I'm going to crash." Sylvia tensed as grass wound itself into her gear and the bike slowed. "Are you *sure* the lake's just ahead?"

"As long as we're on a path, we're heading toward the lake." Wilson slapped another bug. "Go faster, I'm getting eaten alive."

Sylvia gamely pedaled harder, ignoring the long spears of grass that tangled around the gears. How long would it take before Wilson admitted they were lost?

Somehow, she must have taken the wrong path when the trail split. Moment by moment, she and Wilson pedaled deeper into the 125-acre wildlife refuge. This wasn't romantic. It was *suicidal.* She mentally calculated how much food they had and how long it would take before the park rangers came after them. She hoped it was before dark.

"Wilson, I really think we should turn around."

"Just another mile or so," Wilson stated with firm conviction. If she hadn't known him as well as she did, she would have believed he actually knew this for a fact.

Sweat stung her eyes. Huge bugs buzzed past her ears. Her butt alternated between a numbing paralysis and excruciating pain. And then, suddenly, the trail took a hard turn to the left, the meadow fell away, and a grove of hardwoods opened up in front of them. The tall grass gave way to a bed of soft pine needles, and the growth of the trees formed a perfect natural canopy above them. The temperature dropped instantly and the air smelled like pine. She barely had time to appreciate the graceful arch of the old trees before she saw the lake ahead, a glistening patch of blue surrounded by lush forest.

"I see the lake!" Sylvia risked unclenching one hand from the handlebars and gave a thumbs-up signal. "We made it!"

"It's incredible." Wilson's voice rang with excitement. He pulled up alongside her. "I love you, Sylvia."

Suddenly all the aches and pains of the ride seemed inconsequential. He *loved* her. Sylvia grinned so widely it hurt. Here they were, alone, surrounded by a hundred acres of virgin forest. With no distractions, Wilson was becoming romantic, just as she'd hoped.

"I love you, too, Wilson."

They stopped their bikes on a bank overlooking the water. Sylvia measured the lake with her gaze, pleased at the junction of sky and water. No powerboats—nothing mechanical to distract Wilson. Perfect. She unstrapped the picnic lunch from the bike rack as Wilson spread a red-plaid cotton blanket over a thin patch of grass. The silence alone was heady. No kids arguing, no telephone ringing, no noise, nothing except for the slight stir of a breeze through the pines.

She put the paper plates on the blanket and added plastic goblets. The napkins color-coordinated with the blanket, and when she added the bowl of grapes as a centerpiece, she felt certain Martha Stewart would have approved.

Wilson opened the first container. Sylvia frowned when half the potato salad stuck to the lid, no doubt thrown there from the centrifugal force of the ride. "This looks good, Syl."

Sylvia held her plate out as he served her. "It's low-fat, too. Everything is. I want us to be healthy and live a long life *together*."

Wilson smiled. "Absolutely. Did you bring the Fritos?"

Laughing, Sylvia pulled out another container. "Try these pita chips. They're much better than Fritos."

Opening the container, Wilson frowned. "Are they supposed to look like this?"

She peered over his shoulder. "Well, I guess they got a little broken up in the ride. Here, I have a special dip to go with them." She rallied with a smile. "It's called hummus."

Wilson put a chip in his mouth. He reached for another. "These are really good."

She leaned forward, smiling. "Doesn't this remind you of the old days?"

Wilson washed down the chips with a long drink of sweet raspberry iced tea. "Yeah." He squeezed her fingers with affection. "Remember when we went canoeing? That was great."

Great? They'd capsized in the first set of rapids. She'd swallowed half the river before managing to surface, clinging to the canoe as some park ranger shouted at her to let go. Sylvia popped a grape in her mouth. Maybe recalling the past wasn't a good idea, after all. She handed him a container of cold marinated beef, sliced razor thin. Maybe after they ate they would lie on their backs and look up at the vast blue sky. He would reach for her hand, and they would lie there like teenagers and dream aloud.

The beef smelled delicious, and Sylvia added a generous amount to her plate, followed by a large scoop of tri-colored pasta salad. She decorated the edges of her plate with olives and black beans in a cilantro vinaigrette. The food really looked like a work of art.

"We should do this more often." Wilson polished off the entire container of chips and hummus. "Get away—just you and me."

Sylvia smiled. "My thoughts exactly. Starting today, you and I are on a special diet and exercise program." She stopped talking at the look of worry on Wilson's face. "Don't worry, you're going to love the turkey burgers I've got planned for tonight."

Wilson held his hand up. "Quiet." He peered somewhere over her left shoulder. "I think I hear something."

Sylvia held her breath as Wilson strained to hear in the silence. *This is exactly like I imagined, being in the wilderness is sparking Wilson's protective instincts.*

"What is it?"

Wilson shook his head. "Sounded like an animal rooting around."

She smiled. "Maybe a rabbit wants some of my endive salad."

"Endive salad? Pass it over here."

For the next thirty minutes, she and Wilson polished off every bit of the gourmet picnic she'd packed. Placing the final empty container in the cooler, she mentally reviewed all the things they'd talked about: the boys' upcoming Pinewood Derby, the boys' most recent soccer game, Simon's new fascination with bugs, and Tucker's ability to eat half a pizza by himself. Not once, she realized, had they talked about themselves. It was almost as if without the boys they would have had nothing in common. The thought added to her determination to get their date back on track.

Taking her husband's hand, she urged him to lie on his back next to her. "Let's look up at the clouds," she suggested. "I see one that looks like a sheep. What do you see?"

When Wilson remained quiet, she glanced over at him. He had his eyes closed. She nudged him gently. "Are you sleeping?"

"No," he said. "Just relaxing."

She studied the rise and fall of his chest. "Let's talk."

His eyes remained shut. "What about?"

She took a deep breath. It was now or never. "Us." She turned onto her side, facing him. "Are you happy?"

Wilson smiled. "Very happy."

She waited for him to ask her the same question. However, when his hand tucked under his chin, she realized he was going into his sleeping position.

She looked up at the sky in frustration. Some great date. Wilson found her company so invigorating it required a nap; it would be days before she sat comfortably again, and the shrubbery around them looked suspiciously like poison ivy.

She heard something rustle in the distance. There was silence, and then the snap of a branch breaking. "Wilson," she whispered. "I hear something."

"The boys are fine," he muttered. "Go back to sleep."

She shook his arm. "Listen."

The underbrush crunched as something moved closer to them. The small hairs on her arms stood straight up. "Wilson, some animal is coming. I hear it."

Wilson's eyes shot open. "What?" He sat upright and stared hard in the direction of the noise.

"What is it?" Frozen in place, she watched color bloom in her husband's face.

"We're going." Climbing to his feet, Wilson pulled her roughly upright.

"What is it?" She hissed.

Wilson strapped the basket to her bike in record speed then glanced over his shoulder. "Go," he whispered with urgency. "Just *go!*"

Chapter 5

"And then what happened?" Rema leaned forward eagerly, nearly upsetting the pitcher of green tea. "What was after you?"

Sylvia looked around her kitchen table at the expectant expressions of the group. Three days had passed since her infamous date with Wilson, and she couldn't put off the truth any longer. "Well, we jumped on our bikes and pedaled as fast as we could to get out of there."

"What was chasing you?" Rema locked her gaze with Sylvia's. "A bear? A wolf? A bobcat? What?"

Sylvia swallowed. "A wild pig."

"A pig?" Rema repeated in disbelief. "You ran from Wilbur?"

"This wasn't *Charlotte's Web*, Rema. This thing had horns. This long." Sylvia gestured with her hands.

Kelly sat straighter in her seat. "He saved you from a wild boar. Sylvia, don't you see how romantic that is?"

Sylvia shook her head. "Saved me? He nearly ran me off the trail trying to get out of there." She sighed. "In short, the whole date was a disaster."

Rema patted her arm. "You did great. Who could have predicted the pig thing?"

Sylvia sighed and reached for a carrot strip. Dunking it in the low-fat onion dip, she shook her head. "I don't know what I did wrong."

Susan shook her silver-blond head gently. "You didn't do anything wrong. You and Wilson spent time together, and now you have a funny, exciting new story to tell. I think it was a huge success."

Sylvia sipped her diet soda. It wasn't nearly as good as the real stuff. "I didn't even tell you guys what the hummus did to Wilson's digestion. Let's just say it was a good thing we hustled out of the woods."

"Change always feels uncomfortable," Susan stated. "What's Pastor Rick always saying—that God loves us too much to let us stay in the same place? We need to keep growing in our faith. I think as long as you're asking God to help you understand His Word, you'll be fine."

"So what does Sylvia do next?" Rema asked. "Does she keep working on fulfilling Wilson's needs, or does she move on to the next verse?"

All heads turned to Susan, who put on her reading glasses and consulted a manila folder filled with papers. "When my group did this study, we looked at a different verse every week. But I don't think there's a right or wrong way to do this. What are you comfortable with, Sylvia?"

Sylvia shifted on the kitchen chair. The exercise part of the plan wasn't working out as well as she'd hoped. Although Wilson had agreed to take family walks after dinner, so far they hadn't gone on a single one. Every night he'd come home and worked on his laptop.

Sylvia looked around at her friends. "I think," she said slowly, "that I should keep trying to help Wilson lose weight and exercise more, but maybe we should go on to the next verse."

"That's a great idea," Rema agreed. "You need to keep the momentum. If you get bogged down in the first verse, you're never going to get anywhere."

Andrea, wearing yet another power suit, pulled out her legal pad and consulted her notes from the last meeting. "I agree. There are about twenty verses that refer to the Proverbs 31 woman. If Sylvia spends two weeks on each, it'd take her about a year to get through them all. I think she should move on to the next verse."

"It's not a race," Kelly argued. "The important thing is for Sylvia to feel better about her marriage, herself, and her relationship with God." She sipped her herbal concoction and smiled sympathetically at Sylvia. "Some things take time. I'm always telling my patients that getting better is a process."

Sylvia ran her fingers through her hair. "I know," she said. "And even though the date wasn't exactly a romantic success, I think Wilson had fun. When we got back to the car, he laughed harder than I've seen him do in months."

Rema patted Sylvia's arm. "There you go," she said. "I knew it wasn't a total disaster. What's next?"

Sylvia reached for her Bible. She opened the satin pages to Proverbs 31.

> "*'She brings him good, not harm, all the days of her life. She selects wool and flax and works with eager hands. She is like the merchant ships, bringing her food from afar.'*"

Sylvia looked up. "I'll admit it. I don't get how I'm supposed to be like a ship."

"Maybe you're supposed to be like the *Love Boat*," Rema joked and began to hum the opening theme to the show.

"You're supposed to take this seriously," Susan snapped. She pushed her glasses higher on her nose and looked at Kelly and Andrea for support. " 'She brings him good, not harm.' This is what we should be talking about."

"Well, the 'do no harm' part—that sounds like my medical oath," Kelly commented. "So if I translate that to marriage, I think it means our actions, as wives, have consequences. We need to be sure that our choices help our husbands and aren't just selfish ones."

Andrea tapped her pencil on her legal pad. "But honestly, don't our choices have to be selfish sometimes? I mean, sometimes isn't it okay to get take-out even though your husband really wants your chicken tetrazzini for dinner? And, come to think of it, why can't he make the tetrazzini? Or, when your husband turns on Sports Central, and you'd rather watch *Pride and Prejudice*, why does the woman have to concede?" She shook her dark hair. "This verse feels like we have subjugated ourselves as women."

"Andrea has a good point," Rema agreed. "If I didn't stand up for myself, I'd get run over at our house." She tapped her manicured fingernails along the tabletop. "I love Skiezer, but I could be bleeding on the side of the road and he'd drive right past me without even noticing."

"Are you so sure?" Susan argued. "I don't think this verse means you have to be a doormat, or watch Sports Central all the time." She paused and added dryly, "Or be the *Love Boat*." She glanced at Sylvia. "What do you think it means, dear?"

Sylvia swallowed. The last time she'd blurted out an answer she'd ended up in a race with a wild pig. She'd be more careful this time. "Could someone read me the first part of it again? Not the *Love Boat* part. Just the beginning."

" 'She brings him good, not harm, all the days of her life.' "

Sylvia thought of the times in her life when she'd felt closest to Wilson. There were the big events of course, like their wedding and the births of their children. But there were other times, smaller things. Like the time she'd gotten sick. He'd taken care of her, brought her chicken noodle soup, and laid a cool cloth on her forehead. She'd felt so loved. What could she do that would be good for Wilson?

Her gaze drifted beyond the table to the front of the refrigerator, which was covered with the boys' drawings. Hidden nearly out of sight beneath a blue crayon dinosaur, she saw a tattered piece of paper containing a long list of to-do's she'd created for Wilson. She looked away quickly. *No*, she thought, *please Lord, not that*. She didn't know how to do half the chores on it, and the other things were pretty gross.

Their wedding anniversary was in May. Maybe she and Wilson could go shopping together. He could help her pick out a nice new dress. Even as this thought played through her mind, she knew it was wrong. If she wanted to have a better marriage, Wilson needed to work fewer hours, and that included the maintenance work around the house.

"Well," she began, "Wilson does need help with some things that need to be done around the house." She looked at the refrigerator unhappily. "I've made a list. Maybe 'doing good' would be tackling some of those items."

"You're going to take on your own honey-do list?" Rema's eyebrows lifted in shock.

"Why's that so bad?" Andrea asked.

"Because she's setting a precedent," Rema stated firmly. "If she shows him that she's capable of doing man work, then he'll assume she'll do it in the future." She shook her head. "I don't see how that would help her improve things."

"You're right," Andrea agreed. "Once she assumes responsibility of the man list, the chores arguably could be assigned to her." She hesitated a moment. "You could hire someone, Sylvia. A transfer of responsibility, if you will. I've seen plenty of ads in our local paper for a rent-a-husband."

"It wouldn't be the same." Sylvia picked up a piece of celery stuffed with cream cheese, raisins, and walnuts. "It has to be personal—he has to know that I'm trying to help him."

"I think you're on the right track," Susan said. "It should be you doing something for him."

Rema's face wrinkled with worry. "Are you sure about that list, Sylvia?"

Sylvia sighed. "Yes. I've been nagging Wilson about that stuff for weeks—it hasn't helped and all it does is make me feel bad about myself." She frowned. What was on that list? Most of it, she recalled, was heavy, sweaty stuff—fertilize the lawn, clean the gutters. Well, she'd do the best she could. She put on what she hoped was a brave face. "How hard can it be to power wash and change a few light bulbs?"

Chapter 6

Wilson Baxter looked up from his computer at the discreet knock on his office door. Since the door was already open, the noise was a formality designed to get his attention, not his permission to enter.

"Got a second, Wilson?"

"Sure, Bruce." Wilson pushed his chair back from the desk as his boss shut the door behind him. The action more than anything told him the conversation was not only important but also private. His gaze narrowed on the pale, wrinkled face of the man who had control of his career.

Bruce's glossy, black cane thumped lightly as his boss crossed the gray industrial carpet. His boss was only in his fifties but had started using the cane three years ago after his hip replacement.

"They took it." Bruce's distinctive, raspy voice resonated with significance. "It's in legal now."

Although Wilson had expected this—had in fact worked on the proposal to acquire the small savings and loan bank—he was unprepared for the shot of pleasure that rushed through his system. This was his project—*his baby*. He forced himself to assume Bruce's matter-of-fact demeanor. Later, when he got home and told Sylvia, he'd allow himself to beat his fists against his chest and roar like a gorilla.

"That's great news," Wilson said calmly.

"Legal's got the signed contracts," Bruce confirmed. He smoothed his chin thoughtfully. "But we need to take another look at the merger redundancy analysis you did."

"Sure." A couple of key strokes later, he had the requested information on his computer screen. "I'll print you a copy." He knew that Bruce, although well capable of using the program he'd used to create the spreadsheet, preferred to see things in hard copy.

"Thanks, Wilson." Bruce scanned the spreadsheet. "After I've had a chance to review this, you and I are going to have a serious conversation about your future." His boss leaned forward and his deep-set brown eyes had fire in them. "This new bank of ours is going to need a branch manager. Since you've been analyzing its operations for more than a year, I can't think of a better person for that job." He paused to let his words sink in. "Would you be willing to relocate?"

Relocate? Sylvia would kill him. Wilson heard himself reply, "Of course."

"Excellent." Bruce stood. "Of course nothing's set in stone, yet, but it's something to think about." He paused at the door. "Are you free at six? Legal should have something for us by then."

Again, he readily agreed even as he heard the disappointment in Sylvia's voice when he told her he'd be missing yet another family dinner.

Bruce nodded then followed his cane down the hallway to his corner office. From experience, Wilson knew the man would walk slowly, not because of his disability, but because it gave him an excuse to peek through the glass walls into the offices of the other bank employees and see if they were really working.

Bruce might be wily, but he was a financial genius, Wilson conceded. Not only that, but he admired the man's willingness to take risks. In an industry infamous for its conservative nature, Bruce seemed to love a new financial venture as much as any gambler on a riverboat.

Leaning back in his ergonomic computer chair, his gaze fell on Sylvia's picture on his desk. He couldn't wait to tell her that his merger had gone through, and not only that, he was being considered for the position of branch manager.

Branch manager. The word tasted like filet mignon on his tongue. He picked up the phone, smiled, then hung up. This wasn't news to share over the wire. He wanted to look deeply into his wife's beautiful brown eyes and watch them fill with pride. Tonight, after the boys went to bed, he'd suggest a private soak in the hot tub. Sylvia liked to light the citronella candles, pour them both her special batch of iced tea, and lie back in the spa. With the stars overhead, he'd reach for her hand, and—

She'd probably try to drown him. He raked his fingers through his hair then carefully flattened it again to hide the small bald spot. No way was she going to want to move. Not when she loved everything about their town. And lately she'd gotten so prickly about everything. He couldn't believe she'd dyed her hair that awful color and had started making them all eat cereal that tasted like cardboard instead of the chocolate one they all liked.

He studied her picture again, making a mental note to call her and let her know he'd be late for dinner—again. She wouldn't be happy about that either. Well, he'd make it up to her later. The wife of a branch manager was sure to have a lot of perks. He couldn't wait to lay all of them at her feet.

The next time Wilson looked up, it was seven o'clock. Groaning, he realized he'd forgotten to call Sylvia. What was wrong with him? He rubbed his tired eyes. Great. Now he'd be in the doghouse. He picked up the phone to call Sylvia, but Jen Douglas, his boss's executive assistant, sashayed into his office.

"You ready, Wilson?" She was an attractive woman, in her thirties, but her tendency for figure-hugging blouses and dresses always made him a little uncomfortable. "Bruce is waiting for you in the conference room."

"I'll be there in a minute," Wilson said, just as Sylvia picked up. He heard the boys' voices in the background.

"I know I should have called sooner, but I won't be home for a while. I'll tell you about it later, but right now everyone is waiting for me in the conference room." Out of the corner of his eye he saw Jen check her watch. "It shouldn't be too long," he continued. "I'll call you from the road."

To his surprise, she said, "It's okay, honey. Your plate's in the fridge." He heard the sound of Simon and Tucker laughing in the background, and for a moment the noise seemed to come through the receiver and grab his heart. It suddenly seemed like a very long time since he'd seen them or Sylvia. Still, he reminded himself, everything he did was for them, and he'd be home in time to tuck the boys into bed. It wouldn't always be like this, he promised himself as he hung up.

Gathering his papers and laptop, he turned the light off in his office and followed Jen to the conference room.

∞

Sylvia gently replaced the receiver in the cradle. Another late night for Wilson. When had he last been home in time for dinner? She couldn't remember. The new norm was for him to come home just as she was putting the boys to bed.

One minute they were about to fall asleep, and the next they'd be jumping up and down with excitement at the sight of their father, who liked to swing them up in the air or wrestle. Calming them down again took at least forty-five minutes and repeating the whole go-to-bed sequence. She'd tried to explain to Wilson how tired she was at the end of a long day, but he didn't seem to get it.

"Boys," she yelled, "bath time."

"Do we have to?" Tucker shouted from the upstairs game room.

"Yes," Sylvia called back. "Come on down."

"But we're practicing for the Pinewood Derby," Simon called, his seven-year-old voice implied that nothing, especially not a bath, could compete with the importance of the event.

Sylvia climbed halfway up the stairs. All she really wanted to do was get into bed with a cup of hot tea and her romance novel. "You guys," she said, "let's get going. You can work on your racers tomorrow."

"Aw, Mom," Tucker said. "Do I have to?"

"Just five more minutes," Simon pleaded. "It takes that long to fill the tub anyway."

She couldn't argue with his logic. He'd probably turn out to be a lawyer, just like Sylvia's father. Shaking her head, she recalled losing every debate with her dad. Retreating to the bathroom, she turned the hot water spigot on full blast.

Dangling her fingers in the gush of water, she thought about her mother; how easy she had made raising children look.

Maybe it was selective memory, but she couldn't remember either she or her younger brother ever defying their parents. Her father worked long hours as a patent attorney, but it never seemed to faze her mother, who worked equally long hours taking care of her and her brother Tyler.

The water turned warm and then hot. Adjusting the flow, Sylvia remembered wearing the dresses (never jeans) her mother bought her, eating the meals put in front of her (including vegetables), and going to bed without fussing. All of this occurring without her mother raising her voice. How had she accomplished that?

It was a different world then, Sylvia decided. Kids played outside with their neighborhood friends. There weren't as many activities scheduled, so no one was always busy, always on the run. Although she knew her mother had had her share of parental challenges, it still seemed like her mother did everything much better than Sylvia did.

"Tucker, Simon," she hollered above the noise of the water. "The tub's ready."

"Aw gee, Mom," Tucker yelled. "Two more minutes?"

"No!" Sylvia shouted. "You'd better come *now* or else we're not going to have time for a story tonight." She knew this threat was guaranteed to bring them quickly. The boys loved their nightly reading time together almost as much as she did. She pictured the three of them smashed into one twin-sized bed. How could Wilson bear to miss stuff like that?

She heard giggles, the thump of running feet, and then two naked boys dashed into the bathroom and jumped into the tub. Water sloshed against the sides and over the rim.

"Hey," Sylvia warned, "take it easy. This isn't the swimming pool."

Her admonition met with a series of giggles, and then two small heads simultaneously disappeared beneath the surface. Reaching for the shampoo, she couldn't help but smile. They looked like wild sea creatures with their hair flowing like brown seaweed and their arms and legs long and fluid in the water.

Simon surfaced first. Without his glasses, and with his blond hair plastered to his small head, he looked younger, more like the toddler who had peeked out at the world from behind the wall of her legs.

She squirted his head with shampoo, and did the same when Tucker came up for air. Lathering them up, she took her time turning their short hair into horns, spikes, and antennas before swishing it clean in the water.

When she'd been a girl, her hair had been long. Her mother delighting in creating soapy hairdo's for her. Sighing, she wished for the millionth time that her mother were still alive. She needed her counsel more than ever. One thing she was sure of was her mother would have approved of the Proverbs Plan.

"Okay, guys," she declared. "You're clean."

Wrapping each boy in a fluffy towel, Sylvia hugged her sons dry. "Pajama time," she ordered.

"Is Dad going to be home soon?" Simon asked.

Sylvia knelt on the wet bathroom floor. She saw the worry in her son's eyes. "I don't know," she admitted. "But even if you're already asleep, he'll check on you."

Tucker impulsively threw off his towel and ran naked out of the bathroom, shouting to the world that he had escaped from the evil kingdom of Bathtime.

"You'd better be escaping to your bedroom," Sylvia called after him. " 'Cause Mama Dragon is on her way right now."

"How come Daddy has to work so late?" Simon asked.

" 'Cause he loves us so much," Sylvia replied.

"Maybe he shouldn't love us so much," Simon suggested.

Sylvia straightened slowly. Looking in the mirror, she saw her son's worry reflected in her own eyes. She quickly looked away. "There's no such thing as loving someone too much." She touched his nose. "Especially you and Tucker. Now hurry up and get your pajamas on."

After Simon left, she continued to stand in the bathroom. She fingered one of her curls, remembering her mother sitting at the vanity in her bedroom, carefully putting on makeup and styling her hair so she would look nice each evening when her husband came home. No matter how late that was, her parents would have dinner together, privately, in the kitchen.

Maybe this was what had gone wrong in her marriage. Sylvia didn't wear makeup. More than once, she'd even worn the same T-shirt the day after she'd slept in it. Wilson had never seemed to care, and it'd saved her a shirt in the laundry. She'd spent hours helping the boys collect bugs in the backyard instead of worrying about what she looked like, or even, she admitted to herself, if the beds had been made. Now, however, she worried that she'd been so preoccupied with being a mother that she'd let something else precious slip through her fingers.

"Are you coming, Mom?" Tucker yelled, jerking her back to reality.

Well, she decided, she might not be perfect, but she was going to do better. Giving the woman in the mirror a short, determined nod, Sylvia left the room.

Chapter 7

On Friday morning after she dropped the boys at school, Sylvia went straight to the refrigerator and pulled off her honey-do list. The first item was power washing the pool deck and driveway. She had never power washed before, but she'd seen Wilson do it a couple of times and it hadn't seemed too complicated. She'd also gone on the Internet to pick up a few tips.

She rolled the machine out of the garage (which needed organizing, also on Wilson's list) and mixed the bleach solution. Putting on a pair of safety goggles, she set to work.

The tips on the computer said to start nearest to the house, so she pointed the wand at the step next to the back door and pressed the START button. Nothing happened. She checked all the connections and tried again. Nothing.

She pressed the button a second time. It remained dead. Frowning down at the machine, Sylvia decided to treat it like the vacuum, which tended to get temperamental. "This is your last chance," she warned and gave it a third try. When nothing happened, she said, "Okay, then," and when she turned on the machine, she also kicked it with the toe of her Keds. The power washer jerked to life with a roar that made her jump.

"That's the way, baby," she said and directed the narrow blast of water at the concrete. Almost immediately the shade began to lighten. The spray reminded her of the world's strongest Waterpiks, and she made a mental note to tell Rema, who would joke about trying it on Skiezer's teeth.

The wand had a little more kick than she'd expected, but she kept a tight grip and was careful not to leave any lines. The work was monotonous, but then most housework was. This was a nice change from vacuuming or running another endless load of laundry. It wasn't that she minded these chores—they weren't fun, but they were part of her job of caring for her family.

A job that was changing, she silently acknowledged as she widened the area again. When Simon had started kindergarten, it'd only been for half a day. She'd barely gotten him out the door before she was picking him up. But with Tucker, it was different. He spent the whole day at school. Although she had worried he might not be mature enough to handle eight hours of good behavior, Wilson had been adamant things would be fine. So far, he'd been correct. Other than a couple of times Tucker had to "sign the book" for impulsive behavior, he was doing well—solidly in the middle of his class. He wasn't as good a student as Simon, whose teacher had bragged was "scary smart," but Sylvia was fine with that. Having a high IQ came with its own set of problems. Simon was sensitive and tended to cry easily. He had a nervous stomach and sometimes had awful nightmares.

She'd finished the pool deck and was working on the driveway when Rema roared up in her black Suburban. Parking on the curb, Rema hopped out of the SUV. She wig-waggled her way up the driveway on a pair of sandals with three-inch heels.

Sylvia turned off the machine. "Hey," she said. "How does it look?"

Instead of inspecting the pavement, Rema lifted a pair of oversized dark glasses and looked Sylvia over from head to foot. A grin slowly formed on her olive-skinned face. "My gosh," she said. "Are you one hot mama or what?"

"Well, it's like ninety degrees." Sylvia wiped the sweat from her face with the shoulder of her tank top. Like the shorts, her shirt was ancient and a little tight fitting. But she'd wanted to wear something old—something she wouldn't mind getting ruined if she accidentally splashed bleach on it.

"It's the safety goggles," Rema said. "It gives you a brainy-brawny look. I ought to text Wilson a photo."

Sylvia shook her head. "Please don't. I look like a mess—and besides, I don't want to tell him what I'm doing. I think it would defeat the purpose." When Rema's brow furrowed, she added, "he'd feel guilty that I was doing something he always does."

"So you're not going to tell him?"

"Only if he notices."

Rema thought about this for a moment. "Maybe you're right. If Skiezer realized I was power washing, he'd probably have an anxiety attack. He'd think that I did something awful, like go on a shopping spree, and was trying to get on his good side before he found out."

Sylvia laughed. The shopping bag in Rema's hand was proof of her love of the mall. "I'm ready for a break. Why don't we get a soda and sit in the shade for a while? I want to see what you bought."

"Just a quick one," Rema agreed. "I have to get home before Cookie gets bored and chews up something. You know that Oriental rug in my entrance?"

Sylvia nodded and put the wand on the ground. She knew that rug—it was a lovely old wool with navy, red, and gold designs.

"Well, Cookie ate a hole in it. I have a repair person coming after lunch. If he can't fix it, I'm going to have to figure out how to hide it from Skiezer."

Sylvia wasn't surprised. Cookie, who was a black-and-white Border collie, was beautiful but full of energy. She was about nine months old and chewed like a termite. So far Cookie had gnawed down most of the windowsills and the trim along the back door. Skiezer had threatened more than once to take the dog to the pound. Whether or not he'd actually do this wasn't clear to Sylvia, but it scared Rema enough that she tried to hide whatever damage the dog did from her husband.

"Is it a big hole? Maybe you can put the umbrella stand on top of it," Sylvia suggested.

"It's too big." Rema shook her head and sighed. "Skiezer's going to kill me when he finds out that I haven't been crating Cookie when I leave the house. Honestly, Sylvia, if he had to see the look in poor Cookie's eyes when he gets locked in that crate, he wouldn't be able to do it either. And it's too hot to leave him in the backyard."

"Well." Sylvia opened the back door and felt the cool rush of air-conditioning on her skin. "Next time, bring him with you when you come."

Rema slid into the chair and pushed Tucker's bowl of cereal to the side. "Thanks, Sylvia." She lifted the shopping bag onto the table. "This is for you."

Grabbing two diet sodas out of the refrigerator, Sylvia turned around in surprise. "For me? What for?"

Rema smiled. "For the Proverbs Plan. I know you're working on the honey-do list, and I just thought you should have something nice to wear." She pushed the bag toward Sylvia. "Go ahead, open it."

"You didn't have to do this." Sylvia eyed the Ann Taylor logo on the bag and wondered what her friend had been up to.

"I know. It's just my way of helping." Rema smiled. "If you don't like it, we can take it back."

Sylvia pushed aside the tissue wrap and pulled out a pair of cuffed denim shorts. "Oooh, they're cute," she said and held them up, admiring the sparkly designs on the rear pockets. Checking the tag, she saw it was the right size, but then there was little about her that Rema didn't know, and Sylvia loved this.

"Keep going," Rema ordered.

Next Sylvia pulled out a whisper-thin, ribbed, black tank top. The fabric felt deliciously slinky in her hands. "I love it." Looking up, she tried to not look doubtful. "It's the right size, but it looks really small."

"It stretches," Rema said. "I bought a red one for myself, and it's the same size and I'm larger than you. You'll need to wear a push-up. You have one, right?"

Her friend was talking bras of course. "Somewhere," Sylvia said vaguely. It belonged to the life that she had labeled *before children*. Hopefully she hadn't donated it, or worse, outgrown it. She met Rema's gaze. "I can't believe you did this. This is so nice."

"And there's one more thing." Rema's eyes twinkled. "Every outfit needs the right accessories."

There was something leather and heavy at the bottom of the bag. At first she thought it was a belt, but it was too wide. Puzzled, she lifted it out of the bag then laughed.

"A tool belt? You got me my own tool belt?"

Rema's gold earrings swung as she nodded. "Complete with a pink hammer."

"It's so cute!" Sylvia enthusiastically strapped the tool belt around her waist and stuck the hammer in a loop. "I feel so professional," she said, striking a few poses. "Thank you, Rema. You're like my fairy godmother."

Rema shrugged off her thanks. "The receipts are all there in case you want to switch something." She popped the tab to her soda and took a sip. "I'll warn you in advance the tank top is a little lower cut than you're used to wearing. Hence the push-up."

Sylvia held the shirt up against her chest. "I can't wait to try it on—I'll wear it this Saturday when Wilson's home."

Rema nodded approval. "That's exactly what I was thinking." She sipped her soda and a thoughtful expression came into her soft brown eyes. "There's one thing though, that's been bothering me about this whole plan."

Sylvia put the shirt down. "What's that?"

Rema drummed her fingernails along the side of the can then stopped when she realized what she was doing. "I know you want the kind of marriage that you read about in your romance novels, but Sylvia, I honestly don't think it's possible to have that kind of relationship."

Sylvia sighed. "I know nothing is perfect. But I don't want Wilson and I just to be roommates, I want us to be soul mates." She hesitated, wanting to say more, but afraid that doing so would only point out the shortcomings in Rema's relationship with Skiezer.

"I love Skiezer," Rema said as if she'd read Sylvia's mind. "And I complain about him all the time, but deep down inside I know he's going to be there for me. He's not going to cheat on me, or walk out on our family, or come home drunk." She paused. "So what I'm saying, Sylvia, for what it's worth—I think it's better sometimes to accept what you have and not look for more than someone's willing to give you.

"I don't expect Skiezer to meet all my needs—different people play different roles in my life. You're my best friend, and I tell you stuff, Sylvia, that I'd never tell Skiezer in a thousand years. Not because I don't love him, but because he wouldn't understand. Maybe it's a man thing. I honestly don't know. Just go into this with your eyes open, okay?"

Sylvia put her hand over Rema's. "I hear what you're saying, and I love you for saying it. But here's the thing, Rema. I believe that God hears all our prayers and He answers them. Maybe not in the way we want, but in the way it's supposed to be."

Rema sighed. "You say that now, but can you live with it if nothing changes—or things get worse? Whenever I try to make things better with Skiezer, I end up sitting in my closet feeling hopeless. But if I just accept that things are the way they are—it's better." She paused. "Sometimes, Syl, hope is a cruel thing. It makes you hungry all the time and leaves you empty when what you want doesn't happen." Her lips tightened. "This Proverbs Plan—it could backfire on you. I don't want to see you hurt."

Sylvia didn't want to think about being in a marriage where she and Wilson lived in the same house but different worlds, or imagine the loneliness she felt now amplified a thousand times, but she couldn't help it. She was scared, but also determined. "If nothing's there, nothing's there," she said, "and I'll have to figure out how to live with that. But if something's there, and I think there is, I have to go for it, Rema."

Rema sighed. "I thought you'd say that. But if you end up in the closet, Syl, bring your cell and call me. I've had a lot of experience sitting in closets."

Chapter 8

The house was dead quiet as Wilson closed the front door behind him. He strained to hear the boys talking, laughing, possibly fighting, or the sound of footsteps running along the upstairs hallway. He stepped to the foot of the staircase and listened. There wasn't even the faint murmur of Sylvia's voice as she read the boys a nighttime story.

Frowning, Wilson set his briefcase on the floor. He'd known he was cutting it close, but once again the meeting with Bruce had gone longer than he'd been able to control. He hadn't wanted to appear eager to leave, not while the branch manager's position at the new bank was up for grabs, but deep inside he'd been chomping at the bit to get home.

He started up the steps. Even though the boys were sleeping, he'd give them a nighttime kiss. However, halfway up, he met Sylvia, who was starting down. She was wearing a pair of loose-fitting sweat pants, a white T-shirt from their pre-kid vacation in Cancun, and her hair was still damp from the shower. He knew she would smell slightly fruity—like ripe peaches—and feel soft and curvy in his arms. He thought this, and then his mind jumped back to Simon and Tucker.

"Hey," he said. "Is it too late to say good-night to the boys?"

Sylvia put her finger to her lips to shush him. "Yes. I just put them down."

So technically, they weren't sleeping. Wilson hesitated, weighing his need to see his sons with the knowledge that going into their bedrooms might get them excited. While part of him really liked knowing they were happy to see him, another part knew that if the routine was disturbed it could be hours before they'd settle down, and overtired kids tended to have super-sized meltdowns.

Well, it was Friday night. The boys could sleep later tomorrow. He started to go around Sylvia but then stopped himself. Neither boy ever slept late. Tucker, in particular, was an early bird and would probably pounce on him and Sylvia before six in the morning. He promised himself that tomorrow he would make up for the time he hadn't seen them during the week. They'd work on their balsa wood racers, and he would play videogames with them.

He followed Sylvia back down the stairs and into the kitchen. Sinking wearily into a ladder-backed wooden chair, he unbuttoned his shirt as Sylvia pulled his dinner plate out of the refrigerator and stuck it in the microwave. Soon the faint smell of something delicious reached his nostrils.

"What is it?" he asked, stretching out his legs and feeling himself start to relax.

"Lasagna." Sylvia poured him a tall glass of the peach-flavored iced tea he liked. "Vegetable lasagna," she amended. "I tried a new recipe. The boys hated it of course. But it's healthier. I think it was the zucchini they didn't like."

"I'm sure it's great. The boys need to learn to eat their vegetables."

"Tucker was doing pretty well until Simon started calling it puke-chini."

Wilson laughed. He wouldn't admit it to Sylvia, but zucchini wasn't his favorite vegetable either. The microwave pinged, and a moment later Sylvia set a steaming plate in front of him. Zucchini or not, it smelled great, and it'd been hours since he'd had the ham sandwich. He took a big bite and tasted Sylvia's homemade spaghetti sauce, a recipe that had come over with Sylvia's grandmother from Italy.

"Awesome," he said, taking another bite. So far, this was one of the better modifications Sylvia had made to their diet. He knew she wanted both of them to lose some weight, and while he liked how Sylvia looked, every time he looked in the mirror it seemed like the tire around his waist was getting bigger.

"So how was your day?" Sylvia asked, slipping into the seat across from him.

"Busy," Wilson said. He thought about telling her about the conversation he'd had with Bruce Maddox about the merger—specifically about the possibility of a promotion to branch manager of the new bank—but he hesitated. It wasn't a done deal. It wasn't like he'd actually been offered the job. He knew even the suggestion of a move would be unsettling for Sylvia. Why upset her over something that might not happen?

He took another bite of vegetable lasagna and bit into a large chunk of zucchini. He chewed it slowly, realizing that he really wanted to tell Sylvia about the job, and he really wanted her to be proud of him. Maybe he would take her out to dinner, somewhere nice, and he could present it in a way that would make a relocation sound like a good thing.

He realized the room had gotten very quiet. "How about you," he said. "How was your day?"

Sylvia sighed. "Fine," she said. "Took the boys to school, dressed up as Mr. Slice, came home, did housework, went grocery shopping, picked the boys up from school, played Avatar ball in the pool, went over homework, cooked dinner, gave the boys baths, story time, and bed."

The details passed at dizzying speed. "That sounds like a nice day," he said, and his thoughts drifted. There would be other candidates interviewing for the position of course, both from other branches and from other companies. He needed to make sure he stood out. But how? He had an MBA, but then so would many others, and a lot of the guys would be younger than him.

"Wilson?"

He looked up. "Huh?"

"What were you just thinking? You disappeared for a little while."

He smiled apologetically. "Work stuff. I'm sorry." He went to take another bite of the lasagna and discovered he'd eaten all of it.

"You want some more?" Sylvia offered.

He thought about his expanding stomach and shook his head. "No. But that was great." He pushed his plate forward. "Thanks." Now that he'd finished eating, he felt the fatigue of the week setting in. "I'm glad it's the weekend."

"Me, too," Sylvia replied. Standing, she took his plate to the sink and rinsed it off. "You should sleep in tomorrow. I'll get up with the boys."

"No, you should sleep," he said. "I'll get up."

"Honestly, I don't mind." Sylvia set his plate in the dishwasher, and then began wiping down what looked like spotless counters.

His thoughts drifted back to work. While he knew the financial side of the business, he wasn't as familiar with the personnel side. Being good with numbers wasn't going to be enough to guarantee him the job—he needed career-development plans for the existing personnel. Plans that could be tied into new product offerings. He felt strongly that the future of banking lay in online services, and that the key to pulling ahead of the competition lay in installing the most user-friendly software.

He frowned because his ideas would mean powerful servers and desktops with the latest applications. He had to keep the costs down or they'd laugh at him.

He was aware, suddenly, that Sylvia was looking at him. He wondered, guiltily, if she'd asked a question. He let the silence lengthen, and then she turned around and began wiping the counter again. He sensed he'd disappointed her but wasn't sure what he'd done. His mind quickly flashed through a list of possible things he might have missed, like birthdays, anniversaries, an important meeting with the school or a doctor that she might be expecting him to ask about. He couldn't come up with anything—except being late. Again.

"This work stuff. This merger," he amended. "It won't be forever." He forced a smile. "Soon you'll be seeing more of me than you want."

Sylvia tucked a dishtowel onto the bar across the oven. "No problem," she said. "I was wondering if you'd like to watch a movie with me on the couch."

Wilson sighed in relief, grateful she wasn't mad at him. "I'd love that," he said.

It was a romantic comedy, and although he would rather have seen something with more content, he had to admit that Sylvia cuddled next to him was pretty awesome. When his mind started to slip back to work, he forced himself to follow the plot unfolding on the television. Soon, it was hard to keep his eyes open. He fought for a while, but the next thing he knew, Sylvia was nudging him. The movie was over, and it was time for bed.

Chapter 9

It was still dark in the bedroom when a heavy thump hit the bed and Sylvia levitated a couple of inches off the mattress. "Tucker," she groaned, keeping her eyes closed. "That wasn't funny."

The little boy giggled then crawled over to her. Still half-asleep, Sylvia registered his warmth, his little-boy smell, and then the hardness of his skull as it smacked her chin as he made space for himself on the pillow.

She prayed he'd go back to sleep but wasn't really surprised when Tucker whispered, "Is it time to get up?"

Sylvia managed to open one eye. Both of Tucker's big eyes were millimeters from her own. They gleamed almost black in the darkness that was just beginning to lighten in the room. "No," she whispered. "Not until you see some sunlight."

She closed her eyes. Tucker jostled the bed, and then she felt something rolling up the side of her leg and begin climbing her hip. A moment later, Tucker began making a motor-like sound, and she realized he was running his Matchbox car over the side of her body. Her first impulse was to tell him to stop it, but then she realized that if she did this, he'd only move the racetrack to Wilson's body and wake him up.

"Vroom," Tucker whispered hoarsely. "Vroom-vroom."

Sylvia shushed him as the car climbed her hip. She glanced over at her sleeping husband, wondering if he was really sleeping through this or just playing possum. It didn't matter; the Proverbs 31 woman rose before dawn and so would she.

With a sigh, she pushed back the covers. "Come on," she whispered. "I'll put on cartoons for you. But you have to be quiet," she warned.

Tucker happily let her lead him through the semi-darkness to the living room, where she set him up on the couch with a bowl of cereal. Turning on the television, she asked him to stay there while she took a shower and got changed. The little guy's gaze already was glued to the talking construction machines on the set, and he nodded eagerly.

Tiptoeing back into the bedroom, Sylvia headed for the shower. The warm water helped wake her up. Feeling more cheerful and refreshed, she pulled out the outfit Rema had bought her. She felt even better when the old push-up bra still fit. Pulling on the shorts and black tank top, she looked at herself in the mirror.

The copper-colored hair was a mess—but the outfit—it fit perfectly. The tank top was a little lower cut than she normally wore, but it wasn't obscene or anything. It simply showed her curves, which she admitted, had taken on new life in the push-up.

The cuffed denim shorts hugged her hips and ended mid-thigh. The end result was casual but sexy. She felt renewed confidence in herself as she dabbed styling gel in her hair. The final step was to buckle on her new tool belt. The width of the leather made her waist look smaller than it actually was, and the pink hammer looked adorable hanging from its strap.

Wilson sat up in bed as she passed through the room. Blinking sleepily at her, he reached for his glasses on the end table. "Syl, what are you wearing?"

She put her hands on her hips and sucked in her stomach. "Nothing special. Go back to sleep, honey."

Wilson continued to stare at her. "Are you wearing a tool belt?"

"Yes."

His gaze slid over her body and his jaw dropped slightly. With a slight growth of hair covering his chin, he looked manly and adorable. "Is that a new shirt?"

"Yes." Sylvia felt the wire from the push-up digging into her side.

No wonder she'd shoved this bra to the back of her drawer. It was worth it though, to see that look in Wilson's eyes. "I thought I'd fix some things around the house today."

"Come repair me," Wilson invited, tenting the covers.

Sylvia laughed. "Wilson, Tucker is right in the next room."

Wilson looked straight into her eyes. "So what? Just lock the door."

Sylvia hesitated. She was definitely up for some fun, but unlike Wilson, she had no illusions about Tucker being preoccupied for too long. She didn't think it would be too fun being in bed with Wilson as Tucker knocked on the door and begged to be let inside.

Simon wouldn't be asleep much longer either, and if the two of them were banging on the door. . .it'd be totally embarrassing. She crossed the space between herself and Wilson and planted a kiss on his lips. "I'd love to, honey, but I think any second we're going to hear the pitter-patter of little feet."

The words were no sooner out of her mouth when Simon, with Tucker hard on his heels, burst into the room. Both boys jumped on top of Wilson and began wrestling him. As Wilson pretended to be overwhelmed by the attack, Sylvia quietly slipped out of the room.

In the kitchen, she poured herself a hot cup of coffee. After adding a generous amount of cream and sugar, she sat down at the kitchen table and pulled the honey-do list from its magnet.

So far, she'd power washed the driveway, taken the minivan to Sears and gotten the oil changed and new windshield wipers installed. She still needed to tighten the bolts on the toilet seat in the guest bathroom—it tended to swing around when you sat on it—clean the gutters, and fix the washing machine. In addition to all those chores, she still had the usual ones—a house to clean, laundry to wash, grocery shopping, and two young boys to watch.

In fact, all these chores would require a lot of energy. Since she'd be burning a lot of calories, she decided to make blueberry pancakes and bacon for breakfast.

"Watcha wearing, Mom?" Simon walked into the kitchen wearing a pair of Spiderman pajamas. His blond hair stuck straight up from the wrestling, and his thick glasses made his blue eyes look even larger and more owlish than usual. Tucker, as usual, was hard on his older brother's heels.

"It's a belt for weight lifting," Tucker replied, as if this were obvious.

"It's a tool belt," Sylvia corrected gently. "Today I'm going to fix some things around the house. It'll hold my hammer and pliers. That sort of thing."

"Great," Tucker replied. He stuck his fist through one of the smaller loops on the belt. "Can I help?"

Sylvia braced her legs as Tucker attempted to dangle his full weight from her tool belt. "Of course," she said. "But I think your dad wants to spend some time with you today."

"We're going to work on our racers," Simon confirmed. "The derby is next week. We're sanding my car to round the edges and make it more aerodynamic." He said this last word slowly, pronouncing it carefully and a little proudly.

"That sounds good," Sylvia said, cracking an egg into the batter while continuing to balance Tucker, who was proving to have good arm strength.

"*Aero-dy-namic* means the air moving around so my car won't slow it down as much," Simon explained. "Dad told me."

Sylvia gently extracted Tucker's fingers from her belt and immediately felt like she'd lost forty-five pounds as her son's feet touched the ground again. "When you put the wheels on, I have a can of WD-40 in the garage. Your dad uses it on the tires of my bike to make them roll easier. Maybe it'll help your car, too."

Simon's eyes studied her, unblinking. "That's illegal."

"Illegal? You sure?"

"It's in the rules, Mom. Didn't you read them?"

"Of course," Sylvia replied, and dropped a spoonful of batter on the grill to see if it was hot enough. Just where, she wondered, had she put the information package for the Pinewood Derby? Hopefully Simon wouldn't ask for it. "I just don't have them memorized."

"Well I do," Simon stated. "Want to hear?"

"Maybe later," Sylvia said gently.

"Hey Simon," Tucker exclaimed, "*Peter Possum*'s on."

Although Sylvia monitored the amount of TV the boys watched during the week, on Saturday morning she let them have their fill. As the look of delight replaced the worry on Simon's face, she felt herself relax. "Go on," she said, "I'll call you when the pancakes are ready."

After breakfast, Sylvia went right to work. She left Wilson and the boys in front of the television and headed for the laundry room.

The washing machine had been misbehaving for weeks. Whenever it reached the spin cycle it began making a thumping noise that increased exponentially as the machine picked up speed. If she didn't jump on top of it by the third or fourth *whomp, whomp, whomp* it began to inch its way across the floor.

Wilson said he thought the machine was unbalanced. Sylvia had replied that the better word was *deranged*. Wilson had laughed, promised to fix it, and then promptly forgotten all about it.

Looking at the machine, which was sitting about eight inches from the wall, she decided to give Wilson's theory a try. It took some digging, but she found a level in the garage. Placing it on top of the machine, she watched the tiny little bubble slide to the left of the center line. She needed to raise the left side a bit higher.

A block of wood would be too high, but a sheet of leftover balsa wood from the Pinewood Derby racers might do the trick. Wedging it beneath the foot of the washing machine, she then placed the level on the lid. The bubble centered perfectly. Still suspicious, Sylvia turned the dial to the spin cycle and held her breath as the machine jumped to life.

Her muscles tensed as she prepared to jump on top of the lid, but the motor purred smoothly along and the machine stayed right in place. It was still way too far from the wall, but she decided she could live with that.

Feeling pretty good about the way that went, Sylvia peeked into the living room to check on Wilson and the boys. They were camped out on the sofa in front of the television. Wild Bill Hiccup, a tonsil-like creature, was using his tongue to lasso a green creature that Sylvia guessed was some sort of germ. Wilson had his laptop balanced on his knees and was peering intently into the screen.

Sylvia sighed. She didn't want to sound like a nag, but she really wanted Wilson to spend quality time with the boys, not work on his computer. "Hey," she said, "I thought you guys were going to work on your racers."

"Dad says we'll do it after he finishes e-mail," Simon replied. "He has two hundred fifty-eight e-mails in his inbox. A lot are from Jen Douglas."

"She's my boss's administrative assistant," Wilson said. "You really shouldn't be reading my e-mails, Simon."

Sylvia thought of the pretty brunette she'd met at the Christmas party at Wilson's office. Jen was nice, outgoing, and had a killer figure. Part of Sylvia wanted to take a look at those e-mails, but then she reminded herself that she trusted Wilson. She might not always understand him, but she trusted him.

"Sorry, Dad." Simon shrugged. "They're kind of boring anyway. What's a merger?"

"It's when two companies or businesses combine into one business." Wilson shut the lid of his laptop abruptly. "Is this a transformer cartoon?"

Simon laughed. "Dad, Wild Bill Hiccup is a germ hunter. He tracks down germs and then eats them."

Sylvia left them discussing the possibility of science actually developing a soldier-like cell that could attack disease. Maybe Simon would grow up to be a researcher and cure cancer—a disease that had claimed the lives of both her parents within months of each other. Sylvia knew she was a little biased when it came to thinking that God had blessed Simon with remarkable gifts, but still, his mind was like a sponge, and he was fascinated by science.

"I'll be outside if anyone needs me," she said, heading outside to tackle the gutters. It wasn't just that they needed cleaning; it was because Wilson really didn't like doing it. It always put him in a bad mood, and although she had encouraged him to hire someone, so far he wouldn't let her. Wilson's father had always done stuff like that around the house, so she figured Wilson felt he should, too.

It wasn't hard to drag the ladder to the front of the house. From the top rung, she could reach the gutters easily. For a moment though, she paused to enjoy the view. A bright red cardinal perched in a tree just yards from her, and a beautiful garden of wildflowers bloomed in her neighbor's backyard.

The mess in the gutter was less pleasing to her eye. It looked like the bed of pine needles could harbor something slimy and gross, like fat, finger-sucking slugs. Gingerly, she stuck her hand into the gutter.

When nothing bit her, Sylvia started to relax. You couldn't raise two boys and be squeamish. She'd cleaned more than her share of vomit and other gross stuff. *Think of this as mixing a meatloaf. You're at the part when you mix the raw egg in with the hamburger meat.*

While this helped, she suspected it would be a long time before she made meatloaf again. The worst part about the job, she decided, was moving the ladder so often. Going up and down the steps was exhausting. It was like being on an exceptionally wobbly StairMaster. The sun had come out in full, and sweat glued her new top to her body.

She'd really rather be inside, watching Wilson and the boys build their racers or curled up in her favorite chair reading her book. She thought longingly of a glass of sweet tea and air-conditioning. Despite herself, she found herself thinking about what Rema had said. What if she always wanted something that Wilson couldn't give her? What if things got even worse between them? Could she live with that?

"Sylvia," Wilson's voice suddenly boomed. "What are you doing up there?"

Startled, she turned at the sound of his voice. The motion made the ladder wobble, and for one terrible second she feared it would topple backward. She grabbed at the gutter for balance and support and felt something sharp slice her arm.

"Sylvia," Wilson shouted, sounding scared. "You come down right now."

The ladder steadied. When she glanced down, she saw Wilson gripping the steel sides of the ladder tightly. "I'm fine," she said. "You just startled me—that's all."

Her arm stung a little, and when she glanced down, a thin line of blood was trickling from a cut near her wrist. It was a small cut, but fairly deep. It hurt, but what bothered her more was getting blood on both the tank top and cute denim shorts Rema had bought her. She held her arm up and away from her body.

"Sylvia—you're bleeding."

"I'm okay."

"Can you make it down?"

"Of course. It's just a little scratch." Still holding her arm away from her body, she began to back down the ladder slowly.

The cut had started bleeding harder, and when Wilson examined it his lips tightened. "That's not a little scratch. You need stitches." Before she could protest, he whipped off his shirt—a green polo she'd bought him last year for Father's Day—and wrapped it around her arm. "Go wait in the car," he ordered. "I'll get the boys."

Chapter 10

"And then he drove me to the emergency room and waited with me while the doctor stitched me up." Sylvia held out her bandaged arm and all four friends sitting around her kitchen table leaned forward to inspect it. "It took five stitches, and I had to get a tetanus shot." Sylvia held her arms about a foot apart. "The needle was this long."

There was a chorus of long, sympathetic sighs, concerned looks, and voices overlapping that said, "Are you okay, Sylvia? Why didn't you call us?"

"It really wasn't a big deal," Sylvia said, "but I love knowing that if I needed you, you'd all help."

"Of course we would," Andrea said. "Remember when I had the emergency hysterectomy? You did everything for me—took care of my kids, brought me meals, cleaned my house?"

"You've picked up my kids from day care like a hundred times," Kelly said, "when I've had to work late."

"Not to mention all the times I've called you to help with one of my ministries," Susan said. "And you never point out that I've over-committed myself again, even though that's the truth."

Sylvia held up her hand to stop everyone. "You guys are making me sound like a saint, which I'm not. All of you have been great friends to me and helped me out plenty of times. Now, who wants some apple-sauce cake? I know it's a little off the diet list, but I figured apples are healthy, right?"

Everyone took a piece. Sylvia topped off the coffee cups and listened hard for any noises that might indicate Wilson and the boys, who were upstairs, might be on the move. She'd only scheduled the meeting tonight because she'd thought Wilson would be on a business trip. His meetings, however, had been rescheduled.

"I'm sorry you hurt your arm, but Sylvia, I think it's really romantic the way Wilson took care of you." Susan paused to beam at Sylvia. "What better way to show that he loves you?"

"Susan's right," Andrea added with a smile. "Wilson came through for you, Sylvia. This plan is working even better than I thought it would."

Sylvia sighed. "Honestly, it wasn't that romantic. Wilson turned green at the sight of all that blood. The doctor made him sit with his head between his legs while I got stitched up. Luckily some nice nurse kept an eye on the boys."

"You should have paged me," Kelly said. "I would have come and helped you."

Sylvia looked at her whisper-thin friend. As a pediatric surgeon, Kelly already worked terrible hours. Sylvia always felt like if one more thing was added to Kelly's plate, she would break into a million pieces. "I know," she said, "and I appreciate it. But honestly, it wasn't that big of a deal." She reached for a piece of the homemade applesauce cake she'd been unable to resist baking that afternoon.

"Go on, Syl," Rema urged. Her brown eyes sparkled. "Tell the best part."

Sylvia looked over at her friend, who was already grinning in anticipation.

"Well," Sylvia began, taking a deep breath, "the whole way to the hospital we tried to minimize the accident so the boys wouldn't get scared. I thought we did a pretty good job, but when we got to the hospital, the registration lady asked what happened to me. Before Wilson or I could answer, Tucker burst into tears and said really loudly, 'Mommy cut her wrist.' I'm telling you—you could have heard a pin drop in the waiting room."

"They thought Sylvia tried to commit suicide." Rema burst into laughter. She tried to speak but couldn't get anything out. After a few tries, Rema managed to surface and get out, "Tell them, Sylvia." And then she started laughing again.

"The entire room went dead quiet, and registration lady's eyes practically popped out of her head," Sylvia said. "She picked up the telephone, and within a minute there was a doctor taking me back into the examination room."

"I'd pay anything to read the doctor's notes," Rema said, a note of glee in her voice as she wiped her eyes. " 'Note to staff. Do not leave patient unattended in room with exposed gutters.' "

Everyone around the table exploded with laughter. Sylvia tried to hush them—Wilson was, after all, upstairs in his office working.

"So all and all, week two was a success," Andrea said, after everyone had some time to calm down. "What's next?"

Sylvia cut a worried glance at the stairs. Andrea had a loud voice which worked well in the courtroom, but she hoped it wouldn't carry to Wilson. "Maybe we should just call it a night," she said. She lowered her voice. "Now that I've oiled the hinges to Wilson's office door, I can't hear him coming anymore."

"You need to tie a bell around his neck," Rema suggested unhelpfully.

"We'll keep it quick," Andrea said, "but I think we need to look at the next verse."

Susan opened her Bible. Flipping through tissue-thin pages, she looked up when she found the right passage.

" 'She is like the merchant ships, bringing her food from afar. She gets up while it is still night; she provides food for her family and portions for her female servants.' "

"We already talked about the merchant ships part," Rema protested. She dabbed the corner of her eye where her mascara had started to run. "Why are you bringing it up again?"

Andrea tapped her pencil on her legal pad. Her sharp blue eyes blinked. "Because before, we were trying to interpret it in context of the verse preceding it. We never really figured out what it meant. We can't just skip verses that are hard to understand."

"I'm probably being too literal," Kelly mused, "but if I had to paraphrase this, I'd say something like: The Proverbs 31 woman is a good cook and serves her family healthy meals." She shook her head. "I totally get that. You really can't underestimate the value of good nutrition. I see a lot of obese kids, and most of the time it's because they're eating way too much fast food."

Sylvia fervently hoped that her applesauce cake didn't fall into the unhealthy food category. However, she couldn't help but notice Kelly hadn't eaten any of it. She was sipping that herbal concoction in her metal thermos. "I try to serve good meals," Sylvia said, "but sometimes when the boys have activities after school, I really don't have time to cook."

Rema nodded in agreement. "Back when the Bible was written, I'm sure the moms were busy, but they didn't have to factor in carpools, soccer practice, cub scouts, and other activities into their schedules." She forked off another large bite of Sylvia's cake. "I know we could just say no to our kids and not let them do so much stuff—but then they'd be the only ones staying home—they'd have no friends. Not to mention that if you want your kids to play on any of the sports teams in high school, you have to start them young."

Andrea and Kelly exchanged glances. As successful, professional women, both of them worked long hours. For years they had juggled their schedules with their husbands', swapped favors with other parents, and at times hired teenagers to get their kids to music lessons, sports practices, and other stuff.

"Rema's right," Kelly said after a moment. "This verse makes it sound like you can't be a good mother if you rely on takeout."

"Not exactly," Andrea countered. "Look at the text. It says she buys imported foods, brought by ship from distant ports—it doesn't mean she has to cook them. Plus the woman in this verse has servants."

"You have a cleaning lady," Susan pointed out. "Not that I'm suggesting you aren't a great mother," she quickly added.

"In our house," Kelly ventured, "Keith does most of the shopping and cooking, so how does this verse apply to me?"

There was a moment of silence as each woman seemed to ponder the question. The passage didn't seem geared toward a household in which the woman worked and the man stayed at home.

"That's hard," Sylvia agreed. "But the main thing, I think, is that you work hard for your family. That you do the best you can." She crumpled her paper napkin and put it on the table. "That you serve them, even when you'd rather sleep late or put your needs ahead of your family's."

"Excellent," Susan said, giving Sylvia a beaming smile. "When my

Bible study ladies came to this verse, we spent a lot of time focusing on how we, as wives, could make the relationships in our families stronger. I'm not just talking husband-wife. There are siblings, parents, children—not to mention the whole in-law side of things." She paused as Rema, who didn't get along well with her mother-in-law, groaned dramatically. "This is the only verse in the passage that talks about the Proverbs 31 woman in relation to her family." Her gaze came to rest on Sylvia. "Dear," she said, "maybe this week you could try to think of something that you could do as a family."

Sylvia blinked. Just what did they all enjoy? Besides going out to Mexican restaurants and watching television? There were video games, but she didn't think Susan meant playing Xbox 360 would bring them closer together as a family. What they needed, Sylvia considered, was a common goal. Something they could all work toward together.

"Whatever you do, don't do family game night," Rema warned in a gloomy tone of voice. "Or you'll end up sitting in your closet like me."

"What about a family getaway trip to somewhere fun?" Andrea suggested. "Look on the Internet for one of those last-minute getaway deals. Blake and I had a super time in Phoenix."

Sylvia brightened. Planning a spontaneous long weekend with Wilson and the boys sounded fun. But then she thought of the long hours Wilson was putting in at the bank. He'd say he was too busy. And besides, the Pinewood Derby race was the next weekend. She needed something now—not two weeks from now.

She stopped with her cup of coffee halfway to her lips. The Pinewood Derby. Both boys were entered, and Wilson already was involved in helping the boys build their racers. This week she could take a more active role in helping the boys get ready—build a practice track or make team T-shirts or something. The race had been important to Wilson when he was a boy, and he'd been talking it up for months.

Setting her mug on the kitchen table, she smiled at her friends. "I have an idea," she said.

Chapter 11

From his study upstairs, Wilson heard the muffled voices and occasional bursts of laughter coming from the kitchen. He leaned back in his computer chair and stared at the spreadsheet on the screen without really seeing it.

Who would have thought a church group could be so much fun? Usually, the thought of the friends in the Bible study group he and Sylvia attended every other week made him feel good. Yet tonight, hearing the laughter of Sylvia and her friends made his insides churn. It reminded him of the deep roots they'd developed in this town. If he got the promotion he wanted, he'd be taking Sylvia away from the church and all her friends.

Yet were her friends more important than his career?

The question haunted him. Their pastor said that the Lord liked to introduce change into people's lives in order to use them in new ways. It was possible that this promotion was part of God's plan for him. However, Wilson worried that as his responsibilities increased, so would his hours. He closed his eyes and prayed as he had a hundred times. *Please, Lord, if this promotion is Your will for me, let it happen. But if You want me stay in my current role, could You please give me the strength to turn down the job?*

He strained for some sign that God had heard him, but all he heard was another burst of laughter from downstairs.

I know You are a good God, he prayed. *Help me do what's right.*

He opened his eyes and stared again at the spreadsheet on the computer. His business plan for the new bank was getting longer by the minute, but he kept thinking of new things to add—and just that very day the federal government had changed the way banks could charge for their services, which completely threw off the numbers he'd been working with.

He downloaded the new federal government mandate and was puzzling through ways of getting around it, when the door to his study swung open. His oldest son, Simon, stood framed in the doorway. In his Spiderman pajamas and clutching a stuffed monkey so old it looked as if its fur had molted, his son looked small and infinitely vulnerable.

"Dad?"

Wilson pushed back from the computer. Simon's eyes looked glassy, and his cheeks had a reddish hue that meant he was either running a fever or about to cry.

"You okay, buddy?"

The little boy nodded he was fine, but it was clear he wasn't.

"Come here," Wilson said gently.

Still clutching his monkey, Simon slowly closed the distance between them. Leaning forward, he placed his hand on his son's forehead. It was warm, not hot, which meant no fever. He brushed Simon's short blond hair to the side. "What's going on?"

Simon looked up at him with huge blue eyes. "I can't sleep. Mom and her friends are making too much noise."

He smiled as Sylvia's voice rang out with a clear, "No!"

Simon looked at him as if willing Wilson to do something.

"I'll tell them to keep it down." Wilson started to get up, and then settled back in his chair. It was rare that he and Simon had time alone together, mostly because of Wilson's job. Even this past weekend, when he'd consciously decided to give the boys more attention, it hadn't gone as he'd planned.

He studied Simon's face. A hundred new freckles seemed to have popped up overnight against his fair skin. The boy had Sylvia's slender, straight nose and mouth, but Simon had gotten the Baxter blues.

"What do you say we give your mom a little more time with her friends and you hang out here with me?"

Simon nodded.

"So," Wilson began, "how was school today?"

"Good."

"Just good?" Wilson smiled. "You do anything fun?"

Simon shook his head. "No."

He looked harder into his son's face. Simon was pretty verbal and had a really good sense of humor. Usually he had at least one funny observation to make about his day. "You're really quiet," he said. "You sure something isn't wrong?"

Simon glanced over his shoulder as the voices drifted up from below them. "Will you read me a story?"

Wilson nodded. Taking his son's hand, he led the boy back to his room and tucked him beneath his Spiderman comforter. "What story do you want?"

Simon gestured to the children's book of bedtime stories that sat atop a stack of other books. Wilson hesitated. Wasn't that a little young for him? "You sure, buddy?"

"Yes. Read *Davy and Goliath*."

Wilson flipped open the pages to the desired story. He was about to read the first line, when he glanced at Simon, who was biting his lip.

"What is it," Wilson pressed gently. "I can see something's really bothering you." He thought hard. Simon was the consummate overachiever—something Wilson not only related to, but also privately approved. "Something wrong at school? Like a bad test?"

"No." Simon stared hard into Wilson's eyes as if trying, telepathically to tell him something.

"Did you fight with Tucker?"

"No."

Wilson raked his fingers through his hair. "What then?"

Silence, and then, to his surprise, two small tears leaked from the corners of Simon's eyes. Wilson's first thought was to run for Sylvia, but when he started to stand up, Simon shrank back into the pillow. "Dad, don't go."

Wilson sat on the edge of the bed and wiped a wet streak from his son's cheek with his thumb. "I want to help you. I love you very much— whatever you tell me won't change that."

Simon blinked hard. His throat worked, and the color grew even brighter in his face. There was a long silence, and then Simon blurted out, "It's about the race, Dad. It's this weekend and we haven't finished my race car."

Was that it? Wilson worked to arrange his features into a sympathetic expression. "You're going to do great. Don't worry."

Simon blinked up at him. "But you said we'd finish my race car over the weekend and you didn't."

Wilson felt his cell vibrate from its holster around his belt. He was unable to keep his hand from pulling the Velcro open. "Well," he began, trying to ignore the urge to check and see who the caller might be. "Your mommy got hurt. We had to take care of her."

"I know," Simon said. "But the race is this Saturday."

"And we'll finish your car this week—I promise."

"Tomorrow?"

His cell, thankfully, had stopped buzzing. "Yes, tomorrow," Wilson assured him then grimaced. He was going on a two-day business trip. "We'll do it on Friday, and if we don't finish, we'll work on it Saturday. The races aren't until the afternoon." At least he thought they started in the afternoon. Actually he had no idea. Sylvia usually kept track of these things.

Simon looked unconvinced. "What time will you be home on Friday?"

"I have to look at my calendar," Wilson replied, which was true, but it was obviously not the answer Simon wanted. He was about to provide more assurances when he heard the soft chirp from his computer. Despite himself, Wilson's thoughts turned back to the afternoon's visit with the outgoing manager of the bank they were acquiring. The board had offered him a pretty good settlement package. Maybe this was the manager, accepting the offer.

"What if we don't finish?" Simon asked, pulling him back into the present.

"We'll finish. I promise."

"You promised we would finish last weekend," Simon pointed out, "and you didn't."

"Because Mommy cut her arm." Wilson leaned forward and kissed the boy on his forehead. "It's nighttime, and you shouldn't be worrying about anything. Just go to sleep."

His computer pinged again. Something was happening. He felt a strong urge to respond and had to force himself to remain perched on the corner of his son's bed.

The Instant Message could be from Bruce. His boss took pride in his ability to gain a second wind around ten at night. Wilson reminded himself that Simon's well-being came before work. "Everything will be fine. Just go to sleep."

"Tucker's car is faster than mine."

"You're not competing with Tucker," Wilson reminded him. Above everything, he wanted the boys to cheer for each other and value the importance of family.

"I know," Simon said. "I tried loosening the nail holes, to get the wheels to roll faster, but all that's done is made the wheels wobble."

"You need to tighten those axles," Wilson said. "Not loosen them, and then make sure they're absolutely straight. I'll help you."

Simon sighed. "Cross your heart?"

Wilson drew a large X over his chest then grasped Simon's small hands in his own. "Now let's say a quick prayer and then you go to sleep."

"Okay."

Simon took a deep breath and began, "Now I lay me down to sleep. I pray to God my soul to keep. . ."

Something deep inside Wilson stirred at the sound of Simon's childish voice reciting the same prayer he had said as a boy every night of his life. At the end, Simon added a long string of people for God to bless, and then Wilson gave him a final good-night kiss and tiptoed out of the room.

Back in his office, Wilson checked his cell. The message was indeed from Bruce. CALL ME. ASAP. Wilson quickly hit speed dial. As it rang, echoes of the conversation he'd just had with Simon played in his mind. Imagine, his own son worried that he wouldn't have time to help him build his balsa racer.

∽

Simon lay on his back and looked at the glow-in-the-dark constellation above his bed. He knew the names of all the planets and most of the facts about them. He was fascinated by the idea of a universe constantly expanding, extending to infinity. It was like God knew if He didn't keep the universe growing, He might get found, and He didn't want that to happen. God wanted to stay mysterious.

Simon liked mysteries, too, but mostly he liked solving them. He enjoyed learning how things worked and filling his mind with facts that he could call out at will, as if his brain was a microscope he could use to examine the world. He could see things but he didn't have to be in them.

Unlike this Pinewood Derby race.

His dad had won it when he was Simon's age. Simon, himself, had seen the racer in his father's office. It was in a box in the closet, and when Simon found it, his dad had let him take it out and play with it. His dad told him the story of how he and his grandfather had built it together. Simon listened, and from that moment on, he'd decided that when he was the right age, he'd enter the Pinewood Derby, too. He saw himself winning. He saw the look of pride on his dad's face.

He wanted to make his dad proud. Whenever he got a good grade, his mother smothered him in kisses and stuck the paper on the refrigerator. His dad would call him "Rhymin' Simon" and throw him over his shoulder, spinning in circles until Simon's glasses fell off and he wobbled when his dad set him on his feet again.

Yep. The better he did in school, the more they loved him, and he was sure the same went for this upcoming race. He had to win. Had to be the best. If he did, then maybe his dad would start hanging out with him more—the way he used to before "something important" started happening at work. Simon wanted this desperately, even more than the chemistry set he wanted for Christmas. Every night, after he said prayers with his mom and brother, Simon added a silent one: *Please, Lord Jesus, let me win the Pinewood Derby 'cause I miss my dad.*

Chapter 12

Wilson's business trip complicated Sylvia's plan to pull the family together as they prepared for the upcoming Pinewood Derby race. Although she knew practically nothing about building a balsa wood racer, she researched construction tips on the Internet, gamely pulled out the tool box, and offered her services to the boys.

Tucker had been excited to have her help glue the wheels to the axles. Mostly he was interested in getting to the part where he could paint the body of the car. Simon, however, hadn't let her touch his racer. He'd said he wanted to wait for Wilson, who would tighten the axles.

Sylvia had gently suggested that Wilson might get caught up in work, but Simon remained firm in his decision.

Now, seated in the elementary school's conference room, Sylvia shifted in the plastic seat. If only Simon didn't care so much about this race, she wouldn't be so worried. If he won, great. If he didn't, so what? Simon, however, was determined to win. He was used to getting top marks. Used to winning geography and math bees.

Sylvia made a mental note to ask Wilson to tell Simon he'd be proud of him no matter if he won the race or not. Maybe she could talk to him on the phone tonight, after the boys went to bed. It was a conversation she definitely didn't want either boy hearing.

She didn't want to be the nag in the relationship, but honestly, sometimes Wilson could be blind to what was happening directly in front of him. Sometimes she even thought that Wilson encouraged Simon's over-achieving tendencies.

"Sylvia?"

Looking up, Sylvia met the gaze of Casey Armstrong, the president of the PTO. She was a striking woman with red hair, strong facial bones, and a slight southwestern accent. "We were just approving last month's meeting minutes. Since you didn't raise your hand, I assume you have an objection."

Sylvia shook her head and smiled sheepishly. Apparently Wilson wasn't the only one good at tuning out what was happening around him. "No, I approve them."

"Excellent," Casey said. "And now Mr. Allen will give his report."

"Thank you, Mrs. Armstrong." Principal Allen was a tall, thin man with a cleft chin, sparse blond hair, and a passion for ties with cartoon characters on them. "I've only got a couple of things to go over."

Sylvia braced herself. Whenever he said this, it usually meant he was good for at least forty-five minutes. God help them all if he turned on the overhead projector.

"Most everyone is doing really well about adhering to the dismissal procedures," Principal Allen said, "but I thought since you all are leaders of the parent community, we ought to go over them again."

Oh no, Sylvia thought as the principal pulled out a thick manila folder. Next to her Ella King, the head of the teacher appreciation committee, muttered something even worse.

Coming to these meetings was the worst part about being Mr. Slice, but at the same time Sylvia recognized their importance. It gave her a connection to the inner working of the school that she wouldn't have had otherwise.

Although Simon and Tucker were pretty verbal, they couldn't give her complete pictures of their day at school. They couldn't tell her that the school smelled of glue and cleaners, that the assistant vice principal never smiled with her eyes, that you could hear the sweet voices of the children singing as you passed in the hallway in front of the music room.

As the principal droned on, Sylvia mentally planned dinner. She'd make pork chops seasoned with chives and lemon pepper, brown rice, and steamed broccoli, since broccoli gave Wilson gas and he wouldn't be eating dinner with them because of his business trip.

On the other hand, since it was just her and the boys, maybe she'd do takeout. That new burrito place in town was pretty good. The boys loved it, and she'd have more time to spend with them if she didn't have to shop, cook, and clean up.

Amid these thoughts, some small part of her brain registered that the principal was looking directly at her. She quickly arranged her features into an alert, interested look, as if she were paying close attention, even as she continued to mull over what toppings she wanted on her burrito.

The expression, she realized guiltily, was one she used frequently whenever Wilson started talking about investing money. *I can do better,* she promised herself. *I will do better when I listen to him.*

Twenty minutes later, Principal Allen placed the last transparency on the projector. "Are there any questions?" he asked.

There was dead silence. The lights came on, illuminating a room full of silent, semi-comatose women. Someone had to nudge the PTO president, who, although sitting bolt upright, hadn't seemed to have realized the principal had stopped talking. Finally Casey managed to thank Dr. Allen for his presentation and ask for committee reports.

Deanna Williams, who chaired the school beautification committee, stood. "I'm sorry to report that we're having a *serious* drainage problem near the playground entrance."

A heated argument ensued over whether PTO funds should be spent on the necessary repairs or budgeted toward more books for the library.

Both projects seemed worthy, and it soon became apparent that the room was evenly split. As the debate raged, Sylvia slowly raised her hand.

"I could run pizza nights every week instead of every other week. By the end of the year we might have enough with the money left in the budget to put in the drainage ditch *and* buy some new books for the library."

As all gazes turned to her, Sylvia blushed. Being Mr. Slice wasn't exactly a prestigious role in the PTO. In fact, she'd gotten the job because no one else was willing to wear the tights and foam costume. Up until today, she hadn't spoken up much. Mostly she'd been happy to have the vice president of fundraising speak for her. Now, she felt the other women staring at her as if they had never seen her before.

"Great idea," the PTO president declared.

Even as Sylvia reconsidered—volunteering herself for extra work meant that she'd have less time to put into her relationship with Wilson—everyone agreed that the number of pizza nights would be doubled.

"Ladies, we're adjourned," the president declared, and banged the gavel with a flourish.

Glancing at her watch, Sylvia realized it was already lunchtime. If she hurried she might be able to say hello to Tucker in the cafeteria.

The dull roar of voices and the smell of french fries filled her senses as she walked down the hallway to the cafeteria. It also served as the gym, and each day, the cafeteria workers rolled out long tables that spanned the length of the room.

Hundreds of kids sat side by side eating with their classmates. The room was so packed that it was hard to spot Tucker, and for a moment she worried that his class had already finished. But then a small dynamo launched itself into her, and she felt arms wrapping around her waist. "Mommy!" Tucker cried happily.

"Hey sweetie," she said, hugging him back. His enthusiastic greeting thrilled her, but she glanced over the top of his head a little nervously, searching for the lunch monitors. Tucker, in theory, wasn't supposed to get up from his place at the table unless he raised his hand and got permission. If someone spotted him hugging her, he could get in trouble.

Sure enough, his teacher, Linda Chin, was walking toward them with her lips set in a thin, straight line. She was an older woman with small bones; short, straight black hair; and intelligent brown eyes. Sylvia released Tucker. "Quick, go sit down," she whispered.

Tucker didn't need to be told twice. He scurried off as the kindergarten teacher approached. Sylvia braced herself. Mrs. Chin had a reputation not only for being a really good teacher, but also for being on the strict side.

"Hello, Mrs. Baxter," Mrs. Chin said, smiling. Today the teacher was wearing a pair of black slacks and an attractive tunic top in shades of brown and green. "How is your wrist doing? Tucker said you cut it."

Sylvia winced at the choice of words and made a mental note to talk to Tucker again about how he described her injury. She tried to read the expression in the older woman's sharp brown eyes. "Yes," she said. "I cut my arm on the side of a gutter this weekend, but it's doing much better now."

The dark head bobbed. "Tucker told us about it during our story time this morning." Her voice lowered slightly. "He said you had to go to the hospital to get help."

Sylvia smiled and prayed Tucker hadn't made it sound like she needed psychiatric help. "For the stitches," she said.

Again, the head nodded. "I'm glad you're okay." She paused. "I can tell this accident has had an impact on him, so I'm encouraging him to write a short story about it. He's going to draw the pictures, and I'm going to help him write down the words. Isn't that a great idea?"

Sylvia wasn't completely sure if she was smiling or looking horrified. Tucker couldn't draw well and would probably create a stick figure with a bloody arm. Being a boy, Tucker would happily color in as much blood and gore as possible. She imagined the entire family being summoned to the school psychologist's office where they'd probably be handed a pamphlet entitled, "When Mommy Hurts Herself."

"That is a great idea," Sylvia managed. What else could she say? If she protested, it'd only make it look like she had something to hide. "Maybe you could send it home when it's finished? I'd like to see it."

"Of course." Mrs. Chin smiled. "One more thing—I was thinking that Tucker could take Bluebonnet home over the Easter holiday. Would that be all right with you?"

Bluebonnet, a blue parakeet, was the class pet. Getting asked to take her home for the three-day weekend was like winning the kindergarten lottery. Only the students who were high on Mrs. Chin's list of approval were even considered. For the past eight months Tucker had not been asked once to care for the bird, although Sylvia knew for a fact that some kids had gotten Bluebonnet for more than one weekend.

"That'd be great," Sylvia replied. "Tucker will be thrilled."

Mrs. Chin's gaze strayed to Sylvia's bandage before returning to her eyes. "I'd let you have him sooner, but I've already promised several other children."

"That's okay," Sylvia said. "Easter weekend would be perfect."

"Excellent. Pets can be very therapeutic." Mrs. Chin patted Sylvia's arm in a sympathetic gesture. "Take care, Mrs. Baxter."

Chapter 13

Sunlight streamed through the big glass windows as Wilson pushed open the glass doors and stepped into the cavernous room. He stood for a moment, taking in the hushed voices, the almost reverent quiet of a business that played such an important role in people's lives. Where would the world be without banks?

He straightened his shoulders and inhaled the scent of clean, cool air, made even sweeter with the possibility of what could happen here. He knew the blood and guts of this bank, every loan, every investment, every profit, every loss. It had been his life's work for nearly a year. Now, being here and knowing that the acquisition had happened gave him an even deeper connection to the bank. *You could be mine,* he thought.

His gaze strayed to the kiosk in the center of the room. It blocked the tellers' views of who might be standing in the front of the bank. It was a potential security issue, and he'd recommended the bank remove it. He wanted an open sitting area, with the glass-walled offices visible. He wanted to minimize any chance of robbery.

"Hey Wilson," Jen said. Today her long brunette hair was tied in a messy knot and she wore a navy skirt suit that ended just above her knees. She held out a Styrofoam cup. "They've given us an office in the back," she said. "Want some coffee?"

"Sure." Wilson couldn't stop looking around the area, mentally updating the old Burroughs mini-computer system with a client-server, GUI-based system. He felt the furtive stares of the bank employees who tried to pretend that his arrival was business as usual.

Following Jen, he stepped into one of the offices in the back. It held a laminate wood desk, a matching credenza, and a painting of a man standing thigh-deep in water, fishing. The last time he'd gone fishing, Wilson recalled, both boys had refused to let him hook the worms because they couldn't stand to see them hurt. Instead of fishing, he and the boys had hiked an hour until they found the perfect spot for the worms' new home. They'd dug a hole, released the worms, and stopped for ice cream on the way home.

Wilson set his computer bag down and took a sip of coffee. Jen had added just the right amount of cream and sugar, and when he complimented her, she blushed.

"The accountants are in the conference room down the hall," Jen explained. "You need to take a look at these." She set a thick manila envelope on the counter.

Wilson immediately began to thumb through the stack of papers that made up the purchase agreement. Although the basic agreement had been well-established, the implementation schedule constantly changed. He paused at a section Jen had highlighted. His stomach tightened as he recognized the human resources information.

"Bruce wants you to focus on employment contracts. According to our work redundancy analysis, we're looking at a 30 percent overlap between the two banks."

Wilson frowned. "That's a bit higher than we thought."

Jen nodded. "It's mostly middle management that's affected." She leaned close enough to him that he could smell her perfume, a thick scent of roses that tickled his nose. "Bruce wants you to make recommendations for the cuts."

"Oh." Wilson remembered the furtive looks that'd been directed at him when he'd walked into the bank. He'd never fired anyone before and didn't like the idea at all. He pretended to study the documents in front of him, but mostly he was trying to think of a way out of firing anyone. He'd take a hard look at attrition. Maybe he could come up with a very competitive voluntary retirement plan.

"Wilson," Jen said, her voice lowering but nonetheless sounding excited, "I probably shouldn't tell you this, but when I was in Bruce's office, I saw a draft of a new organizational chart. Your name was in the box for the new branch manager!"

The news, although not a complete surprise, hit him like a jolt of electricity. He looked up at her in delight, thinking that Bruce must already have spoken with the other board members. Although he had yet to officially interview for the position, unofficially, it seemed he'd already gotten the promotion.

"You're going to love it here," Jen continued. "I grew up in the next town over."

"*If* I get the job," Wilson pointed out. "I mean, it's not official, so please don't say anything to anyone."

"Of course I wouldn't." Jen walked to the doorway and paused in the frame. "You can't say anything either, but I'm penciled in as the new assistant branch manager." She paused to let this sink in. "*Your* new assistant branch manager."

Wilson blinked. "Congratulations," he said, but inside he was wondering when Bruce had intended to give him the news. He'd thought, as branch manager, he'd have all the control in staffing. Obviously he'd been misled.

Not that Jen wouldn't be great for the job—he had huge respect for her as a professional. But did he want her as his second-in-command? They'd be spending a lot of time together. She was single and undeniably attractive. "*So what,*" a small voice inside him said, "*it's not like you'd let anything happen.*" Jen knew he was happily married, and they'd never discussed anything more personal than her cat, Henry, who left hairballs the size of golf balls on her bed whenever Jen went out of town. Still, how was Sylvia going to feel about that? She trusted him, he assured himself. It wasn't going to be a problem. The real issue was saving as many jobs as he could.

"We'll make a great team." Jen flashed him a smile and headed down the hallway.

Shaking his head to clear his thoughts, Wilson opened his computer bag and pulled out his laptop. By the end of the day, his spirits had improved considerably. The audit was going well, the new disclosures weren't as bad as he feared, and best of all, he'd figured out a way to reduce the number of people who would be let go.

Jen poked her head into his office. "Hey," she said, "it's after five. The auditors have left for the day. How about you and me grab a bite to eat?"

Wilson drew his hand through his hair, brushing over the smooth, small bald spot. He'd planned to work a few more hours and then grab something on his way to the hotel. But the thought of food made his stomach growl, reminding him that he'd only had a small sandwich and chips for lunch.

"I know this great little Tex-Mex place," Jen continued. "It's just a hole-in-the-wall kind of restaurant, but the food is authentic. If you like Mexican food, that is."

Wilson hesitated. "I have a couple of e-mails to send."

Jen took a step closer and lowered her voice. "People are waiting for you to leave before they go home. They don't want you to think they're not hard workers."

Wilson released his breath. He'd been an idiot not to think of that. Of course people were worried about holding on to their jobs. In this economy, who wouldn't be? Still, he hesitated. Jen was a single, attractive woman, and he didn't want rumors to start. "Is there somewhere within walking distance? I'm afraid I still have a lot of work to do tonight."

Jen smiled. "I know the perfect place."

After a day inside, the cool air felt great. He felt himself enjoying the walk as they crossed the street and strolled deeper into the downtown area. He kept the pace slow in deference to Jen's high heels, and she seemed delighted to point out various landmarks.

As they passed the library, he pictured Sylvia, who loved books, spending many happy afternoons taking the boys there.

There was an attractive town center with a green. Every Christmas Eve, Jen explained, people gathered in the town green to sing carols or ride in the horse-drawn carriages. Increasingly, he felt like he, Sylvia, and the boys could be happy here. It was a larger town than the one they were used to, but they would enjoy having more dining and shopping options. It would be a good move for them. The *right* move for them.

At Comida Buena he wolfed down a plate of beef enchiladas. Jen talked about Henry, her cat; he described the Pinewood racers that the boys were building. In the far back of his mind, he realized it felt awkward, dining alone with Jen, but he dismissed the uneasy feeling. He wasn't interested in her as anything but a friend and co-worker. The fact that she was a woman was insignificant. Or at least it should be. In the future it would be easier. There would be other dinners, but team dinners. He'd make sure of that.

Although they ate fairly quickly, when they paid the bill Wilson was dismayed to see it was after eight o'clock. The boys had gone to bed, and once again he'd missed the opportunity to call and say good-night to them. He was angry at himself and didn't talk much on the walk back to the bank to drop Jen at her car.

He dialed Sylvia on his cell on his way to the hotel. The machine picked up, which meant Sylvia probably was still putting the boys to bed. He left a short message explaining that he'd had to work late again, but even to his own ears it sounded lame. Why couldn't he have remembered to call them earlier? It wasn't like he didn't love them—that they weren't more important than work.

God came first in his life, but otherwise, he valued Sylvia and the boys more than anything. He'd always believed that it had been no co-incidence the day he'd stepped into First National and seen a beautiful brunette with big brown eyes and the smile of an angel standing behind the teller's counter. He'd been new to the bank, so she hadn't recognized him as anything but a customer.

"Can I help you, sir?" she'd asked, and he'd been surprised to find that his feet had carried him right up to her.

He'd stood there, awestruck, wanting to extend the moment, and wondering what to say that wouldn't reveal himself as the geek that he was. He silently recognized the irony of having an undergraduate degree in computer science and an MBA in finance and yet he had nothing to say.

In the end, he'd finally held out his hand. "I'm Wilson Baxter," he'd said. "The new guy."

She'd gripped it warmly. "Sylvia Gardano. Welcome."

Wilson had known right away that Sylvia was the one for him. He'd taken it slowly, however, not just because they worked for the same bank, but because he'd never had a serious relationship. It wasn't that he didn't like girls—he did. And it wasn't like he didn't date, because he had. He just didn't let things get serious, never told a girl he loved her. He'd drifted along, letting school and work define his days and waiting for God to send the right girl into his life.

Looking into Sylvia's warm brown eyes, he'd thought the moment had come. It'd taken him a month to ask her out, and even then it was only for lunch. He hadn't wanted to risk coming on too strong, making a mistake or scaring her away.

Things changed one night when, somehow, they'd been talking about college. Hoping to impress her, Wilson rattled off some of his credentials, National Merit Scholar, summa cum laude from Cornell, and a MBA in finance.

Sylvia put her hand on his arm and looked deeply into his eyes. "I like that you're smart," she said, "but you're more than that, Wilson. You're kind. I like how you treat people. You always look pleased to help somebody—like they're the ones who've done you a favor."

Nobody, not even his parents, had ever told him something like that. Oh, he knew his mom and dad loved him, but he knew they also liked to brag about his accomplishments. He liked the way Sylvia saw him. It was almost as if she didn't care if he ever got another award or promotion in his life. He looked into her eyes and said, "I'm falling in love with you, you know."

Which was precisely why, Wilson thought as he walked into his hotel room, he was so determined to give Sylvia the best life possible. With this promotion, he could even give her a membership in the local country club.

He dropped his wallet and keys on the dresser and plopped down wearily on the edge of his bed. He glanced at the floral print on the tan wall, the flat screen television, the blackout shades framed by curtains that had no warmth or charm. He could have been in any hotel anywhere. And where he wanted most to be, he realized, was home.

Chapter 14

Relief washed through Sylvia at the sight of Wilson's Beemer pulling into the driveway. He'd kept his word and come back from his business trip early. A quick glance at the kitchen clock confirmed that it was almost exactly five o'clock. She watched him unload his suitcase and computer bag from the trunk and sling his garment bag over one shoulder.

Meeting him at the front door, she greeted him with a smile and stretched up to kiss him on the lips. "Hey," she said, taking the garment bag off his shoulder, "you made it."

Wilson set his bags inside the front door. "Yeah," he said. "I just beat the Friday rush hour." The words were barely out of his mouth when the boys ran toward him. Launching themselves like small missiles, they jumped the last few feet into Wilson's arms, pushing him back a step. Catching them, Wilson laughed and swung them around in his arms. "I missed you guys," he said.

"We missed you, too," Sylvia said.

Tucker settled himself on Wilson's hip. "A kid in the cafeteria threw up today."

Sylvia met Wilson's gaze and smiled. "There's a stomach virus going around school."

"Uh-oh," Wilson said. He set Simon on the ground. "How about you, Simon? How was your day?"

"It was cool. We're making planets out of paper-mache. Did you know, Dad, that most of the textbooks are wrong? There're more than nine planets."

Sylvia, who had been hearing about Simon's desire to become an astrophysicist since he came home from school, steered them all toward the kitchen. "Come on," she said, "the tacos are ready."

"I love tacos," Tucker, still riding his dad's hip, called out happily. "I bet I can eat more than you can, Simon."

"It isn't a competition," Sylvia warned, even as inside she acknowledged that Tucker was probably right—he would out-eat his older brother. Tucker, although shorter, outweighed Simon. And, at the rate Tucker was growing, he might even be taller than Simon by next year. Already, strangers sometimes mistook the boys for fraternal twins. She knew it had to bother Simon, but whenever she tried to talk to him about how some kids were faster growers than others, she'd see something in his eyes shut down.

Instead of rising to Tucker's challenge, however, Simon looked up at his father. "After dinner, are you going to help me build my racer?"

Wilson ruffled Simon's short blond hair. "Of course," he said. "I'm looking forward to it." Over the boy's shoulder he met Sylvia's gaze. There were dark shadows under his eyes and a tired strain etched around the corners of his mouth. Wilson never slept well in hotels. "Are you tired, honey?"

"A little," Wilson admitted. He loosened his tie. "Mostly I'm just glad to be home."

Sylvia smiled. "Was it productive?"

"Yes." He leaned back against the kitchen counter as she stirred the meat in the skillet. "Jen and I worked on a revised implementation schedule. You wouldn't believe how the new federal regulations are going to complicate things." He took a deep breath. "Those tacos smell great."

"They're turkey meat. Less fat. You eat okay on your trip?"

She looked up in time to see the expression of guilt in Wilson's blue eyes and shook her head. "Admit it. What'd you have for dinner?"

"Beef enchiladas."

He'd always had a fondness for those. She pictured a group going out, Wilson throwing all her attempts at healthy eating to the wind. "Who'd you go with?"

"Just Jen and me."

She lifted her brows. "The two of you?" She didn't want to jump to conclusions, but Jen was single, attractive, and flirty. Was this the reason Wilson had been so distracted lately?

Wilson sighed. "It wasn't like that. Trust me. The restaurant was walking distance to the bank and the most personal thing we talked about was the size of the hairballs her cat hacks up every time she goes out of town." He stepped closer, facing her from across the other side of the island cooktop. "She's a nice lady, but, you are the one I love." He leaned across the distance to plant a kiss on her lips. "Boys, did you know you have the most beautiful mommy in the whole wide world?"

There was a chorus of yeses, and then Tucker launched himself at Wilson, grabbing hold of his lower legs and clinging to him like a monkey. Sylvia shook her head ruefully. Watching her husband interact with her son, she couldn't imagine that the dinner was anything more than Wilson described. While she didn't like it, she'd let it drop. "Daddy! Me and Mom finished my racer. She used her empty board to make the sides smooth."

"Emery board," Simon corrected.

"Fingernail file," she automatically translated. When she'd met Wilson, he hadn't known the difference between eyeliner and mascara. A long time ago he'd sat in the bathroom watching her and talking as she put on her makeup. She'd had a lot of fun teaching him the terminology of beauty products. That was when she was working at the bank and seemed like a lifetime ago. She pulled the tortilla shells out of the oven and filled a bowl with taco meat. "Tucker, get the bowl of lettuce out of the fridge, and Simon would you please put out the cheese and tomatoes?"

"What can I do?" Wilson asked.

Sylvia smiled. "Get yourself something to drink, honey, and have a seat."

When everyone was at the table, she turned to Simon. "Would you give the blessing?"

Simon nodded. Bowing his head, he folded his hands together. "God is great. God is good. God we thank You for this food. Amen."

And thank You, Father, for a meal we are all eating together, Sylvia silently added. *And please bless our marriage and keep Wilson from temptation.*

After dinner, they cleared the table. Sylvia filled the pots and pans in the sink with water to soak while the boys ran to get their racers. Wilson covered the kitchen table with newspaper and retrieved his drill and toolbox from the garage.

Tucker, whose racer already was finished, arrived back at the table first. He wheeled the black-and-white racer, which had been shaped to look like a whale, across the center of the table. "Look, Daddy! Mommy and I painted my car to look like Shamu!"

"Whoa!" Wilson said, giving Sylvia an impressed look. "You did whale—I mean well."

Sylvia laughed. "Thanks but we weren't *fishing* for compliments."

"Are you *fin*-ished?" Wilson asked.

"Yes, that's the end of the *tail*." She grinned as Wilson shook his head.

"No more *spouting* out bad puns," Wilson countered.

Laughing, Sylvia sat down in the kitchen chair and felt herself relax for the first time since Wilson had stepped through the door. This was the old Wilson, participating in conversations and coming up with terrible puns.

"Careful, Tucker," she warned as Tucker nearly smashed his racer into Wilson's toolbox. "I wouldn't push Shamu around too much. I'm not sure how well his wheels are going to hold up."

"Can we attach my wheels now?" Simon asked, holding up the carcass of his racer for Wilson's inspection.

Sylvia's heart caught at the look of vulnerability stamped across Simon's delicate features as he waited for Wilson's answer. Her son's skin was so pale it was nearly translucent. She could see a thin, blue vein on the side of his face near his eye. She found herself holding her breath as Wilson took the car out of Simon's hands and held it up for inspection.

"Well," he said, "before we set the wheels, we need to fill the cuts we made with epoxy glue and let that set."

"Why can't we just glue the axles in now?" Sylvia asked, thinking that was exactly what she'd done with Tucker's car.

Wilson pushed his glasses higher on his face. "You could," he admitted, "but drilling through the epoxy instead of the balsa wood will give us a straighter, more consistent hole."

Sylvia worked to keep her expression neutral. Didn't Wilson realize it was the day before the race and there was still a ton of work that needed to be done? "That sounds great, honey, but won't it take a long time for the glue to dry?"

Wilson was already extracting the bottle of epoxy from his toolbox. "Of course not," he said heartily. "It'll be dry in an hour and a half."

"We still have to attach the wheels, and paint it—"

"Don't worry. We have plenty of time." He gave Simon a reassuring smile. "Your car is going to be the fastest, coolest car out there."

"What about mine?" Tucker demanded. "Will Simon's be faster than mine?"

Wilson took Tucker's car and tested each wheel. "Both your cars will be equally fast."

"Mommy built a track upstairs. We tested it, and my car goes really fast," Tucker said. "Only sometimes it doesn't go completely straight. Once it fell off the track."

Wilson flipped the car over. "I'll have to look at it," he said. "Could be the bolts are tighter on one wheel than another."

He set the car on the table and gave it a small push. The racer rolled easily, but not completely straight. Wilson frowned and repeated the test. "I think we can fix this," he said, "by adding a little more weight to the front of the car and adjusting the screws on the axles."

He pulled out his pliers and set to work on Tucker's car. Wilson didn't notice, but Sylvia did, the slightly, almost haunted look of disappointment in Simon's eyes. "I can do that," she offered, "while you work on Simon's racer."

Wilson was already lost in the task at hand. "We'll do both," he promised.

But by the time Wilson was satisfied with the wheels on Tucker's racer, and the epoxy set, it was past ten o'clock. Restless and whiney, Tucker, who was getting overtired, had started a game of poking Simon in the ribs, although Sylvia had specifically asked him to stop.

Although Simon was usually pretty patient with Tucker, he also was tired, and each time Simon poked him, he yelled more loudly. Once, he had even gone so far as to push Tucker. The happy-little-family moment Sylvia had envisioned was disintegrating by the moment.

"I think Tucker's car is good to go," Wilson said, setting the black-and-white racer on the kitchen table. "Now let's check and see if the epoxy is dry on Simon's."

The words were no sooner out of his mouth when Tucker began running around the kitchen table. Each time he passed Simon, he jabbed him with his finger and laughed.

"You cut that out," Sylvia warned as Tucker streaked past, his blue eyes nearly demonic with mischief. "This is your last warning."

Tucker managed to evade her, circle past Wilson, and come in for a lightning-quick jab at his brother, who howled as if he'd been fatally stabbed.

"Tucker James Baxter! We told you to stop that!" Wilson thundered. He started after Tucker, who laughed and darted into the living room. A moment later, Sylvia heard something crash. She ran into the room in time to see the shattered lamp on the floor. Wilson scooped Tucker under his arm and marched toward the stairs. When Tucker saw her, he began to cry. "Mommy! I'm sorry!"

Sylvia started after them. "Wilson," she said, "he's just overtired."

Wilson didn't pause. "That doesn't excuse him," he said. "I'm putting him to bed, and then I'm coming right back."

She caught one last glimpse of Tucker's red face twisted in misery, and then the two of them disappeared up the stairs. Part of her wanted to go after them, but she knew Wilson would see it as undermining his authority and not trusting him to be a good parent.

She sighed. The lamp lay in pieces on the floor. It had been her parents', and was one of the few pieces she'd kept when she and Wilson had had to close up her parents' house a few years ago.

Kneeling, she picked up the larger pieces, wondering if they could be glued together, and knowing that she should probably just throw the whole thing out. *It's just a lamp,* she told herself, *and not even a particularly valuable one.* Not monetarily. But it was a piece of her past.

She studied the shards, picturing her mother sitting in her overstuffed club chair, reading by the light of this lamp or knitting a pair of socks for someone. Socks—for Pete's sake. Who even knitted anymore?

She shook her head. Her mother would have told her not to worry about one silly little lamp. What was important, she'd have said, was that no one had gotten hurt. But someone had gotten hurt, Sylvia realized. She had.

"Mom?"

Sylvia turned. Simon was standing right behind her, peering over her shoulder.

"Yeah?"

"Will Dad come back downstairs?"

Sylvia didn't answer for a moment. She was still thinking about the lamp, but then she saw the worry in her son's eyes. It was getting late and little progress had been made on Simon's racer. She straightened slowly. "He said he would. Now please stand back so you don't get cut, and let me clean up this mess."

It took awhile before Sylvia was satisfied that there weren't any slivers of porcelain on the floor. She'd given Simon some milk and cookies to eat while she worked, and when she finished cleaning, she was relieved to see that he'd eaten them all.

Together they went upstairs to see what was taking Wilson so long. Sylvia wasn't really surprised to find him asleep next to Tucker in the twin-size bed. Gesturing for Simon to be silent, she slowly backed out of the room and closed the door quietly.

"He'll be up early," she promised Simon as they walked to the adjoining bedroom. "Don't worry. Your racer will be ready." And it would be—even if she had to do it herself.

"The race is at three o'clock," Simon said. "And I have to be there even earlier for inspection."

Sylvia put her hand on the narrow wing of his shoulder blade. It felt so fragile, and at the back of her mind she found herself worrying that he was too thin, that she should make him eat more. "Setting the wheels won't take long." She felt her worry switch to irritation. Wilson could have been less of a perfectionist and spent the evening working on Simon's racer instead of focusing on Tucker's. Tucker honestly didn't care if he won or not. But Simon. Simon was different. He felt things to the bone. He hadn't missed that Tucker was the one who had gotten all Wilson's attention.

"You know," she said carefully, "we love you no matter what, right?"

Simon glanced up at her. The expression in his eyes made him look much older than he was. "I know you do."

"So does Dad," Sylvia said firmly.

It was after eleven-thirty before Sylvia finally got Simon off to bed. In the silence of her bathroom, she washed her face, brushed her teeth, and then slipped on a cotton nightgown worn thin with use.

Padding back into the master bedroom, she glanced around the room at the queen-size bed with its green comforter, pale yellow sheets, and stacks of pillows of every size and shape. A floral, wing-back chair with an ottoman sat near the windows, and atop the dark wood dresser sat an abundance of family pictures.

It was a room more comfortably than expensively furnished. Wilson had let her pick out everything, and she'd tried hard to make it feminine enough to be romantic, and at the same time masculine enough for Wilson to be comfortable.

Unfortunately, right now it was an empty room. Something she acknowledged was beginning to feel more like the norm than the exception. All too often she went to bed while Wilson worked upstairs in his office. Too many nights she read her romance novels until she was too tired to keep her eyes open. She missed the comfort of his presence as sleep slowly came to her—the last minute, sleepy whispers of something he'd forgotten to tell her, or him simply telling her he loved her.

But it wasn't like that anymore. Wilson said it was because he had work, but deep inside Sylvia wondered if he'd simply gotten tired of her. If she couldn't compete with the challenges, excitement, and yes—rewards, of his job. And now maybe even with Jen.

Smoothing back the comforter, she slipped beneath the cool sheets. *Dear God,* she prayed, *I miss my husband. I miss talking to him, and I miss the way things used to be. I know we couldn't live the way we do if Wilson didn't have such a good job, but I don't think You mean for things to be like this. I don't mean to be complaining, Lord—or ungrateful—but sometimes I wonder if this is what You want for me.*

And Simon. I'm scared for him about tomorrow. Please help him understand that he's loved whether he wins or loses. And keep Tucker safe, and help him with the impulse control. Please bless our family and friends with good health. Thank You for always loving us. Amen.

Chapter 15

Wilson cracked open one eye. In the semi-darkness, Tucker's face loomed over him as pale as the moon and so close it looked gigantic. "Go back to sleep, Tuck," he moaned. He attempted to turn onto his side and found himself pressed tightly against a wall, which surprised him because there wasn't any wall next to his side of the bed.

"Dad." Tucker's breath was hot in his ear. "Can I get up now?"

Ask your mom, Wilson started to say and then realized he wasn't in his own bedroom. The evening before slowly came back to him—building the racers in the kitchen and then chasing after Tucker, who'd knocked over the lamp in the living room. After Wilson had given him a lecture about controlling his impulsive behavior, he'd lain down next to Tucker who'd clung to him like a small monkey. In the process of soothing him, Wilson had fallen asleep.

Without his glasses, Wilson had to squint at the bedside clock. "You can get up," he agreed. "But you have to be quiet when we go downstairs so you won't wake your mother." He held up two fingers. "Scout's honor."

Tucker gravely mirrored the gesture. "Scout's honor," he echoed.

In the kitchen, Wilson put on a pot of coffee and cleared a spot on the kitchen table. He set out the Cap'n Crunch and poured Tucker a small glass of orange juice. Tucker immediately attempted to fill his bowl to the point of overflowing with the cereal, and Wilson had to grab the box from him. "Take it easy, buddy," he said.

Sometimes it felt like he was always telling Tucker what to do, correcting his behavior, or arguing with him in a way that he never had to do with Simon. Part of it was the age, of course. Tucker was two years younger. But that was only part of it. Where Simon was thoughtful, Tucker tended to be impulsive; where Simon was gentle, Tucker was rough. Simon followed the rules; Tucker was constantly testing the limits.

He loved both boys equally, but he worried more about his relationship with Tucker. Which was why, last night, he'd been sure to give Tucker a lot of attention. He might have missed helping Tucker put together his car, but he'd been sure to make sure that car was as good as he could make it.

The coffee gurgled from the machine; Tucker slurped his cereal. Wilson saw the backyard slowly become illuminated in the morning light. Today he'd focus on Simon.

"Can I watch a cartoon, Dad?" Tucker asked.

Wilson glanced over at the empty bowl. "After you put away your dishes."

"But what if I want some more later? When Simon wakes up?"

Wilson sipped his coffee and reconsidered. "Okay," he said, "as long as you don't leave your bowl for someone else to put away."

"Okay," Tucker agreed, and then ran into the living room.

Wilson, following more slowly, was in time to watch him vault over the back of the couch. A moment later, Tucker found the two remote controls that operated their television and punched in the correct sequence to get the set working. "It's like we're mission control and trying to launch a rocket out of Cape Canaveral," Sylvia liked to say whenever they settled down to watch the news or a movie.

Sylvia. He glanced at the empty spot on the end table and felt badly for her. He wondered what had happened to the lamp, and if it were repairable or she'd put it in the garbage. It'd belonged to Sylvia's mother, and he remembered how she'd chosen to put it out when they had probably more valuable items stored in the attic. He resolved to ask her about it.

While Tucker watched his cartoon—a show about talking, rainbow-colored ponies—Wilson retrieved his laptop from the hallway. He figured he had just enough time to check his e-mail before Simon woke up and they started work on his son's racer.

He used his remote access code to get into the bank's Intranet and a moment later was pulling down thirty-five new messages. The one marked "urgent" caught his eye immediately. It was from his boss and had been sent at six o'clock that morning. *Just when did Bruce sleep?* he wondered.

Opening the message, he scanned the contents and groaned. The net of it was that Robert Hovers, one of the members on the board of trustees for the bank, was in town for a couple of hours and Bruce had set up a breakfast meeting. Bruce wanted Wilson to take Robert through the latest numbers and the remaining action items in the merger. He also wanted Wilson to bring his résumé.

Wilson shifted on the couch. The last part of the message was only a sentence, but he didn't need Bruce to spell it out. Although technically this was a meeting about the merger, it was really about Wilson—about establishing his credibility and advancing his career. This was his opportunity to gain face time with one of the board members and thereby gain his approval when Bruce nominated him for the branch manager's position.

Wilson hit REPLY then hesitated. Frowning at the screen, he considered telling Bruce that he had a family commitment and declining the meeting. It wasn't like he'd had any advance notice, and Bruce had to respect that if Wilson had to choose between work and family, he'd choose family every time.

At the same time, the meeting was at nine o'clock in the restaurant of a hotel about a half hour away. Wilson would have just enough time to modify the résumé and get to the meeting. He ran his fingers through his hair. He felt the polished skin of a bald spot no larger than a penny—but a bald spot all the same. Time was running out for him, the spot said. If he blew this promotion, there might not ever be another one.

He glanced at his watch with its big face and multiple silver gears showing the different times around the world. Sylvia had given it to him as an anniversary gift, and looking at the time reminded him of her, which usually was a good thing, except for now. But she didn't understand the whole situation—she didn't know about the big promotion. If she did, she'd tell him to go to the meeting.

And, the meeting was at nine o'clock. It wouldn't go more than an hour, which meant he'd be home by 10:30 to help Simon. There'd be plenty of time to finish Simon's racer. He typed Bruce a quick note, and then headed to the guest room where he sometimes changed when he got up earlier than Sylvia. In less than ten minutes he was shaved, dressed, and ready to go. He left Tucker with instructions to let Sylvia sleep a little longer, and then wrote her a quick note which he left on the kitchen table. Ignoring the carcass of Simon's racer that looked at him reproachfully, he grabbed his car keys off the kitchen counter and headed out the door.

∽

"I'm going to kill him," Sylvia announced when she walked into the kitchen and saw Wilson's note scrawled on the back of an envelope.

How could he do this? Go to a meeting on the morning of the Pinewood Derby? How could he not realize how hurtful it would be to Simon to wake up and find that his father had left him with a half-finished race car and the derby only hours away?

"I'll kill him and put him in a hole in the backyard," she stated firmly.

"Kill who?" Simon asked, walking into the room. He was still dressed in his Batman pajamas and his short hair was sticking up in every direction.

"Ah, nobody," Sylvia said and turned the envelope upside-down. "Let's make pancakes." Her mind whirled. Anger at Wilson warred with the need to protect Simon from learning that Wilson had broken his promise to him. Could she delay the breakfast long enough for Wilson to get home? "We'll make chocolate chip ones," she said brightly, and reached into the cabinet for a mixing bowl. "With happy faces. We'll have bacon, too."

Simon's face brightened as she'd hoped it would. "Bacon?"

She nodded. "As many pieces as you like."

Although she'd hoped to keep Simon distracted, the first strips of bacon weren't even out of the package when Simon picked his racer up off the table. "When do you think Dad's going to get up?"

Sylvia froze. It was like the music had stopped and she was the one left holding the hot potato. She didn't want to lie, and yet she didn't want to upset Simon with the truth.

"He's up already," Tucker announced, running into the room with a towel attached to his pajamas like a cape. "I'm hungry," he said, eyeing the strips of bacon dangling from her fingers.

"Dad's awake?" Simon looked around as if he expected his father to pop out of the pantry or from behind the kitchen curtains.

"He went to work," Tucker announced, climbing up on one of the kitchen stools.

Sylvia watched Simon go very still as he digested the news. Very deliberately, he turned so that she couldn't see his face. "It's going to be okay, Simon," she said. "He's coming back in less than an hour."

But he wasn't back at 10:30 as promised, and although Tucker had eaten ten pancakes, Simon had long stopped. He was sitting on the couch, reading a book about the planets, but every few minutes he would glance up at the clock on the mantel and then at the front door.

He was suppressing his anxiety, which was something Wilson tended to do. She studied the top of her son's head and thought how alike he and Wilson were. Tucker tended to be more like Sylvia. She wondered if Wilson saw that, and if it was why he paid more attention to Tucker.

At 11:00, Sylvia suggested that she and Simon, together, drill the axle holes and set the wheels on the racer. Simon shook his head. "I'll wait for Dad," he said. "He promised."

"I'm sure he'll be here soon," Sylvia said, but inside she wasn't sure at all, which said a lot about her confidence in her husband's word. For the first time she had a true inkling of the frustration and unhappiness Rema dealt with on a regular basis with Skiezer. For the first time she looked out the kitchen window at the kidney-shaped pool and wondered if she was strong enough to make the marriage work. When had this double-parent role become the norm?

Dear Lord, she prayed, *help me hold it together.*

She decided to wait until 11:15 and then insist that she and Simon work on the racer. She'd assembled Tucker's, and although his car had pulled to the left before Wilson adjusted the screws, it had been raceable.

At 11:12, however, Wilson breezed through the door, all smiles and apology and eager to get started. He opened his arms, and after the briefest hesitation, Simon walked into them. Over the top of Simon's head their eyes met and he mouthed, "I'm sorry."

Something inside wouldn't let Sylvia accept or even acknowledge his apology. Her lips tightened, and she turned away, swallowing the fury, bitter as a pill in her mouth.

For the next two hours they worked steadily on the racer. Wilson drilled the holes then supervised Simon, who carefully threaded the axle rods through the body of the car. They lubricated the axles and screwed on the wheels.

"You can test it now," Wilson said.

Sylvia held her breath as Simon pushed the car down the center of the table. Something inside relaxed when the car pulled neither to the right or left, and Simon smiled. They weighed the car on her meat scale, and when they saw it was well below the allowed amount, Wilson drilled some more holes in the bottom of the car and they added a few metal washers. Finally, Wilson was satisfied, and Simon pulled out the oil paints.

Sylvia made grilled cheese sandwiches as Simon painstakingly painted the body of his racer black. She tried not to glance at the clock, or urge him not to be so meticulous, but it seemed like time was flying by. The car had to dry before Simon could apply the decals and then there still was that final coat of gloss.

The truth was they never should have left everything to the last minute. She glanced at Wilson, biting back a scathing comment about him going to work instead of starting work on the car earlier. It would only upset Simon, who was happily absorbed in painting.

They used her blow dryer on the cool setting to get the paint to dry faster, and then Simon added the red stripes and the silver decals for the headlights, windows, and windshield. He pasted a large number seven on the car's hood then held the car up for his father's inspection.

"Perfect," Wilson declared. "All we need is the top coat."

While Simon carefully painted the car with the clear polish, Sylvia hauled Tucker upstairs to put on his Cub Scout uniform. After she finished getting him dressed, she grabbed Simon's uniform out of his closet and hurried downstairs. Both Baxter men were still obsessing over the way the car rolled. She glanced at the clock. "Come on," she said, "we have to get going. Put these on," she ordered, handing Simon the clothing.

The trip to the elementary school wasn't far, but parking was a nightmare. They ended up pulling off to the side of the road at the front of a long line of cars that also hadn't been able to fit into the school's lot.

A quick glance at her watch told Sylvia they didn't have a lot of time to make the two o'clock inspection time. She grabbed Tucker's hand, Wilson took Simon's, and they hurried down the street.

By the time they reached the elementary school, Sylvia was sweating, panting, and completely stressed out. The derby was being held in the gym, but the crowd had already overflowed into the hallways. Sylvia's heart sank at the thought of the long line that would be at the inspection station. The information sheet had been very specific about the 2:00 p.m. deadline. The kids could be disqualified if they were late.

She turned to Wilson. "We have to hurry," she said over the dull roar of voices around them.

Wilson nodded and began leading them through the packed crowd. He was the blocker, his large body creating enough space for Sylvia and then the boys to pass through quickly before it closed again.

As they moved deeper into the gym, Sylvia glimpsed the long yellow plywood race tracks, obscured by the parents and kids already standing close by.

When Wilson stopped short, she nearly bumped into his back as they took their place in the inspection line. Peering around his back, Sylvia saw about ten sets of parents and children ahead of them. She looked at her watch and mentally calculated. It was going to be close. Turning to the boys, she gave them a reassuring smile. "Don't worry. We're going to make it."

Tucker nodded. His yellow neckerchief had already slipped out of the metal slide. Hiking her purse higher on her shoulder, Sylvia bent to fix it. More eye level with the kids, she caught Simon's gaze and saw he was clutching his racer protectively to his chest. She reached out to give his shoulder a reassuring squeeze and earned herself a fierce look. Too late she remembered that as a second grader, she wasn't supposed to do anything motherly to Simon in public.

If what Rema said was true, soon Simon wouldn't even want to be seen with her in public.

The line shuffled forward slowly but steadily. Sylvia became even more stressed as the minutes passed. Nobody else got into line behind them. Finally at 1:53 Tucker stepped up and handed the man seated at the inspection station his racer.

Sylvia held her breath as "Shamu" was held close to the inspector's eye, examined from every direction, and then placed on a scale. It passed the weight limitation of five ounces, and Tucker was given an entry number and directed to track one.

"I'll take him," Wilson volunteered when they saw Tucker was in the first heat. "You stay with Simon then meet us at the track."

Sylvia nodded and stepped closer to Simon, who was still clutching his racer protectively.

"Let's take a look," a middle-aged man with dark hair, a broad forehead, and a white goatee smiled encouragingly.

Simon nodded. He started to hand over his racer, but it soon became apparent the car was stuck to his shirt. He looked at Sylvia with an expression of confusion. "Mom?"

Sylvia blinked at the Pinewood Derby racer glued to Simon's uniform. The clear coat they'd applied to the car must not have been completely dry when they'd left the house. Because of the way Simon had been clutching the car, it had bonded to his shirt. She held down the blue fabric. "Pull," she ordered.

Simon set his small jaw, there was a small ripping sound, and then the racer peeled off his shirt. He handed it over to the inspector, who laughed and told Simon that there was no rule that the paint had to be completely dry before the race.

He asked Simon a few questions about the construction, complimented the glue job in the axle holes, and then placed the car on the scale. Sylvia held her breath as the needle swung past the five-ounce limit but then steadied within the accepted weight.

"You pass," the inspector said, "track two, heat nine." He handed back Simon his car and then made some notes in a fat binder. Checking his watch one final time, he closed the binder. "Inspections are closed!" he yelled. "Let the races begin!"

Chapter 16

Sylvia and Simon wiggled their way through the packed gym to track one. The three-lane yellow tracks were about thirty feet long and already surrounded by parents and kids, who pressed around it like passengers awaiting their luggage at an airline's baggage claim area.

Sylvia stood on her tiptoes, craning her neck for a glimpse of Tucker and Wilson. Fortunately Wilson was tall and his light brown hair caught her eye near the front of the track. With Simon in tow, she managed to squeeze her way up to them.

"Everything go okay?" Wilson shifted, allowing Sylvia and Simon a better view of the track. Before Sylvia could answer his question, the crowd roared as the first cars sped down the incline.

"Yeah," she said, struggling to be heard over the cheering. "Simon's car wasn't quite dry and stuck to his shirt, but. . ."

"What?"

She shook her head and raised her voice. "I'll tell you later."

Wilson nodded. "Tucker goes third." His voice, deeper than hers, carried over the dull roar of voices around them. "When's Simon's?"

"Ninth heat," Sylvia shouted, just as the first racers swept under the finish line and the crowd erupted in even louder cheers.

"Good," Wilson said. "Look, Tucker's on deck."

Sylvia followed the direction of Wilson's gaze, and her heartbeat accelerated when she saw her youngest son near the base of a wooden block. Soon it would be his turn, and she couldn't help wanting him to win. Her stomach tightened as the next round of race cars sped down the track.

Tucker wasn't watching though. He was talking to a boy with dark skin and curly black hair standing behind him. Both of them were laughing about something.

Tucker didn't look the least bit nervous, which seemed impossible because Sylvia suddenly felt like jumping out of her skin. She started to whip off a quick prayer and felt Wilson's warm hand wrap around her fingers. She glanced at him and felt the shared love of their son bonding them together. And then Tucker's heat was announced and she was screaming at the top of her lungs as Tucker's car flashed past, head-to-head with two very sleek-looking racers.

Tucker had the middle lane, and as the cars reached the long, flat part of the track, his black-and-white car appeared to be slightly ahead. She jumped up and down—as if that would make it go faster—but she couldn't help herself. But then seconds later, to her joy and disbelief, Tucker's car streaked under the finish line a fraction ahead of both cars.

Sylvia gave a happy jump. "Whoo-hoo! Go Tucker!" She turned to Wilson. "Can you believe that? He won!"

Wilson grinned. "He sure did." He gave Simon a high five then kissed Sylvia on the lips. "Come on," he said, "let's go congratulate the winner."

Sylvia felt the warmth of success shoot through her. All the anxiety about getting to the race on time seemed to leave her, and as they moved toward the finish line, she realized it all was happening just as it said in the Proverbs—they were coming together as a family. She mentally chided herself for having any doubts.

They found Tucker off to the side, talking with an adult volunteer who was recording the race results. It was a best-of-three heat, with winners racing winners.

Sylvia embraced Tucker. "I'm so proud of you," she said, and planted a big kiss on his cheek. (Tucker was younger and thereby less embarrassed by her.)

"Good man," Wilson said, ruffling Tucker's light brown hair and grinning proudly. "I think we might even have a division champion!"

Simon stepped forward. Smiling, he gave his brother a hug. "Congratulations," he said, and the rest of his words were drowned out by the crowd as another set of racers started down the track.

Tucker went off to get back in line for his next heat. Wilson, Sylvia, and Simon squeezed into a small gap near the track to watch. Turning to her, Wilson slipped his arm around her waist and smiled. "It just doesn't get better than this, does it?"

But it did get better, because about fifteen minutes later Tucker won the next heat, and then the finals of his division. After the announcement, Wilson hefted the little boy up on his shoulders and, to Tucker's delight, did a small victory dance.

Sylvia took pictures with her cell phone—she'd forgotten her good camera in the mad dash to the elementary school. "Get in the picture," she urged Simon, who obediently stood beside his dad and Tucker, and if his smile was a little strained, it was understandable. He still had his races to worry about.

Sylvia couldn't help feeling proud of herself as well as of Tucker. They'd built that car together, sanded down the sides with her emery board, and painted it to look like Shamu. And now it had won the kindergarten division. Imagine that!

The races moved along quickly. Soon the first-grade troops were finished and it was the second graders' turn. Sylvia felt herself getting nervous all over again—and it didn't help when she saw Simon's small, pale face peering out from the top of the start of the track.

He was in the lane farthest from them, and she leaned forward as far as she could for a better view. *Dear God,* she prayed as the announcer began the countdown, *please let him win.*

The crowd yelled as the announcer boomed, "Go." All three cars rolled forward at the same time. Sylvia yelled encouragement to Simon's black racer, but almost immediately it seemed to slip behind the other cars. *Maybe when it hits the flat part of the track it'll catch up,* Sylvia told herself. But her hopes were in vain. When the three cars passed under the finish line, Simon's was clearly in third place.

Sylvia shot Wilson a look of distress, and then they all hurried to the finish line. They got there just as Simon retrieved his racer from the track official. Although outwardly, Simon seemed fine, when Sylvia looked into his eyes, she saw a look of dazed disbelief.

"Good job," she said, bending to give him a quick hug and kiss. "I'm proud of you."

Simon shrugged and mumbled something that sounded like, "For what?"

"For participating," Sylvia said, struggling for the right words. "For doing your best."

"My best wasn't good enough," Simon said so softly that if Sylvia hadn't been leaning toward him she wouldn't have heard.

"Yes it was," she said.

"You'll get them in the next heat," Wilson promised. "You just had a fast group."

"Your car was the coolest looking," Tucker added, and Sylvia shot him a grateful smile.

"No it wasn't," Simon said flatly. "The decals on one side came off when my car stuck to my shirt." He looked at Sylvia, as if somehow she could fix everything, and her heart ached because she couldn't. "I want to go home."

"The Baxters never give up," Wilson stated firmly. "There are still two races left."

Simon looked at her again, and this time Sylvia read fear in them. She'd seen this look in his eyes when Wilson had taken them all to the amusement park and asked who wanted to ride "The Thunderbird." Tucker had shouted a mighty "yes" and Simon had gamely agreed. He'd paled as they'd neared the kiddy rollercoaster. The whole ride he'd kept his eyes closed and a death grip on the railing. As soon as he got off the ride, he'd thrown up.

This time, however, it wasn't a scary rollercoaster. Sylvia suspected it was the fear of failing—of losing the race and letting Wilson down. Poor Simon—this race was the main reason he'd joined the Cub Scouts. At the same time, Wilson was essentially right. You didn't give up just because you didn't win.

"It doesn't matter if you win or lose," Sylvia said, hoping to ease some of the pressure. "This is just supposed to be for fun." She nudged Wilson with the tip of her sneaker.

"Your mother is right," Wilson said. "But let me look at the car. Maybe one of the axles needs more lubricant."

More lubricant, however, didn't help Simon's car, which lost all of its remaining races, although coming in a close second in one of them.

Simon, looking almost physically ill from the loss, managed to hold it together and shake hands with the boys who had beaten him.

The ride home was mercifully short but unnaturally quiet. In the backseat, Tucker, clutching a foot-high gold trophy, sat next to a silent and visibly morose Simon. Sylvia wasn't sure what to do. On the one hand, she wanted Tucker to enjoy his victory—take him out for ice cream and shower him with praise. On the other hand, making a big deal out of Tucker's win would only make Simon's loss more painful.

This stunk, Sylvia decided, trying to balance one child's needs over another's. No matter what she did, it would be wrong.

Wilson pulled the minivan into their garage. As soon as he parked, the boys jumped out of the car and ran into the house. Sylvia and Wilson followed more slowly. Before they got into the house, she grabbed Wilson's arm. "You need to talk to him," she said, "make sure he understands that you don't care if he lost."

Pausing, Wilson looked at her. "Of course I don't care if he lost," he said, "but we're not going to baby him. What bothers me is that he's sulking about it. He needs to be more supportive of his brother."

"Wilson, he's seven."

"He's old enough to be a more graceful loser."

In the family room, Simon jumped onto the couch and pulled a plaid throw blanket over his head. Tucker squatted on the rug beside him.

"We can share it," Tucker said, lifting the blanket and attempting to push the trophy into his brother's hands.

"I don't want to!" Simon shoved the trophy away.

"Hey," Wilson said. "Your brother was just trying to be nice." He put his arm around Tucker. "I'm really proud of you." Taking the gold trophy from the little boy's hands, he studied it, smiling. "So where are we going to put that?" Wilson asked. "The mantelpiece maybe?"

"Yes," Tucker agreed, eyes shining.

"The mantelpiece it is then." Wilson shifted an ornate mantel clock and several framed silver photographs to make room. "How's that?"

"We should put both cars on the mantelpiece," Sylvia suggested, "because we're proud of both of you."

"Great idea," Wilson agreed, setting Shamu next to the trophy then looking around for Simon's racer. "Simon—where's your car?"

Simon pulled the crocheted throw blanket up to his chin. "I don't want my car on the mantelpiece. I want to throw it out. It isn't good enough."

"Of course it's good enough," Wilson said. Crossing the room, he crouched, eye level to Simon. "Winning is nice, but it's not everything. In fact losing is sometimes a good thing. It makes you try harder. Next year, we'll redesign your car—try a different shape. We'll sand the axles more carefully." He squeezed Simon's shoulder. "I'll help you. We'll kick some Cub Scout butt."

Sylvia watched tears pool in Simon's eyes and the way he widened his eyes to keep them from spilling out. "You say that, Dad," Simon said, "but you're always working." His voice was thick, filled with tears. He was clenching his fists, and his face was combination of sheet-white and blotchy red.

"Simon," Sylvia said, but gently, "be respectful of your father."

"It's okay." Wilson pulled Simon into his arms and hugged him hard even as the little boy resisted. "Next year will be different," he said. "I promise."

"You promised to help me this year," Simon mumbled. "And you didn't." His breathing became more rapid, and he buried his face into Wilson's shoulder. "You love Tucker more than me."

"Of course I don't," Wilson said, not releasing Simon, who was struggling to get out of his arms and crying. "I love both of you equally. You are my sons."

"No," Simon cried. "No you don't love me."

"Yes I do," Wilson said. "Next year I'm going to help you build another race car. Not because I care if you win or not, but because I like spending time with you."

Simon pulled back. He'd stopped crying and his face looked all at once old and young, wise and slightly jaded. He seemed to search his father's eyes and crumpled, unspeaking into his father's shoulder.

∞

Later, Sylvia sat in the green wing chair in their bedroom trying to read her novel—a romance as usual. It was late—getting the boys to bed had been even more exhausting than usual. Wilson had helped, but then he said he had to check his e-mail and would be right there—but that was a half hour ago. She was determined to stay awake until Wilson came to bed.

She set the book aside when she realized she'd read the same page four times. Crossing her arms, she stared at their bedroom door and wondered how much longer Wilson was going to be. Simon had been disrespectful to Wilson, but essentially he'd been right, and this was what she needed to discuss with Wilson.

He seemed to be taking forever, and she felt fatigue mixing with the anxiety over the day's events. She got up, splashed some water on her face, and was drying it with a towel when Wilson walked through the bedroom door.

He rubbed the skin on his face and said, "What a day."

Sylvia walked into the room. "I know."

"I'm pooped. All I want is to go to sleep."

"Wilson, we need to talk."

This was her cue to him that she had something serious to say. He looked up, surprise and maybe even dread was reflected in his blue eyes. "We do?"

As if he didn't know! "Yes. You broke your promise to Simon—you told him that today would be about building his racer, but then you snuck out to work before we got up. He was looking forward to spending time with you, Wilson, and building that car together. Don't think he's forgotten that you won your Pinewood Derby when you were his age."

Wilson's face tightened. He took a long time answering, which Sylvia viewed as a sign that she was right. "I didn't have a choice," he said at last. "And I didn't break my promise—I did help him put together the race car. Maybe it was rushed, but there's stuff going on at work. . ."

"There's always stuff going on at work," Sylvia said, fatigue making her sharper than she'd normally be. "I don't see what could possibly be more important than your kids."

Wilson took a step toward her, but she moved backward, out of his range and crossed her arms.

"Nothing is more important than you, Simon, and Tucker," Wilson said. "But there are things about the merger that are happening fast now."

She didn't want to hear anything about the merger or the bank. "There are things happening in your family," she said. "Our boys are growing up really fast." She couldn't tell if she was getting through to him or not and shook her head. "I'm beginning to feel like I don't even know you anymore—like we're ships passing in the night."

Something about the word *ship* teased her brain, and she knew in a vague sort of way it had to do with Proverbs 31, but she didn't feel like even trying to be an excellent wife. It was much easier being an angry, righteous wife.

Wilson ran his fingers through his sandy-colored hair, met her gaze, then sighed heavily. "I'm up for a big promotion," he said. "That's why I've been working so hard lately. Bruce has me penciled in for the new branch manager's position, but I have to get approval from the board. I had coffee with one of the members this morning. It ran kind of late."

Sylvia blinked at him. "You what?"

"I'm interviewing for a new job." A proud-looking smile lifted the corners of his mouth. "I've been dying to tell you, but I wasn't sure if it would happen or not."

Sylvia studied his eyes, saw the excitement glowing softly in them. "Branch manager?"

"Yeah," Wilson said. "Of course there'll be other candidates. But I have Bruce's full support, and I think today went well."

"I still can't believe you went on an interview without us even talking about it."

Wilson nodded. "I'm sorry. I should have told you sooner."

"The new job," Sylvia murmured, "would you be taking Bruce's place?"

He shook his head. "No. The new bank."

"The new bank?" Sylvia found the next words hard to get out. "We'd have to relocate?"

Wilson nodded. "Only five hours from here. You'll like it there, Sylvia. With the promotion I'll get a healthy increase and some major perks. We'll be able to afford a bigger house. The schools are great, too—they're rated even higher than the ones here."

Sylvia sank down on the edge of the bed. Dear God, was she hearing this correctly? Wilson had practically accepted a job that required relocation, and he hadn't even discussed it with her before he interviewed for it?

"I know it's a lot to take in," Wilson said, reaching for her hand. "And if you don't want me to take this job, I won't."

Sylvia searched his eyes. She saw the truth in them and knew he really would turn down this job if she said no. But he really wanted it, so how could she ask him to turn it down?

Her heart ached at the thought of leaving Rema and her other friends. The local elementary school was perfect—both boys were thriving there. She loved their church and the friends she'd made there. She and Wilson had a great life here—didn't he see that?

"Couldn't you get a promotion here?"

Wilson shook his head. "Bruce still has years before he retires."

"Oh." Sylvia still couldn't bring herself to tell Wilson she was open to relocating.

"So what do you think, Syl? Are you up for a new town and a new adventure?"

She opened her mouth. Nothing came out. She swallowed and tried again. "I don't know." The habit of supporting him, of supporting his career, made her add, "Maybe."

"Why don't you think about it?" Wilson smiled encouragingly. "We could even drive out there—look at some houses, see the town. Nothing is definite though. All of this is confidential."

"Can I at least tell Rema?"

Wilson hesitated. "Can she keep this private? Just for a little while longer?"

"Yes."

"And you'll keep an open mind?"

Sylvia managed to nod, but she sensed that as far as Wilson was concerned, the decision was already made.

Chapter 17

Sylvia was sitting by the edge of the pool when the latch to the back gate clicked open. Two small boys wearing baggy, knee-length bathing suits with bright Hawaiian prints charged barefoot across the grass. Following at a slower pace, and with the black-and-white Border collie straining at the leash, was Rema.

A cheer went up from Tucker and Simon at the sight of their friends. Sylvia laughed as the small brown bodies launched themselves into the air and cannonballed into the water.

Unclipping the dog, Rema settled on the ledge of the pool beside Sylvia. "Okay. I'm dying to hear it—how did the derby go?"

Sylvia trailed her foot through the water. Although the race had only been yesterday, it already seemed like ages ago. "Depends on whether you ask Simon or Tucker."

The black-and-white dog, Cookie, circled the pool with its feathery tail wagging hard. It barked excitedly as the boys tried to coax it into the water.

Rema followed the direction of Sylvia's gaze. "I didn't have the heart to put him in the crate. I hope it's okay to bring him."

Sylvia nodded. Judging from the way the dog was looking at the boys, she could tell it was dying to get to them. "Can Cookie swim?"

"All dogs can swim," Rema stated confidently. She fell silent though as the dog crouched with its butt high in the air and looked down into the water as if it was trying to judge its depth. As the boys urged him, Cookie slowly slid face-first into the pool. The dog immediately sank below the water.

Rema rose, but before she jumped into the pool, the dog's black-and-white head appeared at the surface line. A moment later, Cookie began paddling furiously toward the boys. It was an odd, almost vertical motion, as if the dog were trying to climb out of the water.

"I told you all dogs could swim," Rema commented. Her eyes, however, never left the dog. "Liam," she shouted, "make sure Cookie knows where the steps are so when he gets tired he can rest."

"Okay, Mom." Liam, Rema's oldest son, two years older than Simon, was one of Simon's best friends. He was a tall, dark-haired kid with Rema's eyes and Skiezer's height and build. He liked the games Simon invented, like Avatar Ball, which was a modified kind of volleyball, but played in the pool with a rubber ball.

"So tell me about the derby," Rema prompted. "What's so big you couldn't tell me on the phone?"

Sylvia sighed and moved her legs in the water. "Basically Tucker won everything and Simon lost everything." She glanced at her sons to make sure they weren't listening. "Simon had a nuclear meltdown, and Wilson and I had an argument."

"Ah, family time," Rema said. Her brown eyes were full of sympathy. "It gets you every time. Family vacation is the worst. Takes me weeks to recover." She peered a little anxiously at Sylvia. "That was supposed to be funny, honey."

"It was. I'm sorry." The stitches in Sylvia's arm where she had cut herself on the gutter itched. She absently scratched at the bandage. She dreaded telling her about Wilson's promotion/move, but she also desperately needed Rema's opinion on what she should do.

"So what happened?" Rema swept back her hair and tied it without any kind of hair tie into a complicated knot.

"First, Wilson went out of town, and then..." Sylvia shrugged. "Oh, I don't know. It's a long story."

"I like long stories," Rema said. "And I don't have to be anywhere until six o'clock soccer practice. So spill it."

As the boys and the dog splashed around the pool, Sylvia told Rema about Wilson slipping out to a business meeting instead of helping with Simon's racer, the stress of getting to the derby on time, Simon's loss and subsequent meltdown when they got home.

"But that's not the worst thing." Sylvia felt herself start to get upset and took a deep breath. "Wilson's up for a big promotion and we might have to move."

"No way," Rema announced firmly. "You're not moving."

"Hopefully not. But it explains why he's been so obsessed with work lately. Rema, he really wants this new job."

Although Rema's eyes were hidden behind a pair of oversize dark glasses, the tightness around her mouth reflected her dismay. "Couldn't he just long-distance commute?"

Sylvia shook her head. "It's like five hours."

"Oh." Rema shook her head as if she still couldn't believe Sylvia's news. "Do the boys know?"

"No. It's still iffy. I promised Wilson you wouldn't tell anyone either."

"Not even Kelly, Andrea, or Susan?"

Sylvia sighed. "Not yet."

"I won't tell a soul," Rema promised. She looked at Sylvia. "Oh my goodness," she said. "You can't move. What would I do without you?"

Both women jerked back as one of the boys threw the rubber Avatar ball and it splashed right in front of them. Cookie, paddling fast, retrieved it, and with his long tail acting like a rudder swam back to the boys.

"What would I do without *you*?" Sylvia looked unhappily at her friend.

"So don't go," Rema stated firmly. "Tell him that you don't want to relocate."

"He did say that if I didn't want to move, he wouldn't make me," Sylvia admitted. "I just feel like since he's the one working, I should support what he wants, and if that means move, I should move."

"Connor," Rema shouted at her youngest son. "Get *off* your brother's back. Do you want to *drown* him?" She turned back to Sylvia. "That's silly. Just because you don't get a paycheck doesn't mean you don't work. Being a stay-at-home mom isn't easy. I've told Skiezer if he had to pay for someone to do the stuff I do every day, he'd be bankrupt."

Sylvia looked away from Rema at the boys playing ball with the dog. They made a picture that seemed to imprint itself all the more in her brain because there might not be many more afternoons like this. "He really wants this job."

Rema shook her head. "*Connor*, I'm *warning* you for the last time. The next time you jump on top of anyone, you're out of the pool for the rest of the day!" She patted Sylvia's leg. "What about you? What do you want?"

Sylvia's ears rang from Rema's shouting. "I want to stay here, but I want Wilson to be happy. If he isn't happy at work, he isn't going to be happy at home. If relocating is what Wilson feels is best for our family, then we should do it."

"What makes you think *he* knows better than you what's good for your family?"

Sylvia blinked. "I don't know," she admitted. "But what if I make him give up the promotion and he ends up resenting me? I don't want something like this getting between us." She paused, watched the dog swim another lap after the ball, then shrugged. "I think it would be easier to deal with the move than deal with the guilt of not moving."

Rema lifted her dark glasses and studied Sylvia's eyes. "That's just hogwash. You need to tell him how you really feel."

"If I tell him how I really feel, he'll turn down the job. I'm kind of hoping that he'll figure out that I wasn't exactly jumping up and down with joy when he told me last night." Sylvia smiled as the boys tried to pull Cookie onto an inflatable raft with them and the whole thing capsized. "And I'm kind of hoping that something will fall through and he won't get the job."

"Wilson's a genius," Rema said flatly. "He'll get the job." She fussed with a strap on her bikini top. "If you want to stay, you're going to have to do something fast."

"Yeah, but what? Pray that he doesn't get the promotion?" Sylvia shook her head. "That doesn't seem right, not when I know Wilson is praying that he gets it." She paused as the boys managed to haul the Border collie onto the raft. Sopping wet, the dog struggled to find its balance and then shook wildly, spraying the boys, who whooped with laughter. Even Simon seemed to have put the whole Pinewood Derby thing behind him and was having fun.

How many afternoons would they have left like this?

Rema's brow furrowed. "Maybe," she said, "what Wilson needs is a wake-up call. Something to remind him of all the good stuff about your life here."

Cocking her head, Sylvia studied her friend's tanned face. "That sounds great, but what?"

Rema thought for a moment. "How about an intervention? We'll call everyone and have them give Wilson reasons why moving is a bad idea. And if he doesn't agree"—she drew a line across her throat—"we'll kill him."

Sylvia shook her head. "The only kind of intervention that would help is Divine intervention." In the back part of her mind, the mom part of her remembered that she needed to defrost hamburger meat for dinner. It would just be her and the boys again—Wilson was working late and planning on grabbing something in the office.

"Well, maybe our group will have an idea. We're still on for Tuesday night at Andrea's house, right?"

Sylvia nodded. She probably would need to get a babysitter though. No way could she count on Wilson getting home at a reasonable hour. "Yeah, although between you and me, I'm beginning to wonder if we should just put the Proverbs Plan on hold. Honestly, I don't think it's working very well."

"We don't know that." Rema's lips straightened into a serious line. "Everything that's happened could be exactly part of God's plan for you."

"I know." Sylvia sighed. "It's just kind of discouraging so far."

"You need a pick-me-up," Rema said. "A new outfit, with shoes, and jewelry—and nothing on sale. It'll help."

Sylvia leaned back on her arms. Shopping was Rema's antidote to just about anything, but Sylvia knew it wasn't the solution for her. She looked up at the fluffy white clouds and watched them morph into different shapes. Just what kind of plan did God have in mind for her? Why did He always have to be so mysterious? And above all, why would He ask her to give up this town, this house—these friends—when it felt like they were the only things holding her together?

∽

Wilson was determined to get home early. He knew Sylvia was upset with him over the way he'd handled the Pinewood Derby thing, and he wanted to make it up to her. Although he had a meeting scheduled, he decided to blow it off. He'd call her from the road to let her know. He'd also stop and buy her a dozen roses. No, he'd get sunflowers. Sylvia loved them.

And Simon—imagine him thinking that Wilson didn't love him

as much as Tucker. He had been tired and disappointed when he'd said that. Wilson was sure he didn't mean it, but he would spend more time with him. Tonight he'd suggest he, Simon, and Tuck play hoops in the driveway.

He was powering down his PC when Bruce stepped into his office. For the next thirty minutes he quizzed Wilson on his plans for an advanced online banking system and the proposed reallocation of personnel.

"Excellent work," Bruce concluded. "You're thinking just like a branch manager. Now all we need to do is increase your visibility with the executive board. You play golf, Wilson?"

Did miniature golf count? Wilson didn't think so. Sports weren't his forte, never had been. "No sir," he said.

"Tennis, then? I used to play three sets twice a week before the hip replacement. Justin Eddelman is looking for a doubles partner."

Wilson could hardly keep a ping-pong rally going. He shook his head. "Sorry, sir."

The older man sighed. "You might want to take some golf or tennis lessons. The higher you go in business, the more you need personal contacts as well as business ones. As many deals are made at the country club as in the boardroom."

When was he going to take golf lessons when he worked more than seventy hours a week? Wilson rubbed his temples. "I'll look into it."

"Sylvia, too," Bruce suggested. "Sunday mornings the wives like to get out. Golf and then brunch afterward. Margie and I used to be practically unbeatable—unless we wanted to be." A sly look formed on his face. "If you know what I mean. Sometimes it's just as important to lose as it is to win."

Wilson thought of Simon, who was far from understanding this lesson.

"You and Sylvia should consider taking golf lessons."

Wilson nodded but doubted this would happen. Judging from her reaction to the prospect of moving, he'd be lucky if she swung at the ball and not his head. *She'll come around,* he assured himself. But the idea of a sport was not entirely a bad one. He saw himself throwing a softball with the boys, maybe shooting hoops with them. They had a basketball net in the driveway, and now both boys were old enough to start playing.

"You can borrow my clubs," Bruce offered. "With my hip, I can't get out there anymore."

"Thank you, sir." He glanced at his watch and struggled to curb his impatience. Bruce didn't seem to realize just how late it was. "Is there anything else you want?"

"No," Bruce replied. "I wanted to tell you that Ron McKensy from the Dallas branch is campaigning hard for that branch manager's job. You have my support, but McKensy is teeing off with Justin Eddelman on Sunday morning."

After Bruce left, Wilson continued to think about Bruce's news. He knew McKensy by reputation, and he would be a tough competitor.

He turned on his PC and settled back into his seat. He needed to present a business plan so dazzling, so profitable, so creative that the board couldn't help but pick him. (Even if he couldn't swing a golf club to save his life.)

Okay, he'd already presented a plan to Bruce, but that plan was outdated now. Today, he'd created a voluntary retirement plan that would significantly reduce the number of layoffs. His mind whirled with ideas, even as his eyes burned with fatigue. He realized there was no way he'd be having dinner with Sylvia tonight, or pretty much any night until things were settled.

It occurred to him suddenly that the more hours he worked at the bank, the more hours Sylvia had to work at home without him. She'd looked tired and certainly hadn't been acting like herself lately at all. Now, with his promotion, there'd be extra work for her as well. She'd have to get their house ready for the market. Plus he'd want her help, too, in picking out the new house.

No doubt about it, Sylvia needed someone to lend a hand cooking, chasing after the boys, and catching up on all the household repairs. Unfortunately, it couldn't be him.

And it couldn't be just anybody, Wilson realized. It had to be someone who loved the boys, a male figure who the boys would respect, and someone Sylvia could trust wholeheartedly.

In short, Wilson realized, she needed his father to visit for a few weeks until everything settled down at work. Although it was late, his dad would be awake. He picked up the telephone and made the necessary plans.

Chapter 18

Andrea Burns lived in one of the newer, more upscale neighborhoods. The houses were big, mostly contemporary brick-and-glass colonials, but there were a few stucco Mediterranean-style homes that sprawled across their large, immaculately landscaped lots.

Whenever Sylvia drove down Andrea's cul-de-sac, she always enjoyed the irony of knowing that while Andrea lived in a 4,000-square-foot mansion, it had been a little wooden cabin that had brought the two of them together.

About four years ago, Sylvia and Rema had gone on a retreat for mothers sponsored by their church. It had been hard leaving the boys with Wilson, but she'd been excited about the prospect of getting away, of meeting other mothers, and studying God's Word in a beautiful lakeside setting.

She hadn't counted on the water being the color of chocolate milk, the cabin smelling of mold, or the family of mice living in the cabinet beneath the sink in the bathroom. But then neither had her four new roommates—Rema, Susan, Kelly, and Andrea.

Their toilet had run continuously, the mattresses felt like they'd been stuffed with rocks, and there was a scary, strange stain in the bathtub, but somehow these things hadn't mattered at all.

Over the weekend something almost magical happened. In that little cabin, everyone had opened up to each other, prayed with and for each other, and talked long into the night.

The bond they'd formed had endured over the years, even though their schedules hadn't always allowed them to get together as frequently as Sylvia would have liked.

Pulling up behind Rema's Suburban, Sylvia parked the minivan. Wilson had asked her not to tell everyone about his possible promotion, but it was going to be really hard. She squared her shoulders and rang the bell.

Andrea opened the massive, solid-wood double doors. As usual, she was wearing one of her fabulous power suits. This one was charcoal gray with a faint navy-and-black weave. Her heels were high, and her gold jewelry impeccable. She took the plate of cookies out of Sylvia's hands and kissed her on the cheek. "Come on in," she said, ushering her into the cool, dark interior of her house.

Sylvia took a seat on a plush, chenille sofa and sipped peach iced tea from a long, tall glass. Rema and Susan were already there. As they waited for Kelly, Sylvia got caught up a little on what had been happening over the past week in her friends' lives.

They were discussing Susan's latest volunteering project—running a youth mission trip—when Kelly called to say that she'd been held up at the hospital and they should start without her.

Settling into a coffee-brown recliner, Andrea turned to Susan. "How about you lead us in prayer?"

Sylvia set her glass down on the glass-topped coffee table. Joining hands with Rema and Andrea, she bowed her head as Susan began.

"Heavenly Father, we thank You so much for the opportunity to get together and study Your Word. Father, we ask that You be with us tonight and that we put aside our wants and our desires in order that we will know Yours more clearly. In Jesus' name. Amen."

Sylvia looked up. "That was beautiful, Susan."

"So," Andrea said, pulling out her leather notebook and opening to a blank page. "Last time you were working on the verse that focused on family. How did the Pinewood Derby go?"

Sylvia wrinkled her nose. "Not exactly as I envisioned," she admitted. "Wilson had to go on a business trip, so there really wasn't much family bonding time." She went on to tell them about Tucker's big win, and Simon's equally big loss.

"But then Tucker shocked me," Sylvia continued, "instead of rubbing it in that he won, he was really kind to Simon and even offered to share the trophy." She felt her eyes tear at the memory. "It was like seeing a glimpse of the man he's going to grow up to be."

"I think that's really awesome," Susan said and reached for one of Sylvia's homemade oatmeal chocolate chip cookies. "Maybe your family didn't come together the way you thought, but it sounds like your boys learned some important life lessons."

"That's what Wilson said. I hope so." Sylvia studied the sprig of mint in her iced tea. Unfortunately Simon had also learned some tough life lessons, namely that his father would sometimes let him down, and that promises could be stretched and bent until they didn't resemble their original shape at all.

"I know it's hard to see your child lose," Andrea offered, "but sometimes it's the best thing that can happen to them. Personally, I've always learned more from the cases I've lost in court than the ones I've won."

Sylvia eased back on the couch as the women offered examples of how their failures actually made them stronger or opened doors to better opportunities. She knew they were right, but they hadn't had to fish Simon's race car out of the trash, or wipe the tears from his face, or try to explain that he wasn't a disappointment to them.

Sipping her tea, Sylvia found her thoughts slipping to her mother. Sylvia's dad had worked long hours, but it hadn't been an issue. Why?

Maybe it was just a different time. Yet when she thought about her mom, the word *content* came to mind. Throughout disappointments and dramas Sylvia's mom had somehow stayed above it all, loving her even when Sylvia felt completely unlovable. Like when that boy Courte Hodges had asked her to the prom—and then unasked her. Sylvia still remembered her mother's arms around her, holding her, telling her that God had something even better planned for her.

But did He? The whole prom thing hadn't worked out. She'd ended up staying home, unhappily playing album after album and trying not to listen to the inner voice that said that her hips were too big and her hair too bushy.

After she'd graduated high school, she'd made it through college and then gone to work, still waiting for that something better to come along. There had been many long, lonely years. When she'd met Wilson, she thought her real life, the one she was supposed to be living, had finally begun.

But now it all felt like the ground beneath her feet was disintegrating. Wilson wasn't in love with her anymore, and she was about to lose her home and her friends. It was prom night all over again.

Sylvia set her glass down. Did it have to be prom night all over again? Did she really have to lose everything? Maybe God wanted her to stop waiting around for Him to fix things and fight for what she wanted.

"Sylvia?"

Sylvia turned toward Susan's voice. Her friend had her Bible open.

"We thought we'd get started on the next verse," Susan said and began to read: " 'She considers a field and buys it; out of her earnings she plants a vineyard.'" Susan paused, but when no one commented, she continued. " 'She sets about her work vigorously; her arms are strong for her tasks. She sees that her trading is profitable, and her lamp does not go out at night.'"

"That's probably enough," Susan said. Her gaze swept around the circle. "Did any of the verses speak to anyone?"

There was a long silence, which didn't surprise Sylvia. She knew she wasn't supposed to think literally—but it was hard to translate buying and planting a vineyard into a suburban Texas town.

"Maybe you'd better read it again," Andrea suggested. "I have an idea, but I'm not sure."

Susan read slowly. Sylvia closed her eyes and tried to concentrate, but she found herself thinking about Wilson and their potential relocation. Maybe the part about buying a field wasn't for growing grapes— maybe it was about building a house and starting a new life somewhere else. She felt her stomach knot.

"The part about the fields," Andrea said, tapping her yellow pad with a polished red fingernail. "It's a metaphor. It's about making good investments and managing them."

"I don't think this verse is just about money," Rema countered. "I think that it's about attitude—of being strong and independent and having the confidence to make decisions without relying on anyone else." She sat up a little straighter on the couch. "I think the Proverbs 31 woman is independent. When she knows a field is the right one for her family, she buys it and develops the land. She doesn't turn it over to her husband and ask what he wants her to do with it." Rema looked straight at Sylvia. "The Proverbs 31 wife is empowered, not submissive."

The look in Rema's dark eyes said Sylvia should tell Wilson to turn down the promotion and not think twice about it. Sylvia pleated the fabric at the hem of her cotton skirt. The decision wasn't that simple. Marriage was about compromise and sometimes sacrifice. "The Proverbs 31 wife would probably sell the field if her husband asked her to."

Rema rolled her eyes. "Then the Proverbs 31 wife would be making a very big mistake. She could be sitting on top of an oil field, especially if she lived in Texas. She should be smart enough to know when her husband is about to make a terrible mistake."

"Even if the house were sitting on an oilfield, the Proverbs 31 wife would have to move anyway," Sylvia pointed out. "You can't grow a vineyard and have an oil well in the same field."

"But then she'd have enough money to buy a new field, right next door to the old one," Rema said firmly. "Because when you find a good field, you should stick with it."

There was a moment of silence. Sylvia studied the confused looks on Susan's and Andrea's faces. She wished she could tell them what she and Rema were really talking about.

"I really don't think this is about fields or grapes," Andrea said. "You both are being too literal." She turned to Susan as if Susan were the referee about to make the call on a play. "What do your notes say the verse about the fields really means?"

Susan adjusted her glasses and consulted her notes. "Well, it says that Andrea was on the right track. The Proverbs 31 wife is enterprising, prudent with money, and energetic." She lifted her gaze to Sylvia. "How do you feel about that?"

Sylvia thought for a moment. "Wilson handles all of our investments. He's really good at that stuff, so I don't worry too much about it."

Translation—the principal's PTO presentations were exciting compared to discussions on stock portfolios, bonds, and mutual funds. Wilson happily spent hours on his computer making sure they invested their money, wisely. Since Sylvia tended to be financially conservative, it wasn't an issue between them. But maybe, she considered, this attitude was part of the reason it felt like they each lived in their own world.

"I guess I could take a more active role," Sylvia said slowly. "Wilson would be thrilled if I showed an interest in managing our money."

"I don't think having a discussion about money is very romantic," Rema said flatly. "In fact, it sounds like a terrible idea to me. The last time Skiezer and I talked about our finances, he tried to put me on a budget and we didn't speak for a week."

The three of them laughed.

"I know talking about money doesn't sound very romantic," Susan said, sipping her iced tea, "but I don't think we should skip this verse, especially considering that Wilson is a banker. He has a passion for finances."

Sylvia picked up another cookie. "He really does," she confirmed. "Give the man a spreadsheet and he's a happy camper."

"This could be a really good thing," Andrea mused, fingering the long strand of pearls that lay on her peach-colored silk blouse. Her blue eyes were bright and intense. Sylvia could almost see her brain spinning.

"I'm thinking that you should ask Wilson to go over your financial situation with you," Andrea began. "Just the two of you, together—no kids. Let him explain the areas he feels best about, your goals for the future, and stuff like that."

"I don't see what good could come from going over their financial portfolio." Rema met Sylvia's gaze. "I think Sylvia needs to be more direct with Wilson, and simply tell him what she wants." Her raised eyebrows implied that what Sylvia wanted was for Wilson to turn down the promotion.

Andrea silenced her with a glare she probably had perfected when she needed to stare down the prosecuting attorney. "The point is that when Wilson starts talking about something he enjoys, he'll open up. He'll get excited about sharing his knowledge with Sylvia, and his defenses will drop. Before you know it, you could be having a really deep, intense conversation that has nothing to do with money." She gestured excitedly. "Passion could lead to passion! Don't you see how amazing this verse is—talking about finances when Wilson's a banker?"

Sylvia tried to look appropriately awed at the connection. Inside she was struggling with the idea of trying so hard to meet Wilson's needs when she was mad at him for dumping this whole promotion thing on her.

Sylvia forced a smile. "You're right. But with Easter around the corner, I'll probably have to wait a little while to plan this." By then she could tell everyone about Wilson's promotion and stop trying to be the Proverbs wife.

Andrea pulled out her Blackberry and punched a few buttons. "You should aim for a Friday or Saturday night—so you can sleep late in the morning. And schedule it for after the boys are in bed. How about the second week in May?"

How about never? Sylvia thought glumly, but forced herself to pull her appointment book out of her purse. She blinked when she saw the date. "But that's our anniversary," she said.

Every year they celebrated it at the same restaurant and each of them ordered the same meal. They'd debate, but skip dessert, and then Wilson would give her a nice card and a charm for her bracelet. It was all very nice, but Sylvia felt a little discouraged thinking about it.

"Sylvia can't talk finances on their anniversary," Rema protested.

"You're forgetting," Andrea said sternly. The gold bracelets on her arm jingled as she gestured. "It could lead to talking about budgeting for a romantic getaway to Hawaii or something." She gave Sylvia an encouraging nod. "You have that pretty little bistro table by the pool. I suggest you invite Wilson to a romantic dinner on your deck." She glanced at Susan. "We'll help. You won't even have to cook."

Once Sylvia had dreamed of going to Italy and looking up her ancestors' homes, but that was a long, long time ago. Everything was different now. She had to bite her lip to keep from blurting out that the conversation might consist of Wilson extolling the joys of his new job until she couldn't take it any longer and pushed him into the pool. However, since Wilson had sworn her to silence about the promotion, she found herself agreeing to Andrea's idea. Secretly, she figured she'd cancel the plans once Wilson's job change became public knowledge.

Chapter 19

Sylvia was hoping Wilson would be awake when she got back from her meeting. She had a lot of questions about where Wilson stood in the interview process. If he got the job, how soon would they have to leave? Would the boys be able to finish out the school year? When would they start looking for a new house?

Wilson was asleep, however—snoring to be exact. Slipping beneath the comforter next to him, she realized that she was still too wired from the evening to sleep. She fumbled for her novel on the bedside table and switched on the tiny reading light. On impulse she picked up her Bible.

"Her lamp does not go out at night," Sylvia recalled as she found her place in the book. Maybe, like her, the Proverbs 31 wife had things on her mind and a husband who snored. She pondered the verse a little longer, and then opened her romance and read until she realized she no longer comprehended any of the words.

There was a cup of coffee and a note sitting on the kitchen table for her the next morning. Taking a sip, Sylvia picked up the scrap of paper with Wilson's handwriting scrawled on it. *I love you, Sylvia*, it stated. *We'll talk more tonight.* He doodled some hearts along the margins. She took a sip of coffee, warm and sweet with just the right amount of milk.

She reread the note then slipped it into the pocket of her robe.

For the next hour, Sylvia dashed around making lunches for the boys and finding lost items. Finally they were out the door. After she dropped the boys off at school, she stopped at the grocery store, picked up more cold cuts and the makings for a spaghetti dinner, then drove home.

In the silent house, she put away the groceries then headed upstairs to gather the laundry. As always, she marveled at the amount of clothing two small children could go through—and then found herself getting sentimental as she stuffed a pair of jeans that had been Simon's and were now Tucker's into the machine.

They weren't babies anymore, and it made her sad to think that part of her life was over. She thought of the ivory-colored crib in the attic. She really should donate it—it wasn't doing anyone good just sitting there. It wasn't like she and Wilson were going to have another child. She evened out the load in the machine. Was this true? Deep down, Sylvia knew she would be thrilled to have another son, or a daughter.

She twisted the dial to the machine and listened to the powerful gush of water filling the drum. When she was pregnant with Tucker, she'd been certain she'd have a girl. The due date was right on her mother's birthday, and she'd seen this as God filling the hole that had opened up inside her at her mother's death. She'd never tell Tucker, but before he was born she'd thought of him as Melanie April.

"Melanie April," Sylvia whispered to herself. She pictured a little girl with plump, rosy cheeks, her auburn, curly hair and Wilson's blue eyes. She could almost feel the chubby weight of her in her arms. Sylvia drew herself up short. She was forty years old. Forty. She was too old for another child. God had blessed her with two healthy, beautiful boys. She couldn't love them more.

Besides, a little girl would grow up, just like a little boy, and soon Sylvia would be at the same point in her life as she was now—the kids in school, a husband who worked long hours, and a house that suddenly felt very empty.

Stepping back from the machine, she told herself to get busy. It would be years before the kids went to college, and only hours before they got back from school. Besides, Easter was a week from Sunday and she had a lot to do before then. Returning to the kitchen, she called Honey-Bee-Ham. When the machine answered, she left her name and number. Hanging up, Sylvia worked the menu. Along with the ham, she'd make honey apples, new potatoes with herbs, sautéed green beans, and a salad with crumbled blue cheese and spicy pecans.

Rema would bring dessert—she always brought banana cream pie and everyone loved it.

Reheating her coffee in the microwave, she sipped it slowly. Wilson had made it for her. She thought of his large hands stirring in the right amount of milk and sugar. It was a small gesture—his making it for her—knowing how she liked it—but it meant something to her.

She touched the note in her pocket. Wilson should have discussed the potential promotion with her before he interviewed for the job, but she knew his heart, and it was good. He wouldn't ask her to relocate lightly. She thought of Rema, who loved Skiezer, but had a difficult marriage. Outwardly they seemed fine—an attractive, successful couple—but Sylvia knew differently. All Rema's jokes aside, bottom line, their arguments had opened up a rift between them. Skiezer and Rema weren't best friends, and at times they weren't friends at all. Sometimes Sylvia wondered if Rema and Skiezer were going to make it. She didn't want that kind of marriage.

Finishing her coffee, Sylvia rinsed her mug and put it in the rack to dry. She didn't want to be at odds with Wilson, and it was clear to her now how badly communication between them had broken down. They needed more time together, which reminded her of the next step in the Proverbs Plan she had promised to take.

She reached for the phone but then had a better idea. For ages Wilson had been asking her to send him an electronic calendar request when she wanted to schedule something with him. She'd never done it before, but today seemed a good day to start. She headed upstairs for the home PC in Wilson's office.

The phone rang just as she was viewing Wilson's calendar on the computer. It was a man from Honey-Bee-Ham. As she confirmed the details of her order, Sylvia blocked off a portion of Wilson's schedule, typed in "Anniversary Dinner" and put the location as "poolside, semi-formal." As a final flourish, she attached an RSVP and tagged the calendar request with an exclamation mark to flag it "high priority" in his inbox.

She hit SEND as she agreed to pick up a 15-pound ham on the Saturday before Easter. Sitting back in the chair, she smiled, pleased with her multi-tasking abilities and imagining the surprise on Wilson's face when he got her meeting request.

She was moving the wet laundry to the dryer when the doorbell rang. Straightening, Sylvia hoped it was Rema. Eager to share the details of her morning, she ran downstairs.

Throwing open the door, Sylvia started to say, "Well I hope you brought your bathing suit," when the words died on her lips. There, standing on her front doorstep wearing a checkered short-sleeve shirt, green shorts, and a pair of calf-high black socks was her father-in-law.

Sylvia's mind raced. Joe wasn't due until a week from Friday. Today was only Wednesday. Had he gotten the dates wrong? She searched his weathered face for a clue, even as she gave him a welcoming smile.

"Joe! This is a lovely surprise!" Never in nine years of marriage had he shown up unannounced on her doorstep. "Is everything okay?"

"Oh yes," he said cheerfully. His blue eyes, the exact shade as Wilson's, peered at her kindly. "Wilson told me about everything that's happening. I thought you could use some extra help."

Three oversize suitcases sat on the porch next to Joe. She stared at their bulging sides and swallowed. It looked more like Joe was moving in with them than spending a few days. "Extra help?" she repeated a little faintly.

Joe beamed. "With the house and the boys. Wilson told me all about the big promotion."

"He did?"

"He said he might have to do some traveling between the banks until things get settled. He sounded so unhappy about leaving you alone, Sylvia, that I knew he needed me to come."

"So Wilson knows you're here?"

"Oh no. It's a surprise. If either of you knew I was coming, you might start fussing—doing extra cleaning or shopping." He straightened his narrow shoulders. "I'm here to work. My tool kit and power tools are in the car." He gestured to an older-model blue Buick parked in front of their house. "Of course, if I'm in the way, I'll just drive home."

Home was a long drive away—fourteen hours to be exact—in the small town in Oklahoma where he had retired from the oil company where he had been working for twenty years. "Of course I want your help," Sylvia said, stepping back and opening the door wider. "Don't just stand there. Come on in."

She reached for one of the suitcases. It was heavy and required both hands to drag it over the threshold. He must have packed a lot of clothes. She pushed back a sense of foreboding. Joe's last visit had been extended several times because every time he was supposed to leave he pretended to be sick.

"You sure I'm not barging in on you in the middle of something?" Joe asked, following her into the cool air-conditioning.

"Absolutely nothing," Sylvia assured him. "Let's get your bags settled in the guest room then have a glass of iced tea."

"Iced tea sounds great," Joe said. "We can put together a list of things you want me to do while I'm here. If you're going to put the house on the market, we should plant some flowers. Petunias or impatiens would be nice in the front. People like flowers. It makes a house look happy."

Sylvia's brow furrowed as she dragged the suitcase up the first step. "Wilson told you we're selling the house?" What else had her husband shared with her father-in-law that he hadn't told her? Maybe she was going to have to reconsider killing him.

"Not exactly," Joe admitted. "But spring is the perfect time to sell. We're already late, but don't worry, there's still time. You sure that suitcase isn't too heavy for you?"

"It's fine," Sylvia assured him. Family photos on the wall tracked her progress up the steps. "What else did Wilson say about the move?"

"Just that he was a little worried about you and the boys because he said it was going to be pretty busy for the next couple of months." Joe paused. "Two young boys can be a handful. Fortunately I'm available for as long as you need me." He chuckled. "I work cheap. All you have to do is feed me. And I like everything."

"But your medical appointments—"

"Any medical care I need, I can get right here, Sylvia. More of my prescriptions are mail order now. And I have a list of referrals from my doctors."

Sylvia reached the landing. "That's great," she managed. "We're glad to have you—and the boys will be so excited when they get home from school and see you."

"I can't wait," Joe replied. "I brought them basketballs. I figure we can put that hoop in your driveway to good use."

The hoop had come with the house. To date, neither boy had been able to throw the ball high enough to play basketball, but Sylvia didn't point this out. "They'll love it," she assured him.

As they passed Wilson's office on their way down the hall they heard a pinging noise. "What's that?" Joe asked.

"It's from the computer," Sylvia replied. "That's the noise it makes when someone sends an e-mail."

The words were barely out of her mouth when the computer chirped again. It made noise several more times on the way to the guestroom. It was still making noise after Sylvia brought up the third suitcase and set out fresh towels for Joe.

Concerned that the machine was malfunctioning, she walked into the office. As she downloaded her e-mail, she was amazed to find she had eighteen new messages. This wasn't normal. She hardly ever got e-mail. But she was more puzzled than concerned when her gaze skimmed the messages and she saw they were all from people at Wilson's bank.

She hesitated. Was this spam or some new computer virus that would infect their PC if she opened up one of the messages? She peered more closely. None of the e-mails had attachments. All of them looked like replies to the calendar request she had sent Wilson.

Saying a quick prayer, Sylvia opened the most recent message. It was from Jen Douglas.

Skimming the content, she realized that Jen was asking her what Sylvia wanted her to bring to the anniversary party, which was surprising, because Sylvia hadn't invited her. She fought the panic building up inside. Had she somehow invited everyone in Wilson's office? And were all these other e-mails acceptances?

"Is everything okay?" Joe asked, walking over to her.

Sylvia had a terrible feeling as she gazed into his steady blue eyes. "I think I goofed," she admitted. "I was trying to schedule something on Wilson's calendar, but it looks like it went to everyone in his office." Sylvia cringed as she saw a reply from Wilson's boss. "What do I do?"

Joe peered over Sylvia's shoulder and studied the list of e-mails. He was a quiet for a few minutes and then straightened slowly. Placing his gnarled hand on her shoulder, he squeezed gently. "There's only one thing you can do," he said gruffly. "Start planning a party. A big party."

Chapter 20

They were hanging plastic eggs in the maple tree in the front yard when Wilson pulled the Beemer into the driveway. Cutting the engine, he sat for a moment taking in the sight of Sylvia in a pair of cutoffs, standing on a ladder straining into the branches of the tree. And then his gaze went to his father. Wilson hadn't expected him to arrive this early, but he was relieved to have his help.

On the lawn, Simon and Tucker were running around and scattering plastic eggs. Not scattering, he realized, but throwing eggs at each other. The eggs were so light, however, they were having trouble reaching each other, which both boys seemed to find hilarious.

Wilson was relieved to see Simon having fun. The boy had been so upset over the Pinewood Derby, but watching him now, it looked like everything was okay.

Stepping out of the car, Wilson walked onto the lawn. The boys spotted him and ran up to him. Crouching, Wilson braced himself as their combined weight slammed into him. If Simon hesitated a second longer than Tucker, it was only because Tucker was rougher and Simon probably didn't want to get in his way.

Holding the boys in a strong hug, Wilson straightened. Growling, he spun them around. They howled with laughter, and Wilson turned even faster.

"Do it again, Daddy," Tucker shouted as he set the boys on the ground.

"First I want to say hi to your Poppy." Wilson still couldn't get over that his father had taken it upon himself to show up so early—but then the day had been full of surprises.

Wilson had been in a meeting when Dale, a rangy, dark-haired kid from accounting, had poked his head into the conference room and asked Wilson if he should bring his swimsuit.

"What are you talking about?" Wilson had asked.

"Your anniversary pool party." Dale, only a couple of years out of college and as smart as they came, had grinned. "Your wife just invited everyone in the bank."

"Ha ha," Wilson had said. "Very funny." But when he'd returned to his office, he'd seen the calendar request Sylvia had sent out. He'd called her immediately, and although she had apologized and tried to explain everything, it still didn't change the fact that now they were entertaining everyone in his office and at a very critical point in the interview process.

"It's great to see you, Dad." Wilson hugged his father then drew back to study him. Shorter than himself, and with a neck fused into a persistent forward tilt, Joe nonetheless looked tan and healthy. His bald head was as freckled and glossy as ever. "You're looking well."

"Thanks, sonny boy," his dad said. "You look pretty good, too."

"Hi, honey." Sylvia stepped from behind his father. "You're just in time to put out Peter Rabbit."

Peter Rabbit was the giant Easter inflatable they stored in the attic. Last year it had consistently blown the fuse, and they had learned to limit the appliances they turned on when Peter was inflated.

"Just let me get changed," he said. "Wait until you see it, Dad, it's the most tacky thing you've ever seen."

"I saw it last year, remember?" Joe smiled at Sylvia. "It's fun, not tacky."

It didn't take long to retrieve the inflatable rabbit from the attic and then to stake it to the ground in the front yard. Everyone cheered when Wilson turned on the power and Peter slowly inflated until it towered above them all. Wilson glanced at Sylvia and felt something solid and strong and happy pass between them. It was Easter, a time of celebration and of rebirth. Some of the anxiety Wilson had been carrying around seemed to leave him. More than ever, anything, especially a new start, in a new town, seemed possible.

It was with this in mind that after dinner—a delicious meal of homemade lasagna, hot, buttery garlic bread, and a crisp salad—that Wilson asked Sylvia if she wanted to go for a short walk around the block. "I'm sure Dad won't mind watching the kids for a little while."

"Go for a long walk," Joe said and winked at the boys. "I'm thinking that it's time Poppy showed you how to build a proper tent in the game room."

The boys cheered.

"Just don't use the flat screen to anchor it," Wilson warned, and then he and Sylvia stepped out the door into the balmy April evening.

It was just getting dark, and lights had come on inside the neighboring houses. As they walked to the end of their cul-de-sac, Wilson reached for Sylvia's hand. "Are you upset about my dad showing up early?"

"No—not really. Not anymore." She paused. "I was at first because it sounded like you'd discussed the promotion with him and it was all settled that we were moving." She glanced sideways at him. "Are you mad about me inviting everyone at the bank to our anniversary?"

He laughed. "No. Actually, everyone's pretty excited about it."

"I know. Just about everyone is coming." They walked a few steps in silence. "I'm really sorry, Wilson. I meant for the invitation to be just for you and me. I hope this doesn't mess up anything about your promotion."

"It won't," Wilson assured her. "In fact, Bruce said he thought business entertaining was good for my image."

"Your image?"

"As a candidate for branch manager."

"Oh." Sylvia walked for a moment in silence. "So this promotion, it's going to happen, isn't it?"

"Maybe." He glanced at her sideways. "Hopefully. Jen saw my name on some organization charts."

"That's great."

Did she really mean it? They walked a moment in silence. Wilson debated telling her what else Jen said. It wasn't going to help his case if he told her Jen had been penciled in as assistant branch manager. On the other hand, he'd already made a mistake in waiting so long to tell her about his possible promotion.

"Jen's been slated for assistant branch manager," he said.

Sylvia didn't speak for a long moment. "At the new bank?"

"It's all still being worked out, but yes, that's the way it's looking."

"You really think it's a good idea for her to be your assistant?"

Although it was something Wilson had wondered himself, he found himself getting defensive. "What do you mean, Sylvia?"

"What do you mean, Sylvia?" She imitated the arguably pompous note in his voice perfectly. "I mean she's a single, attractive woman."

"You have nothing to worry about. I told you. You're the one I love. Besides," he added, "it isn't like this is set in stone. Now there's a guy competing with me from the Dallas office. He's got good credentials and is pushing hard." Wilson shook his head. "It's going to come down to who has the most support from the board of trustees."

"Well," Sylvia said, "they'd be idiots not to give you the job."

He waited, suspecting she had something else to say and wasn't wrong.

"But I still don't like the thought of you and Jen working together every day."

He sighed. "It isn't my choice. But so many things still can change. But you're right and I will suggest that she be given another position."

They'd come to the small park in their neighborhood. Although it was empty now, the swing set, jungle gym, and balance beam gave mute testimony to the presence of children in their neighborhood. Just behind a covered pavilion was a lake stocked with fish and turtles. Wilson himself had brought the boys here to fish, but when Simon had seen the hook, he'd flatly refused. They'd ended up feeding bread to the ducks.

"Don't you think we have a great life here?"

"Absolutely," Wilson agreed. "But we could have a great life somewhere else, too." He hesitated then plunged forward. "I've had the same job for years. And to be honest, I'm ready for a change. The boys are young. This is the time to do it."

Sylvia didn't say anything.

"It could be an adventure," Wilson added. "We could explore a new part of Texas, meet new people. . ." His voice trailed off as Sylvia continued to keep her gaze firmly fixed on the concrete pathway. "The economy is bad," he stated. "When we condense the two banks, there will be job cuts. I want to make sure I stay in a good position to provide for you and the boys."

"So you're saying your job might go away if you don't take this promotion?"

"I don't think I would get laid off," Wilson said, "but it wouldn't be a good career move to turn down this opportunity—if I get it."

"This new job," Sylvia said slowly, "would you have more time to spend with me and the boys?"

"Initially? Probably not," Wilson admitted. "This bank needs a total rehaul. I'm talking physical renovations, personnel changes, new technology—the operating systems are real antiques. The magnitude of the merger is enormous, Syl."

But so was the opportunity. It began to pour out of him then, all the information he'd been storing up, all the plans he'd spent hours forming. He wanted her to understand being a branch manager wasn't an ego booster, it was a chance for him to make a positive impact on a community. To turn something that was failing into something successful. Affect people's lives in a positive way. Build a legacy he could be proud of.

He talked for a long time, and when he finally finished, they had come full circle and were standing at the start to their street. He stopped walking, not wanting their time together to end without hearing he had her full support for the new job.

Turning, he tried to read her face. It was dark, but he thought she looked sad, as if she were digesting bad news. Maybe he was wrong, and it was just the way the shadows played across her face. He'd just given her a lot of information, and they had both been up since six that morning. He ran his fingers through his hair. "So what do you think?"

She shifted her weight, opened her mouth, and then closed it.

"What?" he pressed.

"It's great to see you so excited about something," Sylvia said. "But…"

"But what?"

"But I'm scared if you take this job, you're going to get sucked into work, and the boys and I are never going to see you."

"That's crazy. You and the boys mean everything to me."

Sylvia pinned a gaze on him that even through the semidarkness reached deep inside him. "When you talked about work, Wilson, your voice got really animated, and you went on for like twenty minutes straight."

"Because I wanted you to understand what the job means."

"I get that," Sylvia said. "I just wish you had the same enthusiasm for me and the boys." Her voice lowered. "You never talk about us like that."

"Of course I do," Wilson stated firmly. "You're just not around when I talk about you and the boys."

Sylvia shifted her weight and seemed to consider her words very carefully before speaking. "We're drifting apart, Wilson. Don't you feel it? There's your world and there's mine."

Drifting apart? Wilson leaned forward. What was she talking about? They had a great marriage. He shook his head. "No," he said. "We're not drifting apart. I love you."

"I love you, too, but the most excited you've been about spending time with me is when we were running for our lives from that wild pig."

Wilson almost laughed, but the sheen of tears in her eyes stopped him. "Sylvia, you mean everything to me. You are my total world."

"You say it, but it doesn't *feel* like it." She waved his hands away when he tried to reach for her. "It feels like I'm trying to talk to you, but you don't hear me."

Wilson pulled back as an unexpected rush of defensive anger swept through him. He had just shared his heart with her, and now she was mad at him because he wasn't listening to her? What about her listening to him? He heard the stiffness in his voice as he said, "What are you talking about?"

"Our family. Us. Have you really thought through what moving us will do?"

Wilson frowned. "Of course I have. I've checked out the schools and looked at some possible neighborhoods. I wouldn't ask you to go someplace where I didn't think you or the boys would be happy." He ran his hand through his hair and his fingers went unerringly to the small bald spot. "This promotion will mean more money, Sylvia. We could have a bigger house and take some great vacations. Plus there's college to think about. I know the boys are young, but we need to be saving now."

"I appreciate that," Sylvia said, "But maybe what we really want is to see more of you." She twisted her hands together. "I know you're working really hard. But...I miss you. I don't want to lose you—lose us."

He looked into her eyes and felt the anger drain away. She loved him, and this was all he'd ever wanted. The rest could be worked out. "You'll never lose me," Wilson promised. "You're stuck with me for life, and if I get this job, it'll be a better life." He paused to let this sink in. "This stuff we're going through right now—it's temporary. I won't always work these hours. They'll have to make a decision soon, and after they do, we'll talk and decide together what the best thing is for our family."

"And if it's staying here?"

"Then we stay," Wilson said, but then he couldn't stop himself from adding, "But promise me you'll see the town and look at a few houses before you decide. I think you'll really like it. There're parks for the boys and lots of restaurants and stores."

Sylvia put her hand on his arm and shook her head. "Let's just get through Easter, okay?"

"Okay, but how about a road trip the weekend after?"

"We're going to be busy getting ready for our anniversary party, which reminds me, now that it's a work party, I'm going to need help. I want to tell Andrea, Susan, and Kelly what's going on."

He thought for a moment. Sylvia did need help. Word was already leaking out at work. Although he preferred to wait before they let their friends know, he didn't see any harm. "That'd be fine as long as they know nothing is definite. Now what about house hunting? How about the week after our anniversary? We could bring the boys."

"And that's supposed to talk me into going?"

He laughed. "Okay. The boys can stay home with Dad. But will you at least look?"

"Yes," Sylvia said.

He heard the lack of conviction in her voice but decided it was something that would change once she realized how exciting this opportunity could be for them. Leaning forward, he kissed her lightly on the lips. "You won't regret it," he promised.

Chapter 21

The elementary school let out for a long weekend on Thursday afternoon. Anticipating an even longer car line than usual because of the holiday, Sylvia and Joe drove to the elementary school a half hour earlier than usual. Even so, the car line already backed onto the main road.

It took Sylvia ten minutes after school dismissed before they entered the school's parking lot. As they inched forward, Joe noticed the muddy ditch between the field and the building.

"The playground needs to be releveled," he commented. "Unless you've got a good drainage pipe, after it rains you're going to get a lot of standing water, which means mosquitoes, Sylvia. Mosquitoes carry West Nile."

"I know," Sylvia said. "We're fundraising for it. Wait until you see me in my Mr. Slice outfit."

Joe laughed. "I'm sure you look great." He kept his gaze fixed on the playground. "If I'm still here, I could help with the project. I'm not so old that I've forgotten how to be a good civil engineer."

Sylvia studied the back of his bald head. She wondered if she and Wilson would still live in this town long enough to see it happen. "That'd be great," she said.

They picked up Simon from the line of second graders, and then Sylvia pulled the minivan forward a few more feet and waited as Tucker disentangled himself from a group of boys. When she saw the birdcage, covered with a white cloth, she remembered they were getting another guest for Easter—Bluebonnet, the class pet.

"What you got there?" Joe asked as the doors to the minivan slid shut behind Tucker.

"Bluebonnet," Tucker said proudly. "I get to have him for Easter and write a story and take pictures about what he does at our house."

"Mrs. Chin is very big about reading and writing," Sylvia confirmed as she kept a slow pace with the car moving in front of them. "All the students get a turn taking Bluebonnet home. They keep a journal, and at the end of the year Mrs. Chin combines all the stories into one book with pictures."

"It's so cool," Tucker said. "Can I take a picture of Bluebonnet next to Peter Rabbit?"

He meant, of course, the giant inflatable Easter bunny on their front lawn. "I don't see why not," Sylvia said.

"Simon!" Tucker suddenly yelled. "Stop!"

Sylvia very nearly slammed on the brakes.

"I just want to see what he looks like," Simon said loudly.

"You can't lift his cover! Mrs. Chin said so!"

"I wasn't lifting the cover! I was looking underneath it."

"You'll scare Bluebonnet!"

"Maybe he's scared now and you just can't see it," Simon pointed out. "We should look and see if he's okay."

"Mom!" Tucker shouted. "Make him stop!"

"I'm just trying to help!"

"Simon," Sylvia said sharply. "Leave the bird alone. You can see him later, after he gets settled when we get home. Tucker, stop yelling." They picked up speed as they passed out of the school zone. "And don't forget," she added, because distraction was an essential part of resolving conflicts, "we have three dozen Easter eggs to dye."

"That means we get eighteen each," Simon calculated with impressive speed. There was a pause, and then he added, "Unless you or Poppy want to dye some. In that case it would be—"

"Plenty for everyone," Sylvia said.

"I'm going to dye one blue so that it looks like Bluebonnet," Tucker announced. "It'll look like he's laid an egg."

"He's a boy, Tucker," Simon pointed out. "Boy parakeets can't lay eggs." He hesitated a beat. "Can they mom?"

The way Simon's mind worked, Sylvia could almost predict her son's next question would be how baby parakeets were conceived. Out of the corner of her eye, Sylvia saw Joe grinning widely and guessed he thought the same.

"No they can't," she agreed, and put on her turn signal. "But boy parakeets can help take care of the eggs." She didn't want to raise boys who later in life wouldn't do their part in child raising.

"You mean sit on them and keep them warm?" Tucker exclaimed. "I wonder if Bluebonnet would do that if we put an egg in his cage."

"It'd be way too giant for him to climb onto," Simon said as they turned into the driveway. "It'd be like a chicken trying to sit on a dinosaur's egg."

"Then we could put a blanket over it," Tucker said. "That would keep it warm, wouldn't it, Mom?"

"Honey, there are no baby chickens alive in the eggs we buy from the store."

This silenced both boys from the topic of hatching chickens. Inside the house, Sylvia gave the kids a quick snack of sliced oranges and rice crispy treats. Afterwards, she cleared the kitchen table and Joe spread newspapers over the surface. With Bluebonnet unveiled from the cage cover, watching from his spot on the kitchen counter, Sylvia brought out two boxes of Easter egg dye and then placed two sets of bowls on the table.

Last year, the Easter egg dying session had ended with Tucker having a meltdown when Simon had mixed all the colors together and turned all the dye a muddy brown.

As the boys nearly climbed onto the table watching with interest, she poured water into the bowls, added vinegar, and the small, colored tablets, which immediate began to dissolve.

"Cool!" Tucker shouted as the dye began to dissolve and the bowls filled with an assortment of rainbow colors. "Can I get started?"

Simon already was stirring up the dyes with the thin metal loop for holding the eggs. The loop had always made Sylvia think of a magnifying glass without the glass, and as a child, she had held it up numerous times to look at the world through it.

"Can I have some extra bowls? I want to make some other colors," Simon asked.

Sylvia retrieved the cartons of eggs which she'd hard-boiled earlier and handed Simon four extra mixing bowls. She met Joe's eyes and smiled as the boys eagerly added their eggs to the dye.

Sylvia remembered dying Easter eggs in the cheerful red-and-white kitchen of her childhood. She and Tyler had spent hours bent over the kitchen table, dunking their eggs the darkest shade they could get them. By the time they'd finished, their fingertips had been stained a dark purple color.

She made a mental note to call her brother and wish him a happy Easter. It'd been ages since they'd spoken. Maybe this summer they could all get together—rent a house on the beach or choose a spot halfway between Washington and Texas. She didn't let herself dwell on the fact that they had been talking about this for years and it'd never happened. It'd been that way growing up, too, she reflected. Even then he'd seemed to have his own life that was separate from hers.

Joe nudged her. She followed the direction of his gaze and she watched as Simon pulled his egg out of a bowl of yellow dye. He had created an interesting, marbled effect by covering parts of the egg with his fingers.

"Hold on," Sylvia ordered. "I want to get my camera." She raced off to her bedroom for the Nikon. By the time she got back, all the bowls had eggs in them. Simon was furiously mixing colors like a mad scientist, and Tucker was proudly holding up a robin's-egg blue egg. He'd also gotten blue dye on his fingers, shirt, and eyebrows.

The kitchen table had taken several hits of spilled dye. Joe sat between the boys, happily coloring an egg. He had a smear of red dye on his cheek. Sylvia quickly snapped the picture. She kept taking shots until the boys started to protest and Joe proclaimed he was seeing spots from the flash.

"Come and sit down," he urged her. "Stop taking pictures of everyone having fun and have some fun. Life is too short not to take the time to dye an Easter egg."

Like Mary and Martha, Sylvia thought. A time to work and a time to sit and learn, appreciate the moment. She put down the camera and picked up an egg.

Sylvia decided to celebrate Good Friday with a nice dinner on the back deck. She knew Wilson was working and wouldn't be home until late. Joe, however, volunteered to grill the salmon, which was the only kind of fish the boys would eat. Sylvia made butter noodles and steamed asparagus. By the time Wilson got home, they were ready to eat.

Wilson gave the blessing, which Tucker interrupted with a mighty belch. Although he quickly apologized, Sylvia suspected Tucker had done it on purpose and pinned a look on him that said *"don't do that again."* He shrugged and tried to look innocent, but a smile hovered about his mouth.

The boys ate quickly—Simon loading up on noodles and picking at his fish, and Tucker eating a lion's share of everything. After they'd cleaned up, Wilson turned on the pool lights and the boys jumped into the water.

Sylvia, Wilson, and Joe settled back to watch. The air had cooled, but the pool was heated to eighty-two degrees. Neither boy seemed to feel the slight chill in the air as they splashed around, their skin glossy in the blue lights of the water.

"They're good kids," Joe said, settling deeper into the cushions of the padded chair.

"Most of the time," Sylvia agreed, watching Tucker spit water right into Simon's face through a long, Styrofoam pool noodle. "Tucker needs to learn more self-control."

Simon grabbed the pool noodle and turned it so that the water sprayed back at Tucker. Both boys laughed.

"Maybe we should be a little tougher with Tuck," Wilson said. "Give him more time-outs, or take away his television time."

"Oh he's fine." Joe waved his bony hand dismissively. "He'll grow up in time." He paused. "And he's very funny. I almost laughed when he burped when you were blessing our meal."

"Dad," Wilson said. "That's terrible. I'm glad you didn't encourage him."

Joe shrugged his thin shoulders. "When you get to be my age, you learn that laughter is a wonderful thing. It heals what hurts and makes you feel young."

"I'm glad it makes you feel that way," Wilson said, "but there's a line between funny and disrespectful."

This was true, and while Sylvia agreed with Wilson, she also appreciated Tucker's free spirit. She looked at Joe. It was dark now and he seemed very old and wise. "Was Wilson ever like Tucker when he was growing up?"

"He was a rule follower and a people-pleaser." Joe smiled at Sylvia. "When he was really young, he was a crybaby."

"Gee thanks, Dad, for making me sound so appealing."

"I'm only telling the truth," Joe said, sounding unfazed. "You were very sensitive, but also bright and loving. Alice always said you would make someone a great husband."

"And he does," Sylvia said, and winked at Wilson. "Most of the time."

"You can see," Wilson remarked dryly, "who Tucker takes after."

"I don't burp during the blessing," Sylvia pointed out. "But once I got a terrible case of the hiccups in church." She'd been in her twenties, sitting next to her mother in the pew, and in the middle of the reverend's sermon, she'd started to hiccup. Sylvia's timing had been terrible—every time Reverend Thomas had paused, Sylvia had filled the silence with an uncontrollable hiccup. This had given her mother the giggles, which had given Sylvia the giggles and made her hiccups even worse. Sylvia remembered her mother's face, flooded with color, alive with laughter.

Sylvia had loved this about her mother—her ability to enjoy her life and her faith. She took God seriously without ever taking life too seriously. *I really miss you, Mom,* she thought. *I miss talking to you—and I wish that you were here to see the boys grow up.*

"Oh for goodness sakes! You'll see me in heaven." Sylvia could almost hear her mom's voice—half-assuring, half-scolding—as if she couldn't believe Sylvia had any doubt at all. *"And until then,"* this same voice said, *"you love those boys for me."*

Those boys meant Wilson, too. Her mother had adored him. Sylvia looked at her husband, his eyes crinkling and his teeth bright and even as he laughed at something Joe had said. He seemed more relaxed than he had in ages, maybe because for once he wasn't sucked into work.

"Have you given much thought about house hunting?" Joe asked.

"Not really," Wilson said, exchanging a quick look with Sylvia. "I'm still in the interview stage, Dad."

"It wouldn't hurt to take a look around," Joe said. "Springtime is when most people put their houses on the market. You'd get the best selection if you look now."

"Anyone want coffee?" Sylvia suggested, hoping to change the topic, or at the very least remove herself from the conversation.

She started to rise to her feet but stopped when Joe said, "Please sit, Sylvia, there's something I've been wanting to talk to you both about. Something I've been thinking about ever since Wilson called me."

The serious look on Joe's face gave Sylvia a very bad feeling. Her mind flashed to her father-in-law's health. Last year when he'd visited them, he'd thought he was having a heart attack and Sylvia had taken him to the emergency room. Fortunately it had turned out to be indigestion. She hoped he didn't have cancer, just thinking the word sent a small shiver through her.

"I'm getting older and what time I have, I want to spend with you and my grandkids," Joe said calmly. "When Wilson talked about moving, I thought, why not move, too?" Joe looked from her face to Wilson's. "At first I thought about buying a house close to you, but then I wondered if you would be interested in looking for a house with an in-law apartment. I would be happy to help with the down payment and mortgage."

After a long pause Wilson said, "You want to buy a house with us?"

"I'm just throwing it out there," Joe said. A very slight defensive note crept into his voice. "As you're making your plans, it's something to think about." He patted Sylvia's hand. "I wouldn't be extra work for you, honey. I can cook, clean, and I'm pretty handy around the house." He smiled. "And you'd have a built-in babysitter."

"But Dad, what about Sugar Hill? You've lived there for thirty years—all your doctors are there." Wilson's voice sounded slightly strained, and he cast a definitely anxious look at Sylvia.

"I've gotten great reports from my cardiologist, my internist, my urologist, and my dermatologist. . .*and* my dentist. I'm sure they'll be glad to give me some referrals."

The gazes of both men turned to Sylvia. Joe, living with them full time? She hadn't seen that coming, and although she wasn't completely sure how she felt, she couldn't just squash the hopeful look in his eyes. Ignoring the way Wilson was trying to signal her with his eyes, she smiled at her father-in-law. "I think it's a great idea," she said.

"You do?" Joe beamed.

"Sylvia and I will need to talk more about this, Dad," Wilson said, and cast another look at Sylvia that clearly asked *"What in the world are you thinking?"*

Joe steepled his fingers. "Take all the time you want," he said gravely. He couldn't, however, seem to stop the grin that tugged and tugged then finally stretched into a wide smile. "I think this is going to be the best Easter ever."

Chapter 22

On Easter morning Rema, Skiezer, and their boys arrived a little after eleven. Rema was wearing a cream silk dress with a pale pastel pattern, and her dark hair was swept up in an elegant chignon. Leaning forward to hug her, Sylvia smelled the floral scent of expensive perfume. "You look gorgeous."

"So do you," Rema exclaimed. "That purple is great on you."

"Thanks," Sylvia said. It was one of her favorite dresses—sleeveless with a very slimming A-line shape. She'd paired it with the strand of pearls that Wilson had given her as a wedding gift and a pair of pearl stud earrings. Although the outfit wasn't new, just that morning she'd gotten several compliments at the early service.

She moved forward to hug Skiezer, which proved difficult, not just because he was six foot six and built like a linebacker, but because he was balancing a pie tin and a crystal bowl filled with fruit.

"Happy Easter," she said, and then she saw Connor and Liam behind him. Cookie, the Border collie, danced with excitement on the end of his leash.

"I couldn't leave Cookie in the cage on Easter," Rema said apologetically, pushing the dog down as it jumped on Sylvia to greet her. "I didn't think you'd mind if I brought him."

"Of course not," Sylvia said. "Cookie is part of the family. Aren't you, Cookie?"

The Border collie all but turned itself inside out wagging his tail and squirming all over as Sylvia rubbed behind his ears. Then the dog spotted Simon and Tucker and nearly exploded with joy. The dog loved kids and dragged Connor and Liam toward them. There was a chorus of excited voices and chaos as the dog managed to wrap the leash around them.

"Skiezer, Rema," Sylvia said as the kids untangled themselves and then raced up the stairs with the dog. "You remember Joe Baxter, Wilson's father?"

"Of course," Skiezer said. He was a tall man with a dark complexion, coarse features, and short, curly black hair. "I'd shake your hand, Joe, but you might end up wearing banana cream pie."

"That's no deterrent," Joe said, patting Skiezer's broad shoulder. "Banana cream pie is my favorite." He reached to take the tin from Skiezer. "Can I help you with that?"

"I don't know," Rema teased. "Can we trust you?"

Joe laughed and gave her a kiss. "Happy Easter, sweetheart."

"Happy Easter to you," Rema said. "Sylvia, where's Wilson?"

"Oh, he's in the backyard, finishing hiding the eggs. Joe and I stuffed about two hundred. Come on back—let's put those in the kitchen."

"And I ate as much candy as I stuffed," Joe said, shuffling along with her into the kitchen. "Sylvia got the good stuff—M&M's, Kit Kats, Three Musketeers—you name it. When I was a kid, we hunted hard-boiled eggs. My dad was so good at hiding them that come summer we'd be finding eggs all over the backyard—under bushes, in the garden, everywhere. Not even the raccoons would eat them. Nothing smells as bad as a rotten egg."

"You should try smelling Cookie's breath," Rema said, high heels clicking on the tile floor. "One whiff will knock your socks off. I don't know what that dog eats." Opening the fridge door, she shifted around a few items then gestured for Joe to place the pie inside.

"He eats the same food as us," Skiezer deadpanned.

Rema shot him a death look, and he laughed loudly.

Sylvia laughed and checked the food in the oven. The yam casserole needed about thirty more minutes, and the Honey-Bee ham, delivered yesterday, was warming nicely under its tent of foil. The beans were prepped, and the salads were ready except for the dressing.

Wilson came through the back door, kissed Rema's cheek, and exchanged hey man's and thumps on the back with Skiezer.

"Are we ready?" Sylvia asked.

"Yes." Wilson grinned. "I even put some eggs out on floats in the pool and hid the skimmer."

"It won't stop the kids," Rema predicted. "They'll find a way. Even if they have to swim out to get them." She turned to Skiezer. "Do you have the video camera ready?"

"What video camera?" Skiezer said, and then pretended it hurt when Rema hit him lightly on the shoulder.

Sylvia called up the stairs, "We're ready for the Easter egg hunt." The four boys, with Cookie in the middle, thundered down the stairs. Handing out baskets, Sylvia lined everyone up at the back door by age. Tucker, who was the youngest, went first, followed by Connor and then Simon. Liam went last.

The adults, in unison, gave the countdown, and then Sylvia opened the door. The boys and Cookie charged outside. For the next five minutes, it was like watching a family video in fast-forward. The boys zigzagged around the backyard—grabbing eggs from the flower beds, the crook of the palm trees, the deck chairs, and grass. Cookie ran around barking incessantly and trying unsuccessfully to herd the boys into one group.

The eggs on the floats were the hardest to reach, but Simon used the hose to create a current which brought the float close enough to the side of the pool for the other kids to grab. Wilson had placed a large nest of eggs on top, and the boys quickly divided them.

Afterward, the boys came inside and ran to the game room to count their eggs. Sylvia quickly parboiled the green beans and poured the lemon chive dressing over them. Wilson began carving the ham. Rema, Skiezer, and Joe set out the salads and filled the water goblets.

Finally Sylvia lit the candles and stood back in admiration. The mahogany dining table, which had been her grandmother's, and then her mother's, and now hers, had been expanded with the help of a card table so that it could seat everyone. One tablecloth hadn't been big enough, so Sylvia had bought two matching white linen ones at Target and then overlapped them. The gold-and-white Lenox china was from her wedding, as was the Waterford glassware. The center-piece was a crystal bowl filled with the colorful eggs she and the boys had dyed. The table had looked like this when Sylvia was a girl, and her gaze lingered, remembering her mother bustling about, her father, handsome in his dark suit, asking everyone to join hands so he could give the blessing.

"Okay, everyone," she called, "come and eat."

Soon everyone was crowded around the table, on which every inch of space was covered with dishes of food. Voices overlapped in excitement, and then Wilson said, "Before we start, would anyone like to give the blessing?"

"I would," Joe said.

They all joined hands and bowed their heads. Sylvia gave Tucker a look of warning before she closed her eyes. And then Joe's gravelly voice began.

"Father, we thank You for this Easter Sunday—for the opportunity to be together to celebrate Jesus, who died for us, and then rose again, and taught us so much about love. Because when it comes down to it, the love of You, of friends and family—of all people, really—is all that matters. Please bless this food to our use, and us to Your purpose, and help us be ever mindful of the needs of others. In Jesus' name, amen.

"Okay, everyone," Joe announced, looking up and beaming, "dig in!"

Dishes were passed around and soon everyone's plate was piled high with slices of sweet ham, tangy green beans, honey apples, and herb-flavored new potatoes. The conversation ranged from the morning's sermon, to the unlikely chance of the Astros having a better season, to Skiezer telling funny stories about golfing.

Wilson caught Sylvia's eye. "I've been thinking that Sylvia and I should take some golf lessons."

She smiled back at him. "I don't know if that's such a great idea. Remember when we visited your brother in California and we played miniature golf? We were terrible."

"That was a long time ago," Wilson said. "And we weren't that bad."

"We had to cheat, remember? Hitting it out of the barriers and doing like a zillion do-overs."

"Only on a couple holes, Sylvia," Wilson said. "Technically we didn't cheat, we just took the maximum score and moved on. And the windmill one doesn't count."

"That one was the worst," Sylvia agreed, cutting off a small piece of her ham and enjoying herself tremendously. "It was like playing pinball. Every shot came right back at us. We had the whole course backed up."

There was twittering and laughter from the kids' end of the table.

"It was only ten people or so," Wilson said, "and we asked them if they wanted to play around us."

"Miniature golf is very different from real golf," Skiezer said. He began to explain but was interrupted by the sound of Cookie barking.

"That dog," Rema said. Standing, she folded her napkin on the table. "I'd better make sure he hasn't gotten at the ham bone. He's a genius at opening garbage cans."

"I'll go with you," Sylvia said. "It's just about time for dessert anyway. Anyone want some pie and coffee?"

There was a chorus of yeses. Sylvia followed Rema into the kitchen. She was calculating how many cups of coffee to make but stopped short as she saw Cookie. The dog was standing on his hind legs with his feet on the kitchen counter peering intently into Bluebonnet's cage. His nose was only inches away from the bars of the cage. Cookie woofed, and, as if shot by a gun, Bluebonnet dropped off his perch.

"No!" Rema yelled and jerked Cookie back by the collar. Sylvia raced over to the cage. Bluebonnet lay on his back with his stick-like legs clenched. He twitched once and then didn't move.

"Oh no!" Sylvia said. "I think he's dead."

"Hold on." Rema shoved Cookie out the back door and then rejoined Sylvia. Bending over Sylvia's shoulder, she studied the fallen bird. "Maybe he just fainted, and he'll come around in a few minutes."

Sylvia shook her head. "He's not moving. What are we going to do?"

"Don't panic," Rema said, but her eyes were wide. "Maybe we should poke him with something. See if he moves."

Looking around for something to prod the bird, Sylvia tried not to think about what would happen if Bluebonnet were actually dead. Tucker would be devastated—not to mention twenty-four other kindergartners.

She found a wooden spoon with a long handle and opened the wire cage door. She gently touched the prone parakeet. When Bluebonnet didn't move, she pressed the spoon against its chest in light, gentle pulses.

"What are you doing?"

"CPR," Sylvia said. "But it's not working, and it feels really gross." She definitely was throwing out this spoon afterward. "Rema, what are we going to do?"

"Press harder," Rema stated, leaning over Sylvia's shoulder. "That bird can't be dead. All Cookie did was bark at it."

Sylvia grimly kept doing the compressions with the wooden spoon. *Please, Bluebonnet, don't be dead,* she prayed. *Breathe.*

"Sylvia," Joe's voice startled her. Turning, she saw his bent frame standing in the doorway. "Is everything alright?"

Sylvia continued the CPR. "We don't know—Bluebonnet isn't moving."

Joe crossed the room to peer into the cage. "Holy smoke," he said. "That's one dead bird. What happened?"

"Cookie barked at him," Rema explained. "I think it gave the bird a heart attack." Her face creased with apology. "I'm so sorry, Syl."

"Sylvia, you can stop now," Joe said gently. "He's gone."

"He can't be gone," Sylvia said. "Mrs. Chin is going to kill me."

Joe pulled her arm. "Come on," he said gently. "Let him go."

Sylvia pressed the bird's chest one final time, and then stepped back. Sighing, she wiped her forehead with the sleeve of her shirt. She looked at the kitchen clock and thought, *Time of death: 2:11 p.m.*

"I'm so sorry," Rema repeated.

"It's okay. It wasn't your fault. We'll figure this out."

She was reaching for the cover to the bird's cage when the four boys ran into the kitchen. "Mom," Tucker said, "what's taking so long? We want pie!"

Joe stepped in front of the cage, blocking the view of the dead bird. "We'll be out in a minute, Tuck. All of you can go back to the dining room."

Immediately suspicious, Simon stepped forward and tried to see around Joe. "Why are you putting Bluebonnet's cover on his cage?"

"Because he's taking a nap," Rema answered for Sylvia. She was wearing a wide, and what Sylvia thought was an obviously fake, smile. "And we don't want to wake him."

Liam exchanged looks with his brother. "Can we look at him? I want to see if birds really sleep with their eyes open."

Sylvia couldn't bear the thought of the boys peeking into the cage and seeing the dead bird. "Later," she said. "Right now, we need to cut some big pieces of Aunt Rema's pie. Who wants to add whipped cream to the top?"

The distraction worked. The boys immediately went to the refrigerator and retrieved the can of whipped cream. As Rema cut the pie into generous pieces, the boys took turns shooting the whipped cream into their mouths and then onto the slices of pie. They didn't ask about the bird, and for this, Sylvia was grateful.

Returning to the dining room, Sylvia picked at her pie as the kids wolfed theirs down. She dreaded telling the boys about Bluebonnet. Neither of the boys had been old enough to understand when their grandparents had passed away, so this would be the first time they'd have to deal with death. She wondered how to tell them—and when. She didn't want to ruin their Easter. At the same time, she wasn't sure how long she could hold them off from peering into the cage.

She was still puzzling this when the boys finished dessert and asked to be excused. They ran upstairs, leaving the adults alone at the table. Pushing aside her unfinished dessert, Sylvia leaned forward. "Listen," she said quietly, although the boys were nowhere near enough to hear. "We have a situation."

Chapter 23

The men listened intently as Sylvia explained about the dead parakeet. When she was finished, Skiezer sighed in disgust. "I told Rema not to bring the dog today."

Although nothing changed in Rema's face, Sylvia sensed something inside her friend shrink. "Well it couldn't have been a very healthy bird if all it took was one little woof to kill it," Sylvia stated firmly. "It probably already had a bad heart. Maybe it was about to have a heart attack and Cookie was trying to warn us." She exchanged looks with Rema. "I've heard animals can do that. Sense death."

"We'll pay for another bird of course," Skiezer said. "But unfortunately you're still going to have to deal with telling the kids." He gave Rema a long, hard look. "I'm sure they're going to be very sad."

Rema squirmed visibly. "I'll go with you, Syl, and explain to Mrs. Chin what happened."

"And you should take that dog to obedience school. I've been asking you to do that for weeks." Skiezer turned to Wilson. "You wouldn't believe the hole he chewed in the Oriental rug my mother gave us."

"Maybe he wouldn't have chewed it," Rema said, "if it didn't smell so bad."

"What a minute," Joe said, leaning forward, his wrinkled face earnest. "Do you really have to tell anyone? Why not simply get another blue parakeet—one that looks like Bluebonnet?"

Sylvia sat up a little straighter. The idea had potential. But then Wilson said, "That's lying, Dad. We can't lie to the kids in Tucker's class."

"Are you kidding? We lie to kids all the time. We lie about Santa Claus, the Easter Bunny, the Tooth Fairy, and a lot of other things."

"This isn't the same," Wilson stated with firm conviction.

"Of course it is," Joe said. "The world is scary enough without having to deal with death so young." He kept his gaze level with Wilson's. "Do you really think Sam the Goldfish lived all those years?"

Wilson blinked slowly. "You lied about Sam?"

"You were a little kid. We didn't want you to be sad."

"Just how many Sams were there?"

"I don't remember."

Wilson shook his head. "I always wondered why Sam's color kept changing, but you said it was the drops you added to the water. I can't believe you lied to me, Dad."

"I protected you. Kids will have to deal with death eventually, but why traumatize them if you don't have to?"

"Because it's the right thing to do. What happened was an accident. Kids are tough. They'll deal with the truth a lot better than a cover-up."

"Not if it's a good cover-up," Joe argued. "But we need to move fast."

Wilson raked his hands through his hair and stared at his father as if he couldn't believe what he was hearing. "Dad," he said, "this isn't a goldfish. You're not going to find a bird that looks exactly like Bluebonnet. Even if you could, it wouldn't be right." He glanced at her. "Sylvia?"

She hesitated. "I don't know. Maybe Joe's right."

"You're siding with my father?"

"We need to think about Tucker. He's supposed to keep a journal. What's he supposed to do, write how Bluebonnet dropped like a rock when Cookie barked at him? You think that's going to go over well in story time?"

"I think you and Tucker should ask to speak privately with Mrs. Chin on Monday morning and explain what happened. She'll tell you how she thinks the situation should be handled."

There was a long pause at the table. Wilson's suggestion made sense, but Sylvia dreaded telling Tucker, and she especially dreaded telling his teacher. The last time Mrs. Chin had seen her, she saw her wrist bandaged, and Mrs. Chin had inferred that Sylvia needed therapy. Now she was going to have to admit they'd killed Bluebonnet over the Easter holiday.

Skiezer put his coffee cup down on the table and laced his large hands together. "What Joe says makes sense. One of the guys I golf with is an assistant manager at PetSmart. I say we give him a call, explain the situation, and see if he can help us."

"Excellent," Joe said. "If he has a match, we'll drive over and get it."

"Dad," Wilson said patiently, "I know you're trying to help, but you need to stay out of this."

"We're just finding out if it's an option," Joe said and gave Wilson a determined look. "So relax."

"If you feel strongly, I won't call," Skiezer said, steepling his large hands together. "But since we're replacing the bird anyway, we might as well find out if we can do it today."

"I think we should let him see if we can find another Bluebonnet," Sylvia said. "I'm kind of siding with Joe—I don't think it would be terrible if we swapped out the bird."

Wilson looked at her in disbelief. "Sylvia, we need to talk. In private."

Rema shot her a sympathetic look as Sylvia stood up. Joe squeezed her arm supportively as she moved past him. "Just whistle, honey, if you need me."

In the kitchen, he leaned against the counter and folded his arms. "Is this really how you want to handle this—lie to our children, the kindergarten glass, and Tucker's teacher?"

Sylvia shrugged. "Would it really be so bad to save a lot of kids some grief? And besides, what if everyone blames Tucker?"

"They won't," Wilson said firmly.

"You don't know that," Sylvia argued. "You have no idea what Tucker's world is like. You make these statements blindly. You go to the bank every morning. You don't understand how complicated the problem is or how hard it is to be a kindergartner these days. Kids can be mean, Wilson, and Tuck could get ostracized. This could affect his whole self-esteem."

"His self-esteem will be just fine."

She shifted her weight under his skeptical gaze. "Not everything is black and white, right or wrong."

Wilson folded his arms, and his face took on that awful blankness that it did whenever they argued and he was trying to hide that he was mad at her. "Trying to pass off another parakeet as Bluebonnet is just crazy," he said.

"Is it? How many years did you happily believe you owned the same goldfish?"

There was a long moment of silence. "A long time," Wilson admitted. The corner of his mouth softened. "And to be honest, it was a little traumatic finding out the way I did." He gave her a small smile. "Come on, Sylvia. You know Tucker is going to find out anyway. How will we look as parents then?"

Sylvia rested her hip against the side of the counter. "How about we compromise? We'll tell Tucker and Simon that we took Bluebonnet outdoors to clean his cage and the bird escaped. We'll say we saw him flying south—toward South America. The class could have fun making up stories about his adventures in Rio de Janeiro."

Wilson frowned. "Syl, I appreciate that you're trying to protect Simon and Tucker. But I can't get past the lying part. We need to deal with this head-on." He stepped closer to her and his face was kind and earnest. "They'll be better people because of this."

Sylvia still wasn't convinced. "If it were just our pet, I would agree. But Tucker has to face the whole class. Twenty-four faces are going to look at him like he's a murderer. Do you know how hard that's going to be?"

"They won't be looking at him," Wilson said. "They'll be looking at me because tomorrow morning, I'm going to school with you, and we'll talk to the teacher together."

Sylvia searched his eyes. "Seriously?"

"I have an eight o'clock meeting, but I'll go in a little late."

"And if Mrs. Chin says we can just tell the kids that Bluebonnet flew away, you'll do it?"

"We'll handle it however she wants. But we're telling our kids the truth."

She thought about it then nodded slowly. "Okay—but this might not be as easy as you think it's going to be."

He held her gaze. "Or as bad as you think."

Chapter 24

The next morning Wilson walked into the kindergarten classroom carrying the new parakeet in the cage. His head pounded from lack of sleep, and there was a snot stain on the lapel of his jacket where Tucker's nose had run during his last crying spell.

He hadn't gotten more than a few feet inside the classroom when a skinny, dark-haired boy with baggy shorts and T-shirt with a dinosaur on it spotted him and yelled with the enthusiasm of someone spotting a rock star, "Bluebonnet's here!"

Immediately Wilson was swarmed with kids who tried to lift the canvas cover and peer at the bird inside. He glanced at Sylvia, standing behind him and holding Tucker's hand. She motioned for him to keep going, but just before he did, he caught a glimpse of Tucker, whose face was as white as chalk. His son's blue eyes had the glassy expression of someone walking to his own execution, and he didn't return the smile of reassurance Wilson gave him.

Feeling like a giant, Wilson stepped around the kids and the miniature desks pushed into small clusters with their tiny chairs tucked beneath. The small sink in the corner looked as if he'd have to kneel if he wanted to wash his hands. He spotted Mrs. Chin at her desk in the back of the room and plowed forward with determination.

Their plan had been to get to school early and talk with Mrs. Chin before the other kids arrived, but then he'd seen Sylvia pull the minivan to the side of the road. He'd done the same with his Beemer, and then Tucker had had a long crying session.

It seemed like his younger son had been crying ever since he and Sylvia had broken the news about the bird. Tucker had cried through the funeral service—presided over by Wilson's father, who had read excerpts from Bluebonnet's journal.

That Tucker would spend the night in their bed hadn't surprised him, but Wilson hadn't expected Simon to walk into their room in the middle of the night, pale and shaken, because he'd thought he heard Bluebonnet pecking at his window to get inside. No amount of reassurance could convince him that it was only the wind and a branch.

Behind him, he heard Sylvia say, "Go hang your backpack up, Tuck. It'll be okay."

He turned in time to catch the stricken and slightly panicked look in Tuck's eyes. In that moment, Wilson fully forgave his father for lying all those years about Sam the Goldfish.

Mrs. Chin rose to her feet. "Good morning, Mr. Baxter," she said, and reached for the cage. "I see you brought back our little friend." Her gaze traveled past him. "And Mrs. Baxter—I'm so glad to see your wrist is all healed now."

About five feet tall, small boned, with bright brown eyes, Mrs. Chin seemed a little birdlike herself, and the comparison made Wilson dread his mission even more. "Could we please talk to you privately? Maybe in the hallway?"

"Of course," she said. "Why don't we put Bluebonnet's cage on the counter so you don't have to keep holding it? Besides," she added, smiling, "I know the kids are eager to see him again."

Wilson returned the teacher's smile although he felt himself start to sweat. "I think the bird needs to come with us," he said.

Mrs. Chin pursed her lips and cocked her head. "Oh. Well, we can talk in the hallway."

Once again, Wilson had to thread his way around the cluster of kids who blocked his path and reached for the cage. It crossed Wilson's mind that there was still time to try to pass off the bird without telling anyone, but he squared his shoulders and reminded himself that if he lied now,

Tucker would know it.

He waited for a quiet moment in the hallway, and then said, "I'm very sorry to tell you that there was an unfortunate accident at our house on Easter and Bluebonnet is gone."

"Gone?" Mrs. Chin repeated. "What do you mean, gone?"

Wilson glanced at Sylvia for support. "Gone," he repeated. "As in no longer with us."

There was a moment of silence. Mrs. Chin's silver eyebrows bunched together. "What are you talking about?"

"There was an unfortunate accident," Wilson repeated. "And Bluebonnet didn't make it."

"Didn't make it?"

"He's dead," Wilson said.

"What do you mean he's dead?"

"We think he had a heart attack," Sylvia said. She touched the teacher's thin arm. "We're so sorry."

"Oh." Mrs. Chin's mouth turned down. A look of reproach came into her brown eyes. "What happened?"

Wilson shifted his weight. Out of the corner of his eye, he could feel Sylvia looking at him. He quickly explained about the accident and finished by saying, "Of course we can't replace Bluebonnet, but we thought the kids would handle it better if they had a new friend to meet."

Mrs. Chin drew back the cover and looked at the bird inside. "Well," she said, letting the cover drop, "these things happen."

"We're very sorry," Sylvia said. "Tucker knows what happened, but we've asked him not to tell anyone until we talked to you—to see how you wanted to handle it."

Mrs. Chin took off her glasses, cleaned them on the side of her denim jumper, then replaced them. She looked very disappointed in him. "The class will have to be told of course."

"Yes," Wilson agreed. "But what?"

"That Bluebonnet flew away?" Sylvia suggested in a hopeful tone of voice.

Mrs. Chin shook her head. "I'd rather handle this head-on. It's a tragedy, but it's also a learning opportunity." She was silent a moment then said, "We'll have story time first thing this morning. I'll help you, but you need to answer their questions."

"I'll be glad to answer them," Wilson said, both relieved and impatient. He already was late to an important strategy session with Bruce.

Moments later, he stood with the leaves of a plastic palm tree tickling the back of his neck. Mrs. Chin sat next to him in a rocking chair with the class clustered at her feet. On the other side of the teacher, Sylvia's mouth had a tight, pinched look. Tucker looked like he might throw up.

"Class. . ." Mrs. Chin began.

Wilson found himself thinking of Sam and how much he'd loved that fish. Whenever he walked over to the glass bowl, the fish had recognized him and swam as close to him as the space would allow. Based on all the entries in Bluebonnet's journal, he knew the kids in this class had felt just as strongly about their class pet. He felt himself tearing up a little as Mrs. Chin told the class that Bluebonnet was dead.

He swallowed hard and braced himself as twenty-five sad faces stared at him. A few girls and one of the boys began to cry and were quickly whisked away by Sylvia and Mrs. Chin, leaving him with the rest of the class.

Wilson tugged at his necktie. He wasn't sure what to say, and the silence felt awkward, yet he was afraid of what would happen next. He especially avoided Tucker's eyes.

"Do you have any questions?" he managed. In the back of the room, Sylvia was hugging a girl who was sobbing.

"Did his eyes bleed?" a boy asked, and a roar of outrage rose from the rest of the class. Before Wilson could begin to think about answering it, another boy asked if Bluebonnet might have broken his neck in the fall off his perch. Another asked how he knew Bluebonnet really was dead, and not just in a coma, like a person he'd seen in an episode of *House*.

Another wanted to know if Bluebonnet's body was in the cage Wilson had brought with him—and if he could see it. This made another girl cry. The girl sitting cross-legged next to her began to stroke the crying girl's hair.

Had Cookie been punished for killing Bluebonnet? Why hadn't anyone in class been invited to the funeral; would there be another? Did Wilson believe in bird heaven? The questions came fast and furious, on top of each other. In a matter of moments he'd lost control. He looked for help, but Sylvia and Mrs. Chin were busy comforting other children.

Wilson's armpits grew damp. He'd faced difficult customers, gone head-to-head with peers, and even won some arguments with upper management, but in his entire career he'd never had an audience like this. Waving his arms, he tried to get everyone quiet long enough to answer their questions. "Raise your hands," he said calmly. "If you want me to answer your questions, you have to be quiet."

It wasn't easy, but he finally managed to get their attention. Quickly he explained how Grandpa Joe had read from Bluebonnet's journal at the funeral service and how it would be up to Mrs. Chin if there would be another. No, the dog hadn't been punished. And yes, Wilson believed that God took care of all the creatures He created in life as well as in death.

He was mentally and physically exhausted by the time they left the classroom. Walking back to their cars, he turned to Sylvia. "Dealing with kids is hard—whatever they pay Mrs. Chin, it isn't enough."

∽

"Morning, Wilson," Jen said, looking up from her cubicle as he walked past. "Mr. Maddox said to send you right in."

Wilson had hoped to grab a cup of coffee and take an Advil before he faced his boss, but the look in Jen's eyes told him that Bruce was in one of his moods, and the sooner he met with him, the better.

He tightened his grip on his computer bag, squared his shoulders, and told himself whatever Bruce wanted couldn't be as bad as what he'd just faced at the elementary school.

Inside Bruce Maddox's spacious corner office, his boss was standing in front of a dry-erase board, scribbling notes.

"Good morning," Wilson said.

Bruce kept writing. For a long moment he didn't even acknowledge his presence. Wilson remained standing. He wasn't often late, and he'd had good reason.

"Nice of you to join us," Bruce said, turning slowly. "We had an eight o'clock mandatory strategy meeting with the legal team. I needed you there."

"I'm sorry," Wilson said. "I hope you got my message that I had a family emergency."

Bruce leaned heavily on his cane as he crossed the space to his desk then eased himself into the leather chair. "Sit," he ordered, and when Wilson did, Bruce gave him an expression that was known to make junior employees spill their guts, and more senior ones squirm.

"Family emergency," Bruce prompted as Wilson neither blinked nor spoke. "Are Sylvia and the boys okay?"

"They're fine. The problem is under control now."

Wilson sensed the older man's curiosity, but his boss wasn't the kind of person who was going to be very sympathetic when Wilson explained that he'd skipped an important meeting because of a dead parakeet.

"What happened to your finger?" Bruce asked.

Wilson glanced at the gauze wrapped around his index finger and wondered how his boss would react if he told him that it'd happened when he'd introduced "Bluebell" to the class. Attempting to show how friendly the new bird was, he'd opened the cage door and offered it a treat. The bird had bitten him so hard on the finger that it'd bled. He'd had to use every ounce of self-control not to scream.

"It's nothing," he said. "Tell me about the meeting."

Bruce pushed a paper toward Wilson. "Why are you suggesting that we shut down our main server during business hours?"

For the next hour, Wilson explained about the upgrades to their existing system, which would improve their security as well as enable more functionality, especially online banking applications.

With the need to shut down the server also came an increased need for additional software funds, and although Wilson had already had this discussion with Bruce, he had to go over again the cost of the additional software licenses that would be needed.

It was almost noon by the time they'd gone over everything, and there was still one more thing on Wilson's agenda. "I met with Hovers almost two weeks ago. I thought our meeting went well, but I haven't heard anything. Have you gotten any feedback?"

"Yes," Bruce replied. "He had a few concerns."

Wilson's heart dropped to his shoes, but he managed to keep a straight face. "About what?"

"Your lack of management experience." Bruce laced his fingers together. "He's actually contemplating giving Ken Drivers another chance."

Ken Drivers? Wilson couldn't believe the board would even consider keeping the current branch manager.

"Hovers thinks it would promote stability and keep morale high if they keep him on." Bruce paused. "Plus there wouldn't be any moving expenses."

That was the bottom line—the cost of relocating Wilson and his family. Wilson thought for a moment. He wasn't about to argue anything that would threaten his ability to provide financially for Sylvia and the boys. "Drivers has also nearly driven that bank into the ground. What the board needs, Bruce, is someone new—someone with fresh ideas and an ability to drive profit."

"I totally agree," Bruce said. "However, McKensy's plan for turning around that bank is significantly less expensive than yours."

"Maybe short term," Wilson said, "but I guarantee my long-term outlook has more potential."

Bruce took a sip of coffee and shrugged. "Bottom line, you need more face time with these guys. You need to show them that you have people management as well as technical skills." He held his hand up as Wilson started to argue. "You don't need to convince me—but you need to convince them. And the more they get to know you—both socially and professionally—the better. I think you should invite them to your party next Saturday."

Invite the board? "With all respect," Wilson replied, "wouldn't it seem strange to invite a group of people to my anniversary party when I've never met most of them?"

Bruce waved his bony hand. "This is how it's done at this level, Wilson, and everyone understands. Frankly, they're looking for someone willing to make bold moves—someone who isn't afraid of bucking convention and going after what he wants. You think McKensy hasn't been entertaining them on the golf course and at the country club? You want this job? You're going to have to fight for it."

Wilson frowned. "You make a good point." He fought the urge to tug at his tie which had grown tighter by the minute. "I'll speak with Sylvia."

Bruce leaned back in the chair. "Tell her a formal event would be best. Hire a caterer—Jen will give you some names. No back-yard bar-beque for these people. They expect something catered and classy—something befitting a future branch manager."

"I see," Wilson said, allowing a small amount of sarcasm to slip into his voice. "I'll hire a string quartet and make sure they play only classical music."

"Excellent," Bruce said, not getting his joke at all. "In banking—like life—perception is everything."

Wilson started to argue that he should be getting this promotion based on merit, not on image, but then Jen buzzed and Bruce dismissed Wilson with a wave of his hand.

Back in his office, Wilson studied the picture of Sylvia smiling at him from a dark wood frame on his desk. She wasn't beautiful in the classic sense, but he found the smattering of freckles across her nose and cheekbones, the breadth of her smile, irresistible.

He felt bad about the morning—he hadn't realized, honestly, how traumatic telling the class about the bird would be for Tucker. And he hadn't anticipated that his boss would want to micromanage their anniversary party. She deserved better.

When all this was over, and the job was his, they'd do something really special to celebrate their anniversary. With a good bonus, he'd be in a position to give her something really nice.

Powering up his computer, he logged onto the Internet. He looked at a pair of diamond and pearl earrings, but when he tried to picture her wearing them, they seemed much too fancy.

A new car might be nice, but the minivan was in great shape, and besides, Sylvia really wasn't into cars. What would she like? She loved reading, but he couldn't very well give her a book for their anniversary.

He wanted something that would thrill her, make her realize how much he loved and appreciated her. Something romantic—that would make her think of him and not those guys on the covers of the romance books she read.

He wanted, literally, to take her breath away, and suddenly he knew exactly how to do it.

Chapter 25

On Tuesday night, Sylvia drove to Susan's house for what had become their weekly review of the Proverbs Plan. Susan lived across town, in a patio home off the back end of a golf course.

Cars already filled Susan's driveway when she arrived, so Sylvia parked on the street. She sat in the car for a moment. Her friends probably would think the whole mess-up with the anniversary dinner invitation was funny. And it was—but it was also ironic that the harder she tried to make something right, the more things seemed to go wrong. Like this possible relocation. She really needed to talk to them about it. At the same time she dreaded it.

Walking up the concrete pathway flanked with a variety of flowers and fragrant-smelling herbs—all planted and tended by Susan—Sylvia reminded herself that there would be positive things about moving. That dreading things was often worse than the actuality of them. That she should keep perspective. Plenty of people were struggling with far worse issues.

She didn't knock—Susan would lecture her if she did—and stepped inside a cozy foyer with soft, wheat-colored wall-to-wall carpet and walls the color of honey. Sylvia smelled something warm and chocolaty and resonated with the sound of laughter coming from the kitchen.

"Hello, dear," Susan said, meeting her in the foyer. She kissed Sylvia's cheek. "How are you?"

"Dying to try whatever smells so good," Sylvia said, stepping back with a smile.

"They're chocolate cupcakes with cream filling and caramel fudge icing," Susan said, leading her deeper into the house, where Rema, Andrea, and Kelly were standing around a brown granite island. "I'm baking them for the Meals Ministry at the church—but I made extra, for us."

"And they're great," Andrea said. She looked as if she'd come straight from the courthouse, in an immaculately tailored gray dress with a black belt and cute black cardigan with ruffles. Her high heels put her just shy of six feet, and with her edgy, short haircut, Sylvia imagined her winning every case based on her impeccable style.

She greeted Rema and Kelly, and for the next thirty minutes the women sipped peach iced tea, ate cupcakes, and caught each other up on their Easter holiday.

Kelly, unfortunately, had been on call and spent Easter Sunday in the operating room where she'd taken out a ten-year-old's appendix and then assisted on a surgery repairing a fourteen-year-old's spleen.

Susan and her husband, Dan, whose children were older, had spent their holiday volunteering at a local shelter. Andrea had both sides of the family over for Easter dinner—an event, she admitted, that would not have gone over very well without the help of several bottles of wine.

When Sylvia and Rema recounted their day, the other women whooped with laughter, especially when Sylvia described giving the bird CPR, Joe's solemn eulogy in the backyard, and the grilling Wilson had taken at the elementary school.

"I'm telling you, Wilson has a whole new appreciation for how hard it is to deal with kids," Sylvia concluded, setting her glass down on a coaster.

"So your father-in-law's here," Andrea said, pouring herself more tea and looking at Sylvia with concern. "He's staying with you for how long?"

Sylvia hesitated. The question was more complicated than Andrea realized. A lot depended on whether or not Wilson got promoted and they relocated—a conversation, she admitted, they were both tiptoe-ing around. "I don't know. He's pretty sweet though, so it isn't a big deal."

"It's going to be very hard to put the romance back in your marriage if he's there," Andrea said flatly. She fingered the long strand of pearls at her neck. "No matter how nice he is, he's still Wilson's father, and men tend to regress whenever their parents are around."

"That's so true," Rema agreed, sitting up a little straighter. "When Skiezer is around his parents, all he wants to do is please them. He practically forgets I'm alive—unless he wants me to do something for them. 'Can you take Mom to Walgreens? Can you drop off my dad's dry cleaning?' et cetera, et cetera." She dropped a crumpled wrapper into the garbage can. "But the good news is that when his family comes, he barbeques like a fiend and we eat like kings until they're gone."

This was true. Sylvia and her family had been invited to these feasts more than once and had seen the enormous platters of meat Skiezer grilled. Thanks to Skiezer's cookouts, the boys knew exactly what *carnivore* meant.

"I still think having your in-law around is going to put a damper on the Proverbs Plan," Andrea said. "Will he be gone by your anniversary?"

Sylvia stirred the contents of her glass. "No, but it isn't going to be a problem because there isn't going to be any romantic dinner by the pool."

"What?" Kelly frowned. "I thought you were going to talk about finances and then plan a romantic getaway weekend." She looked at Rema in confusion. "Did I miss something?"

Sylvia shook her head. "No. I messed up. Wilson's been trying to get me to use an electronic calendar, but when I tried to schedule the date on Outlook, I hit the wrong button on the computer," Sylvia said, "and a sent a request to everyone in Wilson's office."

Everyone laughed. "Couldn't Wilson just explain it?" Andrea asked. "And un-invite everyone? Ten years is a big anniversary. I'm sure every-one would understand."

"It's a long story," Sylvia said.

"Why don't we get comfortable?" Susan suggested, and steered them into the adjoining family room.

It was a small area, comfortably filled with a matching, overstuffed floral couch and love seat; two club chairs, slipcovered in a pastel pink color; and a plain pine coffee table. Family photos sat atop a plain white mantelpiece, and an older-looking bookcase held an assortment of knickknacks, books, and more photos.

The plump couch seemed to hug her as Sylvia settled into the cushions. She set her iced tea on a coaster and wondered where to begin.

"Before we start," Susan said, "I think we should pray." Everyone joined hands. Sylvia bowed her head and closed her eyes.

"Heavenly Father," Susan began, "You are good and holy and everything that is right in our lives. We praise You for Your infinite love and wisdom. As we gather here tonight, we ask that You be among us—to help us understand Your Word and enable us to help Sylvia, and also to help ourselves to have better marriages. We ask this in Jesus' name, amen."

Sylvia kept her eyes closed. She let the reminder of God's unconditional love ease her mind. How many times had her mother whispered as she kissed Sylvia good-night, *"God loves you, Sylvie, as I do."*

God has this, she thought, *so why am I worrying so much?* She opened her eyes and looked at the beautiful faces of her friends and suddenly knew exactly where to begin. The words came quickly, and it was a relief to let everything out.

"So after the anniversary, I mean business party," Sylvia concluded, "we'll probably start getting the house ready to put on the market. But you have to keep all this confidential. Wilson doesn't actually have the job."

"Well, maybe this other guy, McKenny, will get the job," Rema said.

"McKensy," Sylvia corrected gently.

"Wilson's a genius," Andrea said. "He'll get the job. I just wish you didn't have to move, Sylvia. We'll miss you so much."

"I'm not gone yet." Sylvia forced a cheerful note into her voice. "Maybe the board of directors will hate us. Wilson says that we need to put on a classy party—hire a caterer and serve pâté or something fancy." She shifted on the couch. "It doesn't sound like us at all, but Wilson really wants us to make a good impression."

Kelly regarded her with thoughtful green eyes. "In Atlanta, my parents used to do a lot of formal entertaining. I hate to see you go, Sylvia, but I'll help you with your party, if you want."

"I know you're super busy," Sylvia said. "I couldn't impose on you."

"It won't be hard," Kelly replied. "It's mostly getting organized and hiring the right people to do the actual work. Let me talk to my mom—I'm sure she can hook us up with a good caterer. Do you have a budget in mind?"

Sylvia shook her head. She and Wilson were doing pretty well, but it wasn't like they could afford an expensive party. "I haven't gotten that far yet. Wilson is still waiting to hear back from the board of directors before we get our final numbers."

"Why does Sylvia even need to hire a caterer?" Rema asked. "We're talking, what, fifty people at the most? We could help her—just like we were planning on doing when it was just she and Wilson."

"What a great idea," Susan exclaimed. "I could easily do the desserts and the flowers."

"Skiezer could do the meat." Rema looked at Sylvia. "I know Wilson said no barbeque but even great chefs like Bobby Flay use the grill. Everybody loves Skiezer's bourbon-glazed chicken and marinated filets. We'll put him in a chef's hat and no one will know that he's really an IT manager."

As Sylvia's mind raced with the possibilities, she heard Andrea add, "I don't cook, but I can make a great fruit punch. Non-alcoholic of course. You can borrow my crystal punch bowl."

Sylvia smiled. "Thanks, Andrea." One of Wilson's best friends in college had died as a result of drinking and driving. Although Wilson hadn't been at that party, even now, more than twenty years later, it still affected him. He never wanted to be responsible for putting someone on the road who might have had a little too much.

"You guys are so sweet to even consider helping me with this party," Sylvia began, "but I'd rather have you come to the party as my friends than as caterers."

"Don't you see, Sylvia," Rema began, "that as much as you've tried to be the Proverbs 31 wife, this is an opportunity for us to be the Proverbs 31 friends. This is our 'go' time. You're our sister, Sylvia. We love you. Let us do this."

Sylvia's throat filled as Rema's words were met with murmurs of agreement from the other women. "We can make it so much more personal," Susan added. "And we'd love to help."

"I'll get my mother's recipes for some appetizers," Kelly volunteered. "Plus I've got a lot of pretty Ironstone serving dishes you can borrow." She looked at Susan. "The pattern has navy blue, orange, and white. Can you make some floral arrangements with those colors?"

"Absolutely."

Andrea turned to a fresh page in her legal pad. "Okay," she said, as if everything had been agreed upon. "We'll make a list and divide up the work."

Chapter 26

It was a little after nine o'clock when Wilson got home. Unlocking the door, he stepped into the foyer. The minute his feet hit the hardwood, he filled his lungs with a deep breath of cool, clean, *home* air. Exhaling, he could almost feel himself shrugging off the last vapors of *bank* air.

The sound of china clinking caught his attention. He spotted Sylvia partially hidden behind the dining room table. She was sitting on the rug and pulling their good china out of the sideboard.

Placing his computer bag on the ground, he walked over to her and kissed her. "Hey honey, what are you doing?"

She looked up at him and smiled. "Inventory."

He glanced at the stacks of gold-and-white serving pieces on the floor beside her. They'd used these at Easter, and he couldn't imagine why she needed to count them now. "Why?"

Sylvia reached deeper into the sideboard and began pulling out white dishes edged with a floral design. They'd never used these plates, but he recognized them as ones they'd inherited from Sylvia's family.

"We're going to need a lot of china for the anniversary party," Sylvia explained. "Here, honey, would you start stacking these on the dining room table? I need to know how many place settings we have."

He set a stack of plates on the wood surface. "I don't think you're going to have enough of either pattern."

"I know," Sylvia said, handing him more plates. "We're going to mix and match."

He hesitated, because she had said this with conviction, as if she already had some kind of plan. "But honey," he said, "shouldn't all the plates be the same pattern?"

Sylvia handed him yet another stack of heavy china. "They don't have to match, Wilson. It'll give our party more charm if we mix the patterns. Kelly has some lovely Ironstone—her parents did a lot of formal entertaining in Atlanta. She's going to show me how to pull everything together. You'll see once we get the right linens."

Wilson shifted his weight. "That's nice, Sylvia, but I don't want this party to look like we've hit a tag sale and picked up a bunch of mismatched china pieces. Bankers like things that match."

Sylvia stopped pulling things out of the sideboard and looked up at him. In her favorite denim shorts and T-shirt from a vacation in Corpus Christi, she looked exactly like the girl he'd married ten years ago. Only that girl had looked a lot happier than the one sitting here now.

"Trust me, Wilson," she said, "this is going to work. You'll like the result."

He rubbed his temples wearily. All the stresses of the day—all the meetings he'd held, all the problems and deadlines and challenges he'd addressed—seemed to return to him like a hundred homing pigeons flapping their wings in his face and fighting for space on his shoulders. He wanted to shoo them all away, shoo this conversation away.

"I don't want this party to be a lot of work for you," he said, congratulating himself for coming up with a reason she couldn't possibly object to. "Seriously, Sylvia, you have my total support to hire a caterer. That way you can enjoy the evening more."

"Don't worry," she assured him. "Andrea, Kelly, Susan, and Rema are going to help me. Susan will do the floral arrangements, Andrea will handle the beverages, Kelly will lend us china. And Skiezer is going to grill for us."

It was the last part that broke him. With his boss's warning not to let this event turn into a backyard barbeque, Wilson felt his stomach knot. "Sylvia, this party. . .it has to be right. We need to make the right impression."

FOREVER *Yours*

"We'll make a great impression," Sylvia promised. "You look tired. Want some dinner?"

"No." He thought hard. "I think we're envisioning two different parties. I'm not talking hamburgers and hot dogs. We're entertaining some very high-level people. They're used to a certain standard."

Sylvia got to her feet slowly. Under the chandelier lights he saw the spark in her usually soft brown eyes. "What are you saying, Wilson, that our friends aren't good enough to help us throw a party?"

"Of course not," he said, backtracking rapidly. "I just think we should get professional help." When she didn't reply, he added, "I don't want it to look like we can't afford to hire a caterer and have to rely on our friends. It's an image thing, Sylvia."

"Is this how it's going to be from now on? How we look is more important than who we are? We have friends willing to help us. That's a blessing, not a liability."

He sighed. "I'm talking one evening, Sylvia. Would it be so hard to do it the way I want?"

She shook her head. "No, it wouldn't. But. . ."

"But what?"

She looked into his eyes. "You're changing, Wilson, getting swept up in work—in being someone else."

Wilson frowned. "That's just plain wrong. I'm not changing. I'm just asking for you to be conscious that my boss's bosses will be coming to our house. I'm not going to get another opportunity like this." He shook his head, increasingly convinced that he was right. "I really don't know why we're arguing about this."

"We're not. Not anymore." Shutting the door to the sideboard gently, she gave him an angry look. "I'll look into a caterer," she said. "But you are changing. You just don't see it." With her back ramrod straight, she left the room.

He'd won, but it gave him no pleasure. Wandering into the kitchen, Wilson pondered the contents of the refrigerator then closed the door. He really wasn't hungry. Maybe he had been a little too critical of Sylvia's plans, but she was definitely out of line saying that he was changing. It stung that she would think that, think the worst of him. All he wanted was to give them a better life and maybe help some other people along the way. Why couldn't she see that?

Still, he didn't like it when Sylvia was mad at him. Truthfully he didn't know a lot about parties and entertaining. He'd grown up solidly middle class, and the most formal it got was Christmas dinner.

Maybe there was a compromise. Sylvia and her friends could handle the party with the help of a caterer. He even had one in mind. Jen had given him the name that very afternoon.

He was about to head upstairs and tell her when his cell rang. The Caller ID told him it was Bruce, and he fought the urge to pitch the phone into the garbage. These late-night calls had to stop. He punched his boss's call over to voicemail. Whatever it was could wait. Yet when the phone rang for the second time, he found himself less annoyed and more concerned. Computers failed all the time, maybe the server had crashed with the new upgrades.

Holding the cell to his ear, he ignored the voice in his head that warned him these calls would only get worse if he became branch manager.

Chapter 27

A few days later, Sylvia knelt beside Joe at the edge of the kidney-shaped flowerbed in the front yard. Digging a hole into the packed earth with her trowel, she then reached behind her for a purple-and-white pansy from one of the flats she and Joe had bought earlier at Home Depot.

"Whenever Alice and I sold a house, we always planted seasonal flowers," Joe said. "People like flowers. It makes a house look happy."

"Our house is going to look very happy." Sylvia patted dirt around the new plant and moved a few inches to her right to dig another hole. She and Joe might have gone a little overboard—they'd stuffed the minivan with flats of pansies, baby's breath, orange poppies, and ornamental grass. They'd also bought brightly colored hibiscus plants for the backyard.

"Have you given any thought to house hunting?" Joe asked.

She glanced sideways at him, but his head was bent, making his profile unreadable. "Not really," she said. "We're thinking of just getting through this party." She stuck another plant in the ground. "What do you think of floating candles in the pool and hanging paper lanterns in the trees? Is that classy or tacky?"

"Classy," Joe instantly replied. "You know, if you want to go house hunting with Wilson, I'd be glad to mind the kids."

"Thanks, Joe, I appreciate that." She sat back on her heels. "You know that we're not saying anything to the kids about moving until we're sure we're really going, right?"

His face was as innocent as a monk's. "Oh sure," he said. "I just thought it might not hurt to look—that way when you're ready to pick a house, you'll already be familiar with the area."

It made sense, and Sylvia remembered her promise to Wilson to check out the new town. "That'd be great," she said, "but I really can't see that we'll have time before the party." She dug around a small root from one of the nearby oaks. "It might be a couple of weeks before we go."

"No problem," Joe said. "I've completely cleared my schedule—canceled my medical appointments and had my mail forwarded." He reached for another plant. "You know, I've been looking around the house, and I was sort of thinking that it could really use a new paint job. Potential buyers like neutral colors. I saw it on HGTV."

Sylvia stopped digging. She liked the granny smith green they'd painted in the kitchen and sunny yellow in the family room. Maybe the red was a little bright in the dining room, but it was cheerful.

"Thanks, Joe," she said. "But I think we'll just leave the paint for now."

"Then how about I get started on the closets? I couldn't help noticing they're really packed. I guess before we do that though, we should make some space in the attic. You've got a lot of boxes up there."

Sylvia sat back on her heels and dusted some of the dirt from her hands. The attic was jammed with stuff—she'd stored a lot of items that'd been in her parents' house that she couldn't bear to get rid of. And there were the boys' childhood things up there—boxes of artwork they'd done in preschool, old toys, their crib, and even that toy horse on springs.

"Thanks, Joe," she said at last, "but I kind of feel like I've got my hands full right now with this party."

"Then I'll definitely put caulking the bathtubs at the top of my list. You don't want to get a water leak."

"I appreciate you want to help, but you don't have to work all the time."

Joe took his time arranging a plant in the hole. "I know," he said. "But I like to feel useful. That's the worst thing about retirement, Sylvia, not feeling useful."

They worked in silence for a moment, and Sylvia thought about what he'd just said. "You still have a lot to give, but it doesn't have to be manual labor," she said. "You know that, right?"

"Oh sure," Joe said casually. "But it's best to stay busy." He stuck a plant in the ground and patted the soil around it. "So I was checking the stickers in your minivan the other day. You're due for an oil change. How about after lunch I take care of that for you?"

Sylvia noticed the shine of sweat and the color beginning to stain the top of Joe's bald head. She put down her trowel. "We'll see," she said, purposefully vague. "I could use a break. How about we go inside and have some iced tea?"

Joe stood up. He was a little wobbly so she steadied him with her arm. "Go slow," she said.

"It's the knees," he said. "They get stuck, but I'm fine now." But he patted her hand as if he liked it on his arm. "By the way," he said, "you have a few prescriptions in your medicine cabinet that have expired. You should throw them out."

Sylvia nearly stopped short. He'd been snooping! In her bathroom!

As if he read her mind, Joe smiled a little sheepishly. "I was looking for an aspirin," he said. "And you weren't around."

∽

After lunch, Sylvia left Joe relaxing on the couch and headed for the grocery store. She was planning on making stuffed chicken breasts and salad for dinner, but as soon as she turned toward the downtown area, her brain started craving something sweet. On impulse she pulled to the shoulder of the road, pulled out her cell, and dialed Rema.

"You feel like meeting at Spoons? I'm dying for some frozen yogurt."

"Give me ten minutes to put on my face," Rema said, "and I'm there."

Something in Sylvia seemed to lighten as she neared the quaint, downtown area. Although past the lunch hour, the sidewalks were busy with shoppers, and she had to circle the square a couple of times before she was able to find a spot. It was a short walk to Spoons, and the door jingled in a welcoming sort of way as she stepped into the air-conditioning.

Rema wasn't far behind and soon swished into the store. She was wearing a short, black skirt of a stretchy material and a tunic top clenched around her middle with a skinny black belt. As usual, her heels were high, her makeup flawless, and big gold hoops dangled from her ears. "I'm so glad you called," she said, greeting Sylvia with a hug. "I was just putting away the Easter decorations and thinking of you."

"I still need to do some of that," Sylvia said, wrinkling her nose. "But I really needed to get out of the house. I'm supposed to be grocery shopping, but I had this sudden craving for something yummy."

"Skip Krogers. You can always make spaghetti," Rema said.

"That's true," Sylvia agreed. Spaghetti was always her "go-to" meal and she always kept extra sauce in the freezer. She liked that Rema knew these things about her.

They walked over to the counter and paused in front of the array of toppings. Sylvia sighed at the tubs of gummy bears, Reese's Pieces, and M&M's. "I'm getting an extra-large," she said. "How about you?"

Rema laughed. "Oh please—as if you have to ask."

They picked up their bowls and headed for the long wall with the shiny silver handles holding back containers of various flavors of home-made frozen yogurt. After circling the choices several times, Sylvia settled for the white raspberry chocolate. Rema favored the peanut butter and fudge. After piling the toppings on high, they paid for their treats and took a seat at a small table for two near the front window.

"This is amazing," Sylvia said, as the frozen yogurt melted in her mouth. "I don't even care how many calories I'm eating or if it goes immediately to my hips."

"It's too bad we can't choose where the fat goes on our bodies," Rema mused and took a bite of her frozen yogurt.

"We'd all look like Barbies."

"And eat like pigs. Somewhere I hope some female scientist is working on this rearrange-your-fat pill."

Sylvia laughed. "It's supposed to be what we look like on the inside that's most important."

"In that case, we're fine." Rema scooped out a generous portion of her dessert. "We should go back for seconds."

"It is good, isn't it?" Sylvia agreed, spooning up just the right amount of Reese's Pieces on her next mouthful. "Can you imagine working here? I would eat them out of business."

Rema smiled. "Either that or you'd get so sick of it that you wouldn't go near it." She licked her spoon clean. "So you going to make me ask you what's bothering you?"

Sylvia looked up. "Why does something have to be bothering me for us to have a yogurt together?"

"Because you always crave something sweet whenever something upsets you. Now, is it something with the boys, Wilson, or Joe?"

Sylvia smoothed the top of her yogurt. Darn her friend for always being able to see right through her. But then, wasn't that why she'd called Rema in the first place? She took another bite of yogurt and swallowed it slowly.

"Tell me it's not that bird, Sylvia."

Sylvia shook her head. "No—that's working out okay." She toyed with the yogurt. "It's nothing big, but last night Wilson and I had a fight—we're hiring caterers now to help with the party—and then this morning. . ." She sighed. "Joe started talking about all the things that needed to be done before we put the house on the market, and then he told me that I had expired aspirin in my medicine cabinet—he said he was just looking for something for a headache, but—"

"He was snooping!"

"In the closets, the attic, and apparently all the bathroom medicine cabinets." She swallowed more yogurt before it turned any mushier. "It's hard to get mad at him though. He's so sweet—honestly I think he just wants to help so we won't make him leave."

"Snooping is not helping. It's meddling. How much longer is he staying?"

Sylvia hesitated. She was pretty sure Rema was about to give her a huge lecture when she told her Joe would be moving in with them. Although outwardly Rema got along well with Skiezer's parents, she also stressed out with each visit, getting frequent headaches and escaping to Sylvia's house as often as she could. "We haven't set a date."

"Maybe you should. Better yet, have Wilson talk to him about going."

Sylvia shook her head. "He doesn't want to go home. He's so lonely there. He wants to feel useful."

"Remember last time he stayed with you? How he pretended to get sick just so he could stay longer? This is a new strategy." Rema's lips tightened. "You'd better be careful or the next thing you know he's going to want to move in with you."

Sylvia kept her gaze on the green peanut M&M melting into the volcano she'd made in her dish.

"Good grief, Sylvia. Tell me you haven't already agreed to let him move in?" When Sylvia didn't reply, Rema leaned forward. "You and Wilson will *never* have any alone time if he does."

Would that be such a bad thing? Sylvia looked up. "You know, when we started the Proverbs Plan, that's what I thought I wanted—more of Wilson. I thought if he would just love me enough, it would make everything okay." Sylvia pushed a gummy worm around in the mush in her bowl. "Now I'm beginning to wonder if it would be enough. Maybe what I want is something that Wilson can't give me."

Rema's brow furrowed. "Sylvia, what are you talking about?"

"I'm not really sure," Sylvia admitted. "It's just. . .oh, I don't know. This whole move is making me look at my life a little differently." She swallowed a spoonful of melting yogurt but barely tasted it. "When we move—and even if we don't—maybe I should think about going back to work. The boys are in school full-time now, and they don't need me as much as they did when they were younger."

"If anything, I think they need you more," Rema stated firmly. "The issues they face get more complicated as they get older. Every time I talk to my sister she tells me how the classes not only get harder, but also there's always some mean kid or friend drama going on. And the whole issue of dating and drugs comes into play much earlier than you think."

"That's true," Sylvia agreed, "but even so, during the day, I can't help them. Right now I can still volunteer in the classroom, but I know that changes. Once the kids hit third or fourth grade, the teachers don't want moms in the classroom—Kelly and Andrea can vouch for that. All they want is someone to change out the bulletin boards in the hallways."

"You're on the PTO," Rema pointed out. "That's the most influential organization in the school." She pointed her spoon at Sylvia. "And that's a lot of kids, especially Simon and Tucker. Don't think your involvement doesn't factor when the school is assigning students to teachers."

Sylvia shook her head. "I don't think so," she said. "I mean, it isn't like I'm a bigwig. For Pete's sake, Rema, I go to classrooms dressed like a slice of pizza."

"And you raise money, Sylvia. Schools need money."

Deep inside Sylvia thought Rema made a good point. Mrs. Chin had been teacher of the year last year, and Simon's teacher, Mr. Powanka, had just received some kind of state award for a science project he'd done with his class. Had volunteering contributed to getting those assignments?

"Besides volunteering," Rema continued. "You're there when Simon and Tucker come home from school. You hear about their day and help with their homework."

Sylvia thought about this. That quick ride home in the minivan was an ideal time to get the boys to talk about their day. Somehow, being together, but not making eye contact, gave the boys the space they needed to open up to her. And although Simon needed no extra help from her with his homework, Tucker had to be monitored or else he'd get distracted and the assignment wouldn't get done.

"Other moms do it," Sylvia pointed out. "They have a job and they run the family and everything turns out fine."

Rema wiped her mouth with a napkin. "It can be done," she conceded. "But is that what you really want?"

Sylvia sighed. "I don't know anymore. It was boring working at the bank, but I liked the people." She'd taken maternity leave with the idea of going back after Simon had been born, but from the moment they'd placed him into her arms, she'd known that he needed her more than anybody in the world. Fortunately Wilson had punched some numbers and figured out a way for them to do it financially.

"We're a dying breed, aren't we?" Rema traced a manicured finger with bright pink polish along the top of the table. "Every day our numbers get fewer. Someday there'll be an exhibit at the museum, or the zoo, and a plaque that reads, 'STAY-AT-HOME MOM.'"

"I hope not," Sylvia said. "I mean, I respect working moms, but I'm glad I was able to be home with Simon and Tucker. It's just now—I'm in kind of a funny place. I don't want to just sit around and wait for the kids to come home from school, but I'm not sure if I'm hirable anymore; or if I am, what I'd do."

Rema fiddled with one of her hoop earrings. Her brown eyes were large and serious, and Sylvia could see that her friend knew exactly what she was talking about.

"First," Rema said, "you're not the kind of person who sits around. Think about all the work you do right now, watching the kids, chauffeuring, cooking, cleaning, et cetera, et cetera. If you worked full-time, who would do those things? Second, and most importantly, you'd miss a thousand moments with the boys that you'd never get back. Is that what you really want?"

"Of course not. I don't want to give up a moment with the boys. But now they're in school all day." She sighed. "Do you ever think about what happens when our kids get older and they don't need us to drive them to lessons or soccer games or their friend's houses? What are we supposed to do then? Everyone will have moved on, but we won't have."

Rema looked a little sad. "You don't know that," she said. "You're looking way too far into the future. For Pete's sake, Sylvia, Tucker is still in kindergarten. You have practically a lifetime with him and Simon. Why worry about this now?"

Sylvia spooned what was left of her semi-melted yogurt and then let it slide off her spoon. "Because if Wilson gets this job, everything is going to change."

Rema leaned forward. "Okay, sometimes I do think about the future. It's really scary, thinking about Skiezer retiring, being home full-time, and driving me crazy. But then I tell myself that when that time comes, something else will happen. Some other door will open. Raising a family is a good job, Sylvia, and will lead to other good things. I don't think God is going to put us out to pasture just because we focused on our kids."

"I know you're right, but I don't want to end up alone."

Both women looked up as the store door jingled and a woman with short white hair, crisp khaki slacks, and a pink sweater set walked into Spoons. She had deep, sad lines engraved in her face. Sylvia's gaze followed her to the front counter then to a table. Obviously she was alone.

The touch of Rema's hand on her arm made her jump. "Stop staring," she whispered. "She isn't you from the future."

Sylvia leaned forward. "How do you know that?"

"Because you and I are going to be little old ladies going out for frozen yogurt together and then complaining about our husbands who are either parked in front of the television or out golfing."

Sylvia sighed. "But what if I move?"

"Then we'll just have to drive farther for our ice cream. But Syl, does Wilson know how you feel about leaving?"

"Sort of," Sylvia said. "But I feel like his mind is made up. He feels like as long as our family is together then that's a home and it doesn't matter where we live."

"That's because he won't have to replicate his world. He'll go to work and come home. He won't have to deal with the million things that you'll have to figure out." She sighed. "Well, it isn't over yet, Sylvia, so don't lose hope."

Sylvia just looked at her.

"There's still the anniversary party," Rema said. "And one more chance for Wilson to see that he's got something here—something worth every bit as much as that promotion."

Chapter 28

On Saturday morning, Sylvia awoke to the smell of bacon. She blinked and looked at the clock. Eight o'clock. She hadn't slept that long in ages—why hadn't Tucker woken her up at six like he always did? She automatically glanced at Wilson's side of the bed. It was empty.

Suddenly the bedroom door cracked open, and Tucker's small face peeked around the corner. "She's awake, Dad," he whispered.

Moments later, the door swung fully open. Three Baxter males with beaming faces carried a huge tray of food into the room. She looked from Tucker to Simon to Wilson, speechless. What was going on?

"What day is today?" Wilson sang the question in a hearty baritone.

"Today is Mommy Day!" The boys sang in a much higher pitch than their father.

Sylvia sat up in bed. "Wilson, this isn't Mother's Day."

Wilson helped the boys lower the tray onto her lap. "I know, this is Mommy Day, a new holiday."

"We made you your favorite breakfast," Tucker exclaimed.

Sylvia glanced down. The tray held a huge plate of scrambled eggs and bacon. There also was a mug of coffee, orange juice, an apple, half a banana, a container of vanilla yogurt, two slices of toast, a bowl of cereal, and a doughnut. It was enough for several Sylvias, and she looked up a little suspiciously.

"You guys," Sylvia began, "what's going on?"

Wilson sank onto the edge of the bed and kissed her forehead. "We're giving you the day off—so think of something you really want to do and go do it!"

Simon bounced onto the bed. Sylvia barely lifted the coffee cup in time before it sloshed into the cereal. She couldn't save the eggs, however, from a splash of orange juice.

"I helped make the eggs," Simon informed her with a huge grin. Climbing over the hills of her legs, he finally reached the top of the bed and kissed her head. She smelled the other half of the banana on his breath.

"I made the cereal," Tucker declared.

"You can't 'make' the cereal," Simon pointed out.

"Well I poured it," Tucker said proudly.

"And you did a great job," Sylvia said. She kissed the top of each boy's head and breathed in their shampoo and little-boy smell. Was there ever a scent so pleasing to the heart?

"We all helped with the bacon," Wilson added. "It's crispy, just the way you like it."

"I still don't understand." Sylvia looked at Wilson. "This is great, but what's going on?"

Wilson's face didn't flinch under her direct gaze. "You've been doing way too much for everyone else. Today, you're supposed to relax completely. The boys and I are getting haircuts and then running some errands. We'll be home around four o'clock."

"But Wilson," Sylvia protested, "we have a lot of work to do around the house to get ready for the party."

"You can make me a list and I'll make sure everything gets done. It's time you had a day off. Boys, kiss your mommy good-bye."

"But where are you going?" Sylvia wished the tray wasn't holding her captive in the bed. "I'll go with you."

"Dad and I have this. The only thing I want you to do today is relax. Go shopping, or get a massage."

"But Wilson," Sylvia protested, "I don't need to do that." Since when was he suggesting massages? "I'll go with you and we'll run by the caterers. I want to show you the linens I picked out..."

Plus they'd hardly seen each other all week. Didn't he want to spend time with her?

Wilson shook his head. "You need a day off—we'll see you later."

"I love you, Mom." Tucker leaned forward to kiss her. "Can I have a piece of bacon?"

"You've already had enough." Wilson pulled the slice from the boy's hand and replaced it on Sylvia's plate. "I'll have my cell turned on if you need me."

"Simon?" Wilson prompted.

"Bye, Mom, love you."

Before Sylvia could utter another word, they ran out the door. For a moment she sat regarding her breakfast and listening to the absolute silence in the house. They really were gone, she decided, which was totally unlike Wilson. The more she thought about it, there had been something funny in his eyes when he'd looked at her—maybe he was happy to have time off from her. The boys to himself.

She picked up her fork and poked at the scrambled eggs. Unless he could grill it, Wilson wasn't very good in the kitchen, which meant that Joe probably had made the eggs.

She nibbled a bite of Cap'n Crunch cereal—Tucker's favorite. She imagined his small hands pouring the cereal and then eating the pieces he spilled.

Wilson and the boys had brought her breakfast in bed before, mostly on her birthday or on Mother's Day, but on those occasions, they'd sat on the bed and kept her company as she ate. Although she knew she should appreciate having a day off, she couldn't help but feel a little abandoned, and a little hurt that Wilson had so casually dismissed her offer to accompany them.

She pushed the tray aside and climbed out of bed. She had a million things that needed to be done before next Saturday's big party. The new flowers in front needed watering, and there were additional plants for the containers around the back deck. The outdoor furniture needed scrubbing and its cushions washed. Plus she really should go up in the attic and look for an additional punch bowl. There was menu stuff to go over, more shopping lists, and she really needed to swing by and pick up the Ironstone dishes from Kelly.

All these things, and more, needed to be done, but as Sylvia carried her tray of food back into the kitchen she found herself puttering around the room, half-heartedly clearing and cleaning while all the time wondering what Wilson, Joe, and the boys were doing.

∞

"Frank's Dry Cleaners, Exxon, Sterling Optical," Joe read aloud. "Walgreens, Wilkerson Animal Clinic, Krogers."

Wilson tightened his grip on the steering wheel. Did his dad really have to read every store sign in sight?

"Panda Express, Exxon, CVS."

"Dad, I'm hungry," Tucker announced.

"You just ate breakfast," Wilson replied.

"Well, I'm hungry again. Can we get something to eat?"

"Sam's, PetSmart, Old Navy. . ."

"Dad." Wilson silenced his father with a quick sideways look. Thankfully Joe stopped reading aloud.

"There's the barbershop," Simon yelled from the backseat. "You just passed it!"

"Hang a U-ey," Tucker advised from the backseat. "But look for cops first."

Joe burst out laughing. "Where'd you hear that from?"

"Aunt Rema," Simon replied. "Once she and Mom made a U-turn and a cop was right there."

"And Aunt Rema said, 'Holy shooting match,'" Tucker exclaimed loudly.

"Tucker James Baxter! Watch what you say!" Wilson ordered, casting a dark glance at his father who was not even trying to hide his grin.

"Why aren't you turning around, Dad?" Simon asked. "We just passed the barbershop."

"We'll hit the barber on the way home," Wilson said. He would get the boys haircuts, but that had just been a cover story.

"So what happened when the cops pulled you over?" Joe asked.

"Oh, Aunt Rema explained we were on our way to the hospital to visit her sick aunt, so the cop let us go."

Wilson shook his head. He didn't approve of the lying, but it was a funny story. He exchanged grins with his father. "They're like Thelma and Louise."

"Who are Thelma and Louise?" Simon asked.

"It's a pop-culture reference," Wilson explained. "Maybe someday you'll see the movie."

They drove farther down Old Elm Street. "Where are we going?" Simon asked.

"You'll see. We're working on a surprise for your mother."

"What surprise?"

"For our anniversary." Wilson glanced at him in the rearview mirror. "So everything we do today is top secret, okay?"

"Right!" The boys yelled in unison.

Wilson turned to his father. "You're up for babysitting, right?"

"Absolutely," his dad agreed.

"Why can't we come on the trip?" Simon asked.

Wilson nearly laughed. "How do you know we're going on a trip?"

"Because Poppy wouldn't have to babysit us if you weren't going somewhere."

"It could be just for a few hours." Wilson enjoyed challenging Simon's mind.

Simon was silent a moment. "If it were only for a few hours, it wouldn't be this big secret."

"You're right," Wilson said. "But that's all I'm going to tell you for now."

Something small and hard pushed into the small of Wilson's back. "Tucker, are those your feet on the back of my seat?"

The boy giggled. "Yeah."

The pressure on his back increased. "Quit it!"

Tucker's restless feet drummed against the back of Wilson's seat again. "I'm really *hungry*."

"Then you should have eaten more breakfast," Wilson said calmly. "And quit kicking the seat." Maybe it was nothing more than the power of suggestion, but suddenly Wilson's stomach began to rumble as well.

"Mason Street, Crossway Boulevard, Tannager."

"Dad," Wilson said a little impatiently, "I thought you were going to stop that."

"I'm not reading the names of stores anymore," Joe replied a little smugly. "These are street signs."

Wilson released his breath slowly. A quick check of his watch informed him he'd been on the road less than fifteen minutes. How was he going to make it all day?

His father's watch beeped. Great. Now he'd have to find someplace to stop so his dad could take his pills. Dad always insisted on taking them with orange juice and a few crackers or cookies. However, his dad merely pressed a small button on his watch to turn off the noise and said nothing.

After a moment, Wilson couldn't stand it anymore. If his dad really needed to take a vitamin or something, maybe he should say something. "Do we need to stop, Dad?"

"Not unless you want to."

"But what about your pills?"

"Oh, I'll take it later," Joe said. "Don't worry about me."

Wilson shot him a quick look to assess the validity of this statement. All he saw was the side of his father's head. The rest of his face was turned in the direction of a cluster of store signs.

"But if you need it. . ." Wilson prompted.

"I'll be fine," Joe said. "That looks like a new office building over there. Do you know what's going in it?"

"No," Wilson said. "You can't just skip taking pills, Dad. It isn't good for you."

"It was just a vitamin, Wilson, so you can relax."

Wilson wondered if his father was telling the truth or just trying not to cause trouble for him. His dad was in pretty good health, but Wilson knew he took medicine for arthritis and a thyroid condition. There might be others, too.

Ahead, the ubiquitous sight of golden arches caught his attention. "McDonald's," Wilson read aloud, sounding, he knew, exactly like his father.

"McDonald's!" three voices shouted in unison.

Without an argument, Wilson put on his blinker, and a cheer went up from the backseat. He smiled. A quick snack wouldn't hurt.

"I want a Happy Meal," Tucker yelled. "A Chicken Nugget Happy Meal."

"It's too early," Simon informed him with the air of an older brother happily imparting superior knowledge. "They're still on breakfast."

"Billions and billions served," Joe read.

"Hot cakes then," Tucker announced. "A Hot Cake Happy Meal."

Wilson pulled into the drive-through and studied the menu. A cup of coffee sounded good, hash browns, because he loved them, and a sausage biscuit because as long as he was here, he might as well.

While he waited his turn, he thought about Sylvia and hoped she was enjoying her day off. Valiantly he tried to ignore the argument in the backseat, which seemed to revolve around the existence of a Hot Cake Happy Meal. Finally, it was his turn to order.

A garbled noise came out of the order box. When it stopped, Wilson gave his order and then turned to his father. "Okay, Dad," he said, "what do you want?"

"Bacon, but ask if they have turkey bacon," his father said, "and an English muffin, but only if it's whole wheat, and butter on the side. Make sure it isn't margarine. Orange juice, with pulp if possible, and oh, and I guess I'll have one of those apple cinnamon Danishes."

Wilson dutifully repeated the instructions, wondering if his voice sounded as garbled to the operator as hers did to him. He then placed Simon's order for an Egg McMuffin meal with apple juice, and then last, but not least, he remembered Tucker's order. "And we'll have an order of flapjacks with butter and syrup. Orange juice, too." As soon as he finished, a chorus of laughter erupted from the backseat.

"What?" Wilson looked over his shoulder. "What's so funny?"

"Flapjacks," Tucker repeated, laughing.

"They're not *flapjacks*," Simon informed him in a voice that struggled to be serious. "They're ho. . ." He tried manfully to control a laugh as Tucker hooted wildly. "Hot cakes."

"Whatever they are, you're going to be wearing them in a minute if you don't stop laughing," Wilson told them. He couldn't believe that something as simple as calling pancakes flapjacks could be so funny.

He pulled up to the cashier's window. A young lady who looked about twelve years old despite the nose piercing and heavy black mascara took his money and handed them their drinks.

"Here's your food," she said for the first time in an audible voice. "Enjoy those *flapjacks*, sir."

Simon and Tucker squealed with such delight that Wilson couldn't help but join in. Handing his father the large paper bag with their food, he swung out of the parking lot.

With a cup of hot coffee in the cup holder and the smell of a sausage biscuit wafting through the air, Wilson felt his spirits improve. He listened to the contented silence of three Baxters eating, and smiled. Hopefully there would be no more feet pummeling his back or recitation of road signs.

Sylvia's minivan purred along under him, not quite as sweetly as his Beemer, but with more than adequate acceleration and handling.

He adjusted the air-conditioning. At nine o'clock, already the temperature had reached the eighties. It'd probably go as high as ninety, and as he turned to comment on this to his father, he realized that they were about to miss the street he wanted.

Making the split-second decision, Wilson turned hard. To its credit, the van leaned into the turn. As it hugged the road, the boys shouted, "Oooooh!" and then, "Aaaahhh!"

"Sorry about that," Wilson apologized as the road straightened. He shot his father a quick look of assessment. "I didn't mean to take that corner so fast."

His dad had his cup of orange juice raised high in the air as if he were making a toast at a dinner party. Some of it had dribbled down his arm. "Are you crazy?"

As Wilson tried to come up with a reasonable explanation, his father added, "That was *great*!"

A chorus of cheers erupted from the backseat. "Yeah, Dad, that was so cool," Tucker shouted. "Can we do it again?"

"No, son," Wilson replied, knowing beyond a doubt that if Sylvia heard he'd nearly put the van on two tires, she'd kill him.

"Can we go back to McDonald's then?" Tucker asked.

"We were just there," Wilson pointed out.

"But I need more maple syrup," the five-year-old explained.

"You have plenty."

"*Had* plenty," Simon corrected with a note of unmistakable glee in his voice.

"Too much sugar is bad for you." Wilson reached for his package of hash browns. They were a little soggy from spilled coffee. "Right, Dad?"

There was a long pause, then his father laughed.

"Dad?" Wilson had a very bad feeling. A quick glance revealed his father looking over his shoulder into the backseat.

"You might want to pull over, son."

Wilson let his breath out very slowly. He knew he didn't want to know why he needed to stop the car.

Unable to contain himself a second longer, his oldest son yelled out, "Tucker's wearing his *flapjacks*, and there's maple syrup all over the backseat."

Wilson groaned.

"Mom's going to kill you," Tucker cried out happily. "She never lets us eat sticky stuff in the car."

Wilson clenched his jaw and assimilated this new information. Things weren't going as planned, but he was a man on a mission, and this mission had to be completed in a matter of hours. He couldn't let himself get discouraged by this minor setback, not when so much needed to be accomplished. Just ahead he spotted the solution and put on his blinker.

"Where are we going?" Simon asked.

"The car wash," Wilson replied.

"Are we washing the car?" Simon asked.

"Yes," Wilson agreed, "but that's not all."

Chapter 29

$\mathcal{S}$ylvia spent the morning working on the pool. She emptied the strainer baskets then got into the water to scrub down the tiles and the volcano rock on the waterfall. As she worked, she knew Wilson would be mad at her—she was supposed to be taking the day off—but it seemed a waste of time to pamper herself when so much needed to be done.

At lunchtime, she made herself a peanut butter and jelly sandwich and ate it at the kitchen table, all the while trying not to imagine four Baxter men all having a great time without her.

Just get busy, she ordered herself. She did a quick vacuum, threw in another load of laundry—did it ever end?—and then looked around her somewhat clean house for something else to do. She read one of her romances until it was time to put the clothes in the dryer, but was too restless to go back to her book. She thought about what else needed to be done, and although she disliked the answer that came to her, she headed upstairs and opened the door to the storage room just off Wilson's office.

It was a room the real estate agent had told them could be converted into another bedroom if they wanted, but she and Wilson had always used it for storage. Now, looking at the piles of stuff, she realized Joe was right. They had accumulated way too much.

She'd seen enough HGTV to know the ropes—things needed to be sorted into three piles: keep, donate, and throw out. It would be a big job—but today was perfect to get started. Without the boys or Wilson home, she could sort through things at her own pace, be sentimental—even cry without anyone knowing.

Promising herself chocolate as a reward, Sylvia got started. A few hours later, she'd made some good progress—paring down the Tupperware containers of the boys' school- and artwork, donating some miscellaneous kitchen items and framed posters that she and Wilson had bought for their first apartment. She only cried once, and that was when she read Simon's handwriting in preschool. He'd filled in a blank that said, "*My mother's name is. . .*" and he'd written, "*Sillveeah.*"

The boys' baby clothes were harder to give up, but Sylvia set them in the pile for the Salvation Army and traveled deeper into the room.

She ignored her mother's sewing machine and did not make eye contact with the rocker where she had spent many hours nursing the boys. Instead, she headed for some boxes that had been shipped to them from her parents' house in Ohio.

Peeling back the shipping tape, she opened a box filled with old photograph albums. Unable to resist, she took an old black one with a broken spine to the gliding rocker and settled herself on the upholstered cushions. On the first page was an old black-and-white photo of her mother grinning from her seat on a tricycle with streamers flowing from the handlebars.

Sylvia smiled at her mom's full head of dark curls, dimples, and mouth like a pink rosebud. Flipping through the pages, she traced her mother's growth—school pictures, then dance recitals, her first communion.

When she finished the album, she opened another and then another until she came to the page and the image she remembered of her mother—taken on her forty-eighth birthday, surrounded by her family and beaming at the camera. Sylvia had taken the shot just as her Uncle Calvin had threatened to moon everyone if they didn't smile like they meant it.

Sudden tears sprang to her eyes. *How did you do it, Mom? Be such a good wife and mother? You really were the Proverbs 31 woman. You made everything seem so easy.*

"*Are you kidding?*" The smiling woman in the photo seemed to say. "*It wasn't always easy, and I certainly wasn't the Proverbs 31 wife. But I was happy, Sylvia. I had a happy life.*"

Sylvia closed the photo album. What was she doing, making up conversations with her mother? It wasn't like her mom was going to be able to help her understand what pieces of her life to hang on to and which to let go. And she didn't just mean the contents of the attic.

The quiet of the house rang in her ears, and Sylvia realized that she could either keep making up things her mother might have said to her or reach out to God. She shut her eyes, and just as she said, "Dear Lord Jesus," a door slammed, and Tucker's little-boy voice wafted into the room, "Mommy-Mommy, we're home!"

Stepping around her piles, Sylvia headed out of the room. As soon as she made it down the stairs, both boys saw her and raced into her arms.

Kissing the tops of their satiny, newly-sheared heads, Sylvia felt her heart literally expanding in her chest. "I missed you guys."

Wilson leaned over the boys to kiss the top of her head. "We missed you, too. Did you have a good day?"

"Yes," Sylvia replied. "How about you?"

Wilson nodded, but didn't quite look her in the eye. "Absolutely."

"Simon broke a glass at the flower shop," Tucker announced.

Sylvia searched Wilson's face. "Flower shop? What were you doing at the florist?"

"Tucker, it was a vase, and you weren't supposed to tell." Simon frowned fiercely at his younger brother. "After what *you* did, I wouldn't talk if I were you."

"What did you do, Tucker?" Sylvia frowned. "You smell like maple syrup." She glanced around. "And where's Joe?" Her gaze found her husband. "Wilson?"

Wilson's face froze over the way it always did when he was trying to keep something from her. "Dad's cleaning out your glove compartment for you—he says there's a bunch of expired inspection papers and insurance cards."

Sylvia relaxed slightly, but something about the look on all their faces told her they were holding something back. "You all okay?"

"We're fine. Just *fine*," Wilson said, so heartedly that Sylvia's antennas went up even higher.

"Something about the car you're not telling me?"

"Nope," Wilson said as the boys giggled.

"You got a speeding ticket?"

The boys broke out into peals of laughter even as Wilson gave her a funny look and said, "Of course not."

"Then what?" Sylvia studied all their faces. "You all look like you're bursting with a secret to tell me."

Tucker squirmed visibly; Simon's eyes blinked in a series of rapid-fire movements. "Spill it," she demanded.

"Dad hosed me off at the car wash."

"Just a little," Wilson said. "To get it off his shirt."

"He spilled maple syrup all over the backseat," Simon announced.

"It wasn't that bad," Wilson said. "We got most of it out."

"What about the glass at the flower shop?"

Wilson shifted. "Okay," he admitted, "we stopped off to order flowers, and Simon did knock over a vase by accident, but it wasn't a big deal."

"But Susan is handling the floral arrangements," Sylvia said. "I told you that."

Wilson shrugged. "The more flowers, the better."

"But what if they don't go together?"

"It'll all be fine, Sylvia. Don't worry. So what did you do while we were gone?"

"But we have a color scheme going," Sylvia said, refusing to change the subject. "You haven't seen the linens yet."

"Dad got all colors," Tucker said, and was immediately given a stern look by his father.

"It'll be fine." Wilson headed for the kitchen. "I'm really thirsty. Boys, do you want a glass of water?"

Sylvia trailed after him. "Don't you trust Susan to do a good job with the floral arrangements?"

"Of course I do," Wilson said. "Let's talk about your day. Did you go get a massage?"

"No," she said. "What else did you do while you were out? And why does Tucker smell like maple syrup?"

"Well," Wilson said, "we went to McDonald's for a snack and some syrup spilled on him."

Simon giggled. Sylvia looked at the color on his normally pale face and the sparkle in his eyes. Whatever had happened, he was highly amused. She was dying to know what it was. "So did you go anywhere else besides the car wash, the barber, and the florist?"

"We went to the mall!" Tucker cried out happily. "But I'm not supposed to tell you what we bought."

Tucker had a hard time keeping secrets and with the right prompting could probably be coaxed into telling her everything. Sylvia smiled warmly at him. "Did Daddy buy something nice for Mommy?"

Tucker looked at his father, and a big guilty smile formed on his face. "We went to the secret store," he admitted.

Sylvia looked at Wilson and felt a small thrill of excitement. He'd bought her something? "Secret store?"

"Oh, Dad saw some fancy shaving cream in the window of that beauty shop." He looked at Simon. "What's it called?"

"Trade Secrets," Simon said, straight-faced. "He bought aftershave."

"Oh," Sylvia said.

Joe walked into the kitchen. He was carrying a small shopping bag from Trade Secret that confirmed Wilson's explanation. "Hello, sweetheart," he said and gave her a kiss. "Your tires might need rotating. I don't think they did it at your last service. At least it wasn't on any of the invoices in your glove compartment."

"Thanks, Joe."

"Mom, I'm hungry," Tucker said. "Can I have a snack?"

Sylvia glanced at her watch and was surprised to see it was so late. She hadn't even thought about what to make for dinner.

"How about I spring for pizza?" Joe suggested.

The boys cheered and began to jump up and down chanting, "Pizza! Pizza!"

"You want to go with Poppy and we'll stop for a movie on the way?"

"I'll go with you, Dad," Wilson offered.

"The boys can tell me how to get there," Joe said. "You go finish up that work you were telling me about so you can watch the movie with us."

Wilson nodded. "Thanks, Dad." He bent to kiss the smooth, warm top of his father's head. "Drive carefully."

Alone in the house with Wilson, Sylvia realized it felt a little awkward. She couldn't remember the last time when it'd been just the two of them, no boys hovering around. She ran her hand through her hair and suddenly wasn't sure what to say to him at all.

He swallowed the remainder of his water and set the glass on the counter. "Well," he said at last. "Dad's right—there are a couple of things I should probably get done before dinner." He turned to leave.

"Wilson?"

"Yeah?"

She searched his face. *We're alone,* she wanted to say, *no kids. We could talk or have some private time.* She opened her mouth but hesitated. Wilson was standing in the doorway, and there was something closed off in his face. It reminded her of the expression and posture a doctor might use to nonverbally communicate the appointment was over. In his mind, she suspected, he'd already gone back to work. She felt disappointment, fear, and then acceptance pass through her.

"Nothing," she said.

∽

Wilson closed his office door then sank wearily into his desk chair. Pushing the skin on his face hard, he sighed in relief. If he'd stayed in the kitchen with Sylvia one second longer, he'd have started spilling the beans. He was as bad as Tucker, who had blurted out the whole secret store thing. Fortunately the whole story about Trade Secrets had been believable—a plot conceived by his father who had suspected someone might crack under Sylvia's questioning. His father's aptitude for deception was becoming alarming, but Wilson had to admit it'd come in handy.

Firing up his PC, he wondered if he was going to be able to hold out for the whole week. Keeping a secret from Sylvia was torture, particularly when he knew she'd be thrilled with his gift. There were still a few things he had to pull together, but he was pleased with the progress he'd made so far.

As his computer began to synchronize, he caught glimpses of the e-mails downloading. There were a lot from Bruce, and most of them marked "urgent." He saw another few RSVPs from board members. Bruce had been right, most of them had accepted his invitation. That was a good sign. A very good sign.

He was about to open a new window and go on the Internet when he glimpsed an e-mail from Peggy Armstrong, a real estate agent he had met once briefly. They'd discussed the kind of house he might be looking for in the future.

When all the mail was downloaded, he opened the real estate agent's note first.

Dear Mr. Baxter,

I enjoyed meeting with you last week and discussing your possible relocation. Since our conversation, a house has come on the market which sounds perfect for you and your family. For your convenience, I have attached photos and the listing information. As we discussed, the housing market here is strong and houses like this one don't last long on the market. If you are interested, I would suggest that you look at it this week. This is probably ahead of your schedule, but as I stated, I felt this house was particularly suited to your needs. Please let me know as soon as possible if you are interested and I will set up a showing.

All Best,
Peggy Armstrong

Wilson clicked on the attachment. When a large redbrick colonial filled the screen, he stared at it for a long time, analyzing every inch of it, and then he went to find Sylvia.

Chapter 30

So you really don't mind watching the boys?"

It was Monday morning, and Sylvia had just called Rema, half hoping that her friend would turn her down and she wouldn't have to go out-of-town house hunting with Wilson and Joe.

"Let me see," Rema said, and Sylvia could almost picture her smiling, playing with one of the dangly earrings she preferred and pretending she had to think about it. "Of course not. My kids will be thrilled."

Sylvia pushed her hair back from her face. "Thanks," she said, and the two women quickly coordinated schedules and arrangements. "We're going to tell the boys that we're going to see where Daddy goes when he travels," Sylvia added. "Simon will be suspicious, but mostly he'll be excited at being able to hang out with Liam."

"Got it." Rema was silent for a moment. "Things are going to start happening fast, aren't they?"

"Wilson thinks they need to make a decision soon. He's got a couple more interviews this week."

"And your anniversary party is on Saturday. Speaking of which, what are you going to wear?"

Sylvia shifted her weight. "I hadn't really thought about it. Maybe that sleeveless black cocktail dress."

"That's cute," Rema said. "But something new is always perky. Macy's is having one of those take-an-extra-twenty-percent-off sales. Maybe we should take a look."

Sylvia looked at the dishes in the rack and the table topped with books, toys, and artwork. The floor probably needed mopping, and there was an entire basket of clothes to iron, especially if she wanted to wear her khaki skirt. But Joe had gone off to Walgreens to refill some prescriptions. The boys wouldn't need her until three o'clock, and besides, how many other opportunities would she have to spend time with Rema? "How about I pick you up in twenty minutes?"

"Perfect," Rema said with a smile in her voice. "I'm ready for a little retail therapy session."

Less than an hour later, Sylvia and Rema pulled into a parking spot near Macy's north entrance. Rema stepped out of the minivan. She was wearing a black leather miniskirt, an animal print tank top, high-heeled ankle boots, and long gold earrings. Sylvia smiled as Rema slung an oversized, red leather handbag over her shoulder and strode like a general toward the entrance doors.

They stepped into the handbag department where Rema was instantly distracted by the display of Fossil bags, a jungle print in particular. After deciding that it had to go home with her, she picked up a plum-colored leather bag with a cross strap. "This would look really cute with the outfit you're wearing."

Sylvia slipped the bag over her shoulder and glanced at herself in the mirror. It did go well with her black capri pants and her white T-shirt with the bold, floral pattern, but then she glanced at the price tag and put the purse back.

Next, they wandered through the shoe department and spent about thirty minutes as Rema debated between silver and gold high heels with tuxedo ruffles down the front, and then ended up buying both. "Skiezer's going to kill me," she confessed. "I'm going to have to sneak everything into the house."

Finally they found their way to the dress department. Rema began looking over the outfits with a professional eye. "You need something classy," she said, "but it also has to be a little romantic, considering that this is an anniversary party."

"I like color, and it has to camouflage my stomach." Sylvia eyed a pretty, bright red dress on display. "Those mannequins have never birthed two children."

"You have a great figure," Rema assured her. "How about this one?" She pulled a midnight blue dress off the rack and held it up for Sylvia's inspection.

Sylvia fingered the chiffon fabric. It had a nice float, but the neckline looked deep. "I'll try it," she said. She found her gaze going again to the bright red dress on the mannequin. Rema, following the direction of her gaze, quickly located the dress and began to sort through the rack for Sylvia's size. "They've only got an eight or a twelve."

"I could try the twelve," Sylvia said, although something in her balked at the idea of going up a dress size.

"Hold on," Rema said, "I've got another idea." The next thing Sylvia knew, her friend was checking the tag on the mannequin and then undressing it. They had to pull the mannequin's arms out of the sockets, but before long the dress was in Rema's arms.

"We can't just leave her like that," Sylvia said, pointing to the nude, armless model. "Let's put her in the twelve."

Working together, the women managed to slip the dress over the mannequin's head and stick the arms back into the body holes.

"Now she kind of looks like a saguaro in a cocktail dress," Rema joked as they stepped back.

"At least she's covered," Sylvia said, grinning. They continued to hunt through dresses and soon Sylvia's arms were full. Heading for the changing room, Sylvia couldn't wait to feel the silken fabric on her body. It had been so long since she'd bought anything that couldn't be machine washed.

Just for one night, she thought, she'd be as romantically dressed as the women on the cover of her romance novels. Wilson and the boys would be stunned to see her in something besides denim. They might even look at her as if she were beautiful.

Dumping her purse onto the floor, Sylvia eagerly kicked off her sandals and then the capri pants and T-shirt. She reached for the midnight blue first. Lifting her arms, she let the silky material slide over her head. Straightening the twisted fabric, her eyes widened. The material exposed an alarming amount of cleavage.

"How are you doing?" Rema called from outside the door.

Sylvia tugged the neckline higher. "It's a little breezy."

"Let me see."

Sylvia stepped into the hallway. Rema took one look at her and laughed. "If you wear that one, I guarantee you'll give one of the men a heart attack, and all the wives will hate you."

Sylvia shook her head. "Not the reaction I'm going for." She stepped back into the room. The next dress, a deep pink with metallic beading around the waist was tight at the hips and a little too short. The third dress, kelly green and short-sleeved, was too matronly. The fourth was a print that was just awful, and when Sylvia stepped out to model it, she said, "I feel like a giant candy cane. Maybe we should give up. I could wear my old, black cocktail dress."

"No way," Rema stated. "We're not leaving here until we find the perfect dress." She handed Sylvia a white dress of a chiffon material. "Try this one."

Sylvia had seen the dress on a rack but passed it up. The fitted bodice was probably going to be too tight, and besides, she wanted color. "I'm not sure I can get into this one."

"I'll help you." Rema stepped into the changing room and lifted the dress above Sylvia's head. For a moment the material caught on her shoulder, and Sylvia had the awful feeling that her arms wouldn't fit through the straps. Rema tugged hard, and the dress magically straightened. "Syl, suck it in." The cold zipper tickled against her ribs. "There," Rema announced, "look in the mirror."

Bracing herself against the prospect of seeing a middle-aged woman wearing a dress that showed only too clearly how gravity was taking its toll, Sylvia lifted her gaze.

The woman who looked back wore a white column dress that hugged the curves of her breasts and hips. Small, white spaghetti straps lay across the smooth, tanned skin of her shoulders. Her exposed arms seemed toned and youthful.

Sylvia studied herself. She hadn't known she had youthful-looking arms. Turning, Sylvia saw the way the fabric draped over her back, exposing the long, straight line of her spine. When she turned her head, her hair flashed copper highlights. *Was this her?*

"Nothing droops?" Sylvia changed angles and glanced anxiously in the mirror. Maybe she was missing something. "I don't look too fat?"

"You look like a movie star. Oh Sylvia, you're so beautiful!"

Sylvia started to reach for the price tag, but Rema slapped her hand away. "It's reasonable, and you're getting it," she stated. "Think of it as an investment in your future and Wilson's. And besides," she added, "every woman should have one dress in her closet that makes her look like a princess."

Sylvia smiled. "I do feel like a princess in this."

In the mirror, Rema beamed back at her. "Mission accomplished," she stated. "Now we celebrate."

"First you've got to get me out of this," Sylvia said, turning so Rema could unzip her. "And then where are we going?"

"Cinnabun," Rema said happily.

"If I eat one of those, I won't be able to get back into this dress. I should go home and do a hundred squats."

"One Cinnabun isn't going to make a bit of difference," Rema stated confidently. "And forget the squats." She unzipped the dress. "Who needs buns of steel when there are sticky buns instead?"

With the dress purchased and carefully placed on a hanger in a plastic case, Rema and Sylvia headed for the food court. They bought coffee and cinnamon buns and found an empty table. Sylvia eyed the creamy slab of cream cheese icing melting on the warm roll and was about to take a bite when her cell rang.

Scrambling within the depths of her purse, she managed to find the phone and answer before it rang into voice mail. Pressing the device to her ear, she heard Joe's gravelly voice say, "Sylvia?"

She felt everything inside go tense. "Is everything okay?"

"Yes," Joe replied, "but the school just called. Simon's running a fever and is in the nurse's office. They want you to come pick him up."

"I'm on my way," Sylvia said. Hanging up the cell, she looked apologetically at Rema. "Simon's sick. I've got to go."

Chapter 31

Wilson shifted the Beemer into REVERSE and carefully backed down his driveway. Next to him, his father filled the space where Sylvia would be sitting if Simon hadn't gotten sick. Although he had improved after a long night, the school policy was that kids had to be fever-free for twenty-four hours before they could return.

He felt a little guilty going without her, but if he didn't, they'd lose the chance to see the house. He was bringing the video camera so Sylvia could see it, too. But it wouldn't be the same, and he knew it.

At the same time, he was really glad that she could be there for Simon, who had looked pale as a ghost, and terribly small and fragile swaddled in blankets on the couch.

As Wilson turned onto the road, his dad opened the map, nearly blocking the right side of Wilson's vision. He didn't say a word. He figured it was better that his father read the map than all the names of the street signs they passed.

Reaching Route 240, Wilson upshifted, and the Beemer surged forward, as if it enjoyed the chance to accelerate as much as he did.

"We go north on I-25," Joe directed, as if Wilson hadn't traveled this route multiple times.

Taking a sip of his burning hot coffee, Wilson prayed Simon felt better soon, and then found his thoughts going back to work. So much of the finance industry was a delicate balancing act, and because of this, bank services and fees were constantly changing. Customers, of course, disliked being charged for things that had been free just the week before. And yet, with federal government regulations so strict, banks couldn't operate the way they had in the past and remain in business.

"We'll stay on I-25 for about sixty miles," Joe stated. "We'll pass that big alligator place. You know, the one we went to last time I visited. Maybe we could stop there."

Wilson remembered. His dad had nearly lost his fingers feeding the alligators bits of dried fish. "I don't think we're going to have time, Dad. We're meeting the Realtor at two and it's a five-hour drive."

"Maybe on the way back, then," his father said. "I want to bring the boys back something. Especially for Simon, the poor kid. I heard him upchucking in the middle of the night."

It had been a hard, long night. "We'll make sure we bring him back something." Wilson hoped they'd have time. Along with the brick colonial, there were a few other houses the Realtor had suggested. He'd make time, Wilson promised himself.

"You think Sylvia has any idea of what you're planning for your anniversary?"

"Not yet," Wilson said. "But she has a sixth sense when it comes to things like this."

His dad laughed. "Tucker was dying to tell her. Aren't you glad I came up with the Trade Secret story?"

"Yes, but I'm beginning to wonder what else you passed off as the truth when I was growing up."

"You turned out okay," Joe said. "That's all that matters."

The scenery flashed by as Wilson considered his father's remark. He didn't agree with it, and yet he knew that his dad loved him, had always loved him, and would always love him. This was the truth of their relationship.

Miles of flat land, dotted with cows and cactus and wire fence filled his gaze. "So, Dad," he said slowly, "about you moving in with us. Are you sure?" He glanced sideways at his father. "You've lived in Sugar Hill for years—all your friends are there."

His dad put another fold in the map in his lap. "Sugar Hill has a lot of happy memories, but I would rather be with you, Sylvia, and the boys."

"What about Stephen and his family? Won't their feelings be hurt if you choose to live with my family instead of theirs?"

"I love your brother," his father said solemnly, "but I couldn't live with them. The last time I visited them, they showed me all these brochures of assisted living facilities. 'Maybe you should think about moving into one now, Dad,' his father mimicked in a falsetto voice, 'so you can still enjoy all the activities.'" His dad made a scoffing noise. "Like chair aerobics is the greatest thing since sliced bread."

Wilson's hands tightened on the steering wheel. He and Stephen, although only two years apart, had never been close. Things had gotten even worse after Stephen married.

"I'm sure they love you, Dad," he said.

"I know," he said. "But I missed a lot when you and Stephen were growing up because I was always working. I can't get those years back, but God willing, I can be a better grandfather."

Wilson was careful not to look at his father. "You were there. Remember that balsa racer we made together?"

"I sure do," his father said. "And next year, I'm going to help Simon build a faster car."

"I don't think Simon will do it," Wilson said. "But maybe Tucker will do it again."

"Simon'll change his mind," his father predicted. "He's like you. He won't be able to resist the challenge."

Wilson allowed the miles to pass in silence as he considered his father's statement. He had been a nerdy little kid and had been only too willing to take on any academic competition. He shifted on the seat. How proud he'd been to bring home another trophy or certificate.

"Next year," his dad mused, "we'll go with a silicone-based paint and more metal in the nose."

"Dad. . ."

"Don't worry. It'll all be legal."

"I'm not worrying about it being legal. I'm worrying about it being what Simon wants."

"If he doesn't want to do it, that's fine," his father assured him. "I just want to give him the chance in case he does. Sometimes people just need a little encouragement."

"I don't want Simon focusing on winning stuff," Wilson said, surprising himself with the words.

"I don't care if he wins or not either," his dad said placidly. "My best memory of building that race car with you is standing around my worktable in the basement and spending time with you."

Time together. Wilson's stomach twisted with regret. Simon had wanted him to help with his Pinewood Derby racer but Wilson had been too busy. *Busy. Busy. Busy.* The words buzzed in his ear like a telephone signal. He'd make it up to Simon, he promised himself, just as soon as this job change was settled.

He turned on the radio, effectively ending the conversation. They stopped for a brief lunch at Wendy's and then drove the remaining distance. Wilson's pulse picked up when he spotted the city limits. He felt like an arrow flying through the air, aimed directly at the center of the target, which was First Federal Bank, located in the heart of the city.

"Walgreen's, Marvelous Cleaners, Valero," his father read.

For once, his dad's habit of reading signs aloud didn't bother Wilson. In fact, he felt a wave of tenderness for the man seated next to him. Dressed in a pair of old green shorts, black socks, and his favorite brown loafers, he looked hopelessly out of fashion and endearingly oblivious to the fact.

"We'll meet the Realtor at her office," Wilson said. "But we'll drive by the bank first."

His dad laughed and slapped him on the leg. "Have I told you how proud I am of you?"

"Only about a million times," Wilson joked, "and technically it's not my bank." But he sat a little taller all the same. Old habits, apparently, died hard.

After his father had admired the bank, they drove straight to the Realtor's office. Peggy Armstrong, a short, heavyset woman with short, black hair and a firm handshake, met them in her office. After she went over a few listings, they all piled into her Lexus.

It was a short drive from the downtown area. Wilson smiled as the brick colonial he'd seen on the Internet came into sight. It was only about five years old and contained more than 4,000 square feet—significantly more than their current home. They paused at the gated entrance. The Realtor punched in a code and the black, wrought iron gate opened with majestic slowness.

Wilson glanced at his dad. "Nice, huh?"

His dad was out of the car as soon as it'd stopped. He headed over to a basketball backboard standing just outside the three-car garage. It looked brand-new, as if not one ball had ever swished through its net.

As if he'd read his thoughts, his dad turned to the agent. "Doesn't look as if anyone ever used this."

The Realtor nodded. "Well, with the country club so close, they probably play golf or tennis instead. Let's go inside."

She ushered them inside a cool, tastefully decorated house with a two-story entranceway that flanked a dining room on his right and a dark, wood-paneled room with built-in shelves that served as an office. Wilson instantly saw himself sitting behind the dark wood desk.

The kitchen was enormous, with stainless steel appliances and a six-burner gas stove that he was sure Sylvia would love. The family room featured an entire side wall of windows overlooking a multi-tiered deck that led to a kidney-shaped pool surrounded by palm trees.

"Isn't this something," his father said, admiring a stone fireplace that rose from floor to ceiling.

The bedrooms were big and spacious, and then his father positively beamed when the Realtor led them into the backyard and showed them a "casita," which was a one-room cottage with its own kitchen and bathroom.

"What do you think?" Peggy Armstrong smiled at Wilson.

"It's perfect," Wilson said. "I love it."

"I thought you would." Peggy's smile grew. "Would you like to make an offer?"

Absolutely, Wilson thought, *Sylvia would love this house*. From the research he'd already done he knew it was well worth the asking price. And yet, what came out of his mouth was, "I'd like to look around a little more."

He walked onto the grass behind the pool. The yard backed into woods, and there wasn't another home in sight. It was quiet, very quiet. Turning, Wilson gazed through the trees at the mansion behind him. It amazed him to think they could afford it, and he tried to imagine himself and Sylvia living there happily. It was much, much grander than they were used to. Well, they'd get used to having all that space in no time, he assured himself.

He walked to the front of the house and again stared at the pristine white net of the basketball hoop. Had it ever been used, or had the man who lived here been too busy to play with his sons? Would he be like that man?

Shielding his eyes, Wilson took another look at the big colonial. It gleamed in the sun like a giant-sized trophy. Was this what the promotion was all about? Climbing to the next rung of success on a ladder that stretched to infinity?

Still, he couldn't help but feel obligated to provide the best possible lifestyle for his family. And if the Lord didn't want him to accept this new job, why did Wilson want it so badly?

Still, he found himself restless, as if he were missing something that was clearly in front of him. He paced about, feeling as if his mind and heart were at war with each other, and realizing that up until now, he'd been so intent on *getting* the position that he hadn't really thought about it being the right thing for him.

Was the job worth giving up all they had?

Analytically, it was. It met the criteria in the categories of finance, career, and adventure. So what was holding him back? He could call Sylvia right now and ask her permission to make an offer.

Wilson reached the perimeter of the property. A few years ago, he'd been in a men's Bible study. One of the group members had been struggling with a decision just like the one Wilson was making. Wilson remembered the pastor advising the man to ask himself two questions.

"Will taking this job help you share your faith with others?" Wilson looked at the distances between the houses. They were much farther apart than in their current neighborhood. Now that he could see the other large, stately homes, there was a definite lack of close neighbors. But surely there would be other church-going families in the area. So yes, technically, he could share his faith.

"Is this new job worth your life?"

This question was harder. Wilson stopped in front of a large oak. He traced the lines on the bark with his finger. "Is this new job worth my life?" he asked aloud.

The selfish part of him reared up immediately, shouting inside his head that it was—and more. For once, Wilson didn't accept that voice and listened harder. Closing his eyes, he heard the leaves flutter against the touch of the wind and the far-off roar of a car. Squirrels chattered in the trees, and a car sped down the street.

It seemed idyllic here, but what would the new job do to him on the inside? Would his soul flourish, or would the very things that seemed so desirable only serve to weigh him down? He'd be making more money, but he'd also be carrying a much bigger mortgage.

Wilson leaned against a towering oak. *Heavenly Father, am I being selfish? Is this promotion what I want or what You want for me? Can our family be happy here? Will all these worries go away once I'm actually in the job?*

Wilson heard the crunch of twigs underfoot, and then his father's voice saying, "Wilson?"

He turned and automatically plastered on a smile intended to cover up these sudden doubts. He could balance the demands of the new job without sacrificing his relationships with the boys and Sylvia. It was only a matter of determination and discipline. "Hey Dad," he said. "Check out this old oak."

"Listen, this house is great," his father said, "but don't let this Realtor lady push you into anything. If it doesn't feel right, it's not."

Wilson shook his head. "I like the house," he said, "but the timing is wrong. I don't even have the job."

"So write a clause into the contract. Give yourself some time," his father urged. "But at least keep the option open. We won't find another house with a casita."

"I just wish Sylvia could see it."

"Well, you're in luck," his father said, pushing the video camera into Wilson's hands. "While you've been out here thinking, I've been filming. All you need to do is upload it."

Chapter 32

Sylvia sat perfectly still on the sofa. Simon's head was in her lap, and they had just finished watching *The Lion King*. She couldn't see her son's face, but the evenness of his breathing suggested he had already fallen asleep, or was about to, and for this she was grateful. Sleep was healing.

He'd had a hard night—they'd all had. The Motrin had brought his fever down, but he'd been achy and nauseous, clingy and unhappy. She'd managed to coax a few sips of water down his throat, but she worried about dehydration. Thankfully his fever had broken, but he'd remained lethargic with little appetite.

Simon twitched a little—Wilson tended to do exactly the same thing when he was falling asleep—and she softly stroked his arm. It was a little after one o'clock. Wilson and Joe were probably still on the road. She was due to pick up Tucker at school at three o'clock, which gave Simon time for a good, long nap.

She heard her cell chirp. Wilson probably had texted her from the road. He'd been disappointed that she couldn't accompany him on the house hunting trip, but promised to video the house and post it on the family web page he had created on the Internet. Sylvia had secretly hoped he'd simply cancel the trip.

Simon's breathing grew increasingly deep and steady. She glanced down at his pale, blond head and felt a wave of tenderness toward him. He seemed so small and fragile, so vulnerable in his bare feet and Batman pajamas. He was a complicated little boy, so full of contrasts—small for his size, and yet years ahead intellectually. So sensitive he wept in movies if anyone (or any animal) died, and yet unyielding in his sense of right and wrong. Not all his peers appreciated his better qualities, and making friends his own age had been challenging.

He stirred a little, and she stroked his hair until he quieted. When Sylvia was a little girl and got sick, her mother sat with her like this for hours, knitting, while Sylvia watched television or played endless rounds of Solitaire. Sylvia's mother brought her icy glasses of ginger ale or warm bowls of noodles and broth. Sometimes it'd felt like getting sick was a treat because everything in the world seemed to stop and her mother focused entirely on her.

Her father, however, wasn't in these memories. *How could he have been*, Sylvia chided herself. He'd been working—providing for his family. Being a patent attorney had been a tough job, and when he came home from work, even as a child, she'd seen his fatigue, the way he'd collapse into his leather recliner and reach for the newspaper.

He'd loved her; she knew this. But he also had been unavailable to her. Maybe she was to blame—she'd been too shy, too young to know how to talk to him and much more comfortable around her mother.

It was a different time, she reminded herself. Fathers were more involved now than when she had been growing up. Wilson wasn't like her father. Hadn't he spent last Saturday doing errands with the boys?

But Sylvia also recognized similarities. Like her mother, Sylvia was a stay-at-home mom, and like her dad, Wilson worked increasingly long hours. Wilson kept saying it was only temporary, but she knew it wasn't. Wilson essentially liked his job. Work seemed to fill some need that she couldn't.

She thought about the Proverbs Plan, how she'd hoped it would help Wilson take notice of her and rekindle the romance that had ebbed from their marriage. Obviously it hadn't worked out the way she'd hoped, but she still believed that through God all things were possible. Just when things seemed the least likely to work out was the time to hold most tightly to her faith.

She stroked Simon's hair but sensed it was more to comfort herself than him. *The Lion King* finished the last credits and Sylvia turned off the set with the remote control. She sat for a moment debating whether to move or not, and then carefully reached for a magazine on the side table. Her Bible was on top of it. She almost pushed it aside but stopped herself. She'd been promising herself to spend more time reading it, particularly Proverbs 31. She opened to the correct spot and read the verses in their entirety.

> *A wife of noble character who can find? She is worth far more than rubies. Her husband has full confidence in her and lacks nothing of value. She brings him good, not harm, all the days of her life. She selects wool and flax and works with eager hands. She is like the merchant ships, bringing her food from afar. She gets up while it is still night; she provides food for her family and portions for her female servants. She considers a field and buys it; out of her earnings she plants a vineyard. She sets about her work vigorously; her arms are strong for her tasks. She sees that her trading is profitable, and her lamp does not go out at night. In her hand she holds the distaff and grasps the spindle with her fingers. She opens her arms to the poor and extends her hands to the needy. When it snows, she has no fear for her household; for all of them are clothed in scarlet. She makes coverings for her bed; she is clothed in fine linen and purple. Her husband is respected at the city gate, where he takes his seat among the elders of the land. She makes linen garments and sells them, and supplies the merchants with sashes. She is clothed with strength and dignity; she can laugh at the days to come. She speaks with wisdom, and faithful instruction is on her tongue. She watches over the affairs of her household and does not eat the bread of idleness. Her children arise and call her blessed; her husband also, and he praises her: "Many women do noble things, but you surpass them all." Charm is deceptive, and beauty is fleeting; but a woman who fears the LORD is to be praised.*

> *Honor her for all that her hands have done, and let her*
> *works bring her praise at the city gate.*

What did these verses really mean? How could she possibly live up to this standard? As Simon continued to sleep in her lap, Sylvia read and reread the verses. She thought about her mother, how in Sylvia's mind, she had embodied so many of these traits. How happy she had seemed—and yet she recognized that her mother had been dealing with many of the same issues she herself faced.

She closed her eyes. *Please God, help Simon feel better, and help me understand what these verses really mean because I feel like everything around me is changing, and maybe I need to change, too.*

Chapter 33

Late that evening, Sylvia was in the kitchen going over a few details for the anniversary party with Rema, Andrea, and Susan when Wilson and Joe returned from the house hunting trip.

It was a little after nine, and Rema's dog, Cookie, sleeping under the table because Rema hadn't wanted to leave him home, barked at the sound of their voices in the foyer. Rema hushed the dog then slipped him a wedge of cheese as Wilson and Joe stepped into the room.

"Hey honey." Wilson dropped his keys and wallet on the counter and crossed the room to give her a kiss. "Hi, ladies," he added, straightening.

"Nice to see you," Rema said. "But I've got to get going." Standing, she turned to Sylvia. "Skiezer will be here early on Saturday morning to start grilling. He's doing ribs and won't be happy unless they're falling off the bone. He's also smoking a turkey breast—I couldn't talk him out of it."

"Tell him thanks," Wilson said. "And please let us reimburse you for the cost of the meat." He glanced at Sylvia. "We really appreciate you all helping us out."

"Wait until you get our bill," Rema said, smiling. "We don't come cheap."

"Tell him if he needs help, I'm pretty handy on the grill," Joe added.

Sylvia thought her father-in-law's posture looked even more bent over than usual and suspected the long ride had been hard on his back. And then she remembered her manners. "Andrea and Susan, have you met my father-in-law, Joe Baxter?"

"Pleasure to meet such lovely ladies," Joe said, extending his hand.

"Nice to meet you, too," Andrea said. In her high heels, she towered above Joe. "I hear you're responsible for that lovely garden in the front of the house."

Joe beamed. "We both planted it."

"It's beautiful," Susan added. "You've got a great eye for color."

"I just look for the healthiest plants, but thank you," Joe said, inclining his head modestly.

"Well, I've got to get going," Andrea said with a sigh. "I've got an early court appearance tomorrow morning." She kissed Sylvia's cheek. "Remember, Blake and I will be here at nine o'clock Saturday morning to help you set everything up, so don't try to do everything yourself."

"Everything is going to be just perfect," Susan added, gathering her purse. "No worries."

With a few more assurances, Sylvia's friends were out the door. After waving them off, Sylvia returned to the kitchen where Wilson was peering into the refrigerator and Joe was leaning against the countertop, arms folded, eyes closed.

"Are you hungry? There's chicken-and-rice soup."

Wilson emerged from the refrigerator with packages of ham and cheese in his hands. "We ate earlier," he admitted. "How's Simon?"

"Much better. He made it through school today, but was really wiped out when he got home." She glanced at Joe whose chin was nearly on his chest. "Why don't you go sit down on the couch?"

"Thanks but I've been sitting all day," Joe said. "I think I'm just going to head upstairs for bed."

"Is he okay?" Sylvia asked after her father-in-law was out of earshot.

Wilson layered ham and cheese on the bread. "Yeah. It was a long drive. Neither of us slept well last night in the hotel either. We were right next to the elevator and it pinged all night."

Sylvia couldn't wait any longer. "Tell me about the house. Did we get it?"

Wilson shook his head. "I don't know yet—they're still considering the offer. It's a nice house, Sylvia, so even though we offered the asking price, they might get a better offer." He took a bite of his sandwich and chewed thoughtfully. "I wrote in a contingency clause so we can always back out of this deal, so don't feel pressure to buy this house if you don't like it."

"I saw the video, and the house looks like a mansion. Can we really afford it?"

Wilson smiled. "Absolutely. I like that my dad would have that little casita in the back."

"It does seem perfect." Sylvia rinsed a plate and put it in the drying rack. "What about the school?"

"That neighborhood feeds into an 'exemplary' school system."

"And what about a church?"

"Several options," Wilson said. "And we're very close to shopping and a really pretty country club with golf, swimming, and tennis."

Sylvia rinsed another plate. She was glad he couldn't see her face. Did he really want to join a country club? It seemed so vastly different— so much more upscale than the life they lived now. She wondered if he had been hiding this part of himself from her, secretly measuring his life by a different standard than the one she'd thought they shared. "That sounds great," she said, "but what happens, honey, if you don't get the job? Will you be okay?"

"I'll be disappointed," Wilson admitted. "But I don't think so many board members would be coming to our party if they weren't serious. Plus I'll have finished all my interviews by Saturday. Bruce was even hinting that they might use our party to announce me."

Sylvia stopped drying a dish. She turned slowly. "Are you sure, Wilson, that this is the right move for us?"

"I don't want to do anything that you don't want to do," Wilson replied. "We can look at other houses if you want."

She took her time setting the china platter, now dried, in the cabinet. She was pretty sure he'd deliberately misunderstood the last question. The last of her hopes that Wilson would see the value of their life here, of seeing how painful a move would be for her, died. "No," she said. "I can't imagine a better house than that one."

Wilson wiped his mouth with a napkin. "I love you, Syl. I'm glad you're up for this."

If he only knew the truth, but he either didn't see it, or else he didn't want to acknowledge it. She felt a little deflated, just like when she'd colored her hair and bought those tight capri pants and Wilson hadn't noticed. She thought about how she had tried to change herself into someone who would be more loveable, more interesting, more compelling. Someone who would inspire Wilson to turn off his computer when he got home and talk to her. Listen to her with all his mind—not just the part that wasn't still churning out something at work—and ask the kind of questions that made her feel fascinating to him.

But this was a fantasy, a pleasant one, but a fantasy all the same. No wonder so few of the romance novels she loved took up the story of what happens after the happily-ever-after. How a relationship could change so gradually it was like aging—you couldn't see it day to day but then one day you looked in the mirror and saw the wrinkles.

Maybe the whole point of Proverbs 31 was not to make Wilson love her more, but to try to be the kind of person God wanted her to be. A woman of faith and character. Maybe she couldn't do all those things in the verses, but it didn't matter how well she did them, only that she try. That's all God wanted from her.

She realized she'd been silent a long time. Putting down the dish, she came to the kitchen table and sat next to Wilson. "Tell me more about the house," she said. "I know it's beautiful, but did it have a good vibe? Or did it feel too elegant for us?"

Something in Wilson's face seemed to relax. "It did feel a little formal," he admitted. "But I think if you were there it would feel like home."

Chapter 34

Saturday morning Sylvia woke up and rolled over to say, "Happy anniversary," but Wilson's side of the bed was empty. The sheets were still warm, so she must have just missed him. She lay in bed looking up at the ceiling and thinking about her wedding day ten years ago. How she'd opened her eyes that cool May morning and felt a rush of excitement—today she was getting married!

She was going to belong to someone—not just anyone, she amended, but Wilson Baxter, who was smarter than anyone she'd ever known, not to mention tall and with those amazing blue eyes that could quite literally pull the breath right out of her.

How precious those moments had been as her mother buttoned up the back of the same white silk-and-lace dress in which she had been married. The ride to the church with her father, never one for words, but who had held her hand the entire way. And the church—walking down that aisle and seeing Wilson standing there—waiting for her—looking at her as if she were the most beautiful woman in the world.

It was a look she couldn't help but hope she'd see on his face again today when he saw her in the white dress. Oh, she knew it was a business party, but it was still their anniversary.

Climbing out of bed she threw on an old pair of denim shorts and a T-shirt. Wandering into the kitchen she looked around for Wilson. He wasn't there.

She turned on the kettle. As she waited for the water to boil, she looked out the kitchen window. It was light enough to see the folding tables and chairs stacked lying on the grass where the caterers had dropped them off the night before.

The water boiled and she dunked a teabag in a mug that the boys had decorated with markers that read, WORLD'S GREATEST MOM. She debated going upstairs to see if Wilson was in his office, but decided against it.

Andrea, Susan, Rema, and Kelly had made her promise not to try to set up the tables and chairs before they got there, and the caterers weren't due until eleven o'clock, but Sylvia restlessly set down her cup and stepped out into the cool April morning.

Reaching for the long pole of the skimmer, she decided to give the pool one last cleaning before she set the set of floating candles in it.

She'd just finished when a black-and-white Border collie charged into the backyard, circled the pool, and ran up to her with its tail wagging hard.

Cookie? Sylvia just had time to think before the dog jumped up on her and strained to lick her face.

"What are you doing here?" Sylvia dodged the long, wet tongue and patted the sides of the dog's silken head. "You get lost?"

"Cookie!" Rema yelled, striding into the backyard in a pair of red shorts and a white tank top. "Come to Mommy right now!" Rema was followed by Skiezer and the boys, who were carrying industrial-sized food trays.

With the excited dog still nearly tripping her as she tried to walk, Sylvia hurried over to help. "Let me take that," she said as Skiezer moved the tray out of her reach.

"Got it," he said in his deep voice that always reminded her of James Earl Jones.

"Sorry about the dog," Rema said, pulling Cookie away from Sylvia. "We figured we'd be here all day. I couldn't figure out anyone to take care of him."

"I told her to leave him in our backyard," Skiezer said, setting the trays down on the black metal dining table near the grill. He wiped his hands on a pair of navy shorts. "Or leave him in the crate."

Rema's eyes narrowed. "It's too long to cage a dog, and if I put him in the backyard, he'd just dig his way out. Besides"—she cast Sylvia a wide smile—"Sylvia doesn't mind."

Sylvia had a brief image of Cookie jumping up on one of the guests but quickly suppressed it. "Of course I don't."

"We'll put him up in one of the bedrooms when the guests arrive," Rema added, as if reading Sylvia's thoughts. "And the boys can watch him." She looked around for Liam and Connor, but they were already gone. Sylvia suspected they'd gone inside the house to play video games with Simon and Tucker.

The back door gave a familiar jingle and Wilson stepped onto the patio. Andrea and Susan were right behind him. "Look who I found," he said, crossing the flagstone to kiss Sylvia's cheek. "Hey," he said, smiling. "Good morning—and happy anniversary."

She smiled. At least he'd remembered. "Happy anniversary," she said. Their gazes met and Sylvia felt something happy stir in her stomach. As soon as they were alone, she'd ask him when he wanted to open the gift she'd gotten him.

"Kelly's running late, but she'll be here in about an hour," Susan said. "And I've got all the flower arrangements in the back of my Suburban."

"The punch doesn't need to be made until right before the party starts," Andrea added, "so you can put me to work on setup."

"Once I get the grill going, I'm going to need some help bringing the fryer around back," Skiezer said. He grinned at Wilson. "We're frying a turkey in a Serrano-jalapeño citrus rub that's got enough kick to jumpstart a Hummer."

Rema rolled her eyes. "You'd better make a lot of punch, Andrea. Skiezer's not kidding. I hope those bankers like spicy food, Wilson."

"I'll make a lot of punch," Andrea promised. "Don't worry."

In her denim cutoffs and ruffled yellow sleeveless top, she looked younger, less formidable, reminding Sylvia less of a highly successful lawyer and more of the woman she'd met at the women's retreat all those years ago—a woman who'd led them all for a midnight "baptismal" swim in that murky brown lake.

For the next several hours, they strung small white lights in the trees, rearranged the outdoor furniture, and ringed the pool with a series of mosquito torches. Wilson worked on the sound system, and Joe appeared midmorning with a flat of petunias, which he squeezed into the already thick flowerbeds.

The rumble of a truck in the driveway announced the caterer's arrival. Soon the backyard was a mass of activity as the tables were rolled out and then set up on the grassy area around the pool. Although Sylvia had argued with Wilson about the need for hiring professionals, she could see that he'd been right. The caterers—a crew of four—two men and two women, obviously knew what they were doing. Effortlessly, it seemed, the snowy white linens and their deep purple accents snapped into place.

Susan anchored the tablecloths with her floral arrangements while Kelly worked on the buffet table, setting out Ironstone serving dishes. Sylvia and Rema went from table to table wrapping the back of the white wooden folding chairs in deep purple tulle.

When Sylvia and Rema tied the last bow, Sylvia stepped back to admire the backyard. Her gaze traveled from the long, rectangular buffet table beneath the shade structure to the six round tables surrounding the pool. She imagined the palms lit up with their delicate white lights and the candles flickering on the tables and in the pool. The whole effect was elegant. Tasteful. Romantic.

"It's perfect," she said to Rema. "I can't believe it's our backyard."

"It really looks great," Rema agreed. "You're going to wow everyone tonight."

"I hope so," Sylvia said. She looked around for Wilson, to see if he liked their newly transformed backyard, but he was nowhere to be seen. "Excuse me a second," she said and went to look for him.

He was in his office, and while that was no big surprise, Sylvia found the door was closed, and for a moment she stared at the silver knob then tried turning it. She hadn't imagined it; the door was locked.

"Wilson?" She knocked gently. "Are you in there?"

"Yes," he yelled back. "Do you need something?"

"Why is this door locked?"

"I'm working," he said loudly. "Is everything okay?"

"Yes, but I want you to come look at the backyard. Make sure you like everything."

"I'm sure it's fine."

She stared at the closed door and frowned. "I hate talking to you through the door. Can you please open it?"

"I'm sorry," Wilson replied, "but I'm right in the middle of something. Let me finish this. I'll be downstairs in five."

His voice was distracted. She pictured him staring into his computer, in cyberspace, a million miles away. She felt like saying, "Oh don't bother," so he would know that she was upset—that he couldn't shut her out and then think she wouldn't notice. It was a big day for him though, and she loved him enough to bite her tongue. Turning, she headed down the stairs to the kitchen to make sandwiches for lunch.

∽

After a quick lunch, Kelly and Andrea headed home to shower and dress. The caterers chased Sylvia out of the kitchen, so she headed to the master bathroom to get cleaned up. She had just finished blow-drying her hair with the diffuser and had slipped on the white column dress when Rema knocked on the bedroom door. "Want some help with your hair and makeup?"

Two hours later, Sylvia inspected herself in the mirror of the master bedroom. Her hair was gathered at the base of her neck in a loose updo. Rema had left some strands loose and enhanced the curls, which framed Sylvia's face in a soft, romantic way.

"You like it?" In the mirror, Rema's face peered anxiously over Sylvia's shoulder.

"Love it," Sylvia said, wanting to touch the curls but knowing if she did, Rema would kill her. "You're a magician. I can't thank you enough."

"All I did was polish you up a bit. You're beautiful, Sylvia. You always were."

Only she wasn't. Her nose was a little too big, and her teeth weren't perfectly straight. She was average in looks, but somehow Rema had transformed her into someone Sylvia barely recognized. Someone with smooth, tanned skin, large brown eyes, and full, coral-colored lips. Maybe it was because she'd been looking at photos recently, but with her hair swept up like this, she could see her mother's cheekbones, and the same shape of her mouth.

Sylvia's gaze found Rema's in the mirror. "Rema, I . . ."

Rema waved her hand. "No," she said very firmly as if she knew Sylvia had been about to tell her that she loved her, but couldn't bear to hear it. "Remember," she added, "you need a face and hair check every twenty minutes, and when they pass out the appetizers, don't eat anything with onions, fish, or spinach."

Sylvia reached for Rema's hand and squeezed it tightly. "I won't," she said.

Rema squeezed Sylvia's hands. "Good luck, honey."

There was a knock on the bedroom door. When Sylvia opened it, Wilson was standing there. His jaw dropped slightly when he saw her, and for a very satisfactory moment he seemed speechless. Finally he said, "Sylvia, you look amazing."

She smiled, stepping back and drawing the door wider so he could see her better. In her high heels, she was eye level with his nose, instead of his chin, and she liked the feeling of being taller, more powerful, and someone who could still surprise him.

Sylvia turned slowly so he could admire the back of the dress. "You like it?"

He nodded tightly. "A lot." The look in his eyes confirmed this. "Sylvia, about our anniversary. . ."

His words were interrupted by laughter, the thump of running feet on the stairs, and then four boys and a dog burst into the bedroom. Rema, coming out of the bathroom, was just in time to intercept Cookie, who had a thin line of drool hanging from his mouth and was making a beeline for Sylvia.

"Liam and Connor!" Rema said sharply. "I told you Cookie has to stay in one of the bedrooms until the party's over."

"It's okay," Sylvia said. She realized that Tucker and Simon were looking at her with big eyes. "Yes, it's me," she said, smiling.

"You look pretty," Simon said a little shyly.

"Yeah, Mom," Tucker added. "You look shiny, even shinier than Daddy's car after he waxes it."

Sylvia smiled at the look of amazement on their features. One of Rema's bobby pins ached where it scraped against her scalp, her ribs pushed hard against the dress, and her feet felt as if they'd been bound for torture in the strappy high heels. However, every bit of the pain vanished in the glow of their praise. She'd wanted to shine like a star in their eyes, and here they were, gazing up at her as if she'd just fallen from the sky. Opening her arms, Sylvia bent, smiling. "I'm still your mom."

Before either boy could step into her embrace, Rema said loudly,

"Sylvia, stop! You're going to mess up your hair, and if their hands are dirty. . .you aren't exactly wearing denim."

Sylvia stiffened. Rema was right; yet part of her didn't care. What good was wearing beautiful clothes if you couldn't touch anyone? What fun was being the brightest star in the universe if her boys couldn't hug her?

"Wave Mommy good-bye." Rema took both boys firmly by the hand. "You're going back upstairs to the game room."

Sylvia turned back to Wilson. "Was there something you wanted to tell me?"

Something unreadable flickered briefly in his eyes. "Just to have fun tonight and be yourself."

Chapter 35

The party was well into swing by six o'clock. Sylvia sipped punch by the side of the pool where she could keep an eye on the guests and still hear the doorbell.

From the stereo speakers, the strains of classical music blended with the sound of voices. There had to be at least forty people—most from the bank—filling in the open spaces of her backyard with brightly colored dresses bumping up against the dark, serious suits of the men.

The white lights outlined the palm trees and the candles in the pool flickered gently. Around her, noises of polite conversation filled the air. The caterers, dressed in black pants and white shirts discreetly moved among the guests, serving trays of stuffed mushrooms and dilled scallop puffs. She spotted Andrea, Susan, Kelly, and Rema, along with their husbands, standing near the buffet table. Her friends looked beautiful in their dresses, and Sylvia felt a wave of gratitude toward them all.

Her gaze turned to Wilson, who stood to the left of her friends talking with the two board members and their wives who had driven in from Houston. The men wore conservative, expensive-looking dark suits. Both women looked as if they'd stepped out of a fashion catalog. The tall blond was wearing a hot pink chiffon dress that Rema whispered she'd seen in a Neiman's catalog for almost a thousand dollars. The other wife had a black, sparkly cocktail dress that probably cost as much as Sylvia's dining room set. As she watched, the women detached themselves from the men and wandered over to the buffet table.

It was strange to think her whole future might be determined tonight by this very party. Wilson had said they were to be themselves, but Sylvia had seen something in his eyes when he'd said it. Maybe he meant they were supposed to be better versions of themselves, to project the executive image fitting a future branch manager.

"Lovely party," a man's voice said. Turning, Sylvia found herself face-to-face with Bruce Maddox, Wilson's boss. He was wearing a dark suit with a pink tie and pink handkerchief sticking out of his breast pocket.

"Thank you," Sylvia murmured, smiling. "It's good to see you again, Bruce."

He looked up at her. His nose was long and bony; his eyes deep set and hard to read. His suit hung more loosely than Sylvia remembered seeing at Christmas, and the hollows under his cheeks seemed more pronounced. She almost asked if he was all right and then remembered Wilson telling her that his boss disliked personal comments.

"I see Justin and Phillip talking to Wilson," Bruce said, "but where are the other two board members?"

Sylvia sipped her punch. "The Abbots said something came up, and I haven't heard from the Wallaces."

"Never mind," Bruce said. "If Wilson gets Bowers, he'll get the job."

"Wilson really appreciates your support for this promotion," Sylvia said. "I know how hard you've been campaigning for him."

"Wilson's like a son to me," Bruce said. "Besides, he's worked hard and he deserves this opportunity. Now you'll have to excuse me, but I have some business to tend to."

Sylvia's gaze followed his back as he wound his way across the crowded patio. He carried a glossy black cane, but she noticed he didn't lean much on it, merely used it to nudge people into making more room for himself—which was good because their backyard really was too small for a party like this. She held her breath as Bruce followed the curve of the pool to the other side. Jen Douglas, beautiful in a black, one-shouldered dress, caught her gaze and waved, before turning back to the group of men who had surrounded her. Sylvia watched her laugh at something one of the men said and felt a little pang. Jen looked so perfect. And while Wilson hadn't said for sure that Jen would be his new assistant, he hadn't said she wouldn't be either.

Sylvia sipped her punch. God had a plan for her—for all of them—a good plan. . .and she had to trust Him. However, it didn't mean she was going to stand idly by and let this woman work side by side with Wilson. It was time to draw the line. If Wilson wanted them to move, he was going to have to get another assistant. She looked up as Rema moved next to her.

"Who's that?" she asked, looking at Jen Douglas.

"Wilson's boss's assistant," Sylvia said. "For now."

"And later?"

"I'll have to get back to you on that."

∽

At the edge of the pool, Wilson sipped fruit punch and offered his opinion about the new BMW series that would be released in the fall. His skin tingled in excitement that Justin Eddelman and Phillip Devall—two of the most powerful men in his company—were standing in his backyard, talking to him.

So far they had discussed cars, golf clubs, and the unlikely possibility of the Astros making the playoffs this year. He was beginning to wonder if the conversation would ever turn to business, specifically his promotion.

His shirt felt damp beneath the suit. He couldn't wait to loosen his tie. Out of the corner of his eye, he glimpsed Sylvia, her white dress nearly glowing in the fading light, talking to Lisa Eddelman and Connie Devall.

"I'm glad to see you value developing relationships outside of the office," Justin Eddelman said, drawing Wilson's full attention back to him. He was a tall, solidly built man with an enviably full head of steel gray hair. He was probably five years younger than Wilson, and yet had three houses, including a ranch in California, and he'd been featured recently in the cover story on the *Financial Times*. "I've always felt team building was key to success."

Wilson nodded gravely. He remembered this quote from the interview in the *Times*. "Sylvia and I enjoy entertaining, and it's a great opportunity to get to meet the spouses."

Justin's heavyset features lifted into a smile. "Yes, you can learn a lot about someone when you understand their personal life."

Wilson sipped his punch. "It's just good to get to know the people you're working with." He put a note of cheerfulness to his voice. "We're all in this together."

"But there's a downside to that," Phillip Devall said. He was a dark-skinned man with a narrow face, close-cropped dark hair, and wire-rimmed glasses. "It's a lot harder to fire someone if you're friends with them. How do you feel about that, Wilson?"

Both men smiled casually, trying to hide the intensity of the question. They were talking, of course, about the job redundancy issues that would occur as the two banks merged. Would Wilson be tough enough to handle the personnel issues?

"Well, I wouldn't feel good about it," Wilson said. "Before I let anyone go, friend or not, I'd work pretty hard to evaluate all potential solutions."

"But you'd do it if you were asked to, correct?" The glass on Phillip Devall's frames looked bulletproof, shielding a set of unyielding brown eyes. He had a reputation for being a tough boss, for firing nonperformers. Rumor had it he'd laid off more than a hundred employees.

Wilson's gaze didn't waver. "What exactly are we talking about, hypothetically of course?"

When Justin named the number, Wilson had to fight not to let his dismay show. What about his business plan which was designed to drive growth at twice the local market rate? Had it been scrapped? "I'm not a hatchet man," he said. "I believe people will perform well if we develop the right game plan. Mine drives growth at twice the local market rate."

"We've seen your plan. You're asking for some sizeable IT investments."

Wilson nodded. He realized he was frowning and forced a smile. This evening was a test of his social skills. "If we want to improve customer satisfaction with more online banking, grow our products and services revenue streams, and be competitive, then that's what we have to do."

"If we go that direction," Phillip argued, "we'd still need to aggressively trim headcount and accelerate the timeline. We can't have the server down during business hours."

He was talking nighttime and weekends, something Wilson had

anticipated but had hoped to avoid by phasing in the changes over time.

"But look, Wilson, Phil and I wouldn't be here if we didn't think you were the right person for the job," Justin said, clasping Wilson on the shoulder. "We're having brunch with Bruce tomorrow morning at the Marriot. Why don't you join us? We can go over a lot of things."

Tomorrow was Sunday. What about church? Wilson looked up as Susan approached, carrying a tray of stuffed mushrooms. Her presence was a welcome distraction. How many times, he wondered, would these men ask him to put the needs of the business before his faith? How many anniversaries, birthdays, soccer games, and cookouts would he miss?

Too many, he feared. And yet, knowing all this, he still felt the familiar pull to climb to the next level, to reach for the trophy now within his grasp.

It'll all work out, he told himself. *Once I've got the new technology and my staff in place, I'll be able to manage my work schedule better. Missing church on one Sunday isn't a big deal. God will understand.*

"What about it, Wilson?" Justin said. "The Marriott at nine?"

∽

It was dark by the time they finished dinner. A soft breeze made the candles on the table flicker and lifted the curls around Sylvia's face. A full moon had come out, and the sight of it reminded her of when Simon and Tucker had been two and four and Wilson had been teaching them the names of the constellations. Simon had looked up at the black velvet sky and said, "The moon looks like God turned His flashlight on."

Next to her, Wilson squeezed her leg. It was his way of telling her that he was pleased with the way the evening was going. Across from her, Connie Devall was talking about a charity event she was hosting for the American Heart Association through the Junior League. It was a good cause, but the dinner tickets were expensive, and it was obviously designed for people with a lot of money. Not that being well-off was bad—and charity work was always great—it just wasn't part of Sylvia's world.

"Anyone ready for dessert and coffee?" Sylvia started to stand, but Wilson's hand on her wrist stopped her.

"Hold on," he said, and then rising to his feet, he lifted a fluted champagne glass. "May I have everyone's attention please?" At first only their table noticed, but after Wilson repeated the request several times, a hush grew over the backyard.

Wilson cleared his throat. "I'd like to thank everyone for coming," he said loudly, "to Sylvia's and my tenth anniversary. Right now I'd like to make a toast to my wife, who makes me feel like the luckiest man on earth." He looked deeply into her eyes. "Sylvia, you are a great wife and mother. You've given me ten wonderful years—the best in my life. I love you, honey." He clinked glasses with her. "Here's to many more years together." Bending, he kissed her on the lips.

Everyone applauded. Sylvia felt herself blush as Wilson pulled away and everyone stared at her. She felt like everyone was expecting her to say something nice back to Wilson, and she could barely get out an awkward, "I love you, too." And then it got very quiet. "How about that cake?" she finally managed, and everyone laughed.

∞

Sylvia was handing out slices of vanilla frosted cake with raspberry filling (purchased at Sam's Club, which she avoided admitting when asked) when the kitchen door opened. Liam, holding Cookie on a leash, stepped onto the patio. As usual, the Border collie was full of energy.

Rearing up on his hind legs, the dog strained against the leash and began to hop, sort of like a kangaroo, in an attempt to free himself. Liam, although tall for his age and strong, had to lean his full weight to hold on to the dog. Sylvia put down the serving piece, but Rema moved faster, and with her purple chiffon dress swirling around her legs, got there first.

"I told you to keep Cookie in the bedroom," Rema hissed.

"But Mom," Liam said, "I think he has to go. Really badly. He was circling and sniffing the carpet."

Rema's lips pursed together before she handed the leash back to her son. "Then take him way in the back behind the trees," she said. "The last thing the guests need to see is a dog bent over pooping." She looked at Sylvia. "Have you got a little baggie?"

"I'll get one." The voice belonged to Simon, who along with Connor and Tucker had appeared on the patio, and they stood in a height line, tallest to shortest, looking a little self-conscious, but a little excited, too, to be part of the party. With the air of someone off to save the world, Simon dashed inside the house.

"Sorry, Sylvia," Rema said.

"Don't worry." Sylvia smiled. "Everything is going great. Boys, did you get enough to eat?"

Tucker, Liam, and Connor nodded soberly. They looked adorable in their khaki pants and a variety of colored polo shirts. Like mini-men. In Tucker, particularly, she could see not only Wilson's extraordinary blue eyes, but also the slight roundness to his face, and the shape of his mouth. Temperamentally, he might be more like her, but physically he was Wilson, minus the glasses. "You want another piece of cake? There's plenty."

Just then, Simon burst out of the back door with an empty grocery bag. The four boys and the dog quickly wound their way through the tables and disappeared into the dark areas of the backyard.

Sylvia lingered in front of the pool. She could see the reflection of her white dress wavering in the silky surface of the water. Around her, the voices of the guests mingled with the strands of classical music. And if she strained, she could hear children's laughter coming from the backyard.

She pictured them moving in a pack with Cookie leading the way, and smiled. Maybe when they moved she would get the boys a dog. She hadn't had one when she was growing up. Her mother had not been an animal person, but Sylvia thought having a dog might be good for the boys. It would teach them about caring for a pet and also be fun. It would also cushion the blow of moving.

God, she said silently, *what happens next—it's all in Your hands.*

"I haven't been to a party as nice as this one for years." The voice belonged to Lisa Eddelman, who had joined her on the flagstone. Lisa was slightly taller than Sylvia, definitely thinner, and had clear, unlined skin and large dark eyes that fixed confidently on Sylvia. "I'm on a mission," she confessed.

"A mission?" Sylvia smiled.

"To recruit you," Lisa admitted. "Justin's very keen on hiring Wilson, but we all know that it's the wife who has to be convinced."

More laughter erupted from the backyard. Tucker's voice shouted with the righteous determination of a younger sibling. "It's my turn, Simon! Give me the leash!"

"I know relocations can be hard—leaving your friends and family—but we're a very social group, Sylvia. We'd keep you busy—you golf, right? And I hear you fundraise for your elementary school. We do lots of charity work through the Junior League. I'd personally be glad to sponsor your membership, and Connie has a lot of pull."

More shouts rang from the backyard. Something was definitely going on back there. As Lisa described luncheons at the club, Sylvia tried to focus, but the snatches of the boys' conversation competed for her attention.

Suddenly Sylvia glimpsed a dog galloping along with its leash tailing behind him. Her heart sank as Liam's voice yelled, "Tucker, why did you let go?" and then, "Get him!"

"Cookie! No!" A shrill voice wailed. It sounded like Simon.

"Will you excuse me a second?" Sylvia stepped onto the grass. Her heels immediately sank into the earth, and pausing, she slipped them off and hiked up the hem of her dress. The backyard wasn't wide, but it was deep. Even so, almost immediately she spotted Cookie, running around like a maniac, trailing his leash. In hot pursuit were the boys, who were shouting at the dog to stop.

It was darker back here—but there was enough moonlight to see the trees and the fence line. Sylvia quickly changed her angle and ran to cut the dog off. It skirted around her, and as it passed, it looked right at her. She could have sworn it was laughing at her.

Great! The last thing she needed was for a big dog to run through their party. Not now, not when Wilson was so close to getting the promotion. She set her jaw. "Boys," she called, "head it off from the pool—try to herd it into the corner."

The dog was faster and more agile than any of them, but fortunately it thought they were playing a game of chase and ran circles around them, staying away from the guests and the pool. Sylvia was out of breath and definitely ready to kill the dog as it continued to evade them. Finally, the leash snagged around the trunk of a crepe myrtle.

Wrapping the leash firmly around her wrist, she led the dog—who was still fresh and full of himself—back toward the house. "You're going back to your room," she told the dog firmly, "before you cause any more trouble."

"Mrs. Baxter," Liam said, as they walked back toward the house. "We're really sorry."

"I didn't mean to let him go," Tucker wailed. "He just pulled really hard then ran away."

Sylvia retrieved her shoes. Her feet were muddy, and she didn't want to think about the hem of her dress—or what her hair was currently doing.

"Mom," Simon added, "he was digging and—"

"That's what they do, dig. Dog's dig," Lisa Eddelman interrupted. She was standing on the edge of the flagstone, and obviously had been watching the whole scene. "Well done, Sylvia," she said, smiling. "You're much faster than my last doubles partner."

Sylvia laughed. She had to tighten her grip on the dog, who began pulling her eagerly toward the board member's wife.

"You know I'm a dog person, don't you," Lisa Eddelman cooed as she bent to pat the squirming dog. Her blond hair gleamed silver beneath the pool spotlights.

"You've been a very bad doggie, haven't you?" Lisa said in a delighted tone. "And what's that in your mouth? Is it your favorite toy?" She put her hand out. "Drop it," she ordered in a commanding voice.

Cookie opened his mouth and dropped the toy into Lisa's open palm, but instead of praising the dog, the board member's wife screamed and dropped the object. Backing away rapidly, she continued to make shrill noises and flapped her hands.

"Lisa?" Sylvia's gaze went from Lisa Eddelman's horrified expression to the small, dark object lying on the flagstone. Her heart seemed to stop as she slowly registered the mothy remains of Bluebonnet.

"Bluebonnet," Tucker cried, and then he began to sob.

"We thought we stopped him in time," Liam said. "I'm so sorry, Mrs. Baxter!"

"It's okay," Sylvia said automatically. She scooped Tucker into her arms and glimpsed Lisa Eddelman kneeling by the side of the pool, splashing water over her arms.

"Simon," she said urgently. "Go get your father."

Chapter 36

After the last guest left, Sylvia turned to Wilson. "I blew it for you, didn't I?" They were standing in the foyer. It was close to midnight and even the caterers had gone. From the family room, she heard the television playing *The Lion King*, although Joe, Simon, and Tucker had long ago fallen asleep on the couch. Sylvia didn't blame them. She was so tired she ached.

Wilson loosened his tie and smiled. "You didn't blow anything for me, Sylvia. That was a great party."

She scrunched up her nose. "Are you serious? Cookie dug up Bluebonnet and dropped her into Lisa Eddelman's hand. She thought she was getting a play toy, not a dead parakeet."

Wilson laughed. "She recovered well," he said. "Although I admit, for a moment, I thought I was going to have to fish her out of the pool."

"She was just trying to wash her hands."

The party had pretty much come to a standstill as Wilson had calmly scooped up the dead bird, talked Lisa Eddelman away from the pool, and then explained to everyone what had happened.

"I don't think Mrs. Eddelman is going to be asking me to join the

Junior League anymore." She studied her husband's face. "I'm sorry we didn't make the impression you were hoping for."

He smiled. "Don't say that. We did fine. And besides, what happened with the dog wasn't your fault."

"I should have told Rema to keep the dog home."

"Because of the dog and the bird, people are going to remember our party for a long time."

"But not in a good way."

"Says who? Sylvia, look at me."

She'd always loved his eyes, the intelligence mixed with kindness. "Everyone had a great time—thanks to your hard work and our friends'. I admit I had doubts, but I can't imagine how we would have done everything without them. We have a lot to be thankful for."

She braced herself, knowing she had to ask, and dreading the disappointment she'd see in his eyes. "The promotion, Wilson."

"What about it?" He tried to look nonchalant, but an excited gleam flickered in his eyes.

"Did you get it?"

Wilson grinned proudly. "You had doubts?"

"Not until Cookie dug up Bluebonnet."

"Actually that clinched it for me," Wilson informed her. "Justin liked seeing firsthand how I handled a stressful situation."

"So you seriously got it?"

The proud smile stretch wider. "Seriously."

Sylvia hugged him hard. "Oh Wilson. I'm so proud of you. Congratulations!" This was it. This was her answer. Maybe it wasn't the answer she'd wanted, but she, Wilson, and the boys were a family, and they would support each other. She'd find a way to stay close to Rema and her friends while building a new life. And she'd plaster the walls of his new office with photos of herself and the kids.

Suddenly they were kissing, and he hadn't kissed her like this in a long time, and even as this registered, her mind whirled. They would be moving. When? Was she really okay with this?

Finally he pulled back. She looked into his eyes. They were dreamy and yet fierce. Strong and gentle. That was the Wilson she had fallen in love with.

"This is so exciting, honey," Sylvia said. "But there's something we need to talk about." She paused, took a breath. "This Jen woman—I trust you completely—but I don't want her to be your assistant. It isn't a good idea."

"It's not going to be a problem."

Sylvia studied his face. "She's getting another job?"

Wilson laughed. "Not exactly."

"Then what?"

"I turned down the job."

What? Sylvia stepped backward so fast she nearly tripped on the hem of her dress. "You what?"

"I turned it down."

She was tired. Maybe she had misunderstood. Her heart began to pound and little chills ran up her arms. "You turned it down? You turned down the position of branch manager?"

"It wasn't right for me. For us."

"But you were so sure. . ."

"I know. I thought I was, too—until tonight. Sylvia, they're looking for someone to fire a lot of people and work nights and weekends. I'm not that person. I hope you're not disappointed."

"Of course not." She stared at him, stunned. "But who are you— and what did you do with my Wilson?"

"I'm still the guy who married you ten years ago and would marry you all over again."

This was something the hero in one of Sylvia's romances would say, and even as it thrilled her to hear it, she couldn't accept that Wilson had actually turned down the promotion. "But what about being passed over, becoming stagnant and all that other stuff you talked about?"

"When I turned down the job, Justin asked me why. I told him that I felt like his vision for the industry was different than mine. I didn't want to downsize and fire people—I wanted to change the fundamental business model. And I told him I didn't want to move." A look of intense satisfaction passed over Wilson's features. "He immediately assumed that I had been interviewing at other companies and said that before I made any changes, we needed to talk again—that the company needed guys like me."

"So we're staying in Sweetwater?" She could barely keep the excitement out of her voice.

"We're staying in Sweetwater." He reached for her hand. "But that's enough business talk. It's our anniversary, and I have a surprise for you."

"And I have a gift for you."

"Mine first."

They tiptoed past Joe who was snoring on the couch with Tucker and Simon sprawled on top of him, their thin limbs so entwined it was hard to separate them.

Wilson's hand gripped hers tightly as they sped up the stairs and past the framed family pictures on the walls. Sylvia had to gather the folds of her long dress in her free hand to keep from tripping over them as they hurried down the hallway.

"Wilson, slow down." But he couldn't, or wouldn't, until they reached the closed door to his office. He came to a stop, and there was a very intense look in his eyes as he swept her off her feet. He fumbled a little with the doorknob, and then it swung open and they stepped inside.

Wilson carried her over the threshold. "Happy anniversary, honey," he said.

The scent of the roses filled her senses. She saw the rose petals forming a giant heart in the middle of the room, and tealight candles flickering from small heart-shaped votives on the bookshelves, the desk, and the credenza. "Oh Wilson," she murmured as he carried her to the center of the heart then gently lowered her to her feet. "Look at the candles!"

"They're battery-operated," he informed her, "because I couldn't be sure what time the party would be over."

Sylvia stood on a carpet of red, pink, and white rose petals. It must have taken a hundred flowers to make up this heart. How soft they felt on her bare feet. How sweet they smelled. "I can't believe you did all this."

"You like it?" Wilson's voice sounded boyishly eager.

She looked into eyes. "Like it? I *love* it."

"We're just getting started," he said, looking very pleased and a little mysterious. "This is for you." He thrust a fat envelope into her hand. "I love you, Sylvia."

"What is this?" Sylvia examined the envelope from every angle. She was dying with curiosity to see what was inside. At the same time she wanted to draw out the tingle of pleasant anticipation. "What did you do?"

"Open it," Wilson urged, "and you'll see."

She fingered the bulky envelope. There was more than just a nice card inside. But what? It seemed almost a shame to rip open the thick, cream-colored envelope, but she slid her fingernail along the seam then pulled out a fat bundle of papers inside, and her heart started to pound. She looked at him in wonder. "You're serious?"

"Very. We'll fly into Rome and rent a car. I was thinking we would head south and stay at bed-and-breakfasts—I've put some brochures in there. I thought you might want to see some of the towns your family comes from."

Sylvia's hands trembled on the pages. They seemed suddenly too fragile, too valuable to trust in her hands. Italy. She'd heard family stories of course, and she couldn't make her grandmother's marinara sauce without thinking of her. But actually going to these places, seeing them with Wilson, was a little overwhelming.

"This is an amazing gift," she said. "I don't know what to say."

Wilson smiled. "Say yes. Just like you did ten years ago."

Sylvia looked at his face, at the worry lines on his forehead that always deepened when something was very important to him. His glasses framed his amazing blue eyes and partially hid faint wrinkles around his eyes. She saw him aging, the lines deepening, the sandy-colored hair receding. And she also saw the handsome young man who had walked into the bank one day and stood staring at her, as if awestruck, and not understanding that he was that someone—that something good her mother had promised would happen in her life.

"Yes," she said. "I will."

Chapter 37

"Hi, Simon," the giant pizza slice blew him a mock kiss as it danced into the second-grade classroom.

"Hey, that doesn't sound like your mom," Will said. He was sitting next to Simon in Mr. Powonka's class, and they had just finished the spelling unit. Both he and Will had gotten one hundred on the test, plus they'd both gotten the bonus word, *aorta*, correct.

Simon shifted on his seat before turning to the boy next to him. He hoped the dancing pizza slice wouldn't do something embarrassing, like hug him in front of everyone. At the same time, he couldn't help sitting a little straighter in his chair. After all, Mr. Slice was a celebrity at their school, and he'd just singled him out.

"I know," he said. "That's my grandfather."

"Hello, everyone," Poppy said, sounding as usual as if he had gravel stuck in his throat. "Are you going to see me in the box tonight?"

"Yes, Mr. Slice!" the entire class shouted at the same time.

"What's our favorite dinner?" The slice of pizza cupped his ear, as if he couldn't hear.

The class took the hint and yelled even louder. "Pizza, Mr. Slice."

"Where's your mom?" Will whispered. Both of them knew if they got caught talking they'd get a lower grade on their weekly conduct report. Will was pretty smart, like Simon, and lately Simon had been thinking of asking him if he wanted to hang out at his house.

"In Italy," Simon replied, "with my dad."

"Remember," Poppy said, "the class that orders the most pizza gets a free pizza party delivered by Mr. Slice." He began to tap dance around the classroom.

"Your grandfather is so cool," Will said. "My grandpa lives in Ohio. I only see him in the summer."

"That's too bad," Simon said. "Poppy used to live in Sugar Hill but he moved in with us."

At first it'd been a little weird having Poppy there all the time. He talked a lot, and once Simon had caught him going through Simon's backpack. But Poppy was always doing some kind of interesting project. Poppy could take things apart then put them back together even better. He'd fixed Mom's favorite lamp and now was working on the vacuum.

"Okay, class," Mr. Powonka said. "Say good-bye to Mr. Slice, he has other classrooms to visit."

"Good-bye, Mr. Slice," Simon called along with his classmates at the top of his lungs.

Mr. Slice pretended he couldn't hear, so Simon took a deep breath and yelled even louder. Just before he left, Poppy gave him a special pat on the shoulder. Simon felt himself turn red but sat up straighter.

If anyone commented on the color in his cheeks, he'd tell them he'd just been touched by a red-hot slice of pizza, which came out of an oven that burned hotter than 700 degrees, more than 600 degrees hotter than the surface of his skin.

At the same time, he knew the facts that rolled so easily off his tongue were not what made him so special.

He was special because God loved him.

He'd prayed for his dad to spend more time with him, and just look what happened. The Lord had not only heard him, but also granted his wish. He treasured that hour in the evening when he, Tucker, Poppy, and his dad shot hoops in the driveway. It didn't matter that he was the worst shot of them all. His dad said not to worry—just have fun playing—and oh, by the way, look over there.

Simon always knew he was just trying to distract him so he could sneak a shot past him. However, Simon *never* fell for it and *always* managed to steal the ball.

The next time, however, he planned to let his dad sneak one past him, just to make him happy, and because Simon, honestly, didn't care who won.

Kim O'Brien grew up in Bronxville, New York. She holds a bachelor's degree in psychology from Emory University in Atlanta, Georgia, and a master's degree in fine arts from Sarah Lawrence College in Bronxville, New York. She worked for many years as a writer, editor, and speechwriter for IBM. She is the author of eight romance novels and seven nonfiction children's books. She's happily married to Michael and has two fabulous daughters, Beth and Maggie. She is active in the Loft Church in The Woodlands, Texas. Kim loves to hear from readers and can be reached through her Facebook author's page.

Major League Dad

by Kathleen Y'Barbo

Dedication

For Jacob Y'Barbo, the real Sam

Prologue

Houston, Texas
August 1

Mason Walker stood on the corner of Prairie and Vine and watched the traffic coming from both directions. In exactly ten minutes Blair Montgomery would walk back into his life just as they'd planned seven months ago on the day of their divorce.

He stared at the hands of the clock atop the bank building and willed them to move faster. Ten minutes became nine, then eight. Finally, with seven minutes left until noon, Mason paused to allow an ambulance to scream past, then crossed Prairie to take his place on the green-and-red bench outside Luigi's Italian Café.

Placing a dozen yellow roses on the seat beside him, Mason glanced at his reflection in the plate glass window that faced downtown. It had taken some fast talking to get his twenty-four-hour pass from the team, and he'd have to miss playing in tonight's game against the Astros, but none of those things mattered. He had a ring in his coat pocket and a goal in his mind.

Tonight he and Blair would take the next step toward becoming husband and wife again, and this time no man or woman, not even

Lettie James, would keep them apart.

The rest of his life—the best of his life—would begin in five minutes.

∞

"ETA five minutes," the emergency medical technician shouted over the roar of the siren. "I have a white, pregnant female, unconscious, victim of auto pedestrian accident. BP is low, pulse rate high. Showing signs of advanced labor."

"Roger that, Unit 14. Any ID?"

"Montgomery," he said as the ambulance turned sharply and lurched forward. "Blair Montgomery."

∞

"Blair Montgomery, please." Mason steeled himself for the tirade he knew Blair's grandmother was about to unleash. Still, with Blair nearly a half hour late, he had to try to find her.

Surely there was an explanation for her tardiness. In their brief phone conversation last week, the only contact he'd had with her since their parting, she'd sounded happy to be seeing him again. She wanted him to see something, something so special, she'd claimed, that she couldn't say what it was over the phone.

"That you, Mason Walker?"

Mason took a deep breath and let it out slowly. "Yes, ma'am, it is. I was just wondering if your granddaughter might be there."

Silence.

"Mrs. James?"

"Yeah, I'm here." She paused. "Look a-here, boy. Blair ain't got no interest in you no more. Just you leave her be, you hear?"

"I can't do that."

"Well, you'd better, or her new husband might not appreciate it."

∞

Lettie James hung up the phone and reached for her car keys. The good Lord hadn't given her Blair only to let her lose her to the likes of a Yankee fool, especially not one who'd never spent a day at hard work or a Sunday inside a church.

Her grandbaby and great-grandbaby deserved better'n that. The nice doctor down at the Hermann Hospital had said Blair would be out of surgery and in recovery soon, so she'd better scoot.

Later on, when Blair was better, she'd break the news to her about

686

that good-for-nothing Mason Walker and how he had called to cancel their little shindig at the Italian place over on Prairie. She'd smart a bit at first, but Grandma Lettie would be there to help pick up the pieces.

"It's all for the best, Blair honey." She closed the door behind her and headed for the Buick. And if her part in this ever came out, she'd just have to tell 'em both she'd done it for love.

After all, the Good Book says that everyone ought to love each other, on account of love covering a multitude of sins.

Chapter 1

Something told Mason Walker to stop, turn around, and look. When he did, he saw her.

At least he thought it was Blair Montgomery. Maybe the combination of Tennessee heat and painkillers he'd taken for his bad knee had hit him too hard. He blinked, shaking his head before training his gaze on her again.

His heart slammed against his chest. It was her. Blair.

She appeared out of nowhere, an image out of his past, painful and still fresh after all these years.

The game.

Mason almost forgot he should be watching the game. A volunteer third-base coach had no business forgetting his responsibilities, even if the only woman he'd ever loved sat fewer than twenty yards away, acting as if she didn't recognize him. Their gazes met, and Blair quickly looked away.

He cast another furtive glance in her direction. From where he stood, she looked every bit as beautiful as the last time he'd seen her.

That day haunted him still.

If only he'd torn up the divorce papers and made her stay instead of allowing her to flee their marriage. If only he'd known the Lord then, maybe—

"Mason! Hey buddy!" Trey demanded. "Get your head in the game!"

He looked up in time to see a pint-sized ballplayer running toward him at full speed. Motioning for him to run for home, he watched as the boy slid past the catcher and rose triumphantly.

"And that's the tie-breaker!" the announcer shouted.

The folks began to cheer as the run ended the game. Mason looked over at the place where Blair had been sitting. She was gone.

"Get a grip, buddy. You look like you've seen a ghost," he heard Trey say. He tried to shake off the image, but all Mason could get rid of was Trey's hold on his shoulder as they walked off the field together.

Without looking back, he climbed into the rented Jeep, gunned the engine, and headed for the interstate. Maybe if he drove fast enough and prayed hard enough, he could leave her memory behind in the tree-shaded ballpark.

Unfortunately, it didn't work. When he opened the door to his Knoxville hotel suite fifteen minutes later, the feeling chased him inside. Now that he'd seen her again, what would he do about it? And what would she say if he tried to contact her? How would she react to his intrusion into her apparently well-ordered suburban life? That was the most disturbing question of all, and for it he had no answer.

After all, it had been nearly ten years.

He hated to think of those days, and most times he squashed the thoughts before they took over. But tonight as he sat in the presidential suite of the most expensive hotel around, he found his usual self-control had eluded him.

His mind, so long closed to that part of his life, now roamed freely down dangerous corridors of the past, and memories rose unbidden to the surface. A door he had shut many years ago now stood wide open. It hurt something awful, but Mason stepped through and let the images swirl around him.

Five minutes after he had arrived in town, Mason had wondered why transferring to this college in the heart of central Texas had ever seemed like a good idea.

Then he found Blair Montgomery and fell in love.

For the better part of four glorious weeks, they had been Mr. and Mrs. Mason Walker, and the sum total of their possessions could have fit easily in the back of his pickup.

Then came the reality that being married was hard and getting a divorce to solve their problems was easy.

How was I ever so naive, Lord? Why did I think everything was so simple? If only I'd known You then.

The phone rang and chased away the fog of memories. Mason walked toward it slowly, hoping whoever it was would give up and go away. Finally, when he reached the desk in the opposite corner of the room, he allowed the phone to ring once more before picking it up.

"Walker, what's this I hear about a baseball camp?"

"Well, good evening, Morty. How's everything out on the coast?" He smiled, knowing his lack of reaction would only increase his agent's anger.

"Good evening, yourself. If you're looking to blow the negotiations on your contract extension with the Honolulu Waves, just keep on doing what you're doing."

Mason allowed a long moment of silence to come between them before answering. "Morty, I have no idea what you're talking about."

"Nice try. I know you're down there working some kiddy camp when you should be up in Montana at that pitiful cabin of yours signing baseballs and letting your knee heal."

"Aw, it's no big deal. I've got a flight out tomorrow." Mason hauled the cordless phone back out onto the patio. "Besides, all I do is stand around and look useful—I promise."

"Don't promise me anything you don't. . ."

Mason set the phone down on the wrought iron-and-glass table, pulled his T-shirt over his head, and let it fall. When he settled into the lounge chair and picked up the phone once more, his agent was still talking.

". . .and with another contract in the works you can't be taking these stupid chances. I'm only looking out for your interests here. You know that, don't you, Mason?"

He closed his eyes, savoring the feel of the sun as it peeked out from behind a particularly ominous-looking cloud. The wind smelled of rain, which made him think of Blair all over again. He frowned and shook his head, as if the thoughts could be easily dislodged.

"Walker, answer me."

A small beep punctuated his agent's outburst. Could Blair have recognized him at the park and traced him through Trey to this hotel?

"Sorry, Morty," he said. "Gotta go. Someone's trying to get through."

"That someone is me, Buddy, and if my message doesn't get through, you're going to be blowing a sweet ten-million-dollar deal."

Another beep.

"Don't even joke about that," Mason said, adding an edge to his voice that he hoped his agent wouldn't miss. "You just get me the money, all right? I'll take care of the rest."

A third beep. Blair could be about to give up.

"I still think—"

"Bye, Morty!" He pushed the button before the enraged man could continue. "Mason Walker here."

"Hey pal, how would you like me to make your day?" Trey paused, obviously waiting for a reaction.

Mason suppressed the desire to do his best Clint Eastwood impression, opting for a simple grunt of agreement instead.

"I found Blair."

A knot formed in his throat, making words impossible.

"Mase? You there?"

Silence.

"Hey, Mase! Did you hear what I said? Talk to me, pal."

"Yeah," he managed. "Uh, sorry. I, uh, I—" He closed his eyes and said a prayer for guidance before he practiced the words in his head. Finally, he attempted the nearly impossible task of saying them aloud. "Where is she?"

"Lives out in Magnolia," he said. "Has a landscape architecture business."

So Blair had gone into the landscape business as she'd planned. Well, good for her. Strange she'd gone all the way from Texas to Tennessee to do it. Maybe her husband had a job transfer.

The husband. He hated to ask, but he had to.

"Is she still married?" He ground out the words, afraid of the answer. The wait for a response nearly killed him.

"Nothing about a husband on the forms. Looks like she's a free agent, buddy."

Finally, Mason managed a ragged breath. "Give me her number." He opened the desk drawer and fished around for a pen. "On second thought just give me her address. This is one reunion that ought to take place face-to-face."

Half an hour later, Mason headed up the freeway with his favorite CD in the stereo and the windows rolled down. As he banged his hand against the steering wheel in time to the music, Mason refused to consider what he might find at his destination. Instead he turned the matter over to the Lord and concentrated on the music and, more rarely, the map.

"Uh-oh," he muttered under his breath when he almost missed the blacktop leading north.

A pair of deer skittered across the road in front of him, causing Mason to slam his foot on the brakes. He pulled the Jeep to the side of the deserted highway, threw it into PARK, and leaned back against the seat. The sounds of the night came at him from all angles, even over the soft purring of the engine.

The deer disappeared from the glow of the headlights, leaving nothing but a dark, empty circle of highway in front of him. He stared hard at that circle and tried to make sense of his scattered thoughts.

Up the road lived the most important woman in his life, the only one who'd managed to love him despite all his faults. The only one who hadn't cared about his batting average or how much money he made.

The only one who'd ever hurt him.

Mason squared his shoulders and kicked the car into DRIVE. Too soon he saw the sign that indicated he'd reached her street.

He eased the car down the road, immediately relieved there were no streetlights to illuminate him. Suppressing the wild desire to cut the headlights and coast the remaining distance to her, Mason touched the accelerator lightly, his gaze fastened on the blue-and-white mailbox bearing the reflective numbers for which he'd been searching.

Whatever possessed him at that moment, he would never know. Without turning his head in the direction of the house, he sped past it, gunning the engine and leaving a spray of black pebbles in his wake.

Safely away from her, he slowed down and removed his foot from the gas, allowing the Jeep to coast to a stop. Before he could think, he threw the vehicle in reverse and turned around, facing back in the direction of her house. He cut the headlights and shut off the engine.

It was crazy, and he knew it, this urge to find her again, especially since she'd obviously spent no energy worrying about where he might be. Mason gave in to the feeling anyway, wanting to see her but not exactly sure what he would say when he did.

Better to do this without her knowing, he decided, as he climbed out of the Jeep and headed toward her house on foot. The sound of his boot heels hitting the road punctuated the soft hum of the crickets.

His strides lengthened when the mailbox came into view again. A moment later, he broke into a run, not realizing it until he had arrived at his destination. Too late he felt his knee start throbbing as the air in his lungs burned like fire.

He leaned against the white picket fence and fought for each gasp of breath forced into his lungs. A movement caught his attention, taking his mind off the excruciating pain shooting through his leg.

Framed by the warm, golden glow of lamplight, he could make out only the dimmest of silhouettes. But he knew it was Blair. He felt her, even before he could see clearly.

As if she'd sensed his presence, she walked toward him. A moment later, her face became visible in the square white picture frame of the window.

White curtains moved against the soft evening breeze, rustling about her as she stood there clutching what looked like a book to her chest. From somewhere inside, soft music floated across the small lawn toward him. Mason took another breath, all physical pain forgotten as he contemplated the image.

A light went on in the room upstairs, drawing his attention away from her. The movement of two shadows played against the creamy window shade until the shade flew open, carving a bright square of light into the front yard only inches from Mason's boots. Instinctively, he stepped back.

A small, fair-haired boy in red-and-white striped pajamas leaned his elbows against the windowsill, his chin tilting skyward. "Up there's Orion." The boy pointed up at the stars, his childish voice carrying across the yard to where Mason stood. The dog beside him looked toward the heavens as if he understood. "And there's the Little Dipper."

Then Blair appeared next to the boy, and Mason was lost once more. Nothing in all the memories he had of Blair prepared him for the sight of her with the tow-headed boy in her arms.

Yet all he could think of was that the boy should have been his. And she should have still been his wife.

Then he realized what had stopped him from stepping back into her life again. She wasn't his wife anymore. That distinction had gone to another.

What was he doing there? Why had he driven all this way to stand in Blair's front yard and act like a lovesick fool?

He was losing it, for sure. And on top of that, his bum knee felt as if it had been mangled under the wheels of a Mack truck. Time to go back to the hotel and speak to the Lord a bit. He'd try to pretend this night had never happened.

"G'night, Mom." The childish voice drifted on the breeze, sinking into his brain and wrapping itself around Mason's battle-scarred heart. "I love you."

" 'Night, sweetie," he heard Blair say. "I love you, too."

The words beckoned to him, pulled him out of the shadows and onto the cracked sidewalk that led to her door. He'd almost reached the doorbell when he realized what he had done and froze.

He closed his eyes and took his fears to the Lord. *Blair and I need to have a real conversation sometime, don't we, Lord? It might as well be now, right?*

When no answer came, Mason extended his index finger until he'd almost touched the doorbell.

"G'night, Daddy." The words floated across the porch like a soft breeze. "Do you know I love you?"

Mason didn't wait around to hear the answer.

Chapter 2

*B*lair prepared Sam for bed while her mind raced and her heart threatened to splinter each time her son said his name.

"*Mason*." So much time had passed, and so much pain still remained. Things were going so well. *Why did You let him see me today at the ballpark, Lord?*

She tossed a damp towel across the hamper and surveyed the tiny bathroom. As usual, Sam had done his best to brush his teeth and wash his face after his bath, but his cleanup had left a little to be desired. Wet footsteps led from the tub to the sink where they stopped at the blue floral rug. A blob of green toothpaste decorated the sink, and the door to the medicine cabinet stood open.

Blair closed the medicine cabinet and caught a glimpse of her haggard expression in the mirror. She snapped off the light.

"Mason Walker called me a slugger today at camp, Mom. He's awesome."

Sam's words echoed in her ears long after the nine-year-old boy had stepped out of the tub and dashed to his room in fresh pajamas with his newly autographed, red baseball cap still on his head. Taking one last look, Blair peeked into the darkened room and saw that, even in his sleep, he still wore the cap. A suspicious lump moved beneath the covers, and Sam lifted a hand to still it. His eyes never opened, although Blair now realized he could not be asleep.

She flipped on the light and tried to look stern. "Get the dog out of the bed, Sam. You know the rules."

Slowly, he peeled the covers back to reveal the mutt he'd hidden there. "Sorry, Bubba," he said. "You gotta go sleep in the kitchen."

The furball slid off the bed and slunk past Blair. She knew he would return as soon as she left the room, but at the moment a misbehaving dog was the least of her worries.

"Wanna say prayers with me, Mom?"

"First, let's talk about something." She stepped over his cleats and bag to straighten the denim quilt and fluff his pillow. Dropping to one knee, she took a deep breath and let it out slowly, hoping the right words would come. "It's about the baseball camp."

"It's so cool." He bolted upright, eyes wide. "I can't believe Mason Walker's really there. I always watch him on television, and once I—"

"Sam, I don't think you can go back to camp tomorrow."

Before she'd finished the statement, tears had begun to gather, both hers and his. She felt another break in the armor surrounding her heart.

His "Why?" came like a soft, sweet whisper.

Why indeed? She certainly couldn't tell him the real reason. "Because I don't think it's a good idea."

A tear slid down his cheek, skirting a path across his freckles to drop onto the denim quilt he clutched beneath his chin. "But why?"

Several perfectly valid reasons came to her mind, first and foremost the distinct possibility her son could once again come into direct contact with his father. Blair forced a smile and blinked back the shimmering of tears threatening to fall.

"Well, I've got so much work to do and—"

"I can help you with your work after camp. You like it when I go on your jobs, and I can water the plants just like you taught me, and I'll even—"

"Sam," she said slowly. "Enough."

His bottom lip trembled, and he sniffed loudly. "But I don't see why I can't go. All we did today was a hitting clinic, then we played a game."

"Well, that sounds like a lot of fun," she offered.

"Yeah, but tomorrow, since Mr. Walker won't be there, we're going to practice pitching and catching, and you know how I wanna learn to catch."

He swiped at his cheek with the quilt, then focused his blue gaze on her. For a split second, she saw his father in his eyes. Looking away, she fumbled with the blankets until the impact of his statement hit her.

"You mean Mr. Walker's not going to be there tomorrow?" She worked at making the words sound as innocent as possible. "I thought he was part of the camp staff."

He straightened his cap and peered at her from under the brim. "Naw, he just came for today on account of his knee is hurt, and he has to go back to his team or something." Making a face, he shook his head. "The Wild Man's not a catcher, Mom."

No, but his friend Trey is.

Intending to tell the boy he would be anywhere but at baseball camp tomorrow, she looked straight at him and somehow said, "You're right. There's no good reason why you can't go."

The smile dawning on his face sealed the cracked edges of her resolve. Of course. Trey might be Mason's friend, but he would be far too busy to care that she had a son at camp. Not allowing Sam to return might cause more consternation, where pretending all was well might keep them above suspicion.

Besides, she reasoned as she pretended not to notice Sam's mutt slinking back into the room, surely she hadn't come this far to be found out now.

"Now can we say prayers, Mom?"

Blair smoothed the quilt around her son. "You go ahead," she whispered through the constriction in her throat. "Tonight I'll just listen and agree."

"Dear Lord, thank You for talking Mom into letting me go to camp tomorrow, and I hope You'll make it as good a day as it was today. Please bless Mom and. . ."

∽

June 21

Last night, when Sam prayed, Blair had felt an unexplainable hope take wing. It stayed with her through the bedtime routine and followed her into the kitchen for cereal and milk at dawn. All through the morning, as she dealt with the details of work, she nurtured that hope.

When tax forms and blueprints for new client Griffin Davenport's atrium could no longer hold her interest, she gave into her worries and took them outside to her potting shed. There she began to give her variegated liriope a long overdue change of containers. Still, even as she sat up to her elbows in peat moss and potting soil, her mind traveled to the ballpark and Sam, and her prayers went with him. Surely God wouldn't let her decision to send Sam there today be a wrong one.

Not after she'd spent half the night crying and the other half in prayer.

That thought alone kept her going. Davenport, a real estate mogul, had proved to be quite an exacting client. "Demanding but fair," she whispered as she reached for her container of pearlite and mixed the tiny white pellets with soil. Garnering his approval was something she did not take lightly. A man in his position could make or break her fledgling career.

Pondering the points of that statement took less than a moment. "Only God can make or break my career," she reminded herself. She wiped the perspiration from her brow and returned to work on the task at hand.

Then, a few minutes before noon, the phone rang, and Mason Walker's voice greeted her with a polite hello. Her good feelings faded, as did her ideas for Griffin Davenport's blueprints. A cold emptiness and an even colder voice, her own, replaced them.

"Mason?" The clay pot in her hand hit the floor. "Sam told me you'd left."

"Yeah, I was supposed to." He paused briefly. "Um, Sam Montgomery—he's yours, right?"

Blair picked her way around the shattered pieces of terra cotta and with a trembling hand reached for the broom. "Yes." The words *and yours* came to mind, and she nearly dropped the phone, too.

"Well, he's a tough guy," Mason said slowly, "but he kind of needs his mom right now."

∞

Mason hung the phone up and eased down beside the injured boy. Still reeling from the sound of the familiar voice, he offered Sam a tentative smile.

He and Blair were bound to run into each other before camp was finished. Now that he knew she would arrive in a few minutes, he fought the urge to run back to his hotel and allow Trey to handle the situation.

But Mason Walker had never backed down from a challenge in his life, and no way would he run off like a beaten dog with his tail between his legs.

After all, he wasn't the one who had failed to show up that day ten years ago.

He looked at the boy and forced another smile as he adjusted the bandage on his bad knee. "Your mom's on the way, kid."

Sam seemed more interested in the pair of squirrels playing chase a few yards away. For a moment, Mason entertained the hope that their time together might be spent in silence. The last thing he needed to do right now was to play nice and hold any sort of conversation with Blair Montgomery's kid.

"Probably breaking the sound barrier to get here, huh?" Sam finally said when the furry pair disappeared into a clump of trees.

"She did sound a little worried."

"Yeah, she worries about me a lot." He gave Mason a serious look. "She says it's 'cause she loves me so much, but ya know what?"

"What?" Mason shifted positions, trying in vain to get comfortable on the rock-hard ground.

"Sometimes I wish she didn't love me so much. I'd get to have a lot more fun."

"Don't ever wish your mom doesn't love you," he said, his voice sharper than he intended. He took a deep breath and let it out slowly. "But, hey, I know what you mean. Sometimes moms don't know what it's like to be a guy."

"I guess." Sam leaned back against the rough trunk of the ancient oak tree and pressed the ice pack to the left side of his face. His gaze landed on the bandage encircling Mason's knee. "What happened to you?"

"A big old catcher named Rock thought I shouldn't score the winning run while he was guarding home."

"Did ya?"

This time Mason's smile was genuine. "Yep."

Sam reached over and touched the bandage. "Does it hurt?"

He shook his head. "It's nothing."

Actually it did, but he would never admit it. The dumb stunt he'd pulled last night had nearly been his undoing, and only by the force of sheer determination had he made it out of bed this morning.

He looked at the little guy next to him. Blair had a great kid, a real ballplayer. Not once had the boy complained about that lump he'd acquired. Even though he had been knocked flat by the pitch, he'd still managed to get up and run the bases.

He'd even stolen third and slid into home head first. Mason smiled. Sam reminded him of himself at that age. To shake the dismal feeling tagging alongside that thought, he snagged Sam's hat, pretended to juggle it, then set it on his head backward.

A pair of dimples flashed as the boy burst into a fit of giggles. Then he asked, "How'd you get the name Wild Man?"

He tried hard to think of a way to steer the conversation away from the name he'd acquired during the first hard year after Blair dumped him—a name that had followed him far longer than he deemed necessary. "How about if we talk about your nickname instead?"

Sam looked up at him with big blue eyes, *his mother's eyes*, Mason thought as he felt his heart lurch. He had spent hours staring into eyes just like those. Quickly, he pushed the memories away.

"I don't have a nickname," the boy said.

"Then we'll have to do something about that, won't we?" He ruffled the boy's straw-colored hair. "Tell me about yourself, and I'll see if I can think of a name for you."

"Cool!" he said, his eyes brightening with interest. "What d'ya wanna know?"

"Everything," Mason answered with a casualness he didn't feel. "Tell me about your mom and dad, school, what you like and don't like, stuff like that."

"Okay, let's see. My mom's pretty cool. She plants flowers for people. That's her job. Sometimes when I don't have school she lets me come along and help." He paused as if he were considering something important. "She gets real mad at Bubba when he gets in the way, so he doesn't get to go with us anymore."

"Is Bubba your brother?" The question sent Sam into peals of laughter. "What?" Mason asked.

"Bubba's my dog," he said through the giggles.

Mason thought back to the image of Sam and the mutt in the

window. If Sam were his son, he'd have a proper dog, something manly like a Labrador retriever or a German shepherd. Definitely not a big dust mop with legs.

And he sure wouldn't be named Bubba.

"Well, do you have any brothers and sisters?" Mason asked.

"Nope. Just me and my mom."

"And your dad?" He knew he shouldn't care about the answer to that question, but he found himself holding his breath until the boy finally spoke.

"Nope. Just me and my mom," he repeated. "My dad's in heaven."

Mason felt himself breathe again, instantly ashamed at the wave of relief that washed over him. Blair was a free agent, just as Trey had claimed.

But why should this fact interest him? It had been too long ago. Why should he care?

Because he couldn't help himself. He corralled his wandering thoughts and focused on the conversation.

"My dad's with Jesus, too," Mason managed to answer. "I miss him." And he did, especially when he put on that uniform and stepped onto the field.

"I never met mine," Sam said matter-of-factly. "He died before I was born."

Mason felt as if he'd been punched in the gut. Why hadn't he kept his mouth shut and not stuck his nose into Blair's business? Now he knew way too much.

Another thought struck him. This boy was at least eight years old, maybe nine. Blair had been a widow a long time. Why hadn't she contacted him in all these years?

Because she'd forgotten all about you by then, man. You were ancient history, a blast from the past.

He shook his head and looked away rather than see himself reflected in those blue eyes. "So your mom took care of you by herself?" he finally managed to say.

"Nope."

"No?"

"Grandma Lettie lived with us until she died; then it was just us."

"Oh?" Mason didn't know whether to be relieved or more irritated. With Lettie James in charge, it was no wonder he'd never even rated as much as a Christmas card from Blair and her cozy little family.

"How long has your grandmother been gone?" Mason asked, not sure why he cared but unwilling to let the silence lengthen. Maybe talking about the demise of the geriatric terrorist might make him feel better, although he knew he'd have to make things right with the Lord on that score later on.

"Grandma Lettie died right before Christmas," he said, wiggling his sneaker-clad feet in time to some imaginary tune. "After that I got to plant flowers with Mom except when I'm at school." He screwed his face into a grimace; then, as quickly as it had come, the expression faded back to seriousness. "I like it better than school, but Mom says I have to go. But I'm a big help, and it's fun mostly."

"Oh yeah?" The question was automatic, barely a grunt.

"Yeah. I liked it better than staying home with Grandma Lettie 'cause Mom lets me play in the dirt. Grandma Lettie used to say my daddy was always rolling around in the dirt and playing games even though he was a grown-up and shouldn't be doing stuff like that." He gave Mason a thoughtful look. "I don't think she liked him much."

Time to steer this conversation out of dangerous waters.

Again.

He searched for a more benign topic. "Let's get back to making up that nickname for you." He pretended to think, although he couldn't have strung two coherent thoughts together at gunpoint. "So, buddy, there's bound to be something special for your name. When's your birthday?"

"It's coming up real soon."

Mason looked away. "Oh yeah?"

"Yeah, it's August second. My mom says since I'm gonna be ten she's gonna take me and the guys to a ball game." Sam tossed the ice pack onto the grass. "This isn't cold anymore."

"Okay, I'll get you another one."

Mason rolled over on all fours and eased himself into a standing position, holding onto the tree trunk for support with one hand, the ice bag in the other.

A thought struck him, the force of it sending him reeling backward against the tree. Mason did the math.

Sam was his son. He had to be. And he was born the same day he and Blair were to meet at Luigi's. But why hadn't Blair told him about the baby she was carrying?

He said something, he must have, for he heard Sam answer, but his brain failed to register the words. Somehow he began to walk, putting one foot in front of the other until he found himself leaning against the burning hot hood of his Jeep in the parking lot.

"Ouch!"

Mason jumped away from the vehicle, slapping the warm bag onto the pain in his arm. It did nothing to dull the burn, but the action temporarily took his mind off the bigger ache that threatened to consume him.

He turned around and examined his face in the dark-tinted side window of the Jeep. No, he still looked the same.

And yet everything about him was different. All he believed to be true about himself had suddenly become skewed. Removing his ball cap, he ran his hand through his hair and pondered the situation.

He was a father.

Somehow he'd given life to a boy he never knew existed. For some reason Blair had judged him unfit for the task of being a father to her son. He banged the ice bag against the side of his leg.

But why? For the life of him he still had no answer.

"Hey Walker! How's the kid?"

The familiar voice jarred his shattered nerves, jerking him back to the present with alarming speed. Twenty yards away, Trey stood waiting for an answer.

"He's fine." Mason hoped he sounded at least vaguely like his normal self as he returned the cap to his head.

Affecting a casual demeanor, he waved the lukewarm ice bag in the air. The last thing he needed to do right then was to try to explain something to Trey that he didn't understand himself.

"Need more ice." He turned away before his buddy could comment.

After he refilled the bag, Mason headed back to wait with Sam for Blair's arrival. As he stepped into the clearing between the snack bar and the stand of oaks and pines that ringed the park, he knew she was already there. He could feel her presence, just like the old days.

And, like the old days, her presence unnerved him. Squaring his shoulders, he plastered a smile on his face and walked toward the spot where he knew he'd find her. *Okay, Lord, walk me through this.*

"Sweetie," he heard her say, "are you sure you're all right? Maybe I need to call Dr. Fraser."

The familiar voice, in the soft tones he remembered all too well, tore at his composure. He felt his breath catch in his throat as he rounded the corner and glimpsed her.

"Aw, Mom, I'm fine," he heard Sam answer.

Frozen in place, Mason felt as if he stared heaven in the face. If anything, the years had been more than kind to Blair, something he hadn't noticed yesterday afternoon at the ballpark or last night in the dim light of her front yard.

But this was no angel, he reminded himself. This was the woman who'd taken his heart and trampled on it, leaving without so much as a backward glance.

"Blair."

When she looked his way, he knew he'd said it aloud. Eyes of rich azure blue widened, then closed, only to open again.

"Mason?"

Had she really said his name, or did he only imagine it?

Mason took a few halting steps toward her. The smile she gave him seemed genuine, if not a little slow in coming. When he returned it, all the hurt and most of the years melted away. He forced himself not to sprint the rest of the distance between them.

But that would mean he cared, that he was anxious to see her, speak to her. That couldn't be it.

"D'you two know each other?"

Sam's voice sliced through his mind, reminding him of what Blair had done to him. As quickly as they had fallen, the barriers went up again around his heart. He knew his smile had disappeared so he hastily looked away, making sure the face that returned to her was as impassive as he could make it.

He opened his mouth to speak, but the words seemed locked in his throat. Instead he turned his attention to the boy. Dimples flashing, Sam eyed the two of them with youthful wonder. Blair looked more than uncomfortable.

"Well, do ya?" Sam repeated.

"Yeah," Mason answered, trying to keep the trembling he felt out of his voice. "Your mom and I go way back."

Chapter 3

He knew.

That's all Blair could think of as she watched Mason ease down into the combination of daylight and shadows. She eyed him critically through the dappled sunlight, watching for the slightest indication. His demeanor was friendly, to be sure, but there was something else. Recognition of some kind, she thought on first glance.

But as quickly as it appeared, it was gone. No, she decided, he had no idea the boy sitting next to him was his child. She relaxed, but only slightly. If he knew she'd seen him yesterday, he must wonder why she hadn't spoken to him. What possible reason could she give for beating a hasty retreat at the first sight of her former husband?

Mason's gaze traveled lightly over her to rest more intently on Sam. He ruffled the boy's hair and winked at him, as if sharing some sort of male-only secret. Blair looked away, unable to stomach the closeness she perceived between the two of them.

She'd gone to such lengths to keep them from meeting, and yet here they were, acting more like the father and son they were than the strangers they should have been. Fear once again rose in a tight knot in her chest. She shoved her hands into her pockets to keep them from shaking. Only her casual behavior could keep Mason from suspecting the obvious.

Dark hair mingled with light as Mason leaned down and whispered something in Sam's ear. Two sets of eyes the color of faded denim gazed in her direction. *How can Mason not know,* she thought as she watched them together? *How can he not see so much of himself in his son?*

Sam's childish laughter bubbled with innocence as he leaned against the ample shoulder of the man who had given him life. Once again, their hair mingled in a pattern of light and dark that captured her attention and held it. Mason made a feeble attempt to keep a straight face, his arm wrapped around his son as he playfully jabbed him with his elbow.

"What?" The word sounded more like a croak than a question, and Blair instantly regretted having spoken.

"Mr. Wild Man said this is the first time he's ever seen you so quiet," Sam said, taking Mason's good-natured roughhousing in stride.

She pulled her hands out of her pockets and smoothed a strand of hair behind her ear. "People change."

"But not you, Blair," Mason said softly.

"Look, Mason, about yesterday." She forced herself to look, really look, into his eyes. What she saw there revealed nothing, so she pressed on with her apology. "I was incredibly rude. I wasn't sure you saw me, but to leave like that—forgive me?"

"Forgive you?" He smiled, then let the corners of his mouth fall and shrugged. "Sure."

He had seen her. Well, the last thing she needed was for Mason to be angry. Better she smooth things out than leave him with any memory of her when he left to rejoin his team.

She frowned. How had he managed to get even one day off, much less the rest of the week? Had something happened?

"Don't you have to play. . . ?" Her voice trailed off. She noticed the bandage on his knee. "Oh, you're hurt."

His big, sturdy hand reached down to touch the wrappings on his knee. "It's nothing," he said.

"He did it running into home," Sam said, a note of authority in his voice. "You should have seen how many guys it took to carry old Rock off the field afterward."

She raised an eyebrow. "Oh, really?"

"Yep," Sam said with a nod. "But that's nothing compared to the time he got hit by a pitch." His gaze swung to Mason, a look of admiration on his face. "I heard all about it when they did that special on you for the Sports Channel. It was cool. You really made him pay, didn't ya, Wild Man?"

Mason looked uncomfortable. "Well, that was another time in my life, before the Lord and I. . ." His voice trailed off as he seemed to be searching for an appropriate answer.

Pulling off the blue ball cap, he ran his hand through his hair in an unconscious ritual she'd seen Sam perform hundreds of times. It broke Blair's heart that something so simple, a gesture done so many times it had most likely become mindless, could affect her so strongly. But everything about Mason Walker had affected her back then.

She stole another look and had to admit it still did. Sam tugged on her arm, bringing her thoughts crashing back to the present.

"Tell Mom like you told me," he implored Mason.

∞

Mason grimaced as he returned his cap to his head. The boy wouldn't rest until he thought of something to say. And from the look on his mother's face she was none too pleased.

Given his current state of mind, Mason could have cared less about Blair's feelings of discomfort. What he did care about, however, was making sure Sam understood. The last thing he wanted to do was give a false impression of what was right to the boy.

To his son.

His thoughts caught on the word and held there until Sam jarred him back to reality with a gentle poke in the ribs. "Hey, something wrong, Mr. Wild Man? You look sad."

"Naw, I'm fine," he said lightly. "It's just that I don't like talking about that stuff. I was a stupid, hot-headed player who did a whole lot of things wrong before Jesus Christ and I paired up. I hardly think your mom's interested in my old war stories."

He picked up the ice bag, weighing it in his hand as he risked another peek at Blair. No smile seemed forthcoming. Quickly, he cast about for another subject. "How's that bump anyway?"

"It don't hurt much, I guess."

"It doesn't hurt much," Blair corrected.

"Yeah, that's what I said." Sam rubbed one grubby finger against the blue-black knot on his freckled cheek and looked up at his mother. "Do I get spaghetti for supper?"

Tilting the corners of her mouth into a wry smile, Blair gave the boy a sideways look.

"Sometimes when I get hurt or have a bad day, she tells me she'll make spaghetti for supper," Sam continued. "I bet your mom used to do the same thing, huh?"

No, but someone else I loved did.

He felt a tug on the sleeve of his shirt. "You're gonna have spaghetti with us, aren't you, Mr. Wild Man?"

Mason didn't miss Blair's sharp intake of breath. "Well, I'd like to, but—"

"I'm sure Mr. Walker already has plans for the evening." A thread of what sounded like panic rose in her voice.

Actually, he did have plans. He planned to fall into bed the minute he hit the empty hotel suite.

But no way would he tell them that.

"C'mon, Mr. Wild Man," Sam said. "My mom makes the best spaghetti in the whole world." He gave Mason a broad smile, with dimples appearing on either side of his mouth. "She'll even pick out the mushrooms if you don't like 'em."

"Sweetheart, Mr. Walker's a busy man. He probably has a plane to catch."

The boy's mother gazed at him expectantly, looking as if she knew he would agree. Mason smiled back and considered how much he would enjoy bursting Blair's bubble and letting her know he'd cashed in his ticket home and planned to stick around awhile.

At least until he could unravel the mystery of instant fatherhood.

"Spaghetti with no mushrooms." He pretended to contemplate the offer, allowing a small bit of joy at Sam's enthusiasm. "Now that's an offer I don't get very often."

"Aw, Mr. Wild Man, just say you're gonna come over," Sam said, the bump obviously forgotten. "We eat at six every day, and if you're late you don't get anything 'cept a peanut butter sandwich. Isn't that right, Mom?"

"That's right, Sam, but—"

"You gotta get all clean, too. Mom's real funny about that. And don't wear your hat at the table either. Mom says it's not polite."

He grudgingly admired the fact Blair cared enough about the boy to set some boundaries and stick by them. It said something about her and the kind of person she intended Sam to be. Unfortunately, the merit paled in comparison to the fact she'd chosen not to share this child with him.

"Please?"

The excitement in Sam's voice was contagious. If only the circumstances had been different.

How would he manage to get through an evening with the two of them? One look at Sam and he knew he'd have to try. "I'll come on one condition," he said, avoiding Blair's steady gaze. "You've got to stop calling me Wild Man."

"But—"

"No buts. Just call me Mason—deal?" He stuck out a hand to shake on it. *And maybe someday you'll call me Dad.*

"Deal!" The boy's pint-sized fingers easily disappeared in Mason's grasp. He was careful not to crush them. Too soon the manly gesture ended, the first agreement struck between father and son.

Mason slid a glance in Blair's direction. To his surprise, she gave him a shy smile.

"So dinner's at six?"

Her smile fell for a split second before she caught it. "It looks that way. Let me give you directions to my house." Blair pulled a small notebook from her purse and scribbled a few lines, then tore out the sheet and handed it to Mason. Without meeting Mason's gaze, she gathered her purse and stood, offering her hand to Sam. "Feel up to a trip to the grocery store, slugger?"

Mason struggled to his feet. "You talking to him or me?" *Where did that come from?*

Her blue eyes widened in shock as a lovely shade of pink crept into her lightly freckled cheeks. "Well, actually—"

"Sorry, ma'am," he said in his best John Wayne voice, arms outstretched. "Sam here says you're awful particular about having clean diners at your table, and right now I don't exactly qualify."

His poor imitation of a cowboy made her laugh, as it always had. Even in the worst of times it seemed he could make her laugh. Somehow he felt that talent might come in handy in the evening ahead. Despite the smile on her face, he had the distinct feeling she hadn't been thrilled he'd accepted the invitation.

But by the time he arrived at the white frame cottage on Whitley Road, freshly shaved and showered and bearing a bouquet of yellow roses, he'd concluded he didn't care how Blair reacted to his presence.

He stepped out of the Jeep, prayed up and determined not to leave this countrified version of Beaver Cleaver's neighborhood until he had the answers he wanted from her. The answers he deserved. She could start by telling him why she'd left without a trace in spite of their promise and finish up with a decent explanation of why she'd seen fit not to tell him of his impending fatherhood. And he wouldn't go anywhere until she did.

He strode past the white picket fence that surrounded the tiny yard, barely noticing the group of pint-sized ragamuffins clustered around the blue-and-white mailbox.

"Hey m—mister, are you really Wild Man W—Walker?" a squeaky voice called, halting his progress in mid-stride.

Mason turned slowly and came face-to-face with a band of kids that numbered almost a half dozen. Armed with various pieces of baseball equipment, they stared expectantly as their spokesman stepped forward and offered a pudgy hand.

"Pleased to meet you, big guy." Mason stifled a smile as he shook the boy's hand. Instantly, his mood improved. "Mason Walker."

A couple of the children elbowed each other, exchanging glances and quiet murmurs before growing silent again. Mason leaned down and smiled at the little fellow. "How can I help you?"

"W—well, see, we heard you might be in the neighborhood, so we th—thought it would be all right"—he colored a bright red as one of his friends poked him from behind—"you see, we really like b—baseball, and we were wondering—"

The Lord knew how much Mason loved children. They were some of the last honest folks left on the planet. He should've had a house full of them to come home to instead of an expensive but empty condo in Waikiki.

He shook his head. Baseball had been good to him. Why would he want to do anything else? His attention returned to the squirming boy. "Whatcha got there?"

"A g—glove."

"Nice glove." He lifted it out of the boy's outstretched hand. "But there's something wrong with it."

Brown eyes widened. "What?"

"Here—take these flowers and let me have a closer look." Mason handed him the roses and pretended to study the well-worn leather a moment, turning it over as he ran his hand over the names that covered its surface. "This has a couple of pretty good ballplayers' autographs on it."

The boy's chest swelled, and he clutched at the lump of flowers, effectively smashing a good portion of the yellow blooms. "Yep. My daddy took me and Sam to see the Astros play last summer, and I got those autographs there. I'm gonna get some more next time we go."

"What's your name?"

"Brian McMinn." A couple of others snickered, and the boy frowned at them before turning back to Mason. "I live right there." He pointed to the house next door. "Me and Sam are best friends."

"Well, Brian, I'll tell you what's wrong with this glove. It's missing my autograph." He lowered his voice and leaned closer to the astonished boy. "I'd be real honored if you'd let me sign my name right here next to that pitcher of theirs. If I remember right, he's the guy who pitched to me when I hit my first big-league home run."

He took the pen offered him and signed his name next to the scribbled signature of the overpaid player who'd almost taken his head off the last time he'd met him on the ball field. The round of *ooh*s and *ahh*s that followed made him all but forget the prima donna pitcher.

Mason handed the glove back to the beaming child. "Thanks. That was a real honor. Anyone else have something they want signed?"

As the rest of the group elbowed for position, he settled on an old painted bench in the shade of a towering oak, leaning his back against its crackled surface. He heard the screen door slam, then Sam's voice as the boy bounded toward them.

"Mr. Wild Man! I mean, Mason!" he shouted. "You're here!" He hugged Mason, then settled down beside him on the bench.

The aroma of garlic and tangy marinara sauce wafted toward Mason on the warm evening breeze as he spent the next half hour talking baseball and signing autographs. Through it all, Sam never gave up his place at Mason's side. When the screen door opened again, he knew it had to be Blair, and he stood to greet her with a promise to the youngsters that he'd be back another day.

The small group dispersed, leaving him alone with Blair and Sam. He looked around, taking in the scenery with a smile.

"I see you still have a way with flowers." He ran his hand over the red and white blooms that spilled out of a hanging basket beneath an ancient oak tree. "Best I remember, your mom could make anything grow," he said to Sam, who trailed behind him as he moved toward the house.

Too soon, Mason reached the porch and Blair. Reminding himself that he was a man on a mission, not a guy on a date, he steeled himself for the encounter, offering her the flowers instead of his hand.

Dressed in a flowing creation of yellow a shade lighter than the roses, she looked as if someone had taken sunshine and wrapped her in it. She accepted the flowers and murmured a word of thanks. Instantly, he resented her for looking so good.

He frowned, not caring that she saw. It would make his job tonight that much tougher if he allowed himself to be distracted.

Lord, let me remember I'm here for Sam. Grant me the strength to do what's right for him.

Still he allowed himself the luxury of one long look, starting with the burnished gold of her hair, this time worn away from her face, a barrette capturing the honeyed strands. The modest cotton dress she'd chosen was perfect, its soft yellow fabric sprigged with tiny blue flowers that matched the color of her eyes.

How many times had those eyes appeared in his dreams, overflowing with tears as she begged him to marry her all over again?

The answer was simple. Too many.

He continued his lazy perusal of her appearance, sure he was in complete control of his emotions. Just a man on a mission.

She spoke, and his concentration shattered. "Go wash for dinner, Sam," she said, watching the boy disappear inside the house before turning her attention to Mason. "Sam's thrilled you could make it."

He could tell she was nervous, and this pleased him. "And you?" Mason spoke before he realized what had happened, the words falling from his lips like the traitorous things they were.

Mason mentally condemned his stupidity. The first thing he said to her, and it came out sounding as if he cared what she thought of him. Which was ridiculous, he reminded himself, because he didn't care. Really, he didn't. He was just a man on a mission.

Only the opinion of the Lord and his son mattered. Blair was merely someone from his past.

"I'm glad, too, Mason." Her voice wrapped around his name and caressed it like a breeze from heaven. "It's been a long time."

Too long. Not that he cared, because he didn't.

Resting one foot on the wide wooden boards of the porch, he leaned against the rail and clutched it with both hands like a lifeline. For a moment, neither of them spoke.

A car passed on the road, kicking up a whirlwind of dust. Still no words were exchanged.

He dared himself to look into her eyes, risking he would feel nothing. He lost.

And when he lost, he lost himself as well. But at the same time he found the part of his soul he had been missing all those years. She had stolen it, taken it long ago without asking.

Sadly, she probably never knew she had it. Even worse, he realized he didn't want it back.

"Whatcha doing' out on the porch? I'm starving in here." Sam stared at him through the screen door.

From where Mason stood, he could tell the boy had combed his hair and changed into a clean shirt. He felt suitably impressed.

Blair moved first, pushing past the barriers his heart had erected, to disappear inside the little frame house. Reluctantly he followed, knowing his mission had fallen sadly into danger.

Chapter 4

Lord, guide my steps, Mason prayed.

Ignoring the pounding of his heart, he stepped inside the cottage. The room unfolded before him, and he felt his world tilt. Nothing in all his imaginings had prepared him for this.

Scattered throughout were touches of a life he thought he'd forgotten. A wild array of flowers in a simple glass jar stood on a little wooden table that had adorned their own tiny living room. In the corner by the window, the brass floor lamp they'd found in a little junk store in East Texas provided a subdued golden light. The lamp had been their first acquisition after the wedding, bought when thirty dollars was a lot of money and the rest of their lives still lay ahead of them.

He crossed the wide-plank oak floor, losing himself in the memories. A leather-bound book about New England gardens he'd purchased for her on a rare trip back home leaned against a container. He moved the book out of the way and picked up the container, a jelly jar he'd filled with bluebonnets and presented to her.

Smiling to himself, he thought about how he'd almost been gored by an old bull when he was picking those flowers. Blair had given him a hard time about that, even though he'd ended up with only a broken nose and a few scratches. Somehow he had known she was pleased he'd cared enough to risk life and limb over a bunch of blue flowers.

After all, they were her favorite. He wondered if she liked them because they matched her eyes.

He paused and savored the moment, remembering all this and more. Then, as quickly as it appeared, his smile faded. As great as things had been, as much as he'd loved her, it hadn't been enough. His love hadn't kept her with him. It hadn't made her stay.

To be fair, they were both guilty, he realized with a start. Each had followed their dreams, even if it seemed as though he had been the only one who'd paid the price in loneliness.

The warm memories turned cold, following the course of his thoughts to the day he learned she'd married someone else.

He could remember every detail, every moment of that day with a clarity that surpassed even his wedding day and his first big league game.

"Done anything dangerous lately?"

Blair's gentle voice jarred him back to the present. He replaced the jelly jar on the shelf before turning to face her. "I'm here, aren't I?"

She stepped into the glow of the lamp, her clean, floral perfume preceding her. He could count every freckle on her nose; yet, despite the hardness in his heart, she wasn't standing nearly as close as he wished.

"Yes, you are."

Her wistful tone caught him off guard, stabbing him with the slightest feeling of guilt for his anger. She seemed to recover quickly, and he wondered if he'd imagined it.

"Are those hands clean?" she asked playfully.

He held them out for her inspection, hoping she would touch them, take them, and close the distance between them, anything but just stand there looking so beautiful. Then she gave him a little half smile, and he sensed she must feel as uncomfortable as he did.

Good.

"Then let's eat." She looked away.

He nodded and offered her his arm, hoping she wouldn't take it and praying she would. When her fingers touched his bare arm just inside the elbow, he felt as if he'd been hit in the stomach by a ninety-mile-an-hour fast ball.

Neither of them moved for what seemed like an eternity.

"Why?" Mason formed the question, giving voice to it before reason forbade it, yet speaking it so quietly he doubted he'd made a sound. Her grip tightened, and he knew she'd heard. He forced himself to look into her eyes and saw them cloud with some unnamed emotion. Somewhere in the house, a clock struck six times. "Blair, why?"

Again it was more of a breath than a question. Her dark, thick lashes flew up at the sound of her name. His hand moved to touch her cheek, running his finger across the smooth line of her jaw. Still she stood frozen, eyes closed.

"You two comin', or do I hafta eat all by myself?" a childish voice called.

"I guess that's our cue," Blair said unevenly, not looking at him. She broke away from his touch and disappeared down the hall leading away from the front door.

Mason caught up with her as she stepped into an airy, old-fashioned kitchen that spanned the rear of the house. At one time the room must have been a porch of some sort, Mason decided, as he followed Blair and watched her place the roses on the dark blue ceramic countertop. A high, wooden ceiling loomed over brilliant white cabinets, while a half dozen hanging plants filled windows behind them. Several copper pots bubbled on the ancient porcelain monstrosity that passed for a stove, their fragrant contents beckoning him forward as Blair removed a loaf of bread from the oven.

He was watching her close the oven door when something caught his attention out the window behind her. Past a broken swing set, he saw a profusion of flowers and Sam's dog sleeping happily in the midst of them. Under other circumstances, he might have laughed.

"May I do anything?" he asked instead.

"You could put the roses in water." She pulled a large bowl of green salad out of the refrigerator. "There's a vase about the right size under the sink."

Their gazes held for a moment over the salad bowl. Blair opened her mouth to speak, then, apparently thinking better of it, carried the blue-and-white container to the table without uttering a word.

Shuffling through the contents under the sink, he finally came upon a rather decrepit-looking green vase. He held it up, fairly certain it hadn't seen use in years. "Don't get a lot of flowers, do you, Blair?"

"Nope." Her voice softened, fading to a murmur as she set the table. "Mine usually come from the yard, and it's generally Sam bringing them to me."

He shoved the flowers into the water and tried not to think of anything but the reason he was standing at her sink.

Watching her under the curtain of his lashes, he felt a familiar stab of emotion. Folding napkins and placing them on the table, Blair obviously had no idea of the picture of domestic happiness she presented to him.

He blinked, focusing his attention on the dark green vase in front of him.

Set the flowers on the counter.

Look out the window.

Do any of a hundred meaningless things to take your mind off her. Just don't let her get to you. Don't fall in love again.

No, he definitely would not fall in love with her again. He couldn't. He'd come tonight only to find out why.

As Sam came bounding into the room, another thought occurred to Mason. Maybe he was also here to get to know his son. He had nearly ten years to make up for, after all. Tomorrow he would get in touch with his lawyer and see what his rights were.

But first he had to get through tonight.

He offered her what he hoped would be a broad smile and placed the vase on the counter next to a red-white-and-blue trivet in the shape of a star. He guessed Sam must have made it because it was lopsided.

"Is there anything else I can do?" he asked.

"Just have a seat," she answered, slipping the crusty bread into a basket. "I hope you don't mind, but Sam and I usually dine informally."

"Of course not. You're talking to a guy who eats the bulk of his meals in a stadium."

Mason eased onto the closest chair, his mind still on that stolen afternoon. He swallowed hard and hoped the direction of his thoughts didn't show on his face.

Amazing, but his memory was a fickle thing. Whole years of his life had gone by without anything special to remember in them; yet every moment of their four-week marriage stood out in his mind as if it were yesterday. He shifted in his chair.

Blair and Sam began filling their plates. Pushing the memories away, he followed suit with a casualness he didn't feel. Sam jabbed a skinny elbow into Mason's ribs.

"Wanna say the blessing?" he whispered.

He winked at Sam to cover his surprise. "Why don't you do the honors, sport?"

He felt Sam grasp his hand tightly. "Thank You, Lord, for Mom's good food and for bringing Mason here tonight," the boy said. "I like him a lot. Amen."

Mason returned the squeeze. "And I like you a lot, too, Sam. Thanks for inviting me."

While being in Blair's presence felt unsettling to say the least, spending time with the boy had proved to be nothing short of delightful. He found himself craving more of it. "Maybe we can get together before I have to leave. Maybe hit the batting cages or grab some burgers," Mason said casually. "Would you like that?"

"Would I?" Sam paused and turned to his mother. "If it's okay with you, Mom."

∞

"When do you leave?" Blair said quickly. A little too quickly, she decided, masking her embarrassment by taking a long drink of water.

"I won't know until tomorrow."

"Oh?" As much as she wanted him to disappear, the thought of his leaving bothered her more than she cared to admit. She took another sip.

"Yeah, I have an MRI scheduled for tomorrow morning. What they find will determine when I play again."

"Oh."

Blair took a bite of spaghetti, surprised to find it had no taste. So he didn't plan a swift exit. She tried hard to pin down exactly how she felt about that, an impossible task given the fact that the object of those mixed feelings sat across the table from her.

"You sound disappointed."

Somehow she swallowed the bite. "No, it's not that. I mean, I'm just surprised—that's all. I thought you would have to wait until it stopped hurting to play again."

"If I wait for that to happen, I may as well quit." He took a bite of salad, washing it down with the rest of his water.

Praying for a steady hand, she reached for the pitcher and refilled his glass. "You mean you'd play hurt?"

As quickly as the words were spoken, Blair wished she could reel them back in. The Mason Walker she'd known so long ago would have played baseball even if he had to drag himself onto the field to do it.

And she had seen him do just that more than a few times.

She hated the memory and wished for some magic words to erase everything related to Mason from her mind. Sadly, she knew nothing short of a miracle would accomplish the feat.

Too many years had passed, and she'd given up praying for that sort of miracle. Most of the time her prayers were for peace and understanding now.

"If the doc says I'm able to play, I play," he said without looking at her.

"Of course."

As Mason turned to speak to Sam, Blair took the opportunity to study him. The years had been good to him, she decided.

A little broader across the shoulders and slightly thicker through the arms, his powerful body could still fill a room with his presence. Brushed away from his face and trimmed to a length slightly below his collar, his gently waving dark hair was showing a few threads of silver at the temples. In the late afternoon sunlight, she realized it only made him more handsome.

He was dressed in a simple white polo shirt and a pair of jeans and still wore his good looks as if he had no idea he possessed them. A thin gold chain, his only jewelry besides a watch, glittered bright against the darkly tanned skin of his neck.

Nothing fancy about Mason Walker, she thought. But there never had been.

He looked in her direction and smiled, dimples flashing, and she felt her knees go weak. Gripping her glass, she took another sip of water and prayed for strength. Still, she couldn't look away.

Age lines crinkled on either side of his amazing blue eyes, fading with his grin as he turned to Sam to answer a question. He refilled his glass and swiveled back in her direction to pour her a generous portion as well.

She nodded, her mouth suddenly dry. "Thank you."

"You're welcome." His direct gaze shifted to Sam, then returned to her.

He picked up the blue-checked napkin and wiped at the corner of his mouth. Her gaze went from the rectangle of cloth in his hand to his eyes that studied her intently.

She wondered if he realized why she loved the color blue so much. *Probably not*, she thought, lowering her gaze to take another bite of the tasteless dinner before her.

Men never noticed things like that.

∞

Halfway though the plate of spaghetti, Mason remembered why he never took his dates to Italian restaurants. Spaghetti made a mess.

He rubbed at the bright red spot on his jeans where a mound of sauce had landed and pretended an interest in the conversation swirling around him. While he watched the spot change to a dull orange, he caught snatches of a story about something Sam did as a baby. His attention piqued.

"Then Grandma told me if I was ever gonna learn how to walk I was gonna have to try harder so she took away my bottle and put it where I couldn't reach it. She said if I wanted it I had to go get it myself."

"He was almost eighteen months old," Blair explained, as if that fact had any relevance.

"So?" Mason's eyes went from the smiling boy to his mother.

"We were desperate." She gave him a look that told him she thought he should understand.

Well, he didn't. Instead his temper rose at the injustice his son had to endure at the hands of those women. He hadn't walked until long past the time he was supposed to, and he'd turned out fine, a fact he was about to point out to both of them when Sam elbowed him.

"Know what I did then?"

"Nope," he answered.

"I got so mad that I stood up and did it." He fairly beamed. "I learned to walk all by myself."

Mason felt his chest swell with pride. "That's great, buddy. You wanted that bottle, and you went for it."

"Nope." He stifled a giggle. "Not even close. Want to guess what I wanted?"

He glanced at Blair. She looked away.

"I give up. What?"

"Anyone want more salad?"

The high-pitched tone in Blair's voice caught him off guard. He noticed the deep pink on her cheeks as she stood and carried the salad bowl to the sink without waiting for an answer. A second later, she returned and began clearing the bread and marinara sauce off the table.

"Guess," Sam said.

Mason tore his attention away from Blair. "What?"

"Samuel Montgomery! That dog has flattened my geraniums again." Blair stood looking out the window, hands on her hips. "Do something with him!"

"Yes ma'am." Sam stuffed the last bite of bread in his mouth and washed it down with a swallow of milk. "It's probably 'cause of Melanie's cat again."

"I hardly think it's the cat's fault that your dog is sleeping in my flower bed." She gave Sam a long look. "And wipe your face. You're wearing half your dinner."

Mason discreetly covered the orange spot on his jeans with his napkin. He noted with dismay that the once-clean cloth now had a bright red stain that matched the one on Sam's chin. Covering it with his hand, he leaned back in his chair and observed the exchange between mother and son.

Sam shrugged. "Aw, he's just tired from watching after us all night." He swiped at the spaghetti sauce on his chin.

"I don't care," she said. "Remove him. Take him for a walk or something, but get him out of my garden."

He shot Mason a knowing look and smiled. "Yes ma'am."

Carrying his plate and glass to the sink, he pulled a bright red cap out of the back pocket of his faded denim shorts and placed it backward on his head. A thick shock of blond hair stuck out through the back of the cap and fell onto his forehead.

"I still get pie, right?" He gave his mother a determined look. " 'Cause it's not my fault Bubba wants to protect us all the time. I told him he's got to be the man of the house when I'm not here."

Mason felt his heart sink. The man of the house should be someone besides a nine-year-old boy or a mutt.

He glanced in Blair's direction. She'd begun washing the dishes, ignoring him and Sam as her hands moved beneath the surface of the sudsy water.

"Yes, you'll still get pie." She looked up from her task. "Now scoot!"

Dropping the cloth onto the counter, she crossed to the table where she began to stack the remaining dishes. Out of the corner of his eye,

Mason saw Sam heading for the door, a bright purple leash in his hand.

A thought occurred to him. "Hey pal. You never told me what made you want to walk so much," he said.

Sam smiled at him, his dimples dancing. With his free hand he opened the door, and his dog bolted onto the porch, then stopped and pranced back to his master's feet.

"A baseball." He leaned over and fastened the leash onto Bubba's collar. "Grandma put my bottle right next to it. Only she didn't know it was there 'cause Mom kept it in a little box with blue flowers on it and let me play with it only when it was just us at home." He shrugged. "I don't think Grandma liked baseball much. Hey, y'know, you never did think of a cool nickname for me."

Mason swallowed hard and hoped his voice still worked. "I didn't?" was all he could manage, and it came out sounding like a croak.

"Nope." The boy stood there while his dog ran in circles around his feet, tangling him in the leash. A pattern of muddy paw prints emerged as the dog slid and jumped about him.

"Well, I guess we'll have to work on that." Mason dropped his gaze to study the floor. "Now go take care of that mutt before your mom tells both of us we don't get pie."

He nodded and smiled broadly, then disappeared off the porch. A little piece of Mason's heart went with him. This time when he looked at Blair, she turned away. He knew without looking she had begun to cry.

Something moved him across the old linoleum tiles of the kitchen floor. When he wrapped his arms around her, all the hurt of the last ten years faded away.

She leaned back against his chest and wiped at her eyes with the dishtowel. "It was your—"

"First home run in the minors. I had to pay the guy who caught it ten bucks to get it back," he said, finishing her sentence.

"And it was the last ten bucks we had until the end of the week," she said quietly.

"I told you it would have to do for an engagement gift until I signed that ten-million-dollar contract and could afford a real wedding." He paused, holding her closer while losing his hold on his feelings. "I can't believe you kept it."

Chapter 5

Blair couldn't believe she'd kept it either.

Those memories and more came flooding back as she closed her eyes and allowed herself a moment to pretend it hadn't been ten years since he'd last held her like this.

"Forgive him, Blair. Forgive him as I have forgiven you."

The dishtowel fell at her feet, and her eyelids slid open. She focused on the towel rather than the man, the situation rather than the words bouncing around in her head. The issue of forgiveness was best dealt with another time.

His fingers encircled her wrist. Imagine the idiocy of leaning into the embrace of the one man she'd made her life's mission to avoid. Where was her brain?

A moment later, she felt his finger lift her chin. In self-defense she closed her eyes.

"Blair, look at me."

Against her better judgment she did.

Was it a trick of the light, or had the years fallen away to reveal the Mason Walker to whom she'd pledged her love and her life all those years ago? She blinked hard, but the image of the young Mason, crooked smile and lock of unruly hair teasing his brow, remained.

Lord, please don't let me fall in love with him again.

The thought sobered her. Forgiveness she'd consider, but love was entirely out of the question. As was standing this close, dredging up these memories, entertaining these thoughts.

"Dessert?" she asked, knowing full well the change of topic was not a smooth one. "I have pie and—"

Then he kissed her, and she was nineteen years old and speechless in his presence again. A girl unsure of herself and yet so sure Mason Walker was her whole world.

Her hands, of their own volition, found his shoulder and held on as he gently pulled away to touch her chin. He met her wavering gaze.

"I shouldn't have done that," he whispered.

Despite the legion of butterflies milling about in her stomach and the taste of marinara sauce on her lips, she somehow smiled. "No, you shouldn't have," she whispered back, although she couldn't think of a single reason why not.

Then he kissed her again. This time she threw out her cautious thoughts and dared to return the kiss.

Kissing Mason Walker brought up so many good memories. She reached for each precious moment as she reached for the back of Mason's neck and tangled her fingers in his hair. She held her memories to the light and relived each one in her mind, allowing the anger and distrust that had built up over the years to disappear. Forgiveness, that elusive decision she'd postponed so long, began to seem like an option.

Lord, what is happening?

The word *forgiveness* entwined with the word *love* and danced about in her mind until she forced them into submission. This was a kiss, nothing more; and if she wanted to kiss Mason Walker in the privacy of her own kitchen in broad daylight, then she could.

Just then the phone rang.

She ignored it. In fact, she wasn't sure she'd heard it. She knew Mason hadn't.

Then the phone rang again. This time the shattering sound broke the moment and their embrace.

"Phone," he whispered, raking a hand through his hair.

Her arms reached for him. "Answering machine," she said softly.

"Good."

A second later, the loud beep punctuated Blair's recorded request for the caller to leave a message. "Hello, Blair. I missed you today."

The distinct drawl carried easily through the quiet house, reminding Blair she hadn't called Griffin Davenport back to reschedule the meeting she'd missed because of Sam's accident.

Blair felt Mason tense beneath her touch. A fraction of a second later, he backed away.

"I'm up for tomorrow at noon if you still are," her client continued. "Just give me a call. You know the number."

Mason's eyes shut tight as the dial tone signaled the end of the message. In the span of half a minute, whatever feelings had passed between them seemed to slip away.

His eyes opened. "Hot date tomorrow?"

"Date? With Mr. Davenport?" She forced a chuckle. "Not hardly."

Mason looked away, apparently studying the table. "I have to get going."

"Mason, I—" She ran out of words and reached out to touch the back of his hand. Still he wouldn't look at her.

Instead, he cleared his throat and smiled faintly, his gaze now focused on some point behind her head. "Thank you for dinner. I'll tell Sam good-bye on my way out."

His footsteps echoed a swift rhythm on the hardwood floor; then the screen door slammed, and voices rose outside, along with the sound of a yapping dog. Sam's high, youthful tones mingled with Mason's deep voice until Blair couldn't stand to listen anymore.

She held her hands over her ears and willed herself to remember why he no longer had a place in her life.

Outside an engine cranked to a start, roaring in her ears along with the pounding of her heart. With all the dignity she could muster, she crossed the linoleum floor, her sandals making a loud slapping noise.

She walked toward the traitorous answering machine, punched the rewind button so hard the box fell off the table, then watched as the old black rotary phone crashed to the floor.

The dial tone shifted to a loud, angry beep. When a message from the phone company cordially warned her the phone was off the hook, she felt the first tear fall.

She gave the phone a good kick and went back to the kitchen to finish the dishes. On the counter a freshly bought apple pie from the best bakery in town mocked her. She fought the urge to throw the pie into the soapy water or, worse, to slice herself a huge chunk of it and drown it in vanilla ice cream.

Instead, she squared her shoulders, picked up the dishtowel from the floor, and headed for the sink and the pots and pans still decorating the counter.

"Oh!" She dabbed at her eyes impatiently. "Well, this was what you wanted. He's gone. Out of your life."

∞

Speeding down the empty country roads, he wished for his favorite black Porsche instead of the slower, less responsive Jeep. More times than he could count, he'd slipped behind the wheel of that little car and outrun his torments, losing himself in the purr of the powerful engine and the strength of prayer until the reason for his troubles had been forgotten.

But the Porsche was back at his home in Honolulu, and he was here, running away from Magnolia, Tennessee, with his tail between his legs.

Despite his intentions to the contrary, his thoughts turned to Blair and the deep feelings she managed to evoke in him. Instantly, he pushed them away.

He reached for his cellular phone. Punching in the number for his attorney's office in Honolulu, he steered the vehicle onto the interstate and waited for the secretary to answer before putting him through to Mike Brighton.

"Mason, how wonderful to hear from you again. I've been meaning to call you."

Lisa. The sound of the junior partner's soft, feminine voice caught him off guard, and he almost rear-ended a slow-moving log truck. Quickly, he swerved and regained his composure. "I really need to speak to the boss man. It's important."

The last person he needed to talk to right now was the woman who'd arrived on his doorstep in Montana two weeks ago declaring her intentions to see to his recuperation personally and privately. Before her high-heeled shoes could touch the front porch, Mason had sent her packing.

"I'm sorry about that little scene up in Montana," she said sweetly. "I just assumed, what with you being such a man of the world, that my offer—"

"Never assume," Mason ground out. He pressed harder on the gas, and the Jeep lurched forward.

Lord, control my tongue and make my words edifying to You. Otherwise, I'm about to lose my temper.

He jerked the wheel to the left in time to pass a minivan loaded with kids and camping equipment, then slowed his speed as the highway became more congested.

"Look, Lisa—it's been real nice talking to you, but I need to speak to Michael pronto."

"Are you sure there's nothing I can help you with?"

He felt only revulsion. "Positive."

After a few parting words, she reluctantly surrendered him to the managing partner. When he heard the masculine voice on the line, he released his tight grip on the steering wheel.

"Mason, good to hear from you, my friend. What can I do for you?"

Briefly he told him about the situation with Blair and Sam. A long pause filled the air as Mason signaled to turn into the hotel parking lot.

"Are you certain?" the attorney asked.

He'd done the math, worked out all the angles. There was no other explanation. And yet what about the Davenport fellow? In his heart, he couldn't consider it. Unless proven otherwise, Mason had to believe Sam was his son.

"I'm positive, Mike."

"Okay. As your attorney and, more important, as your friend, I have to ask you this." He hesitated. "Are you absolutely certain she's not running a scam on you?"

Mason briefly allowed a replay of the kiss they'd shared. Kisses, he amended with a frown. Nothing to get worked up about. He'd have to do a better job of avoiding Blair in the future. "I was married to her once, okay?"

"Oh?"

"The divorce was final just over ten years ago." He paused. "Ten years, get it? That's how old Sam is." Again he hesitated. "She doesn't even know I've figured it out."

"All right then. We have the element of surprise in our favor."

"The element of surprise?" Mason shook his head. "You make it sound like a war, Mike."

"And well it might be. She's obviously gone to great lengths to hide this child from you. It sounds like things could get ugly if we go in unprepared."

"Ugly?" Again he remembered the touch of her lips against his. "No, that's not Blair's style." But was it? He had no idea.

"Fine then. I can only give you preliminary advice based on what you've told me so far. At this juncture, our first course of action is to establish the child's paternity through legal channels. The second step will be to determine your rights and decide whether to pursue custody arrangements. Do you have access to a birth certificate?"

"Nope," he said as he let off on the accelerator.

"Then we'll have to do it the hard way. Do you think the mother is amenable to having DNA testing done on the boy? I could have the papers drawn up and faxed over in the morning. You could have your answer in record time."

Mason grimaced. She might not take kindly to his snooping around looking for proof that Sam was his son, especially if it involved lawyers and blood tests.

Besides, he would never have someone stick a needle in the boy just to prove he was his. Not if he could help it, anyway.

He also had to consider the possibility that Blair might run again. "Is there any other way?"

The attorney's hesitation lasted long enough for Mason to worry. "Nothing that won't take some time," he finally said.

"Time's something I don't have. I have an MRI tomorrow morning, and if that goes okay I could be leaving for a rehab assignment in a couple of days. I'd like to have proof before I go."

He heard the attorney let out a long breath. "Can you stall for time?"

"You have to be kidding."

"Okay, okay. It was a bad suggestion. Let me think of something. Where can I reach you later?"

"You have my cell number. I'll be at the hotel." Mason climbed out of the Jeep and tossed the keys to the valet.

An hour later, he leaned back in the chair in his hotel room and adjusted the bindings on his knee. Then, drumming on the newspaper in his lap, he sipped a glass of orange juice.

A little less painful this evening, his knee still felt stiff. The appointment tomorrow morning loomed large in his mind. He could guess what the outcome of the MRI would be, but what the Waves management would make of it was another thing altogether.

From experience, he knew his return to the team would have nothing to do with any medical tests. When the Waves needed him, they would find an expert to pronounce him fit to play, and he'd return.

He always did.

After all, playing baseball was his job, one that too many other guys would happily take away from him given the chance. Long ago he'd learned to accept the aches and pains and deal with them. A strong belief in the power of prayer had helped, too.

He lifted the heavy glass to his lips. The doctor he'd privately consulted two years ago had warned him if he continued to play he might have permanent knee damage. He'd predicted Mason wouldn't finish the season before his knee gave out, then the guy had practically dared him to prove him wrong.

Well, Mason had shown them all. Not only had he finished that season, but he'd played a couple of more since. He shook his head. The Lord had blessed him with the ability to play ball; he needed to remember that.

He also thought about where he'd learned his work ethic. His unshakable belief in God hadn't taken root until well into his twenties. Before that, the only father he knew was a man whose love of the game superseded any feelings he had for his son.

Every time he swung the bat and watched the ball fly past the outfielder's head and into the bleachers, he thought about his earthly father and the endless tirades that accompanied his coaching, about the stern-faced doctor and his gloom-and-doom predictions. His dad's desire for perfection was something Mason had taken to heart, molding it into a character trait some called a character flaw. Yes, he'd listened to his father and learned never to quit.

For that reason, he'd ignored the doctor. He was a good medical man, the best out there, according to his sources. But when it came to Mason Walker and his desire to play the game of baseball, the guy didn't have a clue.

Just as Mason reached for the remote control, the sound of his cell phone shattered the quiet in the room. He set what was left of his drink on the table and picked up the receiver on the second ring.

"Yes?"

"Mason, it's Michael Brighton again."

"Hey Mike." He picked up a hotel pen from the table and began to scribble on the sports page. "What do you have for me?"

A long pause. Mason colored in a dark blue mustache over the latest contender for the Cy Young pitching award.

"Mike?"

"Sorry, Mason, but I've come up short. I'm going to need more time to get the goods on the woman and her son."

He took a deep breath and tried to remember that he and the lawyer were working on the same side. "Look—I never said anything about getting the goods on Blair. You know me better than that, Mike."

"I regret my unfortunate use of words. Let me rephrase. I'd like to hire a private investigator. Maybe he can get to the bottom of all this."

"No." Mason gripped the pen in his hand and heard it snap. "I don't want anyone snooping around Blair and Sam."

"Then what do you suggest I do?"

He pitched the remains of the broken hotel pen into the wastebasket. "I don't care what you do, Mike, but keep Blair out of this."

"Mason, she's already in this up to her eyeballs."

Ignoring the sarcasm in Brighton's voice, Mason concentrated his gaze on the sports page in his lap. "What is it you need to know?"

"I need something concrete to go on. A birth certificate with your name on it would be ideal. Why don't you see if you can find one in a baby book? Surely the woman keeps that sort of thing lying around. They often do."

"So you want me to waltz into her house and ask to look at the boy's baby book?" The thought of going back there chilled him.

Mason heard him let out a long breath. "I didn't tell you to ask."

The implication of the lawyer's statement hit him hard. "I can't do that." Mason studied the glass before him.

"Look, Mason—we've known each other what, seven, eight years?"

"Yep." He tossed the paper on the floor, picked up the glass, and held it to the light, examining it as if the act of inspection would somehow remove him from the conversation at hand.

"Yet in all these years you've never once mentioned this woman?"

"Yep." Mason replaced the glass on the table and thought of their kiss, albeit one inspired by temporary insanity. He picked up the newspaper again and retrieved another pen from the desk drawer to continue drawing on the paper.

"I don't understand."

Mason said a quick prayer for guidance before speaking his mind. "I know Sam is mine, Mike. A father"—he tested the word on his tongue—"a father knows his son. I want him to know me, too."

The silence was deafening. "What exactly do you want?"

"I want something permanent. I'm afraid she's going to bolt again, Mike, and it'll be another decade before I see my son. I need to be sure that doesn't happen. Legally, I mean."

"Okay." To his credit Mike's reply was soft, almost emotional, and out of character for the man Mason knew.

"I realize that before I go to Blair with this I need to have proof, and I don't think she's going to give me proof willingly. Now, within the bounds of reason, what do you suggest?"

Mason finished his artwork on the Cy Young candidate, then allowed the newspaper to fall to the floor.

"How do you feel about spending more time with the woman?"

How did he feel about it? Scared to death, that's how he felt about it.

He'd walked into her house a man on a mission and left a man on the run. That thought alone made him feel like a fool. Now his lawyer wanted him to step back into the spider's web?

"I'll manage," he said as he hung up the phone, not really sure he would.

⌇

June 22

Blair put away the last of the breakfast dishes and contemplated the spot where she'd stood last night. In Mason's arms she'd forgotten everything she'd promised herself ten years ago. Involuntarily, she touched her lips with her finger, remembering their kiss.

She should never have let Sam talk her into inviting Mason here in the first place.

Not that Mason would likely return, she decided, as she dropped off Sam at camp half an hour later. Trying not to scan the parking lot for the black Jeep, she felt disappointed nonetheless when she didn't see it.

By the time she pulled into the Griffin Davenport Riverwood Center parking lot, she remembered Mason had mentioned something about having an MRI on his knee this morning. The medical tests were the first step in returning to the life he loved, a life in which she and Sam had no part.

"Forget about him, Blair," she muttered, as she set about preparing Riverwood Center's interior landscaping for its grand opening next week.

But forgetting him was impossible, and she knew it. She'd spent half the night dreaming about him and the other half awake trying not to. It seemed as though all rational thought had been suspended and replaced with memories of the handsome, frustrating man from New England.

It was all for the best, she reminded herself. After their disastrous evening together, she knew she would probably never see Mason Walker again

With several hours to kill before picking up Sam from camp, Blair headed home. When she arrived, Mason's Jeep was waiting in the driveway. She eased her van past the dusty black vehicle, then scanned the front yard for some sign of him. Sam's dog followed her up the driveway, staying just far enough away to keep from getting caught under the wheels. Blair pulled around the house and into the narrow shed that served as a garage.

Slamming the vehicle into PARK, she cut the engine and jumped out. Instead of entering the house, she threw her purse inside the back door along with her keys and set out to find her unwanted guest.

Making a complete pass around the house, she finally gave up. Bubba followed her back into the front yard, suddenly interested in the strange vehicle. While the dog sniffed at the tires of the Jeep, Blair put her hand on the hood.

Still warm. He hadn't been here long, wherever he was.

She climbed the steps to the front porch and settled in the old wooden rocker to wait for him. He couldn't have gone far, she reasoned, then reluctantly patted the dog's head.

Bubba dropped down on the gray-painted boards and rolled over, inviting her to scratch his belly. She ignored him, her thoughts churning and the knot in her stomach growing with each passing minute.

For better or worse, Mason Walker was back in her life.

She'd wished for it and prayed against it many times during the long, sleepless hours of the night, but now that it had happened, she wasn't sure how she felt about it. Grandma Lettie always said to be careful of what you wish for because it just might come true.

For once, her grandmother had been right.

But had it been right not to tell him about her pregnancy? Maybe Mason would have welcomed the chance to be a father to Sam. "He's too busy playing games to be a father to that child," her grandmother had been fond of saying. "That boy's got better things to do than change diapers. He don't want you and that baby. He told me so when he called. And here you were in the hospital a-havin' that precious baby."

She hadn't doubted the truth of that statement then, although she'd wondered about it more than once over the years, especially after she committed her life—and the situation—to the Lord. No longer could she blame her choice to leave Mason Walker out of his son's life on her grandmother.

No, the decisions she'd made ten years ago were coming back to haunt her now. She watched a hummingbird flit around the bright orange flowers of the trumpet vine that snaked up one side of the porch while she tried to calm her fears.

Mason's intrusion into their lives was a sudden and, she hoped, short-lived episode. Soon he'd be back in Hawaii with his team, and she could get on with her life. He would never know her secret, and neither would Sam.

That decided, she craned her neck and looked down the road. No sign of him. Where could the man be?

Crossing her arms in front of her, she stopped rocking and leaned one foot on the post. In the distance, a mockingbird landed on the mailbox. Bubba gave a half-hearted yip, and it flew away.

A moment later, the mystery of Mason's whereabouts was solved when she saw him walking up the road toward her house.

Chapter 6

$\mathcal{B}$ubba raised his head, alert to the intruder, and Blair patted him in hopes of keeping him quiet.

Jingling his keys and apparently unaware of her presence, Mason headed for his vehicle, bounding across her lawn with a frown on his face and a cell phone in his hand.

Stuffing the phone into his shirt pocket, he opened the door to the Jeep and had one leg inside the vehicle when Blair finally spoke.

"You're in a hurry," she said evenly.

Mason's dark head jerked up in surprise at the sound of her voice. Shock gave way to a smile, and he turned and walked toward her.

Bubba leaped off the porch and met him halfway. He patted the dog on the head, but his gaze never left Blair.

"Hey. I didn't expect to see you here. Mind if we talk inside?"

"Why?"

Mason turned his back to her and picked up a rock Sam had left on the corner of the porch. In one fluid motion he sent it sailing over the fence and into the road. Bubba jumped to attention and ran after it.

"Because you and I need to talk about some things."

His voice shouldn't have given her pause, but it did. Nothing in his demeanor suggested he had anything of importance to talk to her about.

She stood and gauged the distance between them. Too far and yet far too close.

∽

"All right," she said slowly. "I'll give you ten minutes to tell me why you're here."

She disappeared around the side of the house, and Mason heaved a sigh of relief. *What's she doing at home in the middle of the afternoon?*

"Okay, this is not a problem," he said under his breath.

All he had to do to cover his tracks was to come up with a convincing story as to why he'd driven all the way out here to take a walk. He could do that, he thought. After all, the best media experts in Major League Baseball had trained him. He knew how to say just enough without really saying anything. If he could deal with reporters, it would be a simple matter to work his charm on Blair without actually deceiving her.

He eased his worry down a notch. If Blair was home, Sam might be with her. That made getting caught almost worth it.

Then he stopped himself.

"Oh boy," he whispered. "Is this what you're about now, Walker?"

He hung his head. *Father, I am so ashamed. What do I tell her?*

The front door opened. "You now have nine minutes to explain, and I suspect it will take every bit of that."

Blair's cool, soft voice shook him into action, and he followed her retreating figure inside. As his eyes adjusted to the interior of the house, he heard a curtain snap open, and his head followed the sound.

She stood in the window, her form silhouetted against the bright landscape of flowers and trees outside. Without a word, she sank down onto the window seat and pulled her legs underneath her, crossing them. The look on her face gave away nothing of what she might be thinking.

Mason took a deep breath, let it out slowly, and entered enemy territory with a smile on his face. What he was about to say, he had no idea, but he knew it had better be good. Stalling for time, he took a picture of Sam from the bookshelf. "Cute kid," he said.

"Eight minutes."

"Okay, I'll get to the point. I had an MRI on my knee this morning, and the doctors have cleared me to go back to the team after the break." He walked over to her and dropped into the nearest chair. "I didn't realize how much I missed hanging around with you until last night. I don't want it to end."

∽

His honesty stunned Blair. She found herself looking for something to say in response. Instead, she pushed a strand of hair off her forehead and contemplated the fringe on the brass lamp.

"You've raised a great kid," he said, breaking the silence between them.

Risking a glance in his direction, she felt an unwelcome jolt as their gazes met. "Yes, he is pretty great, isn't he?"

"And you did it alone. That's quite an accomplishment considering. . . ."

She lifted an eyebrow. "Considering?"

"Yes," he said. "Considering you lost your husband. Your second husband, that is. That must have been tough."

Warning bells sounded in her mind. She grabbed the nearest pillow, a floral chintz, and clutched it to her chest. How could he know this? Who had told him?

A car raced by on the narrow country lane, causing him to look out the window. "Care to talk about it?" he asked her.

"No. But you're down to six minutes."

His gaze swung back in her direction. A smile started on his face, growing in its intensity until she fully expected him to laugh aloud. "Fair enough," he said.

He leaned toward her, and Blair had the wildest urge to jump backward. Instead, she calmed herself by clutching the pillow tighter.

Then he touched her arm, and her concentration splintered. A jolt passed through her. She forced herself to ignore it.

"I'm waiting." She tried to sound stern but knew she failed when he smiled again and her heart started beating wildly.

"Okay. We had a good run, didn't we, Blair? I mean—what we had was something special."

"Yes, it was."

Her answer was a shade louder than a whisper, a reflection of her reluctance to answer. She clutched the pillow even tighter, fully expecting it to burst at any minute.

"And our divorce. We blew it by taking the easy way out, didn't we?"

There, the truth was out.

Blair met his gaze, and her shoulders slumped. "There was a time when I would have disagreed with you." She looked away.

"But now?"

Again she focused her attention on him. "But now I know better. As wrong as we were to rush into marriage, we were even more wrong to end it so quickly."

Mason was quiet for a moment. "I don't want to lose touch with you. I know that sounds strange, but not too many people out there can look at me and not see dollar signs." He pulled his hand away and studied it. "Let me get to know you again."

A tight knot formed in her stomach. She took a deep breath and began to count the tiles on the ceiling, exhaling slowly.

"Blair?"

She forced herself to speak, holding back tears. "Why?"

"Do I need a reason?" He paused and seemed to be considering his own question. "History. That's it. Even though it didn't work out between us, we have history." He leaned back in the chair. "Besides, that boy needs a man around."

∞

"Sam's doing just fine." She said the words too fast.

Mason knew he'd made a mistake. *Try again, ace.* "Okay, you want the truth?"

She let out another long sigh. "That would be nice." He heard the dog bark twice, then fall silent. "And you have four minutes."

He took a deep breath and closed his eyes as he prayed for guidance. Then it came to him. *Just say it, get the truth out there and see what happens.*

"Okay, I just love being around him, you know? He's the kid I hope to have someday. I thought I could get in a little practice while I'm here. Find out what it's like to have a son of my own."

There. He'd said it. The truth, or at least a close approximation of it.

Ever since his first conversation with Michael Brighton, he'd been thinking how great it would be to have his son around on a permanent basis—to be a real father to Sam. Mason opened his eyes slightly and peeked at Blair, trying to gauge her reaction. Her fingers had gone white at the knuckles, and the frilly pillow she clutched to her chest was about to pop under the pressure.

She threw the pillow at him and stood abruptly. "I won't be an experiment in family life. Your time's up. Please leave."

Like the veteran infielder he was, he caught the pillow with one hand, dropping it swiftly to the floor with his other hand. And as Blair brushed past him to leave the room, he used his best defensive skills to stop her progress. "Wait."

∞

Blair turned to face Mason. "Wait? That's the best you've got?"

For a moment, she thought he might say something, but all he did was shrug. And despite herself she felt a giggle rising.

It wasn't funny, really, the way he'd shown up out of the blue. But the goofy look on his face made her forget for a moment all that stood between them. He had come in peace, and she'd overreacted, listening to all those terrible things Grandma Lettie had drilled into her brain, instead of giving him a chance.

Blair looked up at him. She couldn't think of the right word to describe him. She caught his attention and laughed again, and this time he joined her. The two of them laughing like kids brought back the best of times, days when the weight of the world had been far away and love had been all they needed to get by.

Blair touched the back of his hand lightly with the tip of her fingers. "Truce?" she heard him say.

"Truce."

She offered him something cold to drink, and he accepted. They walked back to the kitchen and sat at the old familiar table. Over iced tea and leftover pie, Mason began to regale her with tales of his struggle out of the minor leagues, his experiences along the way, and the extraordinary life baseball had given him.

Listening to him talk, a slight trace of his New England roots still evident in his voice, she felt a twinge of some foreign emotion. Jealousy perhaps? She couldn't be sure, but whatever it was, she knew she had no claim on it or him.

He told her about his place in Montana, and she watched his face soften. More years slipped away as he told her of the realization of another of his dreams, the purchase of several prize mares and a new stable of his own. She pictured him on the back of one of his cutting horses, man and animal working as a finely tuned pair, and knew he had all he needed in his life. This time when it came, she recognized the jealousy for what it was and pushed it away.

The fact that he led a full, happy life was as it should be. The fact that the life he led had nothing to do with her was her fault—and her choice—entirely.

By her actions, without his having a say in the matter, she'd given him the ability to lead the life he had. She'd spared him the heartache of giving up his dreams. But most of all neither of them had to watch what they had together slowly die as his resentment of her grew.

The reality of that thought soothed her as much as his close proximity had disconcerted her only moments before. Her aching conscience eased slightly.

Yes, just a couple of old friends spending some time together, she reasoned, as she watched the rise and fall of his chest from her too-close vantage point. *And Sam will be thrilled,* she decided, as she contemplated the fresh, masculine scent of his aftershave, the same fragrance he'd used when they were in love.

She could handle it if he could.

"I've been the one doing all the talking," she heard him say. The words jerked her back into reality with blinding speed. "Tell me about your life, Blair."

"M–my life?" Here it was, the moment of truth. She took a deep breath and let it out slowly. "Oh, I don't know. There's really not a lot to tell."

"Tell me anyway. Start with the day you left for England." His blue eyes, bright and clear, barely blinked. For a disturbing moment, it seemed as if that gaze were trying to peer into her very soul. "I want to know."

"Okay." She took a long drink of iced tea and set the glass back on the table. "I was so excited about the opportunity to study abroad, but when I got there, things were very different from how I'd imagined them."

He looked away. "Tell me about Sam's father."

What could she tell him? "It was all so sudden—and totally unexpected. I'd rather not talk about it."

The smooth, impassive expression on his face softened for a split second. "I see."

A drop of condensation slid down the glass. She watched it, unwilling to lift her gaze to face Mason. *Lord, please give me the right words. Don't let me hurt him any more than I have, but please don't let him find out about Sam.*

"Tell me about your son." His statement startled her.

"Sam's a gift from God, and I could never imagine life without him." That was definitely the truth.

"Any regrets?"

∽

A tear threatened to slide down her cheek. She wiped it away. "What I regret is that I had to lose you," she whispered. The power of that declaration slammed against her chest. She instantly wished she could capture those words and reel them back. Instead, she resumed her desperate dance on the edge of the truth. "Can we not talk about this anymore?"

He shifted positions, leaning slightly toward her, his elbows on the table and his hands cradling his head. "Do you know how long I've wanted to find out about you, Blair? I drove myself crazy for the love of you."

The look on his face told her he hadn't intended to say that. He closed his eyes, opening them slowly only to focus on something on the other side of the kitchen. He lowered his glass, releasing it when it touched the surface of the table.

Then the impact of his words hit home. He loved her?

But Grandma Lettie said. . . .

No, she couldn't consider the implications. He had to be lying. She felt the fragile truce begin to fall apart and scrambled to make things right again. "Hey, everything turned out okay, didn't it?" She forced a smile and reached across the distance to touch his hand. "You have had a great life."

"Yep." Finally, he smiled. "I guess you're right. And so have you."

"Yeah." *Oh Mason, you have no idea.*

Pulling his fingers from beneath hers without warning, Mason stood and checked his watch, a gold and stainless steel Rolex. *Another reminder of the differences in our lives,* she thought. She could pay off all her debts and put braces on Sam's teeth with the amount that timepiece had cost him.

"I'd better go help Trey before he tracks me down." He smiled. "I told him I'd be there by two."

"How is Trey these days?" she asked quickly.

"The same." Mason shrugged. "He retired three years ago, and now he sells mansions to movie stars out in L.A. He does these camps every summer to stay busy."

Blair smiled, thankful for the neutral subject.

They were almost to the door when Mason stopped and touched her lightly on the arm. "Let me bring Sam home after camp today."

She hesitated, trying to accustom herself to the idea. "Okay," she finally said. "If he doesn't mind."

"If he does, I'll call you. Where can I reach you?"

"I'll be home all afternoon. I have an armload of drawings to go over."

"Sounds like you're one busy lady," he said, removing his hand from her arm. "What is it you do?"

"Landscape design," she said. "Residential and commercial. I do office buildings mostly and a couple of restaurants and some private homes."

"For the guy on the phone?"

Was that a frown she saw appear and instantly disappear? She forced back a smile. "Yes, him and others. I plant the plants that everyone ignores, then keep them growing afterward."

He touched a dirt smudge on the hem of her shirt. "That explains this."

"I guess you could say I'm the supervisor and the crew. My business is still in the growing stages." She grinned despite her nervousness. "Pardon the pun."

Mason grinned. "But you're doing what you always wanted to do," he said slowly. "I'm proud of you for making that dream come true."

But how many much more important dreams had died? "Yes" was all she could manage. Then a thought occurred to her. "You never did say why you were here."

She thought she detected a stiffening of his shoulders. His face went blank, then he smiled and shook his head. "I came to talk, that's all."

He stepped out onto the porch and surveyed the front yard. Bubba appeared from out of the shadows of the oak, wagging his tail furiously. "Oh, about tonight."

Her traitorous heart leapt as Mason whirled around to face her.

"Yes?" Oh, great—she sounded too interested. "What about it?"

There, that was better. Interested, but only in a casual, friendly sort of way.

"How about if I get Sam out of your hair and take him into town to a ball game? Trey and I have tickets to the college game, and we came up with an extra one for Sam if you'll let him go. We'll be out of your way all evening, and you can get lots of work done."

Her happiness plummeted. "Great."

"Something wrong?" Mason asked.

"No, nothing." She'd just been offered a rare afternoon and evening off without the responsibilities of parenthood. With Sam occupied, she would get a little extra time to work on projects that might some-day launch her business into the realm of profitability. What could be wrong?

Mason nodded and turned toward the Jeep, then stopped a few feet away and patted Bubba on the head. Mason's blue gaze connected with Blair's over the distance separating them.

"Hey Blair, thanks," he said. "For letting me spend time with Sam, I mean."

"Sure."

He drove away, and she watched him go through a fog of swirling emotions. The man who'd arrived an enemy was leaving a friend, and she needed time to digest this. And fortunately, or unfortunately, time was something that was suddenly in great supply.

Chapter 7

Peanut shells, stray popcorn, and empty cotton candy bags littered the stadium floor behind home plate where Mason, Sam, and Trey sat watching the game. After the ninth inning, when the last batter had been retired and the game ended, Mason stood and stretched.

"Okay, buddy, let's get out of here."

Sam tugged on his sleeve and pointed to the field. "You said I could run the bases."

"I did?" His shoulders sagged. "Sure, slugger." Mason tapped the bill of the boy's red hat and offered him a weak smile. "Go ahead. We'll watch from here."

Trey slapped his back and smiled at him. "Tired?"

"Nah, I'm fine."

Actually, nine innings with a nine-year-old had wiped him out, but in a good way. At this point, the job of major league second baseman looked easy compared to the job of being a dad.

"Hey, Mason!" a childish voice called. "Watch!"

On the other side of the fence, Sam stood poised to run the bases. Pride swelled in Mason's chest as the boy faked a home run swing and took off in the direction of first base. The feeling grew into a full-blown ache as he rounded second. By the time he'd made it to third,

Mason felt his eyes stinging. The twinge in his chest moved upward, lodging in his throat.

A big tear stung his eye as Sam slid into home feet first. Mason tried to hide the tear from Trey with the back of his hand, praying he could contain the rest before they fell.

"Something wrong?" Trey asked.

"Nope," Mason said, wiping the remainder of his emotions off his face. "Just something in my eye." He gripped the back of the seat in front of him, steadying himself.

"Oh. . ." Trey's voice trailed off as Sam trotted across the grass toward them. A look of recognition grew on Trey's face, and Mason felt dread course through him.

"Oh Mase," Trey finally said. "Except for the color of his hair, he's the spitting image of you. He even has your swing."

"You're crazy," Mason heard himself say.

"Crazy like a fox," he answered, returning Sam's wave. "He's got your walk, too." Trey pointed the empty cup in his hand toward Sam for emphasis. "I don't know why I didn't see it before. He's yours, isn't he?"

Briefly, he considered denying it, but he'd known Trey. "Yes," he said. "I'm pretty sure he is."

"Pretty sure, Mase? What does that mean?"

"Okay, he is mine, but Blair doesn't know I figured it out." Saying the words liberated something inside of him. At that moment, shouting his newfound parenthood from the rooftops seemed the next step. A step he'd dearly love to take if only he could.

"So what're you going to do about it?"

"Keep your voice down. I've got to go slow," he said. "I don't want her to run off again. I lost out on the first nine years of Sam's life, and I don't intend to miss any more of them." He gathered up the remains of Sam's souvenirs and started toward him with Trey following a step behind. "I'll find out the truth somehow."

"Buddy, the truth's staring you in the face." He pointed to Sam, who had made his way off the field and stood a few feet from them, absorbed in watching the grounds crew cover the field against the impending rain. "Won't be long before everyone else'll be seeing it, too. Just look at him."

Before Mason could respond, Trey gave him a broad smile and disappeared into the crowd with a shout of good-bye. Mason grabbed

Sam by the hand and went in search of the Jeep with Trey's words weighing heavily on his mind.

"So you've lived here all your life?" Mason asked casually as he pressed the power locks and cranked the ignition.

"Yep," Sam said, playing with the buttons that moved the Jeep's passenger seat.

Mason ignored the urge to tell him to stop. "Born in Tennessee?" he asked, watching the boy out of the corner of his eye.

"I guess." Sam tired of pressing that button and moved to another. "Hey, what does this do?"

The CD player screamed to attention, and a loud guitar solo filled the car. A second later, Mason snapped it off, and silence reigned again. Looking contrite, Sam settled back in his seat and pulled two pieces of candy out of his shirt pocket as Mason steered the Jeep onto the highway.

"Want one?" Sam flipped on the overhead light, temporarily blinding Mason.

"No, thanks," he answered, grasping the steering wheel firmly and focusing on the highway in front of them.

Sam unwrapped both candies and stuffed the sticky paper into the empty ashtray. "Watch this." He opened his mouth, revealing two round orange candies.

"Wow." Up ahead, a sign indicated the number of miles to their destination. Mason prayed for strength. "So the candy's round. That's great."

"No, dontcha see?" He opened his mouth again.

"Yeah, candy." *The boy is easily entertained,* he thought as he flipped off the interior light and turned onto the road leading north. "And it's round."

"No, look. It was red, and now it's orange. In a minute, it'll be yellow."

"Well, how about that?" Mason suppressed a smile. When had the ability to find joy in such simple things as color-changing candy and pushing buttons left him?

Thank You, Lord, for bringing me Sam. And thank You for returning my joy.

Concentrating hard on the candy in his mouth, Sam fell silent. Occasionally, he held it in his hand, checking the progression of colors through the spectrum of the rainbow in the light of the glove compartment. Each time he wiped his hands on something other than the paper napkin Mason had handed him, until finally the candy was gone and Sam fell asleep.

For the first time since he'd picked up the Jeep at Intercontinental Airport, he felt happy he wasn't driving his Porsche. Yet he was still glad the boy was with him.

His mind drifted back to Trey's claim that soon his paternity would become evident. He pondered the idea most of the way back to Magnolia.

By the time his tires crunched the familiar gravel of the driveway, he'd reached a decision. Lifting the boy's sleeping form out of the passenger seat, he carried him to the front door and knocked softly.

Opening the door, he stepped inside.

"Blair?" No answer.

He carried Sam upstairs and into the room at the front of the house where he'd seen him looking at the stars. It was easy to tell the room belonged to a young boy. Baseball posters lined the walls, and stacks of cards stood several inches high on the night stand.

As he settled the boy into bed, he saw that his current card lay on top of the stack. Near the baseball-shaped night-light, a small picture of him in last year's Waves uniform hung on the wall. He smiled.

"Good night, slugger." He removed Sam's cap and hung it on the bedpost, then headed downstairs to find Blair.

∽

"Blair?"

Mason's voice floated toward her, gentle and soft. She smiled and tried to form an answer. Instead only his name escaped her lips.

Blinking heavily, she willed her eyes to focus. And when they did, she was immediately sorry. There stood Mason, both arms crossed in front of his chest, biceps straining against the sleeves of his shirt. On his face was a mischievous grin, marked on either side by deep dimples.

"Sorry, Blair," he said, taming the grin temporarily. "I didn't mean to wake you."

"Wake me?"

She looked around, a puzzled expression on her face. Finally, she realized she was sitting at her desk, a pile of slightly crumpled drawings under her outstretched arm, and the cloud began to lift.

"Was I dreaming?"

Another grin emerged, this one even bigger than the one before. "Yep," he finally said, his blue eyes twinkling. "And it must have been a good one because you said my name." He paused. "Twice."

"I did not!" She sat upright, trying to look dignified in her confusion.

"Afraid so," he said, chuckling. "Not that I blame you."

She tucked a wayward strand of hair behind her ear, refusing to let her embarrassment show. It was time to change the subject.

"Where's Sam?"

"He fell asleep halfway home," he said. "I put him to bed. His room's the one with the baseball posters, right?"

"Yes, thanks," she said softly, trying not to picture Mason's dark head leaning over her sleeping son as he tucked him in.

"It was my pleasure." Even through the fog of her sleepy state, she could tell he meant it.

"Well, I guess I'll say good night then. I have an early start tomorrow. Eight o'clock meeting with my therapist."

She raised an eyebrow.

"Physical therapist," he said quickly.

"I knew that." They shared another smile as the clock struck eleven. "Thanks again for spending time with Sam tonight."

"No problem. Can we do something tomorrow, all three of us? Say six o'clock?"

"Tomorrow?" Fidgeting with a paper on her desk, she tried to swallow her anxiety and nodded. "Sure. What do you want to do?"

"Leave it to me," he said with a smile. "It's my turn to feed you two. Mind if I cook here?"

She mumbled something in agreement, and Mason walked over to the door. She watched him disappear around the corner and into the hall. A second later, he reappeared in the doorway, another mischievous grin on his face.

"Blair?"

"Yes?"

"You still snore."

Before she could deny the claim, he was gone.

∞

June 23

The morning, when it finally dawned, looked dreary, and by noon the gray sky had turned bleak with the possibility of more rain. Blair shoved away the thick stack of drawings and contemplated the pair of hummingbirds flitting outside her window. She stood to lose a small fortune in commissions because she couldn't concentrate, and it was all Mason Walker's fault.

"This is silly." She pulled the drawings back within reach and removed the pencil from its place behind her ear.

Outside the sky threatened a much needed shower, while inside Blair forced her mind back onto the work at hand. She unfurled the drawings and began to fill in the empty spaces with scale models of the plants she planned to use. Half an hour later, the blueprints of Griffin Davenport's private walled garden showed a space that would bloom with bright annuals and perennials, an elegant gazebo, and a lily pond situated in their midst. Satisfied with the results, she transferred the information onto her computer, rolled up the drawing, and began working on the next one.

A few errant raindrops spattered against the windowpane, their uneven cadence contrasting with the ticking of the old Regulator clock in the hall. Unbidden, Mason's face came to her again.

Rain.

It had been raining the first time they'd met. She closed her eyes and tried to picture him as he'd looked that day, but no distinct image would come to her, not as it did before.

Instead, she saw him as he was now, all the lines and imperfections that age had wrought, visible and endearing. The cocky kid he'd been on that first meeting had given way to the man he'd become, a man she had gradually begun to allow back into her heart despite her misgivings.

Thunder rumbled, and the wet pane answered with a small but audible shudder. She opened her eyes and watched the fat drops fill the deep ridges in the ground and clear the dust off the old wooden bench in the front yard.

Rain.

It had been raining the day Sam was born, too. Through a fog of pain she'd called for Mason, knowing somewhere in her dulled mind he would never come. That night she held their child for the first time and listened to the rain. Every drop that fell mocked her, reminding her that Mason would be with her always, yet she would never be with him.

She could never bear to see the hatred in his eyes for saddling him with an unwanted child or even the betrayal on his face for not telling him. She still feared the same reaction. Ten years later, nothing had changed.

Except that he'd found her. Had God put them together again for a reason?

Without warning a bright shaft of sunlight cut across the page, bidding her to follow its path as it traveled over the scars and imperfections of the ancient wood floor toward the antique bookcase in the corner. Out of the shadows a wooden box painted with sprays of bluebonnets seemed to glow with the light that fell across it.

And she knew she had to open it.

Caressing the smooth wooden surface with one fingertip, she took a deep breath and let it out slowly. Another rumble of thunder sounded, this one distant and muted. Slowly she lifted the lid.

Tucked inside a circle of worn green fabric was a dirt-smudged baseball, her engagement present. A smile touched her lips. Warmth spread through her as she pulled the ball out of its nesting place and held it to her cheek. A thousand happy musings flooded her mind.

Joining the recollections of the past were the pictures of the present, images of Mason and Sam together. Suddenly, she couldn't be so sure about the decisions she'd made so long ago. They were adults now, mature people with lives of their own and a son that held them permanently connected.

Didn't he deserve to know?

But how would he react? Would he accept Sam as his son? She pondered this, thinking about what he'd told her about wanting a child of his own someday.

Someday, but not now.

Oh Lord, show me what to do. I want to do Your will, not mine, and I'm having a hard time with it. I have to think of what Your wishes are for Sam. Please give me some sign.

The phone rang, and when she picked it up she heard his voice. "Mason," she said, shoving the box back into the shadows. "I was just thinking about you. I'm glad you called."

Instantly, she cringed, wishing she hadn't said that. What was wrong with her? She sounded like a teenager, all tongue-tied and silly.

"You were?" She heard him chuckle. "Good or bad?"

"I refuse to answer that," she said, recovering her composure. "What's up?"

"It's about tonight."

Her heart fell. "Oh?"

"Yeah, something's come up."

"Oh." The sun hid behind a cloud, echoing her mood. "I understand."

"I'm expecting a conference call at five-thirty, so can we make it a little later, say at seven?"

The room remained cloaked in shadows, but her heart soared. "Sure. Seven it is. Is there anything I can do? Maybe dessert?"

There was a long pause. "Yeah, do you have any more of that pie?"

"You got it," she said softly, hoping that what she'd just heard had been some sort of convoluted male apology for his abrupt departure and hasty assumptions. "See you at seven."

"Hey, Blair?"

She touched the windowpane with one finger and traced the raindrop as it rolled downward. "Yes?"

"I'm glad you were thinking about me."

∽

As he hung up the phone and looked out the rain-splattered front window of the Jeep, he felt a little ashamed he hadn't told her he'd been thinking about her, too. The sad fact was he hadn't been able to get her out of his mind ever since last night.

She had looked innocent and at peace in her slumber while he stood in the doorway and stared, unable to do anything else for a full minute, maybe two. When rational thoughts returned, he'd planned a quick escape, deciding to slip out the door without awakening her.

Then she said his name.

Her voice, hoarse with the effects of whatever she'd been dreaming about, wrenched a knot in his gut when he heard it. He'd moved closer.

Then she said it again.

It irked him that he'd give anything to hear that sleepy voice calling his name just one more time. Surely he didn't really feel that way.

And by the time he reached his hotel room half an hour later, he'd almost convinced himself of that fact. Still, he took his time showering and shaving before looking in the closet for something to wear.

He wanted to give Blair the impression that the evening was no big deal, nothing for which he would dress up. Just another night out.

Discarding several other choices, he put on a pair of starched jeans and a white polo shirt with a Waves logo on the pocket. After consulting the bathroom mirror, he changed into a button-down shirt in a conservative blue-and-white pinstripe, then returned to check out the results, comb in hand.

While standing in front of the mirror, the big one in the dressing room with the fluorescent lights that showed no mercy, he had a startling revelation. The comb fell unnoticed onto the marble counter top as he moved an inch closer, turning his head to each side to confirm his suspicion.

He was going gray.

Strands of silver gleamed bright against his dark hair at each temple, their presence startling under the harsh light. Immediately, he thought of pulling them out, but there were too many. Dying them was out of the question on such short notice.

He braved another look.

Maybe he had more than just a few, but surely no one would notice. Then he saw the wrinkles, a couple of fine lines that etched outward on either side of his eyes. Touching them with his index fingers, he stretched them until they were gone. Then he moved his fingers away, and they were back.

He remembered his agent's recent words, warning him of his advanced age. "*Senior citizen*," he'd called him, and for the first time in his life he felt old. He flexed his knee and wondered which part of his body would go next.

Self-pity was new to Mason and not a feeling he enjoyed, but he was alone in his hotel room and had plenty of time to nurture the feeling. "Snap out of it, Walker."

Falling into the chair beside the bed, he stared hard at the phone.

He looked around the room and felt the walls closing in on him. Finally, he picked up the phone and dialed, knowing if he waited a moment longer he would lose his nerve and regain his powers of reason.

"Blair?"

"Mason?" The sound of that sweet voice saying his name did more than he cared to admit to ease his troubled soul. "What's wrong?"

"Wrong?" He ran a hand through the hair at his temple. "Nothing's wrong. I was just wondering. That is, if you don't mind. . ." His voice trailed off as he tried to find the right words. Nothing casual or clever came to him, so he pressed on anyway. "My plans have changed. May I come over now?"

He found himself holding his breath and quickly let it out. The small silver clock on the dresser read a quarter to four.

"Now? Um, sure."

Relief and dread washed over him in equal parts, mixed with something foreign. Was it anticipation? "Great," he said, stretching his legs to their full length and digging his toes into the plush white carpet.

"I need to pick up Sam from camp at five, but I'll be home after that." She paused. "Is everything all right?"

"Yeah, everything's fine. Everything's great," he said, trying to decipher his mixed feelings. He reached for his socks. "See ya."

"Okay."

"Oh, and Blair?"

"Yes?"

"I've been thinking about you, too." He hung up quickly, unable to believe he'd just said that and wishing he could take it back. Ten minutes later, he headed out the door, not caring that the owner of the Waves and the team's general manager were scheduled for a conference call at five-thirty to discuss his contract.

Let Morty deal with them, he thought. He gunned the engine and slipped into the freeway traffic heading north. That's what his agent was paid to do.

And what Mason got paid to do was play baseball. It had been too many years since anything but showing up at the ballpark had taken much of his time. Back home in Hawaii, he'd simply left his housekeeper a list of things he wanted, and they were there when he came home. Before that he'd been in college, dependent on dorm food, his grocery store outings limited to buying the weekend's ration of beverages and junk food.

Still, grocery shopping couldn't be that big of a deal.

He parked in the nearest place and hurried inside, determined to get in and out of the store quickly and efficiently. His watch read ten after four.

"Sure hope I don't get there before they do," he said as the electric doors of the Biggy Mart swung open and welcomed him inside.

Chapter 8

Nearly five-thirty. Where could Mason be?

The phone rang, and she ran to get it, hoping he hadn't changed his mind. When she heard Griffin Davenport's voice, she sank into the nearest chair with a frown.

The frown deepened when he questioned her about the projects he had assigned, the same items he'd asked about in an e-mail that morning. The man's presence over the phone felt as commanding as it did in person, and Blair wished desperately she had better news for him.

"I'm only looking at the general ideas. I don't expect a completed plan."

She scanned the thick column of blueprints lying rolled up on the top of her desk. What was wrong with her? Any other time she would have jumped at the opportunity to add another project to her list. She flicked an imaginary speck of dust off her best white T-shirt and studied the oak tree outside the window.

"Just fax me what you have."

"Right now?"

Blair thought she heard a chuckle on the other end of the line. "Yes, right now."

Panic surrendered to resignation as she discarded the possibility of

pleading for extra time. If only she'd been able to concentrate this past week, she'd have something more substantial to send him. Just today she'd swept the porch, watered the ferns, lit the vanilla candle on the kitchen window, and performed countless other chores rather than work on the job at hand. Mindless tasks had commanded her attention, but one man had held it, refusing to allow her a single rational thought. Now she had to face the consequences.

"Blair?"

Reluctantly, she answered him. "Yes. I'll fax the preliminaries right away. You'll have a formal proposal on each of the properties in two weeks."

Two weeks? What was she saying? She would have to shake off this cloud of confusion and work almost nonstop to meet that deadline. Thrusting her hand into the pocket of her freshly pressed khaki shorts, she gripped the phone and hoped he would tell her she could have as much time as she needed.

"Two weeks it is," he said.

Her shoulders slumped. So much for hoping.

Twenty minutes later, with Mason still nowhere in sight, Blair said a prayer for God's blessing and thanked Him for the possibility of more work. She started to press the SEND button on her fax machine, then stopped to glance over the documents one last time. If only Mr. Davenport had allowed her more time to do an in-depth analysis of each site before drawing up the preliminary designs.

In her business dealings, Blair prided herself on being professional and in control. *My personal life is another story,* she thought, as she saw the familiar black Jeep coming up the road.

A small fortune in commissions lay in the balance as she closed her eyes and pushed the red button. The machine went to work, the mechanical sound mingling with that of the car door slamming outside.

Turning her back on the fax transmission that could become the assignment of her life, Blair put on a genuine smile and went to meet Mason. When she found him, her smile grew into full-fledged laughter.

With plastic grocery bags dangling from both hands, he was struggling up the back steps with something large and apparently heavy wrapped in brown paper and cradled in the crook of his arm. He dropped the bundles onto the counter with a heavy thud and went back outside without a word.

"Need some help?" she called through the open door after he'd re-peated this process several times.

The mountain of groceries he'd balanced on the counter began to shift. She lunged forward to right them, but not before two packages of carrots and a can of turkey gravy had fallen to the floor. She reached down and picked them up.

"Got it under control," she heard him say. A moment later, he came through the door again, his voice muffled by a package of sour cream-and-onion potato chips balanced on top of another assortment of bags.

A wayward lock of hair fell forward into his eyes, and part of his shirttail was hanging out of his jeans. He looked as if he'd just come back from battle—and lost.

"Where should I put these?"

Blair's eyes scanned the kitchen. Yellow-and-white bags covered every bit of available counter space, and the mysterious brown bundle now filled the porcelain sink. The table overflowed as well. Only the window sill, with the candle flickering, remained uncluttered.

She gestured toward the old Chambers stove. "Over there." She covered her grin with the back of her hand. "I hope that's the last of the bags."

Mason dropped three bags on the table and stepped back to admire his handiwork. A fat red tomato came rolling out, and he fielded it like a pro, tossing it back in one fluid motion. It landed on top of the brown bag and came to rest on the edge of the sink.

"Nothing left but the drinks," he said, glancing quickly around the room. "You get started on the turkey, and I'll clear off the stove as soon as I get the sodas. I'm starved."

"Turkey?"

"Yep." He fairly beamed with pride as he blew the dark lock out of his eyes with an upward breath. "It's my favorite. I bought all the things that go with it, too." His face turned thoughtful, and his brows creased. "I hope you and Sam like turkey because if you don't—"

"No, turkey's fine."

She began digging through the bags in search of the ingredients for turkey sandwiches and found three different types of bread in the first bag alone. The phone rang, and she stopped to answer it.

Before she could continue her search, Sam burst through the door with a carton of orange juice in each hand and his baseball glove balanced atop his red cap.

"Hey Mom, Brian invited me to go with him and his mom and dad to the Pizza Palace," he said as he wedged the cartons of juice between two grocery bags on the counter. "His dad knows the guy who bought it from the guy who used to own it, and he can get us all the tokens we want for free until it closes." Sam took a breath but only long enough to make a face Blair knew she couldn't refuse. "Please, can I go?"

"But Mason's here, and he's brought dinner. You really ought to stay home."

"Aw Mom, Mason's cool and everything, but this is unlimited play in the game room. And we can stay till they close at ten 'cause Mr. McMinn says it's okay." He paused. "Please, Mom. I reeeaally want to go. If you let me, I'll never ask you for anything ever again."

"Yeah, right."

"C'mon, Mom. Mason'll understand." He paused, and she could almost hear the wheels turning. "Hey, maybe he could come, too."

"No," she snapped. Instantly, she softened. "We'll have to talk about this. Mason was counting on your being here, son."

And so was I.

The clock began to strike, and she realized it was only half past six, too many hours before ten. She opened her mouth to tell Sam she'd changed her mind about even considering it. Being alone with Mason Walker wasn't just wrong; it was dangerous.

"Cool! I know he won't mind. I gotta go put on my black shirt so nobody can see me in the virtual terrain hide-and-seek room."

The door slammed shut with a force that made her jump. "Sorry," she heard Mason say. "Didn't mean to do that. It's just that my hands were full and—"

She turned toward him, and he stopped talking midsentence, fixing his gaze on her, then dropped the plastic bags to the floor.

"What's wrong? Has something happened to Sam?"

Everything's wrong. I don't know how to be alone with you. Help me, Lord, to be strong. She realized she must have been frowning and quickly slipped into a smile.

"Nothing. Sam's fine." She took a deep breath and let it out slowly. "But he wants permission to go to the Pizza Palace with Brian."

"Oh?"

Was that the slightest hint of a smile?

"Yes. Something about unlimited virtual terrain. My next-door neighbor knows the new owner."

He ran a hand through his hair and looked interested. "Really? Cool."

"I didn't say he could go yet. Maybe you'd like to postpone dinner."

She tried to decipher the look that passed over his handsome face. Failing that, she leaned her back against the cool tile of the counter and feigned indifference, crossing her arms over her chest and gazing at the candle on the windowsill.

"Now why would I want to do that?" His voice flowed like honey. "I'm starving."

A yam rolled out of a bag and onto the floor, ruining her casual pose. She picked it up and studied it, embarrassed yet grateful for the distraction.

"I mean, if you want to wait until Sam can join us, I'll understand," she said casually. "He did mention that you were invited to go along and play virtual whatchamacallit."

"You trying to get rid of me?"

She glanced up, caught him smiling, and looked down, clutching the yam as if it were made of pure gold.

Please, Lord, guide my words and actions.

"No. I just meant that if you felt uncomfortable about the situation—"

"Situation?" He moved a step closer, and butterflies invaded her stomach. "What situation?" Another step toward her, and she was sure he was close enough to hear the pounding of her heart, although he still stood a good distance away. "Do we have a situation here?"

Yes, we have a huge, confusing, wonderful situation here, she wanted to say. *A situation I've dreamed of and dreaded since the day you came back into my life.* Blair shrugged, rolling the thought back into the files of her mind where it belonged

She swallowed the truth and managed an answer. "No, but I thought—"

"Here's a thought. How about we eat first, then go check out the virtual whatchamacallit?" He looked around the crowded kitchen; then his gaze swung back to her. "How dangerous could that be?"

He punctuated the question with an innocent smile which broadened when, despite her best judgment, she agreed. The Walker dimples taunted her as he turned and began to dig through the bags stacked on the stove.

Finally, she looked away. *Lord, help me. I'm not the same woman he knew ten years ago, and I could never be her again even if I tried.*

Somehow the tomato in her hand slipped to the floor. Ignoring her confusion, Mason moved toward her with purposeful strides. Suddenly, the kitchen shrank.

"Here—let me help."

He brushed past her, leaving the spicy scent of aftershave in his wake. Gooseflesh raised on her arms, and her heart did a flip-flop.

"No, really." Did her voice sound as squeaky to him as it did to her? "I can manage. Why don't you finish unloading the groceries?"

He shrugged and stepped back. "Okay."

She made sure she stayed out of his way as he passed, although the hint of spice drifted toward her.

"Where do you want these?" Mason asked, a half dozen cans stacked in the crook of one arm. A loaf of bread and a package of dinner rolls teetered on top.

"Pantry," she said, exhaling sharply as she spoke the word.

She indicated the direction with her index finger, then began poking nervously at the mysterious item in her sink. Rock hard and cold to the touch, the thing appeared to be frozen. Surely this wasn't the turkey he expected her to prepare.

A thought occurred to her as she began unwrapping the bulky object. "Oh Mason, be careful. There's a broom that keeps—"

"Ouch!" Cans crashed to the floor.

"—falling," she finished, whirling around.

Mason stood in the closet, one hand on his head and the other gripping a long yellow handle. He took a step back and lost his footing on a rolling can. Blair raced to catch him, dodging the broom as it shot out of Mason's hand and whizzed past her head.

Both of them landed in a heap on the floor, their arms and legs tangled and their noses only inches apart. The sound of breaking glass shattered the air as the broom connected with something fragile on the other side of the kitchen.

"Blair?" His eyes were closed; his breath blew warm against her chin.

"Yes?" The word emerged from her lips through a haze.

"Now we have a situation."

She thought she nodded. Numb, though, she wasn't sure until he smiled.

Warm, familiar lips kissed hers lightly. Their lips met again, a feather touch that tested their new and fragile friendship. Now, as with the last time he'd kissed her, all the old feelings came rolling back.

But this time it wasn't a kiss. It was an inferno.

And she could smell the smoke.

Chapter 9

Was that smoke he smelled? "Fire!" Mason flung Blair away from him and ran to the sink and what seemed to be the source of the fire. Side-stepping the still rolling cans, he threw a dishtowel over the miniature bonfire, only to have the towel ignite as well. He reached for the faucet and turned on the water, dousing the flames and splashing soot-colored water everywhere.

Blair peered around his shoulder at the soggy mess.

"What happened?" She clutched his arm to steady herself.

He gave her a dazed look. "Sink. Turkey. Fire."

Their gazes met. Suddenly, she realized she was grasping his sleeve in her hand; she let go and backed away.

"I know," she sputtered. "But how did it start? It's the sink."

"I don't know." He stuck his hand in the murky water and pulled out a blob of grayish-brown wax covered with pieces of charred paper. "What's this?"

She took it from him, holding the object at arm's length. "It's my vanilla candle. The one I keep on the windowsill. But how—"

Her gaze fell on the broken windowpane, the empty windowsill, and finally on the mess in the sink. Several drops of water fell on her shorts, and she brushed them off.

"The broom must have knocked it off the sill and into the sink when you threw it." She handed him the dripping, shapeless blob. "You started the fire."

Sam appeared in the door. "Mason started a fire?" He peered at Mason, confused. "What didja wanna do that for?"

"I did not start a fire. And I didn't throw anything." He leaned toward her until their eyes were level. "I was attacked. It was self-defense."

"Attacked?" She stifled a grin.

Just then they heard a car's horn honking, and Sam gestured toward the door. "Um, I don't have to help clean this up, do I? 'Cause that's probably Brian's dad."

Mason never looked away from her. "You go on, Sam," he said with a smile. "We'll take care of the mess and see you there in a few minutes. Save me a game, okay?"

With a whoop the whole neighborhood must have heard, Sam trotted toward the front door. "We won't be long," Blair called out before she heard the door shut.

Mason inched closer, and the room grew hot. Had the flames rekindled?

"I was attacked," he repeated. "By a broom."

Captured by his ice-blue gaze, she searched her mind for an answer. "Oh" was all she could manage, and that came out sounding more like a squeak than an actual word.

She pushed the dark lock off his face, unaware she was doing so, and saw for the first time the result of his bout with the broom. Her fingers lightly grazed the angry welt that crossed his forehead above his right temple. She felt him tense.

"You're hurt. I'll get you some ice."

"I'm fine, Blair." His voice was low and even.

Mason kept talking, but she couldn't make out the words. She leaned into the silken web of his whisper, allowing him to lull her into a calmness she didn't want to feel. Finally, his gaze returned to her eyes, and an awful, wonderful realization dawned on her.

She had slid sideways into the one feeling she had no right to have. Despite all she thought to be true about Mason Walker and all she could lose if she allowed the feeling to show, she knew without a doubt she had very nearly fallen deeply, hopelessly in love again.

A love she did not deserve.

She wrenched free and stepped away from him, knowing she couldn't risk allowing her emotions to take control. "I'll get that ice."

She'd reached the freezer door when his voice stopped her. "I never forgot you, Blair," he said. "You were always with me." He pointed to his chest with a sooty hand. "Here inside."

At least she thought it was his voice, though she couldn't be certain he'd actually said those words. She searched his face and still couldn't be sure. It was too perfect, the words too close to what she'd been hoping to hear.

"Tell him."

Mason's hand reached for hers across the short distance, and she felt a pull that was more than physical. Their fingers touched, then hands clasped, as the last rays of the sun gave way to dark clouds. Outside the rain had begun again, a light summer shower that held the promise of becoming much more.

In the small kitchen, with the smell of smoke still heavy in the air, Blair felt something pass between them, a current much stronger than electricity, a bond that time and deception could never break. And she knew she had to obey the Lord's urging.

"Mason," she said softly. "Stop. This is wrong." He froze, then slowly released her. Wordless, his gaze captured hers. The smell of smoke tore at her eyes and wreaked havoc on her already delicate stomach. At least she tried to blame it on the smoke. "Let's go outside." She took his hand and led him out to the back porch.

She settled onto the old bench and fought the panic that threatened her. Taking a deep breath, she braved a glance at the man she was about to hurt, wishing with all her heart that things could be different.

Mason stood stiffly, hands stuffed into his front pockets, watching the drops of rain that fell from the eaves of the porch. Light spilled out from the open door and illuminated one side of his face, the other remaining cast in shadows. Dark splotches of soot streaked the front of his shirt, and the shirttail still hung out loosely, giving him the look of a little boy caught playing in his church clothes.

It broke her heart to see how much Sam resembled him. She memorized the moment, storing it away in case there were no more like it, then forced herself to meet his unwavering stare. "I owe you the truth about where I was the day we were supposed to meet outside Luigi's."

❧

"Before you say anything, I want you to know something." He dropped his gaze to study the toe of his boot. *"Tell her,"* he heard the familiar voice of his precious Lord whisper. Slowly, he turned his attention back to Blair.

"Nothing you say will ever make me stop—"

She looked puzzled, vulnerable, and confused. "Stop what?"

Loving you, he wanted to say. "Never mind" came out instead. Someday he would have the courage to say the words. Someday, but not now.

He just couldn't.

She glanced at him, and he felt an ache in his heart.

"Look—I'm not exactly prepared for this," she said. "I never thought we would have this discussion. Could you come and sit by me?"

His feet wouldn't move.

"Please." Her voice wavered. "It might be the last time you come near me."

Oh, great. He could see the tears in her eyes. If she had done him wrong, why did he feel like such a heel? Why didn't he put her out of her misery and tell her he knew about Sam?

Because he had to hear it from her, that's why. Because even though the old feelings had come edging back, a part of him hadn't forgiven her for what she'd done. For what she'd made him miss. And for judging him unworthy of the truth.

"Above all, love each other deeply, because love covers over a multitude of sins. Forgive as I have forgiven. Release her to Me."

With those words echoing in his ears, Mason finally moved his feet in the same direction and took a spot next to her. Leaning forward, he rested his elbows on his knees and cradled his head in his hands, keeping her out of his line of sight.

He couldn't look at her. Not now. Not until he had his emotions under control.

She took a ragged breath, and he heard it, felt it, and tried to ignore it. "I don't know where to start," she whispered. "I've made so many mistakes. Which one do I admit to first?"

A big raindrop hit him on the side of the face. He ignored it, unable to muster the strength to wipe it away.

"I wanted to tell you, first before, then so many times after, but I didn't. I take full responsibility. I made that decision, and I was wrong. So very wrong. Long ago I asked God to forgive me, and now I need to ask you."

"Release her to Me." Mason felt his spine stiffen.

"Mason, please look at me. I was on my way to Luigi's when I stepped out onto Prairie Avenue." She paused. "I was going to tell you about—well, my pregnancy wasn't something I could announce over the phone, and I wanted to make sure you really wanted—"

Again she paused, and another raindrop hit him square in the jaw. The wind blew others to join it. Still he couldn't wipe them away. His shirt collar dampened as he sat quietly and let her continue.

"I found out later that you wouldn't have been there anyway, but that doesn't matter. I still did you wrong, Mason, very wrong."

"Tell her you were there waiting. Don't let her take all the blame."

He tried to speak but couldn't. All he could do was concentrate on the rain pelting his cheek and the drops rolling down his face and pooling on his collar. Then he realized it wasn't rain but tears that ran in streams down his cheeks.

She dipped her head. "Mason, Sam is your son. Our son," she amended. The words hung in the warm, damp air like the rain. Colorless, tasteless, odorless, but still very much there. "Mason, say something."

He tried but couldn't for the waves of peace and comfort washing over him, sweeping away all the anger and pain he'd accumulated over the past ten years.

Thank You, Lord.

She shifted beside him, leaning a bit away. When his gaze moved quickly to meet hers, she recoiled as if he'd hit her. "I'm sorry. I thought—"

"Blair, I was there, sitting on the bench outside Luigi's waiting for you. Then I called your grandmother. She told me you were in love with someone else."

Her gasp spoke volumes. "She told me the same thing about you," Blair whispered. "Oh Mason, I'm so sorry."

The enormity of Lettie's deception rendered him mute. It did not, however, keep him from moving her closer into his arms until he found his voice.

"About Sam," he whispered. "I don't know what to say. God has blessed me with a—" His voice cracked and failed.

"With a son," Blair finished for him. "One you should have met long before now."

Wading in over his head, he could have happily drowned in her arms. The love he felt for Blair thrummed a chorus in his ears, still as strong as ever. Someday she would know how he felt. In the meantime, he knew he would never again hate the rain.

"We should go," Blair said slowly, her voice gentle. "Sam will be wondering what took so long."

Mason nodded, then looked down at his soot-stained shirt. "I don't think I can go like this."

"We're both a mess, aren't we?" Blair laughed and rubbed at the black smudge on her shorts, only making it worse. "At least the soot doesn't show on your dark jeans. I could probably find a T-shirt that would fit, if you don't mind wearing that."

He shook his head. "Thanks, but I think I'll take my chances on whatever I have in my bag in the car."

Blair smiled. "I keep forgetting you jocks don't go anywhere without your well-stocked gym bag."

She disappeared into the house and down the hall while he crossed the yard to the Jeep and pulled a clean shirt out of his bag. Slipping the soot-stained shirt off and buttoning up the fresh one, he wondered how he would spend a whole evening with her without telling her he was falling for her all over again.

Blair emerged a few minutes later in a pair of white slacks and a pink T-shirt that matched the blush on her cheeks. He knew right then that he was a goner.

"Ready?" she asked sweetly.

Mason gazed into her eyes and felt his heart lurch. "Yes," he whispered as he took her hand and led her toward the door.

∽

Blair basked in the warmth of Mason's smile as they strolled out to the car and headed for Magnolia's newest hot spot, the Pizza Palace. Of course, being a small town, the news of Mason Walker's appearance there had spread like a summer cold in sneezing season. The fact that her neighbor Marilee hadn't wasted any time telling anyone who would listen that the superstar had been seen next door probably contributed as well. This much was evident when they walked through the door.

And while Brian's dad, Harley McMinn, had been circumspect in his assessment of Mason, his wife Marilee watched him openly, even speculating on their relationship loudly on more than one occasion during dinner.

Still raw from the evening's confession, Blair sat in silence and listened to Mason's vague answers to Marilee's pointed questions. Beyond sharing the occasional small talk, she and Mason said little to each other; there had been no opportunity.

Before the night ended, Mason had signed autographs for everyone in the place, fended off more than a few bold females, and promised to get tickets to the next Waves game for the Pizza Palace's new owner. Handling the requests for autographs and free tickets seemed as though it came natural to Mason, but Blair sensed that ignoring the women may not have been as easy.

Time after time, whenever a woman approached, Mason would turn his attention to Sam or begin a discussion of some sort with Harley. As the evening wore on, he would occasionally lay his hand across Blair's or brush a lock of hair away from her face.

More than once she caught him watching her, only to smile rather than look away. Even when he seemed busy playing games with Sam, she noticed him looking at her across the restaurant crowd. In those moments, when their gazes met, the room seemed to shrink, and heat flooded her face.

Whatever the reason, whether out of self-defense or because he had a real interest in her and their son, Blair found herself basking in his attention with a happy heart.

This is what I missed, she thought more than once.

Later, after they'd endured the crowd and the virtual-reality games at the Pizza Palace, they returned to put Sam to bed together. While Mason lingered in Sam's room to read the next chapter of a bedtime book, Blair drifted out onto the front porch to try to make sense of the wonderfully confusing day she'd had.

Had she done the right thing by not telling him before? As soon as the thought appeared, she pushed it away. Nothing would mar the happiness she'd found in the past three hours.

"Thank You, Lord," she whispered as she settled onto the rocker and lifted her gaze to the black night sky. "For bringing Mason back into my life."

"Yes, thank You, Lord," she heard a masculine voice say. She jumped to her feet to see Mason standing in the door. "For leading me back to Blair." He looked away, and when his gaze returned to her, his eyes seemed to be shining. "And for our Sam."

Covering her surprise and embarrassment, she offered him her hand as he opened the screen door and stepped outside. He sat down on a nearby chair, took her hand, and lifted her fingers to his lips.

"What're we going to do about this?" His voice sounded rough as sandpaper as he held her fingers against his cheek and smiled shyly at her.

Confused, she shook her head. "About what?"

The smile softened, and his gaze sought hers. "About us."

"Oh" became little more than a breath when Mason touched his finger to her lips and gave her a solemn look.

"It's difficult for me to be here," he said quietly. He looked away as if to collect his thoughts. "Blair, I'm a different man now. Changed."

She refused the urge to question him and pressed a hand to his, waiting silently for him to continue. What seemed like a lifetime later, he did.

"Baseball is important to me. It always was. But God has first place with me now. He's the head coach and general manager of my life. I'm just a base runner."

Her heart soared. "Oh Mason, I'm so glad."

He nodded, almost impatient to continue. "I want to do this right, this thing between us. If there is anything, that is." He studied her fingers, then allowed his gaze to drift back to meet hers. "We have to move slowly and wait for the Lord to guide us."

She smiled, slightly at first, then broader when she realized his meaning. He thought enough of her to wait and seek God's guidance on their relationship this time rather than rush into something that might be wrong. Something like their brief and disastrous marriage ten years ago.

"If only there were more time." He kissed her hand again. "In a few days I'll leave, and you and Sam will go back to the way you were before I came along."

"No," she said quickly. "No matter where you are, we will never be the same. Part of you will always be here." She drew in a breath. "In Sam," she added.

"I need more than that."

The words dangled in the air between them. "I understand," she said.

Mason leaned toward her, then abruptly swung back a step. "I have rehab in the morning, but I'll get to camp before lunch. I'd like it very much if you let me bring Sam home again."

"Sure," she said before she had time to think.

What if he said something to Sam? He wouldn't. Would he?

She opened her mouth to protest, and Mason covered it with a kiss. His hasty retreat seconds later left her reeling, almost as much as his parting words, spoken from the car.

"Let's not do that again," he said. "At least not until we decide on a more permanent relationship."

Blair raised her hand to her lips and, despite herself, blew him a kiss.

∞

Permanent arrangement? Had he really said that?

Mason rolled the idea around in his mind as he raced down the highway toward his hotel. Permanent arrangement, as in what? Suddenly, a picture of Blair sitting beside him on his porch in Montana, Sam astride his favorite cutting horse, came to him.

"Permanent arrangement as in marriage, that's what," he said aloud over the screaming guitar that blared from the speakers.

He snapped off the sound system, the loud music suddenly intrusive. When Mason reached his hotel, he tossed the keys to the valet. Ignoring the youth's curious stare, he entered the hotel lobby with the soot-stained shirt thrown over his shoulder and a smile on his face.

His expansive mood continued, even as he listened to the messages on his voice mail: three calls from his agent, one from Michael Brighton.

Strange—neither the Waves general manager nor the coach had bothered to leave a message. Pushing the SAVE button, he stepped into the bathroom for a hot shower. When he walked out of the steamy room ten minutes later, he heard his cell phone ringing.

He picked it up, hoping it was Blair calling to tell him good night. "Miss me?" he asked and sank into the nearest chair.

"Well, actually I have," Lisa Rivers said.

Mason sat bolt upright, glancing at the clock. "Why are you calling me?" His rudeness should have made him ashamed. It didn't.

The woman laughed. "You're interested in information that might lead to custody of your son. Something damaging that would make the court see that his mother might not be the fit parent to raise him?"

He gripped the phone so hard the plastic receiver nearly snapped. "I never said anything of the sort."

"I'm sorry, Mason. I must have misunderstood."

He could almost hear the sugar dripping from her voice. It sickened him.

"Through some creative computing, which I will deny if put under oath, I was able to obtain a copy of his original birth certificate. Care to know what the boy's birth name was?"

"Look, Lisa—I don't expect you to understand this, but Blair and I won't need your services."

"Really?" Something in her voice put him on his guard once more. " 'Blair and I,' is it?" She paused. "Might I ask why you don't find me worthy of your valuable time? I mean just for future reference. Next time I get dumped, that is."

"You weren't dumped. There never was anything between us in the first place." Mason paused to send up a prayer for patience. "Look— how about joining a church singles' group? You'd meet a much better class of men."

"Maybe I don't want to meet a 'better class of men.'"

"Good-bye." Mason wearily ended the call.

∽

"Oh, I don't think so, Mason."

Lisa pressed the switch to turn off her tape recorder and studied her perfectly manicured pink nails. An hour later, her carefully edited transcript was ready to be faxed. Happily she read her masterpiece, then slipped it into the machine and pressed the button.

Chapter 10

June 24

$\mathscr{B}$lair had heard the humming start late last night and knew she had an incoming fax waiting on her desk. Instead of racing for the machine as she normally would, she strolled to the kitchen and refilled her coffee cup, taking it out onto the back porch. This morning Griffin Davenport, or whomever had sent the late-night fax, would have to wait.

Settling onto the little bench to sip her coffee, Blair allowed her mind to ramble across the events of last night. Her neighbor's greeting carried across the backyard. Adorned in loose denim shorts and a matching top, she wore a broad smile.

"Hi, Marilee. I didn't know you were outside."

"Honey, I don't think you even knew the sun was shining."

"What're you doing up so early?"

"It was either listen to Harley play video games with the boys or head for the yard. I picked the yard." She smiled. "Mind if I grab a cup of coffee?"

"Not at all," she said to her neighbor's retreating back.

"What happened in here?" she heard Marilee call from the kitchen.

"A little accident," she returned. "No big deal. Haven't had a chance to clean it up completely."

"Oh," Marilee replied, settling onto the wooden steps, coffee cup in hand. "So tell me about the cutie."

"Cutie?" Blair stifled a smile.

"Don't play dumb, Blair Montgomery. I saw the looks he gave you last night at the Pizza Palace. He's crazy about you."

"I have no idea what you're talking about." She paused to let the joke sink in. "And I'm kind of crazy about him, too."

They shared a laugh, then lapsed into a companionable silence until Marilee finally spoke. "Seriously, he seems like a real nice guy."

"He is."

"Yeah, well, there aren't too many nice guys out there, so hang on to him."

"Who says there aren't many nice guys out there?" a deep voice called from the driveway.

Blair stood and craned her neck, her stomach doing a flip-flop as she saw Trey Wright turning the corner. Dressed in gray shorts and white T-shirt, a red ball cap covering his overlong tawny hair, he looked every inch the baseball player. He hadn't changed a bit, a fact she hadn't noticed the day she saw him at the ballpark.

"Trey Wright! What are you doing here?"

He covered the distance between them in several long strides, giving Blair a bear hug that lifted her feet off the ground. "Hello, sweetheart. It's been way too long."

She held tight to her coffee cup to keep it from spilling. "It has been, hasn't it?"

"How many more of these do you have hidden around here?" Marilee said.

"Marilee, this is an old friend of mine from college. Meet Trey Wright. Trey, this is my neighbor, Marilee McMinn."

"So, Trey," Blair asked, "what brings you here?"

"Mason Walker, of course."

At the mention of Mason, Blair felt her cheeks grow warm. "Really? What about him?"

"Well, he's been actin' as if he doesn't have the sense the good Lord gave a goose, so I decided to come on out here and take the situation in hand. Make sure he's doin' right by you."

Marilee giggled. "I don't think you have anything to worry about then. She and your friend had a great time last night at the Pizza Palace. There was a room full of people, but Mason Walker had eyes only for Blair."

Blair winced, studying the grass stain on the toe of her tennis shoe as heat flooded into her cheeks with a vengeance. "Is that true?" she heard him ask.

"Anyone want coffee?"

She jumped to her feet and headed back into the kitchen. Unfortunately, they followed her. Both of them.

"What happened?" Trey said, eyeing the sooty mess, the cans that littered the floor, and the burned turkey still floating in brownish-gray water in the sink.

"Mason cooked dinner." Blair took another cup out of the pantry, filled it, and handed it to Trey. As she motioned for them to follow her to the table, she whispered, "Don't ask."

"Ask what?"

Mason stood in the kitchen door. He produced a bag of donuts from behind his back and tossed it to Trey.

"Oh honey, you cooked." Trey glanced over his shoulder at the mess in the sink, then swung his gaze back to Mason. "Again," he added, his eyes twinkling.

When Blair saw Mason look at her, she was sure the fire that had erupted last night still smoldered. She felt herself grow weak and mushy inside.

"Well, it sure is hot in here," Trey said, shattering the silence.

"Definitely," Marilee added, fanning herself.

Mason greeted Trey with a hard slap on the back, then smiled at Blair's neighbor. "My session's cancelled so I thought I'd come by and pick up Sam on my way in." He glanced sideways at Trey. "Looks like someone beat me to it."

Ignoring the neighbor, he headed directly for Blair and kissed her tenderly on the cheek. "Good morning," he whispered.

"Coffee?" Blair asked

"No, thanks." He slid into the chair on Blair's right and wrapped his arm around her. Resisting the urge to wipe the lopsided grin off Trey's face, he reached for a cream-filled donut.

"So, Mase." Trey leaned back in his chair. "I thought I'd track you down and see if you wanted to do a little fishing today. Buddy of mine from prep school's a developer, and he has a sweet little boat docked out at the lake."

"No thanks, Trey," he said, taking Blair's hand in his own. "Blair and I have some business to attend to today."

"Oh!" Marilee swallowed the rest of the donut in one bite.

"Family business," he added.

Trey's gaze met his, and he knew his buddy had caught his message. While visiting with the Lord this morning, he'd come to the decision that the first order of business had to be telling Sam the truth. After that, he and Blair could begin life together without any secrets.

The former catcher pushed away from the table and stood, reaching for another donut. "Okay, well, I guess I'll be going then. You sure you don't want me to take the slugger fishing so the two of you can have some private time?"

"No," they said in unison.

∞

"I knew it! Brian told you about Peter, didn't he?" Sam plopped down on the overstuffed sofa and kicked at a cushion with his foot, sending it flying. "I can't believe my best friend in the whole world ratted on me."

"Who's Peter?" Blair asked.

"The snake Brian told you about."

"Sam, this isn't about a snake," Mason said, leaning against the door frame, his arms crossed in front of him.

Sam's eyes widened as he realized he'd let out a secret. "Oh," he said softly, reaching for the pillow and replacing it on the sofa. "I was keeping him in a coffee can under the porch, but I guess I gotta let him go now, huh?"

Blair nodded. "I doubt if he's happy living in a coffee can, sweetie." She sat next to him on the sofa and tamped down her desire to scold him for keeping a disgusting reptile at all.

Sam appeared to consider her suggestion for a moment. "Yeah, you're probably right."

"Good. Now there's something a lot more important I need to tell you." She wrapped an arm around him. "Something that's very difficult for me. It's about your father."

Sam looked at Mason as if to explain. "He died a long time ago."

Lord, please guide my words and help Sam understand.

"No, Sam, he's very much alive." The boy's blue eyes widened, and she felt the guilt of her omission falling directly on her.

Then his eyes narrowed. "Then why didja tell me he was dead?"

Blair squeezed his shoulder and felt terrible when he pulled away. "I thought it was the right thing to do, but I was wrong. It was a bad mistake, and I'm trying to make it right. Do you understand that?"

"No. You lied." His blond brows creased into a frown, vivid against the tanned skin of his face. "You told me never to lie." He looked at Mason. "Never."

Relying on another quick prayer, she summoned the courage to go on. "What I did was wrong, Sam, very wrong. And I'm so sorry for the hurt that lie has caused. I loved your father with all my heart." She glanced at Mason, saw his encouraging smile, and returned it with one of her own.

Sam gave her a look that nearly broke her heart. "Why?" He shook his head. "Didn't you think he would like me?"

"Oh sweetheart," she said, gathering him into her arms again. "It was nothing like that. I...uh...that is, he—"

"He would have loved you very much," Mason interjected. "And he understands why your mother had to do what she did."

Sam's blond head popped up, and he eyed Mason critically. "How would you know?"

"Because I know."

His soothing voice was closer, though Blair hadn't noticed Mason's movement across the room. His hand joined hers, spanning their son's small back. When her gaze met his, her tears gathered in earnest despite her best efforts.

Mason wrapped his free hand around her, and they formed a tight circle. His head inclined toward hers, his expression tender and his eyes radiating a deep warmth that gave Blair the courage to finish what she'd started.

"Sam, look at me." He did, and his eyes, so like his father's, were two deep pools of blue that gave away nothing of what he might be feeling. "Sweetie, Mason is your father. There never was anyone else. I should have told both of you long ago, but I was afraid." A tidal wave of tears broke loose. "I'm so sorry."

"Be quiet!" The boy shrugged out of their embrace and ran from the room.

"Sam!" Blair jumped to her feet and started after him, but Mason placed his hand on her shoulder and stopped her.

"Let me," he said.

All she could do was nod. After all, who better to speak to her terribly wronged son than his terribly wronged father? She sank back onto the sofa, curled her legs under her, and listened to the sound of Mason's footsteps echoing in the quiet house.

She lifted her gaze to the ceiling. *Oh Lord, help them both to forgive me as You have.*

∞

With each footstep he took, Mason grew less and less sure of what he would say to his son. Words of wisdom failed him, turning him mute as he slipped his hand inside the partly opened door and stepped into the bedroom. *Lord, speak to me and through me.*

To his surprise, Sam sat calmly in the middle of his bed, a notebook open in his lap. As Mason moved closer, he saw the book was filled with pages and pages of baseball cards. A couple of loose cards lay on the multicolored rug beside the bed.

The boy knew he was there, that much was certain, but something kept him from looking up from whatever he was doing. It was pride, Mason guessed, an emotion that seemed to run deep in the veins of the Walker men.

He knocked on the door behind him. No response.

"May I come in?" He watched Sam remove a baseball card from the album and send it sailing.

He tried a different approach. "Need some help with that?"

The boy didn't look up. "Nope," he said.

Mason took that one word as a small victory until he realized what his son was doing. Sam sent another pair of cards flying in his direction. Mason caught one of them and glanced at it.

It was one of his. They were all his.

"Okay, Sam. I get the point."

He dropped the card on the dresser, watching it land next to a picture of a Little League team dressed in red and white. Finding Sam among the motley group of boys, he picked up the photo and pretended to study it.

"I guess you're pretty surprised about all this," he said, returning the picture to the dresser. "I know I was when I found out."

Sam made a big show of turning the pages, never looking up. *At least he'd stopped throwing cards.* Mason took that as another victory for his side. He decided to risk moving closer.

"After the surprise wore off, I was really mad." He sank onto the bed inches away from Sam. "In fact, I was furious with your mom for what she did."

That got his attention. The book slammed shut.

"Yeah?" His gaze met Mason's, then skittered away.

"Yeah." Slowly Mason reached for the album, lifting it out of Sam's lap to place it on the floor. "But then you know what happened?"

Sam pulled his knees up under his chin and wrapped his arms around his legs. He gazed at a Houston Astros baseball poster hanging on the opposite wall.

"What?" he asked grudgingly.

"Well, first off, I prayed and asked God to help me understand what had happened." He paused. "Do you ever pray and ask God to help you with the hard stuff?"

Sam nodded.

"That's good. I guess your mom taught you how to do that, didn't she?"

He nodded again.

Mason folded his hands in his lap and fought the urge to gather the little boy into his arms. "The next thing I did was think about the good part of all this, and that made everything different. I stopped being mad and started being glad."

"What good part?" Sam asked slowly.

"The part where I found out I had a great son." He reached out and patted Sam on the knee. "Now I know you came up with the short end of the deal. Having me for a dad, I mean, but—"

"It's not you, Mason," he said, never looking away from the poster. "It's Mom." Finally, he pried his attention away and focused on Mason. "She lied."

"Yes," he said. "She did." He chose his words carefully. "But I believe her when she said she did it for us, for you and me. She's like that."

"Yeah," Sam admitted. "I guess you're right." He frowned. "But she still lied."

"Yes, she did. But you know what?"

He stretched out to lean on his elbow beside the boy. Fully expecting

Sam to shrink away from him, Mason was surprised when the boy uncurled his legs and settled a few inches away.

"What?"

"The two of us have to forgive just as God forgives." He paused to clear the lump from his throat. "We're a family now."

Sam tilted his head slightly. "We are?"

"Yep. And we have to stick together."

"We do?"

"Sure." Mason rolled onto his back and supported his head in his hands, copying his son's position. "I know there are a lot of things you don't understand right now."

He wriggled a millimeter closer. "Kinda."

"Someday I think you will."

"I guess."

For a long while they lay side by side lost in thought. Finally, Mason spoke. "I love your mom, y'know? Always have, I think." Silence. "Someday I'm going to marry her again if she'll have me."

Sam lifted his head, his eyes open wide. "You and my mom used to be married?"

"Yes, we were," Mason said, "before you were born. And one of these days, when you're older, I'll tell you more about it. But for now, since you're the man of the house, I thought I ought to ask you if it's okay first."

"Oh." A smile lit his face. "Sure." He inched a little closer to Mason. "But you know she's not too hot on baseball."

"Yeah, I know."

"And she says the TV is just a bunch of noise." He scrunched up his nose.

Mason elbowed him playfully in the ribs. "You trying to talk me out of it?"

"Nope." Sam returned his jab with one of his own. "Just thought you ought to know." He paused. "Dad."

"Thanks," he said through the emotions that threatened to overwhelm him. His heart swelling with love, he gathered the boy in his arms and held him tight. "I love you, son."

"Me, too."

Ruffling Sam's hair, he offered him a bittersweet smile. "Maybe we ought to tell your mom everything's all right."

"Yeah, in a minute." He wrapped his little arms around Mason and hugged him tightly. "I don't wanna move yet."

"Me either, son."

∞

Blair couldn't sit still another minute so she tiptoed down the hall toward Sam's room. She had to know how things were going.

The door stood slightly ajar, just enough for her to see Mason lying on his back, his feet hanging a few inches over the end of the bed. Sam snuggled on his shoulder, his little arm extending halfway across his father's broad chest. Both of them were sound asleep, their heads inclined toward each other as if, even in their dreams, they were sharing some special secret.

And both of them were smiling.

She stood and stared, basking in the wonder of the miracle God had wrought. Then she heard a phone ringing and ran to answer it. When she arrived downstairs, she realized it was Mason's cell phone but answered anyway to keep it from waking them.

"Yeah, gimmee Walker," the fast-talking voice said before she could utter a greeting.

"I'm sorry. Mr. Walker's unavailable right now. Could I take a message?"

She heard the man's rude laughter and disliked him immediately. "Yeah, I'll bet he's unavailable, but this is one call he'll want to take. Tell him it's Morty, and I have ten million reasons why he should answer the phone. Think you can remember all that, little lady?"

She opened her mouth to say something, then snapped it shut. Instead, she slipped into her best Southern belle accent. "I'll sure try." She stuck out her tongue at the phone and tiptoed back upstairs to Sam's room.

"Mason," she whispered, tapping his shoulder gently.

He moaned and shrugged away her hand. Sam stretched and rolled onto his side, his eyes still sealed shut.

"Mason," she whispered into his ear. "Telephone. Some man named Morty."

His eyes slanted open, then closed again. "Tell him to go away."

"Believe me—I'd love to tell him that and more." She handed him the phone. "But he says it's important. Something about having ten million reasons for you to talk to him."

In one fluid motion, Mason was out of bed and down the hall. She thought she heard him laugh, but she couldn't be sure. Then the screen door slammed, and she knew he'd gone outside. She picked up the quilt from the end of the bed and covered Sam, closing the door as she left.

From the sound of things, whatever news he'd received must be good. He continued to talk, leaving her no choice but to find something else to do until he finished the call.

She remembered the fax she'd received this morning and went to find it. Griffin Davenport must have thought of more changes to the designs she'd sent him, something that happened on a regular basis these days.

Whatever the changes, she knew she could handle them. With Mason back in her life and the secret of Sam's paternity revealed, she was sure she could handle anything.

Blair stepped into the small office and reached for the document as another loud cheer erupted from the front porch. She smiled. Life was definitely good.

Then she read the fax.

It wasn't from Griffin Davenport.

Chapter 11

Of course, Mason couldn't help but yell, even if he woke up the whole neighborhood. He was entitled. After all these years he'd finally reached his goal of earning ten million dollars—the magic number that told him he'd made it.

So what was the problem? He saw movement out of the corner of his eye and turned to follow it. Blair stood at her desk, a paper in her hand. She turned away, and he studied her back before she stepped away from the window and Mason lost sight of her. Instantly, he felt alone. He shifted positions, moving to another place on the porch where he could see her again. The dog followed, whimpering to be scratched.

Then he knew what the problem was.

If he couldn't stand to be out of her sight for more than a few minutes, how could he be away from her for the rest of the season? Three long months of pain and agony.

And his knee might give him trouble, too.

"Mason? Hello?"

"Yeah, I'm here," he said as he pondered this latest complication.

"So do I tell the boys at the front office we have a done deal?"

He found himself hesitating. "I don't know. I have a couple of people

I need to talk it over with," he heard himself say, surprised at how right the words sounded.

And, Lord, I'll be listening to You, too.

"C'mon, Walker. Quit kidding around. I'm dying here."

Mason leaned against the wooden post on the porch and watched the love of his life reading the paper she held. "I've never been more serious in my life, Morty."

He had a thought, a new and surprising turn of emotions that frightened him almost as much as it excited him. He realized he would gladly do anything she asked, even if it meant giving up the game he loved, to be with her. After all, baseball could hardly compare to Blair.

"Hey Morty. What happens if I don't want to play in the All-Star game?"

Sputtering followed a long string of expletives that Mason barely heard. He was too busy watching Blair. And that bit of freckled shoulder glowing under the light of the lamp as she sank into a chair by the window.

"I'll call you," he said, ending the conversation with the touch of a button.

Leaving the phone on the porch rail, he went inside to tell Blair the good news, to warn her that she might be seeing more of him. When he stepped into the room, her pale, shocked face stopped him.

Without a word, Blair thrust a paper at him. He looked at her, her dark lashes spiked with tears, and felt fear slice through him.

"What's the matter?" He took two steps toward her before she backed away.

"Read it." She turned to face him, her eyes moist but bright with anger. "It's from your lawyer."

"My lawyer?"

The look she gave him sent a chill coursing through his veins. "Just read it. I found it very educational."

He scanned the document, unable to believe the words he read. The conversation he'd had the night before with Lisa Rivers had been edited creatively, giving the impression he had contacted her for the sole purpose of gaining custody of Sam. The conniving woman had even added a little note of her own for Blair, a warning that he was not the man he seemed and that it had taken a weekend trip to his cabin in Montana for her to find this out.

Dull anger bloomed into something more dangerous, more potent. He fought to regain control as the picture became clearer. Crushing the paper with one hand, he sent it sailing across the room; then he walked toward Blair. She cut him off with a sweeping gesture.

"It's true, isn't it?" she asked, her voice half an octave higher than usual. "It's all true."

He felt the rein on his emotions slipping and said a silent prayer for help. "Blair, surely you don't believe that garbage."

"Are you saying you didn't discuss my son with those lawyers?" Her look dared him to tell her anything but the truth.

"Our son," he reminded her, instantly regretting his choice of words. "And, no, I can't deny that I spoke to Mike Brighton about Sam. I'll admit at first I had some concerns—"

"Concerns?" She gestured toward the paper that lay on the floor near the window. "I hardly call trying to take my son away from me having concerns!"

"Do you really believe I'm capable of that?"

She retrieved the fax and held it in front of her, brandishing the white, crumpled paper as if it were a weapon. Finally, she opened it.

"Let's see what you're capable of, Mason." She consulted the paper again, and his heart sank. "Let's see," she said. "How did it go? Oh yes, here it is."

She began to read, and his knees almost buckled. Refusing to give in to the feeling, he squared his shoulders and forced himself to remain standing.

" '. . .that might lead the boy to be placed in your custody. Something damaging that would make the court see that his mother might not be the fit parent to raise him.' " She looked him straight in the eye. "Tell me you didn't have this conversation."

Lying wasn't an option, and he knew it. "I can't, but I can tell you it didn't go down like that. Those were her words, not mine."

"Then she didn't visit you in Hamilton?"

"Yes," he said slowly, "she did, but I sent her away before she even reached the porch."

Blair's expression hardened, and her eyes glazed with what had to be unshed tears. At that moment, he felt lower than pond scum. The biggest idiot on the planet.

"Get out," she said in a voice that gave away nothing.

The words barely left her mouth, so soft was the sound. Yet, in the time it took for her to speak those two words, Mason felt his entire world collapse.

Wild with fear, he closed the distance between them and caught Blair up in his arms. "Don't do this," he said, searching for anything to erase the last five minutes from his life. "Please, Blair. Don't. I love you. Blair!"

But it wasn't Blair he held. Some stranger had taken her place. He could no longer reach her, and that terrified him.

She stood like a statue, her eyes a cold blue and her arms straight down by her side. "Get out," she repeated through clenched teeth.

"Sam," he said, pressing his hand against her back as if the gesture might return his Blair to him. "Think of Sam."

"That's exactly who I'm thinking of. And if you care anything about him you'll do as I ask and leave."

He stepped away from her and saw her push backward as if she were in slow motion. Somehow he moved across the room, distancing himself from her, and stood in the doorway.

"If I care anything about him?" *Get a grip. Try to understand what she must think of you. Try to see how bad this must look.* He grasped the door frame. "I was ready to give up—"

"Stop it! No more lies!"

She stepped toward him, her face a mask of conflicting emotions: anger, hurt, and something else, something he couldn't name. Then she glared at him and turned away.

Disgust. That was what he saw there. That was the emotion he hadn't been able to name. And that hurt more than anything else.

"Sweetheart, look at me." She ignored him, her hands braced on the back of a chair. "I love you. I would never—"

She straightened her shoulders and tightened her grip on the chair. "Leave," she whispered, her plaintive voice tearing at his soul.

He stalled for time while he tried to think of what to do next. No way would he leave—not like this. He had to do something. "Let me call Mike. He'll tell you," he said, knowing he sounded like a teenager making excuses for missing curfew. He didn't care. He was desperate.

"Leave." This time the word was less of a plea and more of a command.

"But I love you. How can I leave you? Give me a chance to prove it." Now he was the one pleading. But he was past caring how he sounded. Beyond the slump of her shoulders, he gauged no discernible reaction. He knew he was about to lose her. "What about Sam?" he said softly. "What will you tell him?"

"I see no need to tell him anything beyond the fact that his father had to leave unexpectedly." She turned to face him, her eyes dry. "I think that's the best thing for all of us under the circumstances." She gave him a cold smile. "That is what you ballplayers do, isn't it? You do what's good for the team."

He could think of nothing to say.

"I won't keep you from Sam," she said. "Have your attorney call me, and we'll set up some sort of visitation schedule. But know this. You will not take Sam away from me."

"This isn't over, Blair," he heard himself say, the words reverberating in his brain until he thought the sound of them would never stop. He was back at his hotel, suitcase in hand, before he realized he could no longer hear them.

As he fastened his seat belt for the long night flight to Honolulu, he gave the matter to God and prayed He would tell him what to do. But as the taxi pulled up in front of his condo on Honolulu's Kalakaua Avenue, he couldn't help but add an additional prayer for God to hurry.

∽

July 2

It was the kiss of a lifetime, one of those great lip-locks you see in the movies, and Blair was in his arms. Then the phone rang, and the dream evaporated into reality. Mason lifted one eye, snapping it shut again when he saw the time. He found the phone and brought it to his ear.

"What?"

"Hi!" came the childish voice. "I got the box of stuff, and it's so cool. I'm wearin' the shirt, and this morning I ate your cereal, and I'd have the cleats on, too, 'cept Mom won't let me wear them in the house 'cause they scratch the floor."

"Hey there, buddy," he said. "Gimme a minute to catch up with you." He shook the cobwebs out of his mind and tried to pry open his eyes.

As the room came into focus, his gaze fell on the clock again. He'd have to figure out a way to explain to the boy the time difference between Tennessee and Hawaii. He rolled over, escaping the shaft of sunlight that threatened on the horizon.

"After I talk to you, I'm gonna show Brian and Uncle Trey. He says I look like you so he's gonna be surprised when I really do look like you. You think my hair's always gonna be this color? It's okay, but I want it to be black like yours, only not with that silver stuff on the side, even if Brian's mom thinks it makes you look 'stinguished.'"

"That's distinguished." Mason shook his head and struggled to keep pace with Sam's rambling one-sided conversation. "Uncle Trey?"

"Yeah, he took me fishing last week. Anyway, I saw a lady on TV that changed her hair, and I asked Mom if I could do that, and she made this face and—"

He paused at his son's mention of Blair. "Hey buddy, how is your mom?"

"I dunno," he said, and Mason was struck by the boy's thoughtful tone. "She misses you a whole bunch."

He sat bolt upright. "Why do you think that?"

As he waited, his mind conjured up all sorts of explanations. She'd cried of course. She'd probably broken down every time she saw a picture of him or heard his name on the news. He saw it all: Blair distraught at the grocery store, crying over the sports page. Blair in tears at the gas station when she heard a couple of guys discussing baseball at the next pump. Blair—

"Didja hear what I said?"

He pulled himself away from the pleasant thoughts. "No, sorry, pal. What was that?"

"I was telling you my mom must miss you 'cause she never says anything about you, and she didn't even watch the Home Run Derby last night even though I told her you were gonna win it. And it was so cool you won. What kind of prize did you get? Was it a big trophy or a lot of money or a car? You probably won a car. Was it a Corvette or a Ferrari or something? Or was it—"

"Slow down, Sam. You're losing me here. Now tell me again about your mom. She misses me because. . ."

He heard Sam take a deep breath and exhale slowly. "Because she never says anything about you, and that's a dead giveaway."

"It is?"

"Yeah, dontcha see? When my turtle was lost I missed it a whole bunch, and whenever I saw another turtle I got real sad so I stopped looking at turtles."

"And?"

"And I found my turtle again, and then I was happy again. It didn't bother me to look at turtles anymore."

This, Mason knew, made perfect sense to a nine-year-old boy. He, however, was more confused than ever. "So what's your suggestion, pal?"

After a long pause, Sam spoke. "Okay, first you gotta get found. Y'know, like let it be a surprise. I was real surprised when I found Skippy, and that made it even better."

"Skippy?"

"The turtle. Anyway, if you sort of pop up like Skippy, then she'd be real glad, and she'd stop throwing the sports page into the trash and running into the bathroom when you come on TV."

Now that last part was interesting. "She throws the sports page in the trash and runs into the bathroom a lot, does she?"

"Only when she sees you. Yesterday I had to dig the paper out from under a whole pile of yucky tissues so I could put it in the cage with. . ."

His mind wandered, losing the last of Sam's sentence in the fog. Tissues? Another interesting fact.

"Yucky, huh?"

"Yeah, I think she has a cold. She's always blowing her nose, 'specially right after she sees you on TV. And sometimes I hear her blowing it at night when she's s'posed to be sleeping."

"Really?" So Blair was crying over him after all.

"I gotta go 'cause she's calling me."

"Okay, son. I'm really glad you called. I'm here for you anytime you need me. Understand?"

"Yeah. I understand."

As tired as he was, Mason found himself reluctant to say good-bye. He searched around for something to keep the boy on the line a little longer. "Hey son, you gonna watch me play today?"

"Are you kidding? 'Course I am. I wish I coulda come see you in person."

"Me, too, pal. Remember our signal?"

"Sure do," Sam answered. "You're gonna lift your glasses and wink, right?" In the background, his mother's voice came closer.

"That's right. You'd better go, buddy."

"Okay," he said, his voice barely louder than a whisper. "I don't want Mom to know I've been talking to you. It might make her sad."

"Yeah." There were no words to tell his son how sad it made Mason. "Talk to you soon."

"Okay," he said. "Oh, and, Dad?"

At the sound of that word he felt a tightness in his chest. "Yeah?" He caught his breath.

"I love you."

"Oh Sam, I love you, too," he managed to say.

⌁

Her heart would heal, she told herself. Blair tried not to listen to what sounded like a ball game going on in the next room. She threw a pencil at the sports page that lined the bottom of her trash can, without noticing whether she'd hit it.

Another rousing cheer went up from the other room. She tried to ignore it as she reached for the nearly empty box of tissues. Against her better judgment, she had allowed Sam to watch every possible minute of media hype leading up to the All-Star game being held this year in Honolulu.

And there had been plenty to watch.

Not being a baseball fan, she'd been shocked at the amount of time devoted to the sport over the past week. *It is indecent,* she decided, *the homage paid to a bunch of game-playing millionaires.* Not a one of them had found the cure for cancer, written a symphony or an unforgettable novel, or even contributed anything of value to justify their places in the world.

Bitter? She considered the idea, then discarded it. *Just the facts,* she thought. *That's all they were.* She picked up another tissue and blew her nose.

With the Lord's help she'd been dealing with this well over the past seven days, she thought, as she aimed the wadded-up tissue at the sports page. Of course, like everything else in her life lately, she just missed the mark.

"Mom, ya gotta see this," Sam called out to her. "Hurry!"

She closed the thick volume of building codes she'd been studying for Mr. Davenport's latest project, a huge renovation and landscape job at a Civil War-era estate called Honey Hill. Shoving her chair loudly across the linoleum in protest, she trudged into the living room to see what part of the monument to stupidity the TV cameras were focused on now.

And there he was in all his glory, the ultimate monument to stupidity—Mason Walker.

Tanned and handsome, he wore a dark-blue baseball cap backward, with a pair of sleek sunglasses cutting a black slash across his face. The shadow of a beard dusted his chin, and his ebony hair touched the neck of his blue Western League All-Stars jersey. A breeze lifted that one errant lock of hair forward, and he pushed it away with the back of his hand.

"Yeah, you know I never get tired of this," he was saying. "It was an honor to be out there playing with those guys today, and I thank God for giving me the privilege."

The camera zoomed in for a close-up. *Another few inches, and I can count his eyelashes,* she thought, looking at the traitorous man with disgust.

"I guess baseball's in my blood," he said. "My dad played the game, and I'm hoping someday my son will get a chance to do the same. Sam's already a decent ballplayer."

Sam squealed with delight. "Didja hear that? Didja? He said my name on TV."

"Oh yes. I heard." How dare he suggest the boy might come close to turning out like him? Not while she was still drawing a breath. Not her child.

Then he lowered his glasses for a split second and winked at her.

Sam squealed in delight. "That's our signal," he said. "He did it like he told me he would."

"Signal?" Try as she might, she couldn't stop staring at the screen.

"Yeah, he told me he'd do it just for me. Look! He did it again! Didja see him?"

Oh yes, she'd seen. Who was she kidding? She'd not only seen it; she'd felt it. One wink from him, and her nerve vanished.

"That's nice."

While the reporter asked him a question about kids and his being a role model, Blair turned to look at Sam. He was chewing happily on a mouthful of popcorn, his gaze fastened on the screen and on the man who would never be his role model as long as she lived. To her disgust, she noticed Sam was wearing a new dark blue baseball jersey, one of those expensive items that must have come from his father.

On the back was the number one along with the name WALKER emblazoned above it in bold letters. Just like the one his dad wore today on television.

Clenching her fists again, she took a deep breath, then exhaled sharply. "Sam, is that what was in the package you got this morning?"

"Yeah. Isn't it cool?"

"Way cool. It was a big box. Anything else in there?" So much for her decision not to pry. "Anything else interesting, that is?"

Sam gave her a funny look. "Uh, I guess not. 'Cept a couple of gloves, a picture, a ball signed by all the Waves which was pretty cool, and the pair of cleats with real spikes on them that you told me I couldn't wear in the house. Oh, and a bunch of cereal boxes with his picture on 'em, and the letter he wrote."

"Letter?"

"Yeah, and he asked about you. Dad misses you, I think."

Dad. The word pierced her heart.

"Oh." She swallowed the lump in her throat, fighting the urge to jump for joy. She pictured him devastated, barely able to share his sadness with his son. "Did he tell you that?"

"Nope." He swung his gaze back to the TV screen and his father. "I just think it."

Joy crashed into disappointment. Blair turned her head to prevent her son from seeing her reaction. Unfortunately, her gaze landed back on the television and Mason.

The man looked straight into the camera and removed his dark glasses. His eyes, their blue irises seeming almost as large as a quarter, looked tired and bloodshot, and the lines around them were more pronounced.

"The knee's fine," he said in response to one of the numerous questions. "A little time off, and I feel like a new man."

A new man indeed. He looked like a man fresh from a party. Or a long night on the town.

∞

Mason sighed deeply and replaced the sunglasses over his tired eyes, trying in vain to listen to the post-game questions the reporters were throwing at him. One by one he answered them, using the trite phrases and meaningless words he'd been taught, giving them the sound bites they needed for the evening news. They lauded his accomplishments, asking him how it felt to be playing ball again after his time away, and he answered, but not with the complete truth.

He would never tell them his time away from the game had been more painful than any injury and more wonderful than playing in any All-Star game. He would never tell them that, in the span of less than a week, his life had been completely and irrevocably changed, an experience second only to the day he let the Lord into his life.

The barrage of questions continued, the circle of people, cameras, and lights forming a tight barrier between him and the playing field he'd just left. He answered them politely and swiftly, not giving much thought to each, yet appearing to consider them before speaking.

"You've about done it all, Mason. You have a home-run record that will probably stand indefinitely, a fat contract on the table for next year, and almost every award a man can win in baseball. Is there anything you can't do?"

Mason jerked his head away from the cameras and lights, pushing away the senseless anger that overtook him as he sought out the face of the man who dared to ask him such a thing. It was just a question, another in the long line of stupid questions he'd been asked.

Why did the answer to that one cut him to the bone?

He replied with some flippant comment about not knowing what lay ahead and being thankful for the things he'd accomplished, or something to that effect. As soon as the words had left his mouth, he forgot them, to avoid thinking about the real answer.

Signaling the end of the interview with a sweep of his hand, he assumed a fake smile and sprinted toward the dugout, reminding himself not to limp. Finally, under the stinging hot spray of the shower, he allowed himself to consider the reporter's painful query.

"Is there anything you can't do?"

He heard the words echo in his mind and hated the answer that accompanied them. He couldn't do a lot of things, and most of them didn't make any difference to him. But the one that mattered, the one he'd give his life for, was to go back in time and change the events of the last ten years. He'd even settle for changing the past couple of weeks.

If he had the gift of time, he would have done things so differently. And he would still have Blair.

But time moved swiftly, and judgments were final. And that was the one thing all the home-run records and ten-million-dollar contracts in the world couldn't change.

He'd had his chance with Blair and blown it. Obviously, he'd misunderstood the Lord's leading on that one. Now it was time to go home and forget her.

And that's exactly what he'd planned to do, except that when he arrived at his hotel she'd left a message in his voice mail and stepped back in his heart as if she'd never left. "Mason," she said sweetly, "Sam wants to talk to you."

That was all. She gave the phone to the boy, and he rambled on about the game and how great it was that he remembered their signal and a few other things he'd hear when he replayed the message. For now he was too busy listening to that silken voice wrap itself around his name.

Without thinking he started dialing her number, then checked the time and almost hung up. He punched in another digit before slamming the receiver down. Seven long days without her and Sam, and it was all his fault.

He had to do something.

Chapter 12

Time had never moved slowly for Blair. She stretched her neck, easing out the kinks with one hand and reaching for the manual of zoning restrictions with the other. It was the end of the first week without Mason, and she'd finally convinced herself that throwing him out had been the right thing to do.

Yesterday she hadn't been so sure, but today her resolve wasn't as weak. He'd called four times over the last seven days, eight hours and twenty-three minutes, and not once had he asked to speak to her.

Allowing Sam to call and congratulate him tonight had been the height of selflessness, she decided. After all, the man was his father. Besides, she thought, if Mason Walker wanted to speak to her, he could do so through their lawyers.

After all, he'd had no problem talking to lawyers before.

That decided, she blotted a big tear off the page she'd been studying, then threw the soggy tissue into the wastebasket on top of the others. She had her work, and she had Sam, and most important she had the Lord. She didn't need anyone or anything else.

Especially not Mason Walker.

She had plenty of ways to keep busy, she thought as she slammed the book shut and contemplated the ceiling. Stomping away from her desk, she headed for the kitchen to do something a little more mindless.

Half an hour later, she answered the phone on the second ring, her fingers dripping from dishwater and her nose stopped up from crying again. A huge knot stuck in her throat at the sound of Mason's voice. After a couple of false starts, she found her voice.

"Sam's asleep, Mason." She brushed her tears away with the dishtowel. "Did you want anything in particular? I could give him the message in the morning."

"Just wanted to talk. You know, thank him for the call." He paused. "I want to spend time with him, Blair," he said. "Can we work something out?"

"Like what?" she said with a gulp.

"We have a long home stand the first week in August. I want him here with me."

"He's too young to fly all that way alone."

"Then come with him," he said casually, taking her completely by surprise.

"I don't think so." She worked to keep her anger in check. After all he'd done, how dare he think she might be interested in flying to Hawaii for a visit? Why, he practically acted as if things were just fine between them.

"Be reasonable, Blair. I miss him and—"

"Reasonable?" Since when had she not been more than reasonable? "I was perfectly content to let you into our lives, and what did you do? You went behind my back and tried to take Sam away from me."

She heard him expel a long breath. "It didn't happen that way. The person who sent that doctored fax was fired and will most likely be disbarred. Besides that, she deliberately deceived you about what went on between us." He paused. "I care deeply for you and for Sam. Doesn't that make any difference?"

She gripped the phone so tight her fingers tingled. "You told me yourself that every word of it was true."

"The words were true, but they were taken out of context. When I realized Sam might be mine, I called a friend—"

"Who happened to be a lawyer."

"Fair enough," he said. "But I wasn't trying to take him away. Read the whole transcript of that conversation, and you'll see. After all that's come between us because of lies, why would I add to that?"

Why indeed? A niggling thought that he might be telling the truth teased her. "All right, Mason, I'd like to read that transcript."

"I'll see that it's sent." He paused, and for a second, she thought he might have hung up the phone. "Blair?"

"Yes?"

Another long pause. "Never mind."

The following morning a courier delivered a thick brown package bearing the return address of a law firm on Bishop Street in Honolulu, Hawaii. The top sheet was a letter, an official-looking document from an attorney named Michael Brighton. Beneath the letter was a file folder containing several more pages.

Scanning each page, she noted places where words seemed familiar. Just as Mason had said, the document in her hands was proof that the fax she received had been edited. In addition, it seemed painfully obvious that he and the lady lawyer had shared something more than an attorney-client relationship in the not-so-distant past.

Jealousy hit her hard even as logic told her she was crazy for caring. She bit her lip and exhaled slowly.

A pale green envelope slid out from beneath the pages and landed in her lap. Blair set the file aside and opened the envelope, taking care not to tear the delicate stationery inside. In neat script beneath the gold letter *R* were a single sentence and a signature.

"You win. Lisa."

Blair tossed the letter into the trash and dumped the contents of the file folder on top of it.

"You can have him, honey," she said as she stalked away. "I don't even want him anymore."

But as the words echoed in the empty room, she knew they were a lie.

⚭

July 18

Mason leaned against the smooth black leather of the desk chair and laced his fingers behind his head. He watched the white-capped breakers pound the Waikiki Beach ten floors below and contemplated his dilemma.

Just looking at that fat file of legal papers made his stomach churn and his head hurt. To compound his troubles, Blair should have received all the proof she needed by now, but he still hadn't heard from her.

He shrugged his shoulders and let the rest of his concerns roll away. "I have ten million reasons for signing this contract with the Waves and only one reason not to," he said to his newly purchased pal, a gawky-looking Labrador retriever puppy named Jake, who lay curled at his feet. "Unfortunately, Blair's not speaking to me right now."

The black ball of fur rolled over and yawned, oblivious to his new owner's internal torment. Mason scooped up the little dog and settled him in his lap. He began to rub the scruff of fur between the puppy's ears, and in minutes, the little guy went limp with sleep.

On the desk in front of him, the contract lay open to the first page that required a signature. "Okay, Lord," he whispered. "It's Your call."

Then it hit him. With amazing clarity, the future lay before him, and he knew what the Lord wanted him to do with it.

After he counted the zeros on the contract twice to convince himself they were all there, he called his contract lawyer. He spoke briefly to Trey next, then phoned his agent to tell him of his decision.

With the reverence befitting such an auspicious occasion, he pulled the contract toward him and squared it on the desk. He picked up the expensive solid silver Mont Blanc pen Morty had given him after signing last year's contract extension and weighed it in his hand.

Jake began to whimper and wiggle, making little snuffing noises in his sleep. A deep sense of peace settled over Mason as he gave the contract one last, long look, then bowed his head to pray again. In his experience, it never hurt to check with the Lord before anything, especially something this important.

That night the Waves won a big victory over their opponent. The final score was due in part to the three home runs Mason hit in his four times at the plate, his best performance of the season.

Life is sweet, he thought to himself as he closed his eyes in the wee hours of the morning. And this time he didn't go to bed alone. Jake lay curled at his feet, soon joining his owner in a chorus of loud snoring.

Mason awakened to the puppy's tail beating a rhythm on his chest. "Today's the day the Lord and I start fixing this problem." He scratched the pup behind his ears, smiled, and reached for the phone.

"Hey," he said in his most cheerful voice when Blair answered. All of a sudden the line went dead. He hit redial. "Blair, we must have been cut off. Look—I just wanted to—" Again the call was disconnected, so he dialed the number a third time.

"Do not hang up," he said in his most commanding voice. To his surprise she complied. "Did you get the transcript?"

"Yes."

"And did you read it?"

"Yes."

"Well, what did you think?"

This time when she hung up he didn't call back. He did, however, make a few more calls. In less than a half hour, his plan was set. Now all he had to do was wait for late September when the Waves played a series within driving distance of Magnolia.

"I can do that."

But as he said it he had little confidence it would be easy.

ဢ

September 22

Sam pointed toward the jumbo jet approaching the terminal. "Is that Dad's plane?"

Blair sighed and nodded, wondering why she'd agreed to this meeting in the first place. She tugged at the neck of her sweater, then leaned against the broad expanse of glass separating her from the runway and tarmac.

She felt a yank on her sleeve. "He loves you, y'know." Sam twisted his face into a serious expression. "He told me so a long time ago. We're gonna be a family."

Knees weakened, Blair sank onto a bench and pulled Sam down beside her. Despite her feelings for the man, she'd been extra careful to keep Sam out of their problems, and she'd trusted Mason to do the same. If planting these false ideas in his head was part of Mason's game plan, she would nip it in the bud.

"Why would you think that, sweetie?"

" 'Cause he told me." His attention returned to the jet now rolling to a stop outside the window. "I just don't know what's taking so long for him to do something about it."

"Maybe you misunderstood," she said slowly. "When did he tell you this?"

"The night I found out he was my dad. Way back in the summer." His gaze rolled back to her for a moment, and she saw Mason's eyes staring back from his innocent little face. "He said that he loved you and that we were gonna be a family, but it doesn't seem like we're a family. Why aren't we like a real family? I never even get to see my dad anymore."

Her heart sank.

What could she say? There were no words that could answer him without destroying the trust he had in his father, something she could never do, no matter what rotten, underhanded things Mason did. So she watched the man outside signal for the walkway to be attached to the plane and changed the subject.

"I bet you and your dad will have a wonderful time today," she said brightly. "It's really great he has a whole day and a half off before the big game tomorrow. You know that whoever wins is going to the World Series."

She'd heard something about it on the sports channel last night. Not that she'd been looking for news of Mason. She'd just been flipping channels, and there he was.

He rolled his eyes. "It's way cool and stuff, but. . ." His voice trailed off as he studied the luggage being unloaded from the plane.

"But?" She wrapped her arm around his little shoulder and gave him a squeeze, then let him wriggle free.

"But I wish you'd go with us. It's not that cold, and I know you don't like fishing, but I could bait the hook for you and take off the fish you catch, and you wouldn't have to touch anything slimy."

"Let's go down to baggage claim."

Blair gathered Sam in her arms and hugged him again before they walked the short distance. She tried to ignore the fact that he'd insisted on wearing the baseball shirt his father had sent him, despite the cooler weather.

A crowd had gathered at the baggage terminal. The time was near, and so was Mason. Her heart began to pound, and her head threatened to do the same.

"Forgive him."

She shook off the words that had become too familiar over the past two months. Sam pulled out of her embrace and smiled. "C'mon and go with us today. Maybe he'll ask ya then."

"Ask me what?" she said.

"To marry you, silly," he said, giving her a playful nudge. "He already asked me if it was okay, and I said yes."

She stared at him in horror. What had the man been telling him? First he'd promised they would be a family and now this. Had he told Sam about the lady lawyer, too?

His devious plan became crystal clear in her mind. He would be the good guy, the one trying to bring the three of them together, and she, by default, would become the bad guy. Well, she wouldn't let that happen.

"Forgive him." This time the words rang louder than ever. She had to work extra hard to press them back into the corner of her mind.

Maybe she'd think about it tonight.

"Forgive him as he and I have forgiven you."

Ouch.

Sam tugged at her elbow. "I figured he'd have done it by now, but maybe he's saving it for a surprise. Sort of like Skippy."

"Skippy? The turtle?"

"Yeah, know how it was such a great surprise when I got him back? Well, maybe that's what Dad's gonna do."

He climbed to his feet in the chair and tried to get a better look at the passengers coming toward them. Blair motioned for him to step down.

"Yes," she said, suppressing a smile. "It was a big surprise when you found Skippy."

How appropriate. He'd found the unfortunate turtle swimming in the toilet.

That image alone kept her sane and slightly amused for the last few minutes before the passengers emerged en masse through the gate. She'd get through this, she knew. Mason hadn't the least amount of hold on her anymore.

She was over him.

Yet the first dark head that appeared in the doorway set her heart fluttering. And it wasn't even Mason. She began to think about what Sam had said, trying to take her mind off the man who even now was making his way toward them from somewhere inside that plane.

He couldn't love her.

The idea was impossible to believe.

After all, it had been more than two months since their last lengthy conversation. Now she heard his voice more often on television than on the phone.

Not that she tried to watch or anything. Because most of the time it was an accident that she saw him. The Waves were winning, and he was about to break some silly record or something—that was all.

In the meantime, he'd spoken to Sam nearly every day.

Sometimes when she heard Sam and Mason talking, she felt a twinge. Was it regret?

Squaring her shoulders, she rose to her feet and pushed away the ridiculous thought. No way. She hadn't done anything to regret. If anyone should have any regrets it should be—

Mason Walker. Rational thoughts scattered when he stepped into the baggage claim area. He looked tired, she decided, as he met Sam halfway and lifted him into his arms. Across the distance their gazes met, and she rocked with the collision.

She couldn't force her limbs to move. Before she could regain her senses, he came toward her, a vision in faded jeans and black leather.

"Hi," he said casually, one arm holding their son, a battered brown leather satchel slung over the other. "It's been a long time."

"Hi," she heard herself say, although not as casually. "Yes, it has. It's been a long time, I mean. Since we've seen each other, that is."

How stupid did that sound? Where were all the witty comments she'd planned in the wee hours of the night when this creature's blue eyes kept her awake?

One look at him, and the grief she'd put herself through disappeared. Gone in the blink of two very blue eyes.

People moved around them, their bright colors and murmuring sounds swirling about as if this were a day like any other. But it wasn't. Mason had returned, and despite her best intentions, she was glad.

She shook her head. No, she couldn't be glad. Mason Walker was up to something. She could sense it. And whatever it was, he would not get away with it.

Still, he did look awfully handsome with his hair slightly mussed as if he'd been sleeping and his face tanned from the Hawaiian sun.

"You okay?" He regarded her with something like amusement.

Avoiding his direct gaze, she could only nod. What was wrong with her? This man tried to steal her child. How could she harbor any thoughts about him? She followed him through the airport and out into the parking garage, trying not to think of the answer to that question. And trying not to think. She did, however, manage a prayer for strength.

"Here it is, right where Trey said he would leave it." Mason stopped short in front of a little black sports car. "Just a sec, and I'll unlock it for you, pal."

"Cool. Look, Mom—it's a Porsche," Sam said.

She mustered a smile. "Looks like someone bought a new toy."

If Mason heard her remark, he ignored it while he stowed his bag in the trunk.

"Wow, Dad!" Sam squealed as he sat down in the front seat and pushed the button on the door. "Where'd you get this cool car?" His seat began to rise, then lower. Then he pushed another button while Blair worked to stretch the seat belt across his middle.

"Sam, cut it out," she said, pushing his hand away and finally connecting the belt. "Sit still and mind your manners. I want you to behave while you're with your"—no, she couldn't say it, not out loud—"while you're with Mason."

"I will." He folded his hands in his lap, the model of good behavior. She saw the twinkle in his eye, however, and for a brief moment pitied Mason.

"Give me a kiss, sweetie. I won't see you until tomorrow." She leaned toward Sam, and he cringed.

"Aw, Mom," he said before allowing her a quick peck on the cheek.

She stood and closed the door, whirling around to come face-to-face with Mason. Taking a step backward in surprise, she felt her foot slip off the curb. Mason caught her, and she landed with her head against his iron-hard shoulder and his arms around her back. The smell of leather mixed with a spicy scent permeated her senses.

With Mason's breath warm against her ear, Blair felt the ice melting somewhere deep inside her. Each rise and fall of his broad chest loosened its grip until only a lingering warmth remained.

It was like coming home. Only she knew this joy was not hers to claim. Obviously, Mason Walker was truly over her. She'd just have to get over him—again.

"Careful," he whispered against her neck. "You might fall and hurt yourself."

Too late, she thought as he released her and stepped away. Not that she'd ever tell him that.

"Are you all right?"

No. "Yes."

"It's good to see you again, Blair." Mason touched her sleeve. "I've missed both of you—a lot."

Their gazes collided, and Blair pulled away. The sincerity she saw in his eyes left her more than a little confused. How could he miss her unless—

Was the lady lawyer with the pale green stationery out of his life now? Had the best woman actually won?

She shook away the ridiculous thought and tried to concentrate on looking casual when she felt anything but that. "Sam's missed you, too," she said as lightly as she could.

Mason grasped her fingers and gently pulled her toward him. "And what about you? Did you miss me?"

"Daaad! Come on!" Sam called.

"I'll have him back by noon." Mason backed away to open the car door and slid inside. "Game's at seven, and I have to get out to the field early. It takes a lot of tape and preparation to get me ready for a game nowadays."

She managed to nod. And as the car sped off, father and son riding with the top down through the crowded airport parking lot, she had to wonder if he'd felt anything when he held her.

Chapter 13

September 23

Blair awoke more exhausted than when she went to bed. Through the night God had dealt with her about her unforgiveness, and this morning she'd finally seen things His way.

The instant she released her pain to Him, the seesaw of her emotions settled down. How dare she hold a grudge against Mason when he'd so easily forgiven her of a much bigger hurt?

Blair smiled and leaned against the porch post. If God wanted the two of them to be more than friends, He would have to do the matchmaking.

As the sun rose over Magnolia, she promised Him she would take the first step to repair the relationship.

Just as soon as He showed her what that step was.

Finishing her coffee, she started working on the last of the plans for Honey Hill, the new project Mr. Davenport had contracted for her to landscape. Under most circumstances, renovating the grounds of the historic property would be an exciting proposition. With Mason Walker as a distraction, the excitement had lessened somewhat.

To that end, Blair placed a call to Hannah Andrews, the new owner of Honey Hill. After discussing everything from the weather to the next time she would bring Sam out to visit, she was able to finalize a list of specifications for finishing the greenhouse. Surprisingly, Mrs. Andrews had little in the way of suggestions for renovating the property. She'd left most of the decisions up to Blair, generally responding with a blithe "whatever you think best, dear."

Barely a month stood between her crew and the projected completion deadline, and at the rate they were going, it would be close. There was so much work left to be done and so little time to waste. Still, she found herself looking up from her work every time she thought she heard a car coming up the road.

When the cloud of dust on the horizon finally produced a little black speck that could be the Porsche, her palms began to sweat. She rushed to the bedroom and took a few swipes at her unruly hair, finally giving up and capturing it in a gold barrette at the nape of her neck.

By the time the rumble of the powerful engine gave way to tires crunching on the driveway, she'd thrown off her old jeans and ratty T-shirt, exchanging them for a casual dress in a cheerful yellow sprinkled with white dots. As the car doors slammed shut, she slipped into her gold sandals and broke into a run, stopping a few steps short of the door.

Taking a deep breath, she wiped her sweaty palms on the back of her dress, then opened the door, feigning surprise.

"Well, hello there, sweetie," she said to Sam, ruffling his hair as he brushed past her with a package under his arm.

"Hi, Mom. Gotta go hook up this neat video game Dad got me. It's a. . ." His words trailed off when he disappeared upstairs and into his room.

And there stood Mason, too close and yet so far away, keys in hand. "I hope you don't mind." He handed her Sam's navy blue Honolulu Waves backpack, and their fingers touched. "I bought him a little something. If you don't want him to have it, I can take it back. I'm sorry, but I didn't think to discuss it with you first."

"No, no, that's fine."

He said something else, but she missed it. Only a brain cell that hadn't been numbed by his presence alerted her to the fact. She shook her head and clasped the backpack a little tighter.

"What?" she said. "I'm sorry."

Please don't let him read my mind. Then he leaned forward, and she felt that magnetic pull again. This time she tried to fight it.

"I said I'd really like it if you and Sam would come to the game tonight. It's for all the marbles, and I'd like it a lot if you were there cheering for us."

"Cheering where?"

Think, Blair, she said to herself. What was it those beautifully chiseled lips were saying? The magnetic pull had begun to win.

"The game," he answered, giving her a look that told her he thought she was as crazy as a loon. "I brought a couple of tickets and arranged a car to pick you up in case you said yes." Then he smiled. "Please."

How many times had she heard him say that word in her dreams? "Yes" was her automatic response. It was a silly sort of whisper, and heat instantly flamed her cheeks. She cleared her throat and risked a look at him. "Sure, we'll go," she said, trying to act as if she hadn't just made a fool of herself.

He touched her hand, the one still gripping the screen door. "Great," he said. "I was afraid you would say no."

"Now why would I say that?"

Blair cringed inwardly. *Oh, wonderful,* she thought, she'd probably even batted her eyes, too. What in the world was happening to her?

One minute he's a despicable creature, and the next minute he has me acting like Scarlett O'Hara to his Rhett Butler. This had nothing to do with the friendship she'd promised God she would pursue.

She pulled her hand away from under his, and the screen door almost hit her in the face. He stopped it in time with the toe of his boot, putting him in even closer proximity to her.

"Well, we did agree to deal with each other only through our lawyers." He backed away, and she caught the door with one hand. "And I think that's probably the right thing to do. After this, I promise I won't bother you anymore."

She felt her hopes spiraling downward and bit her tongue to keep from saying the wrong thing. Slowly a prayer formed in her mind, and she sent it skyward. "You do?"

"No," he said slowly, "actually I don't." Leaning back against the porch rail, he crossed his arms over his chest and met her gaze with an intense look. "I mean, we owe it to Sam to spend a little family time together, don't you think?"

"Family time," she repeated, mindful of her promise to seek this man's friendship. "Yes, well, maybe so."

He nodded. "Definitely. I'm thinking once, maybe twice a week we'll schedule something with Sam—after the season's over, I mean. You know, dinner, fishing, a movie, whatever. Does that work for you?"

She could only echo his nod with one of her own. *Did he say fishing?*

"Good. I'm glad we got that straight." He punctuated the statement with a killer smile, then loped down the porch stairs and across the yard toward the expensive toy that passed for his mode of transportation. "Guess we'll be seeing a lot more of each other once I get moved into my place by the lake."

"The lake?" That was less than five minutes away.

"Yeah," he said, looking down at her over the top of his sunglasses. "Friend of mine's loaning me a place for the off-season. Looks as if we'll be practically neighbors."

He slipped into the car and cranked the engine, then waved as he drove away. As she watched him go, Blair shook her head. The only thing harder than maintaining a friendship with her ex-husband would be reminding herself that a friendship was as far as their relationship could proceed, at least until the Lord told them otherwise.

The smile reappeared later that evening when he stood at home plate and picked her and Sam out of the crowd. While he tipped his hat and winked at Sam, his gaze seemed to linger on Blair. Moments later, he hit his first home run of the night.

"Why are all those men beating on Mason?" she asked Sam over the din of the crowd.

"They're tellin' him he did a good job," Sam said.

"It looks like they're mad at him," she said, knowing that feeling too well. After all, he made loving him so complicated.

Loving him? Where had that come from?

She felt a hand on her shoulder and turned to see a woman of middle age smiling at her.

"I have a theory about that," the woman said. "I think it's because they all wish they'd done it instead of him."

"Makes sense to me," Blair said, sinking back into her seat to wait out the end of the interminably long game.

Every time Mason caught her looking at him, he smiled, and every time he smiled, she felt her stomach flip. When it was over, Mason's team had lost, but just barely.

And all she wanted to do was go home.

Settling into the comfortable limo for the ride back to Magnolia, Blair watched Sam brimming with excitement. His words were a constant stream that soon slowed to the occasional spurt. Before they reached the city limits of Magnolia, Sam had fallen into a deep sleep.

"Lord, what am I going to do about Mason Walker?" she whispered as she traced the curve of her sleeping son's chin.

"Wait and be still."

∞

October 12

As the Honey Hill project neared completion, Blair found she had less and less time to think about waiting, although she saw Mason more and more. At least she saw his car appear in the driveway, and she saw their son disappear into it as she headed off for another day at Honey Hill.

In the evenings, she returned home tired and less than sociable, wanting only a hot bath and a pillow. Sometimes Sam slept over at Mason's place, and other times Mason waited up for her until she arrived, letting Sam sleep in his own bed.

His entire social life seemed to revolve around Sam, giving a final rest to her worries about the lady lawyer. Tonight, as she peeked in on Sam to tell him good night, she caught Mason reading to him.

"Come in and listen, Mom," Sam called. "Dad's just getting to the good part."

She shook her head and took a step backward. "I don't want to intrude on a father-and-son moment."

Mason motioned for her to come in. "You wouldn't want to miss the good part, would you?"

Sinking onto the floor in the corner, she leaned her head against the wall and listened to Mason's deep voice wrap around the vivid prose of

C. S. Lewis. Despite the tiredness that had permeated into her bones, Blair hung on every word until Mason stopped at the end of the chapter and turned to face her.

"This is the part where Sam and I say our prayers. Would you like to join us?"

Sam gave Mason an incredulous look. " 'Course she does, don't you, Mom?"

" 'Course I do," she said, imitating Sam as she climbed to her feet and crossed the room. Against her better judgment, she knelt beside Mason and placed her left hand in his. With her other hand she held tight to Sam. The little boy reached for his dad, completing the circle of prayer.

"You go first, slugger," Mason said to Sam.

The little boy nodded, then cleared his throat. "Lord, thank You for that camping trip I get to go on soon and for fishing with Dad and his friends and for the nice lady with the big house at Mom's new job and for giving me my mom and my dad. . ."

Mason gave Blair's hand a quick squeeze. She cast a sideways glance to return his smile.

". . .and thank You, God, for letting them both be here tonight on account of how much I want them to be married again and live together forever and never get divorced again. Amen."

Blair's breath caught in her throat. Mason's fingers tightened around her hand. She refused to meet his gaze.

"Your turn, Mom."

"Heavenly Father," she said quietly, "thank You for this beautiful day and the star-filled night. Thank You for the blessings we've recognized and those we have failed to notice. Thank You for giving us Sam, and we ask that You hear his prayers and keep him safe through the night. Amen."

"Okay, Dad," Sam said. "Your turn."

"Father God, we come to You a family blessed beyond measure. We thank You for this day and ask that You keep us ever mindful of Your holy presence. Amen." Mason released Blair's hand. "Okay, son, it's bedtime."

"Hey, no fair." Sam scrunched up his face into a scowl and folded his arms over his chest. "You forgot the part about Mom."

Mason cleared his throat and gave Blair a weak smile before

turning to Sam. "Hey, that was supposed to be between us and God, remember?"

"Oh yeah," Sam said.

Blair feigned irritation, her heart beating a furious rhythm and heat rising in her cheeks. "Are you two keeping secrets from me?"

"It's not a secret, 'zackly." Sam looked to his father for agreement. "It's kind of a—"

"It's getting late, Sam. Lights out, or your mom'll be mad at me for keeping you up on a school night."

Mason had tucked Sam in and turned out the lights before Blair could get to her feet. She followed him downstairs to the front door and out onto the porch where she watched him pull his keys from his jeans pocket.

To her surprise he turned to face her. "Blair, you're working too hard."

She shrugged. "I love what I'm doing." The chill of the evening air felt wonderful against the heated skin of her face.

He studied her. "You really do, don't you?"

"Yes," she said, "I really do."

With a nod and a curt "good night," he set off across the yard.

"So what are you and Sam cooking up?" she called when she realized he intended to escape without making any further conversation.

"Wait and you'll see," he returned as he climbed into his car and sped off into the night.

"Wait," she whispered. Every time she took something regarding Mason to the Lord in prayer, she heard the Lord's words: "*Wait and be still.*" Now Mason was adding to it with a similar word of his own.

Exhaustion and the long list of last-minute details for Honey Hill's November eighth deadline waiting on her desk forced her back inside. When she had more time, she'd have to consider what the men in her life might be up to. For now, she'd just have to be still and wait.

∞

October 28

"How's the project?" Mr. Davenport asked, his distinctive twang drawing out the words. "Everything on schedule?"

Blair smiled. "Actually, it looks as if it'll be finished a day early. The painters are done, and all I'm waiting for now is the guys who put in the automatic watering system in the greenhouse. There's a problem with the timer. It goes on and off at all hours."

"But other than that it's all going according to plan?"

"Yes, it's going great. A couple of odd jobs left to be done, but nothing major. Why? Is there something wrong?" She heard the familiar sound of the Porsche pulling into the driveway and lifted the curtains to watch Sam and Mason unload their fishing gear. "You sound a little worried," she said, stepping away from the window to avoid being seen.

"Worried? No."

The screen door slammed, distracting her for a moment. Two voices, both talking at the same time, preceded the father and son into the room.

"You didn't either, Dad," Sam said. "My fish was the biggest."

"Wasn't either," Mason answered. "And we'll never know because they both got away."

"Didn't either. Mine got away, and you never did catch one."

"Did, too," the deeper of the voices replied.

"Did not and dontcha even try to tell me something different."

"Company?" her client asked.

"What?" She watched them walk into the room. "Oh, no, it's just my son and"—she saw Mason's smile and melted inside—"and his dad."

"Well, then, I'll let you go," he said without missing a beat. "I'll see you out at the property in the morning."

She tried to listen, really she did, but Mason's presence made her forget the words as soon as she heard them. "The morning?" she asked, latching on to the only phrase that remained in her memory.

"The meeting is in the morning at Honey Hill," she heard him say. "Ten o'clock." He paused. "Is everything okay?"

Two matching smiles flashed in her direction as Mason picked up his son and hefted him over his shoulder, carrying him out of the room without a backward glance. Sam burst into giggles, and the sound trailed him and his father as they left.

"Fine," she said, feeling the sudden chill of the empty room. "I'm fine. Tomorrow at ten. Honey Hill."

She could hear the sounds of a video game in progress, with both Mason and Sam carrying on a running dialogue punctuated by regular beeps and groans from the computer. Suddenly, the house seemed to shrink.

Escaping out the front door, she sank into the comfortable old rocker and took several deep cleansing breaths of the crisp fall air. Bubba eyed her suspiciously from his patch of sunshine near the mailbox but made no move to join her. She leaned her head back and closed her eyes.

With every creak of the rocker she thanked God for bringing Mason back to her only to beg Him to tell her why with the next conscious thought. Then she asked Him to tell her what to do next, to show her the way.

"Wait and be still. I will make a way."

"I know, but don't You have anything new to report?" When further answers didn't arrive, she prayed for strength.

A couple of more deep breaths and she settled into an easy rhythm, rocking back and forth, with the only sounds around her the chirping of the birds and the occasional truck passing far off on the distant highway. Then she felt it, a subtle change in the air, a whisper on the breeze that only she could hear.

Her eyes opened. Mason Walker stood only inches away, a pained expression on his face. How he got there was a mystery she dared not contemplate.

"What's wrong?"

"Sorry. I didn't mean to bother you." He looked away, shrugging those broad shoulders. "I was about to leave, and I saw you just sitting out here and..."

"And?" She had the strangest notion that his eyes would speak volumes if only he'd look at her.

"Forget it." Without a word, he turned and walked away.

"Lord, please let next week fly by," she whispered as Mason's Porsche disappeared from sight.

∽

October 29

Indeed, the next week did fly by as the big day drew nearer. Twice Blair saw Mason, but only from the front window when he brought Sam home. Her mind filled with a hundred details concerning her work, she tried not to think about him, something so much easier in the light of day.

But at night, when the day's activities slowed to nothing and the darkness closed in, she saw Mason often in her mind. Turning down the covers, she imagined his dark, wavy hair on his own pillow, as it would have been had their marriage continued all these years. Sliding between the white cotton sheets in the shadowy stillness, she felt him just beyond her reach, only inches away from her outstretched hand.

So close yet so far away. Until one night when she reached out and touched a living, breathing body.

"Mom," Sam's little voice said from the other side of the bed. "Can I sleep here tonight? I miss my dad tonight."

At that quiet, vulnerable moment with dreams of him still fresh on her mind, she had to bite her tongue to keep from telling Sam she missed him, ere she pretended she didn't love Mason, had gotten out of hand.

As she held her sleeping son, Blair finally heard the words she'd been waiting for. *"It is time."*

Blair smiled and made a promise to God and herself that she would tell Mason how she felt, no matter what the consequences. And she would do it as soon as the Honey Hill project was finished.

The day before the projected date, Blair's work at Honey Hill was complete. She met one last time with Griffin Davenport and the architect, and their huge success put the three of them in a festive mood. Against her better judgment she agreed to meet them for a get-together after the final run through, one last celebration for a job well done. All that remained by Friday afternoon was a check of the outbuildings and then she could join them.

Clipboard in hand, Blair strolled toward the greenhouse, stopping short at the strange noise she heard. It sounded like snoring.

Striking out across the expanse of bright green grass that divided the newly tilled vegetable garden from the greenhouse, she opened the wood-and-glass door and peeked inside, searching for the offender. No one was around.

Instead, the tropical smell of warm, damp earth greeted her, a few of the hanging ferns still dripping from this morning's watering and the temperature still warm from the softly blowing heaters. She picked her way across the cobblestone floor to the back where the automatic controls were located. Checking the dials to make sure the settings were correct, she pushed the test button and watched while the newly installed automatic watering system burst into action.

Overhead, an assemblage of white painted pipes let loose with gentle streams of water, strategically placed to provide an even coverage for the large expanse of greenhouse interior. From where she stood, it looked to Blair as if someone had captured a rain cloud and set it free inside the room.

Satisfied, she reset the timer and left through the back door, emerging into the cool November afternoon, only to find the source of the loud snoring huddled against the greenhouse's large heating system.

She cleared her throat and waited for a response from the man who should have been painting the stables. Her only answer was a snort followed by a series of resounding snores.

"Mr. Collier," she said loudly.

Again nothing but snoring.

She kneeled down and touched his arm lightly. "Mr. Collier."

This time he opened one eye, regarding her critically from beneath the brim of his dark blue baseball cap. "Yes?" he said slowly.

"Shouldn't you be doing something?"

"I was." His eye shut tight, indicating the conversation was over.

"Mr. Collier?" She counted to ten. Twice. "Mr. Collier!"

He adjusted his cap away from his eyes and glared at her. "What?"

"Are the stables finished?"

"Nope." He resumed his comfortable position. "Can't finish today. They're moving the horses in."

"Horses? No one told me horses would be moved in today."

She consulted the schedule attached to her clipboard. No animals of any kind were supposed to be delivered. Several pallets of Saint Augustine grass to patch the back lawn, four flats of liriope to edge the cutting garden and ten yards of organic mulch for the vegetable garden were all expected this afternoon, but no horses.

"Does Mrs. Andrews know about this?"

"I reckon she does," he said, crossing his arms over his chest. "She's over there right now. Pretty animals they are. You oughta go see 'em."

"I will," she said, heading off in the direction of the stables.

As she rounded the corner, she stopped in her tracks and watched a large brown prancing horse being led into the unfinished stables. She sighed, shaking her head and making a note of her scheduling dilemma as she strode toward the barn.

A herd of horses was not what she needed to deal with right now. Especially not with the all-important deadline looming.

Steel gray hair blowing in the autumn breeze caught Blair's eye, and she knew she'd found Hannah Andrews. The older woman stood to one side, looking for the world like a general instructing the troops. Waving away a man in coveralls bearing a stack of papers, she headed toward Blair with a smile on her face.

"Still at work?" she asked with a smile. "I thought you'd be taking advantage of this beautiful day to spend time with your son. I so enjoyed his visit last weekend."

Blair frowned at the memory of Mason's sudden trip out of town last month, the one that forced her to bring Sam to work with her. Mrs. Andrews made an instant friend in Sam and had kept him entertained all day, much to Blair's relief.

"He's camping with the Scouts this weekend," Blair said. "And when he left he was still talking about the pineapple upside-down cake you let him help you make. I don't know if I thanked you properly for your hospitality. I hadn't intended to bring him, but there was a problem with—"

"Nonsense, Blair. I thoroughly enjoyed the boy." She smiled, her brown eyes twinkling in the bright fall sun. "I haven't had children around in years. It's a pity."

"Yes, they can be a joy, but there are the other times."

"That's true." Mrs. Andrews paused. "So I'll repeat the question. Why are you here when you could be with that darling boy and his father?"

Blair shook her head. "I'm trying my best to meet this schedule, but there's a problem."

"Problem?"

Blair nodded her head in the direction of the stables. "No horse deliveries were on the schedule for today. Is there anything else I should be aware of?"

Mrs. Andrews looked thoughtful. "Well, there is one thing."

She pulled her pencil out and prepared to write. "What's that?"

"Tea. You work entirely too hard." She linked her arm with Blair's. "Let's go have a cup of tea, and you can tell me all about your family."

"Family?"

"Yes," Mrs. Andrews said, practically dragging her toward a table already set for two under the gazebo. "I want to hear all about that adorable imp and his father."

"But the horses—"

"Don't worry about those horses," she said, pushing the back door open. "I've spoken to your Mr. Collier, and he's promised to stay late until the job is finished. I suspect he's gone off somewhere to catch a nap in case he's up late."

An hour later, the big iron gates closed behind Blair, and she drove down the country road with one last look back. "I sure am going to miss this place," she said under her breath as she slowed to a stop at the highway intersection, then headed to join her co-workers in an end-of-the-job celebration.

The Pines, a friendly, open-air restaurant just outside Magnolia, stood virtually empty late on that Friday afternoon. The only other patrons were a pair of leather-clad bikers drinking sodas and watching the news at the end of the bar. Blair paid for her mineral water and slipped into a green plastic patio chair across from Mr. Davenport and the architect, an energetic man by the name of Jack Delaney.

She listened politely as the men discussed various aspects of the real estate market. Soon she found her thoughts more on the decision she'd made a few nights ago than on profits and points. Tomorrow night was the big party, the housewarming at Honey Hill, and she'd decided to ask Mason to be her date.

It had been a big step, admitting he might be long-term commitment material after all, and while she'd accepted the fact in her mind, she wasn't sure she could actually admit it to him. She tried not to think of what he would say, of how he might react. The conversation around her turned to Honey Hill, and she forced herself to join in.

Speculation had run rampant over the party plans, which Mrs. Andrews had rendered top secret. Yesterday the house had been closed to all visitors, and even Blair and the architect hadn't been able to gain admittance. As she left this afternoon, the greenhouse had suffered the same fate, the beautifully leaded glass doors locked, the walls covered in white paper to disguise the goings-on inside.

For the life of her, Blair hadn't the foggiest idea from whom they were hiding the decorations, the location being about as private as any she could imagine. She chalked it up to the peculiarities of the wealthy.

She certainly hadn't learned anything by asking Hannah Andrews.

The mysterious crew of party planners, a varied group wearing badges and carrying clipboards, descended on Honey Hill with the efficiency of a SWAT team, closing the huge metal gates behind them and heading off in the direction of the house. Blair had lagged behind, her curiosity piqued, but she could see nothing of interest.

"I say it's going to be one amazing party," Jack said, raising his glass of iced tea. "Here's to the rich and famous. May they always be in need of a good architect. After all, I have three daughters, and they're marathon shoppers, right down to the five-year-old."

Blair felt Griffin Davenport studying her over his coffee, a faint smile on his perfectly tanned face. "Here, here," he said, his gaze unwavering. "Long live the new mistress of Honey Hill, and may her real-estate requirements be many."

She joined them in their toasts, saying nothing. Once again her mind had wandered elsewhere, caught somewhere between Mason Walker and abject loneliness. Then, in a cloud of dust and a squeal of tires, a car came to a screeching halt inches away from her van and brought her back to the present.

"Some people shouldn't have driver's licenses," she said to Jack who only nodded and smiled.

The car door slammed, but a large tree blocked her view of the driver. Footsteps crunched the gravel, and she knew the menace was about to walk through the door. When he did, she intended to give him a piece of her mind.

When Mason appeared at the entrance to the patio, her mouth went dry, and her brain went numb. Any words she'd intended to say were lost.

Once again she studied him, scuffed boots giving way to a long faded stretch of denim. Beneath the ever-present black leather jacket, he wore a white oxford shirt with a button-down collar that contrasted nicely with the mischievous look he wore on his face.

He'd driven with the top down; this much was obvious from the tangle of dark curls that flowed from the back of his baseball cap. As he leaned against the wooden railing, his arms crossed over his chest.

Then he lifted a finger, moving it to his sunglasses in slow motion. When he pushed the black Ray-Bans on top of his cap, his blue gaze hit her like a pool of ice-cold water on a hot afternoon.

She drank it all in, savoring the smile he gave her and offering him one in return. At least she thought she smiled.

"I'll have whatever the lady's drinking," he said over his shoulder to the bartender.

"Mineral water it is," came the dry response.

"With lime." Mason's gaze slid back to meet hers. For a long moment, time stood still.

"Well, look who's here," Mr. Davenport said then, jumping to his feet to offer Mason a brisk handshake. "I didn't think you were going to show, buddy."

Chapter 14

$\mathcal{M}$ason shook his hand and said something to him, his gaze never leaving Blair's. Then Mr. Davenport introduced him to Jack Delaney, and he spoke again. Still the words did not reach her ears.

"Blair, I'd like you to meet a friend of mine," she heard Mr. Davenport say. "This is Mason Walker."

Mason took a few swaggering strides toward her until their fingers met, sending a shock wave to her brain that jolted her back into reality. She formed an intelligent answer in her mind that never quite materialized.

"Friend?" She stared at Griffin Davenport as if she were seeing him for the first time. Griffin was a businessman, and Mason was a ballplayer. How could the two of them travel in the same circles?

She looked to Mason for confirmation. "You know Mr. Davenport?"

He nodded, and the dimples deepened. "I get around," he said with a shrug.

With catlike grace, Mason slid a straight-backed wooden chair up next to hers and turned it backward. He gave her the most innocent yet guilty look she'd ever seen, and her heart lurched again. It reminded her of Sam.

He sank down next to her. Because of the close space, his leg grazed hers. Every nerve in her jumped to attention, and she fought the urge to scoot away.

"Did Sam get that sleeping bag into the backpack I bought him?" Mason asked. She nodded and watched him sweep his vision away from her toward Mr. Davenport. "He had to carry all this stuff for the camp-out, and he was supposed to fit it all into his backpack so he could hike with it. I tried to tell him he didn't need the big one because it's so bulky, but the boy's stubborn." He nudged her with his leg. "I can't imagine who he gets it from."

"That's right," Mr. Davenport said. "He has the Scout thing. Left right after school, and he's coming back Sunday evening, right? That's all he could talk about at the lake last weekend. And that boy sure loves to talk." He paused and lifted his cup. "That and fish. He's better at it than you are, Walker. And I ought to know."

Before she could think of a reaction to that statement, the conversation veered in the direction of fishing and other things beyond her interest. She heard snatches of it, something about lake temperature and red wigglers, whatever those were, but she remained too surprised to follow it.

One clear truth began to emerge. Griffin Davenport and Mason Walker were on friendly terms—fishing buddy terms, of all things.

"Excuse me," she said evenly.

The male voices continued to swirl around her, paying no heed to her polite words. She tried again with no success.

"Hey!"

Her gaze locked with Mason's, and she automatically shifted into a friendlier disposition. "You've been taking my son fishing with the man who pays my salary, and I didn't know about it?"

He shrugged. "I guess." Mason resumed his debate with Griffin Davenport and the architect as if she hadn't said anything worth considering.

"But you accused me of—" She sputtered and worked to regain her train of thought. "You thought Mr. Davenport was my—" Heat flooded her cheeks when her client began to smile. "Never mind."

Mason leaned toward her and winked. "A good ballplayer always checks out the competition before he takes the field," he whispered.

Filled with the sudden urge to ponder his strange statement in solitude, she stood and touched Mason on the shoulder. Even under the leather jacket, she could feel his muscles jump on contact.

"I should be going. Could I speak to you outside?"

He lowered his drink to the table and gave her a slow smile. "Sure."

"See you tomorrow night," she said to the other men, making her exit as quickly as she could.

Tomorrow night.

Those words lay heavily on her mind as she reached the van, well aware that Mason followed a step behind. She fumbled with her keys, ultimately dropping them. As she leaned over to retrieve them, Mason's hand landed on hers.

His fingers enveloped her hand wrapping it in warmth. When he released her, she dropped the keys again. Fielding them with the expertise of a seasoned baseball veteran, he planted them firmly in her palm, then leaned against the car a few inches away from her. "Drive carefully" was all he said.

"Um, okay. Thanks." She looked away and filled her lungs with the crisp evening air. "How about dinner?" she asked as she exhaled.

Where those words had come from she had no idea. She braved a glance in his direction.

"Dinner?"

"Yes," she said, proud that it had come out sounding like a real word instead of the garbled mess she'd expected. She lifted her gaze to his and braved the impact, never wavering. "Dinner. Tonight."

"Can't." This time he looked away, and she had the distinct impression he felt uncomfortable with the question. "Plans. You know how it is. Late notice and all."

"Sure. It's no big deal."

She wanted to die of embarrassment. Instead, she began to speak, something she regretted almost immediately.

"We all have to eat, and since Sam's away and I was going to anyway and so were you—I mean, I really didn't expect you to—" She affected a casual pose, nearly sliding sideways as she leaned against the freshly waxed surface of the van. "Oh, forget it."

Mason caught her by the arm, pulled her upright, and opened the door for her. She slipped inside and tried to fit the key into the ignition without looking at him. After two failed attempts, he reached over and did it for her.

"There's this thing." She paused. "It's for work. Anyway, I was wondering. . ."

She hoped he'd take the hint and jump right in with a resounding yes. Unfortunately, his handsome face went blank.

"You were wondering what?"

This was not going to be easy. "I was wondering if you'd—" She lost her nerve. "Never mind." If this was what guys went through every time they asked a girl for a date, it was a miracle the human race had survived this long.

"No," he said gently, laying a hand on her arm. "What thing? Do you need help with something for work? Is there anything I can do for you?"

"No."

She shook her head and averted her eyes, finally allowing her gaze to rest on the starched white collar of his shirt. "Never mind," she said, feeling the flush begin as she pulled out of his grasp and turned the ignition. "I changed my mind. No big deal."

But it was a big deal.

Without saying a word, he'd let her know that he no longer thought of her in a romantic way. Their brief time together seemed to be ancient history as far as this guy was concerned. He wouldn't even go to dinner with her, although he was quick to offer help for work.

What a pal.

Well, that was fine by her. She could go to the party alone. There was no shame in that. After all, she'd discovered long ago that no date at all was much better than a bad date.

Especially a bad date with a jock.

And given the uncertain status of their relationship, an evening with Mason might turn out to be a really bad date. She cast a furtive glance at the subject of her daydreams. *Or a really good one,* she thought.

In a flash, she left him standing in the parking lot, putting as much distance as she could between her embarrassment and the source of it. Half a mile from home the tears began. At the back porch, she decided she wouldn't give up that easily.

After all, the Lord had told her it was time to act.

"This is just going to take more time." She ran her hand over the wide porch railing. "But you will be mine, Mason Walker. Just you wait and see."

☙

Blair arrived at Honey Hill the next evening wishing she were any place but at a party. What she really needed to be doing was working on her plans for recapturing Mason's attention, but business was business, and this was a command performance.

When Mrs. Andrews phoned that morning asking her to arrive promptly at six instead of the time of seven-thirty that was printed on the invitation, she'd found it strange. She forced herself to smile as she slipped into her shoes and grabbed her purse. At least she would get to see Honey Hill that much sooner.

But as she backed down the driveway, she felt less and less happy about her decision to attend the party. Even with Sam away on the camping trip, she thought staying home alone might be better than going. Twice she nearly turned back.

Postponing the inevitable, she passed the black iron gates twice before finally coming to a stop at the newly constructed guardhouse to surrender her engraved invitation.

"Drive on up to the house, Miss Montgomery," the guard said. "There'll be a man waiting to park your car."

"Thank you," she said, fighting the butterflies that rose out of nowhere in her stomach.

She drove slowly up the long, winding driveway past the horses that grazed in the pasture, the last rays of the sun disappearing into long purple, orange, and gold streaks behind the pines. Finally, the main house came into view, and Blair slowed to a crawl to admire the breathtaking sight.

Tall columns gleamed a brilliant white against the freshly painted exterior, the glossy foliage of a climbing rose framing either side of the double front doors. Twin chimneys flanked either side of the house, their presence in direct defiance of the architect Delaney's edict that they could never be restored to their former service. Looking at them now, the spires piercing the night sky, she was glad he'd been wrong.

Blair shook off the feeling of foreboding that had been troubling her since her arrival at Honey Hill and appraised the house with a more critical eye. Lights burned in every room, giving it the look of a brightly illuminated dollhouse perched on a carpet of green.

All around her the evidence of her hard work blossomed, literally.

Layers and layers of green were punctuated here and there with bright splashes of color from the ancient camellia bushes, the only flowers in bloom this late in the season. She pictured the gardens as they would look in the spring, acre upon acre of flowers, both wild and cultivated, but all planted by design to complement the beautiful home they surrounded.

For one moment, she allowed herself to savor the pleasure of a job well done. Then a gentleman clad in a severe dark suit stepped out to meet her, ending her pleasant thoughts.

"Welcome to Honey Hill," he said, sweeping the door open with a formal bow. "You're expected, Miss Montgomery. Please follow me."

He led her up the front steps and into the large foyer, its polished marble floor reflecting the candles that shone from the original nineteenth-century chandelier above. She looked around and noticed for the first time that she was the only visitor in the house.

"Am I early?" she asked the retreating butler.

"Early, miss? No, you're quite prompt." He continued his brisk pace down the hall and into the formal parlor. Still no other guests were in evidence.

His heels clicking an even cadence on the marble, he strode through the parlor and opened the large double doors that overlooked the pool and cutting garden, giving way to a thick cluster of yaupon and hollies.

"If you please, Miss Montgomery." He threw open the leaded glass door for her. "You're expected in the greenhouse."

"The greenhouse?"

The dour gentleman almost looked amused. "Shall I escort you?"

"No, I can find it." She stepped out into the cool evening air and pulled her grandmother's antique shawl tight around her shoulders. While the black dress she'd splurged on was long on style, it was short on warmth.

She had nearly lost her nerve and returned it. Twice. Then Mason Walker had turned her down, and she'd made the irrevocable decision to have a great time without him. Well, at least she could dress the part.

She cast a cautious look in that direction. "Are the rest of the guests out there?"

He only smiled and retreated into the house, leaving her with more questions than answers. And a very funny feeling that things were not as they seemed.

Black stiletto heels made for slow going across the paving stones that formed a path between the main house and the secluded greenhouse. Once the pool and patio had disappeared behind her, Blair slipped off the offending shoes and made her way down the twisting, turning path much faster.

At the door to the massive Victorian structure, she stopped, leaning against the freshly painted white wood trim, and slipped back into her shoes. Then she felt it. Someone was nearby.

"Well of course, silly," she said under her breath as she took a tentative step forward. "Mrs. Andrews is waiting for me in there."

But the greenhouse was too dimly lit to be occupied. Or at least it seemed that way from the outside.

She nearly turned back; then she heard the music, a soft soulful sound that seemed to be coming from inside. Putting her ear to the glass, she heard the rise and fall of a saxophone, a rhythm that almost matched the beating of her heart.

When she opened the door, the music swelled, and so did the lump in her throat. Far from being dark, the lush interior basked in the glow of a thousand ivory candles. From the rafters, strings of tiny white lights glittered like lightning bugs on a hot summer night.

Leaving the crisp night air outside, she pulled the door shut and turned to admire the sparkling room. Dark green foliage and a rainbow of hothouse flowers held court with a thousand pinpoints of light.

In the open center of the structure, a table covered in pale cream fabric had been set up with two glasses and a bottle of mineral water chilling in a silver bucket adorned with limes. A gift wrapped in creamy paper and tied with a large silver bow flanked the bucket, a bright profusion of blue and white flowers filling a cut crystal vase behind them.

On either side stood twin chaise lounges thickly padded with a profusion of multicolored chintz pillows. Across from them were two more, forming a tight conversation group that transformed the utilitarian greenhouse into a welcoming space.

One of Mrs. Andrews's more frivolous purchases, Blair had tried to warn her they wouldn't last six months in the warm and humid environment. Seeing them in the glow of the candles, she could understand the reason the woman had insisted on having them.

It was a lovely backdrop for a party, although she couldn't imagine more than twenty or thirty people could have been invited. Any more than that and the guests would be standing elbow to elbow. A movement along the back of the room caught her attention.

"Mrs. Andrews?"

No answer.

She stood still and tried to listen above the music and the pounding of her heart, the urge to run nearly overwhelming her.

"Who's there?" She took a cautious step backward, then another. "Look—it's obvious there's been a mistake. I'll be going now." On the third step backward, she slipped out of her heels. "I'll come back later when the rest of the guests are here."

"Don't go."

The voice filled the room, and her knees went weak. "Mason?"

He stepped into view wearing a black tuxedo and a smile. "Stay. Please?"

She cocked her head to one side and stared at him. "What are you doing here? You said you had plans."

He countered with a look so innocent she knew he had to be guilty of something. "I did. I planned to be here."

Footsteps rang out a warning that he was approaching although she lost him in the play of light and shadows. "Don't tell me you know Mrs. Andrews, too."

"You might say that." Then he materialized beside her, blocking out the light and filling the space with his presence.

"Do you and Sam fish with her, too?"

"No."

She waited for the smile that never appeared; somehow her shawl slipped to the ground, but she couldn't bring herself to look for it.

Soft music filled the silence as she tried to think of something to say. Mason seemed to move closer, inching toward her, although she knew he hadn't moved at all.

"Why am I here?" she finally managed to ask.

"To settle some things." He bridged the gap between them by clasping her hand.

"About Sam?"

"That's part of it."

"I see." She looked down at his fingers, weaving together with hers, and wondered how she'd ever managed to set him free.

"I was thinking—"

She stopped his words with a kiss.

An arm went around her waist, an unyielding steel band covered in velvet that took her breath away. He released her fingers only to capture her completely in the circle of his embrace. Lost in the moment, she almost didn't feel her feet leaving the ground.

"Your knee," she whispered against his lips. "Put me down. How're you going to earn that ten million dollars if you're hurt?"

"I'm not," he said, depositing her on the chaise. "Turned 'em down. I quit baseball for something better."

Another kiss welded her to the spot.

∽

Mason hadn't intended to do that. The kiss, the clutch—neither of them was supposed to happen. This was his party, and he was in charge.

Jumping to his feet, he reached for the bottle of mineral water. After several botched attempts, he opened it despite his shaking hands. Somehow he poured water into the glasses, steeling himself with a deep breath before turning to face Blair. And there she sat, slightly disheveled and so beautiful.

"You planned all of this, didn't you?" she said.

"I'm afraid so. But I can explain."

"You're not dumping me for anyone else?"

"Hardly," he said with a chuckle.

He handed her the glass and sank into the chair beside her, knowing if he came any closer he'd never remember the speech he'd rehearsed over and over in his mind. Studying the rising lime in his glass, he took a deep breath and plunged in.

"Okay, here's the deal. The only thing I want is for you and me and Sam to be a family. I bought this place, and Trey set up the deal with Davenport, a buddy of his from prep school. Hannah Andrews gave up a good job as my housekeeper to sit out here in the middle of nowhere and keep an eye on you while I survived on toast and turkey sandwiches. See—I did it all for you. For us. So we could raise horses and kids."

He chanced a look in her direction, nearly losing his nerve as he saw a tear shimmer in her bluebonnet eyes. "Blair, don't cry. Anything but that."

"Honey Hill is yours? Mrs. Andrews is your housekeeper, and Trey is pals with Griffin Davenport?" Her eyes widened, and he waited for the big explosion. "You set this up?"

He felt like such a jerk for bringing her here under false pretenses. He'd blown it but good—that was for sure.

Too late to turn back now. "Yeah, I did."

He knelt beside her, ignoring the sharp slice of pain that shot upward from his worn-out knee. "I love you, Blair. I can't think of a time in my life when I didn't."

"I love you, too," she whispered.

This time he was the one to silence her with a kiss. And it felt good, he thought, to be back in control.

Okay, so the Lord was in control, but he was definitely on His side. Mason could have kissed Blair longer, but he stopped, reminding himself of the real reason he'd planned this little party. The other party, the one that started in less than an hour, would celebrate the successful completion of his mission with two hundred of their closest friends.

At least he hoped so.

"Blair?"

She looked up, her eyes still moist. "Hmm?"

"About us." Where were the smooth words he'd planned? "I need to ask you something."

She smiled a lazy smile that sent his heart into overdrive. "What?" came out sounding like a whisper.

Mason put a finger beneath her chin and lifted her face until he gazed into her eyes. For what seemed like an eternity, he stared, unable to call forth the speech he'd practiced. Finally, the words came, and he said them quickly before they could vanish again.

"Will you marry me—again?"

Mason handed her the gift and watched in anticipation while she opened it. She lifted the lid of the small wooden box, the one Sam had taken great delight in painting with blue flowers for the occasion, and gasped.

Wrapped in the folds of the worn green fabric was an engagement ring, a large round diamond mounted on a gold band.

"Yes," she said. "I'll marry you—again."

Then the sprinklers came on.

Luigi's Italian Meat Sauce a la Bonnie Sue

½ cup of onion slices
2 tablespoons olive oil or salad oil
1 pound ground beef
2 cloves garlic, minced
2 16-ounce cans (4 cups) tomatoes (I cut these up)
2 8-ounce cans (2 cups) seasoned tomato sauce
1 3-ounce can (½ cup) broiled sliced mushrooms
½ cup chopped parsley
1 ½ teaspoons oregano or sage (I like oregano)
1 teaspoon salt
½ teaspoon thyme
1 bay leaf
1 cup water

In a large skillet, cook onion in hot oil till almost tender. Add meat and garlic; brown lightly. Add remaining ingredients. Simmer uncovered 2 to 2½ hours or till sauce is nice and thick; stir occasionally. Remove bay leaf. Serve over hot spaghetti. Pass bowl of shredded Parmesan cheese. Makes 6 servings. Note: One pound of spaghetti noodles will serve 4 to 6 as a main dish with sauce.

Bestselling author Kathleen Y'Barbo is a Romantic Times Book of the Year winner as well as a multiple Carol Award and RITA nominee of more than fifty novels with almost two million copies in print in the US and abroad. A tenth-generation Texan, she has been nominated for a Career Achievement Award as well a Reader's Choice Award and Book of the Year by Romantic Times magazine.

Kathleen is a paralegal, a proud military wife, and an expatriate Texan cheering on her beloved Texas Aggies from north of the Red River. Connect with her through social media at www.kathleenybarbo.com.

Also available from Barbour Publishing

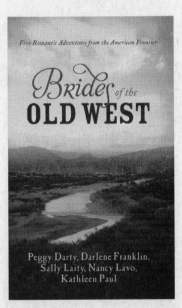

*The American frontier is the stage
for five historical romances.*